Case Studies in

E. M. FORSTER

# Howards End

# Case Studies in Contemporary Criticism
SERIES EDITOR: Ross C Murfin

Case Studies in Contemporary Criticism
SERIES EDITOR: Ross C Murfin, *Southern Methodist University*

# E. M. FORSTER
# *Howards End*

Complete, Authoritative Text with
Biographical and Historical Contexts,
Critical History, and Essays from
Five Contemporary Critical Perspectives

EDITED BY
## Alistair M. Duckworth
*University of Florida*

**Bedford Books**
BOSTON ✻ NEW YORK

**For Bedford Books**
*President and Publisher:* Charles H. Christensen
*General Manager and Associate Publisher:* Joan E. Feinberg
*Managing Editor:* Elizabeth M. Schaaf
*Developmental Editor:* Stephen A. Scipione
*Assistant Managing Editor:* John Amburg
*Production Editor:* Stasia Zomkowski
*Copyeditor:* Tammy Zambo
*Text Designer:* Sandra Rigney, The Book Department
*Cover Design:* Richard Emery Design, Inc.
*Cover Art:* Frederick Frieseke. *Hollyhocks,* c. 1914. Oil on canvas. National Academy of Design, New York.

Library of Congress Catalog Card Number: 96–84932

Manufactured in the United States of America.

1  0  9  8  7  6
f  e  d  c  b  a

*For information, write:* Bedford Books, 75 Arlington Street, Boston, MA 02116
(617–426–7440)

ISBN: 0–312–11182–7 (paperback)
ISBN: 0–312–16292–8 (hardcover)

**Acknowledgments**

The Abinger Edition of *Howards End.* Edited by Oliver Stallybrass. First published by Edward Arnold, Ltd. Copyright © 1910, 1973 the Provost and Scholars of King's College, Cambridge.

Alistair M. Duckworth, "The Critical Fortunes of *Howards End.*" Portions of this essay are included in "A Critical History of *Howards End*" in this volume. Used by permission of Twayne Publishers, an imprint of Simon & Schuster Macmillan from *"Howards End": E. M. Forster's House of Fiction* by Alistair M. Duckworth. Copyright © 1992 by Twayne Publishers.

Elizabeth Langland, "Gesturing Toward an Open Space: Gender, Form, and Language in *Howards End.*" Reprinted from *Out of Bounds: Male Writers and Gender(ed) Criticism,* Laura Claridge and Elizabeth Langland, eds. Amherst: University of Massachusetts Press, 1990. Copyright © 1990 by The University of Massachusetts Press.

*Acknowledgments and copyrights are continued at the back of the book on page 499, which constitutes an extension of the copyright page. It is a violation of the law to reproduce these selections by any means whatsoever without the written permission of the copyright holder.*

# About the Series

Volumes in the Case Studies in Contemporary Criticism series provide college students with an entrée into the current critical and theoretical ferment in literary studies. Each volume reprints the complete text of a classic literary work and presents critical essays that approach the work from different theoretical perspectives, together with the editors' introductions to both the literary work and the critics' theoretical perspectives.

The volume editor of each Case Study has selected and prepared an authoritative text of the classic work, written an introduction to the work's biographical and historical contexts, and surveyed the critical responses to the work since its initial publication. Thus situated biographically, historically, and critically, the work is examined in five critical essays, each representing a theoretical perspective of importance to contemporary literary studies. These essays, prepared especially for undergraduates, show theory in praxis; whether written by established scholars or exceptional young critics, they demonstrate how current theoretical approaches can generate compelling readings of great literature.

As series editor, I have prepared introductions, with bibliographies, to the theoretical perspectives represented in the five critical essays. Each introduction presents the principal concepts of a particular theory in their historical context and discusses the major figures and key works that have influenced their formulation. It is my hope that these introductions will reveal to students that effective criticism is informed by a set of coherent assumptions, and will encourage them to recognize and examine their own assumptions about literature. After each introduction, a selective bibliography presents a partially annotated list of important works from the literature of the particular theoretical perspective, including the most recent and readily available editions and translations of the works cited in the introduction. Finally, I have compiled a glossary of key terms that recur in these volumes and in the discourse of contemporary theory and criticism. We hope that the Case Studies in Contemporary Criticism series will reaffirm the richness of its literary works, even as it introduces invigorating new ways to mine their apparently inexhaustible wealth.

Ross C Murfin
Series Editor
Southern Methodist University

# About This Volume

By kind permission of Dr. Donald Parry, executor of the Forster estate, and of King's College, Cambridge, the estate's proprietors, this volume reprints the text of volume 4 of *The Abinger Edition of E. M. Forster*, edited by Oliver Stallybrass and published by Edward Arnold in London in 1973. Arnold supplied one hundred bound copies of this edition to Holmes and Meier in New York, which issued them in the United States in 1978. The present volume provides the only standard text of *Howards End* commercially available in this country at this time. I have made one emendation to the Abinger text. On page 149 of this edition, I have changed "fire, weather, or music" to "fine weather or music." That Stallybrass intended that this change be made in a future edition of *Howards End* is clear from a statement in his letter to the *Times Literary Supplement* (May 7, 1976: 553) and from an addendum he made in *The Manuscripts of "Howards End": Corrigenda and Addenda* (London: Edward Arnold, 1976, 376); both publications responded to J. H. Stape's review "Editing Forster" (*Essays in Criticism* 36.2 [1976]: 177–81). In the reprinted text I have also noted six significant manuscript variations from the Abinger text; these appear along with other brief notes intended to locate historical and literary references in the novel, identify figures and events, and explain terms whose meanings may no longer be widely understood. For fuller contextual annotations, readers may consult Stallybrass's introduction and annotations in the Abinger edition of *Howards End*. Where my own notes are indebted to Stallybrass, I acknowledge the fact by giving his name.

Part Two of this volume comprises, in addition to my critical history of the novel and Ross Murfin's theoretical introductions, five critical essays on *Howards End*. Each of these essays represents a contemporary mode of reading. The first and last were written especially for this volume. J. H. Stape's "Picturing the Self as Other: *Howards End* as Psychobiography" represents a psychoanalytic approach to a novel read more usually in social and political ways; like other recent critics of Forster, including Elizabeth Langland and J. Hillis Miller in this volume, Stape is interested in the ways in which Forster's homosexual desire informs the novel's plot, themes, and characterization. J. Hillis Miller's "Just Reading *Howards End*" is, so far as I can determine, the first essay to employ a deconstructive approach to *Howards End*. Reading the novel according to the categories of gender, class, nation, and race, Miller is also interested in Forster's appeal to the "unseen," a spiritual reality that individual readers of the novel may or may not interpret as transcending such categories.

The three remaining essays are extracts from books. Peter Widdowson's "*Howards End*: Fiction as History" is taken from his 1977 book of the same title, and Judith Weissman's "*Howards End*: Gasoline and Goddesses" is taken from her 1987 book *Half-Savage and Hardy and Free: Women and Rural Radicalism in the Nineteenth-Century Novel*. These essays, representing cultural and Marxist criticism respectively, offer an interesting comparison. Cultural and Marxist approaches are obviously related in their emphasis on the social and economic aspects of novels; and the essays of both Widdowson and Weissman are indebted to the work of Raymond Williams, a major advocate of the political evaluation of literature in such studies as *The Country and the City* (1973). Yet Widdowson and Weissman differ markedly in their evaluations of Forster's vision in *Howards End*. Widdowson finds Forster's liberalism an inadequate response to the problems of a largely urbanized Edwardian England, while Weissman, equally critical of the liberalism of the Schlegel sisters, finds hope for a radical new economy in the rural community represented by Mrs. Wilcox and the house, Howards End.

Elizabeth Langland's "Gesturing toward an Open Space: Gender, Form, and Language in *Howards End*" first appeared in *Out of Bounds: Male Writers and Gender(ed) Criticism*, a 1990 collection of essays that Langland edited with Laura Claridge. Representing a feminist approach, Langland is aware of the ways in which *Howards End* both inscribes and escapes from gender stereotypes. As her title suggests, however, she is appreciative of Forster's ability to expose culturally constructed forms of masculine and feminine behavior and to value—in the deep affection between the Schlegel sisters, for example, or in the oddly constituted family at the end of the novel—future possibilities of human behavior and relationship.

Reading these excellent and lucid essays, I am more aware than ever of the special pertinence of *Howards End* to the social and political issues of the present moment. The problems of the 1900s—including poverty and welfare, industrial pollution, economic imperialism, women's rights, the duty of the business world to society as a whole, and the social responsibility of intellectuals—are still with us in the 1990s. Forster's achievement is not to have solved problems for which social and political agencies are still seeking solutions, but to have presented these problems to us in wonderfully realistic ways, through characterization, episode, and setting, and to have invited our committed responses. Not the least interesting aspects of the essays in Part Two are the nature, variety, and strength of the commitments made.

## Acknowledgments

I thank, first, the five contributors who have endured with admirable patience the rather long gestation of this volume. One of the contributors was my teacher at Johns Hopkins. Another is my colleague at the University of Florida. With the other three I have enjoyed, at least, epistolary friendships. To J. H. Stape I am most grateful for advice on editorial matters—advice that I fear I was not always able to follow as far as he would have wished; I am also grateful for his prompt and productive responses to the biographical and historical introduction that follows in Part One and to the critical history of the novel in Part Two. To Sears Jayne I owe warm thanks for his scrupulous readings of earlier versions of these essays and for valuable assistance with the annotations. Victor Knight, Christa Zorn-Belde, and John Leavey also gave generously of their time to help me with the annotations. Ross Murfin read and commented constructively on the whole volume and in a dozen other ways showed himself to be the most gracious of series editors. At Bedford Books, Steve Scipione was a patient and supportive presence, as was Stasia Zomkowski during the book's production; I would also like to thank Charles Christensen, Joan Feinberg, Elizabeth Schaaf, and Lori Chong. The Department of English, the College of Liberal Arts and Sciences, and the Division of Sponsored Research of the University of Florida together helped to subsidize a visit to the Modern Archives of King's College, Cambridge, where Jacqueline Cox, the modern archivist, was most accommodating. Donald Parry, provost of King's College, and Gordon Fielden, secretary of the Society of Authors, gave kind and affirmative attention to my request to reprint the text of the Abinger edition. Margaret Ashby, author of *Forster Country* and cofounder of the Friends of Forster Country, graciously gave up most of a Saturday to show my wife and me the beautiful Hertfordshire countryside that Forster loved and described in faithful detail in *Howards End;* and Peter and Ann Newman, of Rooksnest House, provided us with generous access to the lawn, garden, and meadow of "Howards End" and to the remarkably unchanged house itself. Throughout, Emily Jayne Duckworth supported and brightened my work with her wit, warmth, and laughter.

Alistair M. Duckworth
University of Florida

# Contents

# PART ONE

# *Howards End:*
# The Complete Text

# Introduction:
# Biographical and
# Historical Contexts

E. M. Forster was thirty-one when *Howards End* appeared on October 18, 1910. He had already written *Where Angels Fear to Tread* (published in 1905), *The Longest Journey* (1907), and *A Room with a View* (1908). His achievement was remarkable even by the high standards of the Cambridge and Bloomsbury circles with which he had affiliations. Not, on the surface at least, a competitive man, Forster had earned an early reputation, while overtly more ambitious acquaintances such as Lytton Strachey and Virginia Stephen (soon to be Virginia Woolf) remained unknown outside their immediate group. Strachey's fame would come with his iconoclastic *Eminent Victorians*, published in the last year of the First World War (1918); Woolf would not write the modernist novels that made her famous until the 1920s, *Mrs. Dalloway* appearing in 1925 and *To the Lighthouse* in 1927.

Forster's success in 1910 was unexpected and perhaps not entirely pleasing to his friends. He had been a good but not an exceptional student at King's College, Cambridge, between 1897 and 1901. He won prizes, including one for Latin composition and another for an essay entitled "The Novelists of the 18th Century and Their Influence on Those of the 19th"; and he was elected in his fourth year to the "Apostles," an elite secret society that met to discuss philosophical and ethical topics and included among its members brilliant undergraduates such as Leonard Woolf, Lytton Strachey, and J. M. Keynes and distinguished philosopher dons such as Bertrand Russell and G. E. Moore. But Forster took an upper second class in the classical tripos, part 1, when he received his B.A. in June 1900, and after a further year in which he read history, he took a second class in the historical tripos, part 2 (June 1901). These results were not good enough to qualify him for an academic career.

Nor had Forster been a central member of the "Bloomsbury Group," in which, as Keynes famously remarked in his "My Early Beliefs," he appeared as "the elusive colt of a dark horse" (52). The Bloomsbury Group was so named because it first came together at 46 Gordon Square, Bloomsbury, the house in west-central London to which Vanessa and Virginia Stephen had moved in 1904 on the death of their father, Sir Leslie Stephen. The group comprised writers, artists, and art critics. Most were Cambridge men introduced to the Stephen sisters by their brother Thoby (tragically, Thoby died of typhoid in 1906); several were Apostles. Some married (Vanessa and Clive Bell in 1907, and Virginia and Leonard Woolf in 1912); others, such as Keynes and Duncan Grant, had homosexual liaisons; still others, such as Vanessa Bell and Duncan Grant, formed such close artistic and affectionate ties that from 1916 onward they would live, and paint, together in a Sussex farmhouse for the rest of their lives. All forged friendships that survived; all took a keen, and critical, interest in the work of the others.

Shortly after the publication of *Howards End*, Forster gave a well-received paper to the group on "The Feminine Note in Literature," and his relations with Bloomsbury, up to now distant, became closer, especially after Leonard Woolf's return from Ceylon in 1911. But he remained a diffident and occasional presence; it is not easy to imagine Morgan (as Forster's friends called him) shining in the verbally inventive company of Virginia and Vanessa, or excelling in conversations with Desmond McCarthy, the theater reviewer; Maynard Keynes, the expert on Indian currency and finance; Clive Bell, the art critic and future theorist of "significant form"; and Roger Fry, already known as an expert on Italian art and now notorious as the organizer of the first postimpressionist exhibition in London in 1910. Yet with the exception of Fry, who was fifteen years older than Forster and had declined an offer to be director of the National Gallery of Art, none of the group had, in 1910, made a mark on the national scene. Forster, "irritating in his refusal to be great," as Lionel Trilling would later write (9), had beaten them to the post. So it may have appeared in 1910, when Forster had published four novels in five years. So it sometimes appears now, when five of his novels have been made into successful films within an eight-year period.[1]

What in his biographical and historical background explains Forster's achievement at the age of thirty-one? What was the nature of that achievement? And why, having emerged on the national scene as a major novelist with *Howards End*, did he stop publishing novels for fourteen years (*A Passage to India* appeared in 1924) and then for the rest of his long life? To seek answers to these questions, we need to return to Forster's Victorian origins, but first we may note that the continuing appeal of *Howards End* in the 1990s stems from its remarkable relevance to the problems of our own historical present. Forster's concerns in the first decade of the twentieth century remain our concerns in the last, as urbanization threatens the countryside and as the world's irreversible commitment to industry and technology has potentially severe consequences for life on earth. The political attitudes of the Wilcox men in *Howards End* — their commitment to the "classical liberal" principles of a laissez-faire economy, their opposition to the provision of welfare to the poor — are very much alive in post-Thatcherite England and the America of Newt Gingrich; and the indignation of the Schlegel sisters may still strike a chord in liberals of a more humanistic persuasion. We are still seeking Forster's connections, between entrenched male power and emerging female aspirations and between the often separate worlds of culture and business. Liberalism of both hard and soft kinds has taken on a new significance in the aftermath of the demise of communism and the free-market reorientation of socialism; and history, which led Forster in 1946 (during the social revolution of the Labour Party) to admit resignedly that he belonged to "the fag end of Victorian liberalism" ("Challenge" 56), has turned back in the 1990s to canvass again the debates — over taxation and social security, for example — that first appeared at the time of Lloyd George's "People's Budget" in 1909. Sexual politics, too, may explain the continuing interest in his work. Forster was a homosexual, and his novels, including *Howards End*, investigate gender roles and conduct a series of inquiries into marriage as an institution. To be sure, Forster suppressed public knowledge of his homosexuality during his lifetime, and both his homosexuality and its suppression have been controversial

---

[1]Films of Forster's novels are *A Passage to India* (director, David Lean), 1984; *A Room with a View* (director, James Ivory), 1986; *Maurice* (director, James Ivory), 1987; *Where Angels Fear to Tread* (director, Charles Sturridge), 1991; *Howards End* (director, James Ivory), 1992.

topics since the 1970s. Even so, at a time when gay rights are debated in the streets and "queer theory" has arisen in the academy, Forster's sexual politics, like his liberalism, are of much interest.

Edward Morgan Forster was born on January 1, 1879, in London, the only surviving child of Edward Morgan Llewellyn Forster, an architect, and Alice Clara (Lily) Whichelo. His father's mother, Laura Thornton, was the wealthy daughter of Henry Thornton (1760–1815), a banker, member of Parliament, and intimate friend of the philanthropist William Wilberforce. Like Wilberforce, Thornton was an influential member of the evangelical Clapham Sect, a group of nonconformist Christians who crusaded vigorously in the early nineteenth century for the abolition of slavery in the British Empire and for prison reform and were active in missionary work at home and abroad. Forster's unmarried great-aunt, Marianne Thornton (1797–1887), who still resided in Clapham, was a formidable presence in his childhood. She had made the young Lily Whichelo her protégée, paying for her education at a school for young ladies and finding her positions as a governess. While governess at Lord Farrer's home in Abinger Hammer, Surrey, Lily accepted Eddie Forster's proposal, and they were married in 1877. Marianne left Forster a considerable legacy of £8,000 on her death in 1887, the interest on which helped pay for his education and allowed him later to travel and write. Forster believed the legacy to have been "the financial salvation of my life" (*Marianne Thornton* 289), and in 1956 he repaid the debt by writing a biography of his great-aunt.

In "The Challenge of Our Time" (1946), Forster gives a balanced view of the evangelical-liberal heritage that undoubtedly fed into his life of social concern. (Particularly with respect to charity, as Mary Lago has recently demonstrated, he was very much "Clapham's child.") On the one hand, he was respectful of an age that "practised benevolence and philanthropy, was humane and intellectually curious, upheld free speech, had little colour-prejudice, believed that individuals are and should be different, and entertained a sincere faith in the progress of society." On the other, he recognized the blindness of the age into which he was born: "In came the nice fat dividends, up rose the lofty thoughts, and we did not realise that we were exploiting the poor of our own country and the backward races abroad, and getting bigger profits from investments than we should" ("Challenge" 56). Margaret Schlegel in *Howards End* shares Forster's ambivalence about her unearned income when she observes that "independent thoughts are in nine cases out of ten the result of independent means" (121).

Forster's mother's family, although middle class, were neither as rich nor as conventional as his father's. Lily was one of the ten children of Henry Mayle Whichelo, an artist and teacher of drawing, and Forster's Whichelo background surely accounts in part for his artistic and unconventional side. After his father died of tuberculosis in 1880, Forster, not yet two years old, remained close to his maternal grandmother, Louisa Whichelo, a vital and resourceful woman who provided the model for Mrs. Honeychurch in *A Room with a View*. Louisa Whichelo was by no means the only woman other than Forster's mother who played an important role in his childhood. In 1883 Lily took out a lease on Rooksnest, a farmhouse near Stevenage in Hertfordshire, to affirm her independence from Marianne Thornton. But "Aunt Monie," as Marianne was appropriately named, was still an influential presence, as were Forster's Whichelo aunts Georgie, Nellie, and Rosie; his mother's friend Maimie Aylward; his aunt Laura Forster, living at West Hackhurst in Surrey in the house that Forster's father had designed for her; and various older female relatives. Forster grew up, as he later put it, in "a haze of elderly ladies" (Furbank 1:28). Nicknamed "the Important One," he was cuddled and cosseted and made the center of attention. A photograph of him at age five (Furbank 1:16) and a drawing of him at the same age (King 13) show him with long, flowing locks, dressed to resemble Little Lord Fauntleroy.

The years at Rooksnest (1883–93) were happy ones for Forster. Shortly after his very reluctant departure in his fifteenth year, he began a memoir (printed as an appendix in the novel's 1973 Abinger edition) and sketched a map of the house, lawn, garden, and meadow (illustrated in King 14 and Duckworth 57). The details of both precisely establish Rooksnest as the model for Howards End. The map shows the locations of the paddock and the wych elm exactly as they appear in the novel, and the memoir describes the fine view to the west, the vine that covers the house, and even the teeth in the tree (though they are not, as in the novel, pigs' teeth):

About four feet from the ground were three or four fangs stuck deep into the rugged bark. As far as I can make out these were votive offerings of people who had their toothache cured by chewing pieces of the bark, but whether they were their own teeth I don't know and certainly it does not seem likely that they should sacrifice one sound tooth as the price of having one aching one cured. ("Rooksnest" 346–47)

When Margaret Schlegel at last visits Howards End, she enters the space of Forster's childhood: "Drawing-room, dining-room and hall — how petty the names sounded! Here were simply three rooms where children could play and friends shelter from the rain" (179). As the memoir tells us ("Rooksnest" 350), Forster played at Rooksnest with a series of "garden boys," especially one named Ansell who would give his name to the Cambridge undergraduate who debates the objective existence of the cow in the first chapter of *The Longest Journey* and, more appropriately, to the gamekeeper in the short story "Ansell," posthumously published in *The Life to Come* (1972). Written about 1903, "Ansell" describes the adolescent comradeship between Ansell, then a garden boy, and the story's narrator, their subsequent separation when the narrator goes to Cambridge, and the happy renewal of their friendship when the narrator returns to the country and fortuitously loses his books in a river.

The importance of Rooksnest to an understanding of *Howards End* and, indeed, of Forster's whole life, may be understood by reference to Gaston Bachelard's *The Poetics of Space* (1964). Forster's memoir and map resemble the "surveyor's map of . . . lost fields and meadows" that Bachelard invites us all to make, and Rooksnest is "the principle of psychological integration" that he associates with the image of the house. "In the life of a man," Bachelard proposes, "the house thrusts aside contingencies, its councils of continuity are unceasing. Without it, man would be a dispersed being. . . . It is body and soul. It is the human being's first world. Before he is 'cast into the world' . . . man is laid in the cradle of the house" (qtd. in Bachelard 11, 8, 6–7).

Forster was cast into the world from the Rooksnest cradle in 1893 when Lily's lease was not renewed, and she and her son moved to Tonbridge in Kent, where Forster attended Tonbridge School. He was no happier at Tonbridge, where his status as a "day boy" invited the ridicule of the boarders, than he had earlier been at Kent House, a preparatory school in Eastbourne, Sussex, where he had been nicknamed "Mousie" and subjected to bullying, or at The Grange, Stevenage, a weekly boarding school from which he had been quickly removed after suffering rough treatment from his fellow pupils. Forster disliked Tonbridge, a minor but typical public school, for its devotion to athletics, its system of "houses" and the interhouse rivalry that housemasters encouraged, its bullying and cold baths, and its jingoistic patriotism. Long before Lytton Strachey's attack in his portrait of Thomas Arnold in *Eminent Victorians,* Forster satirized the institution of the public school in his description of Sawston in *The Longest Journey*. ("Public" schools were, in fact, private schools purporting to provide superior education to the sons of mostly professional middle-class families that could afford the fees.) Although he recognized that public schools bred practical and efficient leaders who could also be conventionally courteous as adults, Forster blamed them for producing men with what he called "undeveloped hearts." Charles Wilcox in *Howards End* is a typical public school man.

Forster's adolescence was a troubled one, not least because of confusion about gender roles. His childhood had its dark side in this regard (Wyatt-Brown 113–16). Without father or brother, and surrounded by admiring women, he was overprotected by his mother, who may have communicated to him her dissatisfaction with her husband. Despite more than one offer, Lily rejected the idea of remarrying, and Forster thus missed a regular male presence in his early life. Moreover, Lily neglected to tell him the facts of life. She was horrified to discover that he masturbated and urged him to discontinue the "dirty" habit. And when, while at Kent House, he wrote to her obscurely about a sexual encounter he had had with a middle-aged man on the Sussex Downs—an encounter that left him with a feeling of disgust but also of not knowing what had really happened or how to come to terms with it—his mother responded with consternation. Neither she nor the headmaster was capable of overcoming a sense of shock and embarrassment or of providing Forster with the sympathetic support he needed. He was left with the feeling that he was somehow to blame. Something of the headmaster's maladroit attempt to explain the matter and to affirm heterosexuality as a social norm is recalled in the first chapter of *Maurice* (Forster's posthumously published homosexual novel) in the scene on the beach in which Mr. Ducie tries unsuccessfully to explain the mystery of sex to the fourteen-year-old Maurice by drawing diagrams in the sand. Forster was thus unprepared for the often crude world of boys' schools; indeed, he remained naive about sex until well into his adult life, not learning how copulation took place until he was thirty. Even as an undergraduate he played the role of "bright little girl" in correspondence with his mother (Furbank 1: 67).

In his final years at Tonbridge, Forster achieved a degree of academic success and even acceptance, so that when in October 1897 he was admitted as a classics student to King's College, Cambridge, he associated at first mainly with Old Tonbridgians. By his second year, however, he was very much at home in King's. He got on well with his tutors — Oscar Browning, Nathaniel Wedd, and Goldsworthy Lowes Dickinson — and formed a romantic friendship with H. O. Meredith. "H.O.M." sponsored him for membership in the Apostles, then under the influence of G. E. Moore's ethical teaching. Though Forster was never a Moorite and would withdraw into privacy from time to time (Lytton Strachey nicknamed him "the Taupe" [the Mole]), he appreciated the intellectual atmosphere of the meetings, during which Apostles would discuss intensely the nature of truth and the meaning of beauty and hold up for admiration the joys of friendship and "good states of mind."

At King's, Forster was among kindred spirits. With Browning he played duets on the piano; from Wedd he perhaps derived the dislike of aestheticism that is evident in his early novels and his love of Italy (Furbank 1: 58–59), though that love was fostered also by Roger Fry's brilliant lectures on Venetian art. In the company of Dickinson, a scholar of Greek culture and student of political science, he encountered a new intellectual engagement with liberal politics that took on added significance at the time of the Boer War (1899–1902). None of Forster's tutors were religious, despite fellowship in a college whose chapel may lay claim to being the most beautiful in the world. In contact with them, and even more with Meredith, Forster lost whatever Christian faith he had had; henceforth his liberalism, unlike the evangelical liberalism of his Clapham forebears, would make no appeal to the Bible. After returning to King's College in his old age, he became president of the Cambridge Humanists; and at his death in 1970 no religious ceremony was held. Instead, recalling *Howards End*, Forster had instructed that the scherzo from Beethoven's Fifth Symphony be played in the chapel (Furbank 2: 325).

When Forster left Cambridge in the summer of 1901, he had only vague ideas of his future. Wedd had casually suggested to him that he might be a writer, and at Cambridge Forster had already contributed whimsical articles to the college magazine and had begun a novel (now known as "Nottingham Lace"), which anticipates the satire of middle-class stuffiness in *A Room with a View*. Another possible career lay in university extension lecturing. He liked Italian art, knew something of Italian history and literature, and had begun to learn the language. Thus when in October 1901 he left for a year's tour of Italy with his mother, he had more than leisure in mind. On his return, his application to lecture on the Republic of Florence for the Cambridge Local Lectures Board was accepted, and in the years to come he would regularly deliver a series of lectures in different towns on various aspects of

Florentine history, culture, and art. His Italian tour had an even more important result, however: it set him on the path to being a novelist. In May 1902, near Ravello, he was inspired to write his first significant work of fiction, "The Story of a Panic." His experiences of *pensione* life in Italy, and especially of the Pensione Simi in Florence, provided him with the material for *A Room with a View*, a draft of which he wrote while still in Italy; and a visit to Siena and San Gimignano gave him the subject and setting for *Where Angels Fear to Tread*.

Forster, who celebrated his twenty-first birthday on the first day of the twentieth century, spent his twenties in the Edwardian period (1901–10). Because of the subsequent horrors of World War I, the Edwardian period is often viewed as a time of prelapsarian harmony and peace, and Forster's life, it has to be said, gives some support for this view. Reading J. H. Stape's detailed *Chronology*, we can picture Forster leading the "life of cultured but not ignoble ease" (105) enjoyed by the Schlegel siblings in *Howards End*. During the years in which he wrote his first four novels, he traveled extensively on the Continent. In the spring of 1904 he took an educational tour of Greece and Turkey sponsored by the director of the British School of Archaeology at Athens, and in the years that followed he traveled on several occasions to Italy, Austria, Germany, and France. Though he satirizes tourists in his Italian novels and treats John Ruskin, the great authority on Italian art and architecture, with some irony in *Howards End*, Forster was something of a tourist himself (even assigning stars to hotels in his diaries), and he doubtless had Baedeker in his pocket and Ruskin in mind as he conscientiously visited museums, ancient monuments, and churches. He took care to be at the right place at the right time: to be in Naples, for example, to witness the miracle of the liquefaction of San Gennaro's blood (he was disappointed) and to be in Siena for the Palio, the famous horserace around the town square.

In England, too, he was a tireless tourist, exploring on foot parts of Northumberland, Wiltshire, Berkshire, Cornwall, Devon, Dorset, Hampshire, the Isle of Wight, Shropshire, and the Lake District. These expeditions were variously determined by where he was giving extension lectures for Cambridge University; by visits to relatives such as "Uncle Willie" Forster, who had a country house in Northumberland; by visits to friends such as Meredith at Manchester University or "Snow" Wedgwood in Staffordshire; or simply by an interest in the country described by a favorite poet, A. E. Housman, in *A Shropshire Lad*. Like his Italian travels, his English ones influenced his fiction: Figsbury Rings in Wiltshire became the setting of an important scene in *The Longest Journey,* and the Purbeck hills in Dorset provided the occasion for a very Shakespearean praise of England in chapter 19 of *Howards End.* Alongside his pedestrian activities were numerous activities of a more intellectual and cultured kind. In 1904 he and his mother moved to a house ("Harnham") on Monument Green, Weybridge; it would be their home for the next twenty years. Suburban and without any of Rooksnest's sense of heritage, Harnham had the advantage of being close to London and allowing relatively easy access to Cambridge and Oxford. Forster did not disdain Weybridge (he attended and gave papers to its literary society), but he left it often to participate in Apostles' meetings at Cambridge or to attend plays, operas, and concerts. Among musicians, Richard Wagner was an especial favorite; in 1905 in Dresden, Forster attended the *Ring* cycle, and in 1908 at Covent Garden he attended *Götterdämmerung.* Like his travels, these cultural activities provided Forster with rich opportunites for fictional transformation. After hearing Luisa Tetrazzini sing Lucia in Donizetti's *Lucia di Lammermoor* in Florence in 1903, he conceived the opera scene in *Where Angels Fear to Tread;* and a performance of Beethoven's Fifth Symphony in the Queen's Hall in April 1908 inspired him to create that tour de force, the fifth chapter of *Howards End,* though Helen's discovery of goblins in the symphony probably owes more to Wagner than to Beethoven.

Like Tibby Schlegel in *Howards End,* Forster did not have to work for a living, and we get the sense as we note Stape's lists of the many plays and operas he attended and the many books he read — classical literature, history, art history and fiction; in French and Italian as well as English, Greek, and Latin — that he was a man who saw culture as a morally desirable goal in itself. There is a discipline to his reading, touring, and theatergoing that suggests he wished to possess his cultural heritage. Even the work he did in these years was done less for the money or in pursuit of a career (though at first these were never wholly irrelevant considerations because Forster, though independent, was hardly rich) than for his own self-actualization. When in 1904 he undertook to write an introduction and notes for an edition of the *Aeneid,* he was responding to a commission from a friend (Dickinson), but he was also keeping his hand in as a classicist. And when in the spring and summer of 1905 he took a post in Nassenheide, Pomerania, as tutor to the children of Countess von Arnim-Schlagenthin, his motive was less to make money than to learn German, experience German culture, and have an adventure.

True to his Clapham heritage, however, Forster did work to help those less privileged than himself. On his return from Italy in 1902 he began teaching a class in elementary Latin on a voluntary basis at the Working Men's College in London; he would continue to serve the college for a dozen years, writing for the college journal, giving papers, participating in debates, and attending college dinners. In this activity he followed illustrious predecessors such as F. D. Maurice, Ruskin, and Sidney Webb, who set out to provide a full liberal education, modeled on the colleges of Oxford and Cambridge, to working men (Furbank 1:174–75). Forster made friends with students, particularly a printer named Alexander Hepburn, who may have served as one model for Leonard Bast in *Howards End.* In another way Forster's life in the first decade of the twentieth century had a political dimension. Through contact with Cambridge friends, he became a contributor to the *Independent Review,* inaugurated in 1903 to oppose the aggressive imperialism of Joseph Chamberlain, the colonial secretary, and to advocate a constructive social policy in home affairs. It was not so much a Liberal review, Forster wrote in his biography of Dickinson, "as an appeal to Liberalism from the Left to its better self" (115). In the opening number of the journal, Dickinson declared that legislation should pursue the traditional Liberal aim of giving the utmost scope to individual liberty, but that this aim now required a "gradual revolution in all the fundamentals of society, law of property, law of contract, law of marriage" (qtd. in Forster, *Goldsworthy Lowes Dickinson* 115). However much he may have agreed with these sentiments, Forster's own contributions were not political pieces but belletristic articles and fantasy stories such as "The Road from Colonus" and "The Story of the Panic."

Forster's stories in the *Independent Review* hardly seem commensurate with the period of political strife in which they were written; and to some readers, both at the time and later, they seemed escapist, for the Edwardian period, viewed as a whole, was by no means the age of civilization and leisure that Forster's life and fiction suggested. Irish Nationalists were bitterly opposed by Ulster Unionists. Organized labor repeatedly struck for better pay and working conditions. Suffragettes became militant when their demands for equality were refused, and when they were imprisoned for crimes against property they went on hunger strikes; the authorities responded brutally with forcible feeding. Abroad, Germany's expansionist policies alarmed the War Office and the Admiralty, and as a result Parliament committed vast funds to an arms race. At home, conditions in the cities were appalling, as a series of reports from Seebohm Rowntree's *Poverty: A Study of Town Life* (1901) to Sidney and Beatrice Webb's *Minority Report of the Poor Law Commission* (1909) revealed in detail (Colmer 87). In response to the crisis of the time and to the pressures being exerted by a newly powerful Labour Party, the Liberal Party, after its landslide victory in 1905, enacted a series of quasi-socialist measures; these included old-age pensions, unemployment and health insurance, and regulations concerning the hours and conditions of work. Because the revenues to pay for such reforms were to come from an increase in death duties and the income tax and from a new supertax on incomes above £3,000, we can understand why the House of Lords took the imprudent and ultimately self-defeating step of rejecting the 1909 People's Budget proposed by Lloyd George, chancellor of the exchequer.

*Where Angels Fear to Tread* and *A Room with a View* register little sense of the political divisiveness of the times. The "Italian" novels are social comedies of manners aimed at capturing the humor and correcting the excesses of middle-class snobbery, hypocrisy, and sexual repression. They do not seek to be "national" novels and should not be judged as such. *The Longest Journey* is a more serious affair, not only in its criticism of "masculinity" in public schools and public life but also, as Colmer proposes (86), in its concern for England's future. In the character of Stephen Wonham, illegitimate offspring of a farmer and a gentlewoman, a man in touch with his body and with the earth, Forster anticipates the question of *Howards End:* Who shall inherit England? But Stephen is an imperfectly realized figure, and *The Longest Journey* is more concerned with the psychological development of its physically and emotionally crippled hero, Rickie Elliot. *Howards End* is Forster's only serious "national" novel, just as *A Passage to India* is his one serious "international" novel.

Not all critics believe Forster responded adequately to the crisis of the times in *Howards End*. "We are not concerned with the very poor" is the notorious opening sentence of chapter 6, and after all palliations the sentiment sounds condescending, even callous, to many modern ears. Yet Forster was delimiting the range of his subject and expertise (albeit provocatively), not depreciating poverty. Though Margaret Schlegel more than once smells "odours from the abyss" of poverty and despair into which Leonard Bast falls after the worlds of business and culture fail him, no more than her author had she ever experienced the slum life in London—as Jack London had when he wrote *The People of the Abyss* (1903), or as C. F. G. Masterman had when he wrote *From the Abyss: Of Its Inhabitants by One of Them* (1902). Works treating "the abyss" were common at the time, and Masterman's *The Condition of England* (1908), as Peter Widdowson shows (ch. 2), was a major influence on *Howards End*. Masterman was a radical member of Parliament for a constituency in East London, and in his books and articles in the *Independent Review*, he describes the nineteenth-century migration of agricultural laborers to the city, with the consequent demise of rural England and its yeoman class, the growth of slums and suburbia, and the transformation of London into a city of noise and pollution. Together with other writers, he pointed to the general ill health of the poor, whose "weak knees" and "narrow chests" were the result of poor diets, and to the disappointing effects of the national system of education begun in 1870. Forster draws from Masterman in his portraits of Leonard and Jacky Bast, but Leonard is not, when we meet him, one of "the very poor," and Forster's subject is the middle, not the lower classes.

If we grant Forster, to use Henry James's word, his donnée and do not require him to be an urban novelist like George Gissing or a naturalistic novelist like H. G. Wells or Arnold Bennett, the historical range and specification of *Howards End* are impressive. The clash between Schlegels and Wilcoxes, for example, may be seen as a domestic version of the division that occurred within the Liberal Party at the time of the South African War between "little Englanders" who opposed the war and "Imperialists" who supported it. Charles Wilcox brings back a Dutch Bible from the war, and this detail, together with his father's position in the Imperial and West African Rubber Company and his brother Paul's work in Nigeria, places the Wilcoxes among the Liberal Imperialists who made common cause with Joseph Chamberlain in 1903, when he proposed a policy of tariff reform to the consternation of traditional free-trade Liberals. When it comes to the poor, however, Henry Wilcox selfishly appeals to the doctrine of laissez faire, a staple of classical liberalism since the time of Adam Smith, James Mill, and David Ricardo.

*Howards End* is not a statistical abstract or a work of sociology but a novel of domestic realism that contains a wealth of detailed references to Edwardian society: its obsession with games, its dependence on servants, its opposition (in conservative circles) to socialism and feminism, its reception (in progressive circles) of new music (Wagner, Debussy) and new art (Monet), its luxurious London flats and well-appointed country houses, its motorcars and the major social changes they brought about, its fear of Germany's economic challenge, its apprehension of a coming war, and much more (Duckworth 8–11, 65–69). Forster weaves the issues and problems of his day into his fictional fabric with remarkable skill. Consider, to give only one example, how deftly he introduces English-German rivalry into the concert at the Queen's Hall during which music by Elgar, as well as Beethoven, is performed. Edward Elgar in this period was effectively England's composer laureate. *Pomp and Circumstance* marches nos. 1 and 2 date from 1901, and the *Coronation Ode* of 1902 contains the imperialistic text of "Land of Hope and Glory": "Wider still and wider may thy bounds be set. / God who made thee mighty, make thee mightier yet!" Elgar makes considerable use of march rhythms and gives prominence to the brass instruments; his music was thus suited to the chauvinistic mood of an English public aware of trade rivalry with Germany and aware too of Germany's vastly superior musical heritage (Crump 166). At the Queen's Hall the patriotic Mrs. Munt taps her feet to *Pomp and Circumstance,* but Margaret Schlegel dislikes the piece, and the German guests, having heard Beethoven and Brahms, politely leave.

With the publication of *Howards End,* Forster's reputation as a novelist was assured. Even earlier his social life, which included visits or dinners with Henry James, John Galsworthy, and Sir Edward Grey, the foreign affairs minister, had been a measure of his coming reputation. In late 1911 Roger Fry painted his portrait, of which Forster wrote while it was in progress, "Post-Impressionism is at present confined to my lower lip . . . and to my chin, on which soup has apparently dribbled" (qtd. in Furbank 1: 206). And yet, as Furbank has argued, Forster's very success inhibited him as a writer. His next published novel was *A Passage to India* in 1924, and that caused him much travail. *Arctic Summer,* a novel he was working on in 1911, was never completed. Why he should dry up after the facility of his fictional creation between 1903 and 1910 has proved of interest to critics, including J. H. Stape in his essay in this volume. A major reason seems to have been his frustration at not being able to actualize his homosexual desires in either his life or his fiction.

During the years 1900–09, Forster was in love with two men. One was H. O. Meredith, his old friend from King's, with whom he continued to have close ties but from whom he was distanced after Meredith's marriage in 1905, rather as Maurice is distanced by Clive Durham in *Maurice.* The other was Syed Ross Masood, the handsome and extrovert son of a prominent Muslim Indian family, who arrived in England in 1906 to go to Oxford. Forster became his Latin coach, and a strong friendship ensued, one result of which would be Forster's lifelong love of India, which he would visit for extended periods in 1912 and 1921. Soon after the publication of *Howards End*, when it became clear that royalties would pay for his trip to India, Forster declared his love for Masood, who was not shocked but not interested either. Their friendship endured, but Forster had not found "the friend" he increasingly needed in his life. ("Friendship" appears implicitly as a code for homosexual love in *The Longest Journey* and explicitly in *Maurice*.)

Long aware of his "minority" status, Forster seems not fully to have understood his sexual orientation until he visited Edward Carpenter, author of *The Intermediate Sex* (1912), at his home in Millthorpe, Derbyshire, in 1913. A memorable encounter there with Carpenter's working-class companion, George Merrill, inspired him to begin *Maurice*, his novel of homosexual love, which he completed in a first version in 1914 but did not publish during his lifetime. In 1916, while serving with the Red Cross in Alexandria during the First World War, Forster, as he wrote to his close friend Florence Barger, "parted with respectability" (*Selected Letters* 243), and in 1917 he had his first fulfilling homosexual relationship with Mohammed el Adl, an Egyptian tram conductor, who died in 1922 of consumption. From 1930 until his death in 1970, Forster enjoyed a loving friendship with Bob Buckingham, a London policeman—a friendship that survived Buckingham's marriage in 1932.

At the time of *Howards End*, however, his life was one of frustration, exacerbated by a sense that the fictional form he had chosen was incapable of giving direct expression to his desires. Recognizing that a traditional function of the novel of manners had been to resolve moral and social questions by means of the marriage plot, Forster seems to have believed that the effect of novels might be to legislate heterosexual monogamy as a social norm. In his novels he opposes this ideological function by various manipulations of the marriage plot. His critique of marriage is most evident in *The Longest Journey*, but it is evident too in the preference he gives to same-sex relationships, such as those between Gino and Philip in *Where Angels Fear to Tread*, Margaret and Helen Schlegel in *Howards End*, and Aziz and Fielding in *A Passage to India*. Indeed, with the possible exception of *A Room with a View*, he never wrote a novel in which marriage successfully solves the problems raised as it also resolves the plot.

Although Forster's homosexuality goes a fair way toward explaining his writer's block after *Howards End*, it is less helpful as a key to the novel itself. *Howards End* is not, as *The Longest Journey* arguably is, a cryptohomosexual novel, though in Margaret's plea for "eternal differences, planted by God in a single family, so that there may always be colour . . . in the daily gray" (287) the novel may make an appeal for the social acceptance of homosexuality. *Howards End* remains a socially committed work that looks back, on the one hand, to Forster's Clapham forebears and forward, on the other, to a long life of social engagement. As Judith Weissman's Marxist reading in this volume shows, the novel's mythic treatment of Mrs. Wilcox and Howards End and the pastoral nature of its conclusion need not be read as signs of a regressive return to the childhood security of Rooksnest or as an evasion of the "real" problems of Edwardian England. True to his liberal heritage, Forster continued to seek connections, and it is sometimes amusing to read academic critics deploring his lack of productivity. His fiction apart, Forster produced two biographies, 348 articles, reviews, and letters to the press, a pageant play, a book about India, the libretto for Benjamin Britten's *Billy Budd,* many thousands of personal letters, the posthumously published *Commonplace Book,* and more (see Wyatt-Brown 110, with citations). Throughout W. H. Auden's "low, dishonest decade" of the thirties, when the survival of liberalism was endangered by the opposite fanaticisms of fascism and communism, Forster kept the liberal viewpoint alive in articles and speeches. His activities gained him the affection and respect of the younger generation of committed writers, including Auden and Christopher Isherwood. As president of the National Council of Civil Liberties, he fought in the thirties for individual liberty and in the forties against the suppression of free speech on the radio by the British Broadcasting Corporation (BBC). With the BBC, in fact, he had an intimate connection almost from the beginning (in the 1920s) of that august institution. He made 131 broadcasts, including three in 1940 that put him on the Nazis' blacklist. During the Second World War, he broadcast regular talks to India, and after the war, when the BBC's Third Program was created (as a frankly highbrow program devoted to intellectual topics, classical music, and serious literature and drama), he contributed regular talks (Lago, "BBC Broadcasts").

In 1946, after his third and last visit to India (during which he was feted as a public figure), he returned home to West Hackhurst, where he had lived with his mother since 1924. On his mother's death in 1945, the lease on the house, which his Aunt Laura had bequeathed to him, ended, and to Forster's great sadness and anger, he was for a second time forced to leave a house that he loved. But at this point

King's College made him an honorary fellow, and for the last twenty-five years of his life he worked and (from 1953) resided in the college of his youth. Widely esteemed for his achievements as an author and a humanist, he received many honors. Twice, in 1947 and 1949, he came to the United States to give important invited talks, at Harvard University and the American Academy of Arts and Letters respectively. The queen made him a Companion of Honour in 1953 and appointed him to the Order of Merit in 1969. In 1966 he was presented with the gold medal of the Italian Institute. Naturally, his activities lessened as he grew older, but he continued to support liberal causes and was pleased to witness the passage in his lifetime of the 1967 Sexual Offences Act, which, in heeding at last the recommendations of Sir John Wolfenden, removed the threat of legal action against homosexuals.[2] Living at King's in his old age, Forster had come full circle. Not too far from Cambridge was Rooksnest, his childhood home. Despite threats of urban encroachment, the house and its surrounding countryside had survived. In Forster's end was his beginning.

Alistair M. Duckworth

## WORKS CITED

Bachelard, Gaston. *The Poetics of Space.* Trans. Marie Jolas. New York: Orion, 1964.

Colmer, John. *E. M. Forster: The Personal Voice.* London: Routledge, 1975.

Crump, Jeremy. "The Identity of English Music: The Reception of Elgar, 1899–1935." *Englishness: Politics and Culture, 1880–1920.* Ed. Robert Colls and Philip Dodd. London: Croom Helm, 1986. 164–90.

Duckworth, Alistair M. *"Howards End": E. M. Forster's House of Fiction.* New York: Twayne, 1992.

Forster, E. M. "The Challenge of Our Time." 1946. *Two Cheers for Democracy.* New York: Harcourt, 1951. 55–60.

———. *Goldsworthy Lowes Dickinson.* London: Arnold, 1934.

———. *Marianne Thornton, 1797–1887: A Domestic Biography.* London: Arnold, 1956.

---

[2]The recommendations of the 1957 Wolfenden Report—namely that homosexual activity in private between consenting males over the age of 21 should be decriminalized—removed the threat.

————. "Rooksnest." Appendix to *Howards End*. Ed. Oliver Stallybrass. London: Arnold, 1973. 341–51.

————. *Selected Letters of E. M. Forster: Volume One, 1879–1920*. Ed.
Mary Lago and P. N. Furbank. Cambridge, MA: Harvard UP,
1983.

Furbank, P. N. *E. M. Forster: A Life*. 2 vols. in one. Oxford: Oxford
UP, 1979.

Keynes, J. M. "My Early Beliefs." 1949. *The Bloomsbury Group*. Ed.
S. P. Rosenbaum. Toronto: Toronto UP, 1975. 48–64.

King, Francis. *E. M. Forster*. London: Thames, 1978.

Lago, Mary. "The BBC Broadcasts." *E. M. Forster: A Literary Life*.
New York: St. Martin's, 1995. 92–130.

————. "E. M. Forster: Clapham's Child." *Biography* 14.2 (1991):
117–37.

Stape, J. H. *An E. M. Forster Chronology*. London: Macmillan, 1993.

Trilling, Lionel. *E. M. Forster*. 1943. New York: New Directions,
1964.

Widdowson, Peter. *E. M. Forster's "Howards End": Fiction as History*.
London: Chatto, 1977.

Wyatt-Brown, Anne. "A Buried Life: E. M. Forster's Struggle with
Creativity." *Journal of Modern Literature* 10.1 (1983): 109–24.

# Howards End

"Only connect . . ."

## Chapter 1

One may as well begin with Helen's letters to her sister.

Howards End,<br>Tuesday.

Dearest Meg,

It isn't going to be what we expected. It is old and little, and altogether delightful — red brick. We can scarcely pack in as it is, and the dear knows what will happen when Paul (younger son) arrives tomorrow. From hall you go right or left into dining-room or drawing-room. Hall itself is practically a room. You open another door in it, and there are the stairs going up in a sort of tunnel to the first floor. Three bedrooms in a row there, and three attics in a row above. That isn't all the house really, but it's all that one notices — nine windows as you look up from the front garden.

Then there's a very big wych-elm — to the left as you look up — leaning a little over the house, and standing on the boundary between the garden and meadow. I quite love that tree already. Also ordinary elms, oaks — no nastier than ordinary oaks — pear trees, apple trees, and a vine. No silver birches, though. How-

ever, I must get on to my host and hostess. I only wanted to show
that it isn't the least what we expected. Why did we settle that
their house would be all gables and wiggles, and their garden all
gamboge-coloured paths? I believe simply because we associate
them with expensive hotels — Mrs Wilcox trailing in beautiful
dresses down long corridors, Mr Wilcox bullying porters, etc. We
females are that unjust.

I shall be back Saturday; will let you know train later. They are
as angry as I am that you did not come too; really Tibby is too
tiresome, he starts a new mortal disease every month. How could
he have got hay fever in London? And even if he could, it seems
hard that you should give up a visit to hear a schoolboy sneeze.
Tell him that Charles Wilcox (the son who is here) has hay fever
too, but he's brave, and gets quite cross when we inquire after it.
Men like the Wilcoxes would do Tibby a power of good. But you
won't agree, and I'd better change the subject.

This long letter is because I'm writing before breakfast. Oh, the
beautiful vine leaves! The house is covered with a vine. I looked
out earlier, and Mrs Wilcox was already in the garden. She evidently loves it. No wonder she sometimes looks tired. She was
watching the large red poppies come out. Then she walked off the
lawn to the meadow, whose corner to the right I can just see.
Trail, trail, went her long dress over the sopping grass, and she
came back with her hands full of the hay that was cut yesterday —
I suppose for rabbits or something, as she kept on smelling it. The
air here is delicious. Later on I heard the noise of croquet balls,
and looked out again, and it was Charles Wilcox practising; they
are keen on all games. Presently he started sneezing and had to
stop. Then I hear more clicketing, and it is Mr Wilcox practising,
and then, "a-tissue, a-tissue": he has to stop too. Then Evie comes
out, and does some callisthenic exercises on a machine that is
tacked on to a greengage tree — they put everything to use — and
then she says "a-tissue", and in she goes. And finally Mrs Wilcox
reappears, trail, trail, still smelling hay and looking at the flowers. I
inflict all this on you because once you said that life is sometimes
life and sometimes only a drama, and one must learn to distin-
guish tother from which, and up to now I have always put that
down as "Meg's clever nonsense". But this morning, it really does
seem not life but a play, and it did amuse me enormously to watch
the W.s. Now Mrs Wilcox has come in.

I am going to wear [omission]. Last night Mrs Wilcox wore an
[omission], and Evie [omission]. So it isn't exactly a go-as-you-
please place, and if you shut your eyes it still seems the wiggly
hotel that we expected. Not if you open them. The dog-roses are

too sweet. There is a great hedge of them over the lawn — magnificently tall, so that they fall down in garlands, and nice and thin at the bottom, so that you can see ducks through it and a cow. These belong to the farm, which is the only house near us. There goes the breakfast gong. Much love. Modified love to Tibby. Love to Aunt Juley; how good of her to come and keep you company, but what a bore. Burn this. Will write again Thursday.

Helen.

Howards End,<br>Friday.

Dearest Meg,

I am having a glorious time. I like them all. Mrs Wilcox, if quieter than in Germany, is sweeter than ever, and I never saw anything like her steady unselfishness, and the best of it is that the others do not take advantage of her. They are the very happiest, jolliest family that you can imagine. I do really feel that we are making friends. The fun of it is that they think me a noodle, and say so — at least, Mr Wilcox does — and when that happens, and one doesn't mind, it's a pretty sure test, isn't it? He says the most horrid things about women's suffrage so nicely, and when I said I believed in equality he just folded his arms and gave me such a setting down as I've never had. Meg, shall we ever learn to talk less? I never felt so ashamed of myself in my life. I couldn't point to a time when men had been equal,° nor even to a time when the wish to be equal had made them happier in other ways. I couldn't say a word. I had just picked up the notion that equality is good from some book — probably from poetry, or you. Anyhow, it's been knocked into pieces, and, like all people who are really strong, Mr Wilcox did it without hurting me. On the other hand, I laugh at them for catching hay fever. We live like fighting-cocks, and Charles takes us out every day in the motor — a tomb with trees in it, a hermit's house, a wonderful road that was made by the Kings of Mercia — tennis — a cricket match — bridge — and at night we squeeze up in this lovely house. The whole clan's here now — it's like a rabbit warren. Evie is a dear. They want me to stop over Sunday — I suppose it won't matter if I do. Marvellous weather and the air marvellous — views westward to the high ground. Thank you for your letter. Burn this.

Your affectionate<br>Helen.

---

**I couldn't point to a time when men had been equal:** *Women* would seem to make better sense here than *men*.

Howards End,
Sunday.

Dearest dearest Meg,
I do not know what you will say: Paul and I are in love — the younger son who only came here Wednesday.

## Chapter 2

Margaret glanced at her sister's note and pushed it over the breakfast-table to her aunt. There was a moment's hush, and then the floodgates opened.

"I can tell you nothing, Aunt Juley. I know no more than you do. We met — we only met the father and mother — abroad last spring. I know so little that I didn't even know their son's name. It's all so —" She waved her hand and laughed a little.

"In that case it is far too sudden."

"Who knows, Aunt Juley, who knows?"

"But, Margaret dear, I mean, we mustn't be unpractical now that we've come to facts. It *is* too sudden, surely."

"Who knows!"

"But, Margaret dear —"

"I'll go for her other letters," said Margaret. "No, I won't, I'll finish my breakfast. In fact, I haven't them. We met the Wilcoxes on an awful expedition that we made from Heidelberg to Speyer. Helen and I had got it into our heads that there was a grand old cathedral at Speyer — the Archbishop of Speyer was one of the seven electors — you know — 'Speyer, Mainz and Köln'. Those three sees once commanded the Rhine valley and got it the name of Priest Street."

"I still feel quite uneasy about this business, Margaret."

"The train crossed by a bridge of boats, and at first sight it looked quite fine. But oh, in five minutes we had seen the whole thing. The cathedral had been ruined, absolutely ruined, by restoration; not an inch left of the original structure. We wasted a whole day, and came across the Wilcoxes as we were eating our sandwiches in the public gardens. They too, poor things, had been taken in — they were actually stopping at Speyer — and they rather liked Helen insisting that they must fly with us to Heidelberg. As a matter of fact, they did come on next day. We all took some drives together. They knew us well enough to ask Helen to come and see them — at least, I was asked too, but Tibby's illness prevented me, so last Monday she went alone. That's all. You know as much as I do now. It's a young man out of the unknown. She was to have come back Saturday, but put off till Monday, perhaps on account of — I don't know."

She broke off, and listened to the sounds of a London morning. Their house was in Wickham Place, and fairly quiet, for a lofty promontory of buildings separated it from the main thoroughfare. One had the sense of a backwater, or rather of an estuary, whose waters flowed in from the invisible sea, and ebbed into a profound silence while the waves without were still beating. Though the promontory consisted of flats — expensive, with cavernous entrance halls, full of concierges and palms — it fulfilled its purpose, and gained for the older houses opposite a certain measure of peace. These, too, would be swept away in time, and another promontory would arise upon their site, as humanity piled itself higher and higher on the precious soil of London.

Mrs Munt had her own method of interpreting her nieces. She decided that Margaret was a little hysterical, and was trying to gain time by a torrent of talk. Feeling very diplomatic, she lamented the fate of Speyer, and declared that never, never should she be so misguided as to visit it, and added of her own accord that the principles of restoration were ill understood in Germany. "The Germans," she said, "are too thorough, and this is all very well sometimes, but at other times it does not do."

"Exactly," said Margaret; "Germans are too thorough." And her eyes began to shine.

"Of course I regard you Schlegels as English,"° said Mrs Munt hastily — "English to the backbone."

Margaret learned forward and stroked her hand.

"And that reminds me — Helen's letter —"

"Oh yes, Aunt Juley, I am thinking all right about Helen's letter. I know — I must go down and see her. I am thinking about her all right. I am meaning to go down."

"But go with some plan," said Mrs Munt, admitting into her kindly voice a note of exasperation. "Margaret, if I may interfere, don't be taken by surprise. What do you think of the Wilcoxes? Are they our sort? Are they likely people? Could they appreciate Helen, who is to my mind a very special sort of person? Do they care about Literature and Art? That is most important when you come to think of it. Literature and Art. Most important. How old would the son be? She says 'younger son'. Would he be in a position to marry? Is he likely to make Helen happy? Did you gather —"

---

**I regard you Schlegels as English:** The name *Schlegel* recalls the Schlegel brothers, August Wilhelm von Schlegel (1767–1845) and Friedrich von Schlegel (1772–1829), German poets and thinkers.

"I gathered nothing."

They began to talk at once.

"Then in that case —"

"In that case I can make no plans, don't you see."

"On the contrary —"

"I hate plans. I hate lines of action. Helen isn't a baby."

"Then in that case, my dear, why go down?"

Margaret was silent. If her aunt could not see why she must go down, she was not going to tell her. She was not going to say: "I love my dear sister; I must be near her at this crisis of her life." The affections are more reticent than the passions, and their expression more subtle. If she herself should ever fall in love with a man, she, like Helen, would proclaim it from the house-tops, but as she only loved a sister she used the voiceless language of sympathy.

"I consider you odd girls," continued Mrs Munt, "and very wonderful girls, and in many ways far older than your years. But — you won't be offended? — frankly, I feel you are not up to this business. It requires an older person. Dear, I have nothing to call me back to Swanage." She spread out her plump arms. "I am all at your disposal. Let me go down to this house whose name I forget instead of you."

"Aunt Juley" — she jumped up and kissed her — "I must, must go to Howards End myself. You don't exactly understand, though I can never thank you properly for offering."

"I do understand," retorted Mrs Munt, with immense confidence. "I go down in no spirit of interference, but to make inquiries. Inquiries are necessary. Now, I am going to be rude. You would say the wrong thing; to a certainty you would. In your anxiety for Helen's happiness you would offend the whole of these Wilcoxes by asking one of your impetuous questions — not that one minds offending them."

"I shall ask no questions. I have it in Helen's writing that she and a man are in love. There is no question to ask as long as she keeps to that. All the rest isn't worth a straw. A long engagement if you like, but inquiries, questions, plans, lines of action — no, Aunt Juley, no."

Away she hurried, not beautiful, not supremely brilliant, but filled with something that took the place of both qualities — something best described as a profound vivacity, a continual and sincere response to all that she encountered in her path through life.

"If Helen had written the same to me about a shop-assistant or a penniless clerk —"

"Dear Margaret, do come into the library and shut the door. Your good maids are dusting the banisters."

"— or if she had wanted to marry the man who calls for Carter Paterson,° I should have said the same." Then, with one of those turns that convinced her aunt that she was not mad really, and convinced observers of another type that she was not a barren theorist, she added: "Though in the case of Carter Paterson I should want it to be a very long engagement indeed, I must say."

"I should think so," said Mrs Munt; "and, indeed, I can scarcely follow you. Now, just imagine if you said anything of that sort to the Wilcoxes. *I* understand it, but those good people would think you mad. Imagine how disconcerting for Helen! What is wanted is a person who will go slowly, slowly in this business, and see how things are and where they are likely to lead to."

Margaret was down on this.

"But you implied just now that the engagement must be broken off."

"I think probably it must; but slowly."

"Can you break an engagement off slowly?" Her eyes lit up. "What's an engagement made of, do you suppose? I think it's made of some hard stuff, that may snap, but can't break. It is different to the other ties of life. They stretch or bend. They admit of degree. They're different."

"Exactly so. But won't you let me just run down to Howards House, and save you all the discomfort? I will really not interfere, but I do so thoroughly understand the kind of thing you Schlegels want that one quiet look round will be enough for me."

Margaret again thanked her, again kissed her, and then ran upstairs to see her brother.

He was not so well.

The hay fever had worried him a good deal all night. His head ached, his eyes were wet, his mucous membrane, he informed her, in a most unsatisfactory condition. The only thing that made life worth living was the thought of Walter Savage Landor, from whose *Imaginary Conversations* she had promised to read at frequent intervals during the day.

It was rather difficult. Something must be done about Helen. She must be assured that it is not a criminal offence to love at first sight. A telegram to this effect would be cold and cryptic, a personal visit seemed each moment more impossible. Now the doctor arrived, and

**Carter Paterson:** A parcel delivery firm.

said that Tibby was quite bad. Might it really be best to accept Aunt Juley's kind offer, and to send her down to Howards End with a note? Certainly Margaret was impulsive. She did swing rapidly from one decision to another. Running downstairs into the library, she cried: "Yes, I have changed my mind; I do wish that you would go."

There was a train from King's Cross at eleven. At half past ten Tibby, with rare self-effacement, fell asleep, and Margaret was able to drive her aunt to the station.°

"You will remember, Aunt Juley, not to be drawn into discussing the engagement. Give my letter to Helen, and say whatever you feel yourself, but do keep clear of the relatives. We have scarcely got their names straight yet, and, besides, that sort of thing is so uncivilized and wrong."

"So uncivilized?" queried Mrs Munt, fearing that she was losing the point of some brilliant remark.

"Oh, I used an affected word. I only meant would you please only talk the thing over with Helen."

"Only with Helen."

"Because —" But it was no moment to expound the personal nature of love. Even Margaret shrank from it, and contented herself with stroking her good aunt's hand, and with meditating, half sensibly and half poetically, on the journey that was about to begin from King's Cross.

Like many others who have lived long in a great capital, she had strong feelings about the various railway termini. They are our gates to the glorious and the unknown. Through them we pass out into adventure and sunshine, to them, alas! we return. In Paddington all Cornwall is latent and the remoter west; down the inclines of Liverpool Street lie fenlands and the illimitable Broads; Scotland is through the pylons of Euston;° Wessex behind the poised chaos of Waterloo. Italians realize this, as is natural; those of them who are so unfortunate as to serve as waiters in Berlin call the Anhalt Bahnhof the Stazione d'Italia, because by it they must return to their homes. And he is a chilly Londoner who does not endow his stations with some personality, and extend to them, however shyly, the emotions of fear and love.

To Margaret — I hope that it will not set the reader against her — the station of King's Cross had always suggested infinity. Its very situa-

**Margaret was able to drive her aunt to the station:** As Oliver Stallybrass suggests, this presumably means that Margaret accompanied her aunt in a horse-drawn cab. **the pylons of Euston:** As Stallybrass notes, this refers to Philip Hardwick's Doric arch (1846–48), now demolished.

tion — withdrawn a little behind the facile splendours of St Pancras — implied a comment on the materialism of life. Those two great arches, colourless, indifferent, shouldering between them an unlovely clock, were fit portals for some eternal adventure, whose issue might be prosperous, but would certainly not be expressed in the ordinary language of prosperity. If you think this ridiculous, remember that it is not Margaret who is telling you about it; and let me hasten to add that they were in plenty of time for the train; that Mrs Munt secured a comfortable seat, facing the engine, but not too near it; and that Margaret, on her return to Wickham Place, was confronted with the following telegram:

"All over. Wish I had never written. Tell no one. — Helen."

But Aunt Juley was gone — gone irrevocably, and no power on earth could stop her.

## Chapter 3

Most complacently did Mrs Munt rehearse her mission. Her nieces were independent young women, and it was not often that she was able to help them. Emily's daughters had never been quite like other girls. They had been left motherless when Tibby was born, when Helen was five and Margaret herself but thirteen. It was before the passing of the Deceased Wife's Sister Bill,° so Mrs Munt could without impropriety offer to go and keep house at Wickham Place. But her brother-in-law, who was peculiar and a German, had referred the question to Margaret, who with the crudity of youth had answered, No, they could manage much better alone. Five years later Mr Schlegel had died too, and Mrs Munt had repeated her offer. Margaret, crude no longer, had been grateful and extremely nice, but the substance of her answer had been the same. "I must not interfere a third time," thought Mrs Munt. However, of course she did. She learned, to her horror, that Margaret, now of age, was taking her money out of the old safe investments and putting it into Foreign Things, which always smash. Silence would have been criminal. Her own fortune was invested in Home Rails, and most ardently did she beg her niece to imitate her. "Then we should be together, dear." Margaret, out of politeness, invested a few hundreds in the Nottingham

**Deceased Wife's Sister Bill:** Finally enacted into law in 1907 after decades of opposition by the Church of England, this measure legalized marriage between a man and the sister of his dead wife.

and Derby Railway, and, though the Foreign Things did admirably
and the Nottingham and Derby declined with the steady dignity of
which only Home Rails are capable, Mrs Munt never ceased to rejoice,
and to say: "I did manage that, at all events. When the smash comes
poor Margaret will have a nest-egg to fall back upon." This year Helen
came of age, and exactly the same thing happened in Helen's case; she
also would shift her money out of Consols, but she, too, almost without being pressed, consecrated a fraction of it to the Nottingham and
Derby Railway. So far so good, but in social matters their aunt had accomplished nothing. Sooner or later the girls would enter on the
process known as throwing themselves away, and if they had delayed
hitherto it was only that they might throw themselves more vehemently in the future. They saw too many people at Wickham Place —
unshaven musicians, an actress even, German cousins (one knows what
foreigners are), acquaintances picked up at continental hotels (one
knows what they are too). It was interesting, and down at Swanage no
one appreciated culture more than Mrs Munt; but it was dangerous,
and disaster was bound to come. How right she was, and how lucky to
be on the spot when the disaster came!

The train sped northward, under innumerable tunnels. It was only
an hour's journey, but Mrs Munt had to raise and lower the window
again and again. She passed through the South Welwyn Tunnel, saw
light for a moment, and entered the North Welwyn Tunnel, of tragic
fame.° She traversed the immense viaduct whose arches span untroubled meadows and the dreamy flow of Tewin Water. She skirted
the parks of politicians.° At times the Great North Road° accompanied
her, more suggestive of infinity than any railway, awakening, after a
nap of a hundred years, to such life as is conferred by the stench of
motor-cars, and to such culture as is implied by the advertisements of
anti-bilious pills. To history, to tragedy, to the past, to the future, Mrs
Munt remained equally indifferent; hers but to concentrate on the end
of her journey, and to rescue poor Helen from this dreadful mess.

The station for Howards End was at Hilton,° one of the large villages that are strung so frequently along the North Road, and that
owe their size to the traffic of coaching and pre-coaching days. Being

**North Welwyn Tunnel, of tragic fame:** The site of a pileup of three goods trains
(freight trains) in 1866.    **the parks of politicians:** Doubtless including that of the
magnificent Elizabethan Hatfield House, seat of the marquis of Salisbury.    **Great
North Road:** The main road north from London to Grantham, Newark, Doncaster,
Newcastle, and Scotland.    **Hilton:** A fictitious village, based on Stevenage, near
which in fact are six tumuli (Roman burial mounds, once thought to be Danish).

near London, it had not shared in the rural decay, and its long High Street had budded out right and left into residential estates. For about a mile a series of tiled and slated houses passed before Mrs Munt's inattentive eyes, a series broken at one point by six Danish tumuli that stood shoulder to shoulder along the highroad, tombs of soldiers. Beyond these tumuli habitations thickened, and the train came to a standstill in a tangle that was almost a town.

The station, like the scenery, like Helen's letters, struck an indeterminate note. Into which country will it lead, England or Suburbia? It was new, it had island platforms and a subway, and the superficial comfort exacted by businessmen. But it held hints of local life, personal intercourse, as even Mrs Munt was to discover.

"I want a house," she confided to the ticket-boy. "Its name is Howards Lodge. Do you know where it is?"

"Mr Wilcox!" the boy called.

A young man in front of them turned round.

"She's wanting Howards End."

There was nothing for it but to go forward, though Mrs Munt was too much agitated even to stare at the stranger. But remembering that there were two brothers she had the sense to say to him: "Excuse me asking, but are you the younger Mr Wilcox or the elder?"

"The younger. Can I do anything for you?"

"Oh, well" — she controlled herself with difficulty. "Really. Are you? I —" She moved away from the ticket-boy and lowered her voice. "I am Miss Schlegel's aunt. I ought to introduce myself, oughtn't I? My name is Mrs Munt."

She was conscious that he raised his cap and said quite coolly: "Oh, rather; Miss Schlegel is stopping with us. Did you want to see her?"

"Possibly —"

"I'll call you a cab. No; wait a mo." He thought. "Our motor's here. I'll run you up in it."

"That is very kind —"

"Not at all, if you'll just wait till they bring out a parcel from the office. This way."

"My niece is not with you by any chance?"

"No; I came over with my father. He has gone on north in your train. You'll see Miss Schlegel at lunch. You're coming up to lunch, I hope?"

"I should like to come *up*," said Mrs Munt, not committing herself to nourishment until she had studied Helen's lover a little more.

He seemed a gentleman, but had so rattled her round that her powers of observation were numbed. She glanced at him stealthily. To a feminine eye there was nothing amiss in the sharp depressions at the corners of his mouth, nor in the rather box-like construction of his forehead. He was dark, clean-shaven, and seemed accustomed to command.

"In front or behind? Which do you prefer? It may be windy in front."

"In front if I may; then we can talk."

"But excuse me one moment — I can't think what they're doing with that parcel." He strode into the booking-office, and called with a new voice: "Hi! Hi, you there! Are you going to keep me waiting all day? Parcel for Wilcox, Howards End. Just look sharp!" Emerging, he said in quieter tones: "This station's abominably organized; if I had my way, the whole lot of 'em should get the sack. May I help you in?"

"This is very good of you," said Mrs Munt, as she settled herself into a luxurious cavern of red leather, and suffered her person to be padded with rugs and shawls. She was more civil than she had intended, but really this young man was very kind. Moreover, she was a little afraid of him: his self-possession was extraordinary. "Very good indeed," she repeated, adding: "It is just what I should have wished."

"Very good of you to say so," he replied, with a slight look of surprise, which, like most slight looks, escaped Mrs Munt's attention. "I was just tooling my father over to catch the down train."

"You see, we heard from Helen this morning."

Young Wilcox was pouring in petrol, starting his engine, and performing other actions with which this story has no concern. The great car began to rock, and the form of Mrs Munt, trying to explain things, sprang agreeably up and down among the red cushions. "The mater will be very glad to see you," he mumbled. "Hi! I say. Parcel. Parcel for Howards End. Bring it out. Hi!"

A bearded porter emerged with the parcel in one hand and an entry-book in the other. With the gathering whir of the motor these ejaculations mingled: "Sign, must I? Why the ——— should I sign after all this bother? Not even got a pencil on you? Remember next time I report you to the station-master. My time's of value, though yours mayn't be. Here" — here being a tip.

"Extremely sorry, Mrs Munt."

"Not at all, Mr Wilcox."

"And do you object to going through the village? It is rather a longer spin, but I have one or two commissions."

"I should love going through the village. Naturally I am very anxious to talk things over with you."

As she said this she felt ashamed, for she was disobeying Margaret's instructions. Only disobeying them in the letter, surely. Margaret had only warned her against discussing the incident with outsiders. Surely it was not "uncivilized or wrong" to discuss it with the young man himself, since chance had thrown them together.

A reticent fellow, he made no reply. Mounting by her side, he put on gloves and spectacles, and off they drove, the bearded porter — life is a mysterious business — looking after them with admiration.

The wind was in their faces down the station road, blowing the dust into Mrs Munt's eyes. But as soon as they turned into the Great North Road she opened fire. "You can well imagine," she said, "that the news was a great shock to us."

"What news?"

"Mr Wilcox," she said frankly, "Margaret has told me everything — everything. I have seen Helen's letter."

He could not look her in the face, as his eyes were fixed on his work; he was travelling as quickly as he dared down the High Street. But he inclined his head in her direction, and said: "I beg your pardon; I didn't catch."

"About Helen. Helen, of course. Helen is a very exceptional person — I am sure you will let me say this, feeling towards her as you do — indeed, all the Schlegels are exceptional. I come in no spirit of interference, but it was a great shock."

They drew up opposite a draper's. Without replying, he turned round in his seat, and contemplated the cloud of dust° that they had raised in their passage through the village. It was settling again, but not all into the road from which he had taken it. Some of it had percolated through the open windows, some had whitened the roses and gooseberries of the wayside gardens, while a certain proportion had entered the lungs of the villagers. "I wonder when they'll learn wisdom and tar the roads," was his comment. Then a man ran out of the draper's with a roll of oilcloth, and off they went again.

"Margaret could not come herself, on account of poor Tibby, so I am here to represent her and to have a good talk."

---

**contemplated the cloud of dust:** So dusty had English roads become as a result of motor traffic that Lloyd George's budget of 1909 provided £600,000 per year, out of taxes to be levied on petrol and motor licenses, for the tarring of roads.

"I'm sorry to be so dense," said the young man, again drawing up outside a shop. "But I still haven't quite understood."

"Helen, Mr Wilcox — my niece and you."

He pushed up his goggles and gazed at her, absolutely bewildered. Horror smote her to the heart, for even she began to suspect that they were at cross-purposes, and that she had commenced her mission by some hideous blunder.

"Miss Schlegel and myself?" he asked, compressing his lips.

"I trust there has been no misunderstanding," quavered Mrs Munt. "Her letter certainly read that way."

"What way?"

"That you and she —" She paused, then drooped her eyelids.

"I think I catch your meaning," he said stickily. "What an extra-ordinary mistake!"

"Then you didn't the least —" she stammered, getting blood-red in the face, and wishing she had never been born.

"Scarcely, as I am already engaged to another lady." There was a moment's silence, and then he caught his breath and exploded with, "Oh, good God! Don't tell me it's some silliness of Paul's."

"But you are Paul."

"I'm not."

"Then why did you say so at the station?"

"I said nothing of the sort."

"I beg your pardon, you did."

"I beg your pardon, I did not. My name is Charles."

"Younger" may mean son as opposed to father, or second brother as opposed to first. There is much to be said for either view, and later on they said it. But they had other questions before them now.

"Do you mean to tell me that Paul —"

But she did not like his voice. He sounded as if he was talking to a porter, and, certain that he had deceived her at the station, she too grew angry.

"Do you mean to tell me that Paul and your niece —"

Mrs Munt — such is human nature — determined that she would champion the lovers. She was not going to be bullied by a severe young man. "Yes, they care for one another very much indeed," she said. "I dare say they will tell you about it by and by. We heard this morning."

And Charles clenched his fist and cried, "The idiot, the idiot, the little fool!"

Mrs Munt tried to divest herself of her rugs. "If that is your attitude, Mr Wilcox, I prefer to walk."

"I beg you will do no such thing. I take you up this moment to the house. Let me tell you the thing's impossible, and must be stopped."

Mrs Munt did not often lose her temper, and when she did it was only to protect those whom she loved. On this occasion she blazed out. "I quite agree, sir. The thing *is* impossible, and I *will* come up and stop it. My niece is a very exceptional person, and I am not inclined to sit still while she throws herself away on those who will not appreciate her."

Charles worked his jaws.

"Considering she has only known your brother since Wednesday, and only met your father and mother at a stray hotel —"

"Could you possibly lower your voice? The shop-man will overhear."

"Esprit de classe" — if one may coin the phrase — was strong in Mrs Munt. She sat quivering while a member of the lower orders deposited a metal funnel, a saucepan and a garden squirt beside the roll of oilcloth.

"Right behind?"

"Yes, sir." And the lower orders vanished in a cloud of dust.

"I warn you: Paul hasn't a penny; it's useless."

"No need to warn us, Mr Wilcox, I assure you. The warning is all the other way. My niece has been very foolish, and I shall give her a good scolding and take her back to London with me."

"He has to make his way out in Nigeria. He couldn't think of marrying for years, and when he does it must be a woman who can stand the climate, and is in other ways — Why hasn't he told us? Of course he's ashamed. He knows he's been a fool. And so he has — a damned fool."

She grew furious.

"Whereas Miss Schlegel has lost no time in publishing the news."

"If I were a man, Mr Wilcox, for that last remark I'd box your ears. You're not fit to clean my niece's boots, to sit in the same room with her, and you dare — you actually dare — I decline to argue with such a person."

"All I know is, she's spread the thing and he hasn't, and my father's away and I —"

"And all that I know is —"

"Might I finish my sentence, please?"

"No."

Charles clenched his teeth and sent the motor swerving all over the lane.

She screamed.

So they played the game of Capping Families, a round of which is always played when love would unite two members of our race. But they played it with unusual vigour, stating in so many words that Schlegels were better than Wilcoxes, Wilcoxes better than Schlegels. They flung decency aside. The man was young, the woman deeply stirred; in both a vein of coarseness was latent. Their quarrel was no more surprising than are most quarrels — inevitable at the time, incredible afterwards. But it was more than usually futile. A few minutes, and they were enlightened. The motor drew up at Howards End, and Helen, looking very pale, ran out to meet her aunt.

"Aunt Juley, I have just had a telegram from Margaret; I — I meant to stop your coming. It isn't — it's over."

The climax was too much for Mrs Munt. She burst into tears.

"Aunt Juley dear, don't. Don't let them know I've been so silly. It wasn't anything. Do bear up for my sake."

"Paul," cried Charles Wilcox, pulling his gloves off.

"Don't let them know. They are never to know."

"Oh, my darling Helen —"

"Paul! Paul!"

A very young man came out of the house.

"Paul, is there any truth in this?"

"I didn't — I don't —"

"Yes or no, man; plain question, plain answer. Did or didn't Miss Schlegel —"

"Charles dear," said a voice from the garden. "Charles, dear Charles, one doesn't ask plain questions. There aren't such things."

They were all silent. It was Mrs Wilcox.

She approached just as Helen's letter had described her, trailing noiselessly over the lawn, and there was actually a wisp of hay in her hands. She seemed to belong not to the young people and their motor, but to the house, and to the tree that overshadowed it. One knew that she worshipped the past, and that the instinctive wisdom the past can alone bestow had descended upon her — that wisdom to which we give the clumsy name of aristocracy. High-born she might not be. But assuredly she cared about her ancestors, and let them help her. When she saw Charles angry, Paul frightened, and Mrs Munt in tears, she heard her ancestors say: "Separate those human beings who will hurt each other most. The rest can wait." So she did not ask questions. Still less did she pretend that nothing had happened, as a competent society hostess would have done. She said: "Miss Schlegel, would you take your aunt up to your room or to my room, whichever you think best. Paul, do find Evie, and tell her lunch for six, but I'm not sure whether we shall all be downstairs for it." And when they had obeyed her she turned to her elder son, who still stood in the throbbing, stinking car, and smiled at him with tenderness, and without saying a word turned away from him towards her flowers.

"Mother," he called, "are you aware that Paul has been playing the fool again?"

"It is all right, dear. They have broken off the engagement."

"Engagement — !"

"They do not love any longer, if you prefer it put that way," said Mrs Wilcox, stooping down to smell a rose.


## Chapter 4

Helen and her aunt returned to Wickham Place in a state of collapse, and for a little time Margaret had three invalids on her hands. Mrs Munt soon recovered. She possessed to a remarkable degree the power of distorting the past, and before many days were over she had forgotten the part played by her own imprudence in the catastrophe. Even at the crisis she had cried, "Thank goodness, poor Margaret is saved this!" which during the journey to London evolved into "It had to be gone through by someone," which in its turn ripened into the permanent form of "The one time I really did help Emily's girls was over the Wilcox business." But Helen was a more serious patient. New ideas had burst upon her like a thunderclap, and by them and by their reverberations she had been stunned.

The truth was that she had fallen in love, not with an individual, but with a family.

Before Paul arrived she had, as it were, been tuned up into his key. The energy of the Wilcoxes had fascinated her, had created new images of beauty in her responsive mind. To be all day with them in the open air, to sleep at night under their roof, had seemed the supreme joy of life, and had led to that abandonment of personality that is a possible prelude to love. She had *liked* giving in to Mr Wilcox, or Evie, or Charles; she had *liked* being told that her notions of life were sheltered or academic; that Equality was nonsense, Votes for Women nonsense, Socialism nonsense, Art and Literature, except when conducive to strengthening the character, nonsense. One by one the Schlegel fetishes had been overthrown, and, though professing to defend them, she had rejoiced. When Mr Wilcox said that one sound man of business did more good to the world than a dozen of your social reformers, she had swallowed the curious assertion without a gasp, and had leant back luxuriously among the cushions of his motor-car. When Charles said, "Why be so polite to servants? They don't understand it," she had not given the Schlegel retort of "If they don't understand it, I do." No; she had vowed to be less polite to servants in the future. "I am swathed in cant," she thought, "and it is good for me to be stripped of it." And all that she thought or did or breathed was a quiet preparation for Paul. Paul was inevitable. Charles was taken up with another girl, Mr Wilcox was so old, Evie so young, Mrs Wilcox so different. Round the absent brother she began to throw the halo of Romance, to irradiate him with all the splendour of those happy days, to feel that in him she should draw nearest to the robust ideal. He and she were about the same age, Evie said. Most people thought Paul handsomer than his brother. He was certainly a better shot, though not so good at golf. And when Paul appeared, flushed with the triumph of getting through an examination, and ready to flirt with any pretty girl, Helen met him halfway, or more than halfway, and turned towards him on the Sunday evening.

He had been talking of his approaching exile in Nigeria, and he should have continued to talk of it, and allowed their guest to recover. But the heave of her bosom flattered him. Passion was possible, and he became passionate. Deep down in him something whispered: "This girl would let you kiss her; you might not have such a chance again."

That was "how it happened", or, rather, how Helen described it to her sister, using words even more unsympathetic than my own. But the poetry of that kiss, the wonder of it, the magic that there was in life for hours after it — who can describe that? It is so easy for an Englishman to sneer at these chance collisions of human beings. To the insular cynic and the insular moralist they offer an equal opportunity. It is so easy to talk of "passing emotion", and to forget how vivid the emotion was ere it passed. Our impulse to sneer, to forget, is at root a good one. We recognize that emotion is not enough, and that men and women are personalities capable of sustained relations, not mere opportunities for an electrical discharge. Yet we rate the impulse too highly. We do not admit that by collisions of this trivial sort the doors of heaven may be shaken open. To Helen, at all events, her life was to bring nothing more intense than the embrace of this boy who played no part in it. He had drawn her out of the house, where there was danger of surprise and light; he had led her by a path he knew, until they stood under the column of the vast wych-elm.° A man in the darkness, he had whispered "I love you" when she was desiring love. In time his slender personality faded, the scene that he had evoked endured. In all the variable years that followed she never saw the like of it again.

"I understand," said Margaret — "at least, I understand as much as ever is understood of these things. Tell me now what happened on the Monday morning."

"It was over at once."

"How, Helen?"

"I was still happy while I dressed, but as I came downstairs I got nervous, and when I went into the dining-room I knew it was no good. There was Evie — I can't explain — managing the tea-urn, and Mr Wilcox reading *The Times.*"

"Was Paul there?"

"Yes; and Charles was talking to him about Stocks and Shares, and he looked frightened."

By slight indications the sisters could convey much to each other. Margaret saw horror latent in the scene, and Helen's next remark did not surprise her.

"Somehow, when that kind of man looks frightened it is too awful. It is all right for us to be frightened, or for men of another sort — father, for instance; but for men like that! When I saw all the others so placid, and Paul mad with terror in case I said the wrong thing, I felt for a moment that the whole Wilcox family was a fraud, just a wall of newspapers and motor-cars and golf-clubs, and that if it fell I should find nothing behind it but panic and emptiness."

"I don't think that. The Wilcoxes struck me as being genuine people, particularly the wife."

"No, I don't really think that. But Paul was so broad-shouldered; all kinds of extraordinary things made it worse, and I knew that it would never do — never. I said to him after breakfast, when the others were practising strokes, 'We rather lost our heads,' and he looked better at once, though frightfully ashamed. He began a speech about having no money to marry on, but it hurt him to make it, and I stopped

**until they stood under the column of the vast wych-elm:** The autograph manuscript of *Howards End* has "against the column."

him. Then he said: 'I must beg your pardon over this, Miss Schlegel; I can't think what came over me last night.' And I said: 'Nor what over me; never mind.' And then we parted — at least, until I remembered that I had written straight off to tell you the night before, and that frightened him again. I asked him to send a telegram for me, for I knew you would be coming or something; and he tried to get hold of the motor, but Charles and Mr Wilcox wanted it to go to the station; and Charles offered to send the telegram for me, and then I had to say that the telegram was of no consequence, for Paul said Charles might read it, and though I wrote it out several times he always said people would suspect something. He took it himself at last, pretending that he must walk down to get cartridges, and, what with one thing and the other, it was not handed in at the post office until too late. It was the most terrible morning. Paul disliked me more and more, and Evie talked cricket averages till I nearly screamed. I cannot think how I stood her all the other days. At last Charles and his father started for the station, and then came your telegram warning me that Aunt Juley was coming by that train, and Paul — oh, rather horrible — said that I had muddled it. But Mrs Wilcox knew."

"Knew what?"

"Everything, though we neither of us told her a word, and had known all along, I think."

"Oh, she must have overheard you."

"I suppose so, but it seemed wonderful. When Charles and Aunt Juley drove up, calling each other names, Mrs Wilcox stepped in from the garden and made everything less terrible. Ugh! but it has been a disgusting business. To think that —" She sighed.

"To think that because you and a young man meet for a moment there must be all these telegrams and anger," supplied Margaret.

Helen nodded.

"I've often thought about it, Helen. It's one of the most interesting things in the world. The truth is that there is a great outer life that you and I have never touched — a life in which telegrams and anger count. Personal relations, that we think supreme, are not supreme there. There love means marriage settlements; death, death duties. So far I'm clear. But here's my difficulty. This outer life, though obviously horrid, often seems the real one — there's grit in it. It does breed character. Do personal relations lead to sloppiness in the end?"

"Oh, Meg, that's what I felt, only not so clearly, when the Wilcoxes were so competent, and seemed to have their hands on all the ropes."

"Don't you feel it now?"

"I remember Paul at breakfast," said Helen quietly. "I shall never forget him. He had nothing to fall back upon. I know that personal relations are the real life, for ever and ever."

"Amen!"

So the Wilcox episode fell into the background, leaving behind it memories of sweetness and horror that mingled, and the sisters pursued the life that Helen had commended. They talked to each other and to other people, they filled the tall thin house at Wickham Place with those whom they liked or could befriend. They even attended public meetings. In their own fashion they cared deeply about politics, though not as politicians would have us care; they desired that public life should mirror whatever is good in the life within. Temperance, tolerance and sexual equality were intelligible cries to them; whereas they did not follow our Forward Policy in Tibet° with the keen attention that it merits, and would at times dismiss the whole British Empire with a puzzled, if reverent, sigh. Not out of them are the shows of history erected: the world would be a gray, bloodless place were it entirely composed of Miss Schlegels. But, the world being what it is, perhaps they shine out in it like stars.

A word on their origin. They were not "English to the backbone", as their aunt had piously asserted. But, on the other hand, they were not "Germans of the dreadful sort". Their father had belonged to a type that was more prominent in Germany fifty years ago than now. He was not the aggressive German, so dear to the English journalist, nor the domestic German, so dear to the English wit. If one classed him at all it would be as the countryman of Hegel and Kant, as the idealist, inclined to be dreamy, whose Imperialism was the Imperialism of the air. Not that his life had been inactive. He had fought like blazes against Denmark, Austria, France. But he had fought without visualizing the results of victory. A hint of the truth broke on him after Sedan,° when he saw the dyed moustaches of Napoleon going gray; another when he entered Paris, and saw the smashed windows of the Tuileries. Peace came — it was all very immense, one had turned into an Empire — but he knew that some quality had vanished for which not all Alsace-Lorraine could compensate him. Germany a commercial

---

our Forward Policy in Tibet: An imperial trading initiative; compare, on p. 42, "Germany with colonies here and a Forward Policy there."     Sedan: Battle (September 1, 1870) in which the German army defeated the French troops of Emperor Napoleon III. Paris surrendered in 1871 after a 131-day siege; the annexation of Alsace-Lorraine was a consequence of the German victory.

power, Germany a naval power, Germany with colonies here and a
Forward Policy there, and legitimate aspirations in the other place,
might appeal to others, and be fitly served by them; for his own part,
he abstained from the fruits of victory, and naturalized himself in England. The more earnest members of his family never forgave him, and
knew that his children, though scarcely English of the dreadful sort,
would never be German to the backbone. He had obtained work in
one of our provincial universities, and there married Poor Emily (or
*Die Engländerin*, as the case may be), and as she had money they proceeded to London, and came to know a good many people. But his
gaze was always fixed beyond the sea. It was his hope that the clouds
of materialism obscuring the Fatherland would part in time, and the
mild intellectual light re-emerge. "Do you imply that we Germans are
*stupid*, Uncle Ernst?" exclaimed a haughty and magnificent nephew.
Uncle Ernst replied: "To my mind. You use the intellect, but you no
longer care about it. That I call stupidity." As the haughty nephew did
not follow, he continued: "You only care about the things that you
can use, and therefore arrange them in the following order: money,
supremely useful; intellect, rather useful; imagination, of no use at all.
No" — for the other had protested — "your Pan-Germanism is no
more imaginative than is our Imperialism over here. It is the vice of a
vulgar mind to be thrilled by bigness, to think that a thousand square
miles are a thousand times more wonderful than one square mile, and
that a million square miles are almost the same as heaven. *That* is not
imagination. No, it kills it. When their poets over here try to celebrate
bigness they are dead at once, and naturally. Your poets too are dying,
your philosophers, your musicians, to whom Europe has listened for
two hundred years. Gone. Gone with the little courts that nurtured
them — gone with Esterház and Weimar.° What? What's that? Your
universities? Oh yes, you have learned men, who collect more facts
than do the learned men of England. They collect facts, and facts, and
empires of facts. But which of them will rekindle the light within?"

     To all this Margaret listened, sitting on the haughty nephew's
knee.

     It was a unique education for the little girls. The haughty nephew
would be at Wickham Place one day, bringing with him an even
haughtier wife, both convinced that Germany was appointed by God
to govern the world. Aunt Juley would come the next day, convinced

---

**Esterház and Weimar:** Independent courts that were host to musicians such as Haydn,
Bach, and Liszt, and to writers such as Goethe, Herder, and Schiller.

that Great Britain had been appointed to the same post by the same authority. Were both these loud-voiced parties right? On one occasion they had met, and Margaret with clasped hands had implored them to argue the subject out in her presence. Whereat they blushed, and began to talk about the weather. "Papa," she cried — she was a most offensive child — "why will they not discuss this most clear question?" Her father, surveying the parties grimly, replied that he did not know. Putting her head on one side, Margaret then remarked: "To me one of two things is very clear: either God does not know his own mind about England and Germany, or else these do not know the mind of God." A hateful little girl, but at thirteen she had grasped a dilemma that most people travel through life without perceiving. Her brain darted up and down; it grew pliant and strong. Her conclusion was, that any human being lies nearer to the unseen than any organization, and from this she never varied.

Helen advanced along the same lines, though with a more irresponsible tread. In character she resembled her sister, but she was pretty, and so apt to have a more amusing time. People gathered round her more readily, especially when they were new acquaintances, and she did enjoy a little homage very much. When their father died and they ruled alone at Wickham Place, she often absorbed the whole of the company, while Margaret — both were tremendous talkers — fell flat. Neither sister bothered about this. Helen never apologized afterwards, Margaret did not feel the slightest rancour. But looks have their influence upon character. The sisters were alike as little girls, but at the time of the Wilcox episode their methods were beginning to diverge: the younger was rather apt to entice people, and, in enticing them, to be herself enticed; the elder went straight ahead, and accepted an occasional failure as part of the game.

Little need be premised about Tibby. He was now an intelligent man of sixteen, but dyspeptic and difficult.

## Chapter 5

It will be generally admitted that Beethoven's Fifth Symphony is the most sublime noise that has ever penetrated into the ear of man. All sorts and conditions are satisfied by it. Whether you are like Mrs Munt, and tap surreptitiously when the tunes come — of course, not so as to disturb the others; or like Helen, who can see heroes and shipwrecks in the music's flood; or like Margaret, who can only see the music; or like Tibby, who is profoundly versed in counterpoint, and

holds the full score open on his knee; or like their cousin, Fräulein
Mosebach, who remembers all the time that Beethoven is "echt
Deutsch";° or like Fräulein Mosebach's young man, who can remember nothing but Fräulein Mosebach: in any case, the passion of your
life becomes more vivid, and you are bound to admit that such a noise
is cheap at two shillings. It is cheap, even if you hear it in the Queen's
Hall,° dreariest music-room in London, though not as dreary as the
Free Trade Hall, Manchester; and even if you sit on the extreme left of
that hall, so that the brass bumps at you before the rest of the orches-
tra arrives, it is still cheap.

"Who is Margaret talking to?" said Mrs Munt, at the conclusion of
the first movement. She was again in London on a visit to Wickham Place.

Helen looked down the long line of their party, and said that she
did not know.

"Would it be some young man or other whom she takes an interest in?"

"I expect so," Helen replied. Music enwrapped her, and she could
not enter into the distinction that divides young men whom one takes
an interest in from young men whom one knows.

"You girls are so wonderful in always having — oh dear! We
mustn't talk."

For the Andante had begun — very beautiful, but bearing a family
likeness to all the other beautiful Andantes that Beethoven has written,
and, to Helen's mind, rather disconnecting the heroes and shipwrecks
of the first movement from the heroes and goblins of the third. She
heard the tune through once, and then her attention wandered, and
she gazed at the audience, or the organ, or the architecture. Much did
she censure the attenuated Cupids who encircle the ceiling of the
Queen's Hall, inclining each to each with vapid gesture, and clad in
sallow pantaloons, on which the October sunlight struck. "How awful
to marry a man like those Cupids!" thought Helen. Here Beethoven
started decorating his tune, so she heard him through once more, and
then she smiled at her cousin Frieda. But Frieda, listening to Classical
Music, could not respond. Herr Liesecke, too, looked as if wild horses
could not make him inattentive; there were lines across his forehead,
his lips were parted, his pince-nez at right angles to his nose, and he

---

"echt Deutsch": Authentically German.     the Queen's Hall: The Queen's Hall was,
as Stallybrass notes, a casualty of German bombing in World War II. The Free Trade
Hall, also bombed, was rebuilt and reopened in 1951.

had laid a thick, white hand on either knee. And next to her was Aunt
Juley, so British, and wanting to tap. How interesting that row of
people was! What diverse influences had gone to their making! Here
Beethoven, after humming and hawing with great sweetness, said
"Heigho" and the Andante came to an end. Applause, and a round of
wunderschöning and prachtvolleying° from the German contingent.
Margaret started talking to her new young man; Helen said to her
aunt: "Now comes the wonderful movement: first of all the goblins,
and then a trio of elephants dancing"; and Tibby implored the company generally to look out for the transitional passage on the drum.

"On the what, dear?"

"On the *drum,* Aunt Juley."

"No; look out for the part where you think you have done with
the goblins and they come back," breathed Helen, as the music started
with a goblin walking quietly over the universe, from end to end. Others followed him. They were not aggressive creatures; it was that that
made them so terrible to Helen. They merely observed in passing that
there was no such thing as splendour or heroism in the world. After
the interlude of elephants dancing, they returned and made the observation for the second time. Helen could not contradict them, for, once
at all events, she had felt the same, and had seen the reliable walls of
youth collapse. Panic and emptiness! Panic and emptiness! The goblins
were right.

Her brother raised his finger: it was the transitional passage on
the drum.

For, as if things were going too far, Beethoven took hold of the
goblins and made them do what he wanted. He appeared in person.
He gave them a little push, and they began to walk in a major key instead of in a minor, and then — he blew with his mouth and they were
scattered! Gusts of splendour, gods and demigods contending with
vast swords, colour and fragrance broadcast on the field of battle,
magnificent victory, magnificent death! Oh, it all burst before the girl,
and she even stretched out her gloved hands as if it was tangible. Any
fate was titanic; any contest desirable; conqueror and conquered
would alike be applauded by the angels of the utmost stars.

And the goblins — they had not really been there at all? They were
only the phantoms of cowardice and unbelief? One healthy human
impulse would dispel them? Men like the Wilcoxes, or President

**wunderschöning and prachtvolleying:** The narrator's representation of the German
listeners' cries of *wunderschön* (wonderful) and *prachtvoll* (splendid).

Roosevelt,° would say yes. Beethoven knew better. The goblins really
had been there. They might return — and they did. It was as if the
splendour of life might boil over and waste to steam and froth. In its
dissolution one heard the terrible, ominous note, and a goblin, with
increased malignity, walked quietly over the universe from end to end.
Panic and emptiness! Panic and emptiness! Even the flaming ramparts
of the world might fall.

Beethoven chose to make all right in the end. He built the ramparts up. He blew with his mouth for the second time, and again the
goblins were scattered. He brought back the gusts of splendour, the
heroism, the youth, the magnificence of life and of death, and, amid
vast roarings of a superhuman joy, he led his Fifth Symphony to its
conclusion. But the goblins were there. They could return. He had
said so bravely, and that is why one can trust Beethoven when he says
other things.

Helen pushed her way out during the applause. She desired to be
alone. The music had summed up to her all that had happened or
could happen in her career. She read it as a tangible statement, which
could never be superseded. The notes meant this and that to her, and
they could have no other meaning, and life could have no other meaning. She pushed right out of the building, and walked slowly down the
outside staircase, breathing the autumnal air, and then she strolled
home.

"Margaret," called Mrs Munt, "is Helen all right?"

"Oh yes."

"She is always going away in the middle of a programme," said
Tibby.

"The music has evidently moved her deeply," said Fräulein
Mosebach.

"Excuse me," said Margaret's young man, who had for some time
been preparing a sentence, "but that lady has, quite inadvertently,
taken my umbrella."

"Oh, good gracious me! — I am so sorry. Tibby, run after Helen."

"I shall miss the Four Serious Songs if I do."

"Tibby love, you must go."

"It isn't of any consequence," said the young man, in truth a little
uneasy about his umbrella.

"But of course it is. Tibby! Tibby!"

---

President Roosevelt: Theodore Roosevelt, U.S. president (1901–09).

Tibby rose to his feet, and wilfully caught his person on the backs of the chairs. By the time he had tipped up the seat and had found his hat, and had deposited his full score in safety, it was "too late" to go after Helen. The Four Serious Songs had begun, and one could not move during their performance.

"My sister is so careless," whispered Margaret.

"Not at all," replied the young man; but his voice was dead and cold.

"If you would give me your address —"

"Oh, not at all, not at all"; and he wrapped his greatcoat over his knees.

Then the Four Serious Songs rang shallow in Margaret's ears. Brahms, for all his grumbling and grizzling, had never guessed what it felt like to be suspected of stealing an umbrella. For this fool of a young man thought that she and Helen and Tibby had been playing the confidence trick on him, and that if he gave his address they would break into his rooms some midnight or other and steal his walking-stick too. Most ladies would have laughed, but Margaret really minded, for it gave her a glimpse into squalor. To trust people is a lux-ury in which only the wealthy can indulge; the poor cannot afford it. As soon as Brahms had grunted himself out, she gave him her card and said: "That is where we live; if you preferred, you could call for the umbrella after the concert, but I didn't like to trouble you when it has all been our fault."

His face brightened a little when he saw that Wickham Place was W. It was sad to see him corroded with suspicion, and yet not daring to be impolite, in case these well-dressed people were honest after all. She took it as a good sign that he said to her, "It's a fine programme this afternoon, is it not?" for this was the remark with which he had originally opened, before the umbrella intervened.

"The Beethoven's fine," said Margaret, who was not a female of the encouraging type. "I don't like the Brahms, though, nor the Mendelssohn that came first — and ugh! I don't like this Elgar that's coming."

"What, what?" called Herr Liesecke, overhearing. "The 'Pomp and Circumstance' will not be fine?"

"Oh, Margaret, you tiresome girl!" cried her aunt. "Here have I been persuading Herr Liesecke to stop for 'Pomp and Circumstance', and you are undoing all my work. I am so anxious for him to hear what *we* are doing in music. Oh, you mustn't run down our English composers, Margaret."

"For my part, I have heard the composition at Stettin," said Fräulein Mosebach. "On two occasions. It is dramatic, a little."

"Frieda, you despise English music. You know you do. And English art. And English literature, except Shakespeare, and he's a German. Very well, Frieda, you may go."

The lovers laughed and glanced at each other. Moved by a common impulse, they rose to their feet and fled from "Pomp and Circumstance".

"We have this call to pay in Finsbury Circus, it is true," said Herr Liesecke, as he edged past her and reached the gangway just as the music started.

"Margaret —" loudly whispered by Aunt Juley. "Margaret, Margaret! Fräulein Mosebach has left her beautiful little bag behind her on the seat."

Sure enough, there was Frieda's reticule, containing her address-book, her pocket dictionary, her map of London and her money.

"Oh, what a bother — what a family we are! Fr — Frieda!"

"Hush!" said all those who thought the music fine.

"But it's the number they want in Finsbury Circus —"

"Might I — couldn't I —" said the suspicious young man, and got very red.

"Oh, I would be so grateful."

He took the bag — money clinking inside it — and slipped up the gangway with it. He was just in time to catch them at the swing-door, and he received a pretty smile from the German girl and a fine bow from her cavalier. He returned to his seat upsides with the world. The trust that they had reposed in him was trivial, but he felt that it cancelled his mistrust for them, and that probably he would not be "had" over his umbrella. This young man had been "had" in the past — badly, perhaps overwhelmingly — and now most of his energies went in defending himself against the unknown. But this afternoon — perhaps on account of music — he perceived that one must slack off occasionally, or what is the good of being alive? Wickham Place, W., though a risk, was as safe as most things, and he would risk it.

So when the concert was over and Margaret said, "We live quite near; I am going there now. Could you walk round with me, and we'll find your umbrella?" he said "Thank you" peaceably, and followed her out of the Queen's Hall. She wished that he was not so anxious to hand a lady downstairs, or to carry a lady's programme for her — his class was near enough her own for its manners to vex her. But she found him interesting on the whole — everyone interested the Schlegels on the whole at that time — and while her lips talked culture her heart was planning to invite him to tea.

"How tired one gets after music!" she began.

"Do you find the atmosphere of Queen's Hall oppressive?"

"Yes, horribly."

"But surely the atmosphere of Covent Garden is even more oppressive."

"Do you go there much?"

"When my work permits, I attend the gallery for the Royal Opera."

Helen would have exclaimed, "So do I. I love the gallery," and thus have endeared herself to the young man. Helen could do these things. But Margaret had an almost morbid horror of "drawing people out", of "making things go". She had been to the gallery at Covent Garden but she did not "attend" it, preferring the more expensive seats; still less did she love it. So she made no reply.

"This year I have been three times — to *Faust, Tosca,* and —" Was it "Tannhouser" or "Tannhoyser"? Better not risk the word.

Margaret disliked *Tosca* and *Faust*. And so, for one reason and another, they walked on in silence, chaperoned by the voice of Mrs Munt, who was getting into difficulties with her nephew.

"I do in a *way* remember the passage, Tibby, but when every instrument is so beautiful it is difficult to pick out one thing rather than another. I am sure that you and Helen take me to the very nicest concerts. Not a dull note from beginning to end. I only wish that our German friends would have stayed till it finished."

"But surely you haven't forgotten the drum steadily beating on the low C, Aunt Juley?" came Tibby's voice. "No one could. It's unmistakable."

"A specially loud part?" hazarded Mrs Munt. "Of course I do not go in for being musical," she added, the shot failing. "I only care for music — a very different thing. But still I will say this for myself — I do know when I like a thing and when I don't. Some people are the same about pictures. They can go into a picture gallery — Miss Conder can — and say straight off what they feel, all round the wall. I never could do that. But music is so different to pictures, to my mind. When it comes to music I am as safe as houses, and I assure you, Tibby, I am by no means pleased by everything. There was a thing — something about a faun in French° — which Helen went into ecstasies

**something about a faun in French:** *Prélude à l'après-midi d'un faune* (1892–94) by Achille Claude Debussy (1862–1918).

over, but I thought it most tinkling and superficial, and said so, and I
held to my opinion too."

"Do you agree?" asked Margaret. "Do you think music is so different to pictures?"

"I — I should have thought so, kind of," he said.

"So should I. Now my sister declares they're just the same. We
have great arguments over it. She says I'm dense; I say she's sloppy."
Getting under way, she cried: "Now, doesn't it seem absurd to you?
What *is* the good of the arts if they're interchangeable? What *is* the
good of the ear if it tells you the same as the eye? Helen's one aim is to
translate tunes into the language of painting, and pictures into the language of music. It's very ingenious, and she says several pretty things
in the process, but what's gained, I'd like to know? Oh, it's all rubbish, radically false. If Monet's really Debussy, and Debussy's really
Monet, neither gentleman is worth his salt — that's my opinion."

Evidently these sisters quarrelled.

"Now, this very symphony that we've just been having — she
won't let it alone. She labels it with meanings from start to finish;
turns it into literature. I wonder if the day will ever return when music
will be treated as music. Yet I don't know. There's my brother — behind us. He treats music as music, and oh, my goodness! He makes
me angrier than anyone, simply furious. With him I daren't even
argue."

An unhappy family, if talented.

"But, of course, the real villain is Wagner. He has done more than
any man in the nineteenth century towards the muddling of the arts. I
do feel that music is in a very serious state just now, though extraordinarily interesting. Every now and then in history there do come these
terrible geniuses, like Wagner, who stir up all the wells of thought at
once. For a moment it's splendid. Such a splash as never was. But
afterwards — such a lot of mud; and the wells — as it were, they communicate with each other too easily now, and not one of them will run
quite clear. That's what Wagner's done."

Her speeches fluttered away from the young man like birds. If only
he could talk like this, he would have caught the world. Oh, to acquire
culture! Oh, to pronounce foreign names correctly! Oh, to be well-
informed, discoursing at ease on every subject that a lady started! But
it would take one years. With an hour at lunch and a few shattered
hours in the evening, how was it possible to catch up with leisured
women, who had been reading steadily from childhood? His brain
might be full of names, he might even have heard of Monet and

Debussy; the trouble was that he could not string them together into a
sentence, he could not make them "tell", he could not quite forget
about his stolen umbrella. Yes, the umbrella was the real trouble. Behind Monet and Debussy the umbrella persisted, with the steady beat
of a drum. "I suppose my umbrella will be all right," he was thinking.
"I don't really mind about it. I will think about music instead. I suppose my umbrella will be all right." Earlier in the afternoon he had
worried about seats. Ought he to have paid as much as two shillings?
Earlier still he had wondered, "Shall I try to do without a programme?" There had always been something to worry him ever since
he could remember, always something that distracted him in the pursuit of beauty. For he did pursue beauty, and, therefore, Margaret's
speeches did flutter away from him like birds.

Margaret talked ahead, occasionally saying, "Don't you think so?
Don't you feel the same?" And once she stopped, and said, "Oh, do
interrupt me!" which terrified him. She did not attract him, though
she filled him with awe. Her figure was meagre, her face seemed all
teeth and eyes, her references to her sister and her brother were uncharitable. For all her cleverness and culture, she was probably one of
those soulless, atheistical women who have been so shown up by Miss
Corelli.° It was surprising (and alarming) that she should suddenly say:
"I do hope that you'll come in and have some tea."

"I do hope that you'll come in and have some tea. We should be
so glad. I have dragged you so far out of your way."

They had arrived at Wickham Place. The sun had set, and the
backwater, in deep shadow, was filling with a gentle haze. To the right
the fantastic skyline of the flats towered black against the hues of
evening; to the left the older houses raised a square-cut, irregular parapet against the gray. Margaret fumbled for her latchkey. Of course she
had forgotten it. So, grasping her umbrella by its ferrule, she leant
over the area and tapped at the dining-room window.

"Helen! Let us in!"

"All right," said a voice.

"You've been taking this gentleman's umbrella."

"Taken a what?" said Helen, opening the door. "Oh, what's that?
Do come in! How do you do?"

"Helen, you must not be so ramshackly. You took this

---

**Miss Corelli:** Marie Corelli (1855–1924), best-selling British author of more than
thirty three-volume novels, such as *The Sorrows of Satan* (1895), whose heroine dies re-
penting her atheism.

gentleman's umbrella away from Queen's Hall, and he has had the trouble of coming round for it."

"Oh, I am so sorry!" cried Helen, all her hair flying. She had pulled off her hat as soon as she returned, and had flung herself into the big dining-room chair. "I do nothing but steal umbrellas. I am so very sorry! Do come in and choose one. Is yours a hooky or a nobbly? Mine's a nobbly — at least, I *think* it is."

The light was turned on, and they began to search the hall, Helen, who had abruptly parted with the Fifth Symphony, commenting with shrill little cries.

"Don't you talk, Meg! You stole an old gentleman's silk top-hat. Yes, she did, Aunt Juley. It is a positive fact. She thought it was a muff. Oh, heavens! I've knocked the In and Out card down. Where's Frieda? Tibby, why don't you ever — no, I can't remember what I was going to say. That wasn't it, but do tell the maids to hurry tea up. What about this umbrella?" She opened it. "No, it's all gone along the seams. It's an appalling umbrella. It must be mine."

But it was not.

He took it from her, murmured a few words of thanks, and then fled, with the lilting step of the clerk.

"But if you will stop —" cried Margaret. "Now, Helen, how stupid you've been!"

"What ever have I done?"

"Don't you see that you've frightened him away? I meant him to stop to tea. You oughtn't to talk about stealing or holes in an umbrella. I saw his nice eyes getting so miserable. No, it's not a bit of good now." For Helen had darted out into the street, shouting, "Oh, do stop!"

"I dare say it is all for the best," opined Mrs Munt. "We know nothing about the young man, Margaret, and your drawing-room is full of very tempting little things."

But Helen cried: "Aunt Juley, how can you! You make me more and more ashamed. I'd rather he *had* been a thief and taken all the apostle spoons° than that I — well, I must shut the front door, I suppose. One more failure for Helen."

"Yes, I think the apostle spoons could have gone as rent," said Margaret. Seeing that her aunt did not understand, she added: "You remember 'rent'? It was one of father's words — rent to the ideal, to

---

**apostle spoons:** Silver spoons with handles terminating in the figures of the twelve apostles.

his own faith in human nature. You remember how he would trust strangers, and if they fooled him he would say, 'It's better to be fooled than to be suspicious' — that the confidence trick is the work of man, but the want-of-confidence trick is the work of the devil."

"I remember something of the sort now," said Mrs Munt, rather tartly, for she longed to add: "It was lucky that your father married a wife with money." But this was unkind, and she contented herself with "Why, he might have stolen the little Ricketts picture° as well."

"Better that he had," said Helen stoutly.

"No, I agree with Aunt Juley," said Margaret. "I'd rather mistrust people than lose my little Ricketts. There are limits."

Their brother, finding the incident commonplace, had stolen upstairs to see whether there were scones for tea. He warmed the teapot — almost too deftly — rejected the Orange Pekoe° that the parlour-maid had provided, poured in five spoonfuls of a superior blend, filled up with really boiling water, and now called the ladies to be quick or they would lose the aroma.

"All right, Auntie Tibby," called Helen, while Margaret, thoughtful again, said: "In a way, I wish we had a real boy in the house — the kind of boy who cares for men. It would make entertaining so much easier."

"So do I," said her sister. "Tibby only cares for cultured females singing Brahms." And when they joined him she said rather sharply: "Why didn't you make that young man welcome, Tibby? You must do the host a little, you know. You ought to have taken his hat and coaxed him into stopping, instead of letting him be swamped by screaming women."

Tibby sighed, and drew a long strand of hair over his forehead.

"Oh, it's no good looking superior. I mean what I say."

"Leave Tibby alone!" said Margaret, who could not bear her brother to be scolded.

"Here's the house a regular hen-coop!" grumbled Helen.

"Oh, my dear!" protested Mrs Munt. "How can you say such dreadful things? The number of men you get here has always astonished me. If there is any danger it's the other way round."

"Yes, but it's the wrong sort of men, Helen means."

"No, I don't," corrected Helen. "We get the right sort of man,

**Ricketts picture:** Charles Ricketts (1866–1931), British painter, illustrator, and book designer.     **Orange Pekoe:** A large-leaf grade of tea.

but the wrong side of him, and I say that's Tibby's fault. There ought to be a something about the house — an — I don't know what."

"A touch of the W.s, perhaps?"

Helen put out her tongue.

"Who are the W.s?" asked Tibby.

"The W.s are things I and Meg and Aunt Juley know about and you don't, so there!"

"I suppose that ours is a female house," said Margaret, "and one must just accept it. No, Aunt Juley, I don't mean that this house is full of women. I am trying to say something much more clever. I mean that it was irrevocably feminine, even in father's time. Now I'm sure you understand! Well, I'll give you another example. It'll shock you, but I don't care. Suppose Queen Victoria gave a dinner-party, and that the guests had been Leighton, Millais, Swinburne, Rossetti, Meredith, Fitzgerald, etc. Do you suppose that the atmosphere of that dinner would have been artistic? Heavens, no! The very chairs on which they sat would have seen to that. So with our house — it must be feminine, and all we can do is to see that it isn't effeminate. Just as another house that I can mention, but won't, sounded irrevocably masculine, and all its inmates can do is to see that it isn't brutal."

"That house being the W.s' house, I presume," said Tibby.

"You're not going to be told about the W.s, my child," Helen cried, "so don't you think it. And on the other hand I don't the least mind if you find out, so don't you think you've done anything clever, in either case. Give me a cigarette."

"You do what you can for the house," said Margaret. "The drawing-room reeks of smoke."

"If you smoked too, the house might suddenly turn masculine. Atmosphere is probably a question of touch and go. Even at Queen Victoria's dinner-party — if something had been just a little different — perhaps if she'd worn a clinging Liberty tea-gown instead of a magenta satin —"

"With an Indian shawl over her shoulders —"

"Fastened at the bosom with a Cairngorm pin° —"

Bursts of disloyal laughter — you must remember that they are half German — greeted these suggestions, and Margaret said pensively: "How inconceivable it would be if the Royal Family cared about Art." And the conversation drifted away and away, and Helen's

---

**Cairngorm pin:** A pin featuring the yellow or smoky brown variety of quartz crystal found in the Cairngorm mountain region of Scotland.

cigarette turned to a spot in the darkness, and the great flats opposite were sown with lighted windows, which vanished and were relit again, and vanished incessantly. Beyond them the thoroughfare roared gently — a tide that could never be quiet, while in the east, invisible behind the smokes of Wapping, the moon was rising.

"That reminds me, Margaret. We might have taken that young man into the dining-room, at all events. Only the majolica plate — and that is so firmly set in the wall. I am really distressed that he had no tea."

For that little incident had impressed the three women more than might be supposed. It remained as a goblin footfall, as a hint that all is not for the best in the best of all possible worlds,° and that beneath these superstructures of wealth and art there wanders an ill-fed boy, who has recovered his umbrella indeed, but who has left no address behind him, and no name.

## Chapter 6

We are not concerned with the very poor. They are unthinkable, and only to be approached by the statistician or the poet. This story deals with gentlefolk, or with those who are obliged to pretend that they are gentlefolk.

The boy, Leonard Bast, stood at the extreme verge of gentility. He was not in the abyss, but he could see it, and at times people whom he knew had dropped in, and counted no more. He knew that he was poor, and would admit it; he would have died sooner than confess any inferiority to the rich. This may be splendid of him. But he was inferior to most rich people, there is not the least doubt of it. He was not as courteous as the average rich man, nor as intelligent, nor as healthy, nor as lovable. His mind and his body had been alike underfed, because he was poor, and because he was modern they were always craving better food. Had he lived some centuries ago, in the brightly coloured civilizations of the past, he would have had a definite status, his rank and his income would have corresponded. But in his day the angel of Democracy had arisen, enshadowing the classes with leathern wings, and proclaiming, "All men are equal — all men, that is to say, who possess umbrellas," and so he was obliged to assert gentility, lest

---

**all is not for the best in the best of all possible worlds:** A denial of Dr. Pangloss's optimistic claim in Voltaire's *Candide* (1759).

he slipped into the abyss where nothing counts, and the statements of
Democracy are inaudible.

As he walked away from Wickham Place, his first care was to prove
that he was as good as the Miss Schlegels. Obscurely wounded in his
pride, he tried to wound them in return. They were probably not
ladies. Would real ladies have asked him to tea? They were certainly ill-
natured and cold. At each step his feeling of superiority increased.
Would a real lady have talked about stealing an umbrella? Perhaps they
were thieves after all, and if he had gone into the house they would
have clapped a chloroformed handkerchief over his face. He walked on
complacently as far as the Houses of Parliament. There an empty
stomach asserted itself, and told him that he was a fool.

"Evening, Mr Bast."

"Evening, Mr Dealtry."

"Nice evening."

"Evening."

Mr Dealtry, a fellow clerk, passed on, and Leonard stood wondering whether he would take the tram as far as a penny would take him,
or whether he would walk. He decided to walk — it is no good giving
in, and he had spent money enough at Queen's Hall — and he walked
over Westminster Bridge, in front of St Thomas's Hospital, and
through the immense tunnel that passes under the South-Western
main line at Vauxhall. In the tunnel he paused and listened to the roar
of the trains. A sharp pain darted through his head, and he was conscious of the exact form of his eye sockets. He pushed on for another
mile, and did not slacken speed until he stood at the entrance of a road
called Camelia Road, which was at present his home.

Here he stopped again, and glanced suspiciously to right and left,
like a rabbit that is going to bolt into its hole. A block of flats, constructed with extreme cheapness, towered on either hand. Further
down the road two more blocks were being built, and beyond these an
old house was being demolished to accommodate another pair. It was
the kind of scene that may be observed all over London, whatever the
locality — bricks and mortar rising and falling with the restlessness of
the water in a fountain, as the city receives more and more men upon
her soil. Camelia Road would soon stand out like a fortress, and command, for a little, an extensive view. Only for a little. Plans were out
for the erection of flats in Magnolia Road also. And again a few years,
and all the flats in either road might be pulled down, and new buildings, of a vastness at present unimaginable, might arise where they
had fallen.

"Evening, Mr Bast."

"Evening, Mr Cunningham."

"Very serious thing this decline of the birth-rate in Manchester."

"I beg your pardon?"

"Very serious thing this decline of the birth-rate in Manchester," repeated Mr Cunningham, tapping the Sunday paper in which the calamity in question had just been announced to him.

"Ah, yes," said Leonard, who was not going to let on that he had not bought a Sunday paper.

"If this kind of thing goes on the population of England will be stationary in 1960."

"You don't say so."

"I call it a very serious thing, eh?"

"Good evening, Mr Cunningham."

"Good evening, Mr Bast."

Then Leonard entered Block B of the flats, and turned, not upstairs, but down, into what is known to house-agents as a semibasement, and to other men as a cellar. He opened the door, and cried "Hullo!" with the pseudo-geniality of the Cockney. There was no reply. "Hullo!" he repeated. The sitting-room was empty, though the electric light had been left burning. A look of relief came over his face, and he flung himself into the armchair.

The sitting-room contained, besides the armchair, two other chairs, a piano, a three-legged table and a cosy corner. Of the walls, one was occupied by the window, the other by a draped mantelshelf bristling with Cupids. Opposite the window was the door, and beside the door a bookcase, while over the piano there extended one of the masterpieces of Maude Goodman.° It was an amorous and not unpleasant little hole when the curtains were drawn, and the lights turned on, and the gas stove unlit. But it struck that shallow makeshift note that is so often heard in the modern dwelling-place. It had been too easily gained, and could be relinquished too easily.

As Leonard was kicking off his boots he jarred the three-legged table, and a photograph frame, honourably poised upon it, slid sideways, fell off into the fireplace, and smashed. He swore in a colourless sort of way, and picked the photograph up. It represented a young lady called Jacky, and had been taken at the time when young ladies called Jacky were often photographed with their mouths open. Teeth

---

**Maude Goodman:** London painter (fl. 1874–1901) of genre and humorous pictures of children with titles such as *A Little Coquette* and *Like This Grannie*.

of dazzling whiteness extended along either of Jacky's jaws, and positively weighed her head sideways, so large were they and so numerous. Take my word for it, that smile was simply stunning, and it is only you and I who will be fastidious, and complain that true joy begins in the eyes, and that the eyes of Jacky did not accord with her smile, but were anxious and hungry.

Leonard tried to pull out the fragments of glass, and cut his fingers and swore again. A drop of blood fell on the frame, another followed, spilling over onto the exposed photograph. He swore more vigorously, and dashed into the kitchen, where he bathed his hands. The kitchen was the same size as the sitting-room; through it was a bedroom. This completed his home. He was renting the flat furnished: of all the objects that encumbered it none were his own except the photograph frame, the Cupids and the books.

"Damn, damn, damnation!" he murmured, together with such other words as he had learned from older men. Then he raised his hand to his forehead and said, "Oh, damn it all —" which meant something different. He pulled himself together. He drank a little tea, black and silent, that still survived upon an upper shelf. He swallowed some dusty crumbs of a cake. Then he went back to the sitting-room, settled himself anew, and began to read a volume of Ruskin.

"Seven miles to the north of Venice —"

How perfectly the famous chapter opens! How supreme its command of admonition and of poetry! The rich man is speaking to us from his gondola.

"Seven miles to the north of Venice, the banks of sand, which nearer the city rise little above low-water mark, attain by degrees a higher level, and knit themselves at last into fields of salt morass, raised here and there into shapeless mounds, and intercepted by narrow creeks of sea."

Leonard was trying to form his style on Ruskin: he understood him to be the greatest master of English Prose. He read forward steadily, occasionally making a few notes.

"Let us consider a little each of these characters in succession; and first (for of the shafts enough has been said already), what is very peculiar to this church, its luminousness."

Was there anything to be learned from this fine sentence? Could he adapt it to the needs of daily life? Could he introduce it, with modifications, when he next wrote a letter to his brother, the lay-reader? For example —

"Let us consider a little each of these characters in succession; and first (for of the absence of ventilation enough has been said already), what is very peculiar to this flat, its obscurity."

Something told him that the modifications would not do; and that something, had he known it, was the spirit of English Prose. "My flat is dark as well as stuffy." Those were the words for him.

And the voice in the gondola rolled on, piping melodiously of Effort and Self-Sacrifice, full of high purpose, full of beauty, full even of sympathy and the love of men, yet somehow eluding all that was actual and insistent in Leonard's life. For it was the voice of one who had never been dirty or hungry, and had not guessed successfully what dirt and hunger are.

Leonard listened to it with reverence. He felt that he was being done good to, and that if he kept on with Ruskin, and the Queen's Hall concerts, and some pictures by Watts,° he would one day push his head out of the gray waters and see the universe. He believed in sudden conversion, a belief which may be right, but which is peculiarly attractive to a half-baked mind. It is the basis of much popular religion; in the domain of business it dominates the Stock Exchange, and becomes that "bit of luck" by which all successes and failures are explained. "If only I had a bit of luck, the whole thing would come straight. . . . He's got a most magnificent place down at Streatham and a 20-h.p. Fiat, but then, mind you, he's had luck. . . . I'm sorry the wife's so late, but she never has any luck over catching trains." Leonard was superior to these people; he did believe in effort and in a steady preparation for the change that he desired. But of a heritage that may expand gradually he had no conception: he hoped to come to Culture suddenly, much as the Revivalist hopes to come to Jesus. Those Miss Schlegels had come to it; they had done the trick; their hands were upon the ropes, once and for all. And meanwhile his flat was dark as well as stuffy.

Presently there was a noise on the staircase. He shut up Margaret's card in the pages of Ruskin, and opened the door. A woman entered, of whom it is simplest to say that she was not respectable. Her appearance was awesome. She seemed all strings and bell-pulls — ribbons, chains, bead necklaces that clinked and caught — and a boa of azure feathers hung round her neck, with the ends uneven. Her throat was bare, wound with a double row of pearls, her arms were bare to the

---

**some pictures by Watts:** George Frederick Watts (1817–1904) was highly regarded in his time as a painter and sculptor; by 1910, however, his allegorical paintings, with titles such as *Hope* and *Love and Death* had lost much of their appeal. See the note on p. 272.

elbows, and might again be detected at the shoulder, through cheap lace. Her hat, which was flowery, resembled those punnets, covered with flannel, which we sowed with mustard and cress in our childhood, and which germinated here yes, and there no. She wore it on the back of her head. As for her hair, or rather hairs, they are too complicated to describe, but one system went down her back, lying in a thick pad there, while another, created for a lighter destiny, rippled around her forehead. The face — the face does not signify. It was the face of the photograph, but older, and the teeth were not so numerous as the photographer had suggested, and certainly not so white. Yes, Jacky was past her prime, whatever that prime may have been. She was descending quicker than most women into the colourless years, and the look in her eyes confessed it.

"What ho!" said Leonard, greeting the apparition with much spirit, and helping it off with its boa.

Jacky, in husky tones, replied, "What ho!"

"Been out?" he asked. The question sounds superfluous, but it cannot have been really, for the lady answered, "No," adding, "Oh, I am so tired."

"You tired?"

"Eh?"

"I'm tired," said he, hanging the boa up.

"Oh, Len, I am so tired."

"I've been to that classical concert I told you about," said Leonard.

"What's that?"

"I came back as soon as it was over."

"Anyone been round to our place?" asked Jacky.

"Not that I've seen. I met Mr Cunningham outside, and we passed a few remarks."

"What, not Mr Cunningham?"

"Yes."

"Oh, you mean Mr Cunningham."

"Yes. Mr Cunningham."

"I've been out to tea at a lady-friend's."

Her secret being at last given to the world, and the name of the lady-friend being even adumbrated, Jacky made no further experiments in the difficult and tiring art of conversation. She never had been a great talker. Even in her photographic days she had relied upon her smile and her figure to attract, and now that she was

On the shelf,
On the shelf,
Boys, boys, I'm on the shelf,

she was not likely to find her tongue. Occasional bursts of song (of which the above is an example) still issued from her lips, but the spoken word was rare.

She sat down on Leonard's knee, and began to fondle him. She was now a massive woman of thirty-three and her weight hurt him, but he could not very well say anything. Then she said, "Is that a book you're reading?" and he said, "That's a book," and drew it from her unreluctant grasp. Margaret's card fell out of it. It fell face downwards, and he murmured: "Book-marker."

"Len —"

"What is it?" he asked, a little wearily, for she only had one topic of conversation when she sat upon his knee.

"You do love me?"

"Jacky, you know that I do. How can you ask such questions?"

"But you do love me, Len, don't you?"

"Of course I do."

A pause. The other remark was still due.

"Len —"

"Well? What is it?"

"Len, you will make it all right?"

"I can't have you ask me that again," said the boy, flaring up into a sudden passion. "I've promised to marry you when I'm of age, and that's enough. My word's my word. I've promised to marry you as soon as ever I'm twenty-one, and I can't keep on being worried. I've worries enough. It isn't likely I'd throw you over, let alone my word, when I've spent all this money. Besides, I'm an Englishman, and I never go back on my word. Jacky, do be reasonable. Of course I'll marry you. Only do stop badgering me."

"When's your birthday, Len?"

"I've told you again and again, the eleventh of November next. Now get off my knee a bit; someone must get supper, I suppose."

Jacky went through to the bedroom, and began to see to her hat. This meant blowing at it with short sharp puffs. Leonard tidied up the sitting-room, and began to prepare their evening meal. He put a penny into the slot of the gas-meter, and soon the flat was reeking with metallic fumes. Somehow he could not recover his temper, and all the time he was cooking he continued to complain bitterly.

"It really is too bad when a fellow isn't trusted. It makes one feel so wild, when I've pretended to the people here that you're my wife — all right, all right, you *shall* be my wife — and I've bought you the ring to wear, and I've taken this flat furnished, and it's far more than I can afford, and yet you aren't content, and I've also not told the truth when I've written home." He lowered his voice. "He'd stop it." In a tone of horror, that was a little luxurious, he repeated: "My brother'd stop it. I'm going against the whole world, Jacky.

"That's what I am, Jacky. I don't take any heed of what anyone says. I just go straight forward, I do. That's always been my way. I'm not one of your weak knock-kneed chaps. If a woman's in trouble, I don't leave her in the lurch. That's not my street. No, thank you.

"I'll tell you another thing too. I care a good deal about improving myself by means of Literature and Art, and so getting a wider outlook. For instance, when you came in I was reading Ruskin's *Stones of Venice*. I don't say this to boast, but just to show you the kind of man I am. I can tell you, I enjoyed that classical concert this afternoon."

To all his moods Jacky remained equally indifferent. When supper was ready — and not before — she emerged from the bedroom, saying: "But you do love me, don't you?"

They began with a soup square, which Leonard had just dissolved in some hot water. It was followed by the tongue — a freckled cylinder of meat, with a little jelly at the top, and a great deal of yellow fat at the bottom — ending with another square dissolved in water (jelly: pineapple), which Leonard had prepared earlier in the day. Jacky ate contentedly enough, occasionally looking at her man with those anxious eyes, to which nothing else in her appearance corresponded, and which yet seemed to mirror her soul. And Leonard managed to convince his stomach that it was having a nourishing meal.

After supper they smoked cigarettes and exchanged a few statements. She observed that her "likeness" had been broken. He found occasion to remark, for the second time, that he had come straight back home after the concert at Queen's Hall. Presently she sat upon his knee. The inhabitants of Camelia Road tramped to and fro outside the window, just on a level with their heads, and the family in the flat on the ground floor began to sing "Hark, my soul, it is the Lord".

"That tune fairly gives me the hump," said Leonard.

Jacky followed this, and said that, for her part, she thought it a lovely tune.

"No; I'll play you something lovely. Get up, dear, for a minute."

He went to the piano and jingled out a little Grieg. He played badly and vulgarly, but the performance was not without its effect, for Jacky said she thought she'd be going to bed. As she receded, a new set of interests possessed the boy, and he began to think of what had been said about music by that odd Miss Schlegel — the one that twisted her face about so when she spoke. Then the thoughts grew sad and envious. There was the girl named Helen, who had pinched his umbrella, and the German girl who had smiled at him pleasantly, and Herr someone, and Aunt someone, and the brother — all, all with their hands on the ropes. They had all passed up that narrow, rich staircase at Wickham Place, to some ample room, whither he would never follow them, not if he read for ten hours a day. Oh, it was no good, this continual aspiration. Some are born cultured; the rest had better go in for whatever comes easy. To see life steadily and to see it whole° was not for the likes of him.

From the darkness beyond the kitchen a voice called, "Len?"

"You in bed?" he asked, his forehead twitching.

"M'm."

"All right."

Presently she called him again.

"I must clean my boots ready for the morning," he answered.

Presently she called him again.

"I rather want to get this chapter done."

"What?"

He closed his ears against her.

"What's that?"

"All right, Jacky, nothing; I'm reading a book."

"What?"

"What?" he answered, catching her degraded deafness.

Presently she called him again.

Ruskin had visited Torcello by this time, and was ordering his gondoliers to take him to Murano. It occurred to him, as he glided over the whispering lagoons, that the power of Nature could not be shortened by the folly, nor her beauty altogether saddened by the misery, of such as Leonard.

---

**To see life steadily and to see it whole:** Matthew Arnold, in his sonnet "To a Friend," describes Sophocles as a dramatist who "saw life steadily, and saw it whole"; the phrase becomes a leitmotif in the novel.

## Chapter 7

"Oh, Margaret," cried her aunt next morning, "such a most unfortunate thing has happened. I could not get you alone."

The most unfortunate thing was not very serious. One of the flats in the ornate block opposite had been taken furnished by the Wilcox family, "coming up, no doubt, in the hope of getting into London society". That Mrs Munt should be the first to discover the misfortune was not remarkable, for she was so interested in the flats that she watched their every mutation with unwearying care. In theory she despised them — they took away that old-world look — they cut off the sun — flats house a flashy type of person. But, if the truth had been known, she found her visits to Wickham Place twice as amusing since Wickham Mansions had arisen, and would in a couple of days learn more about them than her nieces in a couple of months, or her nephew in a couple of years. She would stroll across and make friends with the porters, and inquire what the rents were, exclaiming for example: "What! A hundred and twenty for a basement? You'll never get it!" And they would answer: "One can but try, madam." The passenger lifts, the provision lifts, the arrangement for coals (a great temptation for a dishonest porter), were all familiar matters to her, and perhaps a relief from the politico-economical-aesthetic atmosphere that reigned at the Schlegels'.

Margaret received the information calmly, and did not agree that it would throw a cloud over poor Helen's life.

"Oh, but Helen isn't a girl with no interests," she exclaimed. "She has plenty of other things and other people to think about. She made a false start with the Wilcoxes, and she'll be as willing as we are to have nothing more to do with them."

"For a clever girl, dear, how very oddly you do talk. Helen'll *have* to have something more to do with them, now that they're all opposite. She may meet that Paul in the street. She cannot very well not bow."

"Of course she must bow. But look here; let's do the flowers. I was going to say, the will to be interested in him has died, and what else matters? I look on that disastrous episode (over which you were so kind) as the killing of a nerve in Helen. It's dead, and she'll never be troubled with it again. The only things that matter are the things that interest one. Bowing, even calling and leaving cards, even a dinner-party — we can do all those things to the Wilcoxes, if they find it agreeable; but the other thing, the one important thing — never again. Don't you see?"

Mrs Munt did not see, and indeed Margaret was making a most questionable statement — that any emotion, any interest, once vividly aroused, can wholly die.

"I also have the honour to inform you that the Wilcoxes are bored with us. I didn't tell you at the time — it might have made you angry, and you had enough to worry you — but I wrote a letter to Mrs W., and apologized for the trouble that Helen had given them. She didn't answer it."

"How very rude!"

"I wonder. Or was it sensible?"

"No, Margaret, most rude."

"In either case one can class it as reassuring."

Mrs Munt sighed. She was going back to Swanage on the morrow, just as her nieces were wanting her most. Other regrets crowded upon her: for instance, how magnificently she would have cut Charles if she had met him face to face. She had already seen him, giving an order to the porter — and very common he looked in a tall hat. But unfortunately his back was turned to her, and though she had cut his back she could not regard this as a telling snub.

"But you will be careful, won't you?" she exhorted.

"Oh, certainly. Fiendishly careful."

"And Helen must be careful, too."

"Careful over what?" cried Helen, at that moment coming into the room with her cousin.

"Nothing," said Margaret, seized with a momentary awkwardness.

"Careful over what, Aunt Juley?"

Mrs Munt assumed a cryptic air. "It is only that a certain family, whom we know by name but do not mention, as you said yourself last night after the concert, have taken the flat opposite from the Mathesons — where the plants are in the balcony."

Helen began some laughing reply, and then disconcerted them all by blushing. Mrs Munt was so disconcerted that she exclaimed, "What, Helen, you don't mind them coming, do you?" and deepened the blush to crimson.

"Of course I don't mind," said Helen a little crossly. "It is that you and Meg are both so absurdly grave about it, when there's nothing to be grave about at all."

"I'm not grave," protested Margaret, a little cross in her turn.

"Well, you look grave; doesn't she, Frieda?"

"I don't feel grave, that's all I can say; you're going quite on the wrong tack."

"No, she does not feel grave," echoed Mrs Munt. "I can bear witness to that. She disagrees —"

"Hark!" interrupted Fräulein Mosebach. "I hear Bruno entering the hall."

For Herr Liesecke was due at Wickham Place to call for the two younger girls. He was not entering the hall — in fact, he did not enter it for quite five minutes. But Frieda detected a delicate situation, and said that she and Helen had much better wait for Bruno down below, and leave Margaret and Mrs Munt to finish arranging the flowers. Helen acquiesced. But, as if to prove that the situation was not delicate really, she stopped in the doorway and said:

"Did you say the Mathesons' flat, Aunt Juley? How wonderful you are! *I* never knew that the woman who laced too tightly's name was Matheson."

"Come, Helen," said her cousin.

"Go, Helen," said her aunt; and continued to Margaret almost in the same breath: "Helen cannot deceive me. She does mind."

"Oh, hush!" breathed Margaret. "Frieda'll hear you, and she can be so tiresome."

"She minds," persisted Mrs Munt, moving thoughtfully about the room, and pulling the dead chrysanthemums out of the vases. "I knew she'd mind — and I'm sure a girl ought to! Such an experience! Such awful coarse-grained people! I know more about them than you do, which you forget, and if Charles had taken *you* that motor drive — well, you'd have reached the house a perfect wreck. Oh, Margaret, you don't know what you are in for. They're all bottled up against the drawing-room window. There's Mrs Wilcox — I've seen her. There's Paul. There's Evie, who is a minx. There's Charles — I saw him to start with. And who would an elderly man with a moustache and a copper-coloured face be?"

"Mr Wilcox, possibly."

"I knew it. And there's Mr Wilcox."

"It's a shame to call his face copper colour," complained Margaret. "He has a remarkably good complexion for a man of his age."

Mrs Munt, triumphant elsewhere, could afford to concede Mr Wilcox his complexion. She passed on from it to the plan of campaign that her nieces should pursue in the future. Margaret tried to stop her.

"Helen did not take the news quite as I expected, but the Wilcox nerve is dead in her really, so there's no need for plans."

"It's as well to be prepared."

"No — it's as well not to be prepared."

"Why?"

"Because —"

Her thought drew being from the obscure borderland. She could not explain in so many words, but she felt that those who prepare for all the emergencies of life beforehand may equip themselves at the expense of joy. It is necessary to prepare for an examination, or a dinner-party, or a possible fall in the price of stock; those who attempt human relations must adopt another method, or fail. "Because I'd sooner risk it," was her lame conclusion.

"But imagine the evenings," exclaimed her aunt, pointing to the Mansions with the spout of the watering-can. "Turn the electric light on here or there, and it's almost the same room. One evening they may forget to draw their blinds down, and you'll see them; and the next, you yours, and they'll see you. Impossible to sit out on the balconies. Impossible to water the plants, or even speak. Imagine going out of the front door, and they come out opposite at the same moment. And yet you tell me that plans are unnecessary, and you'd rather risk it."

"I hope to risk things all my life."

"Oh, Margaret, most dangerous."

"But after all," she continued with a smile, "there's never any great risk as long as you have money."

"Oh, shame! What a shocking speech!"

"Money pads the edges of things," said Miss Schlegel. "God help those who have none."

"But this is something quite new!" said Mrs Munt, who collected new ideas as a squirrel collects nuts, and was especially attracted by those that are portable.

"New for me; sensible people have acknowledged it for years. You and I and the Wilcoxes stand upon money as upon islands. It is so firm beneath our feet that we forget its very existence. It's only when we see someone near us tottering that we realize all that an independent income means. Last night, when we were talking up here round the fire, I began to think that the very soul of the world is economic, and that the lowest abyss is not the absence of love, but the absence of coin."

"I call that rather cynical."

"So do I. But Helen and I, we ought to remember, when we are tempted to criticize others, that we are standing on these islands, and that most of the others are down below the surface of the sea. The poor cannot always reach those whom they want to love, and they can hardly ever escape from those whom they love no longer. We rich can. Imagine the tragedy last June if Helen and Paul Wilcox had been poor people, and couldn't invoke railways and motor-cars to part them."

"That's more like socialism," said Mrs Munt suspiciously.

"Call it what you like. I call it going through life with one's hand spread open on the table. I'm tired of these rich people who pretend to be poor, and think it shows a nice mind to ignore the piles of money that keep their feet above the waves. I stand each year upon six hundred pounds, and Helen upon the same, and Tibby will stand upon eight, and as fast as our pounds crumble away into the sea they are renewed — from the sea, yes, from the sea. And all our thoughts are the thoughts of six-hundred-pounders, and all our speeches; and because we don't want to steal umbrellas ourselves we forget that below the sea people do want to steal them, and do steal them sometimes, and that what's a joke up here is down there reality —"

"There they go — there goes Fräulein Mosebach. Really, for a German she does dress charmingly. Oh — !"

"What is it?"

"Helen was looking up at the Wilcoxes' flat."

"Why shouldn't she?"

"I beg your pardon, I interrupted you. What was it you were saying about reality?"

"I had worked round to myself, as usual," answered Margaret in tones that were suddenly preoccupied.

"Do tell me this, at all events. Are you for the rich or for the poor?"

"Too difficult. Ask me another. Am I for poverty or for riches? For riches. Hurrah for riches!"

"For riches!" echoed Mrs Munt, having, as it were, at last secured her nut.

"Yes. For riches. Money for ever!"

"So am I, and so, I am afraid, are most of my acquaintances at Swanage, but I am surprised that you agree with us."

"Thank you so much, Aunt Juley. While I have talked theories, you have done the flowers."

"Not at all, dear. I wish you would let me help you in more important things."

"Well, would you be very kind? Would you come round with me to the registry office? There's a housemaid who won't say yes but doesn't say no."

On their way thither they too looked up at the Wilcoxes' flat. Evie was in the balcony, "staring most rudely" according to Mrs Munt. Oh yes, it was a nuisance, there was no doubt of it. Helen was proof against a passing encounter, but — Margaret began to lose confidence. Might it reawake the dying nerve if the family were living close against her eyes? And Frieda Mosebach was stopping with them for another fortnight, and Frieda was sharp, abominably sharp, and quite capable of remarking, "You love one of the young gentlemen opposite, yes?" The remark would be untrue, but of the kind which, if stated often enough, may become true; just as the remark "England and Germany are bound to fight" renders war a little more likely each time that it is made, and is therefore made the more readily by the gutter press of either nation. Have the private emotions also their gutter press? Margaret thought so, and feared that good Aunt Juley and Frieda were typical specimens of it. They might, by continual chatter, lead Helen into a repetition of the desires of June. Into a repetition — they could not do more; they could not lead her into lasting love. They were — she saw it clearly — journalism; her father, with all his defects and wrong-headedness, had been Literature, and had he lived he would have persuaded his daughter rightly.

The registry office was holding its morning reception. A string of carriages filled the street. Miss Schlegel waited her turn, and finally had to be content with an insidious "temporary", being rejected by genuine housemaids on the ground of her numerous stairs. Her failure depressed her, and though she forgot the failure the depression remained. On her way home she again glanced up at the Wilcoxes' flat, and took the rather matronly step of speaking about the matter to Helen.

"Helen, you must tell me whether this thing worries you."

"If what?" said Helen, who was washing her hands for lunch.

"The W.s' coming."

"No, of course not."

"Really?"

"Really." Then she admitted that she was a little worried on Mrs Wilcox's account; she implied that Mrs Wilcox might reach backward into deep feelings, and be pained by things that never touched the other members of that clan. "I shan't mind if Paul points at our house and says, 'There lives the girl who tried to catch me.' But she might."

"If even that worries you, we could arrange something. There's no reason we should be near people who displease us or whom we displease, thanks to our money. We might even go away for a little."

"Well, I am going away. Frieda's just asked me to Stettin, and I shan't be back till after the New Year. Will that do? Or must I fly the country altogether? Really, Meg, what has come over you to make such a fuss?"

"Oh, I'm getting an old maid, I suppose. I thought I minded nothing, but really I — I should be bored if you fell in love with the same man twice and" — she cleared her throat — "you did go red, you know, when Aunt Juley attacked you this morning. I shouldn't have referred to it otherwise."

But Helen's laugh rang true, as she raised a soapy hand to heaven and swore that never, nowhere and nohow would she again fall in love with any of the Wilcox family, down to its remotest collaterals.

## Chapter 8

The friendship between Margaret and Mrs Wilcox, which was to develop so quickly and with such strange results, may perhaps have had its beginnings at Speyer, in the spring. Perhaps the elder lady, as she gazed at the vulgar, ruddy cathedral, and listened to the talk of Helen and her husband, may have detected in the other and less charming of the sisters a deeper sympathy, a sounder judgement. She was capable of detecting such things. Perhaps it was she who had desired the Miss Schlegels to be invited to Howards End, and Margaret whose presence she had particularly desired. All this is speculation: Mrs Wilcox has left few clear indications behind her. It is certain that she came to call at Wickham Place a fortnight later, the very day that Helen was going with her cousin to Stettin.

"Helen!" cried Fräulein Mosebach in awestruck tones (she was now in her cousin's confidence) — "his mother has forgiven you!" And then, remembering that in England the newcomer ought not to call before she is called upon, she changed her tone from awe to disapproval, and opined that Mrs Wilcox was "keine Dame".°

"Bother the whole family!" snapped Margaret. "Helen, stop gig-

"keine Dame": No lady.

gling and pirouetting, and go and finish your packing. Why can't the woman leave us alone?"

"I don't know what I shall do with Meg," Helen retorted, collapsing upon the stairs. "She's got Wilcox and Box° upon the brain. Meg, Meg, I don't love the young genterman; I don't love the young genterman, Meg, Meg. Can a body speak plainer?"

"Most certainly her love has died," asserted Fräulein Mosebach.

"Most certainly it has, Frieda, but that will not prevent me from being bored with the Wilcoxes if I return the call."

Then Helen simulated tears, and Fräulein Mosebach, who thought her extremely amusing, did the same. "Oh, boo hoo! Boo hoo hoo! Meg's going to return the call, and I can't. 'Cos why? 'Cos I'm going to German-eye."

"If you are going to Germany, go and pack; if you aren't, go and call on the Wilcoxes instead of me."

"But, Meg, Meg, I don't love the young genterman; I don't love the young — O lud, who's that coming down the stairs? I vow 'tis my brother. O crimini!"

A male — even such a male as Tibby — was enough to stop the foolery. The barrier of sex, though decreasing among the civilized, is still high, and higher on the side of women. Helen could tell her sister all, and her cousin much, about Paul; she told her brother nothing. It was not prudishness, for she now spoke of "the Wilcox ideal" with laughter, and even with a growing brutality. Nor was it precaution, for Tibby seldom repeated any news that did not concern himself. It was rather the feeling that she betrayed a secret into the camp of men, and that, however trivial it was on this side of the barrier, it would become important on that. So she stopped, or rather began to fool on other subjects, until her long-suffering relatives drove her upstairs. Fräulein Mosebach followed her, but lingered to say heavily over the banisters to Margaret, "It is all right — she does not love the young man — he has not been worthy of her."

"Yes, I know; thanks very much."

"I thought I did right to tell you."

"Ever so many thanks."

"What's that?" asked Tibby. No one told him, and he proceeded into the dining-room, to eat Elvas plums.

---

Wilcox and Box: A reference, as Stallybrass points out, to the musical farce *Cox and Box* (1867), adapted by F. C. Burnand and Arthur Sullivan from J. M. Morton's play *Box and Cox* (1847).

That evening Margaret took decisive action. The house was very quiet, and the fog — we are in November now — pressed against the windows like an excluded ghost. Frieda and Helen and all their luggages had gone. Tibby, who was not feeling well, lay stretched on a sofa by the fire. Margaret sat by him, thinking. Her mind darted from impulse to impulse, and finally marshalled them all in review. The practical person, who knows what he wants at once, and generally knows nothing else, will accuse her of indecision. But this was the way her mind worked. And when she did act no one could accuse her of indecision then. She hit out as lustily as if she had not considered the matter at all. The letter that she wrote Mrs Wilcox glowed with the native hue of resolution.° The pale cast of thought was with her a breath rather than a tarnish, a breath that leaves the colours all the more vivid when it has been wiped away.

Dear Mrs Wilcox,
    I have to write something discourteous. It would be better if we did not meet. Both my sister and my aunt have given displeasure to your family, and, in my sister's case, the grounds for displeasure might recur. As far as I know, she no longer occupies her thoughts with your son. But it would not be fair, either to her or to you, if they met, and it is therefore right that our acquaintance, which began so pleasantly, should end.
    I fear that you will not agree with this; indeed, I know that you will not, since you have been good enough to call on us. It is only an instinct on my part, and no doubt the instinct is wrong. My sister would, undoubtedly, say that it is wrong. I write without her knowledge, and I hope that you will not associate her with my discourtesy.
                                            Believe me,
                                            Yours truly,
                                            M. J. Schlegel.

Margaret sent this letter round by the post. Next morning she received the following reply by hand:

Dear Miss Schlegel,
    You should not have written me such a letter. I called to tell you that Paul has gone abroad.
                                            Ruth Wilcox.

Margaret's cheeks burned. She could not finish her breakfast. She was on fire with shame. Helen had told her that the youth was leaving

---

**native hue of resolution:** Like "the pale cast of thought," a borrowing from *Hamlet*.

England, but other things had seemed more important, and she had forgotten. All her absurd anxieties fell to the ground, and in their place arose the certainty that she had been rude to Mrs Wilcox. Rudeness affected Margaret like a bitter taste in the mouth. It poisoned life. At times it is necessary, but woe to those who employ it without due need. She flung on a hat and shawl, just like a poor woman, and plunged into the fog, which still continued. Her lips were compressed, the letter remained in her hand, and in this state she crossed the street, entered the marble vestibule of the flats, eluded the concierges, and ran up the stairs till she reached the second floor.

She sent in her name, and to her surprise was shown straight into Mrs Wilcox's bedroom.

"Oh, Mrs Wilcox, I have made the baddest blunder. I am more, more ashamed and sorry than I can say."

Mrs Wilcox bowed gravely. She was offended, and did not pretend to the contrary. She was sitting up in bed, writing letters on an invalid-table that spanned her knees. A breakfast-tray was on another table beside her. The light of the fire, the light from the window, and the light of a candle-lamp, which threw a quivering halo round her hands, combined to create a strange atmosphere of dissolution.

"I knew he was going to India in November, but I forgot."

"He sailed on the seventeenth for Nigeria, in Africa."

"I knew — I know. I have been too absurd all through. I am very much ashamed."

Mrs Wilcox did not answer.

"I am more sorry than I can say, and I hope that you will forgive me."

"It doesn't matter, Miss Schlegel. It is good of you to have come round so promptly."

"It does matter," cried Margaret. "I have been rude to you; and my sister is not even at home, so there was not even that excuse."

"Indeed?"

"She has just gone to Germany."

"She gone as well," murmured the other. "Yes, certainly, it is quite safe — safe, absolutely, now."

"You've been worrying too!" exclaimed Margaret, getting more and more excited, and taking a chair without invitation. "How perfectly extraordinary! I can see that you have. You felt as I do: Helen mustn't meet him again."

"I did think it best."

"Now why?"

"That's a most difficult question," said Mrs Wilcox, smiling, and a little losing her expression of annoyance. "I think you put it best in your letter — it was an instinct, which may be wrong."

"It wasn't that your son still —"

"Oh no; he often — my Paul is very young, you see."

"Then what was it?"

She repeated: "An instinct which may be wrong."

"In other words, they belong to types that can fall in love, but couldn't live together. That's dreadfully probable. I'm afraid that in nine cases out of ten Nature pulls one way and human nature another."

"These are indeed 'other words'," said Mrs Wilcox. "I had nothing so coherent in my head. I was merely alarmed when I knew that my boy cared for your sister."

"Ah, I have always been wanting to ask you. How *did* you know? Helen was so surprised when our aunt drove up, and you stepped forward and arranged things. Did Paul tell you?"

"There is nothing to be gained by discussing that," said Mrs Wilcox after a moment's pause.

"Mrs Wilcox, were you very angry with us last June? I wrote you a letter and you didn't answer it."

"I was certainly against taking Mrs Matheson's flat. I knew it was opposite your house."

"But it's all right now?"

"I think so."

"You only think? You aren't sure? I do love these little muddles tidied up."

"Oh yes, I'm sure," said Mrs Wilcox, moving with uneasiness beneath the clothes. "I always sound uncertain over things. It is my way of speaking."

"That's all right, and I'm sure too."

Here the maid came in to remove the breakfast-tray. They were interrupted, and when they resumed conversation it was on more normal lines.

"I must say goodbye now — you will be getting up."

"No — please stop a little longer — I am taking a day in bed. Now and then I do."

"I thought of you as one of the early risers."

"At Howards End — yes; there is nothing to get up for in London."

"Nothing to get up for?" cried the scandalized Margaret. "When

there are all the autumn exhibitions, and Ysaye° playing in the afternoon! Not to mention people."

"The truth is, I am a little tired. First came the wedding, and then
Paul went off, and, instead of resting yesterday, I paid a round of
calls."

"A wedding?"

"Yes; Charles, my elder son, is married."

"Indeed!"

"We took the flat chiefly on that account, and also that Paul could
get his African outfit. The flat belongs to a cousin of my husband's,
and she most kindly offered it to us. So before the day came we were
able to make the acquaintance of Dolly's people, which we had not yet
done."

Margaret asked who Dolly's people were.

"Fussell. The father is in the Indian Army — retired; the brother is
in the Army. The mother is dead."

So perhaps these were the "chinless sunburnt men" whom Helen
had espied one afternoon through the window. Margaret felt mildly
interested in the fortunes of the Wilcox family. She had acquired the
habit on Helen's account, and it still clung to her. She asked for more
information about Miss Dolly Fussell that was, and was given it in
even, unemotional tones. Mrs Wilcox's voice, though sweet and compelling, had little range of expression. It suggested that pictures, concerts and people are all of small and equal value. Only once had it
quickened — when speaking of Howards End.

"Charles and Albert Fussell have known one another some time.
They belong to the same club, and are both devoted to golf. Dolly
plays golf too, though I believe not so well, and they first met in a
mixed foursome. We all like her, and are very much pleased. They
were married on the eleventh, a few days before Paul sailed. Charles
was very anxious to have his brother as best man, so he made a great
point of having it on the eleventh. The Fussells would have preferred it
after Christmas, but they were very nice about it. There is Dolly's
photograph — in that double frame."

"Are you quite certain that I'm not interrupting, Mrs Wilcox?"

"Yes, quite."

"Then I will stay. I'm enjoying this."

Dolly's photograph was now examined. It was signed "For dear

Ysaye: Eugène Ysaye (1858–1931), a Belgian violinist.

Mims", which Mrs Wilcox interpreted as "the name she and Charles
had settled that she should call me". Dolly looked silly, and had one of
those triangular faces that so often prove attractive to a robust man.
She was very pretty. From her Margaret passed to Charles, whose features prevailed opposite. She speculated on the forces that had drawn
the two together till God parted them. She found time to hope that
they would be happy.

"They have gone to Naples for their honeymoon."

"Lucky people!"

"I can hardly imagine Charles in Italy."

"Doesn't he care for travelling?"

"He likes travel, but he does see through foreigners so. What he
enjoys most is a motor tour in England, and I think that would have
carried the day if the weather had not been so abominable. His father
gave him a car of his own for a wedding present, which for the present
is being stored at Howards End."

"I suppose you have a garage there?"

"Yes. My husband built a little one only last month, to the west of
the house, not far from the wych-elm, in what used to be the paddock
for the pony."

The last words had an indescribable ring about them.

"Where's the pony gone?" asked Margaret after a pause.

"The pony? Oh, dead, ever so long ago."

"The wych-elm I remember. Helen spoke of it as a very splendid
tree."

"It is the finest wych-elm in Hertfordshire. Did your sister tell you
about the teeth?"

"No."

"Oh, it might interest you. There are pig's teeth stuck into the
trunk, about four feet from the ground. The country people put them
in long ago, and they think that if they chew a piece of the bark it will
cure the toothache. The teeth are almost grown over now, and no one
comes to the tree."

"I should. I love folklore and all festering superstitions."

"Do you think that the tree really did cure toothache, if one believed in it?"

"Of course it did. It would cure anything — once."

"Certainly I remember cases — you see, I lived at Howards End
long, long before Mr Wilcox knew it. I was born there."

The conversation again shifted. At the time it seemed little more
than aimless chatter. She was interested when her hostess explained

that Howards End was her own property. She was bored when too minute an account was given of the Fussell family, of the anxieties of Charles concerning Naples, of the movements of Mr Wilcox and Evie, who were motoring in Yorkshire. Margaret could not bear being bored. She grew inattentive, played with the photograph frame, dropped it, smashed Dolly's glass, apologized, was pardoned, cut her finger thereon, was pitied, and finally said she must be going — there was all the housekeeping to do, and she had to interview Tibby's riding-master.

Then the curious note was struck again.

"Goodbye, Miss Schlegel, goodbye. Thank you for coming. You have cheered me up."

"I'm so glad!"

"I — I wonder whether you ever think about yourself."

"I think of nothing else," said Margaret, blushing, but letting her hand remain in that of the invalid.

"I wonder. I wondered at Heidelberg."

"*I'm* sure!"

"I almost think —"

"Yes?" asked Margaret, for there was a long pause — a pause that was somehow akin to the flicker of the fire, the quiver of the reading-lamp upon their hands, the white blur from the window; a pause of shifting and eternal shadows.

"I almost think you forget you're a girl."

Margaret was startled and a little annoyed. "I'm twenty-nine," she remarked. "That's not so wildly girlish."

Mrs Wilcox smiled.

"What makes you say that? Do you mean that I have been gauche and rude?"

A shake of the head. "I only meant that I am fifty-one, and that to me both of you — read it all in some book or other; I cannot put things clearly."

"Oh, I've got it — inexperience. I'm no better than Helen, you mean, and yet I presume to advise her."

"Yes. You have got it. Inexperience is the word."

"Inexperience," repeated Margaret, in serious yet buoyant tones. "Of course, I have everything to learn — absolutely everything — just as much as Helen. Life's very difficult and full of surprises. At all events, I've got as far as that. To be humble and kind, to go straight ahead, to love people rather than pity them, to remember the submerged — well, one can't do all these things at once, worse luck,

because they're so contradictory. It's then that proportion comes in —
to live by proportion. Don't *begin* with proportion. Only prigs do
that. Let proportion come in as a last resource, when the better things
have failed, and a deadlock — gracious me, I've started preaching!"

"Indeed, you put the difficulties of life splendidly," said Mrs
Wilcox, withdrawing her hand into the deeper shadows. "It is just
what I should have liked to say about them myself."

## Chapter 9

Mrs Wilcox cannot be accused of giving Margaret much information about life. And Margaret, on the other hand, has made a fair show
of modesty, and has pretended to an inexperience that she certainly
did not feel. She had kept house for over ten years; she had entertained, almost with distinction; she had brought up a charming sister,
and was bringing up a brother. Surely, if experience is attainable, she
had attained it.

Yet the little luncheon party that she gave in Mrs Wilcox's honour
was not a success. The new friend did not blend with the "one or two
delightful people" who had been asked to meet her, and the atmosphere was one of polite bewilderment. Her tastes were simple, her
knowledge of culture slight, and she was not interested in the New
English Art Club,° nor in the dividing-line between Journalism and
Literature, which was started as a conversational hare. The delightful
people darted after it with cries of joy, Margaret leading them, and not
till the meal was half over did they realize that the principal guest had
taken no part in the chase. There was no common topic. Mrs Wilcox,
whose life had been spent in the service of husband and sons, had little
to say to strangers who had never shared it, and whose age was half her
own. Clever talk alarmed her, and withered her delicate imaginings; it
was the social counterpart of a motor-car, all jerks, and she was a wisp
of hay, a flower. Twice she deplored the weather, twice criticized the
train service on the Great Northern Railway. They vigorously assented,
and rushed on, and when she inquired whether there was any news of
Helen her hostess was too much occupied in placing Rothenstein° to
answer. The question was repeated: "I hope that your sister is safe in

**New English Art Club:** Founded in 1886 in opposition to the Royal Academy.
**Rothenstein:** William Rothenstein (1872–1945), painter, connoisseur, and from 1894
to 1908 a member of the New English Art Club; his resignation from the latter and his
disagreements with his (and Forster's) friend Roger Fry may explain Margaret's difficulty in "placing" him.

Germany by now." Margaret checked herself and said: "Yes, thank you; I heard on Tuesday." But the demon of vociferation was in her, and the next moment she was off again.

"Only on Tuesday, for they live right away at Stettin. Did you ever know anyone living at Stettin?"

"Never," said Mrs Wilcox gravely, while her neighbour, a young man low down in the Education Office, began to discuss what people who lived at Stettin ought to look like. Was there such a thing as Stettininity? Margaret swept on.

"People at Stettin drop things into boats out of overhanging warehouses. At least, our cousins do, but aren't particularly rich. The town isn't interesting, except for a clock that rolls its eyes, and the view of the Oder, which truly is something special. Oh, Mrs Wilcox, you would love the Oder! The river, or rather rivers — there seem to be dozens of them — are intense blue, and the plain they run through an intensest green."

"Indeed! That sounds like a most beautiful view, Miss Schlegel."

"So I say, but Helen, who will muddle things, says no, it's like music.° The course of the Oder is to be like music. It's obliged to remind her of a symphonic poem. The part by the landing-stage is in B minor, if I remember rightly, but lower down things get extremely mixed. There is a slodgy theme in several keys at once, meaning mudbanks, and another for the navigable canal, and the exit into the Baltic is in C sharp major, pianissimo."

"What do the overhanging warehouses make of that?" asked the man, laughing.

"They make a great deal of it," replied Margaret, unexpectedly rushing off on a new track. "I think it's affectation to compare the Oder to music, and so do you, but the overhanging warehouses of Stettin take beauty seriously, which we don't, and the average Englishman doesn't, and despises all who do. Now don't say 'Germans have no taste' or I shall scream. They haven't. But — but — such a tremendous but! — they take poetry seriously. They do take poetry seriously."

"Is anything gained by that?"

"Yes, yes. The German is always on the lookout for beauty. He may miss it through stupidity, or misinterpret it, but he is always asking beauty to enter his life, and I believe that in the end it will come.

**it's like music:** The autograph manuscript reads, "it sounds like music."

At Heidelberg I met a fat veterinary surgeon whose voice broke with
sobs as he repeated some mawkish poetry. So easy for me to laugh —
I, who never repeat poetry, good or bad, and cannot remember one
fragment of verse to thrill myself with. My blood boils — well, I'm
half German, so put it down to patriotism — when I listen to the
tasteful contempt of the average islander for things Teutonic, whether
they're Böcklin or my veterinary surgeon. 'Oh, Böcklin,' they say; 'he
strains after beauty, he peoples Nature with gods too consciously.' Of
course Böcklin strains, because he wants something — beauty and all
the other intangible gifts that are floating about the world. So his
landscapes don't come off, and Leader's° do."

"I am not sure that I agree. Do you?" said he, turning to Mrs
Wilcox.

She replied: "I think Miss Schlegel puts everything splendidly";
and a chill fell on the conversation.

"Oh, Mrs Wilcox, say something nicer than that. It's such a snub
to be told you put things splendidly."

"I do not mean it as a snub. Your last speech interested me so
much. Generally people do not seem quite to like Germany. I have
long wanted to hear what is said on the other side."

"The other side? Then you do disagree. Oh, good! Give us your
side."

"I have no side. But my husband" — her voice softened, the chill
increased — "has very little faith in the Continent, and our children
have all taken after him."

"On what grounds? Do they feel that the Continent is in bad
form?"

Mrs Wilcox had no idea; she paid little attention to grounds. She
was not intellectual, nor even alert, and it was odd that, all the same,
she should give the idea of greatness. Margaret, zigzagging with her
friends over Thought and Art, was conscious of a personality that
transcended their own and dwarfed their activities. There was no
bitterness in Mrs Wilcox; there was not even criticism; she was lovable,
and no ungracious or uncharitable word had passed her lips. Yet
she and daily life were out of focus: one or the other must show
blurred. And at lunch she seemed more out of focus than usual, and

---

**Böcklin . . . and Leader's:** Arnold Böcklin (1827–1901) and Benjamin William Leader
(1831–1923) were very different landscape painters, as Margaret's comments here and
the narrator's on p. 155 indicate.

nearer the line that divides daily life from a life that may be of greater importance.

"You will admit, though, that the Continent — it seems silly to speak of 'the Continent', but really it is all more like itself than any part of it is like England. England is unique. Do have another jelly first. I was going to say that the Continent, for good or for evil, is interested in ideas. Its literature and art have what one might call the kink of the unseen about them, and this persists even through decadence and affectation. There is more liberty of action in England, but for liberty of thought go to bureaucratic Prussia. People will there discuss with humility vital questions that we here think ourselves too good to touch with tongs."

"I do not want to go to Prussia," said Mrs Wilcox — "not even to see that interesting view that you were describing. And for discussing with humility I am too old. We never discuss anything at Howards End."

"Then you ought to!" said Margaret. "Discussion keeps a house alive. It cannot stand by bricks and mortar alone."

"It cannot stand without them," said Mrs Wilcox, unexpectedly catching on to the thought, and rousing, for the first and last time, a faint hope in the breasts of the delightful people. "It cannot stand without them, and I sometimes think — but I cannot expect your generation to agree, for even my daughter disagrees with me here."

"Never mind us or her. Do say!"

"I sometimes think that it is wiser to leave action and discussion to men."

There was a little silence.

"One admits that the arguments against the suffrage *are* extraordinarily strong," said a girl opposite, leaning forward and crumbling her bread.

"Are they? I never follow any arguments. I am only too thankful not to have a vote myself."

"We didn't mean the vote, though, did we?" supplied Margaret. "Aren't we differing on something much wider, Mrs Wilcox? Whether women are to remain what they have been since the dawn of history; or whether, since men have moved forward so far, they too may move forward a little now. I say they may. I would even admit a biological change."

"I don't know, I don't know."

"I must be getting back to my overhanging warehouse," said the man. "They've turned disgracefully strict."

Mrs Wilcox also rose.

"Oh, but come upstairs for a little. Miss Quested° plays. Do you like MacDowell?° Do you mind him only having two noises? If you must really go, I'll see you out. Won't you even have coffee?"

They left the dining-room, closing the door behind them, and as Mrs Wilcox buttoned up her jacket she said: "What an interesting life you all lead in London!"

"No, we don't," said Margaret, with a sudden revulsion. "We lead the lives of gibbering monkeys. Mrs Wilcox — really — we have something quiet and stable at the bottom. We really have. All my friends have. Don't pretend you enjoyed lunch, for you loathed it, but forgive me by coming again, alone, or by asking me to you."

"I am used to young people," said Mrs Wilcox, and with each word she spoke the outlines of known things grew dim. "I hear a great deal of chatter at home, for we, like you, entertain a great deal. With us it is more sport and politics, but — I enjoyed my lunch very much, Miss Schlegel, dear, and am not pretending, and only wish I could have joined in more. For one thing, I'm not particularly well just today. For another, you younger people move so quickly that it dazes me. Charles is the same, Dolly the same. But we are all in the same boat, old and young. I never forget that."

They were silent for a moment. Then, with a newborn emotion, they shook hands. The conversation ceased suddenly when Margaret re-entered the dining-room: her friends had been talking over her new friend, and had dismissed her as uninteresting.

## Chapter 10

Several days passed.

Was Mrs Wilcox one of the unsatisfactory people — there are many of them — who dangle intimacy and then withdraw it? They evoke our interests and affections, and keep the life of the spirit dawdling round them. Then they withdraw. When physical passion is involved, there is a definite name for such behaviour — flirting — and if carried far enough it is punishable by law. But no law — not public opinion even — punishes those who coquette with friendship, though

---

**Miss Quested:** Perhaps the same Miss (Adela) Quested who appears in *A Passage to India*.    **MacDowell:** Edward Alexander MacDowell (1860–1908), American composer and pianist.

the dull ache that they inflict, the sense of misdirected effort and ex-
haustion, may be as intolerable. Was she one of these?

Margaret feared so at first, for, with a Londoner's impatience, she
wanted everything to be settled up immediately. She mistrusted the
periods of quiet that are essential to true growth. Desiring to book
Mrs Wilcox as a friend, she pressed on the ceremony, pencil, as it were,
in hand, pressing the more because the rest of the family were away,
and the opportunity seemed favourable. But the elder woman would
not be hurried. She refused to fit in with the Wickham Place set, or to
reopen discussion of Helen and Paul, whom Margaret would have uti-
lized as a short cut. She took her time, or perhaps let time take her,
and when the crisis did come all was ready.

The crisis opened with a message: would Miss Schlegel come shopping? Christmas was nearing, and Mrs Wilcox felt behindhand with
the presents. She had taken some more days in bed, and must make up
for lost time. Margaret accepted, and at eleven o'clock one cheerless
morning they started out in a brougham.°

"First of all," began Margaret, "we must make a list and tick off
the people's names. My aunt always does, and this fog may thicken up
any moment. Have you any ideas?"

"I thought we would go to Harrod's or the Haymarket Stores,"
said Mrs Wilcox rather hopelessly. "Everything is sure to be there. I
am not a good shopper. The din is so confusing, and your aunt is
quite right — one ought to make a list. Take my notebook, then, and
write your own name at the top of the page."

"Oh, hooray!" said Margaret, writing it. "How very kind of you to
start with me!" But she did not want to receive anything expensive.
Their acquaintance was singular rather than intimate, and she divined
that the Wilcox clan would resent any expenditure on outsiders; the
more compact families do. She did not want to be thought a second
Helen, who would snatch presents since she could not snatch young
men, nor to be exposed, like a second Aunt Juley, to the insults of
Charles. A certain austerity of demeanour was best, and she added: "I
don't really want a Yuletide gift, though. In fact, I'd rather not."

"Why?"

"Because I've odd ideas about Christmas. Because I have all that
money can buy. I want more people, but no more things."

---

**brougham:** A light, closed carriage named after the Whig politician Lord Brougham
(1778–1868).

"I should like to give you something worth your acquaintance, Miss Schlegel, in memory of your kindness to me during my lonely fortnight. It has so happened that I have been left alone, and you have stopped me from brooding. I am too apt to brood."

"If that is so," said Margaret, "if I have happened to be of use to you, which I didn't know, you cannot pay me back with anything tangible."

"I suppose not, but one would like to. Perhaps I shall think of something as we go about."

Her name remained at the head of the list, but nothing was written opposite it. They drove from shop to shop. The air was white, and when they alighted it tasted like cold pennies. At times they passed through a clot of gray. Mrs Wilcox's vitality was low that morning, and it was Margaret who decided on a horse for this little girl, a golliwog for that, for the rector's wife a copper warming-tray. "We always give the servants money." "Yes, do you, yes, much easier," replied Margaret, but felt the grotesque impact of the unseen upon the seen, and saw issuing from a forgotten manger at Bethlehem this torrent of coins and toys. Vulgarity reigned. Public-houses, besides their usual exhortation against temperance reform, invited men to "Join our Christmas goose club" — one bottle of gin, etc., or two, according to subscription. A poster of a woman in tights heralded the Christmas pantomime, and little red devils, who had come in again that year, were prevalent upon the Christmas-cards. Margaret was no morbid idealist. She did not wish this spate of business and self-advertisement checked. It was only the occasion of it that struck her with amazement annually. How many of these vacillating shoppers and tired shop-assistants realized that it was a divine event that drew them together? She realized it, though standing outside in the matter. She was not a Christian in the accepted sense; she did not believe that God had ever worked among us as a young artisan. These people, or most of them, believed it, and, if pressed, would affirm it in words. But the visible signs of their belief were Regent Street or Drury Lane, a little mud displaced, a little money spent, a little food cooked, eaten and forgotten. Inadequate. But in public who shall express the unseen adequately? It is private life that holds out the mirror to infinity; personal intercourse, and that alone, that ever hints at a personality beyond our daily vision.

"No, I do like Christmas on the whole," she announced. "In its clumsy way, it does approach Peace and Goodwill. But oh, it is clumsier every year."

"Is it? I am only used to country Christmases."

"We are usually in London, and play the game with vigour — carols at the Abbey, clumsy midday meal, clumsy dinner for the maids, followed by Christmas-tree and dancing of poor children, with songs from Helen. The drawing-room does very well for that. We put the tree in the powder-closet, and draw a curtain when the candles are lighted, and with the looking-glass behind it looks quite pretty. I wish we might have a powder-closet in our next house. Of course, the tree has to be very small, and the presents don't hang on it. No; the presents reside in a sort of rocky landscape made of crumpled brown paper."

"You spoke of your 'next house', Miss Schlegel. Then are you leaving Wickham Place?"

"Yes, in two or three years, when the lease expires. We must."

"Have you been there long?"

"All our lives."

"You will be very sorry to leave it."

"I suppose so. We scarcely realize it yet. My father —" She broke off, for they had reached the stationery department of the Haymarket Stores, and Mrs Wilcox wanted to order some private greeting-cards.

"If possible, something distinctive," she sighed. At the counter she found a friend, bent on the same errand, and conversed with her insipidly, wasting much time. "My husband and our daughter are motoring." "Bertha too? Oh, fancy, what a coincidence!" Margaret, though not practical, could shine in such company as this. While they talked, she went through a volume of specimen cards, and submitted one for Mrs Wilcox's inspection. Mrs Wilcox was delighted — so original, words so sweet; she would order a hundred like that, and could never be sufficiently grateful. Then, just as the assistant was booking the order, she said: "Do you know, I'll wait. On second thoughts, I'll wait. There's plenty of time still, isn't there, and I shall be able to get Evie's opinion."

They returned to the carriage by devious paths; when they were in, she said, "But couldn't you get it renewed?"

"I beg your pardon?" asked Margaret.

"The lease, I mean."

"Oh, the lease! Have you been thinking of that all the time? How very kind of you!"

"Surely something could be done."

"No; values have risen too enormously. They mean to pull down Wickham Place, and build flats like yours."

"But how horrible!"

"Landlords are horrible."

Then she said vehemently: "It is monstrous, Miss Schlegel; it isn't right. I had no idea that this was hanging over you. I do pity you from the bottom of my heart. To be parted from your house, your father's house — it oughtn't to be allowed. It is worse than dying. I would rather die than — oh,° poor girls! Can what they call civilization be right, if people mayn't die in the room where they were born? My dear, I am so sorry —"

Margaret did not know what to say. Mrs Wilcox had been over-tired by the shopping, and was inclined to hysteria.

"Howards End was nearly pulled down once. It would have killed me."

"Howards End must be a very different house to ours. We are fond of ours, but there is nothing distinctive about it. As you saw, it is an ordinary London house. We shall easily find another."

"So you think."

"Again my lack of experience, I suppose!" said Margaret, easing away from the subject. "I can't say anything when you take up that line, Mrs Wilcox. I wish I could see myself as you see me — foreshort-ened into a *Backfisch*.° Quite the ingénue. Very charming — wonder-fully well read for my age, but incapable —"

Mrs Wilcox would not be deterred. "Come down with me to Howards End now," she said, more vehemently than ever. "I want you to see it. You have never seen it. I want to hear what you say about it, for you do put things so wonderfully."

Margaret glanced at the pitiless air and then at the tired face of her companion. "Later on I should love it," she continued, "but it's hardly the weather for such an expedition, and we ought to start when we're fresh. Isn't the house shut up, too?"

She received no answer. Mrs Wilcox appeared to be annoyed.

"Might I come some other day?"

Mrs Wilcox leant forward and tapped the glass. "Back to Wickham Place, please!" was her order to the coachman. Margaret had been snubbed.

"A thousand thanks, Miss Schlegel, for all your help."

"Not at all."

"It is such a comfort to get the presents off my mind — the Christmas-cards especially. I do admire your choice."

---

***Backfisch:*** Literally, "baked fish"; as Margaret's comments imply, the word is a deprecia-tory term for a young woman.

It was her turn to receive no answer. In her turn Margaret became annoyed.

"My husband and Evie will be back the day after tomorrow. That is why I dragged you out shopping today. I stayed in town chiefly to shop, but got through nothing, and now he writes that they must cut their tour short, the weather is so bad, and the police traps have been so bad — nearly as bad as in Surrey. Ours is such a careful chauffeur, and my husband feels it particularly hard that they should be treated like road-hogs."

"Why?"

"Well, naturally he — he isn't a road-hog."

"He was exceeding the speed limit, I conclude. He must expect to suffer with the lower animals."

Mrs Wilcox was silenced. In growing discomfort they drove homewards. The city seemed satanic, the narrower streets oppressing like the galleries of a mine. No harm was done by the fog to trade, for it lay high, and the lighted windows of the shops were thronged with customers. It was rather a darkening of the spirit, which fell back upon itself, to find a more grievous darkness within. Margaret nearly spoke a dozen times, but something throttled her. She felt petty and awkward, and her meditations on Christmas grew more cynical. Peace? It may bring other gifts, but is there a single Londoner to whom Christmas is peaceful? The craving for excitement and for elaboration has ruined that blessing. Goodwill? Had she seen any example of it in the hordes of purchasers? Or in herself? She had failed to respond to this invitation merely because it was a little queer and imaginative — she, whose birthright it was to nourish imagination! Better to have accepted, to have tired themselves a little by the journey, than coldly to reply, "Might I come some other day?" Her cynicism left her. There would be no other day. This shadowy woman would never ask her again.

They parted at the Mansions. Mrs Wilcox went in after due civilities, and Margaret watched the tall, lonely figure sweep up the hall to the lift. As the glass doors closed on it she had the sense of an imprisonment. The beautiful head disappeared first, still buried in the muff; the long trailing skirt followed. A woman of undefinable rarity was going up heavenward, like a specimen in a bottle. And into what a heaven — a vault as of hell, sooty black, from which soots descended!

At lunch her brother, seeing her inclined for silence, insisted on talking. Tibby was not ill-natured, but from babyhood something drove him to do the unwelcome and the unexpected. Now he gave her a long account of the day-school that he sometimes patronized. The account was interesting, and she had often pressed him for it before, but she could not attend now, for her mind was focused on the invisible. She discerned that Mrs Wilcox, though a loving wife and mother, had only one passion in life — her house — and that the moment was solemn when she invited a friend to share this passion with her. To answer "another day" was to answer as a fool. "Another day" will do for bricks and mortar, but not for the Holy of Holies into which Howards End had been transfigured. Her own curiosity was slight. She had heard more than enough about it in the summer. The nine windows, the vine and the wych-elm had no pleasant connections for her, and she would have preferred to spend the afternoon at a concert. But imagination triumphed. While her brother held forth she determined to go, at whatever cost, and to compel Mrs Wilcox to go too. When lunch was over she stepped over to the flats.

Mrs Wilcox had just gone away for the night.

Margaret said that it was of no consequence, hurried downstairs, and took a hansom to King's Cross. She was convinced that the escapade was important, though it would have puzzled her to say why. There was question of imprisonment and escape, and, though she did not know the time of the train, she strained her eyes for St. Pancras's clock.

Then the clock of King's Cross swung into sight, a second moon in that infernal sky, and her cab drew up at the station. There was a train for Hilton in five minutes. She took a ticket, asking in her agitation for a single. As she did so, a grave and happy voice saluted her and thanked her.

"I will come if I still may," said Margaret, laughing nervously.

"You are coming to sleep, dear, too. It is in the morning that my house is most beautiful. You are coming to stop. I cannot show you my meadow properly except at sunrise. These fogs" — she pointed at the station roof— "never spread far. I dare say they are sitting in the sun in Hertfordshire, and you will never repent joining them."

"I shall never repent joining you."

"It is the same."

They began the walk up the long platform. Far at its end stood the train, breasting the darkness without. They never reached it. Before imagination could triumph, there were cries of "Mother! Mother!" and a heavy-browed girl darted out of the cloakroom and seized Mrs Wilcox by the arm.

"Evie!" she gasped. "Evie, my pet —"

The girl called: "Father! I say! Look who's here."

"Evie, dearest girl, why aren't you in Yorkshire?"

"No — motor smash — changed plans — father's coming."

"Why, Ruth!" cried Mr Wilcox, joining them. "What in the name of all that's wonderful are you doing here, Ruth?"

Mrs Wilcox had recovered herself.

"Oh, Henry dear! — here's a lovely surprise — but let me introduce — but I think you know Miss Schlegel."

"Oh, yes," he replied, not greatly interested. "But how's yourself, Ruth?"

"Fit as a fiddle," she answered gaily.

"So are we, and so was our car, which ran A1 as far as Ripon, but there a wretched horse and cart which a fool of a driver —"

"Miss Schlegel, our little outing must be for another day."

"I was saying that this fool of a driver, as the policeman himself admits —"

"Another day, Mrs Wilcox. Of course."

"— But as we're insured against third-party risks, it won't so much matter —"

"— Cart and car being practically at right angles —"

The voices of the happy family rose high. Margaret was left alone. No one wanted her. Mrs Wilcox walked out of King's Cross between her husband and her daughter, listening to both of them.


## Chapter 11

The funeral was over. The carriages had rolled away through the soft mud, and only the poor remained. They approached to the newly dug shaft and looked their last at the coffin, now almost hidden beneath the spadefuls of clay. It was their moment. Most of them were women from the dead woman's district, to whom black garments had been served out by Mr Wilcox's orders. Pure curiosity had brought others. They thrilled with the excitement of a death, and of a rapid death, and stood in groups or moved between the graves, like drops of ink. The son of one of them, a woodcutter, was perched high above their heads, pollarding one of the churchyard elms. From where he sat he could see the village of Hilton, strung upon the North Road, with its accreting suburbs; the sunset beyond, scarlet and orange, winking at him beneath brows of gray; the church; the plantations; and behind him an unspoilt country of fields and farms. But he, too, was rolling the event luxuriously in his mouth. He tried to tell his mother down below all that he had felt when he saw the coffin approaching: how he could not leave his work, and yet did not like to go on with it; how he had almost slipped out of the tree, he was so upset; the rooks had cawed, and no wonder — it was as if rooks knew too. His mother claimed the prophetic power herself — she had seen a strange look about Mrs Wilcox for some time. London had done the mischief, said others. She had been a kind lady; her grandmother had been kind, too — a plainer person, but very kind. Ah, the old sort was dying out! Mr Wilcox, he was a kind gentleman. They advanced to the topic again and again, dully, but with exaltation. The funeral of a rich person was to them what the funeral of Alcestis or Ophelia° is to the educated. It was Art; though remote from life, it enhanced life's values, and they witnessed it avidly.

The gravediggers, who had kept up an undercurrent of disapproval — they disliked Charles; it was not a moment to speak of such things, but they did not like Charles Wilcox — the gravediggers finished their work and piled up the wreaths and crosses above it. The sun set over Hilton: the gray brows of the evening flushed a little, and were cleft with one scarlet frown. Chattering sadly to each other, the mourners passed through the lych-gate and traversed the chestnut avenues that led down to the village. The young woodcutter stayed a little longer, poised above the silence and swaying rhythmically. At last the bough fell beneath his saw. With a grunt, he descended, his thoughts dwelling no longer on death, but on love, for he was mating. He stopped as he passed the new grave; a sheaf of tawny chrysanthemums had caught his eye. "They didn't ought to have coloured flowers at buryings," he reflected. Trudging on a few steps, he stopped again, looked furtively at the dusk, turned back, wrenched a chrysanthemum from the sheaf, and hid it in his pocket.

After him came silence absolute. The cottage that abutted on the churchyard was empty, and no other house stood near. Hour after hour the scene of the interment remained without an eye to witness it. Clouds drifted over it from the west; or the church may have been a ship, high-prowed, steering with all its company towards infinity. Towards morning the air grew colder, the sky clearer, the surface of the earth hard and sparkling above the prostrate dead. The woodcutter, returning after a night of joy, reflected: "They lilies, they chrysants; it's a pity I didn't take them all."

Alcestis or Ophelia: Heroines mistreated by men in, respectively, Euripides' *Alcestis* and Shakespeare's *Hamlet*.

Up at Howards End they were attempting breakfast. Charles and Evie sat in the dining-room, with Mrs Charles. Their father, who could not bear to see a face, breakfasted upstairs. He suffered acutely. Pain came over him in spasms, as if it was physical, and, even while he was about to eat, his eyes would fill with tears, and he would lay down the morsel untasted.

He remembered his wife's even goodness during thirty years. Not anything in detail — not courtship or early raptures — but just the un-varying virtue, that seemed to him a woman's noblest quality. So many women are capricious, breaking into odd flaws of passion or frivolity. Not so his wife. Year after year, summer and winter, as bride and mother, she had been the same, he had always trusted her. Her tenderness! Her innocence! The wonderful innocence that was hers by the gift of God. Ruth knew no more of worldly wickedness and wisdom than did the flowers in her garden, or the grass in her field. Her idea of business — "Henry, why do people who have enough money try to get more money?" Her idea of politics — "I am sure that if the mothers of various nations could meet there would be no more wars." Her idea of religion — ah, this had been a cloud, but a cloud that passed. She came of Quaker stock, and he and his family, formerly Dissenters, were now members of the Church of England. The rector's sermons had at first repelled her, and she had expressed a desire for "a more inward light", adding, "not so much for myself as for baby" (Charles). Inward light must have been granted, for he heard no complaints in later years. They brought up their three children without dispute. They had never disputed.

She lay under the earth now. She had gone, and, as if to make her going the more bitter, had gone with a touch of mystery that was all unlike her. "Why didn't you tell me you knew of it?" he had moaned, and her faint voice had answered: "I didn't want to, Henry — I might have been wrong — and everyone hates illnesses." He had been told of the horror by a strange doctor, whom she had consulted during his absence from town. Was this altogether just? Without fully explaining, she had died. It was a fault on her part, and — tears rushed into his eyes — what a little fault! It was the only time she had deceived him in those thirty years.

He rose to his feet and looked out of the window, for Evie had come in with the letters, and he could meet no one's eye. Ah yes — she had been a good woman — she had been steady. He chose the word deliberately. To him steadiness included all praise.

He himself, gazing at the wintry garden, is in appearance a steady man. His face was not as square as his son's, and indeed the chin, though firm enough in outline, retreated a little, and the lips, ambiguous, were curtained by a moustache. But there was no external hint of weakness. The eyes, if capable of kindness and good-fellowship, if ruddy for the moment with tears, were the eyes of one who could not be driven. The forehead, too, was like Charles's. High and straight, brown and polished, merging abruptly into temples and skull, it had the effect of a bastion that protected his head from the world. At times it had the effect of a blank wall. He had dwelt behind it, intact and happy, for fifty years.

"The post's come, father," said Evie awkwardly.

"Thanks. Put it down."

"Has the breakfast been all right?"

"Yes, thanks."

The girl glanced at him and at it with constraint. She did not know what to do.

"Charles says do you want *The Times*?"

"No, I'll read it later."

"Ring if you want anything, father, won't you?"

"I've all I want."

Having sorted the letters from the circulars, she went back to the dining-room.

"Father's eaten nothing," she announced, sitting down with wrinkled brows behind the tea-urn.

Charles did not answer, but after a moment he ran quickly upstairs, opened the door, and said: "Look here, father, you must eat, you know"; and, having paused for a reply that did not come, stole down again. "He's going to read his letters first, I think," he said evasively; "I dare say he will go on with his breakfast afterwards." Then he took up *The Times*, and for some time there was no sound except the clink of cup against saucer and of knife on plate.

Poor Mrs Charles sat between her silent companions, terrified at the course of events, and a little bored. She was a rubbishy little creature, and she knew it. A telegram had dragged her from Naples to the deathbed of a woman whom she had scarcely known. A word from her husband had plunged her into mourning. She desired to mourn inwardly as well, but she wished that Mrs Wilcox, since fated to die, could have died before the marriage, for then less would have been expected of her. Crumbling her toast, and too nervous to ask for the butter, she remained almost motionless, thankful only for this, that her father-in-law was having his breakfast upstairs.

At last Charles spoke. "They had no business to be pollarding those elms yesterday," he said to his sister.

"No indeed."

"I must make a note of that," he continued. "I am surprised that the rector allowed it."

"Perhaps it may not be the rector's affair."

"Whose else could it be?"

"The lord of the manor."

"Impossible."

"Butter, Dolly?"

"Thank you, Evie dear. Charles —"

"Yes, dear?"

"I didn't know one could pollard elms. I thought one only pollarded willows."

"Oh no, one can pollard elms."

"Then why oughtn't the elms in the churchyard to be pollarded?" Charles frowned a little, and turned again to his sister.

"Another point. I must speak to Chalkeley."

"Yes, rather; you must complain to Chalkeley."

"It's no good him saying he is not responsible for those men. He is responsible."

"Yes, rather."

Brother and sister were not callous. They spoke thus, partly because they desired to keep Chalkeley up to the mark — a healthy desire in its way — partly because they avoided the personal note in life. All Wilcoxes did. It did not seem to them of supreme importance. Or it may be as Helen supposed: they realized its importance, but were afraid of it. Panic and emptiness, could one glance behind. They were not callous, and they left the breakfast-table with aching hearts. Their mother never had come in to breakfast. It was in the other rooms, and especially in the garden, that they felt her loss most. As Charles went out to the garage, he was reminded at every step of the woman who had loved him and whom he could never replace. What battles he had fought against her gentle conservatism! How she had disliked improvements, yet how loyally she had accepted them when made! He and his father — what trouble they had had to get this very garage! With what difficulty had they persuaded her to yield them the paddock for it — the paddock that she loved more dearly than the garden itself! The vine — she had got her way about the vine. It still encumbered the south wall with its unproductive branches. And so with Evie, as she stood talking to the cook. Though she could take up her mother's work inside the house, just as the men could take it up without, she felt that something unique had fallen out of her life. Their grief, though less poignant than their father's, grew from deeper roots, for a wife may be replaced: a mother never.

Charles would go back to the office. There was little to do at Howards End. The contents of his mother's will had been long known to them. There were no legacies, no annuities, none of the posthumous bustle with which some of the dead prolong their activities. Trusting her husband, she had left him everything without reserve. She was quite a poor woman — the house had been all her dowry, and the house would come to Charles in time. Her water-colours Mr Wilcox intended to reserve for Paul, while Evie would take the jewelry and lace. How easily she slipped out of life! Charles thought the habit laudable, though he did not intend to adopt it himself, whereas Margaret would have seen in it an almost culpable indifference to earthly fame. Cynicism — not the superficial cynicism that snarls and sneers, but the cynicism that can go with courtesy and tenderness — that was the note of Mrs Wilcox's will. She wanted not to vex people. That accomplished, the earth might freeze over her for ever.

No, there was nothing for Charles to wait for. He could not go on with his honeymoon, so he would go up to London and work — he felt too miserable hanging about. He and Dolly would have the furnished flat while his father rested quietly in the country with Evie. He could also keep an eye on his own little house, which was being painted and decorated for him in one of the Surrey suburbs, and in which he hoped to install himself soon after Christmas. Yes, he would go up after lunch in his new motor, and the town servants, who had come down for the funeral, would go up by train.

He found his father's chauffeur in the garage, said "Morning" without looking at the man's face, and, bending over the car, continued: "Hullo! my new car's been driven!"

"Has it, sir?"

"Yes," said Charles, getting rather red; "and whoever's driven it hasn't cleaned it properly, for there's mud on the axle. Take it off."

The man went for the cloths without a word. He was a chauffeur as ugly as sin — not that this did him disservice with Charles, who thought charm in a man rather rot, and had soon got rid of the little Italian beast with whom they had started.

"Charles —" His bride was tripping after him over the hoar-frost, a dainty black column, her little face and elaborate mourning-hat forming the capital thereof.

"One minute, I'm busy. Well, Crane, who's been driving it, do you suppose?"

"Don't know, I'm sure, sir. No one's driven it since I've been back, but, of course, there's the fortnight I've been away with the other car in Yorkshire."

The mud came off easily.

"Charles, your father's down. Something's happened. He wants you in the house at once. Oh, Charles!"

"Wait, dear, wait a minute. Who had the key of the garage while you were away, Crane?"

"The gardener, sir."

"Do you mean to tell me that old Penny can drive a motor?"

"No, sir; no one's had the motor out, sir."

"Then how do you account for the mud on the axle?"

"I can't, of course, say for the time I've been in Yorkshire. No more mud now, sir."

Charles was vexed. The man was treating him as a fool, and if his heart had not been so heavy he would have reported him to his father. But it was not a morning for complaints. Ordering the motor to be round after lunch, he joined his wife, who had all the while been pouring out some incoherent story about a letter and a Miss Schlegel.

"Now, Dolly, I can attend to you. Miss Schlegel? What does she want?"

When people wrote a letter Charles always asked what they wanted. Want was to him the only cause of action. And the question in this case was correct, for his wife replied: "She wants Howards End."

"Howards End? Now, Crane, just don't forget to put on the Stepney wheel."°

"No, sir."

"Now, mind you don't forget, for I — come, little woman." When they were out of the chauffeur's sight he put his arm round her waist and pressed her against him. All his affection and half his attention — it was what he granted her throughout their happy married life.

"But you haven't listened, Charles —"

"What's wrong?"

"I keep on telling you — Howards End. Miss Schlegel's got it."

**Stepney wheel:** Spare wheel.

"Got what?" said Charles, unclasping her. "What the dickens are you talking about?"

"Now, Charles, you promised not to say those naughty —"

"Look here, I'm in no mood for foolery. It's no morning for it either."

"I tell you — I keep on telling you — Miss Schlegel — she's got it — your mother's left it to her — and you've all got to move out!"

"*Howards End?*"

"*Howards End!*" she screamed, mimicking him, and as she did so Evie came dashing out of the shrubbery.

"Dolly, go back at once! My father's much annoyed with you. Charles" — she hit herself wildly — "come in at once to father. He's had a letter that's too awful."

Charles began to run, but checked himself, and stepped heavily across the gravel path. There the house was — the nine windows, the unprolific vine. He exclaimed "Schlegels again!" and, as if to complete chaos, Dolly said: "Oh no, the matron of the nursing-home has written instead of her."

"Come in, all three of you!" cried his father, no longer inert. "Dolly, why have you disobeyed me?"

"Oh, Mr Wilcox —"

"I told you not to go out to the garage. I've heard you all shouting in the garden. I won't have it. Come in."

He stood in the porch, transformed, letters in his hand.

"Into the dining-room, every one of you. We can't discuss private matters in the middle of all the servants. Here, Charles, here; read these. See what you make."

Charles took two letters, and read them as he followed the procession. The first was a covering note from the matron. Mrs Wilcox had desired her, when the funeral should be over, to forward the enclosed. The enclosed — it was from his mother herself. She had written: "To my husband: I should like Miss Schlegel (Margaret) to have Howards End."

"I suppose we're going to have a talk about this?" he remarked, ominously calm.

"Certainly. I was coming out to you when Dolly —"

"Well, let's sit down."

"Come, Evie, don't waste time, sit down."

In silence they drew up to the breakfast-table. The events of yesterday — indeed, of this morning — suddenly receded into a past so remote that they seemed scarcely to have lived in it. Heavy breath-ings were heard. They were calming themselves. Charles, to steady them further, read the enclosure out loud: "A note in my mother's handwriting, in an envelope addressed to my father, sealed. Inside: 'I should like Miss Schlegel (Margaret) to have Howards End.' No date, no signature. Forwarded through the matron of that nursing-home. Now, the question is —"

Dolly interrupted him. "But I say that note isn't legal. Houses ought to be done by a lawyer, Charles, surely."

Her husband worked his jaw severely. Little lumps appeared in front of either ear — a symptom that she had not yet learned to respect, and she asked whether she might see the note. Charles looked at his father for permission, who said abstractedly: "Give it her." She seized it, and at once exclaimed: "Why, it's only in pencil! I said so. Pencil never counts."

"We know that it is not legally binding, Dolly," said Mr Wilcox, speaking from out of his fortress. "We are aware of that. Legally, I should be justified in tearing it up and throwing it into the fire. Of course, my dear, we consider you as one of the family, but it will be better if you do not interfere with what you do not understand."

Charles, vexed both with his father and his wife, then repeated: "The question is —" He had cleared a space of the breakfast-table from plates and knives, so that he could draw patterns on the table-cloth. "The question is whether Miss Schlegel, during the fortnight we were all away, whether she unduly —" He stopped.

"I don't think that," said his father, whose nature was nobler than his son's.

"Don't think what?"

"That she would have — that it is a case of undue influence. No, to my mind the question is the — the invalid's condition at the time she wrote."

"My dear father, consult an expert if you like, but I don't admit it is my mother's writing."

"Why, you just said it was!" cried Dolly.

"Never mind if I did," he blazed out; "and hold your tongue."

The poor little wife coloured at this, and, drawing her handkerchief from her pocket, shed a few tears. No one noticed her. Evie was scowling like an angry boy. The two men were gradually assuming the manner of the committee-room. They were both at their best when serving on committees. They did not make the mistake of handling human affairs in the bulk, but disposed of them item by item, sharply. Calligraphy was the item before them now, and on it they turned their well-trained brains. Charles, after a little demur, accepted the writing as genuine, and they passed on to the next point. It is the best — perhaps the only — way of dodging emotion. They were the average human article, and had they considered the note as a whole it would have driven them miserable or mad. Considered item by item, the emotional content was minimized, and all went forward smoothly. The clock ticked, the coals blazed higher, and contended with the white radiance that poured in through the windows. Unnoticed, the sun occupied his sky, and the shadows of the tree stems, extraordinarily solid, fell like trenches of purple across the frosted lawn. It was a glorious winter morning. Evie's fox-terrier, who had passed for white, was only a dirty gray dog now, so intense was the purity that surrounded him. He was discredited, but the blackbirds that he was chasing glowed with Arabian darkness, for all the conventional colouring of life had been altered. Inside, the clock struck ten with a rich and confident note. Other clocks confirmed it, and the discussion moved towards its close.

To follow it is unnecessary. It is rather a moment when the commentator should step forward. Ought the Wilcoxes to have offered their home to Margaret? I think not. The appeal was too flimsy. It was not legal; it had been written in illness, and under the spell of a sudden friendship; it was contrary to the dead woman's intentions in the past, contrary to her very nature, so far as that nature was understood by them. To them Howards End was a house: they could not know that to her it had been a spirit, for which she sought a spiritual heir. And — pushing one step further in these mists — may they not have decided even better than they supposed? Is it credible that the possessions of the spirit can be bequeathed at all? Has the soul offspring? A wych-elm tree, a vine, a wisp of hay with dew on it — can passion for such things be transmitted where there is no bond of blood? No; the Wilcoxes are not to be blamed. The problem is too terrific, and they could not even perceive a problem. No; it is natural and fitting that after due debate they should tear the note up and throw it onto their dining-room fire. The practical moralist may acquit them absolutely. He who strives to look deeper may acquit them — almost. For one hard fact remains. They did neglect a personal appeal. The woman who had died did say to them, "Do this," and they answered, "We will not."

The incident made a most painful impression on them. Grief mounted into the brain and worked there disquietingly. Yesterday they had lamented: "She was a dear mother, a true wife; in our absence she neglected her health and died." Today they thought: "She was not as true, as dear, as we supposed." The desire for a more in-ward light had found expression at last, the unseen had impacted on the seen, and all that they could say was "Treachery". Mrs Wilcox had been treacherous to the family, to the laws of property, to her own written word. How did she expect Howards End to be conveyed to Miss Schlegel? Was her husband, to whom it legally belonged, to make it over to her as a free gift? Was the said Miss Schlegel to have a life in-terest in it, or to own it absolutely? Was there to be no compensation for the garage and other improvements that they had made under the assumption that all would be theirs some day? Treacherous! Treacher-ous and absurd! When we think the dead both treacherous and ab-surd, we have gone far towards reconciling ourselves to their depar-ture. That note, scribbled in pencil, sent through the matron, was unbusinesslike as well as cruel, and decreased at once the value of the woman who had written it.

"Ah, well!" said Mr Wilcox, rising from the table. "I shouldn't have thought it possible."

"Mother couldn't have meant it," said Evie, still frowning.

"No, my girl, of course not."

"Mother believed so in ancestors too — it isn't like her to leave anything to an outsider, who'd never appreciate."

"The whole thing is unlike her," he announced. "If Miss Schlegel had been poor, if she had wanted a house, I could understand it a little. But she has a house of her own. Why should she want another? She wouldn't have any use for Howards End."

"That time may prove," murmured Charles.

"How?" asked his sister.

"Presumably she knows — mother will have told her. She got twice or three times into the nursing-home. Presumably she is await-ing developments."

"What a horrid woman!" And Dolly, who had recovered, cried, "Why, she may be coming down to turn us out now!"

Charles put her right. "I wish she would," he said ominously. "I could then deal with her."

"So could I," echoed his father, who was feeling rather in the cold. Charles had been kind in undertaking the funeral arrangements and in telling him to eat his breakfast, but the boy as he grew up was a little dictatorial, and assumed the post of chairman too readily. "I could deal with her, if she comes, but she won't come. You're all a bit hard on Miss Schlegel."

"That Paul business was pretty scandalous, though."

"I want no more of the Paul business, Charles, as I said at the time, and besides, it is quite apart from this business. Margaret Schlegel has been officious and tiresome during this terrible week, and we have all suffered under her, but upon my soul she's honest. She's *not* in collusion with the matron. I'm absolutely certain of it. Nor was she with the doctor, I'm equally certain of that. She did not hide anything from us, for up to that very afternoon she was as ignorant as we are. She, like ourselves, was a dupe —" He stopped for a moment. "You see, Charles, in her terrible pain your poor mother put us all in false positions. Paul would not have left England, you would not have gone to Italy, nor Evie and I into Yorkshire, if only we had known. Well, Miss Schlegel's position has been equally false. Take all in all, she has not come out of it badly."

Evie said: "But those chrysanthemums —"

"Or coming down to the funeral at all —" echoed Dolly.

"Why shouldn't she come down? She had the right to, and she stood far back among the Hilton women. The flowers — certainly we should not have sent such flowers, but they may have seemed the right thing to her, Evie, and for all you know they may be the custom in Germany."

"Oh, I forgot she isn't really English," cried Evie. "That would explain a lot."

"She's a cosmopolitan," said Charles, looking at his watch. "I admit I'm rather down on cosmopolitans. My fault, doubtless. I cannot stand them, and a German cosmopolitan is the limit. I think that's about all, isn't it? I want to run down and see Chalkeley. A bicycle will do. And, by the way, I wish you'd speak to Crane some time. I'm certain he's had my new car out."

"Has he done it any harm?"

"No."

"In that case I shall let it pass. It's not worth while having a row."

Charles and his father sometimes disagreed. But they always parted with an increased regard for one another, and each desired no doughtier comrade when it was necessary to voyage for a little past the emotions. So the sailors of Ulysses voyaged past the Sirens, having first stopped one another's ears with wool.

## Chapter 12

Charles need not have been anxious. Miss Schlegel had never heard of his mother's strange request. She was to hear of it in after years, when she had built up her life differently, and it was to fit into position as the headstone of the corner. Her mind was bent on other questions now, and by her also it would have been rejected as the fantasy of an invalid.

She was parting from these Wilcoxes for the second time. Paul and his mother, ripple and great wave, had flowed into her life and ebbed out of it for ever. The ripple had left no traces behind; the wave had strewn at her feet fragments torn from the unknown. A curious seeker, she stood for a while at the verge of the sea that tells so little, but tells a little, and watched the outgoing of this last tremendous tide. Her friend had vanished in agony, but not, she believed, in degradation. Her withdrawal had hinted at other things besides disease and pain. Some leave our life with tears, others with an insane frigidity; Mrs Wilcox had taken the middle course, which only rarer natures can pursue. She had kept proportion. She had told a little of her grim secret to her friends, but not too much; she had shut up her heart — almost, but not entirely. It is thus, if there is any rule, that we ought to die — neither as victim nor as fanatic, but as the seafarer who can greet with an equal eye the deep that he is entering, and the shore that he must leave.

The last word — whatever it would be — had certainly not been said in Hilton churchyard. She had not died there. A funeral is not death, any more than baptism is birth or marriage union. All three are the clumsy devices, coming now too late, now too early, by which society would register the quick motions of man. In Margaret's eyes Mrs Wilcox had escaped registration. She had gone out of life vividly, her own way, and no dust was so truly dust as the contents of that heavy coffin, lowered with ceremonial until it rested on the dust of the earth, no flowers so utterly wasted as the chrysanthemums that the frost must have withered before morning. Margaret had once said she "loved superstition". It was not true. Few women had tried more earnestly to pierce the accretions in which body and soul are enwrapped. The death of Mrs Wilcox had helped her in her work. She saw a little more clearly than hitherto what a human being is, and to what he may aspire. Truer relationships gleamed. Perhaps the last word would be hope — hope even on this side of the grave.

Meanwhile, she could take an interest in the survivors. In spite of her Christmas duties, in spite of her brother, the Wilcoxes continued to play a considerable part in her thoughts. She had seen so much of them in the final week. They were not "her sort", they were often suspicious and stupid, and deficient where she excelled; but collision with them stimulated her, and she felt an interest that verged into liking, even for Charles. She desired to protect them, and often felt that they could protect her, excelling where she was deficient. Once past the rocks of emotion, they knew so well what to do, whom to send for; their hands were on all the ropes, they had grit as well as grittiness, and she valued grit enormously. They led a life that she could not attain to — the outer life of "telegrams and anger", which had detonated when Helen and Paul had touched in June, and had detonated again the other week. To Margaret this life was to remain a real force. She could not despise it, as Helen and Tibby affected to do. It fostered such virtues as neatness, decision and obedience, virtues of the second rank, no doubt, but they have formed our civilization. They form character, too; Margaret could not doubt it: they keep the soul from becoming sloppy. How dare Schlegels despise Wilcoxes, when it takes all sorts to make a world?

"Don't brood too much," she wrote to Helen, "on the superiority of the unseen to the seen. It's true, but to brood on it is medieval. Our business is not to contrast the two, but to reconcile them."

Helen replied that she had no intention of brooding on such a dull subject. What did her sister take her for? The weather was magnificent. She and the Mosebachs had gone tobogganing on the only hill that Pomerania boasted. It was fun, but overcrowded, for the rest of Pomerania had gone there too. Helen loved the country, and her letter glowed with physical exercise and poetry. She spoke of the scenery, quiet, yet august; of the snow-clad fields, with their scampering herds of deer; of the river and its quaint entrance into the Baltic Sea; of the Oderberge, only three hundred feet high, from which one slid all too quickly back into the Pomeranian plains, and yet these Oderberge were real mountains, with pine-forests, streams, and views complete. "It isn't size that counts so much as the way things are arranged." In another paragraph she referred to Mrs Wilcox sympathetically, but the news had not bitten into her. She had not realized the accessories of death, which are in a sense more memorable than death itself. The atmosphere of precautions and recriminations, and in the midst a human body growing more vivid because it was in pain; the end of that body in Hilton churchyard; the survival of something that suggested hope, vivid in its turn against life's workaday cheerfulness — all these were lost to Helen, who only felt that a pleasant lady could now be pleasant no longer. She returned to Wickham Place full of her own affairs — she had had another proposal — and Margaret, after a moment's hesitation, was content that this should be so.

The proposal had not been a serious matter. It was the work of Fräulein Mosebach, who had conceived the large and patriotic notion of winning back her cousins to the Fatherland by matrimony. England had played Paul Wilcox, and lost; Germany played Herr Förstmeister someone — Helen could not remember his name. Herr Förstmeister lived in a wood, and, standing on the summit of the Oderberge he had pointed out his house to Helen, or, rather, had pointed out the wedge of pines in which it lay. She had exclaimed, "Oh, how lovely! That's the place for me!" and in the evening Frieda appeared in her bedroom. "I have a message, dear Helen," etc., and so she had, but had been very nice when Helen laughed; quite understood — a forest too solitary and damp — quite agreed, but Herr Förstmeister believed he had assurance to the contrary. Germany had lost, but with good humour; holding the manhood of the world, she felt bound to win. "And there will even be someone for Tibby," concluded Helen. "There now, Tibby, think of that; Frieda is saving up a little girl for you, in pigtails and white worsted stockings, but the feet of the stockings are pink, as if the little girl had trodden in strawberries. I've talked too much. My head aches. Now you talk."

Tibby consented to talk. He too was full of his own affairs, for he had just been up to try for a scholarship at Oxford. The men were down,° and the candidates had been housed in various colleges, and had dined in hall. Tibby was sensitive to beauty, the experience was new, and he gave a description of his visit that was almost glowing. The august and mellow university, soaked with the richness of the western counties that it has served for a thousand years, appealed at once to the boy's taste; it was the kind of thing he could understand, and he understood it all the better because it was empty. Oxford is — Oxford; not a mere receptacle for youth, like Cambridge. Perhaps it wants its inmates to love it rather than to love one another; such at all events was to be its effect on Tibby. His sisters sent him there that he might make friends, for they knew that his education had been cranky, and had severed him from other boys and men. He made no friends. His Oxford remained Oxford empty, and he took into life with him, not the memory of a radiance, but the memory of a colour scheme.

It pleased Margaret to hear her brother and sister talking. They did not get on over-well as a rule. For a few moments she listened to them, feeling elderly and benign. Then something occurred to her, and she interrupted:

**The men were down:** The undergraduates were on vacation.

"Helen, I told you about poor Mrs Wilcox; that sad business?"

"Yes."

"I have had a correspondence with her son. He was winding up the estate, and wrote to ask me whether his mother had wanted me to have anything. I thought it good of him, considering I knew her for so little. I said that she had once spoken of giving me a Christmas present, but we both forgot about it afterwards."

"I hope Charles took the hint."

"Yes — that is to say, her husband wrote later on, and thanked me for being a little kind to her, and actually gave me her silver vinaigrette. Don't you think that is extraordinarily generous? It has made me like him very much. He hopes that this will not be the end of our acquaintance, but that you and I will go and stop with Evie some time in the future. I like Mr Wilcox. He is taking up his work — rubber — it is a big business. I gather he is launching out rather. Charles is in it, too. Charles is married — a pretty little creature, but she doesn't seem wise. They took on the flat, but now they have gone off to a house of their own."

Helen, after a decent pause, continued her account of Stettin. How quickly a situation changes! In June she had been in a crisis; even in November she could blush and be unnatural; now it was January, and the whole affair lay forgotten. Looking back on the past six months, Margaret realized the chaotic nature of our daily life, and its difference from the orderly sequence that has been fabricated by historians. Actual life is full of false clues and signposts that lead nowhere. With infinite effort we nerve ourselves for a crisis that never comes. The most successful career must show a waste of strength that might have removed mountains, and the most unsuccessful is not that of the man who is taken unprepared, but of him who has prepared and is never taken. On a tragedy of that kind our national morality is duly silent. It assumes that preparation against danger is in itself a good, and that men, like nations, are the better for staggering through life fully armed. The tragedy of preparedness has scarcely been handled, save by the Greeks. Life is indeed dangerous, but not in the way morality would have us believe. It is indeed unmanageable, but the essence of it is not a battle. It is unmanageable because it is a romance, and its essence is romantic beauty.

Margaret hoped that for the future she would be less cautious, not more cautious, than she had been in the past.

## Chapter 13

Over two years passed, and the Schlegel household continued to lead its life of cultured but not ignoble ease, still swimming gracefully on the gray tides of London. Concerts and plays swept past them, money had been spent and renewed, reputations won and lost, and the city herself, emblematic of their lives, rose and fell in a continual flux, while her shallows washed more widely against the hills of Surrey and over the fields of Hertfordshire. This famous building had arisen, that was doomed. Today Whitehall had been transformed;° it would be the turn of Regent Street tomorrow. And month by month the roads smelt more strongly of petrol, and were more difficult to cross, and human beings heard each other speak with greater difficulty, breathed less of the air, and saw less of the sky. Nature withdrew: the leaves were falling by midsummer; the sun shone through dirt with an admired obscurity.

To speak against London is no longer fashionable. The earth as an artistic cult has had its day, and the literature of the near future will probably ignore the country and seek inspiration from the town. One can understand the reaction. Of Pan and the elemental forces the public has heard a little too much° — they seem Victorian, while London is Georgian — and those who care for the earth with sincerity may wait long ere the pendulum swings back to her again. Certainly London fascinates. One visualizes it as a tract of quivering gray, intelligent without purpose, and excitable without love; as a spirit that has altered before it can be chronicled; as a heart that certainly beats, but with no pulsation of humanity. It lies beyond everything: Nature, with all her cruelty, comes nearer to us than do these crowds of men. A friend explains himself; the earth is explicable — from her we came, and we must return to her. But who can explain Westminster Bridge Road or Liverpool Street in the morning — the city inhaling — or the same thoroughfares in the evening — the city exhaling her exhausted air? We reach in desperation beyond the fog, beyond the very stars, the voids of the universe are ransacked to justify the monster, and stamped with a human face. London is religion's opportunity — not the

---

**Whitehall had been transformed:** By, for example, the new War Office of 1907. Regent Street, the splendid creation of the Regency architect John Nash (1752–1835), was not so much "transformed" as demolished.     **Of Pan . . . too much:** Among writers on the subject was Forster himself with "The Story of a Panic," written in 1902.

decorous religion of theologians, but anthropomorphic, crude. Yes, the continuous flow would be tolerable if a man of our own sort — not anyone pompous or tearful — were caring for us up in the sky.

The Londoner seldom understands his city until it sweeps him, too, away from his moorings, and Margaret's eyes were not opened until the lease of Wickham Place expired. She had always known that it must expire, but the knowledge only became vivid about nine months before the event. Then the house was suddenly ringed with pathos. It had seen so much happiness. Why had it to be swept away? In the streets of the city she noted for the first time the architecture of hurry, and heard the language of hurry on the mouths of its inhabitants — clipped words, formless sentences, potted expressions of approval or disgust. Month by month things were stepping livelier, but to what goal? The population still rose, but what was the quality of the men born? The particular millionaire who owned the freehold of Wickham Place, and desired to erect Babylonian flats upon it — what right had he to stir so large a portion of the quivering jelly? He was not a fool — she had heard him expose socialism — but true insight began just where his intelligence ended, and one gathered that this was the case with most millionaires. What right had such men — but Margaret checked herself. That way lies madness.° Thank goodness she, too, had some money, and could purchase a new home.

Tibby, now in his second year at Oxford, was down for the Easter vacation, and Margaret took the opportunity of having a serious talk with him. Did he at all know where he wanted to live? Tibby didn't know that he did know. Did he at all know what he wanted to do? He was equally uncertain, but when pressed remarked that he should prefer to be quite free of any profession. Margaret was not shocked, but went on sewing for a few minutes before she replied:

"I was thinking of Mr Vyse.° He never strikes me as particularly happy."

"Ye-es," said Tibby, and then held his mouth open in a curious quiver, as if he, too, had thought of Mr Vyse, had seen round, through, over and beyond Mr Vyse, had weighed Mr Vyse, grouped him, and finally dismissed him as having no possible bearing on the subject under discussion. That bleat of Tibby's infuriated Helen. But Helen was now down in the dining-room preparing a speech about

---

**That way lies madness:** Echoes *King Lear* 3.4.21.     **Mr Vyse:** Perhaps the same Mr. (Cecil) Vyse who appears in *A Room with a View*.

political economy. At times her voice could be heard declaiming through the floor.

"But Mr Vyse is rather a wretched, weedy man, don't you think? Then there's Guy. That was a pitiful business. Besides" — shifting to the general — "everyone is the better for some regular work."

Groans.

"I shall stick to it," she continued, smiling. "I am not saying it to educate you; it is what I really think. I believe that in the last century men have developed the desire for work, and they must not starve it. It's a new desire. It goes with a great deal that's bad, but in itself it's good, and I hope that for women, too, 'not to work' will soon become as shocking as 'not to be married' was a hundred years ago."

"I have no experience of this profound desire to which you allude," enunciated Tibby.

"Then we'll leave the subject till you do. I'm not going to rattle you round. Take your time. Only do think over the lives of the men you like most, and see how they've arranged them."

"I like Guy and Mr Vyse most," said Tibby faintly, and leant so far back in his chair that he extended in a horizontal line from knees to throat.

"And don't think I'm not serious because I don't use the traditional arguments — making money, a sphere awaiting you, and so on — all of which are, for various reason, cant." She sewed on. "I'm only your sister. I haven't any authority over you, and I don't want to have any. Just to put before you what I think the truth. You see" — she shook off the pince-nez to which she had recently taken — "in a few years we shall be the same age practically, and I shall want you to help me. Men are so much nicer than women."

"Labouring under such a delusion, why do you not marry?"

"I sometimes jolly well think I would if I got the chance."

"Has nobody arst you?"

"Only ninnies."

"Do people ask Helen?"

"Plentifully."

"Tell me about them."

"No."

"Tell me about your ninnies, then."

"They were men who had nothing better to do," said his sister, feeling that she was entitled to score this point. "So take warning: you must work, or else you must pretend to work, which is what I do. Work, work, work if you'd save your soul and your body. It is honestly a necessity, dear boy. Look at the Wilcoxes, look at Mr Pembroke.° With all their defects of temper and understanding, such men give me more pleasure than many who are better equipped, and I think it is because they have worked regularly and honestly."

"Spare me the Wilcoxes," he moaned.

"I shall not. They are the right sort."

"Oh, goodness me, Meg!" he protested, suddenly sitting up, alert and angry. Tibby, for all his defects, had a genuine personality.

"Well, they're as near the right sort as you can imagine."

"No, no — oh, no!"

"I was thinking of the younger son, whom I once classed as a ninny, but who came back so ill from Nigeria. He's gone out there again, Evie Wilcox tells me — out to his duty."

"Duty" always elicited a groan.

"He doesn't want the money, it is work he wants, though it is beastly work — dull country, dishonest natives, an eternal fidget over fresh water and food. A nation who can produce men of that sort may well be proud. No wonder England has become an Empire."

"*Empire!*"

"I can't bother over results," said Margaret, a little sadly. "They are too difficult for me. I can only look at the men. An Empire bores me, so far, but I can appreciate the heroism that builds it up. London bores me, but what thousands of splendid people are labouring to make London —"

"What it is," he sneered.

"What it is, worse luck. I want activity without civilization. How paradoxical! Yet I expect that is what we shall find in heaven."

"And I," said Tibby, "want civilization without activity, which, I expect, is what we shall find in the other place."

"You needn't go as far as the other place, Tibbikins, if you want that. You can find it at Oxford."

"Stupid —"

"If I'm stupid, get me back to the house-hunting. I'll even live in Oxford if you like — North Oxford. I'll live anywhere except Bournemouth, Torquay and Cheltenham. Oh yes, or Ilfracombe and Swanage and Tunbridge Wells and Surbiton and Bedford. There on no account."

"London, then."

Mr Pembroke: Perhaps the same Mr. (Herbert) Pembroke who appears in *The Longest Journey.*

"I agree, but Helen rather wants to get away from London. However, there's no reason we shouldn't have a house in the country and also a flat in town, provided we all stick together and contribute. Though of course — oh, how one does maunder on, and to think, to think of the people who are really poor. How do they live? Not to move about the world would kill me."

As she spoke, the door was flung open, and Helen burst in in a state of extreme excitement.

"Oh, my dears, what do you think? You'll never guess. A woman's been here asking me for her husband. Her *what?*" (Helen was fond of supplying her own surprise.) "Yes, for her husband, and it really is so."

"Not anything to do with Bracknell?" cried Margaret, who had lately taken on an unemployed of that name to clean the knives and boots.

"I offered Bracknell, and he was rejected. So was Tibby. (Cheer up, Tibby!) It's no one we know. I said: 'Hunt, my good woman; have a good look round, hunt under the tables, poke up the chimney, shake out the antimacassars. Husband? Husband?' Oh, and she so magnificently dressed and tinkling like a chandelier."

"Now, Helen, what did happen really?"

"What I say. I was, as it were, orating my speech. Annie opens the door like a fool, and shows a female straight in on me, with my mouth open. Then we began — very civilly. 'I want my husband, what I have reason to believe it here.' No — how unjust one is. She said 'whom', not 'what'. She got it perfectly. So I said, 'Name, please?' and she said, 'Lan, Miss,' and there we were."

"Lan?"

"Lan or Len. We were not nice about our vowels. Lanoline."

"But what an extraordinary —"

"I said, 'My good Mrs Lanoline, we have some grave misunderstanding here. Beautiful as I am, my modesty is even more remarkable than my beauty, and never, never has Mr Lanoline rested his eyes on mine.'"

"I hope you were pleased," said Tibby.

"Of course," Helen squeaked. "A perfectly delightful experience. Oh, Mrs Lanoline's a dear — she asked for a husband as if he was an umbrella. She mislaid him Saturday afternoon — and for a long time suffered no inconvenience. But all night and all this morning her apprehensions grew. Breakfast didn't seem the same — no, no more did lunch, and so she strolled up to Two, Wickham Place as being the most likely place for the missing article."

"But how on earth —"

"Don't begin how-on-earthing. 'I know what I know,' she kept repeating, not uncivilly, but with extreme gloom. In vain I asked her what she did know. Some knew what others knew, and others didn't, and if they didn't then others again had better be careful. Oh dear, she was incompetent! She had a face like a silk-worm, and the dining-room reeks of orris-root.° We chatted pleasantly a little about husbands, and I wondered where hers was too, and advised her to go to the police. She thanked me. We agreed that Mr Lanoline's a notty, notty man, and hasn't no business to go on the lardy-da. But I think she suspected me up to the last. Bags I writing to Aunt Juley about this. Now, Meg, remember — bags I."

"Bag it by all means," murmured Margaret, putting down her work. "I'm not sure that this is so funny, Helen. It means some horrible volcano smoking somewhere, doesn't it?"

"I don't think so — she doesn't really mind. The admirable creature isn't capable of tragedy."

"Her husband may be, though," said Margaret, moving to the window.

"Oh no, not likely. No one capable of tragedy would have married Mrs Lanoline."

"Was she pretty?"

"Her figure may have been good once."

The flats, their only outlook, hung like an ornate curtain between Margaret and the welter of London. Her thoughts turned sadly to house-hunting. Wickham Place had been so safe. She feared, fantastically, that her own little flock might be moving into turmoil and squalor, into nearer contact with such episodes as these.

"Tibby and I have again been wondering where we'll live next September," she said at last.

"Tibby had better first wonder what he'll do," retorted Helen; and that topic was resumed, but with acrimony. Then tea came, and after tea Helen went on preparing her speech, and Margaret prepared one, too, for they were going out to a discussion society on the morrow. But her thoughts were poisoned. Mrs Lanoline had risen out of the abyss, like a faint smell, a goblin footfall, telling of a life where love and hatred had both decayed.

---

**orris-root:** Fragrant root of the European iris, used in cosmetics.

## Chapter 14

The mystery, like so many mysteries, was explained. Next day, just as they were dressed to go out to dinner, a Mr Bast called. He was a clerk in the employment of the Porphyrion Fire Insurance Company. Thus much from his card. He had come "about the lady yesterday". Thus much from Annie, who had shown him into the dining-room.

"Cheers, children!" cried Helen. "It's Mr Lanoline."

Even Tibby was interested. The three hurried downstairs, to find, not the gay dog they expected, but a young man, colourless, toneless, who had already the mournful eyes above a drooping moustache that are so common in London, and that haunt some streets of the city like accusing presences. One guessed him as the third generation, grandson to the shepherd or ploughboy whom civilization had sucked into the town; as one of the thousands who have lost the life of the body and failed to reach the life of the spirit. Hints of robustness survived in him, more than a hint of primitive good looks, and Margaret, noting the spine that might have been straight, and the chest that might have broadened, wondered whether it paid to give up the glory of the animal for a tailcoat and a couple of ideas. Culture had worked in her own case, but during the last few weeks she had doubted whether it humanized the majority, so wide and so widening is the gulf that stretches between the natural and the philosophic man, so many the good chaps who are wrecked in trying to cross it. She knew this type very well — the vague aspirations, the mental dishonesty, the familiarity with the outsides of books. She knew the very tones in which he would address her. She was only unprepared for an example of her own visiting-card.

"You wouldn't remember giving me this, Miss Schlegel?" said he, uneasily familiar.

"No; I can't say I do."

"Well, that was how it happened, you see."

"Where did we meet, Mr Bast? For the minute I don't remember."

"It was a concert at the Queen's Hall. I think you will recollect," he added pretentiously, "when I tell you that it included a performance of the Fifth Symphony of Beethoven."

"We hear the Fifth practically every time it's done, so I'm not sure — do you remember, Helen?"

"Was it the time the sandy cat walked round the balustrade?"

He thought not.

"Then I don't remember. That's the only Beethoven I ever remember specially."

"And you, if I may say so, took away my umbrella, inadvertently of course."

"Likely enough," Helen laughed, "for I steal umbrellas even oftener than I hear Beethoven. Did you get it back?"

"Yes, thank you, Miss Schlegel."

"The mistake arose out of my card, did it?" interposed Margaret.

"Yes, the mistake arose — it was a mistake."

"The lady who called here yesterday thought that you were calling too, and that she would find you?" she continued, pushing him forward, for, though he had promised an explanation, he seemed unable to give one.

"That's so, calling too — a mistake."

"Then why — ?" began Helen, but Margaret laid a hand on her arm.

"I said to my wife," he continued more rapidly — "I said to Mrs Bast, 'I have to pay a call on some friends,' and Mrs Bast said to me, 'Do go.' While I was gone, however, she wanted me on important business, and thought I had come here, owing to the card, and so came after me, and I beg to tender my apologies, and hers as well, for any inconvenience we may have inadvertently caused you."

"No inconvenience," said Helen; "but I still don't understand."

An air of evasion characterized Mr Bast. He explained again, but was obviously lying, and Helen didn't see why he should get off. She had the cruelty of youth. Neglecting her sister's pressure, she said: "I still don't understand. When did you say you paid this call?"

"Call? What call?" said he, staring as if her question had been a foolish one, a favourite device of those in mid-stream.

"This afternoon call."

"In the afternoon, of course!" he replied, and looked at Tibby to see how the repartee went. But Tibby, himself a repartee, was unsympathetic, and said, "Saturday afternoon or Sunday afternoon?"

"S — Saturday."

"Really!" said Helen; "and you were still calling on Sunday, when your wife came here. A long visit."

"I don't call that fair," said Mr Bast, going scarlet and handsome. There was fight in his eyes. "I know what you mean, and it isn't so."

"Oh, don't let us mind," said Margaret, distressed again by odours from the abyss.

"It was something else," he asserted, his elaborate manner breaking down. "I was somewhere else to what you think, so there!"

"It was good of you to come and explain," she said. "The rest is naturally no concern of ours."

"Yes, but I want — I wanted — have you ever read *The Ordeal of Richard Feverel*?"°

Margaret nodded.

"It's a beautiful book. I wanted to get back to the earth, don't you see, like Richard does in the end. Or have you ever read Stevenson's *Prince Otto*?"°

Helen and Tibby groaned gently.

"That's another beautiful book. You get back to the earth in that. I wanted —" He mouthed affectedly. Then through the mists of his culture came a hard fact, hard as a pebble. "I walked all the Saturday night," said Leonard. "I walked." A thrill of approval ran through the sisters. But culture closed in again. He asked whether they had ever read E. V. Lucas's *Open Road*.

Said Helen, "No doubt it's another beautiful book, but I'd rather hear about *your* road."

"Oh, I walked."

"How far?"

"I don't know, nor for how long. It got too dark to see my watch."

"Were you walking alone, may I ask?"

"Yes," he said, straightening himself; "but we'd been talking it over at the office. There's been a lot of talk at the office lately about these things. The fellows there said one steers by the Pole Star, and I looked it up in the celestial atlas, but once out of doors everything gets so mixed —"

"Don't talk to me about the Pole Star," interrupted Helen, who was becoming interested. "I know its little ways. It goes round and round, and you go round after it."

"Well, I lost it entirely. First of all the street-lamps, then the trees, and towards morning it got cloudy."

Tibby, who preferred his comedy undiluted, slipped from the room. He knew that this fellow would never attain to poetry, and did

---

*The Ordeal of Richard Feverel:* Novel (1859) by George Meredith (1828–1909) in which the hero anticipates Leonard Bast by spending a whole night walking in the woods.   *Prince Otto:* Ultraromantic story (1885) by R. L. Stevenson (1850–1894).

not want to hear him trying. Margaret and Helen remained. Their brother influenced them more than they knew: in his absence they were stirred to enthusiasm more easily.

"Where did you start from?" cried Margaret. "Do tell us more."

"I took the underground to Wimbledon. As I came out of the office I said to myself: 'I must have a walk once in a way. If I don't take this walk now, I shall never take it.' I had a bit of dinner at Wimbledon, and then —"

"But not good country there, is it?"

"It was gas lamps for hours. Still, I had all the night, and being out was the great thing. I did get into woods, too, presently."

"Yes, go on," said Helen.

"You've no idea how difficult uneven ground is when it's dark."

"Did you actually go off the roads?"

"Oh yes. I always meant to go off the roads, but the worst of it is that it's more difficult to find one's way."

"Mr Bast, you're a born adventurer," laughed Margaret. "No professional athlete would have attempted what you've done. It's a wonder your walk didn't end in a broken neck. What ever did your wife say?"

"Professional athletes never move without lanterns and compasses," said Helen. "Besides, they can't walk. It tires them. Go on."

"I felt like R. L. S. You probably remember how in *Virginibus* —"°

"Yes, but the wood. This 'ere wood. How did you get out of it?"

"I managed one wood, and found a road the other side which went a good bit uphill. I rather fancy it was those North Downs, for the road went off into grass, and I got into another wood. That was awful, with gorse bushes. I did wish I'd never come, but suddenly it got light — just while I seemed going under one tree. Then I found a road down to a station, and took the first train I could back to London."

"But was the dawn wonderful?" asked Helen.

With unforgettable sincerity he replied: "No." The word flew again like a pebble from the sling. Down topped all that had seemed ignoble or literary in his talk, down toppled tiresome R. L. S. and the "love of the earth" and his silk top-hat. In the presence of these

---

*Virginibus:* R. L. Stevenson's *Virginibus Puerisque* (1881), a collection of personal essays.

women Leonard had arrived, and he spoke with a flow, an exultation, that he had seldom known.

"The dawn was only gray, it was nothing to mention —"

"Just a gray evening turned upside down. I know."

"— and I was too tired to lift up my head to look at it, and so cold too. I'm glad I did it, and yet at the time it bored me more than I can say. And besides — you can believe me or not as you choose — I was very hungry. That dinner at Wimbledon — I meant it to last me all night like other dinners. I never thought that walking would make such a difference. Why, when you're walking you want, as it were, a breakfast and luncheon and tea during the night as well, and I'd nothing but a packet of Woodbines.° Lord, I did feel bad! Looking back, it wasn't what you may call enjoyment. It was more a case of sticking to it. I did stick. I — I was determined. Oh, hang it all! What's the good — I mean, the good of living in a room for ever? There one goes on day after day, same old game, same up and down to town, until you forget there is any other game. You ought to see once in a way what's going on outside, if it's only nothing particular after all."

"I should just think you ought," said Helen, sitting on the edge of the table.

The sound of a lady's voice recalled him from sincerity, and he said: "Curious it should all come about from reading something of Richard Jefferies."°

"Excuse me, Mr Bast, but you're wrong there. It didn't. It came from something far greater."

But she could not stop him. Borrow° was imminent after Jefferies — Borrow, Thoreau and sorrow. R. L. S. brought up the rear, and the outburst ended in a swamp of books. No disrespect to these great names. The fault is ours, not theirs. They mean us to use them for signposts, and are not to blame if, in our weakness, we mistake the signpost for the destination. And Leonard had reached the destination. He had visited the county of Surrey when darkness covered its amenities, and its cosy villas had re-entered ancient night. Every twelve hours this miracle happens, but he had troubled to go and see for himself. Within his cramped little mind dwelt something

---

**Woodbines:** Cheap cigarettes.   **Richard Jefferies:** Author (1848–1887) of novels and fantasies with rural (Wiltshire) settings.   **Borrow:** George Borrow (1803–1881), author of books of the open road often treating gypsy subjects; in *Lavengro* (1851), as Stallybrass points out, he describes Stonehenge.

that was greater than Jefferies's books — the spirit that led Jefferies to write them; and his dawn, though revealing nothing but monotones, was part of the eternal sunrise that shows George Borrow Stonehenge.

"Then you don't think I was foolish?" he asked, becoming again the naïve and sweet-tempered boy for whom nature had intended him.

"Heavens, no!" replied Margaret.

"Heaven help us if we do!" replied Helen.

"I'm very glad you say that. Now, my wife would never understand — not if I explained for days."

"No, it wasn't foolish!" cried Helen, her eyes aflame. "You've pushed back the boundaries; I think it splendid of you."

"You've not been content to dream as we have —"

"Though we have walked, too —"

"I must show you a picture upstairs —"

Here the door-bell rang. The hansom had come to take them to their evening party.

"Oh, bother, not to say dash — I had forgotten we were dining out; but do, do come round again and have a talk."

"Yes, you must — do," echoed Margaret.

Leonard, with extreme sentiment, replied: "No, I shall not. It's better like this."

"Why better?" asked Margaret.

"No, it is better not to risk a second interview. I shall always look back on this talk with you as one of the finest things in my life. Really. I mean this. We can never repeat. It has done me real good, and there we had better leave it."

"That's rather a sad view of life, surely."

"Things so often get spoiled."

"I know," flashed Helen, "but people don't."

He could not understand this. He continued in a vein which mingled true imagination and false. What he said wasn't wrong, but it wasn't right, and a false note jarred. One little twist, they felt, and the instrument might be in tune. One little strain, and it might be silent for ever. He thanked the ladies very much, but he would not call again. There was a moment's awkwardness, and then Helen said: "Go, then; perhaps you know best; but never forget you're better than Jefferies." And he went. Their hansom caught him up at the corner, passed with a waving of hands, and vanished with its accomplished load into the evening.

London was beginning to illuminate herself against the night. Electric lights sizzled and jagged in the main thoroughfares, gas lamps in the side-streets glimmered a canary gold or green. The sky was a crimson battlefield of spring, but London was not afraid. Her smoke mitigated the splendour, and the clouds down Oxford Street were a delicately painted ceiling, which adorned while it did not distract. She has never known the clear-cut armies of the purer air. Leonard hurried through her tinted corridors, very much part of the picture. His was a gray life, and to brighten it he had ruled off a few corners for Romance. The Miss Schlegels — or, to speak more accurately, his interview with them — were to fill such a corner, nor was it by any means the first time that he had talked intimately to strangers. The habit was analogous to a debauch, an outlet, though the worst of outlets, for instincts that would not be denied. Terrifying him, it would beat down his suspicions and prudence until he was confiding secrets to people whom he had scarcely seen. It brought him many fears and some pleasant memories. Perhaps the keenest happiness he had ever known was during a railway journey to Cambridge, where a decent-mannered undergraduate had spoken to him. They had got into conversation, and gradually Leonard flung reticence aside, told some of his domestic troubles, and hinted at the rest. The undergraduate, supposing they could start a friendship, asked him to "coffee after hall", which he accepted, but afterwards grew shy, and took care not to stir from the commercial hotel where he lodged. He did not want Romance to collide with the Porphyrion, still less with Jacky, and people with fuller, happier lives are slow to understand this. To the Schlegels, as to the undergraduate, he was an interesting creature, of whom they wanted to see more. But they to him were denizens of Romance, who must keep to the corner he had assigned them, pictures that must not walk out of their frames.

His behaviour over Margaret's visiting-card had been typical. His had scarcely been a tragic marriage. Where there is no money and no inclination to violence tragedy cannot be generated. He could not leave his wife, and he did not want to hit her. Petulance and squalor was enough. Here "that card" had come in. Leonard, though furtive, was untidy, and left it lying about. Jacky found it, and then began, "What's that card, eh?" "Yes, don't you wish you knew what that card was?" "Len, who's Miss Schlegel?" etc. Months passed, and the card, now as a joke, now as a grievance, was bandied about, getting dirtier and dirtier. It followed them when they moved from Camelia Road to Tulse Hill. It was submitted to third parties. A few inches of pasteboard, it became the battlefield on which the souls of Leonard and his wife contended. Why did he not say, "A lady took my umbrella, another gave me this that I might call for my umbrella"? Because Jacky would have disbelieved him? Partly, but chiefly because he was sentimental. No affection gathered round the card, but it symbolized the life of culture, that Jacky should never spoil. At night he would say to himself: "Well, at all events, she doesn't know about that card. Yah! Done her there!"

Poor Jacky! She was not a bad sort, and had a great deal to bear. She drew her own conclusion — she was only capable of drawing one conclusion — and in the fullness of time she acted upon it. All the Friday Leonard had refused to speak to her, and had spent the evening observing the stars. On the Saturday he went up, as usual, to town, but he came not back Saturday night, nor Sunday morning, nor Sunday afternoon. The inconvenience grew intolerable, and though she was now of a retiring habit, and shy of women, she went up to Wickham Place. Leonard returned in her absence. The card, the fatal card, was gone from the pages of Ruskin, and he guessed what had happened.

"Well?" he had exclaimed, greeting her with peals of laughter. "I know where you've been, but you don't know where I've been."

Jacky sighed, said, "Len, I do think you might explain," and resumed domesticity.

Explanations were difficult at this stage, and Leonard was too silly — or, it is tempting to write, too sound a chap to attempt them. His reticence was not entirely the shoddy article that a business life promotes, the reticence that pretends that nothing is something, and hides behind the *Daily Telegraph*. The adventurer, also, is reticent, and it is an adventure for a clerk to walk for a few hours in darkness. You may laugh at him, you who have slept nights out on the veldt, with your rifle beside you and all the atmosphere of adventure pat. And you also may laugh who think adventures silly. But do not be surprised if Leonard is shy whenever he meets you, and if the Schlegels rather than Jacky hear about the dawn.

That the Schlegels had not thought him foolish became a permanent joy. He was at his best when he thought of them. It buoyed him as he journeyed home beneath fading heavens. Somehow the barriers of wealth had fallen, and there had been — he could not phrase it — a general assertion of the wonder of the world. "My conviction," says the mystic,° "gains infinitely the moment another soul will believe in it," and they had agreed that there was something beyond life's daily gray. He took off his top-hat and smoothed it thoughtfully. He had hitherto supposed the unknown to be books, literature, clever conversation, culture. One raised oneself by study, and got upsides with the world. But in that quick interchange a new light dawned. Was that "something" walking in the dark among the suburban hills?

He discovered that he was going bareheaded down Regent Street. London came back with a rush. Few were about at this hour, but all whom he passed looked at him with a hostility that was the more impressive because it was unconscious. He put his hat on. It was too big; his head disappeared like a pudding into a basin, the ears bending outwards at the touch of the curly brim. He wore it a little backwards, and its effect was greatly to elongate the face and to bring out the distance between the eyes and the moustache. Thus equipped, he escaped criticism. No one felt uneasy as he titupped along the pavements, the heart of a man ticking fast in his chest.

## Chapter 15

The sisters went out to dinner full of their adventure, and when they were both full of the same subject there were few dinner parties that could stand up against them. This particular one, which was all ladies, had more kick in it than most, but succumbed after a struggle. Helen at one part of the table, Margaret at the other, would talk of Mr Bast and of no one else, and somewhere about the entrée their monologues collided, fell ruining, and became common property. Nor was this all. The dinner party was really an informal discussion club; there was a paper after it, read amid coffee-cups and laughter in the drawing-room, but dealing more or less thoughtfully with some topic of general interest. After the paper came a debate, and in this debate Mr Bast also figured, appearing now as a bright spot in civilization,

**the mystic:** The mystic is Novalis (Friedrich Leopold von Hardenberg, 1722–1801), German Romantic poet and novelist, who in *Fragmente vermischten Inhalts* wrote, "Es ist gewiss, dass eine Meinung sehr viel gewinnt, sobald ich weiss, dass irgend jemand davon überzeugt ist, sie wahrhaft annimmt" [It is certain that an opinion gains very much, as soon as I know that someone else is convinced of it, truly accepts it] (*Novalis Schriften*, ed. Ludwig Tieck and Fr. Schlegel, 5th ed., vol. 2 [Berlin: Reimer, 1837] 139). I have been unable to ascertain whether the citation in *Howards End* is Forster's own creative translation of Novalis or that of another, but it is perhaps worth noting that one of Novalis's editors shares a surname with Margaret and Helen.

now as a dark spot, according to the temperament of the speaker. The subject of the paper had been "How ought I to dispose of my money?" the reader professing to be a millionaire on the point of death, inclined to bequeath her fortune for the foundation of local art galleries, but open to conviction from other sources. The various parts had been assigned beforehand, and some of the speeches were amusing. The hostess assumed the ungrateful role of "the millionaire's eldest son", and implored her expiring parent not to dislocate society by allowing such vast sums to pass out of the family. Money was the fruit of self-denial, and the second generation had a right to profit by the self-denial of the first. What right had "Mr Bast" to profit? The National Gallery was good enough for the likes of him. After property had had its say — a say that is necessarily ungracious — the various philanthropists stepped forward. Something must be done for "Mr Bast": his conditions must be improved without impairing his independence; he must have a free library, or free tennis-courts; his rent must be paid in such a way that he did not know it was being paid; it must be made worth his while to join the Territorials;° he must be forcibly parted from his uninspiring wife, the money going to her as compensation; he must be assigned a Twin Star, some member of the leisured classes who would watch over him ceaselessly (groans from Helen); he must be given food but no clothes, clothes but no food, a third-return ticket to Venice, without either food or clothes when he arrived there. In short, he might be given anything and everything so long as it was not the money itself.

And here Margaret interrupted.

"Order, order, Miss Schlegel!" said the reader of the paper. "You are here, I understand, to advise me in the interests of the Society for the Preservation of Places of Historic Interest or Natural Beauty. I cannot have you speaking out of your role. It makes my poor head go round, and I think you forget that I am very ill."

"Your head won't go round if only you'll listen to my argument," said Margaret. "Why not give him the money itself? You're supposed to have about thirty thousand a year."

"Have I? I thought I had a million."

"Wasn't a million your capital? Dear me! We ought to have settled that. Still, it doesn't matter. Whatever you've got, I order you to give as many poor men as you can three hundred a year each."

the Territorials: Part of Richard Haldane's army reforms, beginning in 1906; the Territorial Force turned the old "Volunteers" and "Yeomanry" into effective fighting units.

"But that would be pauperizing them," said an earnest girl, who liked the Schlegels, but thought them a little unspiritual at times.

"Not if you gave them so much. A big windfall would not pauperize a man. It is these little driblets, distributed among too many, that do the harm. Money's educational. It's far more educational than the things it buys." There was a protest. "In a sense," added Margaret, but the protest continued. "Well, isn't the most civilized thing going the man who has learned to wear his income properly?"

"Exactly what your Mr Basts won't do."

"Give them a chance. Give them money. Don't dole them out poetry books and railway tickets like babies. Give them the wherewithal to buy these things. When your socialism comes it may be different, and we may think in terms of commodities instead of cash. Till it comes give people cash, for it is the warp of civilization, whatever the woof may be. The imagination ought to play upon money and realize it vividly, for it's the — the second most important thing in the world. It is so slurred over and hushed up, there is so little clear thinking — oh, political economy, of course, but so few of us think clearly about our own private incomes, and admit that independent thoughts are in nine cases out of ten the result of independent means. Money: give Mr Bast money, and don't bother about his ideals. He'll pick up those for himself."

She leant back while the more earnest members of the club began to misconstrue her. The female mind, though cruelly practical in daily life, cannot bear to hear ideals belittled in conversation, and Miss Schlegel was asked how ever she could say such dreadful things, and what it would profit Mr Bast if he gained the whole world and lost his own soul. She answered, Nothing, but he would not gain his soul until he had gained a little of the world. Then they said, No, they did not believe it, and she admitted that an overworked clerk may save his soul in the superterrestrial sense, where the effort will be taken for the deed, but she denied that he will ever explore the spiritual resources of this world, will ever know the rarer joys of the body, or attain to clear and passionate intercourse with his fellows. Others had attacked the fabric of society — property, interest, etc.; she only fixed her eyes on a few human beings, to see how, under present conditions, they could be made happier. Doing good to humanity was useless: the many-coloured efforts thereto spreading over the vast area like films and resulting in a universal gray. To do good to one, or, as in this case, to a few, was the utmost she dare hope for.

Between the idealists and the political economists, Margaret had a bad time. Disagreeing elsewhere, they agreed in disowning her, and in keeping the administration of the millionaire's money in their own hands. The earnest girl brought forward a scheme of "personal supervision and mutual help", the effect of which was to alter poor people until they became exactly like people who were not so poor. The hostess pertinently remarked that she, as eldest son, might surely rank among the millionaire's legatees. Margaret weakly admitted the claim, and another claim was at once set up by Helen, who declared that she had been the millionaire's housemaid for over forty years, overfed and underpaid; was nothing to be done for her, so corpulent and poor? The millionaire then read out her last will and testament, in which she left the whole of her fortune to the Chancellor of the Exchequer. Then she died. The serious parts of the discussion had been of higher merit than the playful — in a men's debate is the reverse more general? — but the meeting broke up hilariously enough, and a dozen happy ladies dispersed to their homes.

Helen and Margaret walked the earnest girl as far as Battersea Bridge Station, arguing copiously all the way. When she had gone they were conscious of an alleviation, and of the great beauty of the evening. They turned back towards Oakley Street. The lamps and the plane trees, following the line of the embankment, struck a note of dignity that is rare in English cities. The seats, almost deserted, were here and there occupied by gentlefolk in evening dress, who had strolled out from the houses behind to enjoy fresh air and the whisper of the rising tide. There is something continental about Chelsea Embankment. It is an open space used rightly, a blessing more frequent in Germany than here. As Margaret and Helen sat down, the city behind them seemed to be a vast theatre, an opera-house in which some endless trilogy was performing, and they themselves a pair of satisfied subscribers, who did not mind losing a little of the second act.

"Cold?"

"No."

"Tired?"

"Doesn't matter."

The earnest girl's train rumbled away over the bridge.

"I say, Helen —"

"Well?"

"Are we really going to follow up Mr Bast?"

"I don't know."

"I think we won't."

"As you like."

"It's no good, I think, unless you really mean to know people. The discussion brought that home to me. We got on well enough with him in a spirit of excitement, but think of rational intercourse. We mustn't play at friendship. No, it's no good."

"There's Mrs Lanoline, too," Helen yawned. "So dull."

"Just so, and possibly worse than dull."

"I should like to know how he got hold of your card."

"But he said — something about a concert and an umbrella —"

"Then did the card see the wife —"

"Helen, come to bed."

"No, just a little longer, it is so beautiful. Tell me; oh yes; did you say money is the warp of the world?"

"Yes."

"Then what's the woof?"

"Very much what one chooses," said Margaret. "It's something that isn't money — one can't say more."

"Walking at night?"

"Probably."

"For Tibby, Oxford?"

"It seems so."

"For you?"

"Now that we have to leave Wickham Place, I begin to think it's that. For Mrs Wilcox it was certainly Howards End."

One's own name will carry immense distances. Mr Wilcox, who was sitting with friends many seats away, heard his, rose to his feet, and strolled along towards the speakers.

"It is sad to suppose that places may ever be more important than people," continued Margaret.

"Why, Meg? They're so much nicer generally. I'd rather think of that forester's house in Pomerania than of the fat Herr Förstmeister who lived in it."

"I believe we shall come to care about people less and less, Helen. The more people one knows the easier it becomes to replace them. It's one of the curses of London. I quite expect to end my life caring most for a place."

Here Mr Wilcox reached them. It was several weeks since they had met.

"How do you do?" he cried. "I thought I recognized your voices. What ever are you both doing down here?"

His tones were protective. He implied that one ought not to sit out on Chelsea Embankment without a male escort. Helen resented this, but Margaret accepted it as part of the good man's equipment.

"What an age it is since I've seen you, Mr Wilcox. I met Evie in the Tube, though, lately. I hope you have good news of your son."

"Paul?" said Mr Wilcox, extinguishing his cigarette, and sitting down between them. "Oh, Paul's all right. We had a line from Madeira. He'll be at work again by now."

"Ugh —" said Helen, shuddering from complex causes.

"I beg your pardon?"

"Isn't the climate of Nigeria too horrible?"

"Someone's got to go," he said simply. "England will never keep her trade overseas unless she is prepared to make sacrifices. Unless we get firm in West Africa, Ger — untold complications may follow. Now tell me all your news."

"Oh, we've had a splendid evening," cried Helen, who always woke up at the advent of a visitor. "We belong to a kind of club that reads papers, Margaret and I — all women, but there is a discussion after. This evening it was on how one ought to leave one's money — whether to one's family, or to the poor, and if so how — oh, most interesting."

The man of business smiled. Since his wife's death he had almost doubled his income. He was an important figure at last, a reassuring name on company prospectuses, and life had treated him very well. The world seemed in his grasp as he listened to the river Thames, which still flowed inland from the sea. So wonderful to the girls, it held no mysteries for him. He had helped to shorten its long tidal trough by taking shares in the lock at Teddington, and, if he and other capitalists thought good, some day it could be shortened again. With a good dinner inside him and an amiable but academic woman on either flank, he felt that his hands were on all the ropes of life, and that what he did not know could not be worth knowing.

"Sounds a most original entertainment!" he exclaimed, and laughed in his pleasant way. "I wish Evie would go to that sort of thing. But she hasn't the time. She's taken to breed Aberdeen terriers — jolly little dogs."

"I expect we'd better be doing the same, really."

"We pretend we're improving ourselves, you see," said Helen a little sharply, for the Wilcox glamour is not of the kind that returns, and she had bitter memories of the days when a speech such as he had just made would have impressed her favourably. "We suppose it a good thing to waste an evening once a fortnight over a debate, but, as my sister says, it may be better to breed dogs."

"Not at all. I don't agree with your sister. There's nothing like a debate to teach one quickness. I often wish I had gone in for them when I was a youngster. It would have helped me no end."

"Quickness — ?"

"Yes. Quickness in argument. Time after time I've missed scoring a point because the other man has had the gift of the gab and I haven't. Oh, I believe in these discussions."

The patronizing tone, thought Margaret, came well enough from a man who was old enough to be their father. She had always maintained that Mr Wilcox had a charm. In times of sorrow or emotion his inadequacy had pained her, but it was pleasant to listen to him now, and to watch his thick brown moustache and high forehead confronting the stars. But Helen was nettled. The aim of *their* debates, she implied, was Truth.

"Oh yes, it doesn't much matter what subject you take," said he.

Margaret laughed and said, "But this is going to be far better than the debate itself." Helen recovered herself and laughed too. "No, I won't go on," she declared. "I'll just put our special case to Mr Wilcox."

"About Mr Bast? Yes, do. He'll be more lenient to a special case."

"But, Mr Wilcox, do first light another cigarette. It's this. We've just come across a young fellow, who's evidently very poor, and who seems interest —"

"What's his profession?"

"Clerk."

"What in?"

"Do you remember, Margaret?"

"Porphyrion Fire Insurance Company."

"Oh yes; the nice people who gave Aunt Juley a new hearth-rug. He seems interesting, in some ways very, and one wishes one could help him. He is married to a wife whom he doesn't seem to care for much. He likes books, and what one may roughly call adventure, and if he had a chance — but he is so poor. He lives a life where all the money is apt to go on nonsense and clothes. One is so afraid that circumstances will be too strong for him and that he will sink. Well, he got mixed up in our debate. He wasn't the subject of it, but it seemed to bear on his point. Suppose a millionaire died, and desired to leave money to help such a man. How should he be helped? Should he be given three hundred pounds a year direct, which was Margaret's plan? Most of them thought this would pauperize him. Should he and those like him be given free libraries? I said 'No!' He doesn't want more books to read, but to read books rightly. My suggestion was he should be given something every year towards a summer holiday, but then there is his wife, and they said she would have to go too. Nothing seemed quite right! Now what do you think? Imagine that you were a millionaire, and wanted to help the poor. What would you do?"

Mr Wilcox, whose fortune was not so very far below the standard indicated, laughed exuberantly. "My dear Miss Schlegel, I will not rush in where your sex has been unable to tread. I will not add another plan to the numerous excellent ones that have been already suggested. My only contribution is this: let your young friend clear out of the Porphyrion Fire Insurance Company with all possible speed."

"Why?" said Margaret.

He lowered his voice. "This is between friends. It'll be in the Receiver's hands before Christmas. It'll smash," he added, thinking that she had not understood.

"Dear me, Helen, listen to that. And he'll have to get another place!"

"*Will* have? Let him leave the ship before it sinks. Let him get one now."

"Rather than wait to make sure?"

"Decidedly."

"Why's that?"

Again the Olympian laugh, and the lowered voice. "Naturally the man who's in a situation when he applies stands a better chance, is in a stronger position, than the man who isn't. It looks as if he's worth something. I know by myself (this is letting you into the state secrets) it affects an employer greatly. Human nature, I'm afraid."

"I hadn't thought of that," murmured Margaret, while Helen said: "Our human nature appears to be the other way round. We employ people because they're unemployed. The boot man, for instance."

"And how does he clean the boots?"

"Not well," confessed Margaret.

"There you are!"

"Then do you really advise us to tell this youth — ?"

"I advise nothing," he interrupted, glancing up and down the Embankment, in case his indiscretion had been overheard. "I oughtn't to have spoken — but I happen to know, being more or less behind the scenes. The Porphyrion's a bad, bad concern — now, don't say I said so. It's outside the Tariff Ring."°

"Certainly I won't say. In fact, I don't know what that means."

---

**Tariff Ring:** An alliance of insurance companies.

"I thought an insurance company never smashed," was Helen's contribution. "Don't the others always run in and save them?"

"You're thinking of reinsurance," said Mr Wilcox mildly. "It is exactly there that the Porphyrion is weak. It has tried to undercut, has been badly hit by a long series of small fires, and it hasn't been able to reinsure. I'm afraid that public companies don't save one another for love."

"'Human nature', I suppose," quoted Helen, and he laughed and agreed that it was. When Margaret said that she supposed that clerks, like everyone else, found it extremely difficult to get situations in these days, he replied, "Yes, extremely," and rose to rejoin his friends. He knew by his own office — seldom a vacant post, and hundreds of applicants for it; at present no vacant post.

"And how's Howards End looking?" said Margaret, wishing to change the subject before they parted. Mr Wilcox was a little apt to think one wanted to get something out of him.

"It's let."

"Really. And you wandering homeless in long-haired Chelsea? How strange are the ways of fate!"

"No; it's let unfurnished. We've moved."

"Why, I thought of you both as anchored there for ever. Evie never told me."

"I dare say when you met Evie the thing wasn't settled. We only moved a week ago. Paul has rather a feeling for the old place, and we held on for him to have his holiday there; but, really, it is impossibly small. Endless drawbacks. I forget whether you've been up to it?"

"As far as the house, never."

"Well, Howards End is one of those converted farms. They don't really do, spend what you will on them. We messed away with a garage all among the wych-elm roots, and last year we enclosed a bit of the meadow and attempted a rockery. Evie got rather keen on Alpine plants. But it didn't do — no, it didn't do. You remember, or your sister will remember, the farm with those abominable guinea-fowls, and the hedge that the old woman never would cut properly, so that it all went thin at the bottom. And, inside the house, the beams — and the staircase through a door — picturesque enough, but not a place to live in." He glanced over the parapet cheerfully. "Full tide. And the position wasn't right either. The neighbourhood's getting suburban. Either be in London or out of it, I say; so we've taken a house in Ducie Street, close to Sloane Street,° and a place right down in Shropshire —

***

Sloane Street: The autograph manuscript has "Sloane Square."

Oniton Grange. Ever heard of Oniton? Do come and see us — right
away from everywhere, up towards Wales."

"What a change!" said Margaret. But the change was in her own
voice, which had become most sad. "I can't imagine Howards End or
Hilton without you."

"Hilton isn't without us," he replied. "Charles is there still."

"Still?" said Margaret, who had not kept up with the Charleses.
"But I thought he was still at Epsom. They were furnishing that
Christmas — one Christmas. How everything alters! I used to admire
Mrs Charles from our windows very often. Wasn't it Epsom?"

"Yes, but they moved eighteen months ago. Charles, the good
chap" — his voice dropped — "thought I should be lonely. I didn't
want him to move, but he would, and took a house at the other end of
Hilton, down by the Six Hills. He had a motor, too. There they all
are, a very jolly party — he and she and the two grandchildren."

"I manage other people's affairs so much better than they manage
them themselves," said Margaret as they shook hands. "When you
moved out of Howards End, I should have moved Mr Charles Wilcox
into it. I should have kept so remarkable a place in the family."

"So it is," he replied. "I haven't sold it, and don't mean to."

"No; but none of you are there."

"Oh, we've got a splendid tenant — Hamar Bryce, an invalid. If
Charles ever wanted it — but he won't. Dolly is so dependent on
modern conveniences. No, we have all decided against Howards End.
We like it in a way, but now we feel that it is neither one thing nor the
other. One must have one thing or the other."

"And some people are lucky enough to have both. You're doing
yourself proud, Mr Wilcox. My congratulations."

"And mine," said Helen.

"Do remind Evie to come and see us — Two, Wickham Place. We
shan't be there very long, either."

"You, too, on the move?"

"Next September," Margaret sighed.

"Everyone moving! Goodbye."

The tide had begun to ebb. Margaret leant over the parapet and
watched it sadly. Mr Wilcox had forgotten his wife, Helen her lover;
she herself was probably forgetting. Everyone moving. Is it worth
while attempting the past when there is this continual flux even in the
hearts of men?

Helen roused her by saying: "What a prosperous vulgarian Mr
Wilcox has grown! I have very little use for him in these days. How-

ever, he did tell us about the Porphyrion. Let us write to Mr Bast as soon as ever we get home, and tell him to clear out of it at once."

"Do; yes, that's worth doing. Let us."

"Let's ask him to tea."

## Chapter 16

Leonard accepted the invitation to tea next Saturday. But he was right: the visit proved a conspicuous failure.

"Sugar?" said Margaret.

"Cake?" said Helen. "The big cake or the little deadlies? I'm afraid you thought my letter rather odd, but we'll explain — we aren't odd, really — nor affected, really. We're over-expressive: that's all."

As a lady's lap-dog Leonard did not excel. He was not an Italian, still less a Frenchman, in whose blood there runs the very spirit of persiflage and of gracious repartee. His wit was the Cockney's; it opened no doors into imagination, and Helen was drawn up short by "The more a lady has to say, the better", administered waggishly.

"Oh yes," she said.

"Ladies brighten —"

"Yes, I know. The darlings are regular sunbeams. Let me give you a plate."

"How do you like your work?" interposed Margaret.

He, too, was drawn up short. He would not have these women prying into his work. They were Romance, and so was the room to which he had at last penetrated, with the queer sketches of people bathing upon its walls, and so were the very teacups, with their delicate borders of wild strawberries. But he would not let Romance interfere with his life. There is the devil to pay then.

"Oh, well enough," he answered.

"Your company is the Porphyrion, isn't it?"

"Yes, that's so" — becoming rather offended. "It's funny how things get round."

"Why funny?" asked Helen, who did not follow the workings of his mind. "It was written as large as life on your card, and considering we wrote to you there, and that you replied on the stamped paper —"

"Would you call the Porphyrion one of the big insurance companies?" pursued Margaret.

"It depends what you call big."

"I mean by big a solid, well-established concern, that offers a reasonably good career to its employees."

"I couldn't say — some would tell you one thing and others another," said the employee uneasily. "For my own part" — he shook
his head — "I only believe half I hear. Not that even; it's safer. Those
clever ones come to the worse grief, I've often noticed. Ah, you can't
be too careful."

He drank, and wiped his moustache, which was going to be one of
those moustaches that always droop into teacups — more bother than
they're worth, surely, and not fashionable either.

"I quite agree, and that's why I was curious to know: is it a solid,
well-established concern?"

Leonard had no idea. He understood his own corner of the machine, but nothing beyond it. He desired to confess neither knowledge nor ignorance, and under these circumstances another motion of
the head seemed safest. To him, as to the British public, the Porphyrion was the Porphyrion of the advertisement — a giant, in the
classical style,° but draped sufficiently, who held in one hand a burning
torch, and pointed with the other to St Paul's and Windsor Castle. A
large sum of money was inscribed below, and you drew your own con-
clusions. This giant caused Leonard to do arithmetic and write letters,
to explain the regulations to new clients, and re-explain them to old
ones. A giant was of an impulsive morality — one knew that much. He
would pay for Mrs Munt's hearth-rug with ostentatious haste, a large
claim he would repudiate quietly, and fight court by court. But his
true fighting weight, his antecedents, his amours with other members
of the commercial Pantheon — all these were as uncertain to ordinary
mortals as were the escapades of Zeus. While the gods are powerful,
we learn little about them. It is only in the days of their decadence that
a strong light beats into heaven.

"We were told the Porphyrion's no go," blurted Helen. "We
wanted to tell you; that's why we wrote."

"A friend of ours did think that it is insufficiently reinsured," said
Margaret.

Now Leonard had his clue. He must praise the Porphyrion. "You
can tell your friend," he said, "that he's quite wrong."

"Oh, good!"

The young man coloured a little. In his circle to be wrong was
fatal. The Miss Schlegels did not mind being wrong. They were gen-

a giant, in the classical style: In Greek myth, Porphyrion was a giant who waged war
on Zeus.

uinely glad that they had been misinformed. To them nothing was fatal but evil.

"Wrong, so to speak," he added.

"How 'so to speak'?"

"I mean I wouldn't say he's right altogether."

But this was a blunder. "Then he is right partly," said the elder woman, quick as lightning.

Leonard replied that everyone was right partly, if it came to that.

"Mr Bast, I don't understand business, and I dare say my questions are stupid, but can you tell me what makes a concern 'right' or 'wrong'?"

Leonard sat back with a sigh.

"Our friend, who is also a businessman, was so positive. He said before Christmas —"

"And advised you to clear out of it," concluded Helen. "But I don't see why he should know better than you do."

Leonard rubbed his hands. He was tempted to say that he knew nothing about the thing at all. But a commercial training was too strong for him. Nor could he say it was a bad thing, for this would be giving it away; nor yet that it was good, for this would be giving it away equally. He attempted to suggest that it was something between the two, with vast possibilities in either direction, but broke down under the gaze of four sincere eyes. As yet he scarcely distinguished between the two sisters. One was more beautiful and more lively, but "the Miss Schlegels" still remained a composite Indian god, whose waving arms and contradictory speeches were the product of a single mind.

"One can but see," he remarked, adding, "As Ibsen says, 'things happen'."° He was itching to talk about books and make the most of his romantic hour. Minute after minute slipped away, while the ladies, with imperfect skill, discussed the subject of reinsurance or praised their anonymous friend. Leonard grew annoyed — perhaps rightly. He made vague remarks about not being one of those who minded their affairs being talked over by others, but they did not take the hint. Men might have shown more tact. Women, however tactful elsewhere, are heavy-handed here. They cannot see why we should shroud our incomes and our prospects in a veil. "How much exactly have you, and

As Ibsen says, "things happen": It is hardly likely that the Norwegian dramatist Henrik Ibsen (1828–1906) made this trite saying.

how much do you expect to have next June?" And these were women with a theory, who held that reticence about money matters is absurd, and that life would be truer if each would state the exact size of the golden island upon which he stands, the exact stretch of warp over which he throws the woof that is not money. How can we do justice to the pattern otherwise?

And the precious minutes slipped away, and Jacky and squalor came nearer. At last he could bear it no longer, and broke in, reciting the names of books feverishly. There was a moment of piercing joy when Margaret said, "So *you* like Carlyle," and then the door opened, and "Mr Wilcox, Miss Wilcox" entered, preceded by two prancing puppies.

"Oh, the dears! Oh, Evie, how too impossibly sweet!" screamed Helen, falling on her hands and knees.

"We brought the little fellows round," said Mr Wilcox.

"I bred 'em myself."

"Oh, really! Mr Bast, come and play with puppies."

"I've got to be going now," said Leonard sourly.

"But play with puppies a little first."

"This is Ahab, that's Jezebel,"° said Evie, who was one of those who name animals after the less successful characters of Old Testament history.

"I've got to be going."

Helen was too much occupied with puppies to notice him.

"Mr Wilcox, Mr Ba — must you be really? Goodbye!"

"Come again," said Helen from the floor.

Then Leonard's gorge rose. Why should he come again? What was the good of it? He said roundly: "No, I shan't; I knew it would be a failure."

Most people would have let him go. "A little mistake. We tried knowing another class — impossible." But the Schlegels had never played with life. They had attempted friendship, and they would take the consequences. Helen retorted, "I call that a very rude remark. What do you want to turn on me like that for?" and suddenly the drawing-room re-echoed to a vulgar row.

"You ask me why I turn on you?"

"Yes."

---

**Ahab . . . Jezebel:** As Stallybrass notes, after Ahab's death "the dogs licked up his blood" (1 Kings 22.38); Jezebel was actually eaten by dogs (2 Kings 9.35–36).

"What do you want to have me here for?"

"To help you, you silly boy!" cried Helen. "And don't shout."

"*I* don't want your patronage. *I* don't want your tea. I was quite happy. What do you want to unsettle me for?" He turned to Mr Wilcox. "I put it to this gentleman. I ask you, sir, am I to have my brain picked?"

Mr Wilcox turned to Margaret with the air of humorous strength that he could so well command. "Are we intruding, Miss Schlegel? Can we be of any use, or shall we go?"

But Margaret ignored him.

"I'm connected with a leading insurance company, sir. I receive what I take to be an invitation from these — ladies" (he drawled the word). "I come, and it's to have my brain picked. I ask you, is it fair?"

"Highly unfair," said Mr Wilcox, drawing a gasp from Evie, who knew that her father was becoming dangerous.

"There, you hear that? Most unfair, the gentleman says. There! Not content with" — pointing at Margaret — "you can't deny it." His voice rose: he was falling into the rhythm of a scene with Jacky. "But as soon as I'm useful it's a very different thing. 'Oh yes, send for him. Cross-question him. Pick his brains.' Oh yes. Now, take me on the whole, I'm a quiet fellow: I'm law-abiding, I don't wish any un-pleasantness; but I — I —"

"You," said Margaret — "you — you —"

Laughter from Evie, as at a repartee.

"You are the man who tried to walk by the Pole Star."

More laughter.

"You saw the sunrise."

Laughter.

"You tried to get away from the fogs that are stifling us all — away past books and houses to the truth. You were looking for a real home."

"I fail to see the connection," said Leonard, hot with stupid anger.

"So do I." There was a pause. "You were that last Sunday — you are this today. Mr Bast! I and my sister have talked you over. We wanted to help you; we also supposed you might help us. We did not have you here out of charity — which bores us — but because we hoped there would be a connection between last Sunday and other days. What is the good of your stars and trees, your sunrise and the wind, if they do not enter into our daily lives? They have never entered into mine, but into yours, we thought — haven't we all to struggle against life's daily grayness, against pettiness, against mechanical cheerfulness, against suspicion? I struggle by remembering my friends; others I have known by remembering some place — some beloved place or tree — we thought you one of these."

"Of course, if there's been any misunderstanding," mumbled Leonard, "all I can do is to go. But I beg to state —" He paused. Ahab and Jezebel danced at his boots and made him look ridiculous. "You were picking my brain for official information — I can prove it — I —" He blew his nose and left them.

"Can I help you now?" said Mr Wilcox, turning to Margaret. "May I have one quiet word with him in the hall?"

"Helen, go after him — do anything — *anything* — to make the noodle understand."

Helen hesitated.

"But really —" said their visitor. "Ought she to?"

At once she went.

He resumed. "I would have chimed in, but I felt that you could polish him off for yourselves — I didn't interfere. You were splendid, Miss Schlegel — absolutely splendid. You can take my word for it, but there are very few women who could have managed him."

"Oh yes," said Margaret distractedly.

"Bowling him over with those long sentences was what fetched me," cried Evie.

"Yes, indeed," chuckled her father; "all that part about 'mechanical cheerfulness' — oh, fine!"

"I'm very sorry," said Margaret, collecting herself. "He's a nice creature really. I cannot think what set him off. It has been most unpleasant for you."

"Oh, *I* didn't mind." Then he changed his mood. He asked if he might speak as an old friend, and, permission given, said: "Oughtn't you really to be more careful?"

Margaret laughed, though her thoughts still strayed after Helen. "Do you realize that it's all your fault?" she said. "You're responsible."

"I?"

"This is the young man whom we were to warn against the Porphyrion. We warn him, and — look!"

Mr Wilcox was annoyed. "I hardly consider that a fair deduction," he said.

"Obviously unfair," said Margaret. "I was only thinking how tangled things are. It's our fault mostly — neither yours nor his."

"Not his?"

"No."

"Miss Schlegel, you are too kind."

"Yes, indeed," nodded Evie, a little contemptuously. "You behave much too well to people, and then they impose on you. I know the world and that type of man, and as soon as I entered the room I saw you had not been treating him properly. You must keep that type at a distance. Otherwise they forget themselves. Sad, but true. They aren't our sort, and one must face the fact."

"Ye-es."

"Do admit that we should never have had this outburst if he was a gentleman."

"I admit it willingly," said Margaret, who was pacing up and down the room. "A gentleman would have kept his suspicions to himself."

Mr Wilcox watched her with a vague uneasiness.

"What did he suspect you of?"

"Of wanting to make money out of him."

"Intolerable brute! But how were you to benefit?"

"Exactly. How indeed! Just horrible, corroding suspicion. One touch of thought or of goodwill would have brushed it away. Just the senseless fear that does make men intolerable brutes."

"I come back to my original point. You ought to be more careful, Miss Schlegel. Your servants ought to have orders not to let such people in."

She turned to him frankly. "Let me explain exactly why we like this man, and want to see him again."

"That's your clever way of talking. I shall never believe you like him."

"I do. Firstly, because he cares for physical adventure, just as you do. Yes, you go motoring and shooting; he would like to go camping out. Secondly, he cares for something special *in* adventure. It is quickest to call that special something poetry —"

"Oh, he's one of that writer sort."

"No — oh no! I mean he may be, but it would be loathsome stuff. His brain is filled with the husks of books, culture — horrible; we want him to wash out his brain and go to the real thing. We want to show him how he may get upsides with life. As I said, either friends or the country, some" — she hesitated — "either some very dear person or some very dear place seems necessary to relieve life's daily gray, and to show that it *is* gray. If possible, one should have both."

Some of her words ran past Mr Wilcox. He let them run past. Others he caught and criticized with admirable lucidity.

"Your mistake is this, and it is a very common mistake. This young bounder has a life of his own. What right have you to conclude it is an unsuccessful life, or, as you call it, 'gray'?"

"Because —"

"One minute. You know nothing about him. He probably has his own joys and interests — wife, children, snug little home. That's where we practical fellows" — he smiled — "are more tolerant than you intellectuals. We live and let live, and assume that things are jogging on fairly well elsewhere, and that the ordinary plain man may be trusted to look after his own affairs. I quite grant — I look at the faces of the clerks in my own office, and observe them to be dull, but I don't know what's going on beneath. So, by the way, with London. I have heard you rail against London, Miss Schlegel, and it seems a funny thing to say but I was very angry with you. What do you know about London? You only see civilization from the outside. I don't say in your case, but in too many cases that attitude leads to morbidity, discontent and socialism."

She admitted the strength of his position, though it undermined imagination. As he spoke, some outposts of poetry and perhaps of sympathy fell ruining, and she retreated to what she called her "second line" — to the special facts of the case.

"His wife is an old bore," she said simply. "He never came home last Saturday night because he wanted to be alone, and she thought he was with us."

"With *you?*"

"Yes." Evie tittered. "He hasn't got the cosy home that you assumed. He needs outside interests."

"Naughty young man!" cried the girl.

"Naughty?" said Margaret, who hated naughtiness more than sin. "When you're married, Miss Wilcox, won't you want outside interests?"

"He has apparently got them," put in Mr Wilcox slyly.

"Yes, indeed, father."

"He was tramping in Surrey, if you mean that," said Margaret, pacing away rather crossly.

"Oh, I dare say!"

"Miss Wilcox, he was!"

"M-m-m-m!" from Mr Wilcox, who thought the episode amusing, if risqué. With most ladies he would not have discussed it, but he was trading on Margaret's reputation as an emancipated woman.

"He said so, and about such a thing he wouldn't lie."

They both began to laugh.

"That's where I differ from you. Men lie about their positions and prospects, but not about a thing of that sort."

He shook his head. "Miss Schlegel, excuse me, but I know the type."

"I said before — he isn't a type. He cares about adventures rightly. He's certain that our smug existence isn't all. He's vulgar and hysterical and bookish, but don't think that sums him up. There's manhood in him as well. Yes, that's what I'm trying to say. He's a real man."

As she spoke their eyes met, and it was as if Mr Wilcox's defences fell. She saw back to the real man in him. Unwittingly she had touched his emotions. A woman and two men — they had formed the magic triangle of sex, and the male was thrilled to jealousy, in case the female was attracted by another male. Love, say the ascetics, reveals our shameful kinship with the beasts. Be it so; one can bear that; jealousy is the real shame. It is jealousy, not love, that connects us with the farmyard intolerably, and calls up visions of two angry cocks and a complacent hen. Margaret crushed complacency down because she was civilized. Mr Wilcox, uncivilized, continued to feel anger long after he had rebuilt his defences, and was again presenting a bastion to the world.

"Miss Schlegel, you're a pair of dear creatures, but you really *must* be careful in this uncharitable world. What does your brother say?"

"I forget."

"Surely he has some opinion?"

"He laughs, if I remember correctly."

"He's very clever, isn't he?" said Evie, who had met and detested Tibby at Oxford.

"Yes, pretty well — but I wonder what Helen's doing."

"She is very young to undertake this sort of thing," said Mr Wilcox.

Margaret went out into the landing. She heard no sound, and Mr Bast's topper was missing from the hall.

"Helen!" she called.

"Yes!" replied a voice from the library.

"You in there?"

"Yes — he's gone some time."

Margaret went to her. "Why, you're all alone," she said.

"Yes — it's all right, Meg. Poor, poor creature —"

"Come back to the Wilcoxes and tell me later — Mr W. much concerned, and slightly titillated."

"Oh, I've no patience with him. I hate him. Poor dear Mr Bast!

He wanted to talk literature, and we would talk business. Such a muddle of a man, and yet so worth pulling through. I like him extraordinarily."

"Well done," said Margaret, kissing her, "but come into the drawing-room now, and don't talk about him to the Wilcoxes. Make light of the whole thing."

Helen came and behaved with a cheerfulness that reassured their visitor — this hen at all events was fancy-free.

"He's gone with my blessing," she cried, "and now for puppies."

As they drove away, Mr Wilcox said to his daughter:

"I am really concerned at the way those girls go on. They are as clever as you make 'em, but unpractical — God bless me! One of these days they'll go too far. Girls like that oughtn't to live alone in London. Until they marry, they ought to have someone to look after them. We must look in more often — we're better than no one. You like them, don't you, Evie?"

Evie replied: "Helen's right enough, but I can't stand the toothy one. And I shouldn't have called either of them girls."

Evie had grown up handsome. Dark-eyed, with the glow of youth under sunburn, built firmly and firm-lipped, she was the best the Wilcoxes could do in the way of feminine beauty. For the present, puppies and her father were the only things she loved, but the net of matrimony was being prepared for her, and a few days later she was attracted to a Mr Percy Cahill, an uncle of Mrs Charles's, and he was attracted to her.

## Chapter 17

The Age of Property holds bitter moments even for a proprietor. When a move is imminent, furniture becomes ridiculous, and Margaret now lay awake at nights wondering where, where on earth they and all their belongings would be deposited in September next. Chairs, tables, pictures, books, that had rumbled down to them through the generations, must rumble forward again like a slide of rubbish to which she longed to give the final push, and send it toppling into the sea. But there were all their father's books — they never read them, but they were their father's, and must be kept. There was the marble-topped chiffonier — their mother had set store by it, they could not remember why. Round every knob and cushion in the house sentiment gathered, a sentiment that was at times personal, but more often a faint piety to the dead, a prolongation of rites that might have ended at the grave.

It was absurd, if you came to think of it; Helen and Tibby came to think of it; Margaret was too busy with the house-agents. The feudal ownership of land did bring dignity, whereas the modern ownership of movables is reducing us again to a nomadic horde. We are reverting to the civilization of luggage, and historians of the future will note how the middle classes accreted possessions without taking root in the earth, and may find in this the secret of their imaginative poverty. The Schlegels were certainly the poorer for the loss of Wickham Place. It had helped to balance their lives, and almost to counsel them. Nor is their ground-landlord spiritually the richer. He has built flats on its site, his motor-cars grow swifter, his exposures of socialism more trenchant. But he has spilt the precious distillation of the years, and no chemistry of his can give it back to society again.

Margaret grew depressed; she was anxious to settle on a house before they left town to pay their annual visit to Mrs Munt. She enjoyed this visit, and wanted to have her mind at ease for it. Swanage, though dull, was stable, and this year she longed more than usual for its fresh air and for the magnificent downs that guard it on the north. But London thwarted her; in its atmosphere she could not concentrate. London only stimulates, it cannot sustain; and Margaret, hurrying over its surface for a house without knowing what sort of a house she wanted, was paying for many a thrilling sensation in the past. She could not even break loose from culture, and her time was wasted by concerts which it would be a sin to miss, and invitations which it would never do to refuse. At last she grew desperate; she resolved that she would go nowhere and be at home to no one until she found a house, and broke the resolution in half an hour.

Once she had humorously lamented that she had never been to Simpson's restaurant in the Strand. Now a note arrived from Miss Wilcox, asking her to lunch there. Mr Cahill was coming, and the three would have such a jolly chat, and perhaps end up at the Hippodrome. Margaret had no strong regard for Evie, and no desire to meet her fiancé, and she was surprised that Helen, who had been far funnier about Simpson's, had not been asked instead. But the invitation touched her by its intimate tone. She must know Evie Wilcox better than she supposed, and declaring that she "simply must" she accepted.

But when she saw Evie at the entrance of the restaurant, staring fiercely at nothing after the fashion of athletic women, her heart failed her. Miss Wilcox had changed perceptibly since her engagement. Her voice was gruffer, her manner more downright, and she was inclined to patronize the more foolish virgin. Margaret was silly enough to be pained at this. Depressed at her isolation, she saw not only houses and furniture but the vessel of life itself slipping past her, with people like Evie and Mr Cahill on board.

There are moments when virtue and wisdom fail us, and one of them came to her at Simpson's in the Strand. As she trod the staircase, narrow, but carpeted thickly, as she entered the eating-room, where saddles of mutton were being trundled up to expectant clergymen, she had a strong, if erroneous, conviction of her own futility, and wished she had never come out of her backwater, where nothing happened except art and literature, and where no one ever got married or succeeded in remaining engaged. Then came a little surprise. Father might be of the party — yes, father was. With a smile of pleasure she moved forward to greet him, and her feeling of loneliness vanished.

"I thought I'd get round if I could," said he. "Evie told me of her little plan, so I just slipped in and secured a table. Always secure a table first. Evie, don't pretend you want to sit by your old father, because you don't. Miss Schlegel, come in my side, out of pity. My goodness, but you look tired! Been worrying round after your young clerks?"

"No, after houses," said Margaret, edging past him into the box. "I'm hungry, not tired; I want to eat heaps."

"That's good. What'll you have?"

"Fish pie," said she, with a glance at the menu.

"Fish pie! Fancy coming for fish pie to Simpson's. It's not a bit the thing to go for here."

"Go for something for me, then," said Margaret, pulling off her gloves. Her spirits were rising, and his reference to Leonard Bast had warmed her curiously.

"Saddle of mutton," said he after profound reflection; "and cider to drink. That's the type of thing. I like this place, for a joke, once in a way. It is so thoroughly Old English. Don't you agree?"

"Yes," said Margaret, who didn't. The order was given, the joint rolled up, and the carver, under Mr Wilcox's direction, cut the meat where it was succulent, and piled their plates high. Mr Cahill insisted on sirloin, but admitted that he had made a mistake later on. He and Evie soon fell into a conversation of the "No, I didn't; yes, you did" type — conversation which, though fascinating to those who are engaged in it, neither desires nor deserves the attention of others.

"It's a golden rule to tip the carver. Tip everywhere's my motto."

"Perhaps it does make life more human."

"Then the fellows know one again. Especially in the East, if you tip, they remember you from year's end to year's end."

"Have you been in the East?"

"Oh, Greece and the Levant. I used to go out for sport and business to Cyprus; some military society of a sort there. A few piastres, properly distributed, help to keep one's memory green. But you, of course, think this shockingly cynical. How's your discussion society getting on? Any new utopias lately?"

"No, I'm house-hunting, Mr Wilcox, as I've already told you once. Do you know of any houses?"

"Afraid I don't."

"Well, what's the point of being practical if you can't find two distressed females a house? We merely want a small house with large rooms, and plenty of them."

"Evie, I like that! Miss Schlegel expects me to turn house-agent for her!"

"What's that, father?"

"I want a new home in September, and someone must find it. I can't."

"Percy, do you know of anything?"

"I can't say I do," said Mr Cahill.

"How like you! You're never any good."

"Never any good. Just listen to her! Never any good. Oh, come!"

"Well, you aren't. Miss Schlegel, is he?"

The torrent of their love, having splashed these drops at Margaret, swept away on its habitual course. She sympathized with it now, for a little comfort had restored her geniality. Speech and silence pleased her equally, and while Mr Wilcox made some preliminary inquiries about cheese her eyes surveyed the restaurant, and admired its well-calculated tributes to the solidity of our past. Though no more Old English than the works of Kipling, it had selected its reminiscences so adroitly that her criticism was lulled, and the guests whom it was nourishing for imperial purposes bore the outer semblance of Parson Adams or Tom Jones.° Scraps of their talk jarred oddly on the ear. "Right you are! I'll cable out to Uganda this evening," came from the table behind. "Their Emperor° wants war; well, let him have it," was

---

**Parson Adams or Tom Jones:** Characters in, respectively, *Joseph Andrews* (1742) and *Tom Jones* (1749) by Henry Fielding (1707–1754). **Their Emperor:** The German kaiser Wilhelm II.

the opinion of a clergyman. She smiled at such incongruities. "Next time," she said to Mr Wilcox, "you shall come to lunch with me at Mr Eustace Miles's."°

"With pleasure."

"No, you'd hate it," she said, pushing her glass towards him for some more cider. "It's all proteids and body-buildings, and people come up to you and beg your pardon, but you have such a beautiful aura."

"A what?"

"Never heard of an aura? Oh, happy, happy man! I scrub at mine for hours. Nor of an astral plane?"

He had heard of astral planes, and censured them.

"Just so. Luckily it was Helen's aura, not mine, and she had to chaperon it and do the politenesses. I just sat with my handkerchief in my mouth till the man went."

"Funny experiences seem to come to you two girls. No one's ever asked me about my — what d'ye call it? Perhaps I've not got one."

"You're bound to have one, but it may be such a terrible colour that no one dares mention it."

"Tell me, though, Miss Schlegel, do you really believe in the supernatural and all that?"

"Too difficult a question."

"Why's that? Gruyère or Stilton?"

"Gruyère, please."

"Better have Stilton."

"Stilton. Because, though I don't believe in auras, and think Theosophy's only a halfway-house —"

"— Yet there may be something in it all the same," he concluded, with a frown.

"Not even that. It may be halfway in the wrong direction. I can't explain. I don't believe in all these fads, and yet I don't like saying that I don't believe in them."

He seemed unsatisfied, and said: "So you couldn't give me your word that you *don't* hold with astral bodies and all the rest of it?"

"I could," said Margaret, surprised that the point was of any im-

**Mr Eustace Miles's:** Eustace Miles (1868–1948), author, as Stallybrass notes, of 150 booklets in the series "Milestones on the Road to All-Round Efficiency and Health," and owner, at the time, of a faddish restaurant in Chandos Street, Charing Cross, not far from Simpson's in the Strand.

portance to him. "Indeed, I will. When I talked about scrubbing my aura, I was only trying to be funny. But why do you want this settled?"

"I don't know."

"Now, Mr Wilcox, you do know."

"Yes, I am" — "No, you're not" burst from the lovers opposite. Margaret was silent for a moment, and then changed the subject.

"How's your house?"

"Much the same as when you honoured it last week."

"I don't mean Ducie Street. Howards End, of course."

"Why 'of course'?"

"Can't you turn out your tenant and let it to us? We're nearly demented."

"Let me think. I wish I could help you. But I thought you wanted to be in town. One bit of advice: fix your district, then fix your price, and then don't budge. That's how I got both Ducie Street and Oniton. I said to myself, 'I mean to be exactly here,' and I was, and Oniton's a place in a thousand."

"But I do budge. Gentlemen seem to mesmerize houses — cow them with an eye, and up they come, trembling. Ladies can't. It's the houses that are mesmerizing me. I've no control over the saucy things. Houses are alive. No?"

"I'm out of my depth," he said, and added: "Didn't you talk rather like that to your office-boy?"

"Did I? — I mean I did, more or less. I talk the same way to everyone — or try to."

"Yes, I know. And how much do you suppose that he understood of it?"

"That's his lookout. I don't believe in suiting my conversation to my company. One can doubtless hit upon some medium of exchange that seems to do well enough, but it's no more like the real thing than money is like food. There's no nourishment in it. You pass it to the lower classes, and they pass it back to you, and this you call 'social intercourse' or 'mutual endeavour', when it's mutual priggishness if it's anything. Our friends at Chelsea don't see this. They say one ought to be at all costs intelligible, and sacrifice —"

"Lower classes," interrupted Mr Wilcox, as it were thrusting his hand into her speech. "Well, you do admit that there are rich and poor. That's something."

Margaret could not reply. Was he incredibly stupid, or did he understand her better than she understood herself?

"You do admit that, if wealth was divided up equally, in a few years there would be rich and poor again just the same. The hard-working man would come to the top, the wastrel sink to the bottom."

"Everyone admits that."

"Your socialists don't."

"My socialists do. Yours mayn't; but I strongly suspect yours of being not socialists, but ninepins, which you have constructed for your own amusement. I can't imagine any living creature who would bowl over quite so easily."

He would have resented this had she not been a woman. But women may say anything — it was one of his holiest beliefs — and he only retorted, with a gay smile: "I don't care. You've made two damaging admissions, and I'm heartily with you in both."

In time they finished lunch, and Margaret, who had excused herself from the Hippodrome, took her leave. Evie had scarcely addressed her, and she suspected that the entertainment had been planned by the father. He and she were advancing out of their respective families towards a more intimate acquaintance. It had begun long ago. She had been his wife's friend, and, as such, he had given her that silver vinaigrette as a memento. It was pretty of him to have given that vinaigrette, and he had always preferred her to Helen — unlike most men. But the advance had been astonishing lately. They had done more in a week than in two years, and were really beginning to know each other.

She did not forget his promise to sample Eustace Miles, and asked him as soon as she could secure Tibby as his chaperon. He came, and partook of body-building dishes with humility.

Next morning the Schlegels left for Swanage. They had not succeeded in finding a new home.

**Chapter 18**

As they were seated at Aunt Juley's breakfast-table at The Bays, parrying her excessive hospitality and enjoying the view of the bay, a letter came for Margaret and threw her into perturbation. It was from Mr Wilcox. It announced an "important change" in his plans. Owing to Evie's marriage, he had decided to give up his house in Ducie Street, and was willing to let it on a yearly tenancy. It was a businesslike letter, and stated frankly what he would do for them and what he would not do. Also the rent. If they approved, Margaret was to come up *at once* — the words were underlined, as is necessary when dealing with women — and to go over the house with him. If they disapproved, a wire would oblige, as he should put it into the hands of an agent.

The letter perturbed, because she was not sure what it meant. If he liked her, if he had manœuvred to get her to Simpson's, might this be a manœuvre to get her to London, and result in an offer of marriage? She put it to herself as indelicately as possible, in the hope that her brain would cry, "Rubbish, you're a self-conscious fool!" But her brain only tingled a little and was silent, and for a time she sat gazing at the mincing waves, and wondering whether the news would seem strange to the others.

As soon as she began speaking, the sound of her own voice reassured her. There could be nothing in it. The replies also were typical, and in the buzz of conversation her fears vanished.

"You needn't go, though —" began her hostess.

"I needn't, but hadn't I better? It's really getting rather serious. We let chance after chance slip, and the end of it is we shall be bundled out bag and baggage into the street. We don't know what we *want*, that's the mischief with us —"

"No, we have no real ties," said Helen, helping herself to toast.

"Shan't I go up to town today, take the house if it's the least possible, and then come down by the afternoon train tomorrow, and start enjoying myself. I shall be no fun to myself or to others until this business is off my mind."

"But you won't do anything rash, Margaret?"

"There's nothing rash to do."

"Who *are* the Wilcoxes?" said Tibby, a question that sounds silly, but was really extremely subtle, as his aunt found to her cost when she tried to answer it. "I don't *manage* the Wilcoxes; I don't see where they come *in*."

"No more do I," agreed Helen. "It's funny that we just don't lose sight of them. Out of all our hotel acquaintances, Mr Wilcox is the only one who has stuck. It is now over three years, and we have drifted away from far more interesting people in that time."

"Interesting people don't get one houses."

"Meg, if you start in your honest-English vein, I shall throw the treacle at you."

"It's a better vein than the cosmopolitan," said Margaret, getting up. "Now, children, which is it to be? You know the Ducie Street house. Shall I say yes or shall I say no? Tibby love — which? I'm specially anxious to pin you both."

"It all depends what meaning you attach to the word 'possi — ' "

"It depends on nothing of the sort. Say yes."

"Say no."

Then Margaret spoke rather seriously. "I think," she said, "that our race is degenerating. We cannot settle even this little thing; what will it be like when we have to settle a big one?"

"It will be as easy as eating," returned Helen.

"I was thinking of father. How could he settle to leave Germany as he did, when he had fought for it as a young man, and all his feelings and friends were Prussian? How could he break loose with patriotism and begin aiming at something else? It would have killed me. When he was nearly forty he could change countries and ideals — and we, at our age, can't change houses. It's humiliating."

"Your father may have been able to change countries," said Mrs Munt with asperity, "and that may or may not be a good thing. But he could change houses no better than you can, in fact, much worse. Never shall I forget what poor Emily suffered in the move from Manchester."

"I knew it," cried Helen. "I told you so. It is the little things one bungles at. The big, real ones are nothing when they come."

"Bungle, my dear! You are too little to recollect — in fact, you weren't there. But the furniture was actually in the vans and on the move before the lease for Wickham Place was signed, and Emily took train with baby — who was Margaret then — and the smaller luggage for London, without so much as knowing where her new home would be. Getting away from that house may be hard, but it is nothing to the misery that we all went through getting you into it."

Helen, with her mouth full, cried:

"And that's the man who beat the Austrians, and the Danes, and the French, and who beat the Germans that were inside himself. And we're like him."

"Speak for yourself," said Tibby. "Remember that I am cosmopolitan, please."

"Helen may be right."

"Of course she's right," said Helen.

Helen might be right, but she did not go up to London. Margaret did that. An interrupted holiday is the worst of the minor worries, and one may be pardoned for feeling morbid when a business letter snatches one away from the sea and friends. She could not believe that her father had ever felt the same. Her eyes had been troubling her lately, so that she could not read in the train, and it bored her to look at the landscape, which she had seen but yesterday. At Southampton she "waved" to Frieda; Frieda was on her way down to join them at Swanage, and Mrs Munt had calculated that their trains would cross. But Frieda was looking the other way, and Margaret travelled on to town feeling solitary and old-maidish. How like an old maid to fancy that Mr Wilcox was courting her! She had once visited a spinster — poor, silly and unattractive — whose mania it was that every man who approached her fell in love. How Margaret's heart had bled for the deluded thing! How she had lectured, reasoned, and in despair acquiesced! "I may have been deceived by the curate, my dear, but the young fellow who brings the midday post really is fond of me, and has, as a matter of fact —" It had always seemed to her the most hideous corner of old age, yet she might be driven into it herself by the mere pressure of virginity.

Mr Wilcox met her at Waterloo himself. She felt certain that he was not the same as usual; for one thing, he took offence at everything she said.

"This is awfully kind of you," she began, "but I'm afraid it's not going to do. The house has not been built that suits the Schlegel family."

"What! Have you come up determined not to deal?"

"Not exactly."

"Not exactly? In that case let's be starting."

She lingered to admire the motor, which was new, and a fairer creature than the vermilion giant that had borne Aunt Juley to her doom three years before.

"Presumably it's very beautiful," she said. "How do you like it, Crane?"

"Come, let's be starting," repeated her host. "How on earth did you know that my chauffeur was called Crane?"

"Why, I know Crane: I've been for a drive with Evie once. I know that you've got a parlourmaid called Milton. I know all sorts of things."

"Evie!" he echoed in injured tones. "You won't see her. She's gone out with Cahill. It's no fun, I can tell you, being left so much alone. I've got my work all day — indeed, a great deal too much of it — but when I come home in the evening, I tell you, I can't stand the house."

"In my absurd way, I'm lonely too," Margaret replied. "It's

heartbreaking to leave one's old home. I scarcely remember anything before Wickham Place, and Helen and Tibby were born there. Helen says —"

"You, too, feel lonely?"

"Horribly. Hullo, Parliament's back!"

Mr Wilcox glanced at Parliament contemptuously. The more important ropes of life lay elsewhere. "Yes, they are talking again," said he. "But you were going to say —"

"Only some rubbish about furniture. Helen says it alone endures while men and houses perish, and that in the end the world will be a desert of chairs and sofas — just imagine it! — rolling through infinity with no one to sit upon them."

"Your sister always likes her little joke."

"She says yes, my brother says no, to Ducie Street. It's no fun helping us, Mr Wilcox, I assure you."

"You are not as unpractical as you pretend. I shall never believe it."

Margaret laughed. But she was — quite as unpractical. She could not concentrate on details. Parliament, the Thames, the irresponsive chauffeur, would flash into the field of house-hunting, and all demand some comment or response. It is impossible to see modern life steadily and see it whole, and she had chosen to see it whole. Mr Wilcox saw steadily. He never bothered over the mysterious or the private. The Thames might run inland from the sea, the chauffeur might cancel all passion and philosophy beneath his unhealthy skin. They knew their own business, and he knew his.

Yet she liked being with him. He was not a rebuke, but a stimulus, and banished morbidity. Some twenty years her senior, he preserved a gift that she supposed herself to have already lost — not youth's creative power, but its self-confidence and optimism. He was so sure that it was a very pleasant world. His complexion was robust, his hair had receded but not thinned, the thick moustache and the eyes that Helen had compared to brandy-balls had an agreeable menace in them, whether they were turned towards the slums or towards the stars. Some day — in the millennium — there may be no need for his type. At present, homage is due to it from those who think themselves superior, and who possibly are.

"At all events you responded to my telegram promptly," he remarked.

"Oh, even I know a good thing when I see it."

"I'm glad you don't despise the goods of this world."

"Heavens, no! Only idiots and prigs do that."

"I am glad, very glad," he repeated, suddenly softening and turning to her, as if the remark had pleased him. "There is so much cant talked in would-be intellectual circles. I am glad you don't share it. Self-denial is all very well as a means of strengthening the character. But I can't stand those people who run down comforts. They have usually some axe to grind. Can you?"

"Comforts are of two kinds," said Margaret, who was keeping herself in hand — "those we can share with others, like fine weather or music, and those we can't — food, for instance. It depends."

"I mean reasonable comforts, of course. I shouldn't like to think that you —" He bent nearer; the sentence died unfinished. Margaret's head turned very stupid, and the inside of it seemed to revolve like the beacon in a lighthouse. He did not kiss her, for the hour was half past twelve, and the car was passing by the stables of Buckingham Palace. But the atmosphere was so charged with emotion that people only seemed to exist on her account, and she was surprised that Crane did not realize this, and turn round. Idiot though she might be, surely Mr Wilcox was more — how should one put it? — more psychological than usual. Always a good judge of character for business purposes, he seemed this afternoon to enlarge his field, and to note qualities outside neatness, obedience and decision.

"I want to go over the whole house," she announced when they arrived. "As soon as I get back to Swanage, which will be tomorrow afternoon, I'll talk it over once more with Helen and Tibby, and wire you yes or no."

"Right. The dining-room." And they began their survey.

The dining-room was big, but overfurnished. Chelsea would have moaned aloud. Mr Wilcox had eschewed those decorative schemes that wince, and relent, and refrain, and achieve beauty by sacrificing comfort and pluck. After so much self-colour and self-denial, Margaret viewed with relief the sumptuous dado, the frieze, the gilded wallpaper, amid whose foliage parrots sang. It would never do with her own furniture, but those heavy chairs, that immense sideboard loaded with presentation plate, stood up against its pressure like men. The room suggested men, and Margaret, keen to derive the modern capitalist from the warriors and hunters of the past, saw it as an ancient guest-hall, where the lord sat at meat among his thanes. Even the Bible — the Dutch Bible that Charles had brought back from the Boer War — fell into position. Such a room admitted loot.

"Now the entrance hall."

The entrance hall was paved.

"Here we fellows smoke."

We fellows smoked in chairs of maroon leather. It was as if a motor-car had spawned. "Oh, jolly!" said Margaret, sinking into one of them.

"You do like it?" he said, fixing his eyes on her upturned face, and surely betraying an almost intimate note. "It's all rubbish not making oneself comfortable. Isn't it?"

"Ye-es. Semi-rubbish. Are those Cruikshanks?"

"Gillrays.° Shall we go on upstairs?"

"Does all this furniture come from Howards End?"

"The Howards End furniture has all gone to Oniton."

"Does — however, I'm concerned with the house, not the furniture. How big is this smoking-room?"

"Thirty by fifteen. No, wait a minute. Fifteen and a half."

"Ah, well. Mr Wilcox, aren't you ever amused at the solemnity with which we middle classes approach the subject of houses?"

They proceeded to the drawing-room. Chelsea managed better here. It was sallow and ineffective. One could visualize the ladies withdrawing to it, while their lords discussed life's realities below, to the accompaniment of cigars. Had Mrs Wilcox's drawing-room looked thus at Howards End? Just as this thought entered Margaret's brain, Mr Wilcox did ask her to be his wife, and the knowledge that she had been right so overcame her that she nearly fainted.

But the proposal was not to rank among the world's great love scenes.

"Miss Schlegel" — his voice was firm — "I have had you up on false pretences. I want to speak about a much more serious matter than a house."

Margaret almost answered: "I know —"

"Could you be induced to share my — is it probable —"

"Oh, Mr Wilcox!" she interrupted, holding the piano and averting her eyes. "I see, I see. I will write to you afterwards if I may."

He began to stammer. "Miss Schlegel — Margaret — you don't understand."

"Oh yes! Indeed, yes!" said Margaret.

"I am asking you to be my wife."

So deep already was her sympathy, that when he said, "I am asking you to be my wife," she made herself give a little start. She must show surprise if he expected it. An immense joy came over her. It was indescribable. It had nothing to do with humanity, and most resembled the all-pervading happiness of fine weather. Fine weather is due to the sun, but Margaret could think of no central radiance here. She stood in his drawing-room happy, and longing to give happiness. On leaving him she realized that the central radiance had been love.

"You aren't offended, Miss Schlegel?"

"How could I be offended?"

There was a moment's pause. He was anxious to get rid of her, and she knew it. She had too much intuition to look at him as he struggled for possessions that money cannot buy. He desired comradeship and affection, but he feared them, and she, who had taught herself only to desire, and could have clothed the struggle with beauty, held back, and hesitated with him.

"Goodbye," she continued. "You will have a letter from me — I am going back to Swanage tomorrow."

"Thank you."

"Goodbye, and it's you I thank."

"I may order the motor round, mayn't I?"

"That would be most kind."

"I wish I had written instead. Ought I to have written?"

"Not at all."

"There's just one question —"

She shook her head. He looked a little bewildered, and they parted.

They parted without shaking hands; she had kept the interview, for his sake, in tints of the quietest gray. Yet she thrilled with happiness ere she reached her own house. Others had loved her in the past, if one may apply to their brief desires so grave a word, but those others had been "ninnies" — young men who had nothing to do, old men who could find nobody better. And she had often "loved", too, but only so far as the facts of sex demanded: mere yearnings for the masculine, to be dismissed for what they were worth, with a smile. Never before had her personality been touched. She was not young or very rich, and it amazed her that a man of any standing should take her seriously. As she sat trying to do accounts in her empty house, amidst beautiful pictures and noble books, waves of emotion broke, as if a tide of passion was flowing through the night air. She shook her head, tried to concentrate her attention, and failed. In vain did she repeat: "But I've been through this sort of thing before." She had never been through it; the big machinery, as opposed to the little, had been set in motion, and the idea that Mr Wilcox loved obsessed her before she came to love him in return.

She would come to no decision yet. "Oh, sir, this is so sudden" — that prudish phrase exactly expressed her when her time came. Premonitions are not preparation. She must examine more closely her own nature and his; she must talk it over judicially with Helen. It had been a strange love scene — the central radiance unacknowledged from first to last. She, in his place, would have said, "Ich liebe dich," but perhaps it was not his habit to open the heart. He might have done it if she had pressed him — as a matter of duty, perhaps; England expects every man to open his heart once;° but the effort would have jarred him, and never, if she could avoid it, should he lose those defences that he had chosen to raise against the world. He must never be bothered with emotional talk, or with a display of sympathy. He was an elderly man now, and it would be futile and impudent to correct him.

Mrs Wilcox strayed in and out, ever a welcome ghost; surveying the scene, thought Margaret, without one hint of bitterness.

## Chapter 19

If one wanted to show a foreigner England, perhaps the wisest course would be to take him to the final section of the Purbeck hills, and stand him on their summit, a few miles to the east of Corfe. Then system after system of our island would roll together under his feet. Beneath him is the valley of the Frome, and all the wild lands that come tossing down from Dorchester, black and gold, to mirror their gorse in the expanses of Poole. The valley of the Stour is beyond, unaccountable stream, dirty at Blandford, pure at Wimborne — the Stour, sliding out of fat fields, to marry the Avon beneath the tower of Christchurch. The valley of the Avon — invisible, but far to the north the trained eye may see Clearbury Ring that guards it, and the imagination may leap beyond that onto Salisbury Plain itself, and beyond the Plain to all the glorious downs of central England. Nor is suburbia absent. Bournemouth's ignoble coast cowers to the right, heralding the pine trees that mean, for all their beauty, red houses, and the Stock Exchange, and extend to the gates of London itself. So tremendous is the City's trail! But the cliffs of Freshwater it shall never touch, and

---

England . . . once: An ironical echo of Admiral Nelson's signal before the Battle of Trafalgar: "England expects every man will do his duty."

the island will guard the Island's° purity till the end of time. Seen from the west, the Wight is beautiful beyond all laws of beauty. It is as if a fragment of England floated forward to greet the foreigner — chalk of our chalk, turf of our turf, epitome of what will follow. And behind the fragment lie Southampton, hostess to the nations, and Portsmouth, a latent fire, and all around it, with double and treble collision of tides, swirls the sea. How many villages appear in this view! How many castles! How many churches, vanquished or triumphant! How many ships, railways and roads! What incredible variety of men working beneath that lucent sky to what final end! The reason fails, like a wave on the Swanage beach; the imagination swells, spreads and deepens, until it becomes geographic and encircles England.

So Frieda Mosebach, now Frau Architect Liesecke, and mother to her husband's baby, was brought up to these heights to be impressed, and, after a prolonged gaze, she said that the hills were more swelling here than in Pomerania, which was true, but did not seem to Mrs Munt apposite. Poole harbour was dry, which led her to praise the absence of muddy foreshore at Friedrich Wilhelms Bad, Rügen, where beech trees hang over the tideless Baltic, and cows may contemplate the brine. Rather unhealthy Mrs Munt thought this would be, water being safer when it moved about.

"And your English lakes — Vindermere, Grasmere — are they then unhealthy?"

"No, Frau Liesecke; but that is because they are fresh water, and different. Salt water ought to have tides, and go up and down a great deal, or else it smells. Look, for instance, at an aquarium."

"An aquarium! Oh, *Meesis* Munt, you mean to tell me that fresh aquariums stink less than salt? Why, when Victor, my brother-in-law, collected many tadpoles —"

"You are not to say 'stink'," interrupted Helen; "at least, you may say it, but you must pretend you are being funny while you say it."

"Then 'smell'. And the mud of your Pool down there — does it not smell, or may I say 'stink, ha, ha'?"

"There always has been mud in Poole harbour," said Mrs Munt, with a slight frown. "The rivers bring it down, and a most valuable oyster fishery depends upon it."

"Yes, that is so," conceded Frieda; and another international incident was closed.

the Island's: Refers to the Isle of Wight.

" 'Bournemouth is,' " resumed their hostess, quoting a local rhyme to which she was much attached — " 'Bournemouth is, Poole was, and Swanage is to be, the most important town of all and biggest of the three.' Now, Frau Liesecke, I have shown you Bournemouth, and I have shown you Poole, so let us walk backward a little, and look down again at Swanage."

"Aunt Juley, wouldn't that be Meg's train?"

A tiny puff of smoke had been circuiting the harbour, and now was bearing southwards towards them over the black and the gold.

"Oh, dearest Margaret, I do hope she won't be overtired."

"Oh, I do wonder — I do wonder whether she's taken the house."

"I hope she hasn't been hasty."

"So do I — oh, *so* do I."

"Will it be as beautiful as Wickham Place?" Frieda asked.

"I should think it would. Trust Mr Wilcox for doing himself proud. All those Ducie Street houses are beautiful in their modern way, and I can't think why he doesn't keep on with it. But it's really for Evie that he went there, and now that Evie's going to be married —"

"Ah!"

"You've never seen Miss Wilcox, Frieda. How absurdly matrimonial you are!"

"But sister to that Paul?"

"Yes."

"And to that Charles," said Mrs Munt with feeling. "Oh, Helen, Helen, what a time that was!"

Helen laughed. "Meg and I haven't got such tender hearts. If there's a chance of a cheap house, we go for it."

"Now look, Frau Liesecke, at my niece's train. You see, it is coming towards us — coming, coming; and, when it gets to Corfe, it will actually go *through* the downs on which we are standing, so that, if we walk over, as I suggested, and look down on Swanage, we shall see it coming on the other side. Shall we?"

Frieda assented, and in a few minutes they had crossed the ridge and exchanged the greater view for the lesser. Rather a dull valley lay below, backed by the slope of the coastward downs. They were looking across the Isle of Purbeck and on to Swanage, soon to be the most important town of all, and ugliest of the three. Margaret's train reappeared as promised, and was greeted with approval by her aunt. It came to a standstill in the middle distance, and there it had been planned that Tibby should meet her, and drive her, and a tea-basket, up to join them.

"You see," continued Helen to her cousin, "the Wilcoxes collect houses as your Victor collects tadpoles. They have, one, Ducie Street; two, Howards End, where my great rumpus was; three, a country seat in Shropshire; four, Charles has a house in Hilton; and five, another near Epsom; and six, Evie will have a house when she marries, and probably a pied-à-terre in the country — which makes seven. Oh yes, and Paul a hut in Africa makes eight. I wish we could get Howards End. That was something like a dear little house! Didn't you think so, Aunt Juley?"

"I had too much to do, dear, to look at it," said Mrs Munt, with a gracious dignity. "I had everything to settle and explain, and Charles Wilcox to keep in his place besides. It isn't likely I should remember much. I just remember having lunch in your bedroom."

"Yes, so do I. But, oh dear, dear, how dead it all seems! And in the autumn there began that anti-Pauline movement — you, and Frieda, and Meg, and Mrs Wilcox, all obsessed with the idea that I might yet marry Paul."

"You yet may," said Frieda despondently.

Helen shook her head. "The Great Wilcox Peril will never return. If I'm certain of anything it's of that."

"One is certain of nothing but the truth of one's own emotions."°

The remark fell damply on the conversation. But Helen slipped her arm round her cousin, somehow liking her the better for making it. It was not an original remark, nor had Frieda appropriated it passionately, for she had a patriotic rather than a philosophic mind. Yet it betrayed that interest in the universal which the average Teuton possesses and the average Englishman does not. It was, however illogically, the good, the beautiful, the true, as opposed to the respectable, the pretty, the adequate. It was a landscape of Böcklin's beside a landscape of Leader's, strident and ill-considered, but quivering into supernatural life. It sharpened idealism, stirred the soul. It may have been a bad preparation for what followed.

"Look!" cried Aunt Juley, hurrying away from generalities over the narrow summit of the down. "Stand where I stand, and you will see the pony-cart coming. I see the pony-cart coming."

**One is certain . . . emotions:** An echo of Keats's "I am certain of nothing but of the holiness of the heart's affections" (letter to Benjamin Bailey, November 22, 1817).

They stood and saw the pony-cart coming. Margaret and Tibby were presently seen coming in it. Leaving the outskirts of Swanage, it drove for a little through the budding lanes, and then began the ascent.

"Have you got the house?" they shouted, long before she could possibly hear.

Helen ran down to meet her. The highroad passed over a saddle, and a track went thence at right angles along the ridge of the down.

"Have you got the house?"

Margaret shook her head.

"Oh, what a nuisance! So we're as we were?"

"Not exactly."

She got out, looking tired.

"Some mystery," said Tibby. "We are to be enlightened presently."

Margaret came close up to her and whispered that she had had a proposal of marriage from Mr Wilcox.

Helen was amused. She opened the gate onto the down so that her brother might lead the pony through. "It's just like a widower," she remarked. "They've cheek enough for anything, and invariably select one of their first wife's friends."

Margaret's face flashed despair.

"That type —" She broke off with a cry. "Meg, not anything wrong with you?"

"Wait one minute," said Margaret, whispering always.

"But you've never conceivably — you've never —" She pulled herself together. "Tibby, hurry up through; I can't hold this gate indefinitely. Aunt Juley! I say, Aunt Juley, make the tea, will you, and Frieda; we've got to talk houses, and'll come on afterwards." And then, turning her face to her sister's, she burst into tears.

Margaret was stupefied. She heard herself saying, "Oh, really —" She felt herself touched with a hand that trembled.

"Don't," sobbed Helen, "don't, don't, Meg, don't!" She seemed incapable of saying any other word. Margaret, trembling herself, led her forward up the road, till they strayed through another gate onto the down.

"Don't, don't do such a thing! I tell you not to — don't! I know — don't!"

"What do you know?"

"Panic and emptiness," sobbed Helen. "Don't!"

Then Margaret thought: "Helen is a little selfish. I have never behaved like this when there has seemed a chance of *her* marrying." She said: "But we would still see each other very often, and you —"

"It's not a thing like that," sobbed Helen. And she broke right away and wandered distractedly upwards, stretching her hands towards the view and crying.

"What's happened to you?" called Margaret, following through the wind that gathers at sundown on the northern slopes of hills. "But it's stupid!" And suddenly stupidity seized her, and the immense landscape was blurred. But Helen turned back.

"Meg —"

"I don't know what's happened to either of us," said Margaret, wiping her eyes. "We must both have gone mad." Then Helen wiped hers, and they even laughed a little.

"Look here, sit down."

"All right; I'll sit down if you'll sit down."

"There. (One kiss.) Now, what ever, what ever is the matter?"

"I do mean what I said. Don't; it wouldn't do."

"Oh, Helen, stop saying 'Don't'! It's ignorant. It's as if your head wasn't out of the slime. 'Don't' is probably what Mrs Bast says all the day to Mr Bast."

Helen was silent.

"Well?"

"Tell me about it first, and meanwhile perhaps I'll have got my head out of the slime."

"That's better. Well, where shall I begin? When I arrived at Waterloo — no, I'll go back before that, because I'm anxious you should know everything from the first. The 'first' was about ten days ago. It was the day Mr Bast came to tea and lost his temper. I was defending him, and Mr Wilcox became jealous about me, however slightly. I thought it was the involuntary thing, which men can't help any more than we can. You know — at least, I know in my own case — when a man has said to me, 'So-and-so's a pretty girl,' I am seized with a momentary sourness against so-and-so, and long to tweak her ear. It's a tiresome feeling, but not an important one, and one easily manages it. But it wasn't only this in Mr Wilcox's case, I gather now."

"Then you love him?"

Margaret considered. "It is wonderful knowing that a real man cares for you," she said. "The mere fact of that grows more tremendous. Remember, I've known and liked him steadily for nearly three years."

"But loved him?"

Margaret peered into her past. It is pleasant to analyse feelings while they are still only feelings, and unembodied in the social fabric. With her arm round Helen, and her eyes shifting over the view, as if this county or that could reveal the secret of her own heart, she meditated honestly, and said: "No."

"But you will?"

"Yes," said Margaret, "of that I'm pretty sure. Indeed, I began the moment he spoke to me."

"And have settled to marry him?"

"I had, but am wanting a long talk about it now. What *is* it against him, Helen? You must try and say."

Helen, in her turn, looked outwards. "It is ever since Paul," she said finally.

"But what has Mr Wilcox to do with Paul?"

"But he was there, they were all there that morning when I came down to breakfast, and saw that Paul was frightened — the man who loved me frightened and all his paraphernalia fallen, so that I knew it was impossible, because personal relations are the important thing for ever and ever, and not this outer life of telegrams and anger."

She poured the sentence forth in one breath, but her sister understood it, because it touched on thoughts that were familiar between them.

"That's foolish. In the first place, I disagree about the outer life. Well, we've often argued that. The real point is that there is the widest gulf between my love-making and yours. Yours was romance; mine will be prose. I'm not running it down — a very good kind of prose, but well considered, well thought out. For instance, I know all Mr Wilcox's faults. He's afraid of emotion. He cares too much about success, too little about the past. His sympathy lacks poetry, and so isn't sympathy, really. I'd even say" — she looked at the shining lagoons — "that, spiritually, he's not as honest as I am. Doesn't that satisfy you?"

"No, it doesn't," said Helen. "It makes me feel worse and worse. You must be mad."

Margaret made a movement of irritation.

"I don't intend him, or any man or any woman, to be all my life — good heavens, no! There are heaps of things in me that he doesn't, and shall never, understand."

Thus she spoke before the wedding ceremony and the physical union, before the astonishing glass shade had fallen that interposes between married couples and the world. She was to keep her independence more than do most women as yet. Marriage was to alter her fortunes rather than her character, and she was not far wrong in boasting that she understood her future husband. Yet he did alter her character — a little. There was an unforeseen surprise, a cessation of the winds and odours of life, a social pressure that would have her think conjugally.

"So with him," she continued. "There are heaps of things in him — more especially things that he does — that will always be hidden from me. He has all those public qualities which you so despise and enable all this —" She waved her hand at the landscape, which confirmed anything. "If Wilcoxes hadn't worked and died in England for thousands of years, you and I couldn't sit here without having our throats cut. There would be no trains, no ships to carry us literary people about in, no fields even. Just savagery. No — perhaps not even that. Without their spirit life might never have moved out of protoplasm. More and more do I refuse to draw my income and sneer at those who guarantee it. There are times when it seems to me —"

"And to me, and to all women. So one kissed Paul."

"That's brutal," said Margaret. "Mine is an absolutely different case. I've thought things out."

"It makes no difference thinking things out. They come to the same."

"Rubbish!"

There was a long silence, during which the tide returned into Poole harbour. "One would lose something," murmured Helen, apparently to herself. The water crept over the mud-flats towards the gorse and the blackened heather. Branksea Island lost its immense foreshores, and became a sombre episode of trees. Frome was forced inward towards Dorchester, Stour against Wimborne, Avon towards Salisbury, and over the immense displacement the sun presided, leading it to triumph ere he sank to rest. England was alive, throbbing through all her estuaries, crying for joy through the mouths of all her gulls, and the north wind, with contrary motion, blew stronger against her rising seas. What did it mean? For what end are her fair complexities, her changes of soil, her sinuous coast? Does she belong to those who have moulded her and made her feared by other lands, or to those who have added nothing to her power, but have somehow seen her, seen the whole island at once, lying as a jewel in a silver sea,°

---

**as a jewel in a silver sea:** This phrase, indeed the whole sentence, echoes John of Gaunt's speech in Shakespeare's *Richard II* 2.1.40–41, which begins, "This precious stone set in the silver sea."

sailing as a ship of souls, with all the brave world's fleet accompanying
her towards eternity?


## Chapter 20

Margaret had often wondered at the disturbance that takes place in
the world's waters when Love, who seems so tiny a pebble, slips in.
Whom does Love concern beyond the beloved and the lover? Yet his
impact deluges a hundred shores. No doubt the disturbance is really
the spirit of the generations, welcoming the new generation, and chaf-
ing against the ultimate Fate, who holds all the seas in the palm of her
hand. But Love cannot understand this. He cannot comprehend another's infinity; he is conscious only of his own — flying sunbeam,
falling rose, pebble that asks for one quiet plunge below the fretting
interplay of space and time. He knows that he will survive at the end of
things, and be gathered by Fate as a jewel from the slime, and be
handed with admiration round the assembly of the gods. "Men did
produce this," they will say, and, saying, they will give men immortality. But meanwhile — what agitations meanwhile! The foundations of
Property and Propriety are laid bare, twin rocks; Family Pride floun-
ders to the surface, puffing and blowing, and refusing to be comforted; Theology, vaguely ascetic, gets up a nasty ground-swell. Then
the lawyers are aroused — cold brood — and creep out of their holes.
They do what they can; they tidy up Property and Propriety, reassure
Theology and Family Pride. Half-guineas are poured on the troubled
waters, the lawyers creep back, and, if all has gone well, Love joins one
man and woman together in Matrimony.

Margaret had expected the disturbance, and was not irritated by it.
For a sensitive woman she had steady nerves, and could bear with the
incongruous and the grotesque; and, besides, there was nothing excessive about her love affair. Good humour was the dominant note of her
relations with Mr Wilcox, or, as I must now call him, Henry. Henry
did not encourage Romance, and she was no girl to fidget for it. An
acquaintance had become a lover, might become a husband, but
would retain all that she had noted in the acquaintance; and love must
confirm an old relation rather than reveal a new one.

In this spirit she promised to marry him.

He was in Swanage on the morrow, bearing the engagement ring.
They greeted one another with a hearty cordiality that impressed Aunt
Juley. Henry dined at The Bays, but had engaged a bedroom in the
principal hotel; he was one of those men who know the principal hotel

by instinct. After dinner he asked Margaret if she wouldn't care for a turn on the Parade. She accepted, and could not repress a little tremor; it would be her first real love scene. But as she put on her hat she burst out laughing. Love was so unlike the article served up in books; the joy, though genuine, was different; the mystery an unexpected mystery. For one thing, Mr Wilcox still seemed a stranger.

For a time they talked about the ring; then she said:

"Do you remember the Embankment at Chelsea? It can't be ten days ago."

"Yes," he said, laughing. "And you and your sister were head and ears deep in some quixotic scheme. Ah well!"

"I little thought then, certainly. Did you?"

"I don't know about that; I shouldn't like to say."

"Why, was it earlier?" she cried. "Did you think of me this way earlier? How extraordinarily interesting. Henry! Tell me."

But Henry had no intention of telling. Perhaps he could not have told, for his mental states became obscure as soon as he had passed through them. He misliked the very word "interesting", connoting it with wasted energy and even with morbidity. Hard facts were enough for him.

"I didn't think of it," she pursued. "No; when you spoke to me in the drawing-room, that was practically the first. It was all so different from what it's supposed to be. On the stage, or in books, a proposal is — how shall I put it? — a full-blown affair, a kind of bouquet; it loses its literal meaning. But in life a proposal really is a proposal —"

"By the way —"

"— a suggestion, a seed," she concluded; and the thought flew away into darkness.

"I was thinking, if you didn't mind, that we ought to spend this evening in a business talk; there will be so much to settle."

"I think so too. Tell me, in the first place, how did you get on with Tibby?"

"With your brother?"

"Yes, during cigarettes."

"Oh, very well."

"I am so glad," she answered, a little surprised. "What did you talk about? Me, presumably."

"About Greece too."

"Greece was a very good card, Henry. Tibby's only a boy still, and one has to pick and choose subjects a little. Well done."

"I was telling him I have shares in a currant farm near Calamata."

"What a delightful thing to have shares in! Can't we go there for our honeymoon?"

"What to do?"

"To eat the currants. And isn't there marvellous scenery?"

"Moderately, but it's not the kind of place one could possibly go to with a lady."

"Why not?"

"No hotels."

"Some ladies do without hotels. Are you aware that Helen and I have walked alone over the Apennines, with our luggage on our backs?"

"I wasn't aware, and, if I can manage it, you will never do such a thing again."

She said more gravely: "You haven't found time for a talk with Helen yet, I suppose?"

"No."

"Do, before you go. I am so anxious you two should be friends."

"Your sister and I have always hit it off," he said negligently. "But we're drifting away from our business. Let me begin at the beginning. You know that Evie is going to marry Percy Cahill."

"Dolly's uncle."

"Exactly. The girl's madly in love with him. A very good sort of fellow, but he demands — and rightly — a suitable provision with her. And in the second place, you will naturally understand, there is Charles. Before leaving town, I wrote Charles a very careful letter. You see, he has an increasing family and increasing expenses, and the I. and W. A. is nothing particular just now, though capable of development."

"Poor fellow!" murmured Margaret, looking out to sea, and not understanding.

"Charles being the elder son, some day Charles will have Howards End; but I am anxious, in my own happiness, not to be unjust to others."

"Of course not," she began, and then gave a little cry. "You mean money. How stupid I am! Of course not!"

Oddly enough, he winced a little at the word. "Yes. Money, since you put it so frankly. I am determined to be just to all — just to you, just to them. I am determined that my children shall have no case against me."

"Be generous to them," she said sharply. "Bother justice!"

"I am determined — and have already written to Charles to that effect —"

"But how much have you got?"

"What?"

"How much have you a year? I've six hundred."

"My income?"

"Yes. We must begin with how much you have, before we can settle how much you can give Charles. Justice, and even generosity, depend on that."

"I must say you're a downright young woman," he observed, patting her arm and laughing a little. "What a question to spring on a fellow!"

"Don't you know your income? Or don't you want to tell it me?"

"I —"

"That's all right" — now she patted him — "don't tell me. I don't want to know. I can do the sum just as well by proportion. Divide your income into ten parts. How many parts would you give to Evie, how many to Charles, how many to Paul?"

"The fact is, my dear, I hadn't any intention of bothering you with details. I only wanted to let you know that — well, that something must be done for the others, and you've understood me perfectly, so let's pass on to the next point."

"Yes, we've settled that," said Margaret, undisturbed by his strategic blunderings. "Go ahead; give away all you can, bearing in mind I've a clear six hundred. What a mercy it is to have all this money about one!"

"We've none too much, I assure you; you're marrying a poor man."

"Helen wouldn't agree with me here," she continued. "Helen daren't slang the rich, being rich herself, but she would like to. There's an odd notion, that I haven't yet got hold of, running about at the back of her brain, that poverty is somehow 'real'. She dislikes all organization, and probably confuses wealth with the technique of wealth. Sovereigns in a stocking wouldn't bother her; cheques do. Helen is too relentless. One can't deal in her high-handed manner with the world."

"There's this other point, and then I must go back to my hotel and write some letters. What's to be done now about the house in Ducie Street?"

"Keep it on — at least, it depends. When do you want to marry me?"

She raised her voice, as too often, and some youths, who were also taking the evening air, overheard her. "Getting a bit hot, eh?" said one. Mr Wilcox turned on them, and said sharply, "I say!" There was silence. "Take care I don't report you to the police." They moved away quietly enough, but were only biding their time, and the rest of the conversation was punctuated by peals of ungovernable laughter.

Lowering his voice and infusing a hint of reproof into it, he said: "Evie will probably be married in September. We could scarcely think of anything before then."

"The earlier the nicer, Henry. Females are not supposed to say such things, but the earlier the nicer."

"How about September for us too?" he asked, rather dryly.

"Right. Shall we go into Ducie Street ourselves in September? Or shall we try to bounce Helen and Tibby into it? That's rather an idea. They are so unbusinesslike, we could make them do anything by judicious management. Look here — yes. We'll do that. And we ourselves could live at Howards End or Shropshire."

He blew out his cheeks. "Heavens! How you women do fly round! My head's in a whirl. Point by point, Margaret. Howards End's impossible. I let it to Hamar Bryce on a three years' agreement last March. Don't you remember? Oniton. Well, that is much, much too far away to rely on entirely. You will be able to be down there entertaining a certain amount, but we must have a house within easy reach of town. Only Ducie Street has huge drawbacks. There's a mews behind."

Margaret could not help laughing. It was the first she had heard of the mews behind Ducie Street. When she was a possible tenant it had suppressed itself, not consciously, but automatically. The breezy Wilcox manner, though genuine, lacked the clearness of vision that is imperative for truth. When Henry lived in Ducie Street he remembered the mews; when he tried to let he forgot it; and if anyone had remarked that the mews must be either there or not he would have felt annoyed, and afterwards have found some opportunity of stigmatizing the speaker as academic. So does my grocer stigmatize me when I complain of the quality of his sultanas, and he answers in one breath that they are the best sultanas, and how can I expect the best sultanas at that price? It is a flaw inherent in the business mind, and Margaret may do well to be tender to it, considering all that the business mind has done for England.

"Yes, in summer especially, the mews is a serious nuisance. The smoking-room, too, is an abominable little den. The house opposite has been taken by operatic people. Ducie Street's going down, it's my private opinion."

"How sad! It's only a few years since they built those pretty houses."

"Shows things are moving. Good for trade."

"I hate this continual flux of London. It is an epitome of us at our worst — eternal formlessness; all the qualities, good, bad and indifferent, streaming away — streaming, streaming for ever. That's why I dread it so. I mistrust rivers, even in scenery. Now, the sea —"

"High tide, yes."

"Hoy toid" — from the promenading youths.

"And these are the men to whom we give the vote," observed Mr Wilcox, omitting to add that they were also the men to whom he gave work as clerks — work that scarcely encouraged them to grow into other men. "However, they have their own lives and interests. Let's get on."

He turned as he spoke, and prepared to see her back to The Bays. The business was over. His hotel was in the opposite direction, and if he accompanied her his letters would be late for the post. She implored him not to come, but he was obdurate.

"A nice beginning, if your aunt saw you slip in alone!"

"But I always do go about alone. Considering I've walked over the Apennines, it's common sense. You will make me so angry. I don't the least take it as a compliment."

He laughed, and lit a cigar. "It isn't meant as a compliment, my dear. I just won't have you going about in the dark. Such people about too! It's dangerous."

"Can't I look after myself? I do wish —"

"Come along, Margaret; no wheedling."

A younger woman might have resented his masterly ways, but Margaret had too firm a grip of life to make a fuss. She was, in her own way, as masterly. If he was a fortress she was a mountain peak, whom all might tread, but whom the snows made nightly virginal. Disdaining the heroic outfit, excitable in her methods, garrulous, episodical, shrill, she misled her lover much as she had misled her aunt. He mistook her fertility for weakness. He supposed her "as clever as they make 'em", but no more, not realizing that she was penetrating to the depths of his soul, and approving of what she found there.

And if insight were sufficient, if the inner life were the whole of life, their happiness had been assured.

They walked ahead briskly. The parade and the road after it were well-lighted, but it was darker in Aunt Juley's garden. As they were going up by the side path, through some rhododendrons, Mr Wilcox, who was in front, said "Margaret" rather huskily, turned, dropped his cigar, and took her in his arms.

She was startled, and nearly screamed, but recovered herself at once, and kissed with genuine love the lips that were pressed against her own. It was their first kiss, and when it was over he saw her safely to the door and rang the bell for her, but disappeared into the night before the maid answered it. On looking back, the incident displeased her. It was so isolated. Nothing in their previous conversation had heralded it, and, worse still, no tenderness had ensued. If a man cannot lead up to passion he can at all events lead down from it, and she had hoped, after her complaisance, for some interchange of gentle words. But he had hurried away as if ashamed, and for an instant she was reminded of Helen and Paul.

## Chapter 21

Charles had just been scolding his Dolly. She deserved the scolding, and had bent before it, but her head, though bloody, was unsubdued, and her chirrupings began to mingle with his retreating thunder.

"You've woken the baby. I knew you would. (Rum-ti-foo, Rackety-tackety-Tompkin!) I'm not responsible for what Uncle Percy does, nor for anybody else or anything, so there!"

"Who asked him while I was away? Who asked my sister down to meet him? Who sent them out in the motor day after day?"

"Charles, that reminds me of some poem."

"Does it indeed? We shall all be dancing to a very different music presently. Miss Schlegel has fairly got us on toast."

"I could simply scratch that woman's eyes out, and to say it's my fault is most unfair."

"It's your fault, and five minutes ago you admitted it."

"I didn't."

"You did."

"Tootle, tootle, playing on the pootle!" exclaimed Dolly, suddenly devoting herself to the child.

"It's all very well to turn the conversation, but father would never have dreamt of marrying as long as Evie was there to make him comfortable. But you must needs start match-making. Besides, Cahill's too old."

"Of course, if you're going to be rude to Uncle Percy —"

"Miss Schlegel always meant to get hold of Howards End, and, thanks to you, she's got it."

"I call the way you twist things round and make them hang together most unfair. You couldn't have been nastier if you'd caught me
flirting. Could he, diddums?"

"We're in a bad hole, and must make the best of it. I shall answer
the pater's letter civilly. He's evidently anxious to do the decent thing.
But I do not intend to forget these Schlegels in a hurry. As long as
they're on their best behaviour — Dolly, are you listening? — we'll
behave, too. But if I find them giving themselves airs, or monopolizing my father, or at all ill-treating him, or worrying him with their
artistic beastliness, I intend to put my foot down, yes, firmly. Taking
my mother's place! Heaven knows what poor old Paul will say when
the news reaches him."

The interlude closes. It has taken place in Charles's garden at
Hilton. He and Dolly are sitting in deckchairs, and their motor is regarding them placidly from its garage across the lawn. A short-frocked
edition of Charles also regards them placidly; a perambulator edition is
squeaking; a third edition is expected shortly. Nature is turning out
Wilcoxes in this peaceful abode, so that they may inherit the earth.

## Chapter 22

Margaret greeted her lord with peculiar tenderness on the morrow. Mature as he was, she might yet be able to help him to the building of the rainbow bridge that should connect the prose in us with the
passion. Without it we are meaningless fragments, half monks, half
beasts, unconnected arches that have never joined into a man. With it
love is born, and alights on the highest curve, glowing against the
gray, sober against the fire. Happy the man who sees from either aspect the glory of those outspread wings. The roads of his soul lie clear,
and he and his friends shall find easy going.

It was hard going in the roads of Mr Wilcox's soul. From boyhood
he had neglected them. "I am not a fellow who bothers about my own
inside." Outwardly he was cheerful, reliable and brave; but within, all
had reverted to chaos, ruled, so far as it was ruled at all, by an incom-
plete asceticism. Whether as boy, husband or widower, he had always
the sneaking belief that bodily passion is bad, a belief that is desirable
only when held passionately. Religion had confirmed him. The words
that were read aloud on Sunday to him and to other respectable men
were the words that had once kindled the souls of St Catharine and St
Francis into a white-hot hatred of the carnal. He could not be as the
saints and love the Infinite with a seraphic ardour, but he could be a

little ashamed of loving a wife. "Amabat; amare timebat."° And it was here that Margaret hoped to help him.

It did not seem so difficult. She need trouble him with no gift of her own. She would only point out the salvation that was latent in his own soul, and in the soul of every man. Only connect! That was the whole of her sermon. Only connect the prose and the passion, and both will be exalted, and human love will be seen at its highest. Live in fragments no longer. Only connect, and the beast and the monk, robbed of the isolation that is life to either, will die.

Nor was the message difficult to give. It need not take the form of a "good talking". By quiet indications the bridge would be built and span their lives with beauty.

But she failed. For there was one quality in Henry for which she was never prepared, however much she reminded herself of it: his obtuseness. He simply did not notice things, and there was no more to be said. He never noticed that Helen and Frieda were hostile, or that Tibby was not interested in currant plantations; he never noticed the lights and shades that exist in the grayest conversation, the fingerposts, the milestones, the collisions, the illimitable views. Once — on another occasion — she scolded him about it. He was puzzled, but replied with a laugh: "My motto is Concentrate. I've no intention of frittering away my strength on that sort of thing." "It isn't frittering away the strength," she protested. "It's enlarging the space in which you may be strong." He answered: "You're a clever little woman, but my motto's Concentrate." And this morning he concentrated with a vengeance.

They met in the rhododendrons of yesterday. In the daylight the bushes were inconsiderable and the path was bright in the morning sun. She was with Helen, who had been ominously quiet since the affair was settled. "Here we all are!" she cried, and took him by one hand, retaining her sister's in the other.

"Here we are. Good morning, Helen."

Helen replied, "Good morning, Mr Wilcox."

"Henry, she has had such a nice letter from the queer, cross boy. Do you remember him? He had a sad moustache, but the back of his head was young."

"I have had a letter too. Not a nice one — I want to talk it over with you"; for Leonard Bast was nothing to him now that she had given him her word; the triangle of sex was broken for ever.

"**Amabat; amare timebat**": He loved; he was afraid to love.

"Thanks to your hint, he's clearing out of the Porphyrion."

"Not a bad business that Porphyrion," he said absently, as he took his own letter out of his pocket.

"Not a *bad* —" she exclaimed, dropping his hand. "Surely, on Chelsea Embankment —"

"Here's our hostess. Good morning, Mrs Munt. Fine rhododendrons. Good morning, Frau Liesecke; we manage to grow flowers in England, don't we?"

"Not a *bad* business?"

"No. My letter's about Howards End. Bryce has been ordered abroad, and wants to sublet it. I am far from sure that I shall give him permission. There was no clause in the agreement. In my opinion, subletting is a mistake. If he can find me another tenant, whom I consider suitable, I may cancel the agreement. Morning, Schlegel. Don't you think that's better than subletting?"

Helen had dropped her hand now, and he had steered her past the whole party to the seaward side of the house. Beneath them was the bourgeois little bay, which must have yearned all through the centuries for just such a watering-place as Swanage to be built on its margin. The waves were colourless, and the Bournemouth steamer, drawn up against the pier and hooting wildly for excursionists, gave a further touch of insipidity.

"When there is a sublet I find that damage —"

"Do excuse me, but about the Porphyrion. I don't feel easy — might I just bother you, Henry?"

Her manner was so serious that he stopped, and asked her a little sharply what she wanted.

"You said on Chelsea Embankment, surely, that it was a bad concern, so we advised this clerk to clear out. He writes this morning that he's taken our advice, and now you say it's *not* a bad concern."

"A clerk who clears out of any concern, good or bad, without securing a berth somewhere else first is a fool, and I've no pity for him."

"He has not done that. He's going into a bank in Camden Town, he says. The salary's much lower, but he hopes to manage — a branch of Dempster's Bank. Is that all right?"

"Dempster! My goodness me, yes."

"More right than the Porphyrion?"

"Yes, yes, yes; safe as houses — safer."

"Very many thanks, I'm sorry — if you sublet — ?"

"If he sublets, I shan't have the same control. In theory there should be no more damage done at Howards End; in practice there will be. Things may be done for which no money can compensate. For instance, I shouldn't want that fine wych-elm spoilt. It hangs — Margaret, we must go and see the old place some time. It's pretty in its way. We'll motor down and have lunch with Charles."

"I should enjoy that," said Margaret bravely.

"What about next Wednesday?"

"Wednesday? No, I couldn't well do that. Aunt Juley expects us to stop here another week at least."

"But you can give that up now."

"Er — no," said Margaret, after a moment's thought.

"Oh, that'll be all right. I'll speak to her."

"This visit is a high solemnity. My aunt counts on it year after year. She turns the house upside down for us; she invites our special friends — she scarcely knows Frieda, and we can't leave her on her hands. I missed one day, and she would be so hurt if I didn't stay the full ten."

"But I'll say a word to her. Don't you bother."

"Henry, I won't go. Don't bully me."

"You want to see the house, though?"

"Very much — I've heard so much about it, one way or the other. Aren't there pigs' teeth in the wych-elm?"

"*Pigs' teeth?*"

"And you chew the bark for toothache."

"What a rum notion! Of course not!"

"Perhaps I have confused it with some other tree. There are still a great number of sacred trees in England, it seems."

But he left her to intercept Mrs Munt, whose voice could be heard in the distance; to be intercepted himself by Helen.

"Oh, Mr Wilcox, about the Porphyrion —" she began, and went scarlet all over her face.

"It's all right," called Margaret, catching them up. "Dempster's Bank's better."

"But I think you told us the Porphyrion was bad, and would smash before Christmas."

"Did I? It was still outside the Tariff Ring, and had to take rotten policies. Lately it came in — safe as houses now."

"In other words, Mr Bast need never have left it."

"No, the fellow needn't."

"— and needn't have started life elsewhere at a greatly reduced salary."

"He only says 'reduced'," corrected Margaret, seeing trouble ahead.

"With a man so poor, every reduction must be great. I consider it a deplorable misfortune."

Mr Wilcox, intent on his business with Mrs Munt, was going steadily on, but the last remark made him say: "What? What's that? Do you mean that I'm responsible?"

"You're ridiculous, Helen."

"You seem to think —" He looked at his watch. "Let me explain the point to you. It is like this. You seem to assume, when a business concern is conducting a delicate negotiation, it ought to keep the public informed stage by stage. The Porphyrion, according to you, was bound to say: 'I am trying all I can to get into the Tariff Ring. I am not sure that I shall succeed, but it is the only thing that will save me from insolvency, and I am trying.' My dear Helen —"

"Is that your point? A man who had little money has less — that's mine."

"I am grieved for your clerk. But it is all in the day's work. It's part of the battle of life."

"A man who had little money," she repeated, "has less, owing to us. Under these circumstances I do not consider 'the battle of life' a happy expression."

"Oh come, come!" he protested pleasantly. "You're not to blame. No one's to blame."

"Is no one to blame for anything?"

"I wouldn't say that, but you're taking it far too seriously. Who is the fellow?"

"We have told you about the fellow twice already," said Helen. "You have even met the fellow. He is very poor and his wife is an extravagant imbecile. He is capable of better things. We — we, the upper classes — thought we would help him from the height of our superior knowledge — and here's the result!"

He raised his finger. "Now, a word of advice."

"I require no more advice."

"A word of advice. Don't take up that sentimental attitude over the poor. See that she doesn't, Margaret. The poor are poor, and one's sorry for them, but there it is. As civilization moves forward, the shoe is bound to pinch in places, and it's absurd to pretend that anyone is responsible personally. Neither you, nor I, nor my informant, nor the man who informed him, nor the directors of the Porphyrion,

are to blame for this clerk's loss of salary. It's just the shoe pinching —
no one can help it; and it might easily have been worse."

Helen quivered with indignation.

"By all means subscribe to charities — subscribe to them largely —
but don't get carried away by absurd schemes of Social Reform. I see a
good deal behind the scenes, and you can take it from me that there is
no Social Question — except for a few journalists who try to get a living out of the phrase. There are just rich and poor, as there always
have been and always will be. Point me out a time when men have
been equal —"

"I didn't say —"

"Point me out a time when desire for equality has made them happier. No, no. You can't. There always have been rich and poor. I'm no
fatalist. Heaven forbid! But our civilization is moulded by great impersonal forces" (his voice grew complacent; it always did when he elimi-
nated the personal), "and there always will be rich and poor. You can't
deny it" (and now it was a respectful voice) — "and you can't deny
that, in spite of all, the tendency of civilization has on the whole been
upward."

"Owing to God, I suppose," flashed Helen.

He stared at her.

"You grab the dollars. God does the rest."

It was no good instructing the girl if she was going to talk about
God in that neurotic modern way. Fraternal to the last,° he left her for
the quieter company of Mrs Munt. He thought, "She rather reminds
me of Dolly."

Helen looked out at the sea.

"Don't ever discuss political economy with Henry," advised her
sister. "It'll only end in a cry."

"But he must be one of those men who have reconciled science
with religion," said Helen slowly. "I don't like those men. They are
scientific themselves, and talk of the survival of the fittest, and cut
down the salaries of their clerks, and stunt the independence of all
who may menace their comfort, but yet they believe that somehow
good — it is always that sloppy 'somehow' — will be the outcome,
and that in some mystical way the Mr Basts of the future will benefit
because the Mr Basts of today are in pain."

"He is such a man in theory. But oh, Helen, in theory!"

---

**Fraternal to the last:** The autograph manuscript reads, "Paternal to the last."

"But oh, Meg, what a theory!"

"Why should you put things so bitterly, dearie?"

"Because I'm an old maid," said Helen, biting her lip. "I can't think why I go on like this myself." She shook off her sister's hand and went into the house. Margaret, distressed at the day's beginning, followed the Bournemouth steamer with her eyes. She saw that Helen's nerves were exasperated by the unlucky Bast business beyond the bounds of politeness. There might at any minute be a real explosion, which even Henry would notice. Henry must be removed.

"Margaret!" her aunt called. "Magsy! It isn't true, surely, what Mr Wilcox says, that you want to go away early next week?"

"Not 'want'," was Margaret's prompt reply; "but there is so much to be settled, and I do want to see the Charleses."

"But going away without taking the Weymouth trip, or even the Lulworth?" said Mrs Munt, coming nearer. "Without going once more up Nine Barrows Down?"

"I'm afraid so."

Mr Wilcox rejoined her with, "Good! I did the breaking of the ice."

A wave of tenderness came over her. She put a hand on either shoulder, and looked deeply into the black, bright eyes. What was behind their competent stare? She knew, but was not disquieted.

## Chapter 23

Margaret had no intention of letting things slide, and the evening before she left Swanage she gave her sister a thorough scolding. She censured her, not for disapproving of the engagement, but for throwing over her disapproval a veil of mystery. Helen was equally frank. "Yes," she said, with the air of one looking inwards, "there is a mystery. I can't help it. It's not my fault. It's the way life has been made." Helen in those days was over-interested in the subconscious self. She exaggerated the Punch and Judy aspect of life, and spoke of mankind as puppets, whom an invisible showman twitches into love and war. Margaret pointed out that if she dwelt on this she, too, would eliminate the personal. Helen was silent for a minute, and then burst into a queer speech, which cleared the air. "Go on and marry him. I think you're splendid; and if anyone can pull it off you will." Margaret denied that there was anything to "pull off", but Helen continued: "Yes, there is, and I wasn't up to it with Paul. I can only do what's easy. I can only entice and be enticed. I can't, and won't, attempt difficult relations. If I marry, it will either be a man who's strong enough to boss me or whom I'm strong enough to boss. So I shan't ever marry, for there aren't such men. And heaven help anyone whom I do marry, for I shall certainly run away from him before you can say Jack Robinson. There! Because I'm uneducated. But you, you're different; you're a heroine."

"Oh, Helen! Am I? Will it be as dreadful for poor Henry as all that?"

"You mean to keep proportion, and that's heroic, it's Greek, and I don't see why it shouldn't succeed with you. Go on and fight with him and help him. Don't ask *me* for help, or even for sympathy. Henceforward I'm going my own way. I mean to be thorough, because thoroughness is easy. I mean to dislike your husband, and to tell him so. I mean to make no concessions to Tibby. If Tibby wants to live with me, he must lump me. I mean to love *you* more than ever. Yes, I do. You and I have built up something real, because it is purely spiritual. There's no veil of mystery over us. Unreality and mystery begin as soon as one touches the body. The popular view is, as usual, exactly the wrong one. Our bothers are over tangible things — money, husbands, house-hunting. But heaven will work of itself."

Margaret was grateful for this expression of affection, and answered: "Perhaps." All vistas close in the unseen — no one doubts it — but Helen closed them rather too quickly for her taste. At every turn of speech one was confronted with reality and the absolute. Perhaps Margaret grew too old for metaphysics, perhaps Henry was weaning her from them, but she felt that there was something a little unbalanced in the mind that so readily shreds the visible. The businessman who assumes that this life is everything, and the mystic who asserts that it is nothing, fail, on this side and on that, to hit the truth. "Yes, I see, dear; it's about halfway between," Aunt Juley had hazarded in earlier years. No; truth, being alive, was not halfway between anything. It was only to be found by continuous excursions into either realm, and, though proportion is the final secret, to espouse it at the outset is to ensure sterility.

Helen, agreeing here, disagreeing there, would have talked till midnight, but Margaret, with her packing to do, focused the conversation on Henry. She might abuse Henry behind his back, but please would she always be civil to him in company? "I definitely dislike him, but I'll do what I can," promised Helen. "Do what you can with my friends in return."

This conversation made Margaret easier. Their inner life was so

safe that they could bargain over externals in a way that would have
been incredible to Aunt Juley, and impossible for Tibby or Charles.
There are moments when the inner life actually "pays", when years of
self-scrutiny, conducted for no ulterior motive, are suddenly of practical use. Such moments are still rare in the West; that they come at all
promises a fairer future. Margaret, though unable to understand her
sister, was assured against estrangement, and returned to London with
a more peaceful mind.

The following morning, at eleven o'clock, she presented herself at
the offices of the Imperial and West African Rubber Company. She
was glad to go there, for Henry had implied his business rather than
described it, and the formlessness and vagueness that one associates
with Africa itself had hitherto brooded over the main sources of his
wealth. Not that a visit to the office cleared things up. There was just
the ordinary surface scum of ledgers and polished counters and brass
bars that began and stopped for no possible reason, of electric-light
globes blossoming in triplets, of little rabbit-hutches faced with glass
or wire, of little rabbits. And even when she penetrated to the inner
depths she found only the ordinary table and Turkey carpet, and
though the map over the fireplace did depict a helping of West Africa
it was a very ordinary map. Another map hung opposite, on which the
whole continent appeared, looking like a whale marked out for blub-
ber, and by its side was a door, shut, but Henry's voice came through
it, dictating a "strong" letter. She might have been at the Porphyrion,
or Dempster's Bank, or her own wine-merchant's. Everything seems
just alike in these days. But perhaps she was seeing the Imperial side of
the company rather than its West African, and Imperialism always had
been one of her difficulties.

"One minute!" called Mr Wilcox on receiving her name. He
touched a bell, the effect of which was to produce Charles.

Charles had written his father an adequate letter — more adequate
than Evie's, through which a girlish indignation throbbed. And he
greeted his future stepmother with propriety.

"I hope that my wife — how do you do? — will give you a decent
lunch," was his opening. "I left instructions, but we live in a rough-
and-ready way. She expects you back to tea, too, after you have had a
look at Howards End. I wonder what you'll think of the place. I
wouldn't touch it with tongs myself. Do sit down! It's a measly little
place."

"I shall enjoy seeing it," said Margaret, feeling, for the first time, shy.

"You'll see it at its worst, for Bryce decamped abroad last Monday without even arranging for a charwoman to clear up after him. I never saw such a disgraceful mess. It's unbelievable. He wasn't in the house a month."

"I've more than a little bone to pick with Bryce," called Henry from the inner chamber.

"Why did he go so suddenly?"

"Invalid type; couldn't sleep."

"Poor fellow!"

"Poor fiddlesticks!" said Mr Wilcox, joining them. "He had the impudence to put up notice-boards without so much as saying with your leave or by your leave. Charles flung them down."

"Yes, I flung them down," said Charles modestly.

"I've sent a telegram after him, and a pretty sharp one, too. He, and he in person, is responsible for the upkeep of that house for the next three years."

"The keys are at the farm; we wouldn't have the keys."

"Quite right."

"Dolly would have taken them, but I was in, fortunately."

"What's Mr Bryce like?" asked Margaret.

But nobody cared. Mr Bryce was the tenant, who had no right to sublet; to have defined him further was a waste of time. On his misdeeds they descanted profusely, until the girl who had been typing the strong letter came out with it. Mr Wilcox added his signature. "Now we'll be off," said he.

A motor-drive, a form of felicity detested by Margaret, awaited her. Charles saw them in, civil to the last, and in a moment the offices of the Imperial and West African Rubber Company faded away. But it was not an impressive drive. Perhaps the weather was to blame, being gray and banked high with weary clouds. Perhaps Hertfordshire is scarcely intended for motorists. Did not a gentleman once motor so quickly through Westmorland that he missed it? And if Westmorland can be missed it will fare ill with a county whose delicate structure particularly needs the attentive eye. Hertfordshire is England at its quietest, with little emphasis of river and hill; it is England meditative. If Drayton° were with us again to write a new edition of his incomparable poem, he would sing the nymphs of Hertfordshire as indeterminate of feature, with hair obfuscated by the London smoke. Their

**Drayton:** Michael Drayton (1563–1631), author of the poem *Poly-Olbion*, published in two parts in 1612 and 1622.

eyes would be sad, and averted from their fate towards the northern flats, their leader not Isis or Sabrina, but the slowly flowing Lea. No glory of raiment would be theirs, no urgency of dance; but they would be real nymphs.

The chauffeur could not travel as quickly as he had hoped, for the Great North Road was full of Easter traffic. But he went quite quick enough for Margaret, a poor-spirited creature, who had chickens and children on the brain.

"They're all right," said Mr Wilcox. "They'll learn — like the swallows and the telegraph-wires."

"Yes, but while they're learning —"

"The motor's come to stay," he answered. "One must get about. There's a pretty church — oh, you aren't sharp enough. Well, look out, if the road worries you — right outward at the scenery."

She looked at the scenery. It heaved and merged like porridge. Presently it congealed. They had arrived.

Charles's house on the left; on the right the swelling forms of the Six Hills. Their appearance in such a neighbourhood surprised her. They interrupted the stream of residences that was thickening up towards Hilton. Beyond them she saw meadows and a wood, and beneath them she settled that soldiers of the best kind lay buried. She hated war and liked soldiers — it was one of her amiable inconsistencies.

But here was Dolly, dressed up to the nines, standing at the door to greet them, and here were the first drops of the rain. They ran in gaily, and after a long wait in the drawing-room sat down to the rough-and-ready lunch, every dish in which concealed or exuded cream. Mr Bryce was the chief topic of conversation. Dolly described his visit with the key, while her father-in-law gave satisfaction by chaffing her and contradicting all she said. It was evidently the custom to laugh at Dolly. He chaffed Margaret, too, and Margaret, roused from a grave meditation, was pleased, and chaffed him back. Dolly seemed surprised, and eyed her curiously. After lunch the two children came down. Margaret disliked babies, but hit it off better with the two-year-old, and sent Dolly into fits of laughter by talking sense to him. "Kiss them now, and come away," said Mr Wilcox. She came, but refused to kiss them; it was such hard luck on the little things, she said, and, though Dolly proffered Chorly-worly and Porgly-woggles in turn, she was obdurate.

By this time it was raining steadily. The car came round with the hood up, and again she lost all sense of space. In a few minutes they stopped, and Crane opened the door of the car.

"What's happened?" asked Margaret.

"What do you suppose?" said Henry.

A little porch was close up against her face.

"Are we there already?"

"We are."

"Well, I never! In years ago it seemed so far away."

Smiling, but somehow disillusioned, she jumped out, and her impetus carried her to the front door. She was about to open it, when Henry said: "That's no good; it's locked. Who's got the key?"

As he had himself forgotten to call for the key at the farm, no one replied. He also wanted to know who had left the front gate open, since a cow had strayed in from the road, and was spoiling the croquet lawn. Then he said rather crossly: "Margaret, you wait in the dry. I'll go down for the key. It isn't a hundred yards."

"Mayn't I come too?"

"No; I shall be back before I'm gone."

Then the car turned away, and it was as if a curtain had risen. For the second time that day she saw the appearance of the earth.

There were the greengage trees that Helen had once described, there the tennis lawn, there the hedge that would be glorious with dog-roses in June, but the vision now was of black and palest green. Down by the dell-hole° more vivid colours were awakening, and Lent lilies stood sentinel on its margin, or advanced in battalions over the grass. Tulips were a tray of jewels. She could not see the wych-elm tree, but a branch of the celebrated vine, studded with velvet knobs, had covered the porch. She was struck by the fertility of the soil; she had seldom been in a garden where the flowers looked so well, and even the weeds she was idly plucking out of the porch were intensely green. Why had poor Mr Bryce fled from all this beauty? For she had already decided that the place was beautiful.

"Naughty cow! Go away!" cried Margaret to the cow, but without indignation.

Harder came the rain, pouring out of a windless sky, and spattering up from the notice-boards of the house-agents, which lay in a row

---

dell-hole: In his memoir of his childhood home Rooksnest, printed as an appendix in the Abinger edition of *Howards End* (London: Arnold, 1973), Forster describes "a dell known as the 'dellole' which was a pond when we came but mother had it drained and filled up" (346).

on the lawn where Charles had hurled them. She must have interviewed Charles in another world — where one did have interviews. How Helen would revel in such a notion! Charles dead, all people dead, nothing alive but houses and gardens. The obvious dead, the intangible alive, and — no connection at all between them! Margaret smiled. Would that her own fancies were as clear-cut! Would that she could deal as high-handedly with the world! Smiling and sighing, she laid her hand upon the door. It opened. The house was not locked up at all.

She hesitated. Ought she to wait for Henry? He felt strongly about property, and might prefer to show her over himself. On the other hand, he had told her to keep in the dry, and the porch was beginning to drip. So she went in, and the draught from inside slammed the door behind.

Desolation greeted her. Dirty finger-prints were on the hall windows, flue and rubbish on its unwashed boards. The civilization of luggage had been here for a month, and then decamped. Dining-room and drawing-room — right and left — were guessed only by their wallpapers. They were just rooms where one could shelter from the rain. Across the ceiling of each ran a great beam. The dining-room and hall revealed theirs openly, but the drawing-room's was match-boarded — because the facts of life must be concealed from ladies? Drawing-room, dining-room and hall — how petty the names sounded! Here were simply three rooms where children could play and friends shelter from the rain. Yes, and they were beautiful.

Then she opened one of the doors opposite — there were two — and exchanged wallpapers for whitewash. It was the servants' part, though she scarcely realized that: just rooms again, where friends might shelter. The garden at the back was full of flowering cherries and plums. Further on were hints of the meadow and a black cliff of pines. Yes, the meadow was beautiful.

Penned in by the desolate weather, she recaptured the sense of space which the motor had tried to rob from her. She remembered again that ten square miles are not ten times as wonderful as one square mile, that a thousand square miles are not practically the same as heaven. The phantom of bigness, which London encourages, was laid for ever when she paced from the hall at Howards End to its kitchen and heard the rains run this way and that where the watershed of the roof divided them.

Now Helen came to her mind, scrutinizing half Wessex from the ridge of the Purbeck downs, and saying: "You will have to lose something." She was not so sure. For instance, she would double her kingdom by opening the door that concealed the stairs.

Now she thought of the map of Africa; of empires; of her father; of the two supreme nations, streams of whose life warmed her blood, but, mingling, had cooled her brain. She paced back into the hall, and as she did so the house reverberated.

"Is that you, Henry?" she called.

There was no answer, but the house reverberated again.

"Henry, have you got in?"

But it was the heart of the house beating, faintly at first, then loudly, martially. It dominated the rain.

It is the starved imagination, not the well-nourished, that is afraid. Margaret flung open the door to the stairs. A noise as of drums seemed to deafen her. A woman, an old woman, was descending, with figure erect, with face impassive, with lips that parted and said dryly:

"Oh! Well, I took you for Ruth Wilcox."

Margaret stammered: "I — Mrs Wilcox — I?"

"In fancy, of course — in fancy. You had her way of walking. Good day." And the old woman passed out into the rain.


**Chapter 24**

"It gave her quite a turn," said Mr Wilcox, when retailing the incident to Dolly at tea-time. "None of you girls have any nerves, really. Of course, a word from me put it all right, but silly old Miss Avery — she frightened you, didn't she, Margaret? There you stood clutching a bunch of weeds. She might have said something, instead of coming down the stairs with that alarming bonnet on. I passed her as I came in. Enough to make the car shy. I believe Miss Avery goes in for being a character; some old maids do." He lit a cigarette. "It is their last resource. Heaven knows what she was doing in the place; but that's Bryce's business, not mine."

"I wasn't as foolish as you suggest," said Margaret. "She only startled me, for the house had been silent so long."

"Did you take her for a spook?" asked Dolly, for whom "spooks" and "going to church" summarized the unseen.

"Not exactly."

"She really did frighten you," said Henry, who was far from discouraging timidity in females. "Poor Margaret! And very naturally. Uneducated classes are so stupid."

"Is Miss Avery uneducated classes?" Margaret asked, and found herself looking at the decoration scheme of Dolly's drawing-room.

"She's just one of the crew at the farm. People like that always assume things. She assumed you'd know who she was. She left all the Howards End keys in the front lobby, and assumed that you'd seen them as you came in, that you'd lock up the house when you'd done, and would bring them on down to her. And there was her niece hunting for them down at the farm. Lack of education makes people very casual. Hilton was full of women like Miss Avery once."

"I shouldn't have disliked it, perhaps."

"Or Miss Avery giving me a wedding present," said Dolly.

Which was illogical but interesting. Through Dolly, Margaret was destined to learn a good deal.

"But Charles said I must try not to mind, because she had known his grandmother."

"As usual, you've got the story wrong, my good Dorothea."

"I meant great-grandmother — the one who left Mrs Wilcox the house. Weren't both of them and Miss Avery friends when Howards End, too, was a farm?"

Her father-in-law blew out a shaft of smoke. His attitude to his dead wife was curious. He would allude to her, and hear her discussed, but never mentioned her by name. Nor was he interested in the dim, bucolic past. Dolly was — for the following reason.

"Then hadn't Mrs Wilcox a brother — or was it an uncle? Anyhow, he popped the question, and Miss Avery, she said 'No'. Just imagine, if she'd said 'Yes' she would have been Charles's aunt. (Oh, I say, that's rather good! 'Charlie's Aunt!' I must chaff him about that this evening.) And the man went out and was killed. Yes, I'm certain I've got it right now. Tom Howard — he was the last of them."

"I believe so," said Mr Wilcox negligently.

"I say! Howards End — Howards Ended!" cried Dolly. "I'm rather on the spot this evening, eh?"

"I wish you'd ask whether Crane's ended."

"Oh, Mr Wilcox, how *can* you?"

"Because, if he has had enough tea, we ought to go — Dolly's a good little woman," he continued, "but a little of her goes a long way. I wouldn't live near her if you paid me."

Margaret smiled. Though presenting a firm front to outsiders, no

Wilcox could live near, or near the possessions of, any other Wilcox. They had the colonial spirit, and were always making for some spot where the white man might carry his burden unobserved. Of course, Howards End was impossible, so long as the younger couple were established in Hilton. His objections to the house were plain as daylight now.

Crane had had enough tea, and was sent to the garage, where their car had been trickling muddy water over Charles's. The downpour had surely penetrated the Six Hills by now, bringing news of our restless civilization. "Curious mounds," said Henry, "but in with you now; another time." He had to be up in London by seven — if possible, by six-thirty. Once more she lost the sense of space; once more trees, houses, people, animals, hills, merged and heaved into one dirtiness, and she was at Wickham Place.

Her evening was pleasant. The sense of flux which had haunted her all the year disappeared for a time. She forgot the luggage and the motor-cars, and the hurrying men who know so much and connect so little. She recaptured the sense of space, which is the basis of all earthly beauty, and, starting from Howards End, she attempted to realize England. She failed — visions do not come when we try, though they may come through trying. But an unexpected love of the island awoke in her, connecting on this side with the joys of the flesh, on that with the inconceivable. Helen and her father had known this love, poor Leonard Bast was groping after it, but it had been hidden from Margaret till this afternoon. It had certainly come through the house and old Miss Avery. Through them: the notion of "through" persisted; her mind trembled towards a conclusion which only the unwise have put into words. Then, veering back into warmth, it dwelt on ruddy bricks, flowering plum trees, and all the tangible joys of spring.

Henry, after allaying her agitation, had taken her over his property, and had explained to her the use and dimensions of the various rooms. He had sketched the history of the little estate. "It is so unlucky," ran the monologue, "that money wasn't put into it about fifty years ago. Then it had four — five — times the land — thirty acres at least. One could have made something out of it then — a small park, or at all events shrubberies, and rebuilt the house further away from the road. What's the good of taking it in hand now? Nothing but the meadow left, and even that was heavily mortgaged when I first had to do with things — yes, and the house too. Oh, it was no joke." She saw two women as he spoke, one old, the other young, watching their inheri-

tance melt away. She saw them greet him as a deliverer. "Mismanage-
ment did it — besides, the days for small farms are over. It doesn't
pay — except with intensive cultivation. Small holdings, back to the
land — ah! Philanthropic bunkum. Take it as a rule that nothing pays
on a small scale. Most of the land you see" (they were standing at an
upper window, the only one which faced west) "belongs to the people
at the Park — they made their pile over copper — good chaps. Avery's
Farm, Sishe's — what they call the Common, where you see that ruined oak — one after the other fell in, and so did this, as near as is no
matter." But Henry had saved it; without fine feelings or deep insight,
but he had saved it, and she loved him for the deed. "When I had
more control I did what I could: sold off the two and a half animals,
and the mangy pony, and the superannuated tools; pulled down the
outhouses; drained; thinned out I don't know how many guelder roses
and elder trees; and inside the house I turned the old kitchen into a
hall, and made a kitchen behind where the dairy was. Garage and so
on came later. But one could still tell it's been an old farm. And yet it
isn't the place that would fetch one of your artistic crew." No, it
wasn't; and if he did not quite understand it the artistic crew would
still less: it was English, and the wych-elm that she saw from the window was an English tree. No report had prepared her for its peculiar
glory. It was neither warrior, nor lover, nor god; in none of these roles
do the English excel. It was a comrade, bending over the house,
strength and adventure in its roots, but in its utmost fingers tenderness, and the girth, that a dozen men could not have spanned, became
in the end evanescent, till pale bud clusters seemed to float in the air.
It was a comrade. House and tree transcended any simile of sex. Margaret thought of them now, and was to think of them through many a
windy night and London day, but to compare either to man, to
woman, always dwarfed the vision. Yet they kept within limits of the
human. Their message was not of eternity, but of hope on this side of
the grave. As she stood in the one, gazing at the other, truer relationships had gleamed.

Another touch, and the account of her day is finished. They ventured into the garden for a minute, and to Mr Wilcox's surprise she
was right. Teeth, pigs' teeth, could be seen in the bark of the wych-
elm tree — just the white tips of them showing. "Extraordinary!" he
cried. "Who told you?"

"I heard of it one winter in London," was her answer, for she, too,
avoided mentioning Mrs Wilcox by name.

## Chapter 25

Evie heard of her father's engagement when she was in for a tennis tournament, and her play went simply to pot. That she should marry and leave him had seemed natural enough; that he, left alone, should do the same was deceitful; and now Charles and Dolly said that it was all her fault. "But I never dreamt of such a thing," she grumbled. "Dad took me to call now and then, and made me ask her to Simpson's. Well, I'm altogether off Dad." It was also an insult to their mother's memory; there they were agreed, and Evie had the idea of returning Mrs Wilcox's lace and jewelry "as a protest". Against what it would protest she was not clear; but, being only eighteen, the idea of renunciation appealed to her, the more as she did not care for jewelry or lace. Dolly then suggested that she and Uncle Percy should pretend to break off their engagement, and then perhaps Mr Wilcox would quarrel with Miss Schlegel, and break off his; or Paul might be cabled for. But at this point Charles told them not to talk nonsense. So Evie settled to marry as soon as possible; it was no good hanging about with these Schlegels eyeing her. The date of her wedding was consequently put forward from September to August, and in the intoxication of presents she recovered much of her good humour.

Margaret found that she was expected to figure at this function, and to figure largely; it would be such an opportunity, said Henry, for her to get to know his set. Sir James Bidder would be there, and all the Cahills and the Fussells, and his sister-in-law, Mrs Warrington Wilcox, had fortunately got back from her tour round the world. Henry she loved, but his set promised to be another matter. He had not the knack of surrounding himself with nice people — indeed, for a man of ability and virtue his choice had been singularly unfortunate; he had no guiding principle beyond a certain preference for mediocrity; he was content to settle one of the greatest things in life haphazard, and so, while his investments went right, his friends generally went wrong. She would be told, "Oh, So-and-so's a good sort — a thundering good sort," and find, on meeting him, that he was a brute or a bore. If Henry had shown real affection, she would have understood, for affection explains everything. But he seemed without sentiment. The "thundering good sort" might at any moment become "a fellow for whom I never did have much use, and have less now", and be shaken off cheerily into oblivion. Margaret had done the same as a schoolgirl. Now she never forgot anyone for whom she had once cared; she connected, though the connection might be bitter, and she hoped that some day Henry would do the same.

Evie was not to be married from Ducie Street. She had a fancy for something rural, and, besides, no one would be in London then, so she left her boxes for a few weeks at Oniton Grange, and her banns were duly published in the parish church, and for a couple of days the little town, dreaming between the ruddy hills, was roused by the clang of our civilization, and drew up by the roadside to let the motors pass. Oniton had been a discovery of Mr Wilcox's — a discovery of which he was not altogether proud. It was up towards the Welsh border, and so difficult of access that he had concluded it must be something special. A ruined castle stood in the grounds. But having got there what was one to do? The shooting was bad, the fishing indifferent, and womenfolk reported the scenery as nothing much. The place turned out to be in the wrong part of Shropshire, damn it, and, though he never damned his own property aloud, he was only waiting to get it off his hands, and then to let fly. Evie's marriage was its last appearance in public. As soon as a tenant was found, it became a house for which he never had had much use, and had less now, and, like Howards End, faded into limbo.

But on Margaret Oniton was destined to make a lasting impression. She regarded it as her future home, and was anxious to start straight with the clergy, etc., and, if possible, to see something of the local life. It was a market-town — as tiny a one as England possesses — and had for ages served that lonely valley, and guarded our marches against the Celt. In spite of the occasion, in spite of the numbing hilarity that greeted her as soon as she got into the reserved saloon at Paddington, her senses were awake and watching, and though Oniton was to prove one of her innumerable false starts she never forgot it, nor the things that happened there.

The London party only numbered eight — the Fussells, father and son, two Anglo-Indian ladies° named Mrs Plynlimmon and Lady Edser, Mrs Warrington Wilcox and her daughter, and, lastly, the little girl, very smart and quiet, who figures at so many weddings, and who kept a watchful eye on Margaret, the bride-elect. Dolly was absent — a domestic event detained her at Hilton; Paul had cabled a humorous message; Charles was to meet them with a trio of motors at

**Anglo-Indian ladies:** English women who had spent much of their lives in India as wives of army officers or government officials.

Shrewsbury. Helen had refused her invitation; Tibby had never answered his. The management was excellent, as was to be expected with
anything that Henry undertook; one was conscious of his sensible and
generous brain in the background. They were his guests as soon as
they reached the train: a special label for their luggage; a courier; a
special lunch; they had only to look pleasant and, where possible,
pretty. Margaret thought with dismay of her own nuptials — presumably under the management of Tibby. "Mr Theobald Schlegel and
Miss Helen Schlegel request the pleasure of Mrs Plynlimmon's company on the occasion of the marriage of their sister Margaret." The
formula was incredible, but it must soon be printed and sent, and
though Wickham Place need not compete with Oniton it must feed its
guests properly, and provide them with sufficient chairs. Her wedding
would either be ramshackly or bourgeois — she hoped the latter. Such
an affair as the present, staged with a deftness that was almost beautiful, lay beyond her powers and those of her friends.

The low rich purr of a Great Western express is not the worst background for conversation, and the journey passed pleasantly enough.
Nothing could have exceeded the kindness of the two men. They
raised windows for some ladies, and lowered them for others, they
rang the bell for the servant, they identified the colleges as the train
slipped past Oxford, they caught books or bag-purses in the act of
tumbling onto the floor. Yet there was nothing finicking about their
politeness: it had the Public School touch, and, though sedulous, was
virile. More battles than Waterloo have been won on our playing-
fields, and Margaret bowed to a charm of which she did not wholly
approve, and said nothing when the Oxford colleges were identified
wrongly. "Male and female created He them"; the journey to Shrewsbury confirmed this questionable statement, and the long glass saloon,
that moved so easily and felt so comfortable, became a forcing-house
for the idea of sex.

At Shrewsbury came fresh air. Margaret was all for sight-seeing,
and while the others were finishing their tea at the Raven she annexed
a motor and hurried over the astonishing city. Her chauffeur was not
the faithful Crane, but an Italian, who dearly loved making her late.
Charles, watch in hand, though with a level brow, was standing in
front of the hotel when they returned. It was perfectly all right, he told
her; she was by no means the last. And then he dived into the coffee-
room, and she heard him say, "For God's sake, hurry the women up;
we shall never be off," and Albert Fussell reply, "Not I; I've done my
share," and Colonel Fussell opine that the ladies were getting them-

selves up to kill. Presently Myra (Mrs Warrington's daughter) appeared, and as she was his cousin Charles blew her up a little: she had been changing her smart travelling-hat for a smart motor-hat. Then Mrs Warrington herself, leading the quiet child; the two Anglo-Indian ladies were always last. Maids, courier, heavy luggage, had already gone on by a branch-line to a station nearer Oniton, but there were five hat-boxes and four dressing-bags to be packed in, and five dust-cloaks to be put on, and to be put off at the last moment, because Charles declared them not necessary. The men presided over everything with unfailing good humour. By half past five the party was ready, and went out of Shrewsbury by the Welsh Bridge.

Shropshire had not the reticence of Hertfordshire. Though robbed of half its magic by swift movement, it still conveyed the sense of hills. They were nearing the buttresses that force the Severn eastward and make it an English stream, and the sun, sinking over the sentinels of Wales, was straight in their eyes. Having picked up another guest, they turned southward, avoiding the greater mountains, but conscious of an occasional summit, rounded and mild, whose colouring differed in quality from that of the lower earth, and whose contours altered more slowly. Quiet mysteries were in progress behind those tossing horizons: the west, as ever, was retreating with some secret which may not be worth the discovery, but which no practical man will ever discover.

They spoke of Tariff Reform.°

Mrs Warrington was just back from the Colonies. Like many other critics of Empire, her mouth had been stopped with food, and she could only exclaim at the hospitality with which she had been received, and warn the Mother Country against trifling with young Titans. "They threaten to cut the painter,"° she cried, "and where shall we be then? Miss Schlegel, you'll undertake to keep Henry sound about Tariff Reform? It is our last hope."

Margaret playfully confessed herself on the other side,° and they began to quote from their respective handbooks while the motor carried them deeper into the hills. Curious these were rather than impressive, for their outlines lacked beauty, and the pink fields on their summits suggested the handkerchiefs of a giant spread out to dry. An

---

**Tariff Reform:** A protectionist policy advocated by Colonial Secretary Joseph Chamberlain in 1903, which opposed the free-trade policies of traditional liberal governments; reformers sought to create an imperial trading block by imposing tariffs on trade with countries outside the British Empire.     **to cut the painter:** To cut the rope ("painter") connecting a small boat (a particular colony) to a ship (the mother country).     **on the other side:** In favor of free trade.

occasional outcrop of rock, an occasional wood, an occasional "for-est", treeless and brown, all hinted at wildness to follow, but the main colour was an agricultural green. The air grew cooler; they had sur-mounted the last gradient, and Oniton lay below them with its church, its radiating houses, its castle, its river-girt peninsula. Close to the castle was a gray mansion, unintellectual but kindly, stretching with its grounds across the peninsula's neck — the sort of mansion that was built all over England in the beginning of the last century, while archi-tecture was still an expression of the national character. That was the Grange, remarked Albert, over his shoulder, and then he jammed the brake on, and the motor slowed down and stopped. "I'm sorry," said he, turning round. "Do you mind getting out — by the door on the right. Steady on."

"What's happened?" asked Mrs Warrington.

Then the car behind them drew up, and the voice of Charles was heard saying: "Get out the women at once." There was a concourse of males, and Margaret and her companions were hustled out and re-ceived into the second car. What had happened? As it started off again, the door of a cottage opened, and a girl screamed wildly at them.

"What is it?" the ladies cried.

Charles drove them a hundred yards without speaking. Then he said, "It's all right. Your car just touched a dog."

"But stop!" cried Margaret, horrified.

"It didn't hurt him."

"Didn't really hurt him?" asked Myra.

"No."

"Do *please* stop!" said Margaret, leaning forward. She was stand-ing up in the car, the other occupants holding her knees to steady her. "I want to go back, please."

Charles took no notice.

"We've left Mr Fussell behind," said another; "and Angelo, and Crane."

"Yes, but no woman."

"I expect a little of" — Mrs Warrington scratched her palm — "will be more to the point than one of us!"

"The insurance company see to that," remarked Charles, "and Al-bert will do the talking."

"I want to go back, though, I say!" repeated Margaret, getting angry.

Charles took no notice. The motor, loaded with refugees, continued to travel very slowly down the hill. "The men are there," chorused the others. "Men will see to it."

"The men *can't* see to it.° Oh, this is ridiculous! Charles, I ask you to stop."

"Stopping's no good," drawled Charles.

"Isn't it?" said Margaret, and jumped straight out of the car.

She fell on her knees, cut her gloves, shook her hat over her ear. Cries of alarm followed her. "You've hurt yourself," exclaimed Charles, jumping after her.

"Of course I've hurt myself!" she retorted.

"May I ask what —"

"There's nothing to ask," said Margaret.

"Your hand's bleeding."

"I know."

"I'm in for a frightful row from the pater."

"You should have thought of that sooner, Charles."

Charles had never been in such a position before. It was a woman in revolt who was hobbling away from him, and the sight was too strange to leave any room for anger. He recovered himself when the others caught them up; their sort he understood. He commanded them to go back.

Albert Fussell was seen walking towards them.

"It's all right!" he called. "It wasn't a dog, it was a cat."

"There!" exclaimed Charles triumphantly. "It's only a rotten cat."

"Got room in your car for a little 'un? I cut as soon as I saw it wasn't a dog; the chauffeurs are tackling the girl." But Margaret walked forward steadily. Why should the chauffeurs tackle the girl? Ladies sheltering behind men, men sheltering behind servants — the whole system's wrong, and she must challenge it.

"Miss Schlegel! 'Pon my word, you've hurt your hand."

"I'm just going to see," said Margaret. "Don't you wait, Mr Fussell."

The second motor came round the corner. "It is all right, madam," said Crane in his turn. He had taken to call her madam.

"What's all right? The cat?"

"Yes, madam. The girl will receive compensation for it."

"She was a very ruda girla," said Angelo from the third motor thoughtfully.

**The men *can't* see to it:** The autograph manuscript has "Men *can't* see to it."

"Wouldn't you have been rude?"

The Italian spread out his hands, implying that he had not thought of rudeness, but would produce it if it pleased her. The situation became absurd. The gentlemen were again buzzing round Miss Schlegel with offers of assistance, and Lady Edser began to bind up her hand. She yielded, apologizing slightly, and was led back to the car, and soon the landscape resumed its motion, the lonely cottage disappeared, the castle swelled on its cushion of turf, and they had arrived. No doubt she had disgraced herself. But she felt their whole journey from London had been unreal. They had no part with the earth and its emotions. They were dust, and a stink, and cosmopolitan chatter, and the girl whose cat had been killed had lived more deeply than they.

"Oh, Henry," she exclaimed, "I have been so naughty," for she had decided to take up this line. "We ran over a cat. Charles told me not to jump out, but I would, and look!" She held out her bandaged hand. "Your poor Meg went such a flop."

Mr Wilcox looked bewildered. In evening dress, he was standing to welcome his guests in the hall.

"Thinking it was a dog," added Mrs Warrington.

"Ah, a dog's a companion!" said Colonel Fussell. "A dog'll remember you."

"Have you hurt yourself, Margaret?"

"Not to speak about; and it's my left hand."

"Well, hurry up and change."

She obeyed, as did the others. Mr Wilcox then turned to his son.

"Now, Charles, what's happened?"

Charles was absolutely honest. He described what he believed to have happened. Albert had flattened out a cat, and Miss Schlegel had lost her nerve, as any woman might. She had been got safely into the other car, but when it was in motion had leapt out again, in spite of all that they could say. After walking a little on the road, she had calmed down and had said that she was sorry. His father accepted this explanation, and neither knew that Margaret had artfully prepared the way for it. It fitted in too well with their view of feminine nature. In the smoking-room, after dinner, the Colonel put forward the view that Miss Schlegel had jumped it out of devilry. Well he remembered as a young man, in the harbour of Gibraltar once, how a girl — a handsome girl, too — had jumped overboard for a bet. He could see her now, and all the lads overboard after her. But Charles and Mr Wilcox agreed it was much more probably nerves in Miss Schlegel's case. Charles was depressed. That woman had a tongue. She would bring worse disgrace on his father before she had done with them. He strolled out onto the castle mound to think the matter over. The evening was exquisite. On three sides of him a little river whispered, full of messages from the west; above his head the ruins made patterns against the sky. He carefully reviewed their dealings with this family, until he fitted Helen and Margaret and Aunt Juley into an orderly conspiracy. Paternity had made him suspicious. He had two children to look after, and more coming, and day by day they seemed less likely to grow up rich men. "It is all very well," he reflected, "the pater saying that he will be just to all, but one can't be just indefinitely. Money isn't elastic. What's to happen if Evie has a family? And, come to that, so may the pater. There'll not be enough to go round, for there's none coming in, either through Dolly or Percy. It's damnable!" He looked enviously at the Grange, whose windows poured light and laughter. First and last, this wedding would cost a pretty penny. Two ladies were strolling up and down the garden terrace, and as the syllables "Imperialism" were wafted to his ears he guessed that one of them was his aunt. She might have helped him, if she too had not had a family to provide for. "Everyone for himself," he repeated — a maxim which had cheered him in the past, but which rang grimly enough among the ruins of Oniton. He lacked his father's ability in business, and so had an even higher regard for money; unless he could inherit plenty, he feared to leave his children poor.

As he sat thinking, one of the ladies left the terrace and walked into the meadow; he recognized her as Margaret by the white bandage that gleamed on her arm, and put out his cigar, lest the gleam should betray him. She climbed up the mound in zigzags, and at times stooped down, as if she was stroking the turf. It sounds absolutely incredible, but for a moment Charles thought that she was in love with him, and had come out to tempt him. Charles believed in temptresses, who are indeed the strong man's necessary complement, and having no sense of humour he could not purge himself of the thought by a smile. Margaret, who was engaged to his father, and his sister's wedding-guest, kept on her way without noticing him, and he admitted that he had wronged her on this point. But what was she doing? Why was she stumbling about amongst the rubble and catching her dress in brambles and burrs? As she edged round the keep, she must have got to leeward and smelt his cigar-smoke, for she exclaimed, "Hullo! Who's that?"

Charles made no answer.

"Saxon or Celt?" she continued, laughing in the darkness. "But it

doesn't matter. Whichever you are, you will have to listen to me. I
love this place. I love Shropshire. I hate London. I am glad that this
will be my home. Ah, dear" — she was now moving back towards the
house — "what a comfort to have arrived!"

"That woman means mischief," thought Charles, and compressed
his lips. In a few minutes he followed her indoors, as the ground was
getting damp. Mists were rising from the river, and presently it became
invisible, though it whispered more loudly. There had been a heavy
downpour in the Welsh hills.

## Chapter 26

Next morning a fine mist covered the peninsula. The weather
promised well, and the outline of the castle mound grew clearer each
moment that Margaret watched it. Presently she saw the keep, and the
sun painted the rubble gold, and charged the white sky with blue. The
shadow of the house gathered itself together, and fell over the garden.
A cat looked up at her window and mewed. Lastly the river appeared,
still holding the mists between its banks and its overhanging alders,
and only visible as far as a hill, which cut off its upper reaches.

Margaret was fascinated by Oniton. She had said that she loved it,
but it was rather its romantic tension that held her. The rounded
Druids° of whom she had caught glimpses in her drive, the rivers hurrying down from them to England, the carelessly modelled masses of
the lower hills, thrilled her with poetry. The house was insignificant,
but the prospect from it would be an eternal joy, and she thought of
all the friends she would have to stop in it, and of the conversion of
Henry himself to a rural life. Society, too, promised favourably. The
rector of the parish had dined with them last night, and she found that
he was a friend of her father's, and so knew what to find in her. She
liked him. He would introduce her to the town. While, on her other
side, Sir James Bidder sat, repeating that she only had to give the
word, and he would whip up the county families for twenty miles
round. Whether Sir James, who was Garden Seeds, had promised what
he could perform, she doubted, but so long as Henry mistook them
for the county families when they did call she was content.

Charles and Albert Fussell now crossed the lawn. They were going
for a morning dip, and a servant followed them with their bathing-
dresses. She had meant to take a stroll herself before breakfast, but saw

**Druids:** The Welsh hills.

that the day was still sacred to men, and amused herself by watching their contretemps. In the first place the key of the bathing-shed could not be found. Charles stood by the riverside with folded hands, tragical, while the servant shouted, and was misunderstood by another servant in the garden. Then came a difficulty about a springboard, and soon three people were running backwards and forwards over the meadow with orders and counter-orders and recriminations and apologies. If Margaret wanted to jump from a motor-car, she jumped; if Tibby thought paddling would benefit his ankles, he paddled; if a clerk desired adventure, he took a walk in the dark. But these athletes seemed paralysed. They could not bathe without their appliances, though the morning sun was calling and the last mists were rising from the dimpling stream. Had they found the life of the body after all? Could not the men whom they despised as milksops beat them, even on their own ground?

She thought of the bathing arrangements as they should be in her day — no worrying of servants, no appliances, beyond good sense. Her reflections were disturbed by the quiet child, who had come out to speak to the cat, but was now watching her watch the men. She called, "Good morning, dear," a little sharply. Her voice spread consternation. Charles looked round, and though completely attired in indigo blue vanished into the shed, and was seen no more.

"Miss Wilcox is up —" the child whispered, and then became unintelligible.

"What's that?"

It sounded like, "— cut-yoke — sack-back —"°

"I can't hear."

"— on the bed — tissue-paper —"

Gathering that the wedding-dress was on view, and that a visit would be seemly, she went to Evie's room. All was hilarity here. Evie, in a petticoat, was dancing with one of the Anglo-Indian ladies, while the other was adoring yards of white satin. They screamed, they laughed, they sang, and the dog barked.

Margaret screamed a little too, but without conviction. She could not feel that a wedding was so funny. Perhaps something was missing in her equipment.

Evie gasped: "Dolly is a rotter not to be here! Oh, we would rag just then!" Then Margaret went down to breakfast.

---

**cut-yoke — sack-back:** Terms describing the gatherings and style of Evie's wedding dress; "sack-back" refers to a loose-fitting dress the back of which was not shaped to the figure.

Henry was already installed; he ate slowly and spoke little, and was, in Margaret's eyes, the only member of their party who dodged emotion successfully. She could not suppose him indifferent either to the loss of his daughter or to the presence of his future wife. Yet he dwelt intact, only issuing orders occasionally — orders that promoted the comfort of his guests. He inquired after her hand; he set her to pour out the coffee and Mrs Warrington to pour out the tea. When Evie came down there was a moment's awkwardness, and both ladies rose to vacate their places. "Burton," called Henry, "serve tea and coffee from the sideboard!" It wasn't genuine tact, but it was tact of a sort — the sort that is as useful as the genuine, and saves even more situations at board meetings. Henry treated a marriage like a funeral, item by item, never raising his eyes to the whole, and "Death, where is thy sting? Love, where is thy victory?"° one would exclaim at the close.

After breakfast she claimed a few words with him. It was always best to approach him formally. She asked for the interview, because he was going on to shoot grouse tomorrow, and she was returning to Helen in town.

"Certainly, dear," said he. "Of course I have the time. What do you want?"

"Nothing."

"I was afraid something had gone wrong."

"No; I have nothing to say, but you may talk."

Glancing at his watch, he talked of the nasty curve at the lych-gate. She heard him with interest. Her surface could always respond to his without contempt, though all her deeper being might be yearning to help him. She had abandoned any plan of action. Love is the best, and the more she let herself love him the more chance was there that he would set his soul in order. Such a moment as this, when they sat under fair weather by the walls of their future home, was so sweet to her that its sweetness would surely pierce to him. Each lift of his eyes, each parting of the thatched lip from the clean-shaven, must prelude the tenderness that kills the monk and the beast at a single blow. Disappointed a hundred times, she still hoped. She loved him with too clear a vision to fear his cloudiness. Whether he droned trivialities, as today, or sprang kisses on her in the twilight, she could pardon him, she could respond.

"**Death, where is thy sting? Love, where is thy victory?**": Adapted from lines in the hymn "Abide with Me" by Henry Francis Lyte (1793–1847).

"If there is this nasty curve," she suggested, "couldn't we walk to the church? Not, of course, you and Evie; but the rest of us might very well go on first, and that would mean fewer carriages."

"One can't have ladies walking through the Market Square. The Fussells wouldn't like it; they were awfully particular at Charles's wedding. My — she — one of our party was anxious to walk, and certainly the church was just round the corner, and I shouldn't have minded; but the Colonel made a great point of it."

"You men shouldn't be so chivalrous," said Margaret thoughtfully.

"Why not?"

She knew why not, but said that she did not know. He then announced that, unless she had anything special to say, he must visit the wine-cellar, and they went off together in search of Burton. Though clumsy and a little inconvenient, Oniton was a genuine country house. They clattered down flagged passages, looking into room after room, and scaring unknown maids from the performance of obscure duties. The wedding breakfast must be in readiness when they came back from church, and tea would be served in the garden. The sight of so many agitated and serious people made Margaret smile, but she reflected that they were paid to be serious, and enjoyed being agitated. Here were the lower wheels of the machine that was tossing Evie up into nuptial glory. A little boy blocked their way with pig-pails. His mind could not grasp their greatness, and he said: "By your leave; let me pass, please." Henry asked him where Burton was. But the servants were so new that they did not know one another's names. In the still-room sat the band, who had stipulated for champagne as part of their fee, and who were already drinking beer. Scents of Araby came from the kitchen, mingled with cries. Margaret knew what had happened there, for it happened at Wickham Place. One of the wedding dishes had boiled over, and the cook was throwing cedar shavings to hide the smell. At last they came upon the butler. Henry gave him the keys, and handed Margaret down the cellar stairs. Two doors were unlocked. She, who kept all her wine at the bottom of the linen-cupboard, was astonished at the sight. "We shall never get through it!" she cried, and the two men were suddenly drawn into brotherhood, and exchanged smiles. She felt as if she had again jumped out of the car while it was moving.

Certainly Oniton would take some digesting. It would be no small business to remain herself, and yet to assimilate such an establishment. She must remain herself, for his sake as well as her own, since a shadowy wife degrades the husband whom she accompanies; and she must assimilate for reasons of common honesty, since she had no right to marry a man and make him uncomfortable. Her only ally was the power of Home. The loss of Wickham Place had taught her more than its possession. Howards End had repeated the lesson. She was determined to create new sanctities among these hills.

After visiting the wine-cellar, she dressed, and then came the wedding, which seemed a small affair when compared with the preparations for it. Everything went like one o'clock. Mr Cahill materialized out of space, and was waiting for his bride at the church door. No one dropped the ring or mispronounced the responses, or trod on Evie's train, or cried. In a few minutes the clergymen performed their duty, the register was signed, and they were back in their carriages, negotiating the dangerous curve by the lych-gate. Margaret was convinced that they had not been married at all, and that the Norman church had been intent all the time on other business.

There were more documents to sign at the house, and the breakfast to eat, and then a few more people dropped in for the garden party. There had been a great many refusals, and after all it was not a very big affair — not as big as Margaret's would be. She noted the dishes and the strips of red carpet, that outwardly she might give Henry what was proper. But inwardly she hoped for something better than this blend of Sunday church and fox-hunting. If only someone *had* been upset! But this wedding had gone off so particularly well — "quite like a Durbar"° in the opinion of Lady Edser, and she thoroughly agreed with her.

So the wasted day lumbered forward, the bride and bridegroom drove off, yelling with laughter, and for the second time the sun retreated towards the hills of Wales. Henry, who was more tired than he owned, came up to her in the castle meadow, and, in tones of unusual softness, said that he was pleased. Everything had gone off so well. She felt that he was praising her, too, and blushed; certainly she had done all she could with his intractable friends, and had made a special point of kowtowing to the men. They were breaking camp this evening: only the Warringtons and quiet child would stay the night, and the others were already moving towards the house to finish their packing. "I think it did go off well," she agreed. "Since I had to jump out of the motor, I'm thankful I lighted on my left hand. I am so very glad about it, Henry dear; I only hope that the guests at ours may be half as com-

**quite like a Durbar:** Resembling a highly ceremonial reception of Indian princes by the governor general.

fortable. You must all remember that we have no practical person among us, except my aunt, and she is not used to entertainments on a large scale."

"I know," he said gravely. "Under the circumstances, it would be better to put everything into the hands of Harrod's or Whiteley's, or even to go to some hotel."

"You advise a hotel?"

"Yes, because — well, I mustn't interfere with you. No doubt you want to be married from your old home."

"My old home's falling into pieces, Henry. I only want my new. Isn't it a perfect evening —"

"The Alexandrina isn't bad —"

"The Alexandrina," she echoed, more occupied with the threads of smoke that were issuing from their chimneys, and ruling the sunlit slopes with parallels of gray.

"It's off Curzon Street."

"Is it? Let's be married from off Curzon Street."

Then she turned westward, to gaze at the swirling gold. Just where the river rounded the hill the sun caught it. Fairyland must lie above the bend, and its precious liquid was pouring towards them past Charles's bathing-shed. She gazed so long that her eyes were dazzled, and when they moved back to the house she could not recognize the faces of people who were coming out of it. A parlourmaid was preceding them.

"Who are those people?" she asked.

"They're callers!" exclaimed Henry. "It's too late for callers."

"Perhaps they're town people who want to see the wedding presents."

"I'm not at home yet to townees."

"Well, hide among the ruins, and if I can stop them I will."

He thanked her.

Margaret went forward, smiling socially. She supposed that these were unpunctual guests, who would have to be content with vicarious civility, since Evie and Charles were gone, Henry tired, and the others in their rooms. She assumed the airs of a hostess; not for long. For one of the group was Helen — Helen in her oldest clothes, and dominated by that tense, wounding excitement that had made her a terror in their nursery days.

"What is it?" she called. "Oh, what's wrong? Is Tibby ill?"

Helen spoke to her two companions, who fell back. Then she bore forward furiously.

"They're starving!" she shouted. "I found them starving!"

"Who? Why have you come?"

"The Basts."

"Oh, Helen!" moaned Margaret. "What ever have you done now?"

"He has lost his place. He has been turned out of his bank. Yes, he's done for. We upper classes have ruined him, and I suppose you'll tell me it's the battle of life. Starving. His wife is ill. Starving. She fainted in the train."

"Helen, are you mad?"

"Perhaps. Yes. If you like, I'm mad. But I've brought them. I'll stand injustice no longer. I'll show up the wretchedness that lies under this luxury, this talk of impersonal forces, this cant about God doing what we're too slack to do ourselves."

"Have you actually brought two starving people from London to Shropshire, Helen?"

Helen was checked. She had not thought of this, and her hysteria abated. "There was a restaurant car on the train," she said.

"Don't be absurd. They aren't starving, and you know it. Now, begin from the beginning. I won't have such theatrical nonsense. How dare you! Yes, how dare you!" she repeated, as anger filled her, "bursting into Evie's wedding in this heartless way. My goodness! but you've a perverted notion of philanthropy. Look" — she indicated the house — "servants, people out of the windows. They think it's some vulgar scandal, and I must explain. 'Oh no, it's only my sister screaming, and only two hangers-on of ours, whom she has brought here for no conceivable reason.'"

"Kindly take back that word 'hangers-on'," said Helen, ominously calm.

"Very well," conceded Margaret, who for all her wrath was determined to avoid a real quarrel. "I, too, am sorry about them, but it beats me why you've brought them here, or why you're here yourself."

"It's our last chance of seeing Mr Wilcox."

Margaret moved towards the house at this. She was determined not to worry Henry.

"He's going to Scotland. I know he is. I insist on seeing him."

"Yes, tomorrow."

"I knew it was our last chance."

"How do you do, Mr Bast?" said Margaret, trying to control her voice. "This is an odd business. What view do you take of it?"

"There is Mrs Bast, too," prompted Helen.

Jacky also shook hands. She, like her husband, was shy, and furthermore ill, and furthermore so bestially stupid that she could not grasp what was happening. She only knew that the lady had swept down like a whirlwind last night, had paid the rent, redeemed the furniture, provided them with a dinner and a breakfast, and ordered them to meet her at Paddington next morning. Leonard had feebly protested, and when the morning came had suggested that they shouldn't go. But she, half mesmerized, had obeyed. The lady had told them to, and they must, and their bed-sitting room had accordingly changed into Paddington, and Paddington into a railway carriage, that shook, and grew hot, and grew cold, and vanished entirely, and reappeared amid torrents of expensive scent. "You have fainted," said the lady in an awestruck voice. "Perhaps the air will do you good." And perhaps it had, for there she was, feeling rather better among a lot of flowers.

"I'm sure I don't want to intrude," began Leonard, in answer to Margaret's question. "But you have been so kind to me in the past in warning me about the Porphyrion that I wondered — why, I wondered whether —"

"Whether we could get him back into the Porphyrion again," supplied Helen. "Meg, this has been a cheerful business. A bright evening's work that was on Chelsea Embankment."

Margaret shook her head and returned to Mr Bast.

"I don't understand. You left the Porphyrion because we suggested it was a bad concern, didn't you?"

"That's right."

"And went into a bank instead?"

"I told you all that," said Helen; "and they reduced their staff after he had been in a month, and now he's penniless, and I consider that we and our informant are directly to blame."

"I hate all this," Leonard muttered.

"I hope you do, Mr Bast. But it's no good mincing matters. You have done yourself no good by coming here. If you intend to confront Mr Wilcox, and to call him to account for a chance remark, you will make a very great mistake."

"I brought them. I did it all," cried Helen.

"I can only advise you to go at once. My sister has put you in a false position, and it is kindest to tell you so. It's too late to get to town, but you'll find a comfortable hotel in Oniton, where Mrs Bast can rest, and I hope you'll be my guests there."

"That isn't what I want, Miss Schlegel," said Leonard. "You're very kind, and no doubt it's a false position, but you make me miserable. I seem no good at all."

"It's work he wants," interpreted Helen. "Can't you see?"

Then he said: "Jacky, let's go. We're more bother than we're worth. We're costing these ladies pounds and pounds already to get work for us, and they never will. There's nothing we're good enough to do."

"We would like to find you work," said Margaret rather conventionally. "We want to — I, like my sister. You're only down in your luck. Go to the hotel, have a good night's rest, and some day you shall pay me back the bill, if you prefer it."

But Leonard was near the abyss, and at such moments men see clearly. "You don't know what you're talking about," he said, "I shall never get work now. If rich people fail at one profession, they can try another. Not I. I had my groove, and I've got out of it. I could do one particular branch of insurance in one particular office well enough to command a salary, but that's all. Poetry's nothing, Miss Schlegel. One's thoughts about this and that are nothing. Your money, too, is nothing, if you'll understand me. I mean, if a man over twenty once loses his own particular job, it's all over with him. I have seen it happen to others. Their friends give them money for a little, but in the end they fall over the edge. It's no good. It's the whole world pulling. There always will be rich and poor."

He ceased. "Won't you have something to eat?" said Margaret. "I don't know what to do. It isn't my house, and though Mr Wilcox would have been glad to see you at any other time — as I say, I don't know what to do, but I undertake to do what I can for you. Helen, offer them something. Do try a sandwich, Mrs Bast."

They moved to a long table behind which a servant was still standing. Iced cakes, sandwiches innumerable, coffee, claret-cup, champagne, remained almost intact: their overfed guests could do no more. Leonard refused. Jacky thought she could manage a little. Margaret left them whispering together, and had a few more words with Helen.

She said: "Helen, I like Mr Bast. I agree that he's worth helping. I agree that we are directly responsible."

"No, indirectly. Via Mr Wilcox."

"Let me tell you once for all that if you take up that attitude I'll do nothing. No doubt you're right logically, and are entitled to say a great many scathing things about Henry. Only, I won't have it. So choose."

Helen looked at the sunset.

"If you promise to take them quietly to the George, I will speak to Henry about them — in my own way, mind; there is to be none of this absurd screaming about justice. I have no use for justice. If it was only a question of money, we could do it ourselves. But he wants work, and that we can't give him, but possibly Henry can."

"It's his duty to," grumbled Helen.

"Nor am I concerned with duty. I'm concerned with the characters of various people whom we know, and how, things being as they are, things may be made a little better. Mr Wilcox hates being asked favours; all businessmen do. But I am going to ask him, at the risk of a rebuff, because I want to make things a little better."

"Very well. I promise. You take it very calmly."

"Take them off to the George, then, and I'll try. Poor creatures! but they look tired." As they parted, she added: "I haven't nearly done with you, though, Helen. You have been most self-indulgent. I can't get over it. You have less restraint rather than more as you grow older. Think it over and alter yourself, or we shan't have happy lives."

She rejoined Henry. Fortunately he had been sitting down; these physical matters were important. "Was it townees?" he asked, greeting her with a pleasant smile.

"You'll never believe me," said Margaret, sitting down beside him. "It's all right now, but it was my sister."

"Helen here?" he cried, preparing to rise. "But she refused the invitation. I thought she despised weddings."

"Don't get up. She has not come to the wedding. I've bundled her off to the George."

Inherently hospitable, he protested.

"No; she has two of her protégés with her, and must keep with them."

"Let 'em all come."

"My dear Henry, did you see them?"

"I did catch sight of a brown bunch of a woman, certainly."

"The brown bunch was Helen, but did you catch sight of a sea-green and salmon bunch?"

"What! Are they out beanfeasting?"

"No; business. They wanted to see me, and later on I want to talk to you about them."

She was ashamed at her own diplomacy. In dealing with a Wilcox, how tempting it was to lapse from comradeship, and to give him the

kind of woman that he desired! Henry took the bait at once, and said:
"Why later on? Tell me now. No time like the present."

"Shall I?"

"If it isn't a long story."

"Oh, not five minutes; but there's a sting at the end of it, for I
want you to find the man some work in your office."

"What are his qualifications?"

"I don't know. He's a clerk."

"How old?"

"Twenty-five, perhaps."

"What's his name?"

"Bast," said Margaret, and was about to remind him that they had
met at Wickham Place, but stopped herself. It had not been a successful meeting.

"Where was he before?"

"Dempster's Bank."

"Why did he leave?" he asked, still remembering nothing.

"They reduced their staff."

"All right; I'll see him."

It was the reward of her tact and devotion through the day. Now
she understood why some women prefer influence to rights. Mrs Plynlimmon, when condemning suffragettes, had said: "The woman who
can't influence her husband to vote the way she wants ought to be
ashamed of herself." Margaret had winced, but she was influencing
Henry now, and though pleased at her little victory she knew that she
had won it by the methods of the harem.

"I should be glad if you took him," she said, "but I don't know
whether he's qualified."

"I'll do what I can. But, Margaret, this mustn't be taken as a
precedent."

"No, of course — of course —"

"I can't fit in your protégés every day. Business would suffer."

"I can promise you he's the last. He — he's rather a special case."

"Protégés always are."

She let it stand at that. He rose with a little extra touch of complacency, and held out his hand to help her up. How wide the gulf between Henry as he was and Henry as Helen thought he ought to be!
And she herself — hovering as usual between the two, now accepting
men as they are, now yearning with her sister for Truth. Love and
Truth — their warfare seems eternal. Perhaps the whole visible world

rests on it, and, if they were one, life itself, like the spirits when Prospero was reconciled to his brother,° might vanish into air, into thin air.

"Your protégé has made us late," said he. "The Fussells will just be starting."

On the whole she sided with men as they are. Henry would save the Basts as he had saved Howards End, while Helen and her friends were discussing the ethics of salvation. His was a slapdash method, but the world has been built slapdash, and the beauty of mountain and river and sunset may be but the varnish with which the unskilled artificer hides his joins. Oniton, like herself, was imperfect. Its apple trees were stunted, its castle ruinous. It, too, had suffered in the border warfare between the Anglo-Saxon and the Celt, between things as they are and as they ought to be. Once more the west was retreating, once again the orderly stars were dotting the eastern sky. There is certainly no rest for us on the earth. But there is happiness, and as Margaret descended the mound on her lover's arm she felt that she was having her share.

To her annoyance, Mrs Bast was still in the garden; the husband and Helen had left her there to finish her meal while they went to engage rooms. Margaret found this woman repellent. She had felt, when shaking her hand, an overpowering shame. She remembered the motive of her call at Wickham Place, and smelt again odours from the abyss — odours the more disturbing because they were involuntary. For there was no malice in Jacky. There she sat, a piece of cake in one hand, an empty champagne-glass in the other, doing no harm to anybody.

"She's overtired," Margaret whispered.

"She's something else," said Henry. "This won't do. I can't have her in my garden in this state."

"Is she —" Margaret hesitated to add "drunk". Now that she was going to marry him, he had grown particular. He discountenanced risqué conversations now.

Henry went up to the woman. She raised her face, which gleamed in the twilight like a puff-ball.

"Madam, you will be more comfortable at the hotel," he said sharply.

Jacky replied: "If it isn't Hen!"

**like the spirits . . . brother:** Shakespeare's *Tempest* 4.1.148–58.

"Ne crois pas que le mari lui ressemble," apologized Margaret. "Il est tout à fait différent."°

"Henry!" she repeated, quite distinctly.

Mr Wilcox was much annoyed. "I can't congratulate you on your protégés," he remarked.

"Hen, don't go. You do love me, dear, don't you?"

"Bless us, what a person!" sighed Margaret, gathering up her skirts.

Jacky pointed with her cake. "You're a nice boy, you are." She yawned. "There now, I love you."

"Henry, I am awfully sorry."

"And pray why?" he asked, and looked at her so sternly that she feared he was ill. He seemed more scandalized than the facts demanded.

"To have brought this down on you."

"Pray don't apologize."

The voice continued.

"Why does she call you 'Hen'?" said Margaret innocently. "Has she ever seen you before?"

"Seen Hen before!" said Jacky. "Who hasn't seen Hen? He's serving you like me, my dear. These boys! You wait — still, we love 'em."

"Are you now satisfied?" Henry asked.

Margaret began to grow frightened. "I don't know what it is all about," she said. "Let's come in."

But he thought she was acting. He thought he was trapped. He saw his whole life crumbling. "Don't you indeed?" he said bitingly. "I do. Allow me to congratulate you on the success of your plan."

"This is Helen's plan, not mine."

"I now understand your interest in the Basts. Very well thought out. I am amused at your caution, Margaret. You are quite right — it was necessary. I am a man, and have lived a man's past. I have the honour to release you from your engagement."

Still she could not understand. She knew of life's seamy side as a theory; she could not grasp it as a fact. More words from Jacky were necessary — words unequivocal, undenied.

"So that —" burst from her, and she went indoors. She stopped herself from saying more.

"Ne crois . . . différent": "Don't think that the husband resembles her. He is quite different." Margaret's French is idiomatic, unlike the French of her future husband on p. 254.

"So what?" asked Colonel Fussell, who was getting ready to start in the hall.

"We were saying — Henry and I were just having the fiercest argument, my point being —" Seizing his fur coat from a footman, she offered to help him on. He protested, and there was a playful little scene.

"No, let me do that," said Henry, following.

"Thanks so much! You see — he has forgiven me!"

The Colonel said gallantly: "I don't expect there's much to forgive."

He got into the car. The ladies followed him after an interval. Maids, courier and heavier luggage had been sent on earlier by the branch-line. Still chattering, still thanking their host and patronizing their future hostess, the guests were borne away.

Then Margaret continued: "So that woman has been your mistress?"

"You put it with your usual delicacy," he replied.

"When, please?"

"Why?"

"When, please?"

"Ten years ago."

She left him without a word. For it was not her tragedy: it was Mrs Wilcox's.


## Chapter 27

Helen began to wonder why she had spent a matter of eight pounds in making some people ill and others angry. Now that the wave of excitement was ebbing, and had left her, Mr Bast and Mrs Bast stranded for the night in a Shropshire hotel, she asked herself what forces had made the wave flow. At all events, no harm was done. Margaret would play the game properly now, and, though Helen disapproved of her sister's methods, she knew that the Basts would benefit by them in the long run.

"Mr Wilcox is so illogical," she explained to Leonard, who had put his wife to bed, and was sitting with her in the empty coffee-room. "If we told him it was his duty to take you on, he might refuse to do it. The fact is, he isn't properly educated. I don't want to set you against him, but you'll find him a trial."

"I can never thank you sufficiently, Miss Schlegel," was all that Leonard felt equal to.

"I believe in personal responsibility. Don't you? And in personal everything. I hate — I suppose I oughtn't to say that — but the Wilcoxes are on the wrong tack surely. Or perhaps it isn't their fault. Perhaps the little thing that says 'I' is missing out of the middle of their heads, and then it's a waste of time to blame them. There's a nightmare of a theory° that says a special race is being born which will rule the rest of us in the future just because it lacks the little thing that says 'I'. Had you heard that?"

"I get no time for reading."

"Had you thought it, then? That there are two kinds of people — our kind, who live straight from the middle of their heads, and the other kind who can't, because their heads have no middle? They can't say 'I'. They *aren't* in fact, and so they're supermen. Pierpont Morgan° has never said 'I' in his life."

Leonard roused himself. If his benefactress wanted intellectual conversation, she must have it. She was more important than his ruined past. "I never got on to Nietzsche," he said. "But I always understood that those supermen were rather what you may call egoists."

"Oh no, that's wrong," replied Helen. "No superman ever said 'I want', because 'I want' must lead to the question, 'Who am I?' and so to Pity and to Justice. He only says 'want'. 'Want Europe' if he's Napoleon; 'want wives' if he's Bluebeard; 'want Botticelli' if he's Pierpont Morgan. Never the 'I'; and if you could pierce through him you'd find panic and emptiness in the middle."

Leonard was silent for a moment. Then he said: "May I take it, Miss Schlegel, that you and I are both the sort that say 'I'?"

"Of course."

"And your sister too?"

"Of course," repeated Helen, a little sharply. She was annoyed with Margaret, but did not want her discussed. "All presentable people say 'I'."

"But Mr Wilcox — he is not perhaps —"

"I don't know that it's any good discussing Mr Wilcox either."

"Quite so, quite so," he agreed. Helen asked herself why she had snubbed him. Once or twice during the day she had encouraged him to criticize, and then had pulled him up short. Was she afraid of him presuming? If so, it was disgusting of her.

There's a nightmare of a theory: The theory of Friedrich Nietzsche (1844–1900) in works such as *Beyond Good and Evil* (1886) and *Thus Spake Zarathustra* (1883–92). Pierpont Morgan: John Pierpont Morgan (1837–1913), immensely rich American railway magnate and financier whom Forster's friend Roger Fry advised on the purchase of European art masterpieces.

But he was thinking the snub quite natural. Everything she did was natural, and incapable of causing offence. While the Miss Schlegels were together he had felt them scarcely human — a sort of admonitory whirligig. But a Miss Schlegel alone was different. She was in Helen's case unmarried, in Margaret's about to be married, in neither case an echo of her sister. A light had fallen at last into this rich upper world, and he saw that it was full of men and women, some of whom were more friendly to him than others. Helen had become "his" Miss Schlegel, who scolded him and corresponded with him, and had swept down yesterday with grateful vehemence. Margaret, though not unkind, was severe and remote. He would not presume to help her, for instance. He had never liked her, and began to think that his original impression was true, and that her sister did not like her either. Helen was certainly lonely. She, who gave away so much, was receiving too little. Leonard was pleased to think that he could spare her vexation by holding his tongue and concealing what he knew about Mr Wilcox. Jacky had announced her discovery when he fetched her from the lawn. After the first shock, he did not mind for himself. By now he had no illusions about his wife, and this was only one new stain on the face of a love that had never been pure. To keep perfection perfect, that should be his ideal, if the future gave him time to have ideals. Helen, and Margaret for Helen's sake, must not know.

Helen disconcerted him by turning the conversation to his wife. "Mrs Bast — does she ever say 'I'?" she asked, half mischievously, and then, "Is she very tired?"

"It's better she stops in her room," said Leonard.

"Shall I sit up with her?"

"No, thank you; she does not need company."

"Mr Bast, what kind of woman is your wife?"

Leonard blushed up to his eyes.

"You ought to know my ways by now. Does that question offend you?"

"No, oh no, Miss Schlegel, no."

"Because I love honesty. Don't pretend your marriage has been a happy one. You and she can have nothing in common."

He did not deny it, but said shyly: "I suppose that's pretty obvious; but Jacky never meant to do anybody any harm. When things went wrong, or I heard things, I used to think it was her fault, but, looking back, it's more mine. I needn't have married her, but as I have I must stick to her and keep her."

"How long have you been married?"

"Nearly three years."

"What did your people say?"

"They will not have anything to do with us. They had a sort of family council when they heard I was married, and cut us off altogether."

Helen began to pace up and down the room. "My good boy, what a mess!" she said gently. "Who are your people?"

He could answer this. His parents, who were dead, had been in trade; his sisters had married commercial travellers; his brother was a lay-reader.

"And your grandparents?"

Leonard told her a secret that he had held shameful up to now. "They were just nothing at all," he said — "agricultural labourers and that sort."

"So! From which part?"

"Lincolnshire mostly, but my mother's father — he, oddly enough, came from these parts round here."

"From this very Shropshire. Yes, that is odd. My mother's people were Lancashire. But why do your brother and your sisters object to Mrs Bast?"

"Oh, I don't know."

"Excuse me, you do know. I am not a baby. I can bear anything you tell me, and the more you tell me the more I shall be able to help. Have they heard anything against her?"

He was silent.

"I think I have guessed now," said Helen very gravely.

"I don't think so, Miss Schlegel; I hope not."

"We must be honest, even over these things. I have guessed. I am frightfully, dreadfully sorry, but it does not make the least difference to me. I shall feel just the same to both of you. I blame, not your wife for these things, but men."

Leonard left it at that — so long as she did not guess the man. She stood at the window and slowly pulled up the blinds. The hotel looked over a dark square. The mists had begun. When she turned back to him her eyes were shining.

"Don't you worry," he pleaded. "I can't bear that. We shall be all right if I get work. If I could only get work — something regular to do. Then it wouldn't be so bad again. I don't trouble after books as I used. I can imagine that with regular work we should settle down again. It stops one thinking."

"Settle down to what?"

"Oh, just settle down."

"And that's to be life!" said Helen, with a catch in her throat. "How can you, with all the beautiful things to see and do — with music — with walking at night —"

"Walking is well enough when a man's in work," he answered. "Oh, I did talk a lot of nonsense once, but there's nothing like a bailiff in the house to drive it out of you. When I saw him fingering my Ruskins and Stevensons, I seemed to see life straight real, and it isn't a pretty sight. My books are back again, thanks to you, but they'll never be the same to me again, and I shan't ever again think night in the woods so wonderful."

"Why not?" asked Helen, throwing up the window.

"Because I see one must have money."

"Well, you're wrong."

"I wish I was wrong, but — the clergyman — he has money of his own, or else he's paid; the poet or the musician — just the same; the tramp — he's no different. The tramp goes to the workhouse in the end, and is paid for with other people's money. Miss Schlegel, the real thing's money, and all the rest is a dream."

"You're still wrong. You've forgotten Death."

Leonard could not understand.

"If we lived for ever, what you say would be true. But we have to die, we have to leave life presently. Injustice and greed would be the real things if we lived for ever. As it is, we must hold to other things, because Death is coming. I love Death — not morbidly, but because He explains. He shows me the emptiness of Money. Death and Money are the eternal foes. Not Death and Life. Never mind what lies behind Death, Mr Bast, but be sure that the poet and the musician and the tramp will be happier in it than the man who has never learned to say: 'I am I.'"

"I wonder."

"We are all in a mist — I know, but I can help you this far — men like the Wilcoxes are deeper in the mist than any. Sane, sound Englishmen! Building up empires, levelling all the world into what they call common sense. But mention Death to them and they're offended, because Death's really imperial, and He cries out against them for ever."

"I am as afraid of Death as anyone."

"But not of the idea of Death."

"But what is the difference?"

"Infinite difference," said Helen, more gravely than before.

Leonard looked at her wondering, and had the sense of great

things sweeping out of the shrouded night. But he could not receive them, because his heart was still full of little things. As the lost umbrella had spoilt the concert at Queen's Hall, so the lost situation was obscuring the diviner harmonies now. Death, Life and Materialism were fine words, but would Mr Wilcox take him on as a clerk? Talk as one would, Mr Wilcox was king of this world, the superman, with his own morality, whose head remained in the clouds.

"I must be stupid," he said apologetically.

While to Helen the paradox became clearer and clearer. "Death destroys a man; the idea of Death saves him."° Behind the coffins and the skeletons that stay the vulgar mind lies something so immense that all that is great in us responds to it. Men of the world may recoil from the charnel-house that they will one day enter, but Love knows better. Death is his foe, but his peer, and in their age-long struggle the thews of Love have been strengthened, and his vision cleared, until there is no one who can stand against him.

"So never give in," continued the girl, and restated again and again the vague yet convincing plea that the Invisible lodges against the Visible. Her excitement grew as she tried to cut the rope that fastened Leonard to the earth. Woven of bitter experience, it resisted her. Presently the waitress entered and gave her a letter from Margaret. Another note, addressed to Leonard, was inside. They read them, listening to the murmurings of the river.

## Chapter 28

For many hours Margaret did nothing; then she controlled herself, and wrote some letters. She was too bruised to speak to Henry; she could pity him, and even determine to marry him, but as yet all lay too deep in her heart for speech. On the surface the sense of his degradation was too strong. She could not command voice or look, and the gentle words that she forced out through her pen seemed to proceed from some other person.

"My dearest boy," she began, "this is not to part us. It is everything or nothing, and I mean it to be nothing. It happened long before we ever met, and even if it had happened since, I should be writing the same, I hope. I do understand."

---

"**Death destroys a man; the idea of Death saves him**": A saying attributed to Michelangelo, as Stallybrass notes.

But she crossed out "I do understand"; it struck a false note. Henry could not bear to be understood. She also crossed out "It is everything or nothing." Henry would resent so strong a grasp of the situation. She must not comment; comment is unfeminine.

"I think that'll about do," she thought.

Then the sense of his degradation choked her. Was he worth all this bother? To have yielded to a woman of that sort was everything, yes, it was, and she could not be his wife. She tried to translate his temptation into her own language, and her brain reeled. Men must be different, even to want to yield to such a temptation. Her belief in comradeship was stifled, and she saw life as from that glass saloon on the Great Western, which sheltered male and female alike from the fresh air. Are the sexes really races, each with its own code of morality, and their mutual love a mere device of Nature's to keep things going? Strip human intercourse of the proprieties, and is it reduced to this? Her judgement told her no. She knew that out of Nature's device we have built a magic that will win us immortality. Far more mysterious than the call of sex to sex is the tenderness that we throw into that call; far wider is the gulf between us and the farmyard than between the farmyard and the garbage that nourishes it. We are evolving, in ways that Science cannot measure, to ends that Theology dares not contemplate. "Men did produce one jewel," the gods will say, and, saying, will give us immortality. Margaret knew all this, but for the moment she could not feel it, and transformed the marriage of Evie and Mr Cahill into a carnival of fools, and her own marriage — too miserable to think of that, she tore up the letter, and then wrote another:

Dear Mr Bast,

I have spoken to Mr Wilcox about you, as I promised, and am sorry to say that he has no vacancy for you.

Yours truly,
M. J. Schlegel.

She enclosed this in a note to Helen, over which she took less trouble than she might have done; but her head was aching, and she could not stop to pick her words:

Dear Helen,

Give him this. The Basts are no good. Henry found the woman drunk on the lawn. I am having a room got ready for you here, and will you please come round at once on getting this? The Basts are not at all the type we should trouble about. I may go round to them myself in the morning, and do anything that is fair.

M.

In writing this, Margaret felt that she was being practical. Something might be arranged for the Basts later on, but they must be silenced for the moment. She hoped to avoid a conversation between the woman and Helen. She rang the bell for a servant, but no one answered it; Mr Wilcox and the Warringtons were gone to bed, and the kitchen was abandoned to saturnalia. Consequently she went over to the George herself. She did not enter the hotel, for discussion would have been perilous, and, saying that the letter was important, she gave it to the waitress. As she recrossed the square she saw Helen and Mr Bast looking out of the window of the coffee-room, and feared she was already too late. Her task was not yet over; she ought to tell Henry what she had done.

This came easily, for she saw him in the hall. The night wind had been rattling the pictures against the wall, and the noise had disturbed him.

"Who's there?" he called, quite the householder.

Margaret walked in and past him.

"I have asked Helen to sleep," she said. "She is best here; so don't lock the front door."

"I thought someone had got in," said Henry.

"At the same time I told the man that we could do nothing for him. I don't know about later, but now the Basts must clearly go."

"Did you say that your sister is sleeping here, after all?"

"Probably."

"Is she to be shown up to your room?"

"I have naturally nothing to say to her; I am going to bed. Will you tell the servants about Helen? Could someone go to carry her bag?"

He tapped a little gong, which had been bought to summon the servants.

"You must make more noise than that if you want them to hear."

Henry opened a door, and down the corridor came shouts of laughter. "Far too much screaming there," he said, and strode towards it. Margaret went upstairs, uncertain whether to be glad that they had met, or sorry. They had behaved as if nothing had happened, and her deepest instincts told her that this was wrong. For his own sake, some explanation was due.

And yet — what would an explanation tell her? A date, a place, a few details, which she could imagine all too clearly. Now that the first shock was over, she saw that there was every reason to premise a Mrs Bast. Henry's inner life had long lain open to her — his intellectual confusion, his obtuseness to personal influence, his strong but furtive passions. Should she refuse him because his outer life corresponded? Perhaps. Perhaps, if the dishonour had been done to her, but it was done long before her day. She struggled against the feeling. She told herself that Mrs Wilcox's wrong was her own. But she was not a barren theorist. As she undressed, her anger, her regard for the dead, her desire for a scene, all grew weak. Henry must have it as he liked, for she loved him, and some day she would use her love to make him a better man.

Pity was at the bottom of her actions all through this crisis. Pity, if one may generalize, is at the bottom of woman. When men like us, it is for our better qualities, and however tender their liking we dare not be unworthy of it, or they will quietly let us go. But unworthiness stimulates woman. It brings out her deeper nature, for good or for evil.

Here was the core of the question. Henry must be forgiven, and made better by love; nothing else mattered. Mrs Wilcox, that unquiet yet kindly ghost, must be left to her own wrong. To her everything was in proportion now, and she, too, would pity the man who was blundering up and down their lives. Had Mrs Wilcox known of his trespass? An interesting question, but Margaret fell asleep, tethered by affection, and lulled by the murmurs of the river that descended all the night from Wales. She felt herself at one with her future home, colouring it and coloured by it, and awoke to see, for the second time, Oniton Castle conquering the morning mists.

## Chapter 29

"Henry dear —" was her greeting.

He had finished his breakfast, and was beginning *The Times*. His sister-in-law was packing. She knelt by him and took the paper from him, feeling that it was unusually heavy and thick. Then, putting her face where it had been, she looked up in his eyes.

"Henry dear, look at me. No, I won't have you shirking. Look at me. There. That's all."

"You're referring to last evening," he said huskily. "I have released you from your engagement. I could find excuses, but I won't. No, I won't. A thousand times no. I'm a bad lot, and must be left at that."

Expelled from his old fortress, Mr Wilcox was building a new one. He could no longer appear respectable to her, so he defended himself instead in a lurid past. It was not true repentance.

"Leave it where you will, boy. It's not going to trouble us; I know what I'm talking about, and it will make no difference."

"No difference?" he inquired. "No difference, when you find that I am not the fellow you thought?" He was annoyed with Miss Schlegel here. He would have preferred her to be prostrated by the blow, or even to rage. Against the tide of his sin flowed the feeling that she was not altogether womanly. Her eyes gazed too straight; they had read books that are suitable for men only. And though he had dreaded a scene, and though she had determined against one, there was a scene, all the same. It was somehow imperative.

"I am unworthy of you," he began. "Had I been worthy, I should not have released you from your engagement. I know what I am talking about. I can't bear to talk of such things. We had better leave it."

She kissed his hand. He jerked it from her, and, rising to his feet, went on: "You, with your sheltered life, and refined pursuits, and friends, and books, you and your sister, and women like you — I say, how can you guess the temptations that lie round a man?"

"It is difficult for us," said Margaret; "but if we are worth marrying we do guess."

"Cut off from decent society and family ties, what do you suppose happens to thousands of young fellows overseas? Isolated. No one near. I know by bitter experience, and yet you say it makes 'no difference'."

"Not to me."

He laughed bitterly. Margaret went to the sideboard and helped herself to one of the breakfast dishes. Being the last down, she turned out the spirit-lamp that kept them warm. She was tender, but grave. She knew that Henry was not so much confessing his soul as pointing out the gulf between the male soul and the female, and she did not desire to hear him on this point.

"Did Helen come?" she asked.

He shook his head.

"But that won't do at all, at all! We don't want her gossiping with Mrs Bast."

"Good God, no!" he exclaimed, suddenly natural. Then he caught himself up. "Let them gossip. My game's up, though I thank you for your unselfishness — little as my thanks are worth."

"Didn't she send me a message or anything?"

"I heard of none."

"Would you ring the bell, please?"

"What to do?"

"Why, to inquire."

He swaggered up to it tragically, and sounded a peal. Margaret poured herself out some coffee. The butler came, and said that Miss Schlegel had slept at the George, so far as he had heard. Should he go round to the George?

"I'll go, thank you," said Margaret, and dismissed him.

"It is no good," said Henry. "Those things leak out; you cannot stop a story once it has started. I have known cases of other men — I despised them once, I thought that *I'm* different, *I* shall never be tempted. Oh, Margaret —" He came and sat down near her, improvising emotion. She could not bear to listen to him. "We fellows all come to grief once in our time. Will you believe that? There are moments when the strongest man — 'Let him who standeth, take heed lest he fall.' That's true, isn't it? If you knew all, you would excuse me. I was far from good influences — far even from England. I was very, very lonely, and longed for a woman's voice. That's enough. I have told you too much already for you to forgive me now."

"Yes, that's enough, dear."

"I have" — he lowered his voice — "I have been through hell."

Gravely she considered this claim. Had he? Had he suffered tortures of remorse, or had it been "There! That's over. Now for respectable life again"? The latter, if she read him rightly. A man who has been through hell does not boast of his virility. He is humble and hides it, if, indeed, it still exists. Only in legend does the sinner come forth penitent, but terrible, to conquer pure woman by his resistless power. Henry was anxious to be terrible, but had not got it in him. He was a good average Englishman, who had slipped. The really culpable point — his faithlessness to Mrs Wilcox — never seemed to strike him. She longed to mention Mrs Wilcox.

And bit by bit the story was told her. It was a very simple story. Ten years ago was the time, a garrison town in Cyprus the place. Now and then he asked her whether she could possibly forgive him, and she answered: "I have already forgiven you, Henry." She chose her words carefully, and so saved him from panic. She played the girl, until he could rebuild his fortress and hide his soul from the world. When the butler came to clear away, Henry was in a very different mood — asked the fellow what he was in such a hurry for, complained of the noise last night in the servants' hall. Margaret looked intently at the butler. He, as a handsome young man, was faintly attractive to her as a woman — an attraction so faint as scarcely to be perceptible, yet the skies would have fallen if she had mentioned it to Henry.

On her return from the George the building operations were complete, and the old Henry fronted her, competent, cynical and kind. He had made a clean breast, had been forgiven, and the great thing now was to forget his failure, and to send it the way of other unsuccessful investments. Jacky rejoined Howards End and Ducie Street, and the vermilion motor-car, and the Argentine Hard Dollars, and all the things and people for whom he had never had much use, and had less now. Their memory hampered him. He could scarcely attend to Margaret, who brought back disquieting news from the George. Helen and her clients had gone.

"Well, let them go — the man and his wife, I mean, for the more we see of your sister the better."

"But they have gone separately — Helen very early, the Basts just before I arrived. They have left no message. They have answered neither of my notes. I don't like to think what it all means."

"What did you say in the notes?"

"I told you last night."

"Oh — ah — yes! Dear, would you like one turn in the garden?"

Margaret took his arm. The beautiful weather soothed her. But the wheels of Evie's wedding were still at work, tossing the guests outwards as deftly as they had drawn them in, and she could not be with him long. It had been arranged that they should motor to Shrewsbury, whence he would go north, and she back to London with the Warringtons. For a fraction of time she was happy. Then her brain recommenced.

"I am afraid there has been gossiping of some kind at the George. Helen would not have left unless she had heard something. I mismanaged that. It is wretched. I ought to have parted her from that woman at once."

"Margaret!" he exclaimed, loosing her arm impressively.

"Yes — yes, Henry?"

"I am far from a saint — in fact, the reverse — but you have taken me, for better or worse. Bygones must be bygones. You have promised to forgive me. Margaret, a promise is a promise. Never mention that woman again."

"Except for some practical reason — never."

"Practical! You practical!"

"Yes, I'm practical," she murmured, stooping over the mowing-machine and playing with the grass which trickled through her fingers like sand.

He had silenced her, but her fears made him uneasy. Not for the first time, he was threatened with blackmail. He was rich and supposed to be moral; the Basts knew that he was not, and might find it profitable to hint as much.

"At all events, you mustn't worry," he said. "This is a man's business." He thought intently. "On no account mention it to anybody."

Margaret flushed at advice so elementary, but he was really paving the way for a lie. If necessary he would deny that he had ever known Mrs Bast, and prosecute her for libel. Perhaps he never had known her. Here was Margaret, who behaved as if he had not. There the house. Round them were half a dozen gardeners, clearing up after his daughter's wedding. All was so solid and spruce that the past flew up out of sight like a spring-blind, leaving only the last five minutes unrolled.

Glancing at these, he saw that the car would be round during the next five, and plunged into action. Gongs were tapped, orders issued, Margaret was sent to dress, and the housemaid to sweep up the long trickle of grass that she had left across the hall. As is Man to the Universe, so was the mind of Mr Wilcox to the minds of some men — a concentrated light upon a tiny spot, a little Ten Minutes moving self-contained through its appointed years. No pagan he, who lives for the Now, and may be wiser than all philosophers. He lived for the five minutes that have passed, and the five to come; he had the business mind.

How did he stand now, as his motor slipped out of Oniton and breasted the great round hills? Margaret had heard a certain rumour, but was all right. She had forgiven him, God bless her, and he felt the manlier for it. Charles and Evie had not heard it, and never must hear. No more must Paul. Over his children he felt great tenderness, which he did not try to track to a cause; Mrs Wilcox was too far back in his life. He did not connect her with the sudden aching love that he felt for Evie. Poor little Evie! He trusted that Cahill would make her a decent husband.

And Margaret? How did she stand? She had several minor worries. Clearly her sister had heard something. She dreaded meeting her in town. And she was anxious about Leonard, for whom they certainly were responsible. Nor ought Mrs Bast to starve. But the main situation had not altered. She still loved Henry. His actions, not his disposition, had disappointed her, and she could bear that. And she loved her future home. Standing up in the car, just where she had leapt from it two days before, she gazed back with deep emotion upon Oniton. Besides the Grange and the Castle keep, she could now pick out the church and the black-and-white gables of the George. There was the bridge, and the river nibbling its green peninsula. She could even see the bathing-shed, but while she was looking for Charles's new springboard the forehead of the hill rose up and hid the whole scene.

She never saw it again. Day and night the river flows down into England, day after day the sun retreats into the Welsh mountains, and the tower chimes "See the Conquering Hero".° But the Wilcoxes have no part in the place, nor in any place. It is not their names that recur in the parish register. It is not their ghosts that sigh among the alders at evening. They have swept into the valley and swept out of it, leaving a little dust and a little money behind.

## Chapter 30

Tibby was now approaching his last year at Oxford. He had moved out of college, and was contemplating the Universe, or such portions of it as concerned him, from his comfortable lodgings in Long Wall. He was not concerned with much. When a young man is untroubled by passions and sincerely indifferent to public opinion, his outlook is necessarily limited. Tibby neither wished to strengthen the position of the rich nor to improve that of the poor, and so was well content to watch the elms nodding behind the mildly embattled parapets of Magdalen. There are worse lives. Though selfish, he was never cruel; though affected in manner, he never posed. Like Margaret, he disdained the heroic equipment, and it was only after many visits that men discovered Schlegel to possess a character and a brain. He had done well in Mods,° much to the surprise of those who attended lectures and took proper exercise, and was now glancing disdainfully at Chinese in case he should some day consent to qualify as a Student Interpreter. To him thus employed Helen entered. A telegram had preceded her.

the tower chimes "See the Conquering Hero": Oniton is based on Clun in Shropshire, but its chiming clock is based on the clock in nearby Ludlow, described by A. E. Housman in poem 3 of *A Shropshire Lad* (1896). See Philip Gardner, "E. M. Forster and the Possession of England," *Modern Language Quarterly* 42.2 (1981): 168.
Mods: Examinations on the first part of the classical degree course at Oxford.

He noticed, in a distant way, that his sister had altered. As a rule he found her too pronounced, and had never come across this look of appeal, pathetic yet dignified — the look of a sailor who has lost everything at sea.

"I have come from Oniton," she began. "There has been a great deal of trouble there."

"Who's for lunch?" said Tibby, picking up the claret, which was warming in the hearth. Helen sat down submissively at the table. "Why such an early start?" he asked.

"Sunrise or something — when I could get away."

"So I surmise. Why?"

"I don't know what's to be done, Tibby. I am very much upset at a piece of news that concerns Meg, and do not want to face her, and I am not going back to Wickham Place. I stopped here to tell you this."

The landlady came in with the cutlets. Tibby put a marker in the leaves of his Chinese Grammar and helped them. Oxford — the Oxford of the vacation — dreamed and rustled outside, and indoors the little fire was coated with gray where the sunshine touched it. Helen continued her odd story.

"Give Meg my love and say that I want to be alone. I mean to go to Munich or else Bonn."

"Such a message is easily given," said her brother.

"As regards Wickham Place and my share of the furniture, you and she are to do exactly as you like. My own feeling is that everything may just as well be sold. What does one want with dusty economic books, which have made the world no better, or with mother's hideous chiffoniers? I have also another commission for you. I want you to deliver a letter." She got up. "I haven't written it yet. Why shouldn't I post it, though?" She sat down again. "My head is rather wretched. I hope that none of your friends are likely to come in."

Tibby locked the door. His friends often found it in this condition. Then he asked whether anything had gone wrong at Evie's wedding.

"Not there," said Helen, and burst into tears.

He had known her hysterical — it was one of her aspects with which he had no concern — and yet these tears touched him as something unusual. They were nearer the things that did concern him, such as music. He laid down his knife and looked at her curiously. Then, as she continued to sob, he went on with his lunch.

The time came for the second course, and she was still crying. Apple charlotte was to follow, which spoils by waiting. "Do you mind

Mrs Martlett coming in?" he asked, "or shall I take it from her at the door?"

"Could I bathe my eyes, Tibby?"

He took her to his bedroom, and introduced the pudding in her absence. Having helped himself, he put it down to warm in the hearth. His hand stretched towards the Grammar, and soon he was turning over the pages, raising his eyebrows scornfully, perhaps at human nature, perhaps at Chinese. To him thus employed Helen returned. She had pulled herself together, but the grave appeal had not vanished from her eyes.

"Now for the explanation," she said. "Why didn't I begin with it? I have found out something about Mr Wilcox. He has behaved very wrongly indeed, and ruined two people's lives. It all came on me very suddenly last night; I am very much upset, and I do not know what to do. Mrs Bast —"

"Oh, those people!"

Helen seemed silenced.

"Shall I lock the door again?"

"No, thanks, Tibbikins. You're being very good to me. I want to tell you the story before I go abroad. You must do exactly what you like — treat it as part of the furniture. Meg cannot have heard it yet, I think. But I cannot face her and tell her that the man she is going to marry has misconducted himself. I don't even know whether she ought to be told. Knowing as she does that I dislike him, she will suspect me, and think that I want to ruin her match. I simply don't know what to make of such a thing. I trust your judgement. What would you do?"

"I gather he has had a mistress," said Tibby.

Helen flushed with shame and anger. "And ruined two people's lives. And goes about saying that personal actions count for nothing, and there always will be rich and poor. He met her when he was trying to get rich out in Cyprus — I don't wish to make him worse than he is, and no doubt she was ready enough to meet him. But there it is. They met. He goes his way and she goes hers. What do you suppose is the end of such women?"

He conceded that it was a bad business.

"They end in two ways: either they sink till the lunatic asylums and the workhouses are full of them, and cause Mr Wilcox to write letters to the papers complaining of our national degeneracy, or else they entrap a boy into marriage before it is too late. She — I can't blame her."

"But this isn't all," she continued after a long pause, during which the landlady served them with coffee. "I come now to the business that took us to Oniton. We went all three. Acting on Mr Wilcox's advice, the man throws up a secure situation and takes an insecure one, from which he is dismissed. There are certain excuses, but in the main Mr Wilcox is to blame, as Meg herself admitted. It is only common justice that he should employ the man himself. But he meets the woman, and, like the cur that he is, he refuses, and tries to get rid of them. He makes Meg write. Two notes came from her late that evening — one for me, one for Leonard, dismissing him with barely a reason. I couldn't understand. Then it comes out that Mrs Bast had spoken to Mr Wilcox on the lawn while we left her to get rooms, and was still speaking about him when Leonard came back to her. This Leonard knew all along. He thought it natural he should be ruined twice. Natural! Could you have contained yourself?"

"It is certainly a very bad business," said Tibby.

His reply seemed to calm his sister. "I was afraid that I saw it out of proportion. But you are right outside it, and you must know. In a day or two — or perhaps a week — take whatever steps you think fit. I leave it in your hands."

She concluded her charge.

"The facts as they touch Meg are all before you," she added; and Tibby sighed and felt it rather hard that, because of his open mind, he should be empanelled to serve as a juror. He had never been interested in human beings, for which one must blame him, but he had had rather too much of them at Wickham Place. Just as some people cease to attend when books are mentioned, so Tibby's attention wandered when "personal relations" came under discussion. Ought Margaret to know what Helen knew the Basts to know? Similar questions had vexed him from infancy, and at Oxford he had learned to say that the importance of human beings has been vastly overrated by specialists. The epigram, with its faint whiff of the 'eighties, meant nothing. But he might have let it off now if his sister had not been ceaselessly beautiful.

"You see, Helen — have a cigarette — I don't see what I'm to do."

"Then there's nothing to be done. I dare say you are right. Let them marry. There remains the question of compensation."

"Do you want me to adjudicate that too? Had you not better consult an expert?"

"This part is in confidence," said Helen. "It has nothing to do with Meg, and do not mention it to her. The compensation — I do not see who is to pay it if I don't, and I have already decided on the minimum sum. As soon as possible I am placing it to your account, and when I am in Germany you will pay it over for me. I shall never forget your kindness, Tibbikins, if you do this."

"What is the sum?"

"Five thousand."

"Good God alive!" said Tibby, and went crimson.

"Now, what is the good of driblets? To go through life having done one thing — to have raised one person from the abyss; not these puny gifts of shillings and blankets — making the gray more gray. No doubt people will think me extraordinary."

"I don't care a damn what people think!" cried he, heated to unusual manliness of diction. "But it's half what you have."

"Not nearly half." She spread out her hands over her soiled skirt. "I have far too much, and we settled at Chelsea last spring that three hundred a year is necessary to set a man on his feet. What I give will bring in a hundred and fifty between two. It isn't enough."

He could not recover. He was not angry or even shocked, and he saw that Helen would still have plenty to live on. But it amazed him to think what haycocks people can make of their lives. His delicate intonations would not work, and he could only blurt out that the five thousand pounds would mean a great deal of bother for him personally.

"I didn't expect you to understand me."

"I? I understand nobody."

"But you'll do it?"

"Apparently."

"I leave you two commissions, then. The first concerns Mr Wilcox, and you are to use your discretion. The second concerns the money, and is to be mentioned to no one, and carried out literally. You will send a hundred pounds on account tomorrow."

He walked with her to the station, passing through those streets whose serried beauty never bewildered him and never fatigued. The lovely creature raised domes and spires into the cloudless blue, and only the ganglion of vulgarity round Carfax° showed how evanescent was the phantom, how faint its claim to represent England. Helen, rehearsing her commission,° noticed nothing; the Basts were on her brain, and she retold the crisis in a meditative way which might have

---

Carfax: An intersection of four streets at the center of Oxford.   Helen, rehearsing her commission: The autograph manuscript has "commissions."

made other men curious. She was seeing whether it would hold. He
asked her once why she had taken the Basts right into the heart of
Evie's wedding. She stopped like a frightened animal and said, "Does
that seem to you so odd?" Her eyes, the hand laid on the mouth, quite
haunted him, until they were absorbed into the figure of St Mary the
Virgin, before whom he paused for a moment on the walk home.

It is convenient to follow him in the discharge of his duties. Margaret summoned him the next day. She was terrified at Helen's flight,
and he had to say that she had called in at Oxford. Then she said: "Did
she seem worried at any rumour about Henry?" He answered, "Yes."
"I knew it was that!" she exclaimed. "I'll write to her." Tibby was
relieved.

He then sent the cheque to the address that Helen gave him, and
stated that later on he was instructed to forward five thousand pounds.
An answer came back, very civil and quiet in tone — such an answer as
Tibby himself would have given. The cheque was returned, the legacy
refused, the writer being in no need of money. Tibby forwarded this
to Helen, adding in the fullness of his heart that Leonard Bast seemed
somewhat a monumental person after all. Helen's reply was frantic. He
was to take no notice. He was to go down at once and say that she
commanded acceptance. He went. A scurf of books and china orna-
ments awaited him. The Basts had just been evicted for not paying
their rent, and had wandered no one knew whither. Helen had begun
bungling with her money by this time, and had even sold out her
shares in the Nottingham and Derby Railway. For some weeks she did
nothing. Then she reinvested, and, owing to the good advice of her
stockbrokers, became rather richer than she had been before.

## Chapter 31

Houses have their own ways of dying, falling as variously as the
generations of men, some with a tragic roar, some quietly but to an af-
terlife in the city of ghosts, while from others — and thus was the
death of Wickham Place — the spirit slips before the body perishes. It
had decayed in the spring, disintegrating the girls more than they
knew, and causing either to accost unfamiliar regions. By September it
was a corpse, void of emotion, and scarcely hallowed by the memories
of thirty years of happiness. Through its round-topped doorway passed
furniture, and pictures, and books, until the last room was gutted and
the last van had rumbled away. It stood for a week or two longer,
open-eyed, as if astonished at its own emptiness. Then it fell. Navvies

came, and spilt it back into the gray. With their muscles and their beery good temper, they were not the worst of undertakers for a house which had always been human, and had not mistaken culture for an end.

The furniture, with a few exceptions, went down into Hertfordshire, Mr Wilcox having most kindly offered Howards End as a warehouse. Mr Bryce had died abroad — an unsatisfactory affair — and as there seemed little guarantee that the rent would be paid regularly he cancelled the agreement, and resumed possession himself. Until he re-let the house, the Schlegels were welcome to stack their furniture in the garage and lower rooms. Margaret demurred, but Tibby accepted the offer gladly; it saved him from coming to any decision about the future. The plate and the more valuable pictures found a safer home in London, but the bulk of the things went country-ways, and were entrusted to the guardianship of Miss Avery.

Shortly before the move, our hero and heroine were married. They have weathered the storm, and may reasonably expect peace. To have no illusions and yet to love — what stronger surety can a woman find? She had seen her husband's past as well as his heart. She knew her own heart with a thoroughness that commonplace people believe impossible. The heart of Mrs Wilcox was alone hidden, and perhaps it is superstitious to speculate on the feelings of the dead. They were married quietly — really quietly, for as the day approached she refused to go through another Oniton. Her brother gave her away, her aunt, who was out of health, presided over a few colourless refreshments. The Wilcoxes were represented by Charles, who witnessed the marriage settlement, and by Mr Cahill. Paul did send a cablegram. In a few minutes, and without the aid of music, the clergyman made them man and wife, and soon the glass shade had fallen that cuts off married couples from the world. She, a monogamist, regretted the cessation of some of life's innocent odours; he, whose instincts were polygamous, felt morally braced by the change, and less liable to the temptations that had assailed him in the past.

They spent their honeymoon near Innsbruck. Henry knew of a reliable hotel there, and Margaret hoped for a meeting with her sister. In this she was disappointed. As they came south, Helen retreated over the Brenner, and wrote an unsatisfactory postcard from the shores of the Lake of Garda, saying that her plans were uncertain and had better be ignored. Evidently she disliked meeting Henry. Two months are surely enough to accustom an outsider to a situation which a wife has accepted in two days, and Margaret had again to regret her sister's lack of self-control. In a long letter she pointed out the need of charity in sexual matters: so little is known about them; it is hard enough for those who are personally touched to judge; then how futile must be the verdict of society. "I don't say there is no standard, for that would destroy morality; only that there can be no standard until our impulses are classified and better understood." Helen thanked her for her kind letter — rather a curious reply. She moved south again, and spoke of wintering in Naples.

Mr Wilcox was not sorry that the meeting failed. Helen left him time to grow skin over his wound. There were still moments when it pained him. Had he only known that Margaret was awaiting him — Margaret, so lively and intelligent, and yet so submissive — he would have kept himself worthier of her. Incapable of grouping the past, he confused the episode of Jacky with another episode that had taken place in the days of his bachelorhood. The two made one crop of wild oats, for which he was heartily sorry, and he could not see that those oats are of a darker stock which are rooted in another's dishonour. Unchastity and infidelity were as confused to him as to the Middle Ages, his only moral teacher. Ruth (poor old Ruth!) did not enter into his calculations at all, for poor old Ruth had never found him out.

His affection for his present wife grew steadily. Her cleverness gave him no trouble, and, indeed, he liked to see her reading poetry or something about social questions; it distinguished her from the wives of other men. He had only to call, and she clapped the book up and was ready to do what he wished. Then they would argue so jollily, and once or twice she had him in quite a tight corner, but as soon as he grew really serious she gave in. Man is for war, woman for the recreation of the warrior,° but he does not dislike it if she makes a show of fight. She cannot win in a real battle, having no muscles, only nerves. Nerves make her jump out of a moving motor-car, or refuse to be married fashionably. The warrior may well allow her to triumph on such occasions; they move not the imperishable plinth of things that touch his peace.

Margaret had a bad attack of these nerves during the honeymoon. He told her — casually, as was his habit — that Oniton Grange was

Man . . . warrior: Possibly borrowed from Nietzsche's *Thus Spake Zarathustra* (1883–92). See Thomas Mulvey, "A Paraphrase of Nietzsche in Forster's *Howards End*," *Notes and Queries* 12.2 (1972): 52.

let. She showed her annoyance, and asked rather crossly why she had not been consulted.

"I didn't want to bother you," he replied. "Besides, I have only heard for certain this morning."

"Where are we to live?" said Margaret, trying to laugh. "I loved the place extraordinarily. Don't you believe in having a permanent home, Henry?"

He assured her that she misunderstood him. It is home life that distinguishes us from the foreigner. But he did not believe in a damp home.

"This is news. I never heard till this minute that Oniton was damp."

"My dear girl!" — he flung out his hand — "Have you eyes? Have you a skin? How could it be anything but damp in such a situation? In the first place, the Grange is on clay, and built where the castle moat must have been; then there's that detestable little river, steaming all night like a kettle. Feel the cellar walls; look up under the eaves. Ask Sir James or anyone. Those Shropshire valleys are notorious. The only possible place for a house in Shropshire is on a hill; but, for my part, I think the county is too far from London, and the scenery nothing special."

Margaret could not resist saying, "Why did you go there, then?"

"I — because —" He drew his head back and grew rather angry. "Why have we come to the Tyrol, if it comes to that? One might go on asking such questions indefinitely."

One might; but he was only gaining time for a plausible answer. Out it came, and he believed it as soon as it was spoken.

"The truth is, I took Oniton on account of Evie. Don't let this go any further."

"Certainly not."

"I shouldn't like her to know that she nearly let me in for a very bad bargain. No sooner did I sign the agreement than she got engaged. Poor little girl! She was so keen on it all, and wouldn't even wait to make proper inquiries about the shooting. Afraid it would get snapped up — just like all of your sex. Well, no harm's done. She has had her country wedding, and I've got rid of my house to some fellows who are starting a preparatory school."

"Where shall we live, then, Henry? I should enjoy living somewhere."

"I have not yet decided. What about Norfolk?"

Margaret was silent. Marriage had not saved her from the sense of flux. London was but a foretaste of this nomadic civilization which is altering human nature so profoundly, and throws upon personal relations a stress greater than they have ever borne before. Under cosmopolitanism, if it comes, we shall receive no help from the earth. Trees and meadows and mountains will only be a spectacle, and the binding force that they once exercised on character must be entrusted to Love alone. May Love be equal to the task!

"It is now what?" continued Henry. "Nearly October. Let us camp for the winter in Ducie Street, and look out for something in the spring."

"If possible, something permanent. I can't be as young as I was, for these alterations don't suit me."

"But, my dear, which would you rather have — alterations or rheumatism?"

"I see your point," said Margaret, getting up. "If Oniton is really damp, it is impossible, and must be inhabited by little boys. Only, in the spring, let us look before we leap. I will take warning by Evie, and not hurry you. Remember that you have a free hand this time. These endless moves must be bad for the furniture, and are certainly expensive."

"What a practical little woman it is! What's it been reading? Theo — theo — how much?"

"Theosophy."

So Ducie Street was her first fate — a pleasant enough fate. The house, being only a little larger than Wickham Place, trained her for the immense establishment that was promised in the spring. They were frequently away, but at home life ran fairly regularly. In the morning Henry went to the business, and his sandwich — a relic this of some prehistoric craving — was always cut by her own hand. He did not rely upon the sandwich for lunch, but liked to have it by him in case he grew hungry at eleven. When he had gone, there was the house to look after, and the servants to humanize, and several kettles of Helen's to keep on the boil. Her conscience pricked her a little about the Basts; she was not sorry to have lost sight of them. No doubt Leonard was worth helping, but being Henry's wife she preferred to help someone else. As for theatres and discussion societies, they attracted her less and less. She began to "miss" new movements, and to spend her spare time rereading or thinking, rather to the concern of her Chelsea friends. They attributed the change to her marriage, and perhaps some deep instinct did warn her not to travel further from her husband than was inevitable. Yet the main cause lay deeper still; she had outgrown stimulants, and was passing from words to things. It was doubtless a pity not to keep up with Wedekind or John,° but some closing of the gates is inevitable after thirty, if the mind itself is to become a creative power.

## Chapter 32

She was looking at plans one day in the following spring — they had finally decided to go down into Sussex and build — when Mrs Charles Wilcox was announced.

"Have you heard the news?" Dolly cried, as soon as she entered the room. "Charles is so ang — I mean he is sure you know about it, or, rather, that you don't know."

"Why, Dolly!" said Margaret, placidly kissing her. "Here's a surprise! How are the boys and the baby?"

Boys and the baby were well, and in describing a great row that there had been at the Hilton Tennis Club Dolly forgot her news. The wrong people had tried to get in. The rector, as representing the older inhabitants, had said — Charles had said — the tax-collector had said — Charles had regretted not saying — and she closed the description with, "But lucky you, with four courts of your own at Midhurst."

"It will be very jolly," replied Margaret.

"Are those the plans? Does it matter me seeing them?"

"Of course not."

"Charles has never seen the plans."

"They have only just arrived. Here is the ground floor — no, that's rather difficult. Try the elevation. We are to have a good many gables and a picturesque skyline."

"What makes it smell so funny?" said Dolly, after a moment's inspection. She was incapable of understanding plans or maps.

"I suppose the paper."

"And *which* way up is it?"

"Just the ordinary way up. That's the skyline, and the part that smells strongest is the sky."

"Well, ask me another. Margaret — oh — what was I going to say? How's Helen?"

"Quite well."

---

**Wedekind or John:** Frank Wedekind (1864–1918), German dramatist; Augustus John (1878–1961), British painter.

"Is she never coming back to England? Everyone thinks it's awfully odd she doesn't."

"So it is," said Margaret, trying to conceal her vexation. She was getting rather sore on this point. "Helen is odd, awfully. She has now been away eight months."

"But hasn't she any address?"

"A poste restante somewhere in Bavaria is her address. Do write her a line. I will look it up for you."

"No, don't bother. That's eight months she has been away, surely?"

"Exactly. She left just after Evie's wedding. It would be eight months."

"Just when baby was born, then?"

"Just so."

Dolly sighed, and stared enviously round the drawing-room. She was beginning to lose her brightness and good looks. The Charleses were not well off, for Mr Wilcox, having brought up his children with expensive tastes, believed in letting them shift for themselves. After all, he had not treated them generously. Yet another baby was expected, she told Margaret, and they would have to give up the motor. Margaret sympathized, but in a formal fashion, and Dolly little imagined that the stepmother was urging Mr Wilcox to make them a more liberal allowance. She sighed again, and at last the particular grievance was remembered. "Oh yes," she cried, "that is it: Miss Avery has been unpacking your packing-cases."

"Why has she done that? How unnecessary!"

"Ask another. I suppose you ordered her to."

"I gave no such orders. Perhaps she was airing the things. She did undertake to light an occasional fire."

"It was far more than an air," said Dolly solemnly. "The floor sounds covered with books. Charles sent me to know what is to be done, for he feels certain you don't know."

"Books!" cried Margaret, moved by the holy word. "Dolly, are you serious? Has she been touching our books?"

"Hasn't she, though! What used to be the hall's full of them. Charles thought for certain you knew of it."

"I am very much obliged to you, Dolly. What can have come over Miss Avery? I must go down about it at once. Some of the books are my brother's, and are quite valuable. She had no right to open any of the cases."

"I say she's dotty. She was the one that never got married, you know. Oh, I say, perhaps she thinks your books are wedding presents to herself. Old maids are taken that way sometimes. Miss Avery hates us all like poison ever since her frightful dust-up with Evie."

"I hadn't heard of that," said Margaret. A visit from Dolly had its compensations.

"Didn't you know she gave Evie a present last August, and Evie returned it, and then — oh, goloshes! You never read such a letter as Miss Avery wrote."

"But it was wrong of Evie to return it. It wasn't like her to do such a heartless thing."

"But the present was so expensive."

"Why does that make any difference, Dolly?"

"Still, when it costs over five pounds — I didn't see it, but it was a lovely enamel pendant from a Bond Street shop. You can't very well accept that kind of thing from a farm-woman. Now, can you?"

"You accepted a present from Miss Avery when you were married."

"Oh, mine was old earthenware stuff — not worth a half-penny. Evie's was quite different. You'd have to ask anyone to the wedding who gave you a pendant like that. Uncle Percy and Albert and father and Charles all said it was quite impossible, and when four men agree what is a girl to do? Evie didn't want to upset the old thing, so thought a sort of joking letter best, and returned the pendant straight to the shop to save Miss Avery trouble."

"But Miss Avery said —"

Dolly's eyes grew round. "It was a perfectly awful letter. Charles said it was the letter of a madman. In the end she had the pendant back again from the shop and threw it into the duck-pond."

"Did she give any reasons?"

"We think she meant to be invited to Oniton, and so climb into society."

"She's rather old for that," said Margaret pensively. "May not she have given the present to Evie in remembrance of her mother?"

"That's a notion. Give everyone their due, eh? Well, I suppose I ought to be toddling. Come along, Mr Muff — you want a new coat, but I don't know who'll give it you, I'm sure"; and addressing her apparel with mournful humour Dolly moved from the room.

Margaret followed her to ask whether Henry knew about Miss Avery's rudeness.

"Oh yes."

"I wonder, then, why he let me ask her to look after the house."

"But she's only a farm-woman," said Dolly, and her explanation proved correct. Henry only censured the lower classes when it suited him. He bore with Miss Avery as with Crane — because he could get good value out of them. "I have patience with a man who knows his job," he would say, really having patience with the job, and not the man. Paradoxical as it may sound, he had something of the artist about him: he would pass over an insult to his daughter sooner than lose a good charwoman for his wife.

Margaret judged it better to settle the little trouble herself. Parties were evidently ruffled. With Henry's permission, she wrote a pleasant note to Miss Avery, asking her to leave the cases untouched. Then, at the first convenient opportunity, she went down herself, intending to repack her belongings and store them properly in the local warehouse; the plan had been amateurish and a failure. Tibby promised to accompany her, but at the last moment begged to be excused. So, for the second time in her life, she entered the house alone.

## Chapter 33

The day of her visit was exquisite, and the last of unclouded happiness that she was to have for many months. Her anxiety about Helen's extraordinary absence was still dormant, and as for a possible brush with Miss Avery — that only gave zest to the expedition. She had also eluded Dolly's invitation to luncheon. Walking straight up from the station, she crossed the village green and entered the long chestnut avenue that connects it with the church. The church itself stood in the village once. But it there attracted so many worshippers that the Devil, in a pet, snatched it from its foundations, and poised it on an inconvenient knoll, three-quarters of a mile away. If this story is true, the chestnut avenue must have been planted by the angels. No more tempting approach could be imagined for the lukewarm Christian, and if he still finds the walk too long the Devil is defeated all the same, Science having built Holy Trinity, a Chapel of Ease, near the Charleses, and roofed it with tin.

Up the avenue Margaret strolled slowly, stopping to watch the sky that gleamed through the upper branches of the chestnuts, or to finger the little horseshoes on the lower branches. Why has not England a great mythology? Our folklore has never advanced beyond daintiness, and the greater melodies about our countryside have all issued through the pipes of Greece. Deep and true as the native imagination can be, it seems to have failed here. It has stopped with the witches and the fairies. It cannot vivify one fraction of a summer field, or give names to half a dozen stars. England still waits for the supreme moment of her literature — for the great poet who shall voice her, or, better still, for the thousand little poets whose voices shall pass into our common talk.

At the church the scenery changed. The chestnut avenue opened into a road, smooth but narrow, which led into the untouched country. She followed it for over a mile. Its little hesitations pleased her. Having no urgent destiny, it strolled downhill or up as it wished, taking no trouble about the gradients, nor about the view, which nevertheless expanded. The great estates that throttle the south of Hertfordshire were less obtrusive here, and the appearance of the land was neither aristocratic nor suburban. To define it was difficult, but Margaret knew what it was not: it was not snobbish. Though its contours were slight, there was a touch of freedom in their sweep to which Surrey will never attain, and the distant brow of the Chilterns towered like a mountain. "Left to itself," was Margaret's opinion, "this county would vote Liberal." The comradeship, not passionate, that is our highest gift as a nation was promised by it, as by the low brick farm where she called for the key.

But the inside of the farm was disappointing. A most finished young person received her. "Yes, Mrs Wilcox; no, Mrs Wilcox; oh yes, Mrs Wilcox, Auntie received your letter quite duly. Auntie has gone up to your little place at the present moment. Shall I send the servant to direct you?" Followed by: "Of course, Auntie does not *generally* look after your place; she only does it to oblige a neighbour as something exceptional. It gives her something to do. She spends quite a lot of her time there. My husband says to me sometimes, 'Where's Auntie?' I say: 'Need you ask? She's at Howards End.' Yes, Mrs Wilcox. Mrs Wilcox, could I prevail upon you to accept a piece of cake? Not if I cut it for you?"

Margaret refused the cake, but unfortunately this acquired her gentility in the eyes of Miss Avery's niece.

"I cannot let you go on alone. Now don't. You really mustn't. I will direct you myself if it comes to that. I must get my hat. Now" — roguishly — "Mrs Wilcox, don't you move while I'm gone."

Stunned, Margaret did not move from the best parlour, over which the touch of *art nouveau* had fallen. But the other rooms looked in keeping, though they conveyed the peculiar sadness of a rural interior. Here had lived an elder race, to which we look back with disquietude. The country, which we visit at week-ends, was really a home to it, and the graver sides of life, the deaths, the partings, the yearnings for love, have their deepest expression in the heart of the fields. All was not sadness. The sun was shining without. The thrush sang his two syllables on the budding guelder rose. Some children were playing uproariously in heaps of golden straw. It was the presence of sadness at all that surprised Margaret, and ended by giving her a feeling of completeness. In these English farms, if anywhere, one might see life steadily and see it whole, group in one vision its transitoriness and its eternal youth, connect — connect without bitterness until all men are brothers. But her thoughts were interrupted by the return of Miss Avery's niece, and were so tranquillizing that she suffered the interruption gladly.

It was quicker to go out by the back door, and, after due explanations they went out by it. The niece was now mortified by innumerable chickens, who rushed up to her feet for food, and by a shameless and maternal sow. She did not know what animals were coming to. But her gentility withered at the touch of the sweet air. The wind was rising, scattering the straw and ruffling the tails of the ducks as they floated in families over Evie's pendant. One of those delicious gales of spring, in which leaves still in bud seem to rustle, swept over the land and then fell silent. "Georgie," sang the thrush. "Cuckoo," came furtively from the cliff of pine trees. "Georgie, pretty Georgie," and the other birds joined in with nonsense. The hedge was a half-painted picture which would be finished in a few days. Celandines grew on its banks, lords-and-ladies and primroses in the defended hollows; the wild rose bushes, still bearing their withered hips, showed also the promise of blossom. Spring had come, clad in no classical garb, yet fairer than all springs; fairer even than she who walks through the myrtles of Tuscany° with the graces before her and the zephyr behind.

The two women walked up the lane full of outward civility. But Margaret was thinking how difficult it was to be earnest about furniture on such a day, and the niece was thinking about hats. Thus engaged, they reached Howards End. Petulant cries of "Auntie!" severed the air. There was no reply, and the front door was locked.

"Are you sure that Miss Avery is up here?" asked Margaret.

"Oh, yes, Mrs Wilcox, quite sure. She is here daily."

Margaret tried to look in through the dining-room window, but the curtain inside was drawn tightly. So with the drawing-room and

**fairer even . . . Tuscany:** A reference to the figure of Flora in Botticelli's painting *Primavera.*

the hall. The appearance of these curtains was familiar, yet she did not remember them being there on her other visit; her impression was that Mr Bryce had taken everything away. They tried the back. Here again they received no answer, and could see nothing; the kitchen window was fitted with a blind, while the pantry and scullery had pieces of wood propped up against them, which looked ominously like the lids of packing-cases. Margaret thought of her books, and she lifted up her voice also. At the first cry she succeeded.

"Well, well!" replied someone inside the house. "If it isn't Mrs Wilcox come at last!"

"Have you got the key, Auntie?"

"Madge, go away," said Miss Avery, still invisible.

"Auntie, it's Mrs Wilcox —"

Margaret supported her. "Your niece and I have come together —"

"Madge, go away. This is no moment for your hat."

The poor woman went red. "Auntie gets more eccentric lately," she said nervously.

"Miss Avery!" called Margaret. "I have come about the furniture. Could you kindly let me in?"

"Yes, Mrs Wilcox," said the voice, "of course." But after that came silence. They called again without response. They walked round the house disconsolately.

"I hope Miss Avery is not ill," hazarded Margaret.

"Well, if you'll excuse me," said Madge, "perhaps I ought to be leaving you now. The servants need seeing to at the farm. Auntie is so odd at times." Gathering up her elegancies, she retired defeated, and, as if her departure had loosed a spring, the front door opened at once.

Miss Avery said, "Well, come right in, Mrs Wilcox!" quite pleasantly and calmly.

"Thank you so much," began Margaret, but broke off at the sight of an umbrella-stand. It was her own.

"Come right into the hall first," said Miss Avery. She drew the curtain, and Margaret uttered a cry of despair. For an appalling thing had happened. The hall was fitted up with the contents of the library from Wickham Place. The carpet had been laid, the big work-table drawn up near the window; the bookcases filled the wall opposite the fireplace, and her father's sword — this is what bewildered her particularly — had been drawn from its scabbard and hung naked amongst the sober volumes. Miss Avery must have worked for days.

"I'm afraid this isn't what we meant," she began. "Mr Wilcox and

I never intended the cases to be touched. For instance, these books are my brother's. We are storing them for him and for my sister, who is abroad. When you kindly undertook to look after things, we never expected you to do so much."

"The house has been empty long enough," said the old woman.

Margaret refused to argue. "I dare say we didn't explain," she said civilly. "It has been a mistake, and very likely our mistake."

"Mrs Wilcox, it has been mistake upon mistake for fifty years. The house is Mrs Wilcox's, and she would not desire it to stand empty any longer."

To help the poor decaying brain, Margaret said:

"Yes, Mrs Wilcox's house, the mother of Mr Charles."

"Mistake upon mistake," said Miss Avery. "Mistake upon mistake."

"Well, I don't know," said Margaret, sitting down in one of her own chairs. "I really don't know what's to be done." She could not help laughing.

The other said: "Yes, it should be a merry house enough."

"I don't know — I dare say. Well, thank you very much, Miss Avery. Yes, that's all right. Delightful."

"There is still the parlour." She went through the door opposite and drew a curtain. Light flooded the drawing-room and the drawing-room furniture from Wickham Place. "And the dining-room." More curtains were drawn, more windows were flung open to the spring. "Then through here —" Miss Avery continued passing and repassing through the hall. Her voice was lost, but Margaret heard her pulling up the kitchen blind. "I've not finished here yet," she announced, returning. "There's still a deal to do. The farm-lads will carry your great wardrobes upstairs, for there is no need to go into expense at Hilton."

"It is all a mistake," repeated Margaret, feeling that she must put her foot down. "A misunderstanding. Mr Wilcox and I are not going to live at Howards End."

"Oh, indeed. On account of his hay fever?"

"We have settled to build a new home for ourselves in Sussex, and part of this furniture — my part — will go down there presently." She looked at Miss Avery intently, trying to understand the kink in her brain. Here was no maundering old woman. Her wrinkles were shrewd and humorous. She looked capable of scathing wit and also of high but unostentatious nobility.

"You think that you won't come back to live here, Mrs Wilcox, but you will."

"That remains to be seen," said Margaret, smiling. "We have no intention of doing so for the present. We happen to need a much larger house. Circumstances oblige us to give big parties. Of course, some day — one never knows, does one?"

Miss Avery retorted: "Some day! Tcha! Tcha! Don't talk about some day. You are living here now."

"Am I?"

"You are living here, and have been for the last ten minutes, if you ask me."

It was a senseless remark, but with a queer feeling of disloyalty Margaret rose from her chair. She felt that Henry had been obscurely censured. They went into the dining-room, where the sunlight poured in upon her mother's chiffonier, and upstairs, where many an old god peeped from a new niche. The furniture fitted extraordinarily well. In the central room — over the hall, the room that Helen had slept in four years ago — Miss Avery had placed Tibby's old bassinet.

"The nursery," she said.

Margaret turned away without speaking.

At last everything was seen. The kitchen and lobby were still stacked with furniture and straw, but, as far as she could make out, nothing had been broken or scratched. A pathetic display of ingenuity! Then they took a friendly stroll in the garden. It had gone wild since her last visit. The gravel sweep was weedy, and grass had sprung up at the very jaws of the garage. And Evie's rockery was only bumps. Perhaps Evie was responsible for Miss Avery's oddness. But Margaret suspected that the cause lay deeper, and that the girl's silly letter had but loosed the irritation of years.

"It's a beautiful meadow," she remarked. It was one of those open-air drawing-rooms that have been formed, hundreds of years ago, out of the smaller fields. So the boundary hedge zigzagged down the hill at right angles, and at the bottom there was a little green annex — a sort of powder-closet for the cows.

"Yes, the maidy's well enough," said Miss Avery, "for those, that is, who don't suffer from sneezing." And she cackled maliciously. "I've seen Charlie Wilcox go out to my lads in hay time — oh, they ought to do this — they mustn't do that — he'd learn them to be lads. And just then the tickling took him. He has it from his father, with other things. There's not one Wilcox that can stand up against a field in June — I laughed fit to burst while he was courting Ruth."

"My brother gets hay fever too," said Margaret.

"This house lies too much on the land for them. Naturally, they

were glad enough to slip in at first. But Wilcoxes are better than nothing, as I see you've found."

Margaret laughed.

"They keep a place going, don't they? Yes, it is just that."

"They keep England going, it is my opinion."

But Miss Avery upset her by replying: "Ay, they breed like rabbits.
Well, well, it's a funny world. But He who made it knows what He
wants in it, I suppose. If Mrs Charlie is expecting her fourth, it isn't
for us to repine."

"They breed and they also work," said Margaret, conscious of
some invitation to disloyalty, which was echoed by the very breeze and
by the songs of the birds. "It certainly is a funny world, but so long as
men like my husband and his sons govern it I think it'll never be a bad
one — never really bad."

"No, better'n nothing," said Miss Avery, and turned to the
wych-elm.

On their way back to the farm she spoke of her old friend much
more clearly than before. In the house Margaret had wondered
whether she quite distinguished the first wife from the second. Now
she said: "I never saw much of Ruth after her grandmother died, but
we stayed civil. It was a very civil family. Old Mrs Howard never spoke
against anybody, nor let anyone be turned away without food. Then it
was never 'Trespassers will be prosecuted' in their land, but would
people please not come in? Mrs Howard was never created to run a
farm."

"Had they no men to help them?" Margaret asked.

Miss Avery replied: "Things went on until there were no men."

"Until Mr Wilcox came along," corrected Margaret, anxious that
her husband should receive his dues.

"I suppose so; but Ruth should have married a — no disrespect to
you to say this, for I take it you were intended to get Wilcox anyway,
whether she got him first or no."

"Whom should she have married?"

"A soldier!" exclaimed the old woman. "Some real soldier."

Margaret was silent. It was a criticism of Henry's character far
more trenchant than any of her own. She felt dissatisfied.

"But that's all over," she went on. "A better time is coming now,
though you've kept me long enough waiting. In a couple of weeks I'll
see your lights shining through the hedge of an evening. Have you ordered in coals?"

"We are not coming," said Margaret firmly. She respected Miss

Avery too much to humour her. "No. Not coming. Never coming. It has all been a mistake. The furniture must be repacked at once, and I am very sorry, but I am making other arrangements, and must ask you to give me the keys."

"Certainly, Mrs Wilcox," said Miss Avery, and resigned her duties with a smile.

Relieved at this conclusion, and having sent her compliments to Madge, Margaret walked back to the station. She had intended to go to the furniture warehouse and give directions for removal, but the muddle had turned out more extensive than she expected, so she decided to consult Henry. It was as well that she did this. He was strongly against employing the local man whom he had previously recommended, and advised her to store in London after all.

But before this could be done an unexpected trouble fell upon her.

### Chapter 34

It was not unexpected entirely. Aunt Juley's health had been bad all the winter. She had had a long series of colds and coughs, and had been too busy to get rid of them. She had scarcely promised her niece "to really take my tiresome chest in hand" when she caught a chill and developed acute pneumonia. Margaret and Tibby went down to Swanage. Helen was telegraphed for, and the spring party that after all gathered in that hospitable house had all the pathos of fair memories. On a perfect day,when the sky seemed blue porcelain, and the waves of the discreet little bay beat gentlest of tattoos upon the sand, Margaret hurried up through the rhododendrons, confronted again by the senselessness of Death. One death may explain itself, but it throws no light upon another; the groping inquiry must begin anew. Preachers or scientists may generalize, but we know that no generality is possible about those whom we love; not one heaven awaits them, not even one oblivion. Aunt Juley, incapable of tragedy, slipped out of life with odd little laughs and apologies for having stopped in it so long. She was very weak; she could not rise to the occasion, or realize the great mystery which all agree must await her; it only seemed to her that she was quite done up — more done up than ever before; that she saw and heard and felt less every moment; and that, unless something changed, she would soon feel nothing. Her spare strength she devoted to plans: could not Margaret take some steamer expeditions? Were mackerel cooked as Tibby liked them? She worried herself about Helen's absence, and also that she should be the cause of Helen's return. The nurses seemed to think such interests quite natural, and perhaps hers was an average approach to the Great Gate. But Margaret saw Death stripped of any false romance; whatever the idea of Death may contain, the process can be trivial and hideous.

"Important — Margaret dear, take the Lulworth when Helen comes."

"Helen won't be able to stop, Aunt Juley. She has telegraphed that she can only get away just to see you. She must go back to Germany as soon as you are well."

"How very odd of Helen! Mr Wilcox —"

"Yes, dear?"

"Can he spare you?"

Henry wished her to come, and had been very kind. Yet again Margaret said so.

Mrs Munt did not die. Quite outside her will, a more dignified power took hold of her and checked her on the downward slope. She returned, without emotion, as fidgety as ever. On the fourth day she was out of danger.

"Margaret — important," it went on: "I should like you to have some companion to take walks with. Do try Miss Conder."

"I have been a little walk with Miss Conder."

"But she is not really interesting. If only you had Helen."

"I have Tibby, Aunt Juley."

"No, but he has to do his Chinese. Some real companion is what you need. Really, Helen is odd."

"Helen is odd, very," agreed Margaret.

"Not content with going abroad, why does she want to go back there at once?"

"No doubt she will change her mind when she sees us. She has not the least balance."

That was the stock criticism about Helen, but Margaret's voice trembled as she made it. By now she was deeply pained at her sister's behaviour. It may be unbalanced to fly out of England, but to stop away eight months argues that the heart is awry as well as the head. A sick-bed could recall Helen, but she was deaf to more human calls; after a glimpse at her aunt, she would retire into her nebulous life behind some poste restante. She scarcely existed; her letters had become dull and infrequent; she had no wants and no curiosity. And it was all put down to poor Henry's account! Henry, long pardoned by his wife, was still too infamous to be greeted by his sister-in-law. It was morbid, and, to her alarm, Margaret fancied that she could trace the growth of morbidity back in Helen's life for nearly four years. The flight from Oniton; the unbalanced patronage of the Basts; the explosion of grief up on the downs — all connected with Paul, an insignificant boy whose lips had kissed hers for a fraction of time. Margaret and Mrs Wilcox had feared that they might kiss again. Foolishly: the real danger was reaction. Reaction against the Wilcoxes had eaten into her life until she was scarcely sane. At twenty-five she had an idée fixe. What hope was there for her as an old woman?

The more Margaret thought about it the more alarmed she became. For many months she had put the subject away, but it was too big to be slighted now. There was almost a taint of madness. Were all Helen's actions to be governed by a tiny mishap, such as may happen to any young man or woman? Can human nature be constructed on lines so insignificant? The blundering little encounter at Howards End was vital. It propagated itself where graver intercourse lay barren; it was stronger than sisterly intimacy, stronger than reason or books. In one of her moods Helen had confessed that she still "enjoyed" it in a certain sense. Paul had faded, but the magic of his caress endured. And where there is enjoyment of the past there may also be reaction — propagation at both ends.

Well, it is odd and sad that our minds should be such seed-beds, and we without power to choose the seed. But man is an odd, sad creature as yet, intent on pilfering the earth, and heedless of the growths within himself. He cannot be bored about psychology. He leaves it to the specialist, which is as if he should leave his dinner to be eaten by a steam-engine. He cannot be bothered to digest his own soul. Margaret and Helen have been more patient, and it is suggested that Margaret has succeeded — so far as success is yet possible. She does understand herself, she has some rudimentary control over her own growth. Whether Helen has succeeded one cannot say.

The day that Mrs Munt rallied Helen's letter arrived. She had posted it at Munich, and would be in London herself on the morrow. It was a disquieting letter, though the opening was affectionate and sane.

Dearest Meg,
    Give Helen's love to Aunt Juley. Tell her that I love and have loved her ever since I can remember. I shall be in London Thursday.
    My address will be care of the bankers. I have not yet settled on

a hotel, so write or wire to me there and give me detailed news. If Aunt Juley is much better, or if, for a terrible reason, it would be no good my coming down to Swanage, you must not think it odd if I do not come. I have all sorts of plans in my head. I am living abroad at present, and want to get back as quickly as possible. Will you please tell me where our furniture is. I should like to take out one or two books; the rest are for you.

Forgive me, dearest Meg. This must read like rather a tiresome letter, but all letters are from your loving

Helen.

It was a tiresome letter, for it tempted Margaret to tell a lie. If she wrote that Aunt Juley was still in danger her sister would come. Unhealthiness is contagious. We cannot be in contact with those who are in a morbid state without ourselves deteriorating. To "act for the best" might do Helen good, but would do herself harm, and, at the risk of disaster, she kept her colours flying a little longer. She replied that their aunt was much better, and awaited developments.

Tibby approved of her reply. Mellowing rapidly, he was a pleasanter companion than before. Oxford had done much for him. He had lost his peevishness, and could hide his indifference to people and his interest in food. But he had not grown more human. The years between eighteen and twenty-two, so magical for most, were leading him gently from boyhood to middle age. He had never known youngmanliness, that quality which warms the heart till death, and gives Mr Wilcox an imperishable charm. He was frigid — through no fault of his own, and without cruelty. He thought Helen wrong, and Margaret right, but this family trouble was for him what a scene behind footlights is for most people. He had only one suggestion to make, and that was characteristic.

"Why don't you tell Mr Wilcox?"

"About Helen?"

"Perhaps he has come across that sort of thing."

"He would do all he could, but —"

"Oh, you know best. But he is practical."

It was the student's belief in experts. Margaret demurred for one or two reasons. Presently Helen's answer came. She sent a telegram requesting the address of the furniture, as she would now return at once. Margaret replied, "Certainly not; meet me at the bankers at four." She and Tibby went up to London. Helen was not at the bankers, and they were refused her address. Helen had passed into chaos.

Margaret put her arm round her brother. He was all that she had left, and never had he seemed more unsubstantial.

"Tibby love, what next?"

He replied: "It is extraordinary."

"Dear, your judgement's often clearer than mine. Have you any notion what's at the back?"

"None, unless it's something mental."

"Oh — that!" said Margaret. "Quite impossible." But the suggestion had been uttered, and in a few minutes she took it up herself. Nothing else explained. And London agreed with Tibby. The mask fell off the city, and she saw it for what it really is — a caricature of infinity. The familiar barriers, the streets along which she moved, the houses between which she had made her little journeys for so many years, became negligible suddenly. Helen seemed one with the grimy trees and the traffic and the slowly flowing slabs of mud. She had accomplished a hideous act of renunciation and returned to the One. Margaret's own faith held firm. She knew the human soul will be merged, if it be merged at all, with the stars and the sea. Yet she felt that her sister had been going amiss for many years. It was symbolic the catastrophe should come now, on a London afternoon, while rain fell slowly.

Henry was the only hope. Henry was definite. He might know of some paths in the chaos that were hidden from them, and she determined to take Tibby's advice and lay the whole matter in his hands. They must call at his office. He could not well make it worse. She went for a few moments into St Paul's, whose dome stands out of the welter so bravely, as if preaching the gospel of form. But, within, St Paul's is as its surroundings — echoes and whispers, inaudible songs, invisible mosaics, wet footmarks crossing and recrossing the floor. *Si monumentum requiris, circumspice:*° it points us back to London. There was no hope of Helen here.

Henry was unsatisfactory at first. That she had expected. He was overjoyed to see her back from Swanage, and slow to admit the growth of a new trouble. When they told him of their search, he only chaffed Tibby and the Schlegels generally, and declared that it was "just like Helen" to lead her relatives a dance.

"That is what we all say," replied Margaret. "But why *should* it be just like Helen? Why should she be allowed to be so queer, and to grow queerer?"

---

*Si monumentum requiris, circumspice:* "If you require a monument, look around you"; the epitaph for Sir Christopher Wren, architect of St. Paul's Cathedral.

"Don't ask me. I'm a plain man of business. I live and let live. My advice to you both is, don't worry. Margaret, you've got black marks again under your eyes. You know that's strictly forbidden. First your aunt — then your sister. No, we aren't going to have it. Are we, Theobald?" He rang the bell. "I'll give you some tea, and then you go straight to Ducie Street. I can't have my girl looking as old as her husband."

"All the same, you have not quite seen our point," said Tibby.

Mr Wilcox, who was in good spirits, retorted: "I don't suppose I ever shall." He leant back, laughing at the gifted but ridiculous family, while the fire flickered over the map of Africa. Margaret motioned to her brother to go on. Rather diffident, he obeyed her.

"Margaret's point is this," he said. "Our sister may be mad."

Charles, who was working in the inner room, looked round.

"Come in, Charles," said Margaret kindly. "Could you help us at all? We are again in trouble."

"I'm afraid I cannot. What are the facts? We are all mad more or less, you know, in these days."

"The facts are as follows," replied Tibby, who had at times a pedantic lucidity. "The facts are that she has been in England for three days and will not see us. She has forbidden the bankers to give us her address. She refuses to answer questions. Margaret finds her letters colourless. There are other facts, but these are the most striking."

"She has never behaved like this before, then?" asked Henry.

"Of course not!" said his wife, with a frown.

"Well, my dear, how am I to know?"

A senseless spasm of annoyance came over her. "You know quite well that Helen never sins against affection," she said. "You must have noticed that much in her, surely."

"Oh yes; she and I have always hit it off together."

"No, Henry — can't you see? — I don't mean that."

She recovered herself, but not before Charles had observed her. Stupid and attentive, he was watching the scene.

"I was meaning that when she was eccentric in the past one could trace it back to the heart in the long run. She behaved oddly because she cared for someone, or wanted to help them. There's no possible excuse for her now. She is grieving us deeply, and that is why I am sure that she is not well. 'Mad' is too terrible a word, but she is not well. I shall never believe it. I shouldn't discuss my sister with you if I thought she was well — trouble you about her, I mean."

Henry began to grow serious. Ill-health was to him something perfectly definite. Generally well himself, he could not realize that we sink to it by slow gradations. The sick had no rights; they were outside the pale; one could lie to them remorselessly. When his first wife was seized, he had promised to take her down into Hertfordshire, but meanwhile arranged with a nursing-home instead. Helen, too, was ill. And the plan that he sketched out for her capture, clever and well-meaning as it was, drew its ethics from the wolf-pack.

"You want to get hold of her?" he said. "That's the problem, isn't it? She has got to see a doctor."

"For all I know she has seen one already."

"Yes, yes; don't interrupt." He rose to his feet and thought intently. The genial, tentative host disappeared, and they saw instead the man who had carved money out of Greece and Africa, and bought forests from the natives for a few bottles of gin. "I've got it," he said at last. "It's perfectly easy. Leave it to me. We'll send her down to Howards End."

"How will you do that?"

"After her books. Tell her that she must unpack them herself. Then you can meet her there."

"But, Henry, that's just what she won't let me do. It's part of her — whatever it is — never to see me."

"Of course you won't tell her you're going. When she is there, looking at the cases, you'll just stroll in. If nothing is wrong with her, so much the better. But there'll be the motor round the corner, and we can run her up to a specialist in no time."

Margaret shook her head. "It's quite impossible."

"Why?"

"It doesn't seem impossible to me," said Tibby; "it is surely a very tippy plan."

"It is impossible, because —" She looked at her husband sadly. "It's not the particular language that Helen and I talk, if you see my meaning. It would do splendidly for other people, whom I don't blame."

"But Helen doesn't talk," said Tibby. "That's our whole difficulty. She won't talk your particular language, and on that account you think she's ill."

"No, Henry; it's sweet of you, but I couldn't."

"I see," he said; "you have scruples."

"I suppose so."

"And sooner than go against them you would have your sister suffer. You could have got her down to Swanage by a word, but you had scruples. And scruples are all very well. I am as scrupulous as any man alive, I hope; but when it is a case like this, when there is a question of madness —"

"I deny it's madness."

"You said just now —"

"It's madness when I say it, but not when you say it."

Henry shrugged his shoulders. "Margaret! Margaret!" he groaned. "No education can teach a woman logic. Now, my dear, my time is valuable. Do you want me to help you or not?"

"Not in that way."

"Answer my question. Plain question, plain answer. Do —"

Charles surprised them by interrupting. "Pater, we may as well keep Howards End out of it," he said.

"Why, Charles?"

Charles could give no reason; but Margaret felt as if, over tremendous distances, a salutation had passed between them.

"The whole house is at sixes and sevens," he said crossly. "We don't want any more mess."

"Who's 'we'?" asked his father. "My boy, pray, who's 'we'?"

"I am sure I beg your pardon," said Charles. "I appear always to be intruding."

By now Margaret wished she had never mentioned her trouble to her husband. Retreat was impossible. He was determined to push the matter to a satisfactory conclusion, and Helen faded as he talked. Her fair, flying hair and eager eyes counted for nothing, for she was ill, without rights, and any of her friends might hunt her. Sick at heart, Margaret joined in the chase. She wrote her sister a lying letter, at her husband's dictation; she said the furniture was all at Howards End, but could be seen on Monday next at 3.00 p.m., when a charwoman would be in attendance. It was a cold letter, and the more plausible for that. Helen would think she was offended. And on Monday next she and Henry were to lunch with Dolly, and then ambush themselves in the garden.

After they had gone, Mr Wilcox said to his son: "I can't have this sort of behaviour, my boy. Margaret's too sweet-natured to mind, but I mind for her."

Charles made no answer.

"Is anything wrong with you, Charles, this afternoon?"

"No, pater; but you may be taking on a bigger business than you reckon."

"How?"

"Don't ask me."

## Chapter 35

One speaks of the moods of spring, but the days that are her true children have only one mood: they are all full of the rising and dropping of winds, and the whistling of birds. New flowers may come out, the green embroidery of the hedges increase, but the same heaven broods overhead, soft, thick and blue, the same figures, seen and unseen, are wandering by coppice and meadow. The morning that Margaret had spent with Miss Avery, and the afternoon she set out to entrap Helen, were the scales of a single balance. Time might never have moved, rain never have fallen, and man alone, with his schemes and ailments, was troubling Nature until he saw her through a veil of tears.

She protested no more. Whether Henry was right or wrong, he was most kind, and she knew of no other standard by which to judge him. She must trust him absolutely. As soon as he had taken up a business, his obtuseness vanished. He profited by the slightest indications, and the capture of Helen promised to be staged as deftly as the marriage of Evie.

They went down in the morning as arranged, and he discovered that their victim was actually in Hilton. On his arrival he called at all the livery-stables in the village, and had a few minutes' serious conversation with the proprietors. What he said, Margaret did not know — perhaps not the truth; but news arrived after lunch that a lady had come by the London train, and had taken a fly° to Howards End.

"She was bound to drive," said Henry. "There will be her books."

"I cannot make it out," said Margaret for the hundredth time.

"Finish your coffee, dear. We must be off."

"Yes, Margaret, you know you must take plenty," said Dolly.

Margaret tried, but suddenly lifted her hand to her eyes. Dolly stole glances at her father-in-law which he did not answer. In the silence the motor came round to the door.

"You're not fit for it," he said anxiously. "Let me go alone. I know exactly what to do."

"Oh yes, I am fit," said Margaret, uncovering her face. "Only most frightfully worried. I cannot feel that Helen is really alive. Her letters and telegrams seem to have come from someone else. Her voice isn't in them. I don't believe your driver really saw her at the station. I wish I'd never mentioned it. I know that Charles is vexed. Yes, he is —"

a **fly:** A light horse-drawn cab.

She seized Dolly's hand and kissed it. "There, Dolly will forgive me. There. Now we'll be off."

Henry had been looking at her closely. He did not like this breakdown.

"Don't you want to tidy yourself?" he asked.

"Have I time?"

"Yes, plenty."

She went to the lavatory by the front door, and as soon as the bolt slipped Mr Wilcox said quietly:

"Dolly, I'm going without her."

Dolly's eyes lit up with vulgar excitement. She followed him on tiptoe out to the car.

"Tell her I thought it best."

"Yes, Mr Wilcox, I see."

"Say anything you like. All right."

The car started well, and with ordinary luck would have got away. But Porgly-woggles, who was playing in the garden, chose this moment to sit down in the middle of the path. Crane, in trying to pass him, ran one wheel over a bed of wallflowers. Dolly screamed. Margaret, hearing the noise, rushed out hatless, and was in time to jump on the footboard. She said not a single word; he was only treating her as she had treated Helen, and her rage at his dishonesty only helped to indicate what Helen would feel against them. She thought: "I deserve it; I am punished for lowering my colours." And she accepted his apologies with a calmness that astonished him.

"I still consider you are not fit for it," he kept saying.

"Perhaps I was not at lunch. But the whole thing is spread clearly before me now."

"I was meaning to act for the best."

"Just lend me your scarf, will you. This wind takes one's hair so."

"Certainly, dear girl. Are you all right now?"

"Look! My hands have stopped trembling."

"And have quite forgiven me? Then listen. Her cab should already have arrived at Howards End. (We're a little late, but no matter.) Our first move will be to send it down to wait at the farm, as, if possible, one doesn't want a scene before servants. A certain gentleman" — he pointed at Crane's back — "won't drive in, but will wait a little short of the front gate, behind the laurels. Have you still the keys of the house?"

"Yes."

"Well, they aren't wanted. Do you remember how the house stands?"

"Yes."

"If we don't find her in the porch, we can stroll round into the garden. Our object —"

Here they stopped to pick up the doctor.

"I was just saying to my wife, Mansbridge, that our main object is not to frighten Miss Schlegel. The house, as you know, is my property, so it should seem quite natural for us to be there. The trouble is evidently nervous — wouldn't you say so, Margaret?"

The doctor, a very young man, began to ask questions about Helen. Was she normal? Was there anything congenital or hereditary? Had anything occurred that was likely to alienate her from her family?

"Nothing," answered Margaret, wondering what would have happened if she had added: "Though she did resent my husband's immorality."

"She always was highly strung," pursued Henry, leaning back in the car as it shot past the church. "A tendency to spiritualism and those things, though nothing serious. Musical, literary, artistic, but I should say normal — a very charming girl."

Margaret's anger and terror increased every moment. How dare these men label her sister! What horrors lay ahead! What impertinences that shelter under the name of science! The pack was turning on Helen, to deny her human rights, and it seemed to Margaret that all Schlegels were threatened with her. Were they normal? What a question to ask! And it is always those who know nothing about human nature, who are bored by psychology and shocked by physiology, who ask it. However piteous her sister's state, she knew that she must be on her side. They would be mad together if the world chose to consider them so.

It was now five minutes past three. The car slowed down by the farm, in the yard of which Miss Avery was standing. Henry asked her whether a cab had gone past. She nodded, and the next moment they caught sight of it, at the end of the lane. The car ran silently like a beast of prey. So unsuspicious was Helen that she was sitting in the porch, with her back to the road. She had come. Only her head and shoulders were visible. She sat framed in the vine, and one of her hands played with the buds. The wind ruffled her hair, the sun glorified it; she was as she had always been.

Margaret was seated next to the door. Before her husband could prevent her, she slipped out. She ran to the garden gate, which was shut, passed through it, and deliberately pushed it in his face. The noise alarmed Helen. Margaret saw her rise with an unfamiliar movement, and, rushing into the porch, learned the simple explanation of all their fears — her sister was with child.

"Is the truant all right?" called Henry.

She had time to whisper: "Oh, my darling —" The keys of the house were in her hand. She unlocked Howards End and thrust Helen into it. "Yes, all right," she said, and stood with her back to the door.

## Chapter 36

"Margaret, you look upset!" said Henry.

Mansbridge had followed. Crane was at the gate, and the flyman had stood up on the box. Margaret shook her head at them; she could not speak any more. She remained clutching the keys, as if all their future depended on them. Henry was asking more questions. She shook her head again. His words had no sense. She heard him wonder why she had let Helen in. "You might have given me a knock with the gate," was another of his remarks. Presently she heard herself speaking. She, or someone for her, said; "Go away." Henry came nearer. He repeated: "Margaret, you look upset again. My dear, give me the keys. What are you doing with Helen?"

"Oh, dearest, do go away, and I will manage it all."

"Manage what?"

He stretched out his hand for the keys. She might have obeyed if it had not been for the doctor.

"Stop that at least," she said piteously; the doctor had turned back, and was questioning the driver of Helen's cab. A new feeling came over her: she was fighting for women against men. She did not care about rights, but if men came into Howards End it should be over her body.

"Come, this is an odd beginning," said her husband.

The doctor came forward now, and whispered two words to Mr Wilcox — the scandal was out. Sincerely horrified, Henry stood gazing at the earth.

"I cannot help it," said Margaret. "Do wait. It's not my fault. Please all four of you to go away now."

Now the flyman was whispering to Crane.

"We are relying on you to help us, Mrs Wilcox," said the young doctor. "Could you go in and persuade your sister to come out?"

"On what grounds?" said Margaret, suddenly looking him straight in the eyes.

Thinking it professional to prevaricate, he murmured something about a nervous breakdown.

"I beg your pardon, but it is nothing of the sort. You are not qualified to attend my sister, Mr Mansbridge. If we require your services, we will let you know."

"I can diagnose the case more bluntly if you wish," he retorted.

"You could, but you have not. You are, therefore, not qualified to attend my sister."

"Come, come, Margaret!" said Henry, never raising his eyes. "This is a terrible business, an appalling business. It's doctor's orders. Open the door."

"Forgive me, but I will not."

"I don't agree."

Margaret was silent.

"This business is as broad as it's long," contributed the doctor. "We had better all work together. You need us, Mrs Wilcox, and we need you."

"Quite so," said Henry.

"I do not need you in the least," said Margaret.

The two men looked at each other anxiously.

"No more does my sister, who is still many weeks from her confinement."

"Margaret, Margaret!"

"Well, Henry, send your doctor away. What possible use is he now?"

Mr Wilcox ran his eye over the house. He had a vague feeling that he must stand firm and support the doctor. He himself might need support, for there was trouble ahead.

"It all turns on affection now," said Margaret. "Affection. Don't you see?" Resuming her usual methods, she wrote the word on the house with her finger. "Surely you see. I like Helen very much, you not so much. Mr Mansbridge doesn't know her. That's all. And affection, when reciprocated, gives rights. Put that down in your notebook, Mr Mansbridge. It's a useful formula."

Henry told her to be calm.

"You don't know what you want yourselves," said Margaret, folding her arms. "For one sensible remark I will let you in. But you cannot make it. You would trouble my sister for no reason. I will not permit it. I'll stand here all the day sooner."

"Mansbridge," said Henry in a low voice, "perhaps not now."

The pack was breaking up. At a sign from his master, Crane also went back into the car.

"Now, Henry, you," she said gently. None of her bitterness had been directed at him. "Go away now, dear. I shall want your advice later, no doubt. Forgive me if I have been cross. But, seriously, you must go."

He was too stupid to leave her. Now it was Mr Mansbridge who called in a low voice to him.

"I shall soon find you down at Dolly's," she called, as the gate at last clanged between them. The fly moved out of the way, the motor backed, turned a little, backed again, and turned in the narrow road. A string of farm carts came up in the middle; but she waited through all, for there was no hurry. When all was over and the car had started, she opened the door. "Oh, my darling!" she said. "My darling, forgive me." Helen was standing in the hall.

## Chapter 37

Margaret bolted the door on the inside. Then she would have kissed her sister, but Helen, in a dignified voice, that came strangely from her, said:

"Convenient! You did not tell me that the books were unpacked. I have found nearly everything that I want."

"I told you nothing that was true."

"It has been a great surprise, certainly. Has Aunt Juley been ill?"

"Helen, you wouldn't think I'd invent that?"

"I suppose not," said Helen, turning away, and crying a very little. "But one loses faith in everything after this."

"We thought it was illness, but even then — I haven't behaved worthily."

Helen selected another book.

"I ought not to have consulted anyone. What would our father have thought of me?"

She did not think of questioning her sister, nor of rebuking her. Both might be necessary in the future, but she had first to purge a greater crime than any that Helen could have committed — that want of confidence that is the work of the devil.

"Yes, I am annoyed," replied Helen. "My wishes should have been respected. I would have gone through this meeting if it was necessary, but after Aunt Juley recovered it was not necessary. Planning my life, as I now have to do —"

"Come away from those books," called Margaret. "Helen, do talk to me."

"I was just saying that I have stopped living haphazard. One can't go through a great deal of — " she missed out the noun — "without planning one's actions in advance. I am going to have a child in June, and in the first place conversations, discussions, excitement, are not good for me. I will go through them if necessary, but only then. In the second place I have no right to trouble people. I cannot fit in with England as I know it. I have done something that the English never pardon. It would not be right for them to pardon it. So I must live where I am not known."

"But why didn't you tell me, dearest?"

"Yes," replied Helen judicially. "I might have, but decided to wait."

"I believe you would never have told me."

"Oh yes, I should. We have taken a flat in Munich."

Margaret glanced out of the window.

"By 'we' I mean myself and Monica. But for her, I am and have been and always wish to be alone."

"I have not heard of Monica."

"You wouldn't have. She's an Italian — by birth at least. She makes her living by journalism. I met her originally on Garda. Monica is much the best person to see me through."

"You are very fond of her, then."

"She has been extraordinarily sensible with me."

Margaret guessed at Monica's type — "Italiano inglesiato"° they had named it: the crude feminist of the South, whom one respects but avoids. And Helen had turned to it in her need!

"You must not think that we shall never meet," said Helen, with a measured kindness. "I shall always have a room for you when you can be spared, and the longer you can be with me the better. But you haven't understood yet, Meg, and of course it is very difficult for you. This is a shock to you. It isn't to me, who have been thinking over our futures for many months, and they won't be changed by a slight con-tretemps such as this. I cannot live in England."

"Helen, you've not forgiven me for my treachery. You *couldn't* talk like this to me if you had."

"Oh, Meg dear, why do we talk at all?" She dropped a book and sighed wearily. Then, recovering herself, she said: "Tell me, how is it that all the books are down here?"

---

"**Italiano inglesiato**": A variant on *inglese Italianato* (the Italianized Englishman), a suspect figure since the time of the Elizabethan dramatists.

"Series of mistakes."

"And a great deal of the furniture has been unpacked."

"All."

"Who lives here, then?"

"No one."

"I suppose you are letting it, though."

"The house is dead," said Margaret, with a frown. "Why worry on about it?"

"But I am interested. You talk as if I had lost all my interest in life. I am still Helen, I hope. Now this hasn't the feel of a dead house. The hall seems more alive even than in the old days, when it held the Wilcoxes' own things."

"Interested, are you? Very well, I must tell you, I suppose. My husband lent it on condition we — but by a mistake all our things were unpacked, and Miss Avery, instead of —" She stopped. "Look here, I can't go on like this. I warn you, I won't. Helen, why should you be so miserably unkind to me, simply because you hate Henry?"

"I don't hate him now," said Helen. "I have stopped being a schoolgirl, and, Meg, once again, I'm not being unkind. But as for fitting in with your English life — no, put it out of your head at once. Imagine a visit from me at Ducie Street! It's unthinkable."

Margaret could not contradict her. It was appalling to see her quietly moving forward with her plans, not bitter or excitable, neither asserting innocence nor confessing guilt, merely desiring freedom and the company of those who would not blame her. She had been through — how much? Margaret did not know. But it was enough to part her from old habits as well as old friends.

"Tell me about yourself," said Helen, who had chosen her books, and was lingering over the furniture.

"There's nothing to tell."

"But your marriage has been happy, Meg?"

"Yes, but I don't feel inclined to talk."

"You feel as I do."

"Not that, but I can't."

"No more can I. It is a nuisance, but no good trying."

Something had come between them. Perhaps it was society, which henceforward would exclude Helen. Perhaps it was a third life, already potent as a spirit. They could find no meeting-place. Both suffered acutely, and were not comforted by the knowledge that affection survived.

"Look here, Meg, is the coast clear?"

"You mean that you want to go away from me?"

"I suppose so — dear old lady! It isn't any use. I knew we should have nothing to say. Give my love to Aunt Juley and Tibby, and take more yourself than I can say. Promise to come and see me in Munich later."

"Certainly, dearest."

"For that is all we can do."

It seemed so. Most ghastly of all was Helen's common sense: Monica had been extraordinarily good for her.

"I am glad to have seen you and the things." She looked at the bookcase lovingly, as if she was saying farewell to the past.

Margaret unbolted the door. She remarked: "The car has gone, and here's your cab."

She led the way to it, glancing at the leaves and the sky. The spring had never seemed more beautiful. The driver, who was leaning on the gate, called out, "Please, lady, a message," and handed her Henry's visiting-card through the bars.

"How did this come?" she asked.

Crane had returned with it almost at once.

She read the card with annoyance. It was covered with instructions in domestic French. When she and her sister had talked she was to come back for the night to Dolly's. "Il faut dormir sur ce sujet." While Helen was to be found "une confortable chambre à l'hotel." The final sentence displeased her greatly until she remembered that the Charleses had only one spare room, and so could not invite a third guest.

"Henry would have done what he could," she interpreted.

Helen had not followed her into the garden. The door once open, she lost her inclination to fly. She remained in the hall, going from bookcase to table. She grew more like the old Helen, irresponsible and charming.

"This *is* Mr Wilcox's house?" she inquired.

"Surely you remember Howards End?"

"Remember? I who remember everything! But it looks to be ours now."

"Miss Avery was extraordinary," said Margaret, her own spirits lightening a little. Again she was invaded by a slight feeling of disloyalty. But it brought her relief, and she yielded to it. "She loved Mrs Wilcox, and would rather furnish her house with our things than think of it empty. In consequence here are all the library books."

"Not all the books. She hasn't unpacked the art books, in which she may show her sense. And we never used to have the sword here."

"The sword looks well, though."

"Magnificent."

"Yes, doesn't it?"

"Where's the piano, Meg?"

"I warehoused that in London. Why?"

"Nothing."

"Curious, too, that the carpet fits."

"The carpet's a mistake," announced Helen. "I know that we had it in London, but this floor ought to be bare. It is far too beautiful."

"You still have a mania for underfurnishing. Would you care to come into the dining-room before you start? There's no carpet there."

They went in, and each minute their talk became more natural.

"Oh, *what* a place for mother's chiffonier!" cried Helen.

"Look at the chairs, though."

"Oh, look at them! Wickham Place faced north, didn't it?"

"North-west."

"Anyhow, it is thirty years since any of those chairs have felt the sun. Feel. Their dear little backs are quite warm."

"But why has Miss Avery made them set to partners? I shall just —"

"Over here, Meg. Put it so that anyone sitting will see the lawn."

Margaret moved a chair. Helen sat down in it.

"Ye-es. The window's too high."

"Try a drawing-room chair."

"No, I don't like the drawing-room so much. The beam has been match-boarded. It would have been so beautiful otherwise."

"Helen, what a memory you have for some things! You're perfectly right. It's a room that men have spoilt through trying to make it nice for women. Men don't know what we want —"

"And never will."

"I don't agree. In two thousand years they'll know."

"But the chairs show up wonderfully. Look where Tibby spilt the soup."

"Coffee. It was coffee surely."

Helen shook her head. "Impossible. Tibby was far too young to be given coffee at that time."

"Was father alive?"

"Yes."

"Then you're right and it must have been soup. I was thinking of much later — that unsuccessful visit of Aunt Juley's, when she didn't realize that Tibby had grown up. It was coffee then, for he threw it down on purpose. There was some rhyme, 'Tea, coffee — coffee, tea,' that she said to him every morning at breakfast. Wait a minute — how did it go?"

"I know — no, I don't. What a detestable boy Tibby was!"

"But the rhyme was simply awful. No decent person could have put up with it."

"Ah, that greengage tree," cried Helen, as if the garden was also part of their childhood. "Why do I connect it with dumb-bells? And there come the chickens. The grass wants cutting. I love yellow-hammers —"°

Margaret interrupted her. "I have got it," she announced.

> "Tea, tea, coffee, tea,
> Or chocolaritee.

That every morning for three weeks. No wonder Tibby was wild."

"Tibby is moderately a dear now," said Helen.

"There! I knew you'd say that in the end. Of course he's a dear."

A bell rang.

"Listen! What's that?"

Helen said, "Perhaps the Wilcoxes are beginning the siege."

"What nonsense — listen!"

And the triviality faded from their faces, though it left something behind — the knowledge that they never could be parted because their love was rooted in common things. Explanations and appeals had failed; they had tried for a common meeting-ground, and had only made each other unhappy. And all the time their salvation was lying round them — the past sanctifying the present; the present, with wild heart-throb, declaring that there would after all be a future, with laughter and the voices of children. Helen, still smiling, came up to her sister. She said: "It is always Meg." They looked into each other's eyes. The inner life had paid.

Solemnly the clapper tolled. No one was in the front. Margaret went to the kitchen, and struggled between packing-cases to the window. Their visitor was only a little boy with a tin can. And triviality returned.

"Little boy, what do you want?"

"Please, I am the milk."

"Did Miss Avery send you?" said Margaret, rather sharply.

"Yes, please."

---

**yellowhammers**: Finches.

"Then take it back and say we require no milk." While she called to Helen: "No, it's not the siege, but possibly an attempt to provision us against one."

"But I like milk," cried Helen. "Why send it away?"

"Do you? Oh, very well. But we've nothing to put it in, and he wants the can."

"Please, I'm to call in the morning for the can," said the boy.

"The house will be locked up then."

"In the morning would I bring eggs, too?"

"Are you the boy whom I saw playing in the stacks last week?"

The child hung his head.

"Well, run away and do it again."

"Nice little boy," whispered Helen. "I say, what's your name? Mine's Helen."

"Tom."

That was Helen all over. The Wilcoxes, too, would ask a child its name, but they never told their names in return.

"Tom, this one here is Margaret. And at home we've another called Tibby."

"Mine are lop-eareds," replied Tom, supposing Tibby to be a rabbit.

"You're a very good and rather a clever little boy. Mind you come again — isn't he charming?"

"Undoubtedly," said Margaret. "He is probably the son of Madge, and Madge is dreadful. But this place has wonderful powers."

"What do you mean?"

"I don't know."

"Because I probably agree with you."

"It kills what is dreadful and makes what is beautiful live."

"I do agree," said Helen, as she sipped the milk. "But you said that the house was dead not half an hour ago."

"Meaning that I was dead. I felt it."

"Yes, the house has a surer life than we, even if it was empty, and, as it is, I can't get over that for thirty years the sun has never shone full on our furniture. After all, Wickham Place was a grave. Meg, I've a startling idea."

"What is it?"

"Drink some milk to steady you."

Margaret obeyed.

"No, I won't tell you yet," said Helen, "because you may laugh or be angry. Let's go upstairs first and give the rooms an airing."

They opened window after window, till the inside, too, was rustling to the spring. Curtains blew, picture frames tapped cheerfully. Helen uttered cries of excitement as she found this bed obviously in its right place, that in its wrong one. She was angry with Miss Avery for not having moved the wardrobes up. "Then one would see really." She admired the view. She was the Helen who had written the memorable letters four years ago. As they leant out, looking westward, she said: "About my idea. Couldn't you and I camp out in this house for the night?"

"I don't think we could well do that," said Margaret.

"Here are beds, tables, towels —"

"I know; but the house isn't supposed to be slept in, and Henry's suggestion was —"

"I require no suggestions. I shall not alter anything in my plans. But it would give me so much pleasure to have one night here with you. It will be something to look back on. Oh, Meg lovey, do let's!"

"But, Helen, my pet," said Margaret, "we can't without getting Henry's leave. Of course, he would give it, but you said yourself that you couldn't visit at Ducie Street now, and this is equally intimate."

"Ducie Street is his house. This is ours. Our furniture, our sort of people coming to the door. Do let us camp out, just one night, and Tom shall feed us on eggs and milk. Why not? It's a moon."

Margaret hesitated. "I feel Charles wouldn't like it," she said at last. "Even our furniture annoyed him, and I was going to clear it out when Aunt Juley's illness prevented me. I sympathize with Charles. He feels it's his mother's house. He loves it in rather an untaking way. Henry I could answer for — not Charles."

"I know he won't like it," said Helen. "But I am going to pass out of their lives. What difference will it make in the long run if they say, 'And she even spent the night at Howards End'?"

"How do you know you'll pass out of their lives? We have thought that twice before."

"Because my plans —"

"— which you change in a moment."

"Then because my life is great and theirs are little," said Helen, taking fire. "I know of things they can't know of, and so do you. We *know* that there's poetry. We *know* that there's death. They can only take them on hearsay. We know this is our house, because it feels ours. Oh, they may take the title-deeds and the door-keys, but for this one night we are at home."

"It would be lovely to have you once more alone," said Margaret. "It may be a chance in a thousand."

"Yes, and we could talk." She dropped her voice. "It won't be a very glorious story. But under that wych-elm — honestly, I see little happiness ahead. Cannot I have this one night with you?"

"I needn't say how much it would mean to me."

"Then let us."

"It is no good hesitating. Shall I drive down to Hilton now and get leave?"

"Oh, we don't want leave."

But Margaret was a loyal wife. In spite of imagination and poetry — perhaps on account of them — she could sympathize with the technical attitude that Henry would adopt. If possible, she would be technical, too. A night's lodging — and they demanded no more — need not involve the discussion of general principles.

"Charles may say no," grumbled Helen.

"We shan't consult him."

"Go if you like; I should have stopped without leave."

It was the touch of selfishness, which was not enough to mar Helen's character, and even added to its beauty. She would have stopped without leave, and escaped to Germany the next morning. Margaret kissed her.

"Expect me back before dark. I am looking forward to it so much. It is like you to have thought of such a beautiful thing."

"Not a thing, only an ending," said Helen rather sadly; and the sense of tragedy closed in on Margaret again as soon as she left the house.

She was afraid of Miss Avery. It is disquieting to fulfil a prophecy, however superficially. She was glad to see no watching figure as she drove past the farm, but only little Tom, turning somersaults in the straw.

## Chapter 38

The tragedy began quietly enough, and, like many another talk, by the man's deft assertion of his superiority. Henry heard her arguing with the driver, stepped out and settled the fellow, who was inclined to be rude, and then led the way to some chairs on the lawn. Dolly, who had not been "told", ran out with offers of tea. He refused them, and ordered her to wheel baby's perambulator away, as they desired to be alone.

"But the diddums can't listen; he isn't nine months old," she pleaded.

"That's not what I was saying," retorted her father-in-law.

Baby was wheeled out of earshot, and did not hear about the crisis till later years. It was now the turn of Margaret.

"Is it what we feared?" he asked.

"It is."

"Dear girl," he began, "there is a troublesome business ahead of us, and nothing but the most absolute honesty and plain speech will see us through." Margaret bent her head. "I am obliged to question you on subjects we'd both prefer to leave untouched. As you know, I am not one of your Bernard Shaws° who consider nothing sacred. To speak as I must will pain me, but there are occasions — we are husband and wife, not children. I am a man of the world, and you are a most exceptional woman."

All Margaret's senses forsook her. She blushed, and looked past him at the Six Hills, covered with spring herbage. Noting her colour, he grew still more kind.

"I see that you feel as I felt when — my poor little wife! Oh, be brave! Just one or two questions, and I have done with you. Was your sister wearing a wedding-ring?"

Margaret stammered a "No".

There was an appalling silence.

"Henry, I really came to ask a favour about Howards End."

"One point at a time. I am now obliged to ask for the name of her seducer."

She rose to her feet and held the chair between them. Her colour had ebbed, and she was gray. It did not displease him that she should receive his question thus.

"Take your time," he counselled her. "Remember that this is far worse for me than for you."

She swayed; he feared she was going to faint. Then speech came, and she said slowly: "Seducer? No; I do not know her seducer's name."

"Would she not tell you?"

"I never even asked her who seduced her," said Margaret, dwelling on the hateful word thoughtfully.

---

one of your Bernard Shaws: George Bernard Shaw (1856–1950), Irish dramatist known for his critique of conventional morality in plays such as *Mrs. Warren's Profession* (performed 1902).

"That is singular," Then he changed his mind. "Natural perhaps, dear girl, that you shouldn't ask. But until his name is known nothing can be done. Sit down. How terrible it is to see you so upset! I knew you weren't fit for it. I wish I hadn't taken you."

Margaret answered: "I like to stand, if you don't mind, for it gives me a pleasant view of the Six Hills."

"As you like."

"Have you anything else to ask me, Henry?"

"Next you must tell me whether you have gathered anything. I have often noticed your insight, dear. I only wish my own was as good. You may have guessed something, even though your sister said nothing. The slightest hint would help us."

"Who is 'we'?"

"I thought it best to ring up Charles."

"That was unnecessary," said Margaret, growing warmer. "This news will give Charles disproportionate pain."

"He has at once gone to call on your brother."

"That too was unnecessary."

"Let me explain, dear, how the matter stands. You don't think that I and my son are other than gentlemen? It is in Helen's interests that we are acting. It is still not too late to save her name."

Then Margaret hit out for the first time. "Are we to make her seducer marry her?" she asked.

"If possible. Yes."

"But, Henry, suppose he turned out to be married already? One has heard of such cases."

"In that case he must pay heavily for his misconduct, and be thrashed within an inch of his life."

So her first blow missed. She was thankful of it. What had tempted her to imperil both of their lives? Henry's obtuseness had saved her as well as himself. Exhausted with anger, she sat down again, blinking at him as he told her as much as he thought fit. At last she said: "May I ask you my question now?"

"Certainly, my dear."

"Tomorrow Helen goes to Munich —"

"Well, possibly she is right."

"Henry, let a lady finish. Tomorrow she goes; tonight, with your permission, she would like to sleep at Howards End."

It was the crisis of his life. Again she would have recalled the words as soon as they were uttered. She had not led up to them with

sufficient care. She longed to warn him that they were far more important than he supposed. She saw him weighing them, as if they were a
business proposition.

"Why Howards End?" he said at last. "Would she not be more
comfortable, as I suggested, at the hotel?"

Margaret hastened to give him reasons. "It is an odd request, but
you know what Helen is and what women in her state are." He
frowned, and moved irritably. "She has the idea that one night in your
house would give her pleasure and do her good. I think she's right.
Being one of those imaginative girls, the presence of all our books and
furniture soothes her. This is a fact. It is the end of her girlhood. Her
last words to me were 'A beautiful ending'."

"She values the old furniture for sentimental reasons, in fact."

"Exactly. You have quite understood. It is her last hope of being
with it."

"I don't agree there, my dear! Helen will have her share of the
goods wherever she goes — possibly more than her share, for you are
so fond of her that you'd give her anything of yours that she fancies,
wouldn't you? And I'd raise no objection. I could understand it if it
was her old home, because a home, or a house" — he changed the
word, designedly; he had thought of a telling point — "because a
house in which one has once lived becomes in a sort of way sacred, I
don't know why. Associations and so on. Now Helen has no associations with Howards End, though I and Charles and Evie have. I do not
see why she wants to stay the night there. She will only catch cold."

"Leave it that you don't see," cried Margaret. "Call it fancy. But
realize that fancy is a scientific fact. Helen is fanciful, and wants to."

Then he surprised her — a rare occurrence. He shot an unexpected bolt. "If she wants to sleep one night, she may want to sleep
two. We shall never get her out of the house, perhaps."

"Well?" said Margaret, with the precipice in sight. "And suppose
we don't get her out of the house? Would it matter? She would do no
one any harm."

Again the irritated gesture.

"No, Henry," she panted, receding. "I didn't mean that. We will
only trouble Howards End for this one night. I take her to London
tomorrow —"

"Do you intend to sleep in a damp house, too?"

"She cannot be left alone."

"That's quite impossible! Madness. You must be here to meet
Charles."

"I have already told you that your message to Charles was unnecessary, and I have no desire to meet him."

"Margaret — my Margaret —"

"What has this business to do with Charles? If it concerns me little, it concerns you less, and Charles not at all."

"As the future owner of Howards End," said Mr Wilcox, arching his fingers, "I should say that it did concern Charles."

"In what way? Will Helen's condition depreciate the property?"

"My dear, you are forgetting yourself."

"I think you yourself recommended plain speaking."

They looked at each other in amazement. The precipice was at their feet now.

"Helen commands my sympathy," said Henry. "As your husband, I shall do all for her that I can, and I have no doubt that she will prove more sinned against than sinning. But I cannot treat her as if nothing has happened. I should be false to my position in society if I did."

She controlled herself for the last time. "No, let us go back to Helen's request," she said. "It is unreasonable, but the request of an unhappy girl. Tomorrow she will go to Germany, and trouble society no longer. Tonight she asks to sleep in your empty house — a house which you do not care about, and which you have not occupied for over a year. May she? Will you give my sister leave? Will you forgive her — as you hope to be forgiven, and as you have actually been forgiven? Forgive her for one night only. That will be enough."

"As I have actually been forgiven — ?"

"Never mind for the moment what I mean by that," said Margaret. "Answer my question."

Perhaps some hint of her meaning did dawn on him. If so, he blotted it out. Straight from his fortress he answered: "I seem rather unaccommodating, but I have some experience of life, and know how one thing leads to another. I am afraid that your sister had better sleep at the hotel. I have my children and the memory of my dear wife to consider. I am sorry, but see that she leaves my house at once."

"You have mentioned Mrs Wilcox."

"I beg your pardon?"

"A rare occurrence. In reply, may I mention Mrs Bast?"

"You have not been yourself all day," said Henry, and rose from his seat with face unmoved. Margaret rushed at him and seized both his hands. She was transfigured.

"Not any more of this!" she cried. "You shall see the connection if it kills you, Henry! You have had a mistress — I forgave you. My sister has a lover — you drive her from the house. Do you see the connection? Stupid, hypocritical, cruel — oh, contemptible! — a man who insults his wife when she's alive and cants with her memory when she's dead. A man who ruins a woman for his pleasure, and casts her off to ruin other men. And gives bad financial advice, and then says he is not responsible. These men are you. You can't recognize them, because you cannot connect. I've had enough of your unweeded kindness. I've spoilt you long enough. All your life you have been spoilt. Mrs Wilcox spoiled you. No one has ever told you what you are — muddled, criminally muddled. Men like you use repentance as a blind, so don't repent. Only say to yourself: 'What Helen has done, I've done.'"

"The two cases are different," Henry stammered. His real retort was not quite ready. His brain was still in a whirl, and he wanted a little longer.

"In what way different? You have betrayed Mrs Wilcox, Helen only herself. You remain in society, Helen can't. You have had only pleasure, she may die. You have the insolence to talk to me of differences, Henry?"

Oh, the uselessness of it! Henry's retort came.

"I perceive you are attempting blackmail. It is scarcely a pretty weapon for a wife to use against her husband. My rule through life has been never to pay the least attention to threats, and I can only repeat what I said before: I do not give you and your sister leave to sleep at Howards End."

Margaret loosed his hands. He went into the house, wiping first one and then the other on his handkerchief. For a little she stood looking at the Six Hills, tombs of warriors, breasts of the spring. Then she passed out into what was now the evening.


## Chapter 39

Charles and Tibby met at Ducie Street, where the latter was staying. Their interview was short and absurd. They had nothing in common but the English language, and tried by its help to express what neither of them understood. Charles saw in Helen the family foe. He had singled her out as the most dangerous of the Schlegels, and, angry as he was, looked forward to telling his wife how right he had been. His mind was made up at once: the girl must be got out of the way before she disgraced them further. If occasion offered she might be married to a villain or, possibly, to a fool. But this was a concession to morality, it formed no part of his main scheme. Honest and hearty was

Charles's dislike, and the past spread itself out very clearly before him; hatred is a skilful compositor. As if they were heads in a notebook, he ran through all the incidents of the Schlegels' campaign: the attempt to compromise his brother, his mother's legacy, his father's marriage, the introduction of the furniture, the unpacking of the same. He had not yet heard of the request to sleep at Howards End; that was to be their master-stroke and the opportunity for his. But he already felt that Howards End was the objective, and, though he disliked the house, was determined to defend it.

Tibby, on the other hand, had no opinions. He stood above the conventions; his sister had a right to do what she thought right. It is not difficult to stand above the conventions when we leave no hostages among them; men can always be more unconventional than women, and a bachelor of independent means need encounter no difficulties at all. Unlike Charles, Tibby had money enough; his ancestors had earned it for him, and if he shocked the people in one set of lodgings he had only to move into another. His was the leisure without sympathy — an attitude as fatal as the strenuous: a little cold culture may be raised on it, but no art. His sisters had seen the family danger, and had never forgotten to discount the gold islets that raised them from the sea. Tibby gave all the praise to himself, and so despised the struggling and the submerged.

Hence the absurdity of the interview; the gulf between them was economic as well as spiritual. But several facts passed; Charles pressed for them with an impertinence that the undergraduate could not withstand. On what date had Helen gone abroad? To whom? (Charles was anxious to fasten the scandal on Germany.) Then, changing his tactics, he said roughly: "I suppose you realize that you are your sister's protector?"

"In what sense?"

"If a man played about with my sister, I'd send a bullet through him, but perhaps you don't mind."

"I mind very much," protested Tibby.

"Who d'ye suspect, then? Speak out, man. One always suspects someone."

"No one. I don't think so." Involuntarily he blushed. He had remembered the scene in his Oxford rooms.

"You are hiding something," said Charles. As interviews go, he got the best of this one. "When you saw her last, did she mention anyone's name? Yes or no!" he thundered, so that Tibby started.

"In my rooms she mentioned some friends called the Basts —"

"Who are the Basts?"

"People — friends of hers at Evie's wedding."

"I don't remember. But, by great Scott! I do. My aunt told me about some tagrag. Was she full of them when you saw her? Is there a man? Did she speak of the man? Or — look here — have you had any dealings with him?"

Tibby was silent. Without intending it, he had betrayed his sister's confidence; he was not enough interested in human life to see where things will lead to. He had a strong regard for honesty, and his word, once given, had always been kept up to now. He was deeply vexed, not only for the harm he had done Helen, but for the flaw he had discovered in his own equipment.

"I see — you are in his confidence. They met at your rooms. Oh, what a family, what a family! God help the poor pater —"

And Tibby found himself alone.

## Chapter 40

Leonard — he would figure at length in a newspaper report, but that evening he did not count for much. The foot of the tree was in shadow, since the moon was still hidden behind the house. But above, to right, to left, down the long meadow the moonlight was streaming. Leonard seemed not a man, but a cause.

Perhaps it was Helen's way of falling in love — a curious way to Margaret, whose agony and whose contempt of Henry were yet imprinted with his image. Helen forgot people. They were husks that had enclosed her emotion. She could pity, or sacrifice herself, or have instincts, but had she ever loved in the noblest way, where man and woman, having lost themselves in sex, desire to lose sex itself in comradeship?

Margaret wondered, but said no word of blame. This was Helen's evening. Troubles enough lay ahead of her — the loss of friends and social advantages, the agony, the supreme agony, of motherhood, which is even yet not a matter of common knowledge. For the present let the moon shine brightly and the breezes of the spring blow gently, dying away from the gale of the day, and let the earth, who brings increase, bring peace. Not even to herself dare she blame Helen. She could not assess her trespass by any moral code; it was everything or nothing. Morality can tell us that murder is worse than stealing, and group most sins in an order all must approve, but it cannot group Helen. The surer its pronouncements on this point, the surer may we be that morality is not speaking. Christ was evasive when they questioned Him. It is those that cannot connect who hasten to cast the first stone.

This was Helen's evening — won at what cost, and not to be marred by the sorrows of others. Of her own tragedy Margaret never uttered a word.

"One isolates," said Helen slowly. "I isolated Mr Wilcox from the other forces that were pulling Leonard downhill. Consequently, I was full of pity, and almost of revenge. For weeks I had blamed Mr Wilcox only, and so, when your letters came —"

"I need never have written them," sighed Margaret. "They never shielded Henry. How hopeless it is to tidy away the past, even for others!"

"I did not know that it was your own idea to dismiss the Basts."

"Looking back, that was wrong of me."

"Looking back, darling, I know that it was right. It is right to save the man whom one loves. I am less enthusiastic about justice now. But we both thought you wrote at his dictation. It seemed the last touch of his callousness. Being very much wrought up by this time — and Mrs Bast was upstairs. I had not seen her, and had talked for a long time to Leonard — I had snubbed him for no reason, and that should have warned me I was in danger. So when the notes came I wanted us to go to you for an explanation. He said that he guessed the explanation — he knew of it, and you mustn't know. I pressed him to tell me. He said no one must know; it was something to do with his wife. Right up to the end we were Mr Bast and Miss Schlegel. I was going to tell him that he must be frank with me when I saw his eyes, and guessed that Mr Wilcox had ruined him in two ways, not one. I drew him to me. I made him tell me. I felt very lonely myself. He is not to blame. He would have gone on worshipping me. I want never to see him again, though it sounds appalling. I wanted to give him money and feel finished. Oh, Meg, the little that is known about these things!"

She laid her face against the tree.

"The little, too, that is known about growth! Both times it was loneliness, and the night, and panic afterwards. Did Leonard grow out of Paul?"

Margaret did not speak for a moment. So tired was she that her attention had actually wandered to the teeth — the teeth that had been thrust into the tree's bark to medicate it. From where she sat she could see them gleam. She had been trying to count them. "Leonard is a better growth than madness," she said. "I was afraid that you would react against Paul until you went over the verge."

"I did react until I found poor Leonard. I am steady now. I shan't ever *like* your Henry, dearest Meg, or even speak kindly about him, but all that blinding hate is over. I shall never rave against Wilcoxes any more. I understand how you married him, and you will now be very happy."

Margaret did not reply.

"Yes," repeated Helen, her voice growing more tender, "I do at last understand."

"Except Mrs Wilcox, dearest, no one understands our little movements."

"Because in death — I agree."

"Not quite. I feel that you and I and Henry are only fragments of that woman's mind. She knows everything. She is everything. She is the house, and the tree that leans over it. People have their own deaths as well as their own lives, and even if there is nothing beyond death we shall differ in our nothingness. I cannot believe that knowledge such as hers will perish with knowledge such as mine. She knew about realities. She knew when people were in love, though she was not in the room. I don't doubt that she knew when Henry deceived her."

"Good night, Mrs Wilcox," called a voice.

"Oh, good night, Miss Avery."

"Why should Miss Avery work for us?" Helen murmured.

"Why, indeed?"

Miss Avery crossed the lawn and merged into the hedge that divided it from the farm. An old gap, which Mr Wilcox had filled up, had reappeared, and her track through the dew followed the path that he had turfed over, when he improved the garden and made it possible for games.

"This is not quite our house yet," said Helen. "When Miss Avery called, I felt we are only a couple of tourists."

"We shall be that everywhere, and for ever."

"But affectionate tourists —"

"But tourists who pretend each hotel is their home."

"I can't pretend very long," said Helen. "Sitting under this tree one forgets, but I know that tomorrow I shall see the moon rise out of Germany. Not all your goodness can alter the facts of the case. Unless you will come with me."

Margaret thought for a moment. In the past year she had grown so fond of England that to leave it was a real grief. Yet what detained

her? No doubt Henry would pardon her outburst, and go on blustering and muddling into a ripe old age. But what was the good? She had
just as soon vanish from his mind.

"Are you serious in asking me, Helen? Should I get on with your
Monica?"

"You would not, but I am serious in asking you."

"Still, no more plans now. And no more reminiscences."

They were silent for a little. It was Helen's evening.

The present flowed by them like a stream. The tree rustled. It had
made music before they were born, and would continue after their
deaths, but its song was of the moment. The moment had passed. The
tree rustled again. Their senses were sharpened, and they seemed to
apprehend life. Life passed. The tree rustled again.

"Sleep now," said Margaret.

The peace of the country was entering into her. It has no com-
merce with memory, and little with hope. Least of all is it concerned
with the hopes of the next five minutes. It is the peace of the present,
which passes understanding. Its murmur came "now", and "now"
once more as they trod the gravel, and "now" as the moonlight fell
upon their father's sword. They passed upstairs, kissed, and amidst the
endless iterations fell asleep. The house had enshadowed the tree at
first, but as the moon rose higher the two disentangled, and were clear
for a few moments at midnight. Margaret awoke and looked into the
garden. How incomprehensible that Leonard Bast should have won
her this night of peace! Was he also part of Mrs Wilcox's mind?

## Chapter 41

Far different was Leonard's development. The months after Oniton, whatever minor troubles they might bring him, were all overshadowed by Remorse. When Helen looked back she could philosophize,
or she could look into the future and plan for her child. But the father
saw nothing beyond his own sin. Weeks afterwards, in the midst of
other occupations, he would suddenly cry out, "Brute — you brute, I
couldn't have —" and be rent into two people who held dialogues. Or
brown rain would descend, blotting out faces and the sky. Even Jacky
noticed the change in him. Most terrible were his sufferings when he
awoke from sleep. Sometimes he was happy at first, but grew conscious of a burden hanging to him and weighing down his thoughts
when they would move. Or little irons scorched his body. Or a sword
stabbed him. He would sit at the edge of his bed, holding his heart

and moaning, "Oh, what *shall* I do, what ever *shall* I do?" Nothing brought ease. He could put distance between him and the trespass, but it grew in his soul.

Remorse is not among the eternal verities. The Greeks were right to dethrone her. Her action is too capricious, as though the Erinyes° selected for punishment only certain men and certain sins. And of all means to regeneration Remorse is surely the most wasteful. It cuts away healthy tissues with the poisoned. It is a knife that probes far deeper than the evil. Leonard was driven straight through its torments and emerged pure, but enfeebled — a better man, who would never lose control of himself again, but also a smaller man, who had less to control. Nor did purity mean peace. The use of the knife can become a habit as hard to shake off as passion itself, and Leonard continued to start with a cry out of dreams.

He built up a situation that was far enough from the truth. It never occurred to him that Helen was to blame. He forgot the intensity of their talk, the charm that had been lent him by sincerity, the magic of Oniton under darkness and of the whispering river. Helen loved the absolute. Leonard had been ruined absolutely, and had appeared to her as a man apart, isolated from the world. A real man, who cared for adventure and beauty, who desired to live decently and pay his way, who could have travelled more gloriously through life than the Juggernaut car that was crushing him. Memories of Evie's wedding had warped her, the starched servants, the yards of uneaten food, the rustle of overdressed women, motor-cars oozing grease on the gravel, rubbish from a pretentious band. She had tasted the lees of this on her arrival; in the darkness, after failure, they intoxicated her. She and the victim seemed alone in a world of unreality, and she loved him absolutely, perhaps for half an hour.

In the morning she was gone. The note that she left, tender and hysterical in tone, and intended to be most kind, hurt her lover terribly. It was as if some work of art had been broken by him, some picture in the National Gallery slashed out of its frame.° When he recalled her talents and her social position, he felt that the first passer-by had a right to shoot him down. He was afraid of the waitress and the porters

---

the **Erinyes:** Avenging deities (or furies) in Greek myth who brought retribution on those who violated norms of natural piety and hospitality or who were guilty of perjury or homicide.     **some picture . . . slashed:** As Velázquez's *Venus at Her Mirror* ("the Rokeby Venus") was slashed in seven places by a suffragette in 1914.

at the railway station. He was afraid at first of his wife, though later he was to regard her with a strange new tenderness, and to think: "There is nothing to choose between us, after all."

The expedition to Shropshire crippled the Basts permanently. Helen in her flight forgot to settle the hotel bill, and took their return tickets away with her; they had to pawn Jacky's bangles to get home, and the smash came a few days afterwards. It is true that Helen offered him five thousand pounds, but such a sum meant nothing to him. He could not see that the girl was desperately righting herself, and trying to save something out of the disaster, if it was only five thousand pounds. But he had to live somehow. He turned to his family, and degraded himself to a professional beggar. There was nothing else for him to do.

"A letter from Leonard," thought Blanche, his sister; "and after all this time." She hid it, so that her husband should not see, and when he had gone to his work read it with some emotion, and sent the prodigal a little money out of her dress allowance.

"A letter from Leonard!" said the other sister, Laura, a few days later. She showed it to her husband. He wrote a cruel, insolent reply, but sent more money than Blanche, so Leonard soon wrote to him again.

And during the winter the system was developed. Leonard realized that they need never starve, because it would be too painful for his relatives. Society is based on the family, and the clever wastrel can exploit this indefinitely. Without a generous thought on either side, pounds and pounds passed. The donors disliked Leonard, and he grew to hate them intensely. When Laura censured his immoral marriage, he thought bitterly: "She minds that! What would she say if she knew the truth?" When Blanche's husband offered him work, he found some pretext for avoiding it. He had wanted work keenly at Oniton, but too much anxiety had shattered him, he was joining the unemployable. When his brother, the lay-reader, did not reply to a letter, he wrote again, saying that he and Jacky would come down to his village on foot. He did not intend this as blackmail. Still, the brother sent a postal order, and it became part of the system. And so passed his winter and his spring.

In the horror there are two bright spots. He never confused the past. He remained alive, and blessed are those who live, if it is only to a sense of sinfulness. The anodyne of muddledom, by which most men blur and blend their mistakes, never passed Leonard's lips —

> And if I drink oblivion of a day,
> So shorten I the stature of my soul.°

It is a hard saying, and a hard man wrote it, but it lies at the root of all character.

And the other bright spot was his tenderness for Jacky. He pitied her with nobility now — not the contemptuous pity of a man who sticks to a woman through thick and thin. He tried to be less irritable. He wondered what her hungry eyes desired — nothing that she could express, or that he or any man could give her. Would she ever receive the justice that is mercy — the justice for by-products that the world is too busy to bestow? She was fond of flowers, generous with money, and not revengeful. If she had borne him a child he might have cared for her. Unmarried, Leonard would never have begged; he would have flickered out and died. But the whole of life is mixed. He had to provide for Jacky, and went down dirty paths that she might have a few feathers and the dishes of food that suited her.

One day he caught sight of Margaret and her brother. He was in St Paul's. He had entered the cathedral partly to avoid the rain and partly to see a picture that had educated him in former years.° But the light was bad, the picture ill-placed, and Time and Judgement were inside him now. Death alone still charmed him, with her lap of poppies, on which all men shall sleep. He took one glance, and turned aimlessly away towards a chair. Then down the nave he saw Miss Schlegel and her brother. They stood in the fairway of passengers, and their faces were extremely grave. He was perfectly certain that they were in trouble about their sister.

Once outside — and he fled immediately — he wished that he had spoken to them. What was his life? What were a few angry words, or even imprisonment? He had done wrong — that was the true terror. Whatever they might know, he would tell them everything he knew. He re-entered St Paul's. But they had moved in his absence, and had gone to lay their difficulties before Mr Wilcox and Charles.

The sight of Margaret turned remorse into new channels. He desired to confess, and though the desire is proof of a weakened nature, which is about to lose the essence of human intercourse, it did not take an ignoble form. He did not suppose that confession would bring

---

**"And if I drink . . . soul"**: From sonnet 12 of *Modern Love* (1862) by George Meredith (1828–1909).    **a picture that had educated him in former years**: *Time, Death, and Judgment* (1866) by George Frederick Watts (1817–1904). See the note on p. 59.

him happiness. It was rather that he yearned to get clear of the tangle. So does the suicide yearn. The impulses are akin, and the crime of suicide lies rather in its disregard for the feelings of those whom we leave behind. Confession need harm no one — it can satisfy that test — and though it was un-English, and ignored by our Anglican cathedral, Leonard had a right to decide upon it.

Moreover, he trusted Margaret. He wanted her hardness now. That cold, intellectual nature of hers would be just, if unkind. He would do whatever she told him, even if he had to see Helen. That was the supreme punishment she could exact. And perhaps she would tell him how Helen was. That was the supreme reward.

He knew nothing about Margaret, not even whether she was married to Mr Wilcox, and tracking her out took several days. That evening he toiled through the wet to Wickham Place, where the new flats were now appearing. Was he also the cause of their move? Were they expelled from society on his account? Thence to a public library, but could find no satisfactory Schlegel in the directory. On the morrow he searched again. He hung about outside Mr Wilcox's office at lunch-time, and, as the clerks came out said: "Excuse me, sir, but is your boss married?" Most of them stared, some said, "What's that to you?" but one, who had not yet acquired reticence, told him what he wished. Leonard could not learn the private address. That necessitated more trouble with directories and tubes. Ducie Street was not discovered till the Monday, the day that Margaret and her husband went down on their hunting expedition to Howards End.

He called at about four o'clock. The weather had changed, and the sun shone gaily on the ornamental steps — black and white marble in triangles. Leonard lowered his eyes to them after ringing the bell. He felt in curious health: doors seemed to be opening and shutting inside his body, and he had been obliged to sleep sitting up in bed, with his back propped against the wall. When the parlourmaid came he could not see her face; the brown rain had descended suddenly.

"Does Mrs Wilcox live here?" he asked.

"She's out," was the answer.

"When will she be back?"

"I'll ask," said the parlourmaid.

Margaret had given instructions that no one who mentioned her name should ever be rebuffed. Putting the door on the chain — for Leonard's appearance demanded this — she went through to the smoking-room, which was occupied by Tibby. Tibby was asleep. He had had a good lunch. Charles Wilcox had not yet rung him up for the distracting interview. He said drowsily: "I don't know. Hilton. Howards End. Who is it?"

"I'll ask, sir."

"No, don't bother."

"They have taken the car to Howards End," said the parlourmaid to Leonard.

He thanked her, and asked whereabouts that place was.

"You appear to want to know a good deal," she remarked. But Margaret had forbidden her to be mysterious. She told him against her better judgement that Howards End was in Hertfordshire.

"Is it a village, please?"

"Village! It's Mr Wilcox's private house — at least, it's one of them. Mrs Wilcox keeps her furniture there. Hilton is the village."

"Yes. And when will they be back?"

"Mr Schlegel doesn't know. We can't know everything, can we?" She shut him out, and went to attend to the telephone, which was ringing furiously.

He loitered away another night of agony. Confession grew more difficult. As soon as possible he went to bed. He watched a patch of moonlight cross the floor of their lodging, and, as sometimes happens when the mind is overtaxed, he fell asleep for the rest of the room, but kept awake for the patch of moonlight. Horrible! Then began one of those disintegrating dialogues. Part of him said: "Why horrible? It's ordinary light from the moon." "But it moves." "So does the moon." "But it is a clenched fist." "Why not?" "But it is going to touch me." "Let it." And, seeming to gather motion, the patch ran up his blanket. Presently a blue snake appeared; then another, parallel to it. "Is there life in the moon?" "Of course." "But I thought it was uninhabited." "Not by Time, Death, Judgement and the smaller snakes." "Smaller snakes!" said Leonard indignantly and aloud. "What a notion!" By a rending effort of the will he woke the rest of the room up. Jacky, the bed, their food, their clothes on the chair, gradually entered his consciousness, and the horror vanished outwards, like a ring that is spreading through water.

"I say, Jacky, I'm going out for a bit."

She was breathing regularly. The patch of light fell clear of the striped blanket, and began to cover the shawl that lay over her feet. Why had he been afraid? He went to the window, and saw that the moon was descending through a clear sky. He saw her volcanoes, and the bright expanses that a gracious error has named seas. They paled, for the sun, who had lit them up, was coming to light the earth. Sea of

Serenity, Sea of Tranquillity, Ocean of the Lunar Storms, merged into one lucent drop, itself to slip into the sempiternal dawn. And he had been afraid of the moon!

He dressed among the contending lights, and went through his money. It was running low again, but enough for a return ticket to Hilton. As it clinked Jacky opened her eyes.

"Hullo, Len! What ho, Len!"

"What ho, Jacky! See you again later."

She turned over and slept.

The house was unlocked, their landlord being a salesman at Covent Garden. Leonard passed out and made his way down to the station. The train, though it did not start for an hour, was already drawn up at the end of the platform, and he lay down in it and slept. With the first jolt he was in daylight; they had left the gateways of King's Cross, and were under blue sky. Tunnels followed, and after each the sky grew bluer, and from the embankment at Finsbury Park he had his first sight of the sun. It rolled along behind the eastern smokes — a wheel, whose fellow was the descending moon — and as yet it seemed the servant of the blue sky, not its lord. He dozed again. Over Tewin Water it was day. To the left fell the shadow of the embankment and its arches; to the right Leonard saw up into the Tewin woods and towards the church, with its wild legend of immortality.° Six forest trees — that is a fact — grow out of one of the graves in Tewin churchyard. The grave's occupant — that is the legend — is an atheist, who declared that if God existed six forest trees would grow out of her grave. These things in Hertfordshire; and further afield lay the house of a hermit — Mrs Wilcox had known him — who barred himself up, and wrote prophecies, and gave all he had to the poor. While, powdered in between, were the villas of businessmen, who saw life more steadily, though with the steadiness of the half-closed eye. Over all the sun was streaming, to all the birds were singing, to all the primroses were yellow, and the speedwell blue, and the country, however they interpreted her, was uttering her cry of "now". She did not free Leonard yet, and the knife plunged deeper into his heart as the train drew up at Hilton. But remorse had become beautiful.

Hilton was asleep or, at the earliest, breakfasting. Leonard noticed

---

the church, with its wild legend of immortality: The "atheist" of the legend, as Stallybrass notes, was Lady Anne Grimston, who died in 1710; the "hermit," as Margaret Ashby notes in *Forster Country* (Stevenage: Flaunden, 1991), was James Lucas (1813–1874), a hermit who lived on the outskirts of Stevenage and was once visited by Dickens.

the contrast when he stepped out of it into the country. Here men had been up since dawn. Their hours were ruled, not by a London office, but by the movements of the crops and the sun. That they were men of the finest type only the sentimentalist can declare. But they kept to the life of daylight. They are England's hope. Clumsily they carry forward the torch of the sun, until such time as the nation sees fit to take it up. Half clodhopper, half board-school prig, they can still throw back to a nobler stock, and breed yeomen.

At the chalk-pit a motor passed him. In it was another type whom Nature favours — the Imperial. Healthy, ever in motion, it hopes to inherit the earth. It breeds as quickly as the yeoman, and as soundly; strong is the temptation to acclaim it as a super-yeoman, who carries his country's virtue overseas. But the Imperialist is not what he thinks or seems. He is a destroyer. He prepares the way for cosmopolitanism, and though his ambitions may be fulfilled the earth that he inherits will be gray.

To Leonard, intent on his private sin, there came the conviction of innate goodness elsewhere. It was not the optimism which he had been taught at school. Again and again must the drums tap and the goblins stalk over the universe before joy can be purged of the superficial. It was rather paradoxical, and arose from his sorrow. Death destroys a man, but the idea of death saves him — that is the best account of it that has yet been given. Squalor and tragedy can beckon to all that is great in us, and strengthen the wings of love. They can beckon; it is not certain that they will, for they are not love's servants. But they can beckon, and the knowledge of this incredible truth comforted him.

As he approached the house all thought stopped. Contradictory notions stood side by side in his mind. He was terrified but happy, ashamed, but had done no sin. He knew the confession: "Mrs Wilcox, I have done wrong," but sunrise had robbed its meaning, and he felt rather on a supreme adventure.

He entered a garden, steadied himself against a motor-car that he found in it, found a door open and entered a house. Yes, it would be very easy. From a room to the left he heard voices, Margaret's amongst them. His own name was called aloud, and a man whom he had never seen said, "Oh, is he there? I am not surprised. I now thrash him within an inch of his life."

"Mrs Wilcox," said Leonard, "I have done wrong."

The man took him by the collar and cried, "Bring me a stick." Women were screaming. A stick, very bright, descended. It hurt him, not where it descended, but in the heart. Books fell over him in a shower. Nothing had sense.

"Get some water," commanded Charles, who had all through kept very calm. "He's shamming. Of course I only used the blade. Here, carry him out into the air."

Thinking that he understood these things, Margaret obeyed him. They laid Leonard, who was dead, on the gravel; Helen poured water over him.

"That's enough," said Charles.

"Yes, murder's enough," said Miss Avery, coming out of the house with the sword.

## Chapter 42

When Charles left Ducie Street he had caught the first train home, but had no inkling of the newest development until late at night. Then his father, who had dined alone, sent for him, and in very grave tones inquired for Margaret.

"I don't know where she is, pater," said Charles. "Dolly kept back dinner nearly an hour for her."

"Tell me when she comes in."

Another hour passed. The servants went to bed, and Charles visited his father again, to receive further instructions. Mrs Wilcox had still not returned.

"I'll sit up for her as late as you like, but she can hardly be coming. Isn't she stopping with her sister at the hotel?"

"Perhaps," said Mr Wilcox thoughtfully — "perhaps."

"Can I do anything for you, sir?"

"Not tonight, my boy."

Mr Wilcox liked being called sir. He raised his eyes and gave his son more open a look of tenderness than he usually ventured. He saw Charles as little boy and strong man in one. Though his wife had proved unstable his children were left to him.

After midnight he tapped on Charles's door. "I can't sleep," he said. "I had better have a talk with you and get it over."

He complained of the heat. Charles took him out into the garden, and they paced up and down in their dressing-gowns. Charles became very quiet as the story unrolled; he had known all along that Margaret was as bad as her sister.

"She will feel differently in the morning," said Mr Wilcox, who had of course said nothing about Mrs Bast. "But I cannot let this kind of thing continue without comment. I am morally certain that she is with her sister at Howards End. The house is mine — and, Charles, it will be yours — and when I say that no one is to live there I mean that no one is to live there. I won't have it." He looked angrily at the moon. "To my mind this question is connected with something far greater, the rights of property itself."

"Undoubtedly," said Charles.

Mr Wilcox linked his arm in his son's, but somehow liked him less as he told him more. "I don't want you to conclude that my wife and I had anything of the nature of a quarrel. She was only overwrought, as who would not be? I shall do what I can for Helen, but on the understanding that they clear out of the house at once. Do you see? That is a *sine qua non.*"

"Then at eight tomorrow I may go up in the car?"

"Eight or earlier. Say that you are acting as my representative, and, of course, use no violence, Charles."

On the morrow, as Charles returned, leaving Leonard dead upon the gravel, it did not seem to him that he had used violence. Death was due to heart-disease. His stepmother herself had said so, and even Miss Avery had acknowledged that he only used the flat of the sword. On his way through the village he informed the police, who thanked him, and said there must be an inquest. He found his father in the garden shading his eyes from the sun.

"It has been pretty horrible," said Charles gravely. "They were there, and they had the man up there with them too."

"What — what man?"

"I told you last night. His name was Bast."

"My God! Is it possible?" said Mr Wilcox. "In your mother's house! Charles, in your mother's house!"

"I know, pater. That was what I felt. As a matter of fact, there is no need to trouble about the man. He was in the last stages of heart-disease, and just before I could show him what I thought of him he went off. The police are seeing about it at this moment."

Mr Wilcox listened attentively.

"I got up there — oh, it couldn't have been more than half past seven. The Avery woman was lighting a fire for them. They were still upstairs. I waited in the drawing-room. We were all moderately civil and collected, though I had my suspicions. I gave them your message, and Mrs Wilcox said, 'Oh yes, I see; yes,' in that way of hers."

"Nothing else?"

"I promised to tell you, 'with her love', that she was going to Germany with her sister this evening. That was all we had time for."

Mr Wilcox seemed relieved.

"Because by then I suppose the man got tired of hiding, for suddenly Mrs Wilcox screamed out his name. I recognized it, and went for him in the hall. Was I right, pater? I thought things were going a little too far."

"Right, my dear boy? I don't know. But you would have been no son of mine if you hadn't. Then did he just — just — crumple up as you said?" He shrank from the simple word.

"He caught hold of the bookcase, which came down over him. So I merely put the sword down and carried him into the garden. We all thought he was shamming. However, he's dead right enough. Awful business!"

"Sword?" cried his father, with anxiety in his voice. "What sword? Whose sword?"

"A sword of theirs."

"What were you doing with it?"

"Well, didn't you see, pater, I had to snatch up the first thing handy. I hadn't a riding-whip or stick. I caught him once or twice over the shoulders with the flat of their old German sword."

"Then what?"

"He pulled over the bookcase, as I said, and fell," said Charles, with a sigh. It was no fun doing errands for his father, who was never quite satisfied.

"But the real cause was heart-disease? Of that you're sure?"

"That or a fit. However, we shall hear more than enough at the inquest on such unsavoury topics."

They went in to breakfast. Charles had a racking headache, consequent on motoring before food. He was also anxious about the future, reflecting that the police must detain Helen and Margaret for the inquest and ferret the whole thing out. He saw himself obliged to leave Hilton. One could not afford to live near the scene of a scandal — it was not fair on one's wife. His comfort was that the pater's eyes were opened at last. There would be a horrible smash-up, and probably a separation from Margaret; then they would all start again, more as they had been in his mother's time.

"I think I'll go round to the police-station," said his father when breakfast was over.

"What for?" cried Dolly, who had still not been "told".

"Very well, sir. Which car will you have?"

"I think I'll walk."

"It's a good half-mile," said Charles, stepping into the garden. "The sun's very hot for April. Shan't I take you up, and then, perhaps, a little spin round by Tewin?"

"You go on as if I didn't know my own mind," said Mr Wilcox fretfully. Charles hardened his mouth. "You young fellows' one idea is to get into a motor. I tell you, I want to walk; I'm very fond of walking."

"Oh, all right; I'm about the house if you want me for anything. I thought of not going up to the office today, if that is your wish."

"It is, indeed, my boy," said Mr Wilcox, and laid a hand on his sleeve.

Charles did not like it; he was uneasy about his father, who did not seem himself this morning. There was a petulant touch about him — more like a woman. Could it be that he was growing old? The Wilcoxes were not lacking in affection; they had it royally, but they did not know how to use it. It was the talent in the napkin, and, for a warm-hearted man, Charles had conveyed very little joy. As he watched his father shuffling up the road, he had a vague regret — a wish that something had been different somewhere — a wish (though he did not express it thus) that he had been taught to say "I" in his youth. He meant to make up for Margaret's defection, but knew that his father had been very happy with her until yesterday. How had she done it? By some dishonest trick, no doubt — but how?

Mr Wilcox reappeared at eleven, looking very tired. There was to be an inquest on Leonard's body tomorrow, and the police required his son to attend.

"I expected that," said Charles. "I shall naturally be the most important witness there."


## Chapter 43

Out of the turmoil and horror that had begun with Aunt Juley's illness and was not even to end with Leonard's death, it seemed impossible to Margaret that healthy life should re-emerge. Events succeeded in a logical, yet senseless, train. People lost their humanity, and took values as arbitrary as those in a pack of playing-cards. It was natural that Henry should do this and cause Helen to do that, and then think her wrong for doing it; natural that she herself should think him wrong; natural that Leonard should want to know how Helen was, and come, and Charles be angry with him for coming — natural, but unreal. In this jangle of causes and effects what had become of their true selves? Here Leonard lay dead in the garden, from natural causes; yet life was a deep, deep river, death a blue sky, life was a house, death a wisp of hay, a flower, a tower, life and death were anything and everything, except this ordered insanity, where the king takes the queen, and the ace the king. Ah, no; there was beauty and adventure behind, such as the man at her feet had yearned for; there was hope this side of the grave; there were truer relationships beyond the limits that fetter us now. As a prisoner looks up and sees stars beckoning, so she, from the turmoil and horror of those days, caught glimpses of the diviner wheels.

And Helen, dumb with fright, but trying to keep calm for the child's sake, and Miss Avery, calm, but murmuring tenderly, "No one ever told the lad he'll have a child" — they also reminded her that horror is not the end. To what ultimate harmony we tend she did not know, but there seemed great chance that a child would be born into the world, to take the great chances of beauty and adventure that the world offers. She moved through the sunlit garden, gathering narcissi, crimson-eyed and white. There was nothing else to be done; the time for telegrams and anger was over, and it seemed wisest that the hands of Leonard should be folded on his breast and be filled with flowers. Here was the father; leave it at that. Let squalor be turned into tragedy, whose eyes are the stars, and whose hands hold the sunset and the dawn.

And even the influx of officials, even the return of the doctor, vulgar and acute, could not shake her belief in the eternity of beauty. Science explained people, but could not understand them. After long centuries among the bones and muscles it might be advancing to knowledge of the nerves, but this would never give understanding. One could open the heart to Mr Mansbridge and his sort without discovering its secrets to them, for they wanted everything down in black and white, and black and white was exactly what they were left with.

They questioned her closely about Charles. She never suspected why. Death had come, and the doctor agreed that it was due to heart-disease. They asked to see her father's sword. She explained that Charles's anger was natural, but mistaken. Miserable questions about Leonard followed, all of which she answered unfalteringly. Then back to Charles again. "No doubt Mr Wilcox may have induced death," she said; "but if it wasn't one thing it would have been another, as you yourselves know." At last they thanked her, and took the sword and the body down to Hilton. She began to pick up the books from the floor.

Helen had gone to the farm. It was the best place for her, since she had to wait for the inquest. Though, as if things were not hard enough, Madge and her husband had raised trouble; they did not see why they should receive the offscourings of Howards End. And, of course, they were right. The whole world was going to be right, and amply avenge any brave talk against the conventions. "Nothing matters," the Schlegels had said in the past, "except one's self-respect and that of one's friends." When the time came, other things mattered terribly. However, Madge had yielded, and Helen was assured of peace for one day and night, and tomorrow she would return to Germany.

As for herself, she determined to go too. No message came from Henry; perhaps he expected her to apologize. Now that she had time to think over her own tragedy, she was unrepentant. She neither forgave him for his behaviour nor wished to forgive him. Her speech to him seemed perfect. She would not have altered a word. It had to be uttered once in a life, to adjust the lopsidedness of the world. It was spoken not only to her husband, but to thousands of men like him — a protest against the inner darkness in high places that comes with a commercial age. Though he would build up his life without her, she could not apologize. He had refused to connect, on the clearest issue that can be laid before a man, and their love must take the consequences.

No, there was nothing more to be done. They had tried not to go over the precipice, but perhaps the fall was inevitable. And it comforted her to think that the future was certainly inevitable: cause and effect would go jangling forward to some goal doubtless, but to none that she could imagine. At such moments the soul retires within, to float upon the bosom of a deeper stream, and has communion with the dead, and sees the world's glory not diminished, but different in kind to what she has supposed. She alters her focus until trivial things are blurred. Margaret had been tending this way all the winter. Leonard's death brought her to the goal. Alas! that Henry should fade away as reality emerged, and only her love for him should remain clear, stamped with his image like the cameos we rescue out of dreams.

With unfaltering eye she traced his future. He would soon present a healthy mind to the world again, and what did he or the world care if he was rotten at the core? He would grow into a rich, jolly old man, at times a little sentimental about women, but emptying his glass with anyone. Tenacious of power, he would keep Charles and the rest dependent, and retire from business reluctantly and at an advanced age. He would settle down — though she could not realize this. In her eyes Henry was always moving and causing others to move, until the ends of the earth met. But in time he must get too tired to move, and settle down. What next? The inevitable word. The release of the soul to its appropriate Heaven.

Would they meet in it? Margaret believed in immortality for herself. An eternal future had always seemed natural to her. And Henry believed in it for himself. Yet would they meet again? Are there not rather endless levels beyond the grave, as the theory that he had censured teaches? And his level, whether higher or lower, could it possibly be the same as hers?

Thus gravely meditating, she was summoned by him. He sent up Crane in the motor. Other servants passed like water, but the chauffeur remained, though impertinent and disloyal. Margaret disliked Crane, and he knew it.

"Is it the keys that Mr Wilcox wants?" she asked.

"He didn't say, madam."

"You haven't any note for me?"

"He didn't say, madam."

After a moment's thought she locked up Howards End. It was pitiable to see in it the stirrings of warmth that would be quenched for ever. She raked out the fire that was blazing in the kitchen, and spread the coals in the gravelled yard. She closed the windows and drew the curtains. Henry would probably sell the place now.

She was determined not to spare him, for nothing new had happened as far as they were concerned. Her mood might never have altered from yesterday evening. He was standing a little outside Charles's gate, and motioned the car to stop. When his wife got out he said hoarsely: "I prefer to discuss things with you outside."

"It will be more appropriate in the road, I am afraid," said Margaret. "Did you get my message?"

"What about?"

"I am going to Germany with my sister. I must tell you now that I shall make it my permanent home. Our talk last night was more important than you have realized. I am unable to forgive you and am leaving you."

"I am extremely tired," said Henry, in injured tones. "I have been walking about all the morning, and wish to sit down."

"Certainly, if you will consent to sit on the grass."

The Great North Road should have been bordered all its length with glebe. Henry's kind had filched most of it. She moved to the scrap opposite, wherein were the Six Hills. They sat down on the further side, so that they could not be seen by Charles or Dolly.

"Here are your keys," said Margaret. She tossed them towards him. They fell on the sunlit slope of grass, and he did not pick them up.

"I have something to tell you," he said gently.

She knew this superficial gentleness, this confession of hastiness, that was only intended to enhance her admiration of the male.

"I don't want to hear it," she replied. "My sister is going to be ill. My life is going to be with her now. We must manage to build up something, she and I and her child."

"Where are you going?"

"Munich. We start after the inquest, if she is not too ill."

"After the inquest?"

"Yes."

"Have you realized what the verdict at the inquest will be?"

"Yes, heart-disease."

"No, my dear; manslaughter."

Margaret drove her fingers through the grass. The hill beneath her moved as if it was alive.

"Manslaughter," repeated Mr Wilcox. "Charles may go to prison. I dare not tell him. I don't know what to do — what to do. I'm broken — I'm ended."

No sudden warmth arose in her. She did not see that to break him was her only hope. She did not enfold the sufferer in her arms. But all through that day and the next a new life began to move. The verdict was brought in. Charles was committed for trial. It was against all reason that he should be punished, but the law, being made in his image, sentenced him to three years' imprisonment. Then Henry's fortress gave way. He could bear no one but his wife, he shambled up to Margaret afterwards and asked her to do what she could with him. She did what seemed easiest — she took him down to recruit at Howards End.

### Chapter 44

Tom's father was cutting the big meadow. He passed again and again amid whirring blades and sweet odours of grass, encompassing with narrowing circles the sacred centre of the field. Tom was negotiating with Helen.

"I haven't any idea," she replied. "Do you suppose baby may, Meg?"

Margaret put down her work and regarded them absently. "What was that?" she asked.

"Tom wants to know whether baby is old enough to play with hay?"

"I haven't the least notion," answered Margaret, and took up her work again.

"Now, Tom, baby is not to stand; he is not to lie on his face; he is not to lie so that his head wags; he is not to be teased or tickled; and he is not to be cut into two or more pieces by the cutter. Will you be as careful as all that?"

Tom held out his arms.

"That child is a wonderful nursemaid," remarked Margaret.

"He is fond of baby. That's why he does it!" was Helen's answer. "They're going to be lifelong friends."

"Starting at the ages of six and one?"

"Of course. It will be a great thing for Tom."

"It may be a greater thing for baby."

Fourteen months had passed, but Margaret still stopped at Howards End. No better plan had occurred to her. The meadow was being re-cut, the great red poppies were reopening in the garden. July would follow with the little red poppies among the wheat, August with the cutting of the wheat. These little events would become part of her, year after year. Every summer she would fear lest the well should give out, every winter lest the pipes should freeze; every westerly gale might blow the wych-elm down and bring the end of all things, and so she could not read or talk during a westerly gale. The air was tranquil now. She and her sister were sitting on the remains of Evie's rockery, where the lawn merged into the field.

"What a time they all are!" said Helen. "What can they be doing inside?" Margaret, who was growing less talkative, made no answer. The noise of the cutter came intermittently, like the breaking of waves. Close by them a man was preparing to scythe out one of the dell-holes.

"I wish Henry was out to enjoy this," said Helen. "This lovely weather and to be shut up in the house! It's very hard."

"It has to be," said Margaret. "The hay fever is his chief objection against living here, but he thinks it worth while."

"Meg, is or isn't he ill? I can't make out."

"Not ill. Eternally tired. He has worked very hard all his life, and noticed nothing. Those are the people who collapse when they do notice a thing."

"I suppose he worries dreadfully about his part of the tangle."

"Dreadfully. That is why I wish Dolly had not come, too, today. Still, he wanted them all to come. It has to be."

"Why does he want them?"

Margaret did not answer.

"Meg, may I tell you something? I like Henry."

"You'd be odd if you didn't," said Margaret.

"I usen't to."

"Usen't!" She lowered her eyes a moment to the black abyss of the past. They had crossed it, always excepting Leonard and Charles. They were building up a new life, obscure, yet gilded with tranquillity. Leonard was dead; Charles had two years more in prison. One usen't always to see clearly before that time. It was different now.

"I like Henry because he does worry."

"And he likes you because you don't."

Helen sighed. She seemed humiliated, and buried her face in her hands. After a time she said: "About love" — a transition less abrupt than it appeared.

Margaret never stopped working.

"I mean a woman's love for a man. I supposed I should hang my life onto that once, and was driven up and down and about as if something was worrying through me. But everything is peaceful now; I seem cured. That Herr Förstmeister, whom Frieda keeps writing about, must be a noble character, but he doesn't see that I shall never marry him or anyone. It isn't shame or mistrust of myself. I simply couldn't. I'm ended. I used to be so dreamy about a man's love as a girl, and think that for good or evil love must be the great thing. But it hasn't been; it has been itself a dream. Do you agree?"

"I do not agree. I do not."

"I ought to remember Leonard as my lover," said Helen, stepping down into the field. "I tempted him, and killed him, and it is surely the least I can do. I would like to throw out all my heart to Leonard on such an afternoon as this. But I cannot. It is no good pretending. I am forgetting him." Her eyes filled with tears. "How nothing seems to match — how, my darling, my precious —" She broke off. "Tommy!"

"Yes, please?"

"Baby's not to try and stand — there's something wanting in me. I see you loving Henry, and understanding him better daily, and I know that death wouldn't part you in the least. But I — is it some awful, appalling criminal defect?"

Margaret silenced her. She said: "It is only that people are far more different than is pretended. All over the world men and women are worrying because they cannot develop as they are supposed to develop. Here and there they have the matter out, and it comforts them. Don't fret yourself, Helen. Develop what you have; love your child. I do not love children. I am thankful to have none. I can play with their beauty and charm, but that is all — nothing real, not one scrap of what there ought to be. And others — others go further still, and move outside humanity altogether. A place, as well as a person, may catch the glow. Don't you see that all this leads to comfort in the end? It is part of the battle against sameness. Differences — eternal differences, planted by God in a single family, so that there may always be colour; sorrow perhaps, but colour in the daily gray. Then I can't have you worrying about Leonard. Don't drag in the personal when it will not come. Forget him."

"Yes, yes, but what has Leonard got out of life?"

"Perhaps an adventure."

"Is that enough?"

"Not for us. But for him."

Helen took up a bunch of grass. She looked at the sorrel, and the red and white and yellow clover, and the quaker grass, and the daisies, and the bents that composed it. She raised it to her face.

"Is it sweetening yet?" asked Margaret.

"No, only withered."

"It will sweeten tomorrow."

Helen smiled. "Oh, Meg, you are a person," she said. "Think of the racket and torture this time last year. But now I couldn't stop unhappy if I tried. What a change — and all through you!"

"Oh, we merely settled down. You and Henry learned to understand one another and to forgive, all through the autumn and the winter."

"Yes, but who settled us down?"

Margaret did not reply. The scything had begun, and she took off her pince-nez to watch it.

"You!" cried Helen. "You did it all, sweetest, though you're too stupid to see. Living here was your plan — I wanted you; he wanted you; and everyone said it was impossible, but you knew. Just think of our lives without you, Meg — I and baby with Monica, revolting by theory, he handed about from Dolly to Evie. But you picked up the pieces, and made us a home. Can't it strike you — even for a moment — that your life has been heroic? Can't you remember the two months after Charles's arrest, when you began to act, and did all?"

"You were both ill at the time," said Margaret. "I did the obvious things. I had two invalids to nurse. Here was a house, ready-furnished and empty. It was obvious. I didn't know myself it would turn into a permanent home. No doubt I have done a little towards straightening the tangle, but things that I can't phrase have helped me."

"I hope it will be permanent," said Helen, drifting away to other thoughts.

"I think so. There are moments when I feel Howards End peculiarly our own."

"All the same, London's creeping."

She pointed over the meadow — over eight or nine meadows, but at the end of them was a red rust.

"You see that in Surrey and even Hampshire now," she continued. "I can see it from the Purbeck downs. And London is only part of something else, I'm afraid. Life's going to be melted down, all over the world."

Margaret knew that her sister spoke truly. Howards End, Oniton, the Purbeck downs, the Oderberge, were all survivals, and the melting-pot was being prepared for them. Logically, they had no right to be alive. One's hope was in the weakness of logic. Were they possibly the earth beating time?

"Because a thing is going strong now, it need not go strong for ever," she said. "This craze for motion has only set in during the last hundred years. It may be followed by a civilization that won't be a movement, because it will rest on the earth. All the signs are against it now, but I can't help hoping, and very early in the morning in the garden I feel that our house is the future as well as the past."

They turned and looked at it. Their own memories coloured it now, for Helen's child had been born in the central room of the nine. Then Margaret said, "Oh, take care — !" for something moved behind the window of the hall, and the door opened.

"The conclave's breaking at last. I'll go."

It was Paul.

Helen retreated with the children far into the field. Friendly voices greeted her. Margaret rose, to encounter a man with a heavy black moustache.

"My father has asked for you," he said with hostility.

She took her work and followed him.

"We have been talking business," he continued, "but I daresay you knew all about it beforehand."

"Yes, I did."

Clumsy of movement — for he had spent all his life in the saddle — Paul drove his foot against the paint of the front door. Mrs Wilcox gave a little cry of annoyance. She did not like anything scratched; she stopped in the hall to take Dolly's boa and gloves out of a vase.

Her husband was lying in a great leather chair in the dining-room, and by his side, holding his hand rather ostentatiously, was Evie. Dolly, dressed in purple, sat near the window. The room was a little dark and airless; they were obliged to keep it like this until the carting of the hay. Margaret joined the family without speaking; the five of them had met already at tea, and she knew quite well what was going to be said. Averse to wasting her time, she went on sewing. The clock struck six.

"Is this going to suit everyone?" said Henry in a weary voice. He used the old phrases, but their effect was unexpected and shadowy. "Because I don't want you all coming here later on and complaining that I have been unfair."

"It's apparently got to suit us," said Paul.

"I beg your pardon, my boy. You have only to speak, and I will leave the house to you instead."

Paul frowned ill-temperedly, and began scratching at his arm. "As I've given up the outdoor life that suited me, and have come home to look after the business, it's no good my settling down here," he said at last. "It's not really the country, and it's not the town."

"Very well. Does my arrangement suit you, Evie?"

"Of course, father."

"And you, Dolly?"

Dolly raised her faded little face, which sorrow could wither but not steady. "Perfectly splendidly," she said. "I thought Charles wanted it for the boys, but last time I saw him he said no, because we cannot possibly live in this part of England again. Charles says we ought to change our name, but I cannot think what to, for Wilcox just suits Charles and me, and I can't think of any other name."

There was a general silence. Dolly looked nervously round, fearing that she had been inappropriate. Paul continued to scratch his arm.

"Then I leave Howards End to my wife absolutely," said Henry. "And let everyone understand that; and after I am dead let there be no jealousy and no surprise."

Margaret did not answer. There was something uncanny in her triumph. She, who had never expected to conquer anyone, had charged straight through these Wilcoxes and broken up their lives.

"In consequence, I leave my wife no money," said Henry. "That is her own wish. All that she would have had will be divided among you. I am also giving you a great deal in my lifetime, so that you may be independent of me. That is her wish, too. She also is giving away a great deal of money. She intends to diminish her income by half during the next ten years; she intends when she dies to leave the house to her — to her nephew, down in the field. Is all that clear? Does everyone understand?"

Paul rose to his feet. He was accustomed to natives, and a very little shook him out of the Englishman. Feeling manly and cynical, he said: "Down in the field? Oh, come! I think we might have had the whole establishment, piccaninnies included."

Mrs Cahill whispered: "Don't, Paul. You promised you'd take care." Feeling a woman of the world, she rose and prepared to take her leave.

Her father kissed her. "Goodbye, old girl," he said; "don't you worry about me."

"Goodbye, dad."

Then it was Dolly's turn. Anxious to contribute, she laughed nervously, and said: "Goodbye, Mr Wilcox. It does seem curious that Mrs Wilcox should have left Margaret Howards End, and yet she get it, after all."

From Evie came a sharply drawn breath. "Goodbye," she said to Margaret, and kissed her.

And again and again fell the word, like the ebb of a dying sea.

"Goodbye."

"Goodbye, Dolly."

"So long, father."

"Goodbye, my boy; always take care of yourself."

"Goodbye, Mrs Wilcox."

"Goodbye."

Margaret saw their visitors to the gate. Then she returned to her husband and laid her head in his hands. He was pitiably tired. But Dolly's remark had interested her. At last she said: "Could you tell me,

Henry, what was that about Mrs Wilcox having left me Howards End?"

Tranquilly he replied: "Yes, she did. But that is a very old story. When she was ill and you were so kind to her she wanted to make you some return, and, not being herself at the time, scribbled 'Howards End' on a piece of paper. I went into it thoroughly, and, as it was clearly fanciful, I set it aside, little knowing what my Margaret would be to me in the future."

Margaret was silent. Something shook her life in its inmost recesses, and she shivered.

"I didn't do wrong, did I?" he asked, bending down.

"You didn't, darling. Nothing has been done wrong."

From the garden came laugher. "Here they are at last!" exclaimed Henry, disengaging himself with a smile. Helen rushed into the gloom, holding Tom by one hand and carrying her baby on the other. There were shouts of infectious joy.

"The field's cut!" Helen cried excitedly — "The big meadow! We've seen to the very end, and it'll be such a crop of hay as never!"

WEYBRIDGE, 1908–1910

PART TWO

*Howards End:*
A Case Study in
Contemporary Criticism

# A Critical History of
# *Howards End*

From the novel's first appearance, critics recognized that *Howards End* differed from Forster's three earlier novels in the scope of its social critique and the ambition of the goals announced in the epigraph, "Only connect . . .". Though not all have agreed with Lionel Trilling's 1943 verdict that *Howards End* is "undoubtedly" Forster's masterpiece (114), many preferring *A Passage to India* instead, few have denied it the status of a major work. Written a year after C. F. G. Masterman's sociological study *The Condition of England*, Forster's novel came to be seen, as Trilling most eloquently describes, as a novel about England's fate, with the house, Howards End, symbolizing England itself. For Trilling, the question at the heart of the novel was, Who shall inherit England? Early reviewers hardly pitched their commentaries at this level, but they were warmly appreciative of Forster's serious intentions, divided on the question of Mrs. Wilcox's mysticism, and astutely critical of the novel's shortcomings, especially the contrivances of the plot and the characterization of Leonard Bast.

*Howards End* was published on October 18, 1910. The first printing of 2,500 copies was followed by impressions of 1,000, 3,000, and 2,500 copies in November and 1,000 copies in December (Kirkpatrick 15). As the *World* reviewer noted, congratulating Forster on "the tremendous strides" he had taken since *A Room with a View*, *Howards End* was "one of the sensations of the autumn season" (qtd. in

Gardner 154). Archibald Marshall in the *Daily Mail* considered that Forster, with *Howards End*, had "arrived": "It stands out head and shoulders above the great mass of fiction now claiming a hearing" (qtd. in Gardner 143, 145). "There is no doubt about it whatever," wrote the reviewer of the *Daily Telegraph*, "Mr. E. M. Forster is one of the great novelists." "Never," the reviewer went on to say with reference to the Schlegel sisters, "has an intellectual atmosphere been better transferred to paper" (qtd. in Gardner 130). Considered with its three predecessors, wrote the *Athenaeum* critic, "*Howards End* assures its author a place amongst the handful of living authors who count" (qtd. in Gardner 151). The *Athenaeum* reviewer, we now know, was Clive Bell (Rosenbaum 474), but, typically for Bloomsbury, he was not one simply to puff a friend. Anticipating one of Virginia Woolf's criticisms, Bell complained that the protagonists were points of view rather than characters, and, voicing a common opinion, he found the episodes of Margaret's courtship and Helen's seduction unconvincing. But Bell also put his finger on an aspect of the novel that is as impressive to many present-day readers as it must have been to Bell, the husband of Vanessa Stephen and close friend of her sister Virginia: "The great thing in the book is the sisters' affection for each other; personal relationships, except those between lovers, have never, we venture to say, been more beautiful or more real" (qtd. in Gardner 151).

Writing as Jacob Tonson in *New Age*, the prominent Edwardian novelist Arnold Bennett, whose novel *Clayhanger* was also published in 1910, remarked "that no novel for very many years has been so discussed by the *élite* as Mr. Forster's *Howards End*." Bennett's praise laid a burden on Forster that may have contributed to the writer's block that set in after *Howards End*. The young Forster could become, in Bennett's opinion, "the most fashionable novelist in England in ten years time," or better, "if . . . he writes solely to please himself, forgetting utterly the existence of the *élite*, he may produce some first-class literature" (qtd. in Gardner 156). Bennett's use of *élite* on no fewer than six occasions in a short review may have been a straw in the wind. Soon would occur the bitter debate between H. G. Wells and Henry James on the nature of the novel, a debate exacerbated by Wells's satire, in *Boon* (1915), of James's finely nuanced style and supersubtle depictions of states of consciousness; then, in 1924, Virginia Woolf would publish her polemical pamphlet *Mr. Bennett and Mrs. Brown*, in which Bennett would be classed, together with Wells and John Galsworthy, as an Edwardian "materialist."

To which side did Forster belong? Was the novel a form of art, dedicated to registering subjective complexities, or a critique of life, immersed in the realistic details of the outer world? If Bennett, in January 1911, seems to be warning Forster against the aestheticism of the Bloomsbury elite, Woolf in her 1927 *Atlantic Monthly* article "The Novels of E. M. Forster" is bothered by Forster's materialism, his commitment to life over art: "He sees beauty . . . imprisoned in a fortress of brick and mortar whence he must extricate her. Hence he is always constrained to build the cage — society in all its intricacy and triviality — before he can free the prisoner" (165). Woolf's article — still one of the best, and best-written, appreciations of his novels — caused Forster pain, and it is not hard to see why. She compares him invidiously with Ibsen, noting that both writers try to combine realism and mysticism; but Woolf points out that whereas Ibsen succeeds, Forster fails in crucial scenes (like Leonard's death) to fuse the real and the mystical or to animate "a dense, compact body of observation with a spiritual light" (175), as he almost does in *A Passage to India*. In *Aspects of the Novel* (1927), Forster gave a sideward glance at Woolf and Bloomsbury when he praised Wells and disparaged James, and in his 1941 Rede Lecture, delivered in the Senate House at Cambridge after Woolf's suicide, he qualified his praise by criticizing Woolf for being incapable of lifelike characterization in the manner of Jane Austen, George Eliot, and none other than Arnold Bennett.

Despite Wilfred Stone's argument that Forster, in *Aspects of the Novel*, was "trying to do for the novel what [Roger] Fry tried to do for the plastic arts" (102), Forster exhibits few of the formal characteristics that we associate with the high phase of modernism that feeds into the twentieth-century novel from Flaubert and James: rather than making the author invisible, limiting the point of view, and consistently dramatizing his ideas by incorporating them into the actual speeches or represented thoughts of his characters, Forster is often an intrusive presence in *Howards End*. This was another of Woolf's criticisms. Even while praising *Howards End* for its structure, characterization, atmosphere, moral discrimination, humor, and social observation, she objected to its didactic designs on the reader: "We are tapped on the shoulder. We are to notice this, to take heed of that. Margaret or Helen, we are made to understand, is not speaking simply as herself; her words have another and a larger intention" (172).

Forster is clearly not a modernist author like Woolf. From Jane Austen, a major influence, he learned "the possibilities of domestic humor" (qtd. in Stone 375), and in other ways his fiction belongs to the tradition of the "socio-moral" novel (Bradbury, *Forster* 6), a tradition to which he gave new life and that he handed on to later English novelists such as Angus Wilson, Malcolm Bradbury, and Margaret Drabble. The tradition is alive today in David Lodge's *Nice Work* (1988), in which a student wears a T-shirt with the slogan "Only Connect"; the male protagonist is named Wilcox; and the "connection" to be achieved, in a postimperial and postindustrial Britain demoralized by unemployment and urban blight, is that between the practical, male world of the factory and the theoretical (and feminist) world of the university. Yet Forster's fiction is not to be confined to the novel-of-manners tradition either. As Daniel R. Schwarz has shown, Forster altered the novel of manners by rejecting marriage as a formal resolution. Nor does Forster easily fit with the social realism of the Edwardians, though early and more recent readers have compared *Howards End* to the country-house fiction of Wells, Galsworthy, and others (Gardner 134, 135, 155, 158; Brooker and Widdowson). When R. A. Scott-James described Forster's method in his 1910 review in the *Daily News,* he saw it as "a sort of bridge between that of Mr. Conrad and that of Mr. Galsworthy" (qtd. in Gardner 135). Forster hardly achieves (or seeks to achieve) Conrad's philosophical intensity, but *Howards End* is often Conradian in vision: the goblins that Helen imagines haunting the universe in Beethoven's Fifth Symphony are a figure for the nihilism that threatens civilized ideals, and the "panic and emptiness" that Helen sees behind the arrogant front put up by the Wilcox men place them in the company of the hollow men in the *Heart of Darkness.*

Woolf was the only major contemporary novelist to comment at any length on Forster's fiction. D. H. Lawrence somewhat puzzlingly criticized Forster's portrayal of the Wilcoxes in a 1922 letter to Forster: "But I think you *did* make a nearly deadly mistake in glorifying those *business* people in *Howards End.* Business is no good" (qtd. in Gardner 190). And Katherine Mansfield noted sarcastically in a 1917 journal entry that she "could never be perfectly certain whether Helen was got with child by Leonard Bast or by his fatal forgotten umbrella." She also decided that *Howards End* was "not good enough. E. M. Forster never gets any further than warming the teapot. He's a rare fine hand at that. Feel this teapot. Is it not beautifully warm? Yes, but there ain't going to be no tea" (qtd. in Gardner 162). But precisely what Mansfield dismissed in Forster, Christopher Isherwood, in *Lions and Shadows: An Education in the Twenties* (1938), admired: "The whole of Forster's technique is based on the tea-table; instead of trying to screw all his scenes up to the highest possible pitch, he tones them down until they sound like mothers'-meeting gossip. . . . In fact, there's actually *less* emphasis on the big scenes than on the unimportant ones: that's what's so utterly terrific" (qtd. in Rosenbaum 478–79).

Academic criticism of *Howards End* is not much in evidence in the two or three decades following the publication of the novel. Two figures of consequence in pre–World War II Cambridge, however — each a critic of Bloomsbury, each a close reader of texts — did find Forster worthy of significant engagement. In a 1927 article, I. A. Richards discovered two themes in *Howards End:* on the one hand, a half-mystical preoccupation "with the continuance of life, from parent to child, with the quality of life in the sense of blood or race"; and on the other, "the presentation of a sociological thesis . . . concerning the relations of certain prominent classes in Modern England" (18, 19). In the conflict between these themes, Richards detected an "elusive weakness" evident in the character of Leonard Bast, who supports the sociological thesis in his early relations with the Wilcoxes and the Schlegels but becomes a "dummy" in the later episodes that lead to his death and to the subsequent birth of his and Helen's child at Howards End. In an essay appearing in *Scrutiny* in 1938, F. R. Leavis, like Richards before him, found fault with the novel's symbolism; for Leavis, the house, the wych elm, Mrs. Wilcox, and Miss Avery together comprised a vague and sentimental ideal. Yet Leavis, who elsewhere fiercely repudiated Bloomsbury's claim to represent the Cambridge ethos, granted to Forster "a real and very fine distinction" (34). Recognizing that Forster was "pre-eminently a novelist of civilized personal relations" and thus in the line of Jane Austen and George Meredith, Leavis also approvingly discovered in Forster "a radical dissatisfaction with civilization . . . that prompts references to D. H. Lawrence" (35).

Leavis's *Scrutiny* piece was a response to the first book-length study of Forster, by Rose Macaulay, which had also appeared in 1938. Five years later appeared an altogether more significant book, Lionel Trilling's *E. M. Forster.* Forster had enjoyed something of a cult following in England, and Trilling's book made him known in the United States as well. It also cast Forster, in the middle of World War II, as an artist-hero, "one of those who raise the shield of Achilles, which is the moral intelligence of art, against the panic and emptiness which make their onset when the will is tired of its own excess" (184). Seldom have critic and author been in more accord. Trilling, author of

*The Liberal Imagination* (1955), recognized in Forster a kindred
spirit, a liberal who was "deeply at odds with the liberal mind" (13).
Liberal in his critique of soldiers, bureaucrats, the British Empire,
business, public schools, and in his affirmation of spontaneity, sexual
fulfillment, and intelligence, Forster departed from liberalism in his refusal to believe that good and evil can be easily separated. Like
Hawthorne, he had an unremitting concern with "moral realism,
which is not the awareness of morality itself but of the contradictions,
paradoxes, and dangers of living the moral life" (Trilling 11–12).

Trilling admired Forster's irony and complexity, finding these
virtues lacking in contemporary American literature. Casting his net
wide, he also admired Forster's dialogue with the great books of the
past. In chapter 7 he compares *Howards End* to Dickens's *Our Mutual Friend* and James's *The Princess Casamassima* as one of the great
comments on class struggle. In a discussion of Mr. Wilcox, he refers to
Plato's *Republic.* Mrs. Wilcox recalls Chaucer's patient Griselda,
Shakespeare's countess in *All's Well That Ends Well,* and the biblical
Ruth, sick at heart amid the alien corn. Margaret and Helen have the
names of the heroines in the two parts of Goethe's *Faust* (on this
point Forster disagreed), and Leonard and Helen's child is Goethe's
Euphorion. Elsewhere in the same chapter we read of Montaigne,
Erasmus, Milton, and Matthew Arnold. The range of Trilling's erudi-
tion is remarkable, as is his habit of moving seamlessly from fictional
instance to cultural history and back again. Thus, the Schlegel sisters
exemplify the dilemma of the intellectual in the modern world: they
participate in the "politics of conscious altruism" but are ironically limited by their very "articulateness," which separates them from both the
Wilcoxes and the Basts of the world and severely hampers their social
effectiveness (122–25).

No subsequent writer on Forster could ignore Trilling's study, but
later scholars would provide a far more specific accounting of the social, historical, and intellectual backgrounds of *Howards End,* and
some would dispute Trilling's affirmation of Forster's nuanced liberalism. In John Beer's book (1962) and in the major studies of Frederick
C. Crews (1962) and Wilfred Stone (1966), the Romantic, Victorian,
and Edwardian contexts of Forster's thought were recovered in convincing detail. Beer argued that Forster belonged to the romantic tradition of William Blake, Samuel Taylor Coleridge, and Percy Bysshe
Shelley. Crews incisively described Forster's liberal heritage, divided
between the laissez-faire principles of classical liberalism (reductively
parroted by Henry Wilcox in *Howards End*) and the more "socialist"

liberalism of John Stuart Mill. Stone saw Forster as following Mill in trying to reconcile the analytic rationality of the Enlightenment with the creative imagination of the Romantic writers. In Stone's interpretation, Matthew Arnold is of particular importance to *Howards End*, not only in his pursuit of Sophocles' goal of seeing life steadily and seeing it whole, but also in the hope he expresses in *Culture and Anarchy* that culture can oppose the forces of selfishness and materialism and bring society to an awareness of its ideal destiny. *Howards End*, for Stone, is "the most explicit test of Arnold's notion of culture in our literature" (239).

The studies of Crews, Stone, and others benefited from books that Forster published following Trilling's study, especially *Two Cheers for Democracy* (1951), a collection of sixty-six essays, and *Marianne Thornton* (1956), his biography of his great-aunt. Scholars could now learn a great deal about Forster's heritage and milieu, although the secret of his homosexuality (unknown to Trilling in 1943, known but not revealed by Stone in 1966) would be kept from the public until after Forster's death in 1970 and the publication of *Maurice* in 1971. What Crews, Stone, and others investigated in the 1960s were contexts such as the Clapham Sect, the group of early nineteenth-century Evangelicals from whom Forster derived a social conscience if not their Christian faith; Cambridge in its brilliant period at the turn of the twentieth century, when J. M. E. McTaggart, the idealist philosopher, and Nathaniel Wedd and Goldsworthy Lowes Dickinson, Forster's tutors at King's, were arguably of more real importance to Forster than was the Bertrand Russell of *Principia Mathematica* or the G. E. Moore of *Principia Ethica;* and the Bloomsbury Group, comprising Lytton Strachey, J. M. Keynes, the Stephen sisters, and others with whom (though he was never a central figure and claimed never to have read Moore's work) Forster may have shared a general faith in Moore's "good," defined in terms of complex wholes of consciousness that derive from an intense perception of beauty in art or nature, or from personal relationships.

Crews and Stone were first-rate scholars, but they were critics too. Stone's chapter in *The Cave and the Mountain* exhibits the blend of historical scholarship and close textual analysis that characterized criticism in the period. It remains an essential work but is depressing reading for admirers of *Howards End*. Using Dickinson's distinction between "Red-bloods" and "Mollycoddles," Stone argues that Forster is not an impartial mediator in the contest between the world of practical action and the world of art and thought. Unlike Clive Bell earlier and some feminist critics later, he is unimpressed by Forster's relinquishing of the hero role to the women in the novel. Forster's "fictional transvestism" (237), like the preference he shows for the aesthetic Tibby Schlegel over the red-blooded Henry Wilcox (252), suggests, in Stone's view, that the contest is rigged. As for the novel's conclusion, it suggests that Forster did not really want "connection" at all: "The malignancy inherent in a spiritual-esthetic withdrawal is a subject Forster knows well. . . . But in fictionalizing the problem, he has presented a moral failure as a triumph — and, in the name of much that is beautiful and fine, has become the partisan of much that is sick and corrupt" (266).

Crews also depreciated *Howards End*. In his argument, *A Passage to India* becomes Forster's "sole claim on posterity" (178), while *Howards End* testifies to the bankruptcy of liberal humanism in the modern world. Writing at a time when formalist critics equated fictional achievement with a novelist's ability to integrate plot, character, theme, and imagery, Crews preferred *Passage* to *Howards End* because in the former, "resources of plot and symbolism work in harmony toward a single end" (179). That end entailed Forster's realization of "the destructive ironies" of the humanism in *Howards End*, his movement away from "the fashionable slogans of sexual equality, self-expression, and even social responsibility," and his achievement of a vision that placed him among "those great writers who have looked steadily, with humor and compassion, at the permanent ironies of the human condition" (179–80).

Academic criticism of Forster increased from 1960 onward. In his monumental bibliography of writings about Forster between 1905 and 1975, Frederick P. W. McDowell provides full and detailed annotations for nearly two thousand entries, fifteen of which are books and 469 of which pertain to *Howards End*. In his 1991 *Guide to Research*, Claude J. Summers provides detailed and sometimes pungent annotations for almost thirteen hundred entries, which include some twenty books and essay collections on Forster published since 1975, as well as five hundred items that did not appear in McDowell. Observing the huge body of Forster criticism available in 1985, Alan Wilde proposed that Forster had "called forth and controlled precisely the kind of criticism he has received" (1). Wilde's proposal is particularly true of fine early studies by E. K. Brown (1950) and James McConkey (1958), which apply to Forster's novels the critical categories of Forster's own *Aspects of the Novel* (1927), but it is generally true, too, of other studies. George H. Thomson's *The Fiction of E. M. Forster* (1967), for example, is typical of its decade in its discovery of archetypal and romance elements in *Howards End*, but in his detailed analysis of the hay and the wych elm, Thomson uncovers symbolic meanings strategically deposited by the author. Wilde's proposal is also pertinent to a number of good studies of the 1970s and 1980s that remained largely unaffected by the seismic shifts that occurred in academic criticism as a result of the application of Marxist, feminist, and deconstructive theories to literature. Much Forster criticism in this period retains the traditional critical objectives of close reading and the recovery of informing biographical and historical contexts, or revisits such questions as the relation of satire to romance, or of the realistic to the pastoral, in *Howards End*. A general virtue of this criticism is that it rehabilitates *Howards End* from the depreciations of Crews and Stone. In an essay in *Possibilities* (1973), for example, Malcolm Bradbury praises Forster for his blend of moral commitment and skepticism and for the social and emotional wholeness he seeks to achieve in *Howards End*, a novel that provides its readers with both social comedy and a serious inquiry into the state of the nation.

When Forster died in 1970, he was widely regarded as a saint of humanism (in 1969 the queen had awarded him the Order of Merit). In 1971 *Maurice*, his novel of homosexual love, was published, and in 1972 *The Life to Come*, a collection of short stories, more than half of which had homosexual themes, appeared. Also in 1972, the Abinger edition of Forster's works was initiated under the editorship of Oliver Stallybrass. In 1973 Stallybrass brought out *Howards End*, complete with Forster's memoir of Rooksnest (the original of Howards End), an introduction, and annotations; the same year saw the publication of *The Manuscripts of "Howards End,"* which correlated the manuscripts of the novel with the final printing of the novel in Forster's lifetime. A little later appeared P. N. Furbank's two-volume authorized biography (1977–78), Forster's *Commonplace Book* (facsimile edition, 1978), and two volumes of selected letters edited by Mary Lago and Furbank (1983–85).

Here was a trove of new material to be explored. The revelations concerning Forster's homosexual life and writings caused controversy in the press and in some critical circles, as I will discuss, but Forster scholars tended to assimilate the new material into received assessments of Forster's achievement. John Colmer (1975), John Sayre Martin (1976), and Glen Cavaliero (1979), for example, all treated with sensitivity the posthumous short stories as part of larger studies, while Norman Page (1977) devoted a monograph to them. Regarding

*Howards End,* however, Forster criticism conformed to familiar patterns, often tilling more finely the ground broken by Trilling, Crews, and Stone. Colmer and Cavaliero usefully place the novel in the context of Edwardian fiction, particularly "condition-of-England" novels by Galsworthy, Wells, Lawrence, Jack London, and Howard Overing Sturgis; Martin is illuminating on the sea and river imagery in *Howards End.* In *The Short Narratives of E. M. Forster* (1988), Judith Scherer Herz typifies the positive disposition of Forster scholars by arguing for the high achievement of Forster's short pieces (comprising essays, broadcasts, and *Commonplace Book* fragments as well as stories) and by associating Forster with Montaigne, the essayist whom Forster himself admired in his most famous essay, "What I Believe" (1939).

Outside Forster circles, however, the cat had been put among the pigeons by the posthumous publication of Forster's homosexual novel and stories. He was attacked from the right and the left. In a 1971 *Commentary* essay, Cynthia Ozick argued that Forster's liberal views in the major novels were devalued after the appearance of *Maurice.* In "Forster's Cramp" (1972), Samuel Hynes proposed that while Forster's homosexuality as such was not the critic's business, the homosexuality of his imagination was another matter; the latter negatively affected the novels, he argued, most obviously in Forster's failure to represent heterosexual relations and marriage in convincing ways. For Denis Altman in 1977, it was not Forster's homosexuality but his suppression of it that posed the problem; with *Maurice* particularly in mind, Altman argued that Forster's position was compromised by the socially induced guilt that led him to accept social opprobrium as a given and to seek freedom for homosexuals only in escape or fantasy. Other gay liberationists, surely insensitive to the pressures of English history, deplored Forster's refusal to come out of the closet in his lifetime. In Andrew Hodges and David Hutter's *With Downcast Gaze: Aspects of Homosexual Self-Oppression* (1974), Forster was the only gay author to be singled out by name for attack (Dellamora 162). In "'The Flesh Educating the Spirit,'" on the other hand, Claude Summers rated *Maurice* the first masterpiece of gay liberation. It was one thing to defend Forster's integrity; however, it was quite another to deny that the posthumous fiction had no bearing on how the major novels should be read. What had puzzled Trilling ("though we hear much about the transcendent values of sexual love, we are never shown a happy marriage" [115–16]) now seemed explicable, as in Colmer's succinct proposal that Forster was "an interesting case of the creative tension between a personal ideology only belatedly raised to full consciousness and an alien social ideology enshrined in a literary form to which he was strongly attracted on stylistic grounds" ("Marriage" 113).

The sexual politics of Forster's fiction also provided a focus of interest to feminist critics who, from the 1970s onward, were conducting a general scrutiny of representations of women in the fictional canon. Feminist criticism of Forster came in both hostile and appreciative forms. Some critics found in *Maurice,* the letters, and the *Commonplace Book* instances of Forster's misogyny, while others recalled still earlier evidence of hostility to women in *The Longest Journey,* particularly in the characterization of Agnes Pembroke. To such critics, Forster's commitment to women's rights seemed lukewarm at best. In "Liberty, Sorority, Misogyny" (1983), Jane Marcus, a champion of Virginia Woolf, resented Forster's obituary comments on Woolf's feminism and his depreciation of her most radical feminist work, *Three Guineas.* In her pioneering *Women and Fiction: Feminism and the Novel, 1880–1920* (1979), Patricia Stubbs was less antagonistic but still critical. Conceding that Margaret and Helen in *Howards End* are to some degree feminists, Stubbs judged the novel deficient because it failed to show women at work and accepted "the traditionally rigid separation between male and female psychological characteristics" (219).

As one would expect, more favorable views appeared among Forster specialists. Herz, for example, rebutted Marcus's attack in *Short Narratives* (145–47). But appreciations of Forster's depictions of women also came from feminist scholars such as Carolyn Heilbrun who, ironically enough in view of the Woolf-Forster rivalry, used the idea of "androgyny," which Woolf had put forward in *A Room of One's Own,* to read Forster positively. In her *Toward a Recognition of Androgyny* (1973), Heilbrun recognized the great importance Forster grants to "feminine" values in *Howards End* — in the intimacy of the Schlegel sisters, in Margaret's friendship with Mrs. Wilcox, in Mrs. Wilcox herself, and in the novel's conclusion, which does not give us a "gelded" Henry Wilcox, as Trilling proposed, but a man who learns in the end to be open to the feminine spirit. In *Forster's Women* (1975), another study that recognizes androgynous strains in Forster, Bonnie Finkelstein was appreciative of Forster's feminism, particularly in *Howards End.* Commenting on Margaret's speech to Tibby in praise of work, in which Margaret hopes that for women "not to work" will soon be as shocking as "not to be married" was a hundred years earlier, Finkelstein comments: "Margaret's belief in work is related to her attraction to Mr. Wilcox, but it also expresses the heart of feminism" (94).

Not all of Forster's women in *Howards End* are as positively portrayed as Mrs. Wilcox and the Schlegel sisters (of Dolly Wilcox, Forster writes, "She was a rubbishy little creature, and she knew it" [92]), but that *Howards End* is remarkable for its sympathetic female characters has been recognized, and usually applauded, from its first publication. True, Forster does not frontally address the women's issues of his time, as H. G. Wells does in *Ann Veronica* (1909), or as G. B. Shaw does in such plays as *Mrs. Warren's Profession* (1894) and *Man and Superman* (1903). Margaret and Helen are not suffragettes, nor do they attend university or contemplate careers in business, medicine, or law. Mrs. Wilcox, a touchstone of value in the novel, goes just about as far from feminism as a woman can decently go. Yet, as Malcolm Page shows in a helpful and balanced discussion (32–37), Forster both knows and cares about women's issues in *Howards End*, and, as Elizabeth Langland shows in her feminist essay reprinted in this volume, he is a superb analyst of social constructions of masculine and feminine behavior.

Forster's role as a social and political novelist was not forgotten in this period of critical interest in the sexual aspects of his fiction. In 1977 Peter Widdowson devoted a significant book to *Howards End*, an extract of which appears in this volume. Writing in the decade in which Raymond Williams wrote *The Country and the City* (1973) and superseded F. R. Leavis as the major literary voice of social criticism in England, Widdowson shares with Williams a determination to evaluate fiction in terms of its ability to represent a whole way of life. Thus, Widdowson is critical of what Forster excludes — the city of London and the poor — in a novel purporting to be about England. For the same reason he finds unconvincing Forster's elegiac tributes to the English countryside; four-fifths of the population of England, as C. F. G. Masterman pointed out in *The Condition of England* (1909), was urban. In common with many earlier critics, Widdowson finds the plot of the novel contrived and the characterization of Leonard Bast unsatisfactory. He also observes a disparity between the novel's vision, upheld by myth and symbol, and its social realism. "The rich ambiguity," he writes, "the fundamental *irresolution* of *Howards End* are key factors in its importance as a novel" (12). Like Crews, then, he reads *Howards End* as testifying to the failure of liberal humanism, but, unlike Crews, he identifies this failure as political rather than metaphysical, a fictional realization of the economic and class basis of liberalism's values and their consequent inadequacy to the twentieth-century world. Along with Trilling and Crews, Widdowson is required reading for those interested in *Howards End* in relation to liberalism.

One critic who adopts a similar perspective is Paul Delany. In his "'Islands of Money': Rentier Culture in E. M. Forster's *Howards End*" (1988), Delany uncovers the connection between money and value in the novel, while demonstrating how the rentier culture of the Schlegels is parasitic on imperial investment; like Widdowson, he finds the pastoralism of the ending an evasive rather than authentic resolution of the problem of money that Forster shared with his character Margaret.

In my own study of *Howards End* (1992), I attempted to mitigate Widdowson's critique (much of which seems unassailable) by loosening the novel from its damaging identification with liberal humanism. Using Mikhail Bakhtin's idea of the dialogic imagination, I found in Forster's superb ability to mimic speech a realistic critique of the historical limitations of the Schlegel sisters' humanitarianism as well as, more obviously, of the Wilcox men's social Darwinism; and in an analysis of the intrusive and provocative narrator, I found an author who invited a dialogical response, not from "the reader" considered as the target of an imperfectly delivered political message, but from "readers" whose plurality and diversity is assumed and addressed in the novel itself. Forster's liberal humanism remains (he manifestly prefers the Schlegels, and Margaret especially, to the Wilcoxes), but he is perfectly aware not only of the powerlessness of rentier intellectuals but also of their financial complicity in the oppressive system they critique.

A somewhat similar way of approaching Forster's liberalism is evident in Daniel Born's "Private Gardens, Public Swamps: *Howards End* and the Revaluation of Liberal Guilt" (1992). Now that the doctrines of classical liberalism have achieved renewed life, Born proposes that we should listen to Forster's voice, the voice "that stands implicitly behind Schlegelian liberalism, but often subjects it to scathing interrogation" (145). He sees Forster's novel as a gloss on and critique of the pragmatic liberalism of the contemporary philosopher Richard Rorty. Although Born finds much relevance to Forster in Rorty's argument (in *Contingency, Irony, and Solidarity* [1989]) concerning the incommensurability of private and public worlds — of aesthetic self-realization, on the one hand, and commitment to public justice, on the other — he disagrees with Rorty's view that bourgeois capitalism should be recognized as the form of polity best actualized even though it is a form irrelevant to most of society's problems. Aware, along with

Widdowson and Delany, that *Howards End* provides us with a "pastoral escape hatch" (152) and that the sloughing off of Jacky Bast in the novel too conveniently prevents the "abyss" from being brought to the hayfield, Born is critical of Margaret (and of Rorty too) for giving up the goal of "connecting" private and public worlds. Forster's lesson, he concludes, is that "the liberal imagination retains its vitality only so long as we are able to revalue, and not dispense with, liberal guilt" (159).

What of the future of Forster criticism? It may be doubted that his fiction will long sustain the close attention to patterns, symbols, and irony that made Forster a magnet for academic criticism in the 1960s and 1970s. Formalism is a paradigm lost among the current generation of academic critics; those who continue to pay close attention to the structure and texture of Forster's fiction, such as Alan Wilde in "Injunctions and Disjunctions" (1987), may use the old "new critical" vocabulary of irony and tension, but they no longer assume unity as a criterion of fiction. To this extent, at least, deconstruction has had its effect on criticism of Forster (although in more specific forms, deconstruction seems to have passed by Forster entirely, with the welcome exception of J. Hillis Miller's essay written for this volume). The Modern Language Association's annual bibliography, that stock market of literary reputation, shows that academic interest in Forster has fallen in recent years. Compared with Faulkner, Joyce, or Woolf, Forster receives relatively little scholarly attention; and *Howards End* is interpreted less often than *A Passage to India,* doubtless because of the latter novel's accessibility to postcolonial critical analysis. Yet the enduring general appeal of Forster's narratives is attested to by the continuing healthy sale of his novels, not only in Britain and North America but throughout the world. *Howards End* alone has been translated into a dozen foreign languages.

Forster's novels have also proved very successful when adapted for the screen. It may well be that more people today have seen the 1992 Merchant-Ivory film of *Howards End* than have read the novel, though it is surely also the case that the film has brought new readers to the novel. The success of the award-winning film owes much to its lush re-creation of the Edwardian age, evident in the camera's lingering fascination with period costumes, motorcars, architecture, and scenery. James Ivory's direction remains generally faithful to Forster's narrative, and in adapting the novel for the screen, Ruth Prawer Jhabvala sensibly did not try to improve on Forster's superb skills as a creator of dialogue. Emma Thompson is a thoroughly convincing Margaret Schlegel, and Anthony Hopkins a brisk, if perhaps too sympathetic, Henry Wilcox. Vanessa Redgrave's performance, though mannered, suggests Mrs. Wilcox's ethereal spirit. Thus the themes of "connection" — between past and present, rich and poor, man and woman, businessman and intellectual — are, to an extent, communicated to the film's audience. In one instance, the sexual "connection" between Leonard Bast and Helen Schlegel, the film improves on the book by providing a plausible seduction scene. What does not translate so well from novel to film are Forster's social and moral themes. The film is not much interested in the symbolic resonance of Howards End, the house at the heart of the novel's values, nor does it rise to the challenge of staging the concert at the Queen's Hall during which Beethoven's Fifth Symphony assumes in the novel its considerable thematic importance. In the novel the narrator plays a crucial role, a role that the film does not (and could not without an awkward use of voice-over) reproduce. Through commentaries, descriptions, addresses to the reader, and the indirect representations of characters' thoughts, the narrator gives both a meditative and a dialogical character to the novel that the film, for all its fine compensations in the form of visual, verbal, and musical enactments, cannot provide.

Forster's posthumous cinematic success owes much to his basic fictional virtues: his ability to tell a good story, to make us want, as he put it in *Aspects of the Novel,* to know what happens next; his engagement of significant human issues, typically by way of oppositions in belief and behavior; his creation of "round" characters, to use one of the terms he has bequeathed to criticism; and his wonderful power of imitating speech and, through such imitation, of revealing not only psychological motivation but also socially conditioned attitudes. Such fictional virtues define Forster as a major novelist and *Howards End* as a classic novel, but what may be most impressive, and most enduring, about *Howards End* is its openness to the ideological demands that different readers and different generations of readers have made on it. The interest that Born and others have shown in *Howards End* in relation to the neoliberalism of Rorty suggests that Forster can no longer be dismissively labeled a liberal humanist. Forster's politics no longer seem superannuated as we see the welfare state rolled back and hear politicians sound more and more like Henry Wilcox chiding Helen for taking up a "sentimental attitude over the ▓▓▓▓▓▓ 8⌋ Nor, in this era of ozone depletion, does his oppos▓▓▓ ▓▓▓tcar seem as politically regressive as it once did. Ecologicäl c▓▓▓▓▓ay ind in *Howards End* (and in *The Longest Journey, Maurice,* ▓▓▓▓▓rstⱼr's pageant plays of the 1930s) ample support for a green cause. Roger Bowen's fine "A Version of Pastoral: E. M. Forster as Country Guardian" (1976) may serve as a starting point for such critics, who may also be heartened to learn that, as a result of concerted action by the Friends of Forster Country, Rooksnest and the surrounding countryside have recently been saved from suburban development. The "red rust" of London that Helen Schlegel sees menacing Howards End (288) has not yet obliterated Forster's childhood house (the model of Howards End) or his Blakean vision of a green, eternal England.

More studies, too, may be expected of Forster as a homosexual (or "homotextual") writer (Nelson 311). Summers's view that Forster embodied more fully than any other writer of his generation a modern gay liberationist perspective ("Flesh") is likely to be tested by the critical resituating of all his fiction, not only *Maurice* and the posthumous stories, in the context of the works of Havelock Ellis, John Addington Symonds, and Edward Carpenter, who variously sought to understand and liberate "the intermediate sex" (Nelson 312). "Only connect" is likely to remain the epigraph of future Forster criticism: only connect the public man and the private man, his life and his texts, his time and our own, and we will live in fragments no longer. Until the achievement of that utopia, we may look forward to a film of *The Longest Journey*, the only one of Forster's six novels not yet adapted for the screen.

Alistair M. Duckworth

## WORKS CITED

Altman, Denis. "The Homosexual Vision of E. M. Forster." *Cahiers d'études et de recherches Victoriennes et Edouardiennes* 4–5 (1977): 85–95.

Beer, John B. *The Achievement of E. M. Forster*. New York: Barnes, 1962.

Born, Daniel. "Private Gardens, Public Swamps: *Howards End* and the Revaluation of Liberal Guilt." *Novel* 25.2 (1992): 141–59.

Bowen, Roger. "A Version of Pastoral: E. M. Forster as Country Guardian." *South Atlantic Quarterly* 75.1 (1976): 36–54.

Bradbury, Malcolm. "E. M. Forster as Victorian and Modern: *Howards End* and *A Pa*▓▓▓" (1▓▓▓▓▓▓▓▓ *Possibilities: Essays on the State of the Novel*. Lon▓o▓ ▓▓▓▓▓ 91–120.

——, ed. *Forster: A* ▓▓ ▓▓ ▓▓▓ ▓▓▓▓▓ *Essays*. Englewood Cliffs: Prentice, 1966.

Brooker, Peter, and Peter Widdowson. "A Literature for England." *Englishness: Politics and Culture, 1880–1920*. Ed. Robert Colls and Philip Dodd. London: Croom Helm, 1986. 116–63.

Brown, E. K. *Rhythm in the Novel*. Toronto: U of Toronto P, 1950.

Cavaliero, Glen. *A Reading of E. M. Forster*. Totowa: Rowan, 1979.

Colmer, John. *E. M. Forster: The Personal Voice*. London: Routledge, 1975.

———. "Marriage and Personal Relations in Forster's Fiction." *E. M. Forster: Centenary Revaluations*. Ed. Judith Scherer Herz and Robert K. Martin. London: Macmillan, 1982. 113–23.

Crews, Frederick C. *E. M. Forster: The Perils of Humanism*. Princeton: Princeton UP, 1962.

Delany, Paul. "'Islands of Money': Rentier Culture in E. M. Forster's *Howards End*." *English Literature in Transition, 1880–1920*. 31.3 (1988): 285–96.

Dellamora, Richard. "Textual Politics/Sexual Politics." *Modern Language Quarterly* 54.1 (1993): 155–64.

Duckworth, Alistair M. *"Howards End": E. M. Forster's House of Fiction*. Twayne's Masterwork Studies. Ser. 93. New York: Twayne, 1992.

Finkelstein, Bonnie Blumenthal. *Forster's Women: Eternal Differences*. New York: Columbia UP, 1975.

Gardner, Philip, ed. *E. M. Forster: The Critical Heritage*. London: Routledge, 1973.

Heilbrun, Carolyn. *Toward a Recognition of Androgyny*. New York: Knopf, 1973.

Herz, Judith Scherer. *The Short Narratives of E. M. Forster*. New York: St. Martin's, 1988.

Herz, Judith Scherer, and Robert K. Martin, eds. *E. M. Forster: Centenary Revaluations*. London: Macmillan, 1982.

Hynes, Samuel. "Forster's Cramp." *Edwardian Occasions: Essays on English Writing in the Early Twentieth Century*. New York: Oxford UP, 1972. 114–22.

Kirkpatrick, B. J. *A Bibliography of E. M. Forster*. 2nd ed. Soho Bibliographies 19. Oxford: Clarendon, 1985.

Leavis, F. R. "E. M. Forster." 1938. Bradbury, *Forster* 34–47.

Lodge, David. *Nice Work*. New York: Viking, 1988.

Marcus, Jane. "Liberty, Sorority, Misogyny." *The Representation of Women in Fiction*. Ed. Carolyn G. Heilbrun and Margaret R. Higonnet. Baltimore: Johns Hopkins UP, 1983. 60–97.

Martin, John Sayre. *E. M. Forster: The Endless Journey*. Cambridge: Cambridge UP, 1976.

McConkey, James. *The Novels of E. M. Forster*. Ithaca: Cornell UP, 1958.

McDowell, Frederick P. W. *E. M. Forster: An Annotated Bibliography of Writings about Him*. De Kalb: Northern Illinois UP, 1976.

Nelson, Scott R. "Narrative Inversion: The Textual Construction of Homosexuality in E. M. Forster's Novels." *Style* 26.2 (1992): 310–26.

Ozick, Cynthia. "Forster as Homosexual." *Commentary* Dec. 1971: 81–85.

Page, Malcolm. *"Howards End."* Critics Debate Ser. London: Macmillan, 1993.

Page, Norman. *E. M. Forster's Posthumous Fiction*. English Literary Studies Monograph Ser. 10. Victoria, BC: U of Victoria, 1977.

Richards, I. A. "A Passage to Forster: Reflections on a Novelist." 1927. Bradbury, *Forster* 15–20.

Rosenbaum, S. P. *Edwardian Bloomsbury: The Early Literary History of the Bloomsbury Group*. Vol. 2. New York: St. Martin's, 1994.

Schwarz, Daniel R. "The Originality of E. M. Forster." *Modern Fiction Studies* 29 (1983): 623–41.

Stone, Wilfred. *The Cave and the Mountain: A Study of E. M. Forster*. London: Oxford UP, 1966.

Stubbs, Patricia. *Women and Fiction: Feminism and the Novel, 1880–1920*. New York: Barnes, 1979.

Summers, Claude J. *E. M. Forster: A Guide to Research*. New York: Garland, 1991.

———. "'The Flesh Educating the Spirit': E. M. Forster's Gay Fictions." *Gay Fictions: Wilde to Stonewall, Studies in a Male Homosexual Literary Tradition*. New York: Continuum, 1990. 79–112.

Thomson, George H. *The Fiction of E. M. Forster*. Detroit: Wayne State UP, 1967.

Trilling, Lionel. *E. M. Forster*. 1943. New York: New Directions, 1964.

Widdowson, Peter. *E. M. Forster's "Howards End": Fiction as History*. London: Chatto/Sussex UP, 1977.

Wilde, Alan, ed. *Critical Essays on E. M. Forster*. Boston: G. K. Hall, 1985.

———. "Injunctions and Disjunctions." *Horizons of Assent: Modernism, Postmodernism, and the Ironic Imagination*. Philadelphia: U of Pennsylvania P, 1987. 50–89.

Woolf, Virginia. "The Novels of E. M. Forster." 1927. *The Death of the Moth and Other Essays*. New York: Harcourt, 1942. 162–75.

# Psychoanalytic Criticism
# and
# *Howards End*

## WHAT IS PSYCHOANALYTIC CRITICISM?

It seems natural to think about literature in terms of dreams. Like dreams, literary works are fictions, inventions of the mind that, although based on reality, are by definition not literally true. Like a literary work, a dream may have some truth to tell, but, like a literary work, it may need to be interpreted before that truth can be grasped. We can live vicariously through romantic fictions, much as we can through daydreams. Terrifying novels and nightmares affect us in much the same way, plunging us into an atmosphere that continues to cling, even after the last chapter has been read — or the alarm clock has sounded.

The notion that dreams allow such psychic explorations, of course, like the analogy between literary works and dreams, owes a great deal to the thinking of Sigmund Freud, the famous Austrian psychoanalyst who in 1900 published a seminal essay, *The Interpretation of Dreams*. But is the reader who feels that Emily Brontë's *Wuthering Heights* is dreamlike — who feels that Mary Shelley's *Frankenstein* is nightmarish — necessarily a Freudian litera█████ To some extent the answer has to be yes. We are all Freudians,█████whether or not we have read a single work by Freud. At one time ██ █nother, most of us have referred to ego, libido, complexes, uncons█ ██us desires, and sexual

313

repression. The premises of Freud's thought have changed the way the Western world thinks about itself. Psychoanalytic criticism has influenced the teachers our teachers studied with, the works of scholarship and criticism they read, and the critical and creative writers *we* read as well.

What Freud did was develop a language that described, a model that explained, a theory that encompassed human psychology. Many of the elements of psychology he sought to describe and explain are present in the literary works of various ages and cultures, from Sophocles' *Oedipus Rex* to Shakespeare's *Hamlet* to works being written in our own day. When the great novel of the twenty-first century is written, many of these same elements of psychology will probably inform its discourse as well. If, by understanding human psychology according to Freud, we can appreciate literature on a new level, then we should acquaint ourselves with his insights.

Freud's theories are either directly or indirectly concerned with the nature of the unconscious mind. Freud didn't invent the notion of the unconscious; others before him had suggested that even the supposedly "sane" human mind was conscious and rational only at times, and even then at possibly only one level. But Freud went further, suggesting that the powers motivating men and women are *mainly* and *normally* unconscious.

Freud, then, powerfully developed an old idea: that the human mind is essentially dual in nature. He called the predominantly passional, irrational, unknown, and unconscious part of the psyche the *id*, or "it." The *ego*, or "I," was his term for the predominantly rational, logical, orderly, conscious part. Another aspect of the psyche, which he called the *superego*, is really a projection of the ego. The superego almost seems to be outside of the self, making moral judgments, telling us to make sacrifices for good causes even though self-sacrifice may not be quite logical or rational. And, in a sense, the superego *is* "outside," since much of what it tells us to do or think we have learned from our parents, our schools, or our religious institutions.

What the ego and superego tell us *not* to do or think is repressed, forced into the unconscious mind. One of Freud's most important contributions to ꞓy criticʒ the psyche, the theory of repression, goes something like  really, hat lies in the unconscious mind has been put there by ʳˡʸ, s, which acts as a censor, driving underground unconscious ʳ a scious thoughts or instincts that it deems unacceptable. Censor materials often involve infantile sexual desires,

Freud postulated. Repressed to an unconscious state, they emerge only in disguised forms: in dreams, in language (so-called Freudian slips), in creative activity that may produce art (including literature), and in neurotic behavior.

According to Freud, all of us have repressed wishes and fears; we all have dreams in which repressed feelings and memories emerge disguised, and thus we are all potential candidates for dream analysis. One of the unconscious desires most commonly repressed is the childhood wish to displace the parent of our own sex and take his or her place in the affections of the parent of the opposite sex. This desire really involves a number of different but related wishes and fears. (A boy — and it should be remarked in passing that Freud here concerns himself mainly with the male — may fear that his father will castrate him, and he may wish that his mother would return to nursing him.) Freud referred to the whole complex of feelings by the word *oedipal,* naming the complex after the Greek tragic hero Oedipus, who unwittingly killed his father and married his mother.

Why are oedipal wishes and fears repressed by the conscious side of the mind? And what happens to them after they have been censored? As Roy P. Basler puts it in *Sex, Symbolism, and Psychology in Literature* (1975), "from the beginning of recorded history such wishes have been restrained by the most powerful religious and social taboos, and as a result have come to be regarded as 'unnatural,'" even though "Freud found that such wishes are more or less characteristic of normal human development":

> In dreams, particularly, Freud found ample evidence that such wishes persisted. . . . Hence he conceived that natural urges, when identified as "wrong," may be repressed but not obliterated. . . . In the unconscious, these urges take on symbolic garb, regarded as nonsense by the waking mind that does not recognize their significance. (14)

Freud's belief in the significance of dreams, of course, was no more original than his belief that there is an unconscious side to the psyche. Again, it was the extent to which he developed a theory of how dreams work — and the extent to which that theory helped him, by analogy, to understand far more than just dreams — that made him unusual, important, and influential beyond the perimeters of medical schools and psychiatrists' offices.

The psychoanalytic approach to literature not only rests on the theories of Freud; it may even be said to have *begun* with Freud, who was interested in writers, especially those who relied heavily on symbols. Such writers regularly cloak or mystify ideas in figures that make sense only when interpreted, much as the unconscious mind of a neurotic disguises secret thoughts in dream stories or bizarre actions that need to be interpreted by an analyst. Freud's interest in literary artists led him to make some unfortunate generalizations about creativity; for example, in the twenty-third lecture in *Introductory Lectures on Psycho-Analysis* (1922), he defined the artist as "one urged on by instinctive needs that are too clamorous" (314). But it also led him to write creative literary criticism of his own, including an influential essay on "The Relation of a Poet to Daydreaming" (1908) and "The Uncanny" (1919), a provocative psychoanalytic reading of E. T. A. Hoffmann's supernatural tale "The Sandman."

Freud's application of psychoanalytic theory to literature quickly caught on. In 1909, only a year after Freud had published "The Relation of a Poet to Daydreaming," the psychoanalyst Otto Rank published *The Myth of the Birth of the Hero*. In that work, Rank subscribes to the notion that the artist turns a powerful, secret wish into a literary fantasy, and he uses Freud's notion about the "oedipal" complex to explain why the popular stories of so many heroes in literature are so similar. A year after Rank had published his psychoanalytic account of heroic texts, Ernest Jones, Freud's student and eventual biographer, turned his attention to a tragic text: Shakespeare's *Hamlet*. In an essay first published in the *American Journal of Psychology*, Jones, like Rank, makes use of the oedipal concept: he suggests that Hamlet is a victim of strong feelings toward his mother, the queen.

Between 1909 and 1949, numerous other critics decided that psychological and psychoanalytic theory could assist in the understanding of literature. I. A. Richards, Kenneth Burke, and Edmund Wilson were among the most influential to become interested in the new approach. Not all of the early critics were committed to the approach; neither were all of them Freudians. Some followed Alfred Adler, who believed that writers wrote out of inferiority complexes, and others applied the ideas of Carl Gustav Jung, who had broken with Freud over Freud's emphasis on sex and who had developed a theory of the *collective* unconscious. According to Jungian theory, a great work of literature is not a disguised expression of its author's personal, repressed wishes; rather, it is a manifestation of desires once held by the whole human race but now repressed because of the advent of civilization.

It is important to point out that among those who relied on Freud's models were a number of critics who were poets and novelists as well. Conrad Aiken wrote a Freudian study of American literature, and poets such as Robert Graves and W. H. Auden applied Freudian insights when writing critical prose. William Faulkner, Henry James, James Joyce, D. H. Lawrence, Marcel Proust, and Toni Morrison are only a few of the novelists who have either written criticism influenced by Freud or who have written novels that conceive of character, conflict, and creative writing itself in Freudian terms. The poet H.D. (Hilda Doolittle) was actually a patient of Freud's and provided an account of her analysis in her book *Tribute to Freud*. By giving Freudian theory credibility among students of literature that only they could bestow, such writers helped to endow earlier psychoanalytic criticism with a largely Freudian orientation that has begun to be challenged only in the last two decades.

The willingness, even eagerness, of writers to use Freudian models in producing literature and criticism of their own consummated a relationship that, to Freud and other pioneering psychoanalytic theorists, had seemed fated from the beginning; after all, therapy involves the close analysis of language. René Wellek and Austin Warren included "psychological" criticism as one of the five "extrinsic" approaches to literature described in their influential book *Theory of Literature* (1942). Psychological criticism, they suggest, typically attempts to do at least one of the following: provide a psychological study of an individual writer; explore the nature of the creative process; generalize about "types and laws present within works of literature"; or theorize about the psychological "effects of literature upon its readers" (81). Entire books on psychoanalytic criticism began to appear, such as Frederick J. Hoffman's *Freudianism and the Literary Mind* (1945).

Probably because of Freud's characterization of the creative mind as "clamorous" if not ill, psychoanalytic criticism written before 1950 tended to psychoanalyze the individual author. Poems were read as fantasies that allowed authors to indulge repressed wishes, to protect themselves from deep-seated anxieties, or both. A perfect example of author analysis would be Marie Bonaparte's 1933 study of Edgar Allan Poe. Bonaparte found Poe to be so fixated on his mother that his repressed longing emerges in his stories in images such as the white spot on a black cat's breast, said to represent mother's milk.

A later generation of psychoanalytic critics often paused to analyze the characters in novels and plays before proceeding to their authors. But not for long, since characters, both evil and good, tended to be seen by these critics as the author's potential selves or projections of various repressed aspects of his or her psyche. For instance, in *A*

*Psychoanalytic Study of the Double in Literature* (1970), Robert Rogers begins with the view that human beings are double or multiple in nature. Using this assumption, along with the psychoanalytic concept of "dissociation" (best known by its result, the dual or multiple personality), Rogers concludes that writers reveal instinctual or repressed selves in their books, often without realizing that they have done so.

In the view of critics attempting to arrive at more psychological insights into an author than biographical materials can provide, a work of literature is a fantasy or a dream — or at least so analogous to daydream or dream that Freudian analysis can help explain the nature of the mind that produced it. The author's purpose in writing is to gratify secretly some forbidden wish, in particular an infantile wish or desire that has been repressed into the unconscious mind. To discover what the wish is, the psychoanalytic critic employs many of the terms and procedures developed by Freud to analyze dreams.

The literal surface of a work is sometimes spoken of as its "manifest content" and treated as a "manifest dream" or "dream story" would be treated by a Freudian analyst. Just as the analyst tries to figure out the "dream thought" behind the dream story — that is, the latent or hidden content of the manifest dream — so the psychoanalytic literary critic tries to expose the latent, underlying content of a work. Freud used the words *condensation* and *displacement* to explain two of the mental processes whereby the mind disguises its wishes and fears in dream stories. In condensation, several thoughts or persons may be condensed into a single manifestation or image in a dream story; in displacement, an anxiety, a wish, or a person may be displaced onto the image of another, with which or whom it is loosely connected through a string of associations that only an analyst can untangle. Psychoanalytic critics treat metaphors as if they were dream condensations; they treat metonyms — figures of speech based on extremely loose, arbitrary associations — as if they were dream displacements. Thus figurative literary language in general is treated as something that evolves as the writer's conscious mind resists what the unconscious tells it to picture or describe. A symbol is, in Daniel Weiss's words, "a meaningful concealment of truth as the truth promises to emerge as some frightening or forbidden idea" (20).

In a 1970 article entitled "The 'Unconscious' of Literature," Norman Holland, a literary critic trained in psychoanalysis, succinctly sums up the attitudes held by critics who would psychoanalyze authors, but without quite saying that it is the *author* that is being analyzed by the psychoanalytic critic. "When one looks at a poem psychoanalytically," he writes, "one considers it as though it were a dream or as though some ideal patient [were speaking] from the couch in iambic pentameter." One "looks for the general level or levels of fantasy associated with the language. By level I mean the familiar stages of childhood development — oral [when desires for nourishment and infantile sexual desires overlap], anal [when infants receive their primary pleasure from defecation], urethral [when urinary functions are the locus of sexual pleasure], phallic [when the penis or, in girls, some penis substitute is of primary interest], oedipal." Holland continues by analyzing not Robert Frost but Frost's poem "Mending Wall" as a specifically oral fantasy that is not unique to its author. "Mending Wall" is "about breaking down the wall which marks the separated or individuated self so as to return to a state of closeness to some Other" — including and perhaps essentially the nursing mother ("'Unconscious'" 136, 139).

While not denying the idea that the unconscious plays a role in creativity, psychoanalytic critics such as Holland began to focus more on the ways in which authors create works that appeal to *our* repressed wishes and fantasies. Consequently, they shifted their focus away from the psyche of the author and toward the psychology of the reader and the text. Holland's theories, which have concerned themselves more with the reader than with the text, have helped to establish another school of critical theory: reader-response criticism. Elizabeth Wright explains Holland's brand of modern psychoanalytic criticism in this way: "What draws us as readers to a text is the secret expression of what we desire to hear, much as we protest we do not. The disguise must be good enough to fool the censor into thinking that the text is respectable, but bad enough to allow the unconscious to glimpse the unrespectable" (117).

Holland is one of dozens of critics who have revised Freud significantly in the process of revitalizing psychoanalytic criticism. Another such critic is R. D. Laing, whose controversial and often poetical writings about personality, repression, masks, and the double or "schizoid" self have (re)blurred the boundary between creative writing and psychoanalytic discourse. Yet another is D. W. Winnicott, an "object relations" theorist who has had a significant impact on literary criticism. Critics influenced by Winnicott and his school have questioned the tendency to see reader/text as an either/or construct; instead, they have seen reader and text (or audience and play) in terms of a *relationship* taking place in what Winnicott calls a "transitional" or "potential" space — space in which binary terms such as *real* and *illusory, objective* and *subjective,* have little or no meaning.

Psychoanalytic theorists influenced by Winnicott see the transitional or potential reader/text (or audience/play) space as being *like* the space entered into by psychoanalyst and patient. More important, they also see it as being similar to the space between mother and infant: a space characterized by trust in which categorizing terms such as *knowing* and *feeling* mix and merge and have little meaning apart from one another.

Whereas Freud saw the mother-son relationship in terms of the son and his repressed oedipal complex (and saw the analyst-patient relationship in terms of the patient and the repressed "truth" that the analyst could scientifically extract), object-relations analysts see both relationships as *dyadic* — that is, as being dynamic in both directions. Consequently, they don't depersonalize analysis or their analyses. It is hardly surprising, therefore, that contemporary literary critics who apply object-relations theory to the texts they discuss don't depersonalize critics or categorize their interpretations as "truthful," at least not in any objective or scientific sense. In the view of such critics, interpretations are made of language — itself a transitional object — and are themselves the mediating terms or transitional objects of a relationship.

Like critics of the Winnicottian school, the French structuralist theorist Jacques Lacan focuses on language and language-related issues. He treats the unconscious *as* a language and, consequently, views the dream not as Freud did (that is, as a form and symptom of repression) but rather as a form of discourse. Thus we may study dreams psychoanalytically to learn about literature, even as we may study literature to learn more about the unconscious. In Lacan's seminar on Poe's "The Purloined Letter," a pattern of repetition like that used by psychoanalysts in their analyses is used to arrive at a reading of the story. According to Wright, "the new psychoanalytic structural approach to literature" employs "analogies from psychoanalysis . . . to explain the workings of the text as distinct from the workings of a particular author's, character's, or even reader's mind" (125).

Lacan, however, did far more than extend Freud's theory of dreams, literature, and the interpretation of both. More significantly, he took Freud's whole theory of psyche and gender and added to it a crucial third term — that of language. In the process, he both used and significantly developed Freud's ideas about the oedipal stage and complex.

Lacan points out that the pre-oedipal stage, in which the child at first does not even recognize its independence from its mother, is also a pre*verbal* stage, one in which the child communicates without the medium of language, or — if we insist on calling the child's communications a language — in a language that can only be called *literal*. ("Coos," certainly, cannot be said to be figurative or symbolic.) Then, while still in the pre-oedipal stage, the child enters the *mirror* stage.

During the mirror period, the child comes to view itself and its mother, later other people as well, *as* independent selves. This is the stage in which the child is first able to fear the aggressions of another, to desire what is recognizably beyond the self (initially the mother), and, finally, to want to compete with another for the same desired object. This is also the stage at which the child first becomes able to feel sympathy with another being who is being hurt by a third, to cry when another cries. All of these developments, of course, involve projecting beyond the self and, by extension, constructing one's own self (or "ego" or "I") as others view one — that is, as *another*. Such constructions, according to Lacan, are just that: constructs, products, artifacts — fictions of coherence that in fact hide what Lacan calls the "absence" or "lack" of being.

The mirror stage, which Lacan also refers to as the *imaginary* stage, is fairly quickly succeeded by the oedipal stage. As in Freud, this stage begins when the child, having come to view itself as self and the father and mother as separate selves, perceives gender and gender differences between its parents and between itself and one of its parents. For boys, gender awareness involves another, more powerful recognition, for the recognition of the father's phallus as the mark of his difference from the mother involves, at the same time, the recognition that his older and more powerful father is also his rival. That, in turn, leads to the understanding that what once seemed wholly his and even indistinguishable from himself is in fact someone else's: something properly desired only at a distance and in the form of socially acceptable *substitutes*.

The fact that the oedipal stage roughly coincides with the entry of the child into language is extremely important for Lacan. For the linguistic order is essentially a figurative or "Symbolic" order; words are not the things they stand for but are, rather, stand-ins or substitutes for those things. Hence boys, who in the most critical period of their development have had to submit to what Lacan calls the "Law of the Father" — a law that prohibits direct desire for and communicative intimacy with what has been the boy's whole world — enter more easily into the realm of language and the Symbolic order than do girls, who have never really had to renounce that which once seemed continuous with the self: the mother. The gap that has been opened up for boys, which includes the gap between signs and what they substitute — the gap marked by the phallus and encoded with the boy's sense of his maleness — has not opened up for girls, or has not opened up in the same way, to the same degree.

For Lacan, the father need not be present to trigger the oedipal stage; nor does his phallus have to be seen to catalyze the boy's (easier) transition into the Symbolic order. Rather, Lacan argues, a child's recognition of its gender is intricately tied up with a growing recognition of the system of names and naming, part of the larger system of substitutions we call language. A child has little doubt about who its mother is, but who is its father, and how would one know? The father's claim rests on the mother's *word* that he is in fact the father; the father's relationship to the child is thus established through language and a system of marriage and kinship — names — that in turn is basic to rules of everything from property to law. The name of the father (*nom du père*, which in French sounds like *non du père*) involves, in a sense, nothing of the father — nothing, that is, except his word or name.

Lacan's development of Freud has had several important results. First, his sexist-seeming association of maleness with the Symbolic order, together with his claim that women cannot therefore enter easily into the order, has prompted feminists not to reject his theory out of hand but, rather, to look more closely at the relation between language and gender, language and women's inequality. Some feminists have gone so far as to suggest that the social and political relationships between male and female will not be fundamentally altered until language itself has been radically changed. (That change might begin dialectically, with the development of some kind of "feminine language" grounded in the presymbolic, literal-to-imaginary communication between mother and child.)

Second, Lacan's theory has proved of interest to deconstructors and other poststructuralists, in part because it holds that the ego (which in Freud's view is as necessary as it is natural) is a product or construct. The ego-artifact, produced during the mirror stage, *seems* at once unified, consistent, and organized around a determinate center. But the unified self, or ego, is a fiction, according to Lacan. The yoking together of fragments and destructively dissimilar elements takes its psychic toll, and it is the job of the Lacanian psychoanalyst to "deconstruct," as it were, the ego, to show its continuities to be contradictions as well.

In the essay that follows, J. H. Stape reads *Howards End* in terms of "its creator's psychology," which he defines as one in which "the social and the instinctive exist in a near-perpetual conflict that is occasionally eased and negotiated by violence." Although Stape in no way rejects the prevailing critical view of the novel as "an extended inquiry into the political and social conditions of Edwardian England," he maintains that "*Howards End* is also a psychological self-portrait." He further claims that "the application of psychoanalytic techniques . . . reveals how an author's unconscious experience is reflected in and mediated through language and symbol."

Stape's own psychoanalytic technique involves analyzing the text and the author's life in tandem, searching the novel for clues to the author's formative and recurring psychological experiences while looking to the author's private history for clues to the novel's psychological origins. He finds similarities between Howards End (the house) and Rooksnest, the farmhouse where Forster grew up with his widowed mother — and without "a counterbalancing male presence." Although Stape acknowledges that "the explanatory power" of Freud's oedipal theory "appears too simplistic to contemporary students of sexual psychology," he nonetheless makes use of that theory to a considerable degree, grounding the "'feminine' value system" that pervades the novel in the unusual closeness that developed between Forster and his mother at Rooksnest. Ultimately, however, Stape goes beyond Freud, complicating our understanding of Forster and the "sexual psychology" of *Howards End* in the process. He argues that the tensions reflected in Forster's life and art, the frustrated longing that makes "the novel's pleas for 'connection' . . . resonantly and poignantly personal," are primarily rooted not in oedipal but rather in homosexual desire.

In his extraordinarily wide-ranging argument, Stape touches on Jungian dream theory and Jaroslav Havelka's theory that creative individuals liberate themselves through the invention of doubles. He examines the problematic nature of Forster's male characters, the overlap between Margaret's voice and that of the narrator, and the essentially "homosocial" bond between the novel's two sisters. In the final stage of his argument, Stape turns to the relationship between Leonard and Jacky Bast, analyzing their "cramped basement flat" in terms of its psychological symbolism, rather than simply in socioeconomic terms as most previous critics have done.

At no time, however, are Forster's life and experiences relegated to the status of mere background (let alone expunged entirely, as they would be from a discussion of novelistic symbolism by formalists or

New Critics). Indeed, Stape implicitly demonstrates how difficult it is
to separate literature and life, especially when practicing psychoanalytic
criticism. He reminds us that readers can and should ask questions that
probe and elucidate this complex and elusive relationship. What was
Forster *doing* while writing *Howards End?* "Reading Walt Whitman, of
whose homoeroticism Forster was aware through the writings of Edward Carpenter, the period's champion of 'homogenic love,'" and
writing "The Machine Stops," a "dystopian short story" in which "an
emotionally absent mother figure . . . dominates, and the protagonist . . .
longs for and identifies with an idealized male." Psychoanalytic analysis, Stape claims, focuses "on the private experience" that engenders
"the publicly circulated text." Whether its "orientation" is that of
"Freudian symbol hunting . . . , Jungian archetypes . . . , Lacanian
analysis . . . , or Winnicottian object-relations theory," psychoanalytic
criticism "seeks to account for and enrich understanding of a work's
widest, occasionally concealed, context and to illumine the way in
which its structure, characters, and thematics dynamically project
aspects of its writer's shifting inner world." Stape's analysis provides
just such an illuminative account, patiently but revealingly connecting
symbols, characters, and the relationships between characters, not
only to one another but also to Forster's literary and psychological
experiences.

Ross C Murfin

## PSYCHOANALYTIC CRITICISM:
## A SELECTED BIBLIOGRAPHY

### Some Short Introductions to Psychological
### and Psychoanalytic Criticism

Holland, Norman. "The 'Unconscious' of Literature: The Psychoanalytic Approach." *Contemporary Criticism*. Ed. Malcolm Bradbury
and David Palmer. Stratford-upon-Avon Studies 12. New York:
St. Martin's, 1971. 131–53.

Natoli, Joseph, and Frederik L. Rusch, comps. *Psychocriticism: An
Annotated Bibliography*. Westport: Greenwood, 1984.

Scott, Wilbur. *Five Approaches to Literary Criticism*. London: Collier-
Macmillan, 1962. See the essays by Burke and Gorer as well as
Scott's introduction to the section "The Psychological Approach:
Literature in the Light of Psychological Theory."

Wellek, René, and Austin Warren. *Theory of Literature*. New York: Harcourt, 1942. See the chapter "Literature and Psychology" in pt. 3, "The Extrinsic Approach to the Study of Literature."

Wright, Elizabeth. "Modern Psychoanalytic Criticism." *Modern Literary Theory: A Comparative Introduction*. Ed. Ann Jefferson and David Robey. Totowa: Barnes, 1982. 113–33.

### Freud, Lacan, and Their Influence

Basler, Roy P. *Sex, Symbolism, and Psychology in Literature*. New York: Octagon, 1975. See especially 13–19.

Bowie, Malcolm. *Lacan*. Cambridge: Harvard UP, 1991.

Clément, Catherine. *The Lives and Legends of Jacques Lacan*. Trans. Arthur Goldhammer. New York: Columbia UP, 1983.

Freud, Sigmund. *Introductory Lectures on Psycho-Analysis*. Trans. Joan Riviere. London: Allen, 1922.

Gallop, Jane. *Reading Lacan*. Ithaca: Cornell UP, 1985.

Hoffman, Frederick J. *Freudianism and the Literary Mind*. Baton Rouge: Louisiana State UP, 1945.

Hogan, Patrick Colm, and Lalita Pandit, eds. *Lacan and Criticism: Essays and Dialogue on Language, Structure, and the Unconscious*. Athens: U of Georgia P, 1990.

Kazin, Alfred. "Freud and His Consequences." *Contemporaries*. Boston: Little, 1962. 351–93.

Lacan, Jacques. *Écrits: A Selection*. Trans. Alan Sheridan. New York: Norton, 1977.

——. *Feminine Sexuality: Lacan and the École Freudienne*. Ed. Juliet Mitchell and Jacqueline Rose. Trans. Rose. New York: Norton, 1985.

——. *The Four Fundamental Concepts of Psychoanalysis*. Trans. Alan Sheridan. London: Penguin, 1980.

Macey, David. *Lacan in Contexts*. New York: Verso, 1988.

Meisel, Perry, ed. *Freud: A Collection of Critical Essays*. Englewood Cliffs: Prentice, 1981.

Muller, John P., and William J. Richardson. *Lacan and Language: A Reader's Guide to "Écrits."* New York: International UP, 1982.

Porter, Laurence M. *"The Interpretation of Dreams": Freud's Theories Revisited*. Twayne's Masterwork Studies Ser. Boston: G. K. Hall, 1986.

Reppen, Joseph, and Maurice Charney. *The Psychoanalytic Study of Literature*. Hillsdale: Analytic, 1985.

Schneiderman, Stuart. *Jacques Lacan: The Death of an Intellectual Hero*. Cambridge: Harvard UP, 1983.

———. *Returning to Freud: Clinical Psychoanalysis in the School of Lacan*. New Haven: Yale UP, 1980.

Selden, Raman. *A Reader's Guide to Contemporary Literary Theory*. 2nd ed. Lexington: U of Kentucky P, 1989. See "Jacques Lacan: Language and the Unconscious."

Sullivan, Ellie Ragland. *Jacques Lacan and the Philosophy of Psychoanalysis*. Champaign: U of Illinois P, 1986.

Sullivan, Ellie Ragland, and Mark Bracher, eds. *Lacan and the Subject of Language*. New York: Routledge, 1991.

Trilling, Lionel. "Art and Neurosis." *The Liberal Imagination*. New York: Scribner's, 1950. 160–80.

Wilden, Anthony. "Lacan and the Discourse of the Other." In Lacan, *Speech and Language in Psychoanalysis*. Trans. Wilden. Baltimore: Johns Hopkins UP, 1981. (Published as *The Language of the Self* in 1968.) 159–311.

Zizek, Slavoj. *Looking Awry: An Introduction to Jacques Lacan through Popular Culture*. Cambridge: MIT P, 1991.

### Psychoanalysis, Feminism, and Literature

Chodorow, Nancy. *The Reproduction of Mothering: Psychoanalysis and the Sociology of Gender*. Berkeley: U of California P, 1978.

Gallop, Jane. *The Daughter's Seduction: Feminism and Psychoanalysis*. Ithaca: Cornell UP, 1982.

Garner, Shirley Nelson, Claire Kahane, and Madelon Sprengnether. *The (M)other Tongue: Essays in Feminist Psychoanalytic Interpretation*. Ithaca: Cornell UP, 1985.

Grosz, Elizabeth. *Jacques Lacan: A Feminist Introduction*. New York: Routledge, 1990.

Irigaray, Luce. *The Speculum of the Other Woman*. Trans. Gillian C. Gill. Ithaca: Cornell UP, 1985.

———. *This Sex Which Is Not One*. Trans. Catherine Porter. Ithaca: Cornell UP, 1985.

Jacobus, Mary. "Is There a Woman in This Text?" *New Literary History* 14 (1982): 117–41.

Kristeva, Julia. *The Kristeva Reader*. Ed. Toril Moi. New York: Columbia UP, 1986. See especially the selection from *Revolution in Poetic Language*, 89–136.

Mitchell, Juliet. *Psychoanalysis and Feminism.* New York: Random, 1974.

Mitchell, Juliet, and Jacqueline Rose. "Introduction I" and "Introduction II." Lacan, *Feminine Sexuality: Jacques Lacan and the École Freudienne.* New York: Norton, 1985. 1–26, 27–57.

Sprengnether, Madelon. *The Spectral Mother: Freud, Feminism, and Psychoanalysis.* Ithaca: Cornell UP, 1990.

## Psychological and Psychoanalytic Studies of Literature

Bettelheim, Bruno. *The Uses of Enchantment: The Meaning and Importance of Fairy Tales.* New York: Knopf, 1976. Although this book is about fairy tales instead of literary works written for publication, it offers model Freudian readings of well-known stories.

Crews, Frederick C. *Out of My System: Psychoanalysis, Ideology, and Critical Method.* New York: Oxford UP, 1975.

———. *Relations of Literary Study.* New York: MLA, 1967. See the chapter "Literature and Psychology."

Diehl, Joanne Feit. "Re-Reading *The Letter:* Hawthorne, the Fetish, and the (Family) Romance." *Nathaniel Hawthorne, The Scarlet Letter.* Ed. Ross C Murfin. Case Studies in Contemporary Criticism Ser. Ed. Ross C Murfin. Boston: Bedford–St. Martin's, 1991. 235–51.

Hallman, Ralph. *Psychology of Literature: A Study of Alienation and Tragedy.* New York: Philosophical Library, 1961.

Hartman, Geoffrey, ed. *Psychoanalysis and the Question of the Text.* Baltimore: Johns Hopkins UP, 1978. See especially the essays by Hartman, Johnson, Nelson, and Schwartz.

Hertz, Neil. *The End of the Line: Essays on Psychoanalysis and the Sublime.* New York: Columbia UP, 1985.

Holland, Norman N. *Dynamics of Literary Response.* New York: Oxford UP, 1968.

———. *Poems in Persons: An Introduction to the Psychoanalysis of Literature.* New York: Norton, 1973.

Kris, Ernest. *Psychoanalytic Explorations in Art.* New York: International, 1952.

Lucas, F. L. *Literature and Psychology.* London: Cassell, 1951.

Natoli, Joseph, ed. *Psychological Perspectives on Literature: Freudian Dissidents and Non-Freudians: A Casebook.* Hamden: Archon Books–Shoe String, 1984.

Phillips, William, ed. *Art and Psychoanalysis.* New York: Columbia UP, 1977.

Rogers, Robert. *A Psychoanalytic Study of the Double in Literature.* Detroit: Wayne State UP, 1970.

Skura, Meredith. *The Literary Use of the Psychoanalytic Process.* New Haven: Yale UP, 1981.

Strelka, Joseph P. *Literary Criticism and Psychology.* University Park: Pennsylvania State UP, 1976. See especially the essays by Lerner and Peckham.

Weiss, Daniel. *The Critic Agonistes: Psychology, Myth, and the Art of Fiction.* Ed. Eric Solomon and Stephen Arkin. Seattle: U of Washington P, 1985.

### Lacanian Psychoanalytic Studies of Literature

Collings, David. "The Monster and the Imaginary Mother: A Lacanian Reading of *Frankenstein.*" *Mary Shelley, Frankenstein.* Ed. Johanna M. Smith. Case Studies in Contemporary Criticism Ser. Ed. Ross C Murfin. Boston: Bedford–St. Martin's, 1992. 245–58.

Davis, Robert Con, ed. *The Fictional Father: Lacanian Readings of the Text.* Amherst: U of Massachusetts P, 1981.

―――. "Lacan and Narration." *Modern Language Notes* 5 (1983): 848–59.

Felman, Shoshana, ed. *Jacques Lacan and the Adventure of Insight: Psychoanalysis in Contemporary Culture.* Cambridge: Harvard UP, 1987.

―――. *Literature and Psychoanalysis: The Question of Reading: Otherwise.* Baltimore: Johns Hopkins UP, 1982.

Froula, Christine. "When Eve Reads Milton: Undoing the Canonical Economy." *Canons.* Ed. Robert von Hallberg. Chicago: U of Chicago P, 1984. 149–75.

Homans, Margaret. *Bearing the Word: Language and Female Experience in Nineteenth-Century Women's Writing.* Chicago: U of Chicago P, 1986.

Mellard, James. *Using Lacan, Reading Fiction.* Urbana: U of Illinois P, 1991.

Muller, John P., and William J. Richardson, eds. *The Purloined Poe: Lacan, Derrida, and Psychoanalytic Reading.* Baltimore: Johns Hopkins UP, 1988. Includes Lacan's seminar on Poe's "The Purloined Letter."

## Psychoanalytic Approaches to *Howards End*

Armstrong, Paul B. "E. M. Forster's *Howards End:* The Existential Crisis of the Liberal Imagination." *Mosaic* 8.1 (1974): 183–99.

Dellamora, Richard. "Textual Politics/Sexual Politics." *Modern Language Quarterly* 54.1 (1993): 155–64.

Golden, Kenneth L. "Jung, Modern Dissociation, and Forster's *Howards End.*" *CLA Journal* 29 (1985): 221–31.

Hanquart, Evelyne. "The Evolution of the Mother-Figure in E. M. Forster's Fictional World." *Approaches to E. M. Forster: A Centenary Volume.* Ed. Vasant A. Shahane. Atlantic Highlands: Humanities, 1981. 59–69.

Hultberg, Peer. "The Faithless Mother: An Aspect of the Novels of E. M. Forster." *Narcissism and the Text: Studies in Literature and the Psychology of the Self.* Ed. Lynne Layton and Barbara Schapiro. New York: New York UP, 1986. 233–54.

Nelson, Scott R. "Narrative Inversion: The Textual Construction of Homosexuality in E. M. Forster's Novels." *Style* 26.2 (1992): 310–26.

Rosecranz, Barbara. "Forster's Comrades." *Partisan Review* 47 (1980): 590–603.

Wyatt-Brown, Anne M. "A Buried Life: E. M. Forster's Struggle with Creativity." *Journal of Modern Literature* 10.1 (1983): 109–24.

―――. *"Howards End:* Celibacy and Stalemate." *Psychohistory Review* 12 (1983): 26–33.

## A PSYCHOANALYTIC PERSPECTIVE

## J. H. STAPE

### Picturing the Self as Other:
### *Howards End* as Psychobiography

## 1

The famous opening sentence of *Howards End,* "One may as well begin with Helen's letters to her sister," introduces and with disarming casualness problematizes the theme of origins at the beginning of a work obsessively concerned with antecedents. The poised, Jane

Austenish tones lull the reader into a characteristically Forsterian sense of false complacency that is almost immediately undermined as the plot proper begins with Paul Wilcox and Helen Schlegel's kiss in the garden. This offstage act of passion (its narration is deferred until chapter 4) reverberates until the novel's conclusion. The scene introduces thematic material developed throughout, focalizing the attraction and collision between the Wilcoxes' "masculine" concerns of self-sufficiency, independence, and power, represented by motorcars, clock time, and business, and the Schlegels' antithetically "feminine" world of high culture, "the inner life," connectedness, and "personal relations" (40). The night realm of instinct and sexuality is contrasted with the day world of social containment in which marriage and domesticity control emotion.

Paul and Helen's "muddle," to use a Forsterian term, lies in Paul's inability to give social form to basic instincts; in seeing himself bound to a career and money-making before he can marry, he identifies wholly with social constructions of masculinity. Repressed or deferred desire leads to the violence of his kiss, whereas internalized cultural models engender conflict, for, whatever its greater freedom, the Edwardian period maintained much Victorian public reticence about emotion and erotic expression. But this scene and the Wilcoxes' consequent response to it also point to basic structures in its creator's psychology: the social and the instinctive exist in a near-perpetual conflict that is occasionally eased and negotiated by violence. The two main elements of the collision between Paul and Helen figure in Forster's earlier writing, for instance, in the sublimated rape of "The Story of a Panic" and George's sudden kissing of Lucy in *A Room with a View;* they recur later in the Marabar Caves episode of *A Passage to India* and in "The Other Boat" (1957), where the angst occasioned by racial and cultural "otherness" results in sexual violence, imagined in the one case, actual in the other. The manuscripts of *Howards End* show that in revising the Paul-Helen scene, Forster deemphasized its physicality, a revision consistent with others he made while polishing the novel, partly to heighten the theme of comradeship, but partly to further the repression of the physical (Forster, *Manuscripts* 23; Stape, "Leonard's" 126). Critics of *Howards End* have mostly concentrated on its thematics, narrative technique, and sociopolitics, yet a psychoanalytic approach reveals the Paul-Helen scene as a key to some of the novel's central tensions.

The application of psychoanalytic techniques to literary works reveals how an author's unconscious experience is reflected in and mediated through language and symbol. Flexibly pursued, it permits a variety of insights into a work's thematics and may also affect judgment about its final achievement. *Howards End* has received only some criticism of this kind,[1] though it offers a compendium of information about the man who, between the ages of twenty-nine and thirty-one, drew upon his personal experience to produce a classic exemplum of Edwardian fiction. One critic has argued that "though not directly autobiographical," the novel "examines Forster's *economic* origins" (Delany 285). More precisely, it addresses the origins of his emotional life, his values, and his attitudes toward himself and his society. While primarily an extended inquiry into the political and social conditions of Edwardian England, *Howards End* is also a psychological self-portrait. At both manifest and latent levels the novel reveals Forster's preoccupations during the relatively brief period of its genesis and drafting, as well as fundamental aspects of his sexual psychology.

Psychoanalytical criticism openly targets both "the teller" *and* "the tale," to recall D. H. Lawrence's terms; or, as Norman Holland has observed, it treats the work "as though it were a dream" or "some ideal patient" speaking (136). This kind of critical inquiry is an exercise in retrieval and etiology, a search for a work's origins in the writer's private history. At the same time, the application of this methodology helps to define and highlight the individual writer's complicated relationship to his or her specific social milieu. The "author," then, persists as a practical construct despite recent theorizing about the existence of a polyphonic self and social collaboration in the production of texts.

Psychoanalytic readings, with their primary focus on the private experience behind the publicly circulated text, justify themselves by exposing facets of artistic production that might otherwise remain inaccessible or only partially revealed. Whatever the orientation of such analysis — Freudian symbol hunting in the 1950s, Jungian archetypes in the 1960s, Lacanian analysis in the 1970s, or Winnicottian object-relations theory in the 1980s — it seeks to account for and enrich understanding of a work's widest, occasionally concealed, context and to illumine the way in which its structure, characters, and thematics dynamically project aspects of its writer's shifting inner world.

---

[1]Stone and Golden offer Jungian readings. Armstrong focuses on existential psychology.

2

For Forster the writing of *Howards End,* which he began in June 1908 and finished in July 1910, comprised a prolonged backward glance at the circumstances and experiences of his childhood and early adolescence. Howards End recreates some of the atmosphere and actual features of Rooksnest, a modest red-brick villa, once a farmhouse, near Stevenage, Hertfordshire, where his newly widowed mother, Lily Forster, established a home from 1883 to 1893.[2] Like the Schlegels' Wickham Place ("Ours is a female house," declares Margaret [54]), Rooksnest was exclusively feminine, lacking, aside from the visiting garden boy or tutor, a counterbalancing male presence. Lily Forster was at its core and continued to remain at the center of her son's life until her death in advanced old age in 1945, when Forster himself was in his mid-sixties. Forster's childhood at Stevenage — his mother's warmth and affection, their relative isolation, the closeness of their house to the natural environment — provided him, he believed, a bedrock for his life and work. At the same time, as Francis King has observed, a solitary upbringing and an overly close mother made for "the classic Freudian recipe for subsequent confusion" about sexual identity (5).

While the explanatory power of this "Freudian recipe" for the Oedipus complex now appears too simplistic to contemporary students of sexual psychology, the novel undeniably describes an unbalanced sexual environment based on Forster's memories. Ruth Wilcox, its mother figure, and Margaret Schlegel, her heir, contrast with a group of inadequate or negative males who in some cases border on caricature. Masculinity and the male impulse appear to be inimical to the novel's "feminine" value system, which esteems connectedness, feeling, and intuition. The sex lines are too obviously demarcated by a "sheep-and-goats" polarity that critics have generally faulted in Forster's fiction, the origins of which may partly lie in late-Victorian discourse about the double.[3]

---

[2]Ashby discusses the period of the Forsters' residence at Stevenage and provides a number of photographs of Rooksnest.

[3]Discourse about dualism that pervaded late-nineteenth-century thought and writing emerged in psychoanalytic theory as the phenomenon of the "split personality" (Heller et al.). Summers suggests that *Howards End* treats various "dualities of existence," including "the inner life and the outer life, the past and the present, the body and the soul, the masculine and the feminine, the city and the country, the visible and the invisible, the prose and the passion, life and death" (106–07).

The idealized, even sentimentalized, depiction of Mrs. Wilcox and of the feminine might in part represent an overcompensation for Forster's ambivalent feelings toward his mother and his resentment (largely repressed) of her influence on him. He was, moreover, fully aware that the central drama of this work — intimate relations between men and women — was composed against the grain of his deepest private longings and interests. In a 1907 essay entitled "Pessimism in Literature," Forster observed how early twentieth-century social changes problematized the fictional presentation of women and marriage. In 1911 he resentfully characterized heterosexual relations as "the only subject that I both can and may treat" (qtd. in Stape, *E. M. Forster* 41). (In old age he also commented with annoyance about the "swish of the skirts" and "non-sexual embraces" in *Howards End* [Forster, *Commonplace* 204].) Fully conscious of his homosexuality at this stage of his life, he found public self-expression censored by societally imposed models ingrained first by his mother and reinforced by his society. Moreover, and crucially, during the two years he was writing the novel, he was one-sidedly in love with Syed Ross Masood, a handsome and charismatic young Indian whom he had tutored in Latin. His day-to-day occupation, however, was to fashion a highly detailed depiction of a society that refused to acknowledge his sexual desires and criminalized their expression. Forster took refuge in fantasy that covertly articulates this alienation and his obsessive anxieties about exclusion and continuity, themes he had already explored in *The Longest Journey*. At the same time, in writing about affective relationships he was locating or attempting to claim some space for himself in a society hostile to his inclinations, and in this respect, writing served to lessen a sense of alienation.[4]

Self-division of this kind often prompts heightened self-awareness, and, for the homosexual, necessarily deepens a perception of isolation and displacement. As Charles Taylor has argued, the self is constituted not in objective descriptions but only in interpretations located in a community "outside" it (33–34). Societal hostility, then, toward homosexual love may thus give rise to tensions and anxieties that find

[4]Whereas Rosenbaum finds homosexuality "not much in evidence" (477), Duckworth draws attention to the characterization of "Auntie Tibby," a possible homosexual scandal involving one of the Schlegels' acquaintances, and a possible lesbian relationship between Helen and her friend Monica (81–83). In a note to the Abinger edition of *Howards End*, Stallybrass suggests that with the hindsight of *Maurice*, Margaret's set piece about "eternal differences" can be read as "a concealed plea for charity towards homosexuals" (364). See Bakshi for a useful placing of Forster's novels within Edwardian constructions of homosexuality.

relief in aggression, actual or projected, ranging from suicide to displaced activities that could include the writing of fiction in which a
self-image dies of heart disease. The consequences of this pattern of
displacement for Forster's work are diversely registered, not least in
the compensatory idealization of the feminine in *Howards End* and in
the novel's dualities and divisions. In addition to their obvious social
and political significance, the novel's pleas for "connection" are resonantly and poignantly personal.

The frustrating and even disabling lack of connection in Forster's
emotional life finds partial expression in *Howards End* but is more
overtly signaled in "The Machine Stops," a dystopian short story
Forster completed in 1908, after he had already begun drafting the
novel. This intriguing exercise in science fiction is not only a critical response to the faith in a technological future that, in Forster's view,
H. G. Wells expressed in novels such as *The Day of the Comet* (1906);
but it is also a significant key to *Howards End,* which was written concurrently with "The Machine Stops" and shares some of its thematic
materials. These are sometimes, however, presented in reverse: an
emotionally absent mother figure (Vashti), dominates, and the protagonist (Vashti's son, Kuno) longs for and identifies with an idealized
male, the hero of the constellation Orion.[5] The story's ending, like
that of *Howards End,* ushers in a new time after the violent destruction
of the old order; and, allowing for the different fictional modes, the
fate of Kuno is similar to that of Leonard Bast: both unsuccessfully
strive for upward "expansion" and desire to break out of the confines
set for them. Kuno's attempts to emerge from emotional paralysis
(without an "egression permit" he escapes to the surface of the earth
from his underground cell) place his life in jeopardy and end in his
maiming. Psychologically, the story's key concern is escape and separation from the maternal, which is symbolized by the emotionally cata-
tonic Vashti and the womb-like underground world. Kuno longs
simultaneously to escape and to receive his mother's love. Her rejection of him propels him to seek freedom — and maleness. As S. P.
Rosenbaum has observed, Vashti has replaced physical reality, specifically the body, with aesthetic experience (336), a fear that Forster reg-
isters throughout his writings and that haunts *Howards End.* Tellingly,
Kuno's longing for a male figure who represents independence and

[5]The story's homoeroticism is implied in an entry Forster made in his diary for January 11, 1908: "Orion, a ghost, but the sight of him gives physical joy as if a man of the
kind I care for was in heaven" (qtd. in Herz 153).

self-sufficiency, a version of the "wholeness" that *Howards End* frequently alludes to, activates the tentacles of Kuno's society to confine him. The "mending-machine," a policing apparatus with which his mother identifies, symbolically if not actually castrates Kuno. The act assures the jealous mother's hold over her son, and the apocalyptic conclusion, as the machine finally stops, is an image of psychic disintegration, although the neglected claims of the body are asserted by the dying kiss of son and mother as their world collapses around them.

"The Machine Stops" perhaps too clearly dramatizes Forster's frustration with his emotional situation and with his inability to change it. The story's ending is a fantasized murder-suicide, and as Flaubert had claimed of Emma Bovary, so Forster could have said of his protagonist: "Kuno, *c'est moi.*" Elements of this foreshortened psychological self-portrait are introduced into and reworked in the more expansive structure of *Howards End,* which articulates the guilt consequent upon the adult son's attempt to break away from the romance that he and his mother have collaborated in and that he senses he has outgrown.

If "The Machine Stops" provides signal clues to Forster's psychological condition at the time of the writing of *Howards End,* his activities during this period provide an explanatory context for the novel's psychological concerns.[6] Its original inspiration, in June 1908, came from reading Walt Whitman, of whose homoeroticism Forster was aware through the writings of Edward Carpenter, the period's champion of "homogenic love." The next twenty-four months were turbulent as Forster's love for Masood gained urgency, alternately tormenting him and providing the occasional satisfaction of loving, if not being loved in return. During these two years Forster supplemented his inherited income by teaching at the Working Men's College and lecturing for Cambridge University's extension program. These activities brought him closely into touch with young men longing for "culture" and "betterment." These commitments provided him with considerable material for Leonard Bast, whose uneasy contact with the Schlegels' world of cultured ease — Forster's own world — has earlier roots. In the depiction of Leonard, Forster returns to a sharply drawn conflict that he had already fictionalized in "Ansell" (1901), between "instinct," represented by Ansell, a character named after a Rooksnest garden boy, and "culture," represented by his bookish self. In both

---

[6]For detailed discussions of Forster's life during the writing of *Howards End,* see Furbank 1: 160–87; Beauman 216–25; and Stape, *E. M. Forster* 31–38.

this early short story and *Howards End,* the conflict between the aesthetic and the physical is closely linked to the eroticization of difference, a pervasive theme in Forster's writing.

In *Howards End* this motif receives its fullest expression in the sexual (mis)connection between Leonard and Helen, a scene that echoes and plays variations upon the Paul-Helen encounter. The episode has been severely criticized, faulted on the one hand for being unprepared and on the other for its lack of realism. Samuel Hynes claims that Forster was unable to portray heterosexual love convincingly (115). From another perspective, the scene's symbolic imperatives tend to overwhelm the novel's dominant realism. These are only partial explanations, however, for the episode's failure also lies in complex personal factors. It is a wish fulfillment of Forster's necessarily frustrated desire simultaneously to break down and to maintain class barriers, a situation that mirrors his actual experiences with the eroticized Others by whom he wished to be dominated sexually and whom he reciprocally dominated socially and intellectually.[7] This dynamic operated obviously in his contacts with men attending the Working Men's College. It also existed embryonically in his friendship with Masood (the racial Other) and was later fully acted out both with Mohammed el Adl, the young Egyptian with whom Forster fell in love in Alexandria, and in the pattern of his intense involvement with working-class men. Helen, no less than Leonard, is a sexual outlaw, crossing boundaries marked out by society, and in this sense she is a covert self-portrait.

The pattern of breaking down and maintaining barriers also informs the attempted connection between Margaret Schlegel and Henry Wilcox. Though the "otherness" of class distinction is considerably more subtle in this instance, the opposition between the aesthetic and the physical recurs, along with the pattern of subdued or displaced violence. Henry's brusque and unexpected first kiss is a piece of masculine stage bravado: he "said 'Margaret' rather huskily, turned, dropped his cigar, and took her in his arms" while the "startled" Margaret "nearly screamed" (166). Their essential incompatibility and repeated failures to communicate yield only a forced connection that, in the view of early reviewers and later critics, mars the novel, particularly at its conclusion. Lionel Trilling, for instance, appositely commented that the final connection is forged at the cost of too thorough a "gelding" of the male (135). The division of the male characters, to recall the terms of Forster's friend Goldsworthy Lowes Dickinson, into

[7]See Rahman and Salter for discussions of Forster's sexuality.

"Red-bloods" and "Mollycoddles" (195) also represents extremes and oppositions in Forster's sexual psychology. Although useful dramatically, the split nonetheless risks straightforward caricature: Tibby's exaggerated aestheticism finds its opposite in Charles Wilcox's stagy masculinity. In presenting characters in these ways, *Howards End* displays the genesis of compositional and aesthetic problems in intimate psychological factors.

The most problematic male representation is, however, Leonard Bast, a character through whom, whatever the obvious and extremely marked differences in class, temperament, and experience, Forster essays an oblique self-portrait of aspects of himself as an outsider. Jung's theory that dream figures invariably represent projections of the dreamer can be extrapolated to fictional characters. This basic proposition finds its echo in Jaroslav Havelka's formulation that the ego of the creative individual experiences omnipotence in inventing doubles that liberate him or her from real-life limitations (Slochower 215–16). Not only Leonard, then, but all the novel's characters may rehearse the author's conscious and unconscious identifications, conflicts, and wish fulfillments.

Forster's identification with his female characters establishes his problematic integration into Edwardian constructions of masculinity, particularly their emphasis on the nexus of money and power. While the novel severely criticizes these constructions, it is, of course, far from engaging in reductive polemic. The main positive characters, Mrs. Wilcox and Margaret (who are, in one sense, a single composite character since Margaret later literally becomes "Mrs. Wilcox"), embody and counsel "feminine" values. Critics have frequently noted how Margaret's voice blends and merges with Forster's own to the degree that she becomes "an extension of himself" (Rivenberg 171). The psychological implications of this narrative technique remain to be explored, but it is not surprising that more than one reviewer thought that a woman had written the novel (Beauman 223–24), and it has also been argued, although on a misreading of syntax, that the narrator is in fact a woman (Roby).

The main sexual problem Forster poses, however, and one that many readers feel is never satisfactorily resolved, is how to achieve a balance between the sexes in his loaded opposition between power and feeling. The novel nowhere argues a simple reversal of established sexual or political hegemonies; its epigraph, "Only connect . . ." (unlike the wording in Margaret's "sermon" [168]), may be read not as an imperative but, as the ellipsis indicates, a subjunctive, a condition expressing hope. The balance that the novel's plot appears to aspire to, however, remains more wished for than actualized. The tableau of connection — Henry, Margaret, and Helen holding hands at Howards End — is a symbolic substitute for a working out of the novel's sexual politics. Moreover, the closest and arguably most successful and fulfilled relationship (Alistair M. Duckworth characterizes it as the novel's "central value" [75] and most "convincing union" [79]) remains that between the two Schlegel sisters. This deeply emotional bond between similarities rather than opposites is in a broad sense homosocial rather than heterosocial and creates a subtext that in a displaced fashion voices Forster's homosexual identity.

Constrained to depict heterosexual relationships, Forster manages to do so mainly formally, and both contemporary and more recent critics have noted that his description lacks conviction. The exclusion of adult males from the new scheme of things at the end of the novel evokes the unbalanced sexual situation of Forster's Rooksnest childhood, and the male-female conflict remains intact. Margaret is married to a broken man, and Helen vows to remain single (as did Lily Forster, who declined at least one proposal of marriage during the period she and her son lived at Rooksnest). Contradicting the rhetoric of connection, then, the female and the feminine dominate. But whereas Anne Wright asserts that the "movement towards a female line of inheritance, together with the symbolic emasculation of the male figures, points to an endorsement of female power" (25–26), a psychoanalytic reading might contrarily observe how Forster's inability to separate his identity from his mother affects and ultimately hamstrings some of his handling of character, plot, and theme. Feminist readings are also inclined to miss the extent to which the novel's women characters project essentially male and homosexual dynamics and to underplay the fact that the power attained by emasculation is that of the devouring mother.[8] In love with Masood, resentful of his mother's restricting influence, and confronting matter that in a real sense was, and remained, at one remove, Forster produced a work of fissures and tensions that longs for resolution but fails to attain it. This lack of unity of effect mirrors psychogenetic factors, and thus readings focusing on the novel's failed liberalism tend to underemphasize or exclude from con-

---

[8]Finkelstein offers the most comprehensive feminist approach to Forster's work, though many of her observations have now been dated by later feminist theory. Wyatt-Brown sees the women characters as reflecting Forster's "positive" feelings about women, and Margaret as the product of Forster's memories of his mother and her friend Maimie Synott.

sideration the intrapersonal dynamics that generate and determine narrative strategies and thematics.[9]

## 3

Howards End is often viewed as a stable center of traditional rural values opposed to the flux and rootlessness of London. In psychoanalytic terms, however, the places of the novel suggest other possibilities. Thus, for instance, while Leonard and Jacky Bast's life in a cramped basement flat obviously forms part of the novel's social realism and its concern with questions of class, in psychoanalytic terms, the couple's basement further represents a relegated and marginalized sexuality, one positioned under the surface that Forster was forced to produce in dealing with his society. A symbol of the unconscious, the basement shelters those parts of the self that lie beneath the public persona and are subversive of it. The alliance between Leonard and Jacky lacks legal sanction and is lived in self-consciously defiant opposition to collective mores. "A fallen woman," Jacky is importantly situated in the discussion of the class wars as a representation of working-class culture, yet, more significantly, she is a means through which Forster articulates fears about the social legitimacy and "placement" of his own emotional and erotic desires. At this stage in his life, these desires were given, at best, partial expression, mainly through fantasy; his love of and strong sexual attraction to Masood were staged mostly within the socially and personally imposed conditions of concealment and duplicity. While the Basts' further exile in their eviction from this flat on the margins of "respectability" dramatizes the extent of Leonard's financial collapse (thanks in part to the bad advice given by Mr. Wilcox), it significantly places them outside society altogether, a theme repeated by Helen's self-exile and one that Forster returns to in his openly homosexual novel, *Maurice*, written in 1913–14 but not published until after his death.

The Basts' appearance at the wedding feast of Evie Wilcox and Percy Cahill enacts a fundamental opposition between the legitimate and the illegitimate, the socially conventional and the socially outlawed, with the further irony that Henry, who bases his life on externals, has had a hidden life — his affair with Jacky in Cyprus — that cannot be spoken of. In attempting to deal with it, Margaret retreats into

[9]See Page's study of *Howards End* 50–52, on the novel's heterogeneous generic allegiances and critical responses to them.

conventionality, forcing out "gentle words" that seem "to proceed from some other person" (210). More important, however, is the coerced silence of Leonard and Jacky, perhaps most obvious in Margaret's attempt to exclude them from Oniton, that represents the general condition of homosexuality in the period of the novel. The inability to articulate, registered in the Basts' impoverished speech modes, is not surprisingly a recurrent motif. Another attempted exclusion — Henry's refusal to allow Helen to stay overnight at Howards End — highlights Forster's concerns about "legitimacy" and sanity. The hostile portrait of the insensitive and misogynistic Mr. Mansbridge, the significantly named doctor whom Henry enlists to control Helen, encodes Forster's anxiety that the text too openly reveals his inner conflicts.

Leonard's death at Howards End is a retribution on the part of society for his transgression of orthodox sexual norms, possibly even for his identification with "feminine" values and interests. That his death is exacted by Charles Wilcox, the novel's most conventional male character, has widely been viewed as crucial. Charles, who identifies almost exclusively with societal values, assumes the role of society's chivalric avenger of Helen, the "wronged" woman. But Leonard, in addition to suffering physically, suffers mentally: convinced of his guilt, he longs for "confession" (274), for speech that would free him from his inner burden, end his isolation, and effect his reintegration into society. In his insomnia-induced reveries, he has visions of "a clenched fist" of moonlight (274) and "the smaller snakes" (274). The latter, resembling the mending-machine's wormlike tentacles in "The Machine Stops" or the "small snakes" of the Marabar Cave in *A Passage to India,* represent a repressed desire for punishment that, as Roy P. Basler points out, takes on "symbolic garb" because it is "regarded as nonsense by the waking mind" (14).

Whatever its melodramatic aspects and thematic relevance to the social issues that Forster treats, Leonard's death scene fully dramatizes Forster's fears and concerns about his own emotional life. Though Leonard fails to complete his confession, Forster, even if not wholly aware of it, symbolically succeeds and, in doing so, eloquently articulates his own dilemma. The scene addresses his fear that aestheticism, symbolized by the bookcase that tumbles down upon Leonard, would eventually deaden him to instinct and the physical, a topic also addressed in the ironized portrait of Tibby, who retreats from life into literature, food, and "Oxford." Leonard's death from heart disease emphasizes a basic lack of vitality: in the end his internal mechanisms are simply unable to supply him the energy needed to sustain life.

Like the death of another self-image, that of Rickie Elliot in *The Longest Journey*, Leonard's is a ritual sacrifice for a potentially more vital self, for the son who is his reincarnation and who will claim an inheritance, actual and spiritual, that Leonard himself could never possess. A reading stressing the encoding of collective psychology might view his death as an offering made to ensure harvest, an enactment of the agrarian myth that Sir James Frazer explicates in *The Golden Bough*, which Forster knew (Stape, *E. M. Forster* 26). A more Freudian approach, however, might read the death as a return to and devouring by the *mater magna*, Mother Earth herself. At the same time, the national myth that the novel inscribes, the victory of rural (Mother) England, is assured. Leonard's death thus consummates the oedipal yearnings feared yet desired throughout the novel.

The novel's coda has widely been commented upon as a fantasy that achieves through symbolism the connections between Schlegels and Wilcoxes that do not occur in the "real world." Its terms are also essentially autobiographical, as the "newly widowed" Helen and her infant son settle at Howards End, with Helen's son destined to become its eventual owner. In psychological terms, the ending reenacts the premature and sudden death of Forster's father and the subsequent installation of Lily Forster and her young son at Rooksnest. Moreover, it provides a compensation for his father's abandonment of him by death and for Forster's later traumatic double exile — from his mother's unqualified affection and from a beloved place — experienced in early adolescence.

Seen in these terms, the ending embodies a longing for childhood simplicities and dependency. The outside world is closed out, at least provisionally, and the mother-and-son romance finds its wish fulfillment. Despite contrary pulls, Forster opted finally — and however unconsciously — for security and silence. Tied to his mother, sexually frustrated, muzzled about the meaning of his life, he experienced a series of creative false starts after completing *Howards End*. He abandoned his next novel, *Arctic Summer* (1911), wrote homoerotic short stories and *Maurice* (1913–14), not for publication but for private satisfaction, and in 1914–15 attempted but could not finish a book about Samuel Butler (of whose homosexuality he was aware). The writing of *Howards End* may rightly be seen as a turning point in its author's career as his most ambitious and most fully achieved fiction to date, but it also represents the climax of an acute crisis of identity. While Forster may well have found public acclaim problematic and possibly inhibiting, this alone is unlikely to have so crippled him as to block further writing, as has been suggested (Wilkinson 166; Furbank 1: 191). Taken as a psychological document, *Howards End* amply signals regression, a desire for explicitly maternal protection from the encroaching "red rust" of adult concern and for the sustaining and all-encompassing nurturing received in childhood. The rooted home, set in a verdant and fecund countryside, which the novel explicitly represents as maternal and static, attains mythic stature. As Terry Eagleton has written, "an original lost object — the mother's body . . . drives forward the narrative of our lives, impelling us to pursue substitutes for this lost paradise in the endless metonymic movement of desire" (185). Having retrieved the "lost object," at least in fantasy, Forster is riven by insecurities about keeping it, for at the conclusion of the novel, "London" — the outside world with its demands and compromises — threatens. The "goblins" (the phrase itself recalls childhood fears) cannot disappear simply by one's wishing they would, and their distant presence at the novel's end gives to the triumphant cries celebrating plentiful harvest a somber, even sinister, note.

## WORKS CITED

Armstrong, Paul B. "E. M. Forster's *Howards End:* The Existential Crisis of the Liberal Imagination." *Mosaic* 8.1 (1974): 183–99.

Ashby, Margaret. *Forster Country.* Stevenage, Eng.: Flaunden, 1991.

Bakshi, Parminder. "The Politics of Desire: E. M. Forster's Encounters with India." *"A Passage to India."* Ed. Tony Davies and Nigel Wood. Theory in Practice Ser. Buckingham, Eng.: Open UP, 1994. 23–64.

Basler, Roy P. *Sex, Symbolism, and Psychology in Literature.* New York: Octagon, 1975.

Beauman, Nicola. *Morgan: A Biography of E. M. Forster.* London: Hodder, 1993; New York: Knopf, 1994.

Delany, Paul. "'Islands of Money': Rentier Culture in E. M. Forster's *Howards End.*" *English Literature in Transition, 1880–1920* 31.3 (1988): 285–96.

Dickinson, Goldsworthy Lowes. *Appearances: Notes of Travel East and West.* Garden City: Doubleday, 1914.

Duckworth, Alistair M. *"Howards End": E. M. Forster's House of Fiction.* Twayne's Masterwork Studies Ser. 93. New York: Twayne, 1992.

Eagleton, Terry. *Literary Theory: An Introduction.* Minneapolis: U of Minnesota P, 1983.

Finkelstein, Bonnie Blumenthal. *Forster's Women: Eternal Differences.* New York: Columbia UP, 1975.

Forster, E. M. "Ansell." 1901. *The Life to Come and Other Stories.* Ed. Oliver Stallybrass. London: Arnold, 1972; New York: Norton, 1973. 1–9.

——. *Commonplace Book.* Ed. Philip Gardner. Stanford: Stanford UP, 1985.

——. "The Machine Stops." 1909. *The Eternal Moment and Other Stories.* London: Sidgwick, 1928. 1–61.

——. *The Manuscripts of "Howards End".* Ed. Oliver Stallybrass. London: Arnold, 1973.

——. "Pessimism in Literature." 1907. *Albergo Empedocle and Other Writings.* Ed. George H. Thomson. New York: Liveright, 1971. 129–45.

Furbank, P. N. *E. M. Forster: A Life.* 2 vols. London: Secker, 1978–1979.

Golden, Kenneth L. "Jung, Modern Dissociation, and Forster's *Howards End.*" *CLA Journal* 29 (1985): 221–31.

Heller, Thomas C., et al., eds. *Reconstructing Individualism: Autonomy, Individuality, and the Self in Western Thought.* Stanford: Stanford UP, 1986.

Herz, Judith Scherer. *The Short Narratives of E. M. Forster.* London: Macmillan, 1988.

Holland, Norman. "The 'Unconscious' of Literature: The Psychoanalytic Approach." *Contemporary Criticism.* Ed. Malcolm Bradbury and David Palmer. Stratford-upon-Avon Studies 12; New York: St. Martin's, 1971. 131–53.

Hynes, Samuel. "Forster's Cramp." *Edwardian Occasions: Essays on English Writing in the Early Twentieth Century.* London: Routledge, 1972. 114–22.

King, Francis. *E. M. Forster and His World.* London: Thames, 1978.

Page, Malcolm. *"Howards End."* The Critics Debate Series. London: Macmillan, 1993.

Rahman, Tariq. *"Maurice* and *The Longest Journey:* A Study of E. M. Forster's Deviation from the Representation of Male Homosexuality in Literature." *Studies in English Literature* (Tokyo) (1990): 57–75.

Rivenberg, Paul R. "The Role of the Essayist-Commentator in *Howards End.*" *E. M. Forster: Centenary Revaluations.* Ed. Judith

Scherer Herz and Robert K. Martin. Toronto: U of Toronto P; London: Macmillan, 1982. 167–76.

Roby, Kinley E. "Irony and the Narrative Voice in *Howards End*." *Journal of Narrative Technique* 2 (1972): 116–24.

Rosenbaum, S. P. *Edwardian Bloomsbury: The Early Literary History of the Bloomsbury Group.* Vol. 2. London: Macmillan; New York: St. Martin's, 1994.

Salter, Donald. "'That Is My Ticket': The Homosexual Writings of E. M. Forster." *London Magazine* Feb.–Mar. 1975: 5–33.

Slochower, Harry. "Contemporary Psychoanalytic Theories on Creativity in the Arts." *Literary Criticism and Psychology.* Ed. Joseph P. Strelka. University Park: Pennsylvania State UP, 1976. 207–22.

Stape, J. H. *An E. M. Forster Chronology.* London: Macmillan, 1993.

———. "Leonard's 'Fatal Forgotten Umbrella': Sexuality and the Manuscripts of *Howards End*." *Journal of Modern Literature* 9 (1981–82): 123–32.

Stone, Wilfred. *The Cave and the Mountain: A Study of E. M. Forster.* Stanford: Stanford UP, 1966.

Summers, Claude J. *E. M. Forster.* New York: Ungar, 1983.

Taylor, Charles. *Sources of the Self: The Making of the Modern Identity.* Cambridge: Harvard UP, 1989.

Trilling, Lionel. *E. M. Forster.* Norwalk, CT: New Directions, 1943.

Wilkinson, L. P. "The Later Years." *E. M. Forster: Interviews and Recollections.* Ed. J. H. Stape. London: Macmillan; New York: St. Martin's, 1993. 161–79.

Wright, Anne. *Literature of Crisis, 1910–22: "Howards End," "Heartbreak House," "Women in Love," and "The Waste Land."* London: Macmillan, 1984.

Wyatt-Brown, Anne M. "*Howards End:* Celibacy and Stalemate." *Psychohistory Review* 12 (Fall 1983): 26–33.

# Cultural Criticism

# and

# *Howards End*

## WHAT IS CULTURAL CRITICISM?

What do you think of when you think of culture? The opera or
ballet? A performance of a Mozart symphony at Lincoln Center or a
Rembrandt show at the De Young Museum in San Francisco? Does
the phrase "cultural event" conjure up images of young people in jeans
and T-shirts — or of people in their sixties dressed formally? Most
people hear "culture" and think "high culture." Consequently, when
they first hear of cultural criticism, most people assume it is more formal than, well, say, formalism. They suspect it is "highbrow," in both
subject and style.

Nothing could be further from the truth. Cultural critics oppose
the view that culture refers exclusively to high culture, Culture with a
capital *C*. Cultural critics want to make the term refer to popular, folk,
urban, and mass (mass-produced, -disseminated, -mediated, and
-consumed) culture, as well as to that culture we associate with the so-
called classics. Raymond Williams, an early British cultural critic whose
ideas will later be described at greater length, suggested that "art and
culture are ordinary"; he did so not to "pull art down" but rather
to point out that there is "creativity in all our living. . . . We create
our human world as we have thought of art being created" (*Revolution* 37).

Cultural critics have consequently placed a great deal of emphasis on what Michel de Certeau has called "the practice of everyday life." Rather than approaching literature in the elitist way that academic literary critics have traditionally approached it, cultural critics view it more as an anthropologist would. They ask how it emerges from and competes with other forms of discourse (science, for instance, or television) within a given culture. They seek to understand the social contexts in which a given text was written, and under what conditions it was — and is — produced, disseminated, read, and used.

Contemporary cultural critics are as willing to write about *Star Trek* as they are to analyze James Joyce's *Ulysses,* a modern literary classic full of allusions to Homer's *Odyssey.* And when they write about *Ulysses,* they are likely to view it as a collage reflecting and representing cultural forms common to Joyce's Dublin, such as advertising, journalism, film, and pub life. Cultural critics typically show how the boundary we tend to envision between high and low forms of culture — forms thought of as important on one hand and relatively trivial on the other — is transgressed in all sorts of exciting ways within works on both sides of the putative cultural divide.

A cultural critic writing about a revered classic might contrast it with a movie, or even a comic-strip version produced during a later period. Alternatively, the literary classic might be seen in a variety of other ways: in light of some more common form of reading material (a novel by Jane Austen might be viewed in light of Gothic romances or ladies' conduct manuals); as the reflection of some common cultural myths or concerns (*Adventures of Huckleberry Finn* might be shown to reflect and shape American myths about race and concerns about juvenile delinquency); or as an example of how texts move back and forth across the alleged boundary between "low" and "high" culture. For instance, one group of cultural critics has pointed out that although Shakespeare's history plays probably started off as popular works enjoyed by working people, they were later considered "highbrow" plays that only the privileged and educated could appreciate. That view of them changed, however, due to later film productions geared toward a national audience. A film version of *Henry V* produced during World War II, for example, made a powerful, popular, patriotic statement about England's greatness during wartime (Humm, Stigant, and Widdowson 6–7). More recently, cultural critics have analyzed the "cultural work" accomplished cooperatively by Shakespeare and Kenneth Branagh in the latter's 1992 film production of *Henry V.*

In combating old definitions of what constitutes culture, of course, cultural critics sometimes end up contesting old definitions of what constitutes the literary canon, that is, the once-agreed-upon honor roll of Great Books. They tend to do so, however, neither by adding books (and movies and television sitcoms) *to* the old list of texts that every "culturally literate" person should supposedly know nor by substituting some kind of counterculture canon. Instead, they tend to critique the very *idea* of canon.

Cultural critics want to get us away from thinking about certain works as the "best" ones produced by a given culture. They seek to be more descriptive and less evaluative, more interested in relating than in rating cultural products and events. They also aim to discover the (often political) reasons *why* a certain kind of aesthetic or cultural product is more valued than others. This is particularly true when the product in question is one produced since 1945, for most cultural critics follow Jean Baudrillard (*Simulations,* 1981) and Andreas Huyssen (*The Great Divide,* 1986) in thinking that any distinctions that may once have existed between high, popular, and mass culture collapsed after the end of World War II. Their discoveries have led them beyond the literary canon, prompting them to interrogate many other value hierarchies. For instance, Pierre Bourdieu in *Distinction: A Social Critique of the Judgment of Taste* (1984 [1979]) and Dick Hebdige in *Hiding the Light: On Images and Things* (1988) have argued that definitions of "good taste" — which are instrumental in fostering and reinforcing cultural discrimination — tell us at least as much about prevailing social, economic, and political conditions as they do about artistic quality and value.

In an article entitled "The Need for Cultural Studies," four groundbreaking cultural critics have written that "Cultural Studies should . . . abandon the goal of giving students access to that which represents a culture." A literary work, they go on to suggest, should be seen in relation to other works, to economic conditions, or to broad social discourses (about childbirth, women's education, rural decay, and so on) within whose contexts it makes sense. Perhaps most important, critics practicing cultural studies should counter the prevalent notion of culture as some preformed whole. Rather than being static or monolithic, culture is really a set of interactive *cultures,* alive and changing, and cultural critics should be present- and even future-oriented. They should be "resisting intellectuals," and cultural studies should be "an emancipatory project" (Giroux et al. 478–80).

The paragraphs above are peppered with words like *oppose, counter, deny, resist, combat, abandon,* and *emancipatory.* What such words quite accurately suggest is that a number of cultural critics view themselves in political, even oppositional, terms. Not only are they likely to take on the literary canon, they are also likely to oppose the institution of the university, for that is where the old definitions of culture as high culture (and as something formed, finished, and canonized) have been most vigorously preserved, defended, and reinforced.

Cultural critics have been especially critical of the departmental structure of universities, which, perhaps more than anything else, has kept the study of the "arts" relatively distinct from the study of history, not to mention from the study of such things as television, film, advertising, journalism, popular photography, folklore, current affairs, shoptalk, and gossip. By maintaining artificial boundaries, universities have tended to reassert the high/low culture distinction, implying that all the latter subjects are best left to historians, sociologists, anthropologists, and communication theorists. Cultural critics have taken issue with this implication, arguing that the way of thinking reinforced by the departmentalized structure of universities keeps us from seeing the aesthetics of an advertisement as well as the propagandistic elements of a work of literature. Cultural critics have consequently mixed and matched the analytical procedures developed in a variety of disciplines. They have formed — and encouraged other scholars to form — networks and centers, often outside of those enforced departmentally.

Some initially loose interdisciplinary networks have, over time, solidified to become cultural studies programs and majors. As this has happened, a significant if subtle danger has arisen. Richard Johnson, who along with Hebdige, Stuart Hall, and Richard Hoggart was instrumental in developing the Center for Contemporary Cultural Studies at Birmingham University in England, has warned that cultural studies must not be allowed to turn into yet another traditional academic discipline — one in which students encounter a canon replete with soap operas and cartoons, one in which belief in the importance of such popular forms has become an "orthodoxy" (39). The only principles that critics doing cultural studies can doctrinally espouse, Johnson suggests, are the two that have thus far been introduced: the principle that "culture" has been an "inegalitarian" concept, a "tool" of "condescension," and the belief that a new, "interdisciplinary (and even antidisciplinary)" approach to *true* culture (that is, to the forms in which culture currently lives) is required now that history, art, and the communications media are so complex and interrelated (42).

The object of cultural study should not be a body of works assumed to comprise or reflect a given culture. Rather, it should be human consciousness, and the goal of that critical analysis should be to understand and show how that consciousness is itself forged and formed, to a great extent, by cultural forces. "Subjectivities," as Johnson has put it, are "produced, not given, and are . . . objects of inquiry" inevitably related to "social practices," whether those involve factory rules, supermarket behavior patterns, reading habits, advertisements, myths, or languages and other signs to which people are exposed (44–45).

Although the United States has probably contributed more than any other nation to the *media* through which culture is currently expressed, and although many if not most contemporary practitioners of cultural criticism are North American, the evolution of cultural criticism and, more broadly, cultural studies has to a great extent been influenced by theories developed in Great Britain and on the European continent.

Among the Continental thinkers whose work allowed for the development of cultural studies are those whose writings we associate with structuralism and poststructuralism. Using the linguistic theory of Ferdinand de Saussure, structuralists suggested that the structures of language lie behind all human organization. They attempted to create a *semiology* — a science of signs — that would give humankind at once a scientific and holistic way of studying the world and its human inhabitants. Roland Barthes, a structuralist who later shifted toward poststructuralism, attempted to recover literary language from the isolation in which it had been studied and to show that the laws that govern it govern all signs, from road signs to articles of clothing. Claude Lévi-Strauss, an anthropologist who studied the structures of everything from cuisine to villages to myths, looked for and found recurring, common elements that transcended the differences within and between cultures.

Of the structuralist and poststructuralist thinkers who have had an impact on the evolution of cultural studies, Jacques Lacan is one of three whose work has been particularly influential. A structuralist psychoanalytic theorist, Lacan posited that the human unconscious is structured like a language and treated dreams not as revealing symptoms of repression but, rather, as forms of discourse. Lacan also argued that the ego, subject, or self that we think of as being natural (our individual human nature) is in fact a product of the social order and its symbolic systems (especially, but not exclusively, language). Lacan's thought has served as the theoretical underpinning for cultural critics seeking to show the way in which subjectivities are produced by social discourses and practices.

Jacques Derrida, a French philosopher whose name has become synonymous with poststructuralism, has had an influence on cultural criticism at least as great as that of Lacan. The linguistic focus of structuralist thought has by no means been abandoned by poststructuralists, in spite of their opposition to structuralism's tendency to find universal patterns instead of textual and cultural contradictions. Indeed, Derrida has provocatively asserted that *"there is nothing outside the text"* (*Grammatology* 158), by which he means something like the following: we come to know the world through language, and even our most worldly actions and practices (the Gulf War, the wearing of condoms) are dependent upon discourses (even if they deliberately contravene those discourses). Derrida's "deconstruction" of the world/text distinction, like his deconstruction of so many of the hierarchical oppositions we habitually use to interpret and evaluate reality, has allowed cultural critics to erase the boundaries between high and low culture, classic and popular literary texts, and literature and other cultural discourses that, following Derrida, may be seen as manifestations of the same textuality.

Michel Foucault is the third Continental thinker associated with structuralism and/or poststructuralism who has had a particularly powerful impact on the evolution of cultural studies — and perhaps *the* strongest influence on American cultural criticism and the so-called new historicism, an interdisciplinary form of cultural criticism whose evolution has often paralleled that of cultural criticism. Although Foucault broke with Marxism after the French student uprisings of 1968, he was influenced enough by Marxist thought to study cultures in terms of power relationships. Unlike Marxists, however, Foucault refused to see power as something exercised by a dominant class over a subservient class. Indeed, he emphasized that power is not just repressive power, that is, a tool of conspiracy by one individual or institution against another. Power, rather, is a whole complex of forces; it is that which produces what happens.

Thus even a tyrannical aristocrat does not simply wield power but is empowered by "discourses" — accepted ways of thinking, writing, and speaking — and practices that embody, exercise, and amount to power. Foucault tried to view all things, from punishment to sexuality, in terms of the widest possible variety of discourses. As a result, he traced what he called the "genealogy" of topics he studied through texts that more traditional historians and literary critics would have overlooked, examining (in Lynn Hunt's words) "memoirs of deviants, diaries, political treatises, architectural blueprints, court records, doctors' reports — appl[ying] consistent principles of analysis in search of moments of reversal in discourse, in search of events as loci of the conflict where social practices were transformed" (Hunt 39). Foucault tended not only to build interdisciplinary bridges but also, in the process, to bring into the study of culture the "histories of women, homosexuals, and minorities" — groups seldom studied by those interested in Culture with a capital C (Hunt 45).

Of the British influences on cultural studies and criticism, two stand out prominently. One, the Marxist historian E. P. Thompson, revolutionized the study of the industrial revolution by writing about its impact on human attitudes, even consciousness. He showed how a shared cultural view, specifically that of what constitutes a fair or just price, influenced crowd behavior and caused such things as the "food riots" of the eighteenth and nineteenth centuries (during which the women of Nottingham repriced breads in the shops of local bakers, paid for the goods they needed, and carried them away). The other, even more important early British influence on contemporary cultural criticism and cultural studies was Raymond Williams, who coined the phrase "culture is ordinary." In works like *Culture and Society: 1780–1950* (1958) and *The Long Revolution* (1961) Williams demonstrated that culture is not fixed and finished but, rather, living and evolving. One of the changes he called for was the development of a common socialist culture.

Although Williams dissociated himself from Marxism during the period 1945–58, he always followed the Marxist practice of viewing culture in relation to ideologies, which he defined as the "residual," "dominant," or "emerging" ways of viewing the world held by classes or individuals holding power in a given social group. He avoided dwelling on class conflict and class oppression, however, tending instead to focus on people as people, on how they experience the conditions in which they find themselves and creatively respond to those conditions through their social practices. A believer in the resiliency of the individual, Williams produced a body of criticism notable for what Stuart Hall has called its "humanism" (63).

As is clearly suggested in several of the preceding paragraphs, Marxism is the background to the background of cultural criticism.

What isn't as clear is that some contemporary cultural critics consider themselves Marxist critics as well. It is important, therefore, to have some familiarity with certain Marxist concepts — those that would have been familiar to Foucault, Thompson, and Williams, plus those espoused by contemporary cultural critics who self-identify with Marxism. That familiarity can be gained from an introduction to the works of four important Marxist thinkers: Mikhail Bakhtin, Walter Benjamin, Antonio Gramsci, and Louis Althusser.

Bakhtin was a Russian, later a Soviet, critic so original in his thinking and wide ranging in his influence that some would say he was never a Marxist at all. He viewed literary works in terms of discourses and dialogues *between* discourses. The narrative of a novel written in a society in flux, for instance, may include an official, legitimate discourse, plus others that challenge its viewpoint and even its authority. In a 1929 book on Dostoyevsky and the 1940 study *Rabelais and His World,* Bakhtin examined what he calls "polyphonic" novels, each characterized by a multiplicity of voices or discourses. In Dostoyevsky the independent status of a given character is marked by the difference of his or her language from that of the narrator. (The narrator's language may itself involve a dialogue involving opposed points of view.) In works by Rabelais, Bakhtin finds that the (profane) languages of Carnival and of other popular festivities play against and parody the more official discourses of the magistrates and the church. Bakhtin's relevance to cultural criticism lies in his suggestion that the dialogue involving high and low culture takes place not only between classic and popular texts but also between the "dialogic" voices that exist within all great books.

Walter Benjamin was a German Marxist who, during roughly the same period, attacked fascism and questioned the superior value placed on certain traditional literary forms that he felt conveyed a stultifying "aura" of culture. He took this position in part because so many previous Marxist critics (and, in his own day, Georg Lukács) had seemed to prefer nineteenth-century realistic novels to the modernist works of their own time. Benjamin not only praised modernist movements, such as dadaism, but also saw as promising the development of new art forms utilizing mechanical production and reproduction. These forms, including photography, radio, and film, promised that the arts would become a more democratic, less exclusive, domain. Anticipating by decades the work of those cultural critics interested in mass-produced, mass-mediated, and mass-consumed culture, Benjamin analyzed the meanings and (defensive) motivations behind words like *unique* and *authentic* when used in conjunction with mechanically reproduced art.

Antonio Gramsci, an Italian Marxist best known for his *Prison Notebooks* (first published in 1947), critiqued the very concept of literature and, beyond that, of culture in the old sense, stressing the importance of culture more broadly defined and the need for nurturing and developing proletarian, or working-class, culture. He argued that all intellectual or cultural work is fundamentally political and expressed the need for what he called "radical organic" intellectuals. Today's cultural critics urging colleagues to "legitimate the notion of writing reviews and books for the general public," to "become involved in the political reading of popular culture," and more generally to "repoliticize" scholarship have viewed Gramsci as an early precursor (Giroux et al. 482).

Gramsci related literature to the ideologies — the prevailing ideas, beliefs, values, and prejudices — of the culture in which it was produced. He developed the concept of "hegemony," which refers at once to the process of consensus-formation and to the authority of the ideologies so formed, that is to say, their power to shape the way things look, what they would seem to mean, and, therefore, what reality *is* for the majority of people. But Gramsci did not see people, even poor people, as the helpless victims of hegemony, as ideology's pathetic robots. Rather, he believed that people have the freedom and power to struggle against and shape ideology, to alter hegemony, to break out of the weblike system of prevailing assumptions and to form a new consensus. As Patrick Brantlinger has suggested in *Crusoe's Footprints: Cultural Studies in Britain and America* (1990), Gramsci rejected the "intellectual arrogance that views the vast majority of people as deluded zombies, the victims or creatures of ideology" (100).

Of those Marxists who, after Gramsci, explored the complex relationship between literature and ideology, the French Marxist Louis Althusser had a significant impact on cultural criticism. Unlike Gramsci, Althusser tended to portray ideology as being in control of people, and not vice versa. He argued that the main function of ideology is to reproduce the society's existing relations of production, and that that function is even carried out in literary texts. In many ways, though, Althusser is as good an example of how Marxism and cultural criticism part company as he is of how cultural criticism is indebted to Marxists and their ideas. For although Althusser did argue that literature is relatively autonomous — more independent of ideology than, say, church, press, or state — he meant literature in the high cultural sense, certainly not the variety of works that present-day cultural critics routinely examine alongside those of Tolstoy and Joyce, Eliot and Brecht. Popular fictions, Althusser assumed, were mere packhorses designed (however unconsciously) to carry the baggage of a culture's ideology, or mere brood mares destined to reproduce it.

Thus, while a number of cultural critics would agree both with Althusser's notion that works of literature reflect certain ideological formations and with his notion that, at the same time, literary works may be relatively distant from or even resistant to ideology, they have rejected the narrow limits within which Althusser and some other Marxists (such as Georg Lukács) have defined literature. In "Marxism and Popular Fiction" (1986), Tony Bennett uses *Monty Python's Flying Circus* and another British television show, *Not the 9 O'clock News*, to argue that the Althusserian notion that all forms of culture belong "among [all those] many material forms which ideology takes . . . under capitalism" is "simply not true." The "entire field" of "popular fiction" — which Bennett takes to include films and television shows as well as books — is said to be "replete with instances" of works that do what Bennett calls the "work" of "distancing." That is, they have the effect of separating the audience from, not rebinding the audience to, prevailing ideologies (249).

Although Marxist cultural critics exist (Bennett himself is one, carrying on through his writings what may be described as a lovers' quarrel with Marxism), most cultural critics are not Marxists in any strict sense. Anne Beezer, in writing about such things as advertisements and women's magazines, contests the "Althusserian view of ideology as the construction of the subject" (qtd. in Punter 103). That is, she gives both the media she is concerned with and their audiences more credit than Althusserian Marxists presumably would. Whereas they might argue that such media make people what they are, she points out that the same magazines that, admittedly, tell women how to please their men may, at the same time, offer liberating advice to women about how to preserve their independence by not getting too serious romantically. And, she suggests, many advertisements advertise their status as ads, just as many people who view or read them see advertising as advertising and interpret it accordingly.

The complex sort of analysis that Beezer has brought to bear on women's magazines and advertisements has been focused on paperback romance novels in *Loving with a Vengeance* (1982) and *Reading the Romance* (1984) by Tania Modleski and Janice A. Radway, respectively. Radway, a feminist cultural critic who uses but ultimately

goes beyond Marxism, points out that many women who read romances do so in order to carve out a time and space that is wholly their
own, not to be intruded upon by husbands or children. Although
many such novels end in marriage, the marriage is usually between a
feisty and independent heroine and a powerful man she has "tamed,"
that is, made sensitive and caring. And why do so many of these stories
involve such heroines and end as they do? Because, as Radway demonstrates through painstaking research into publishing houses, book-
stores, and reading communities, their consumers *want* them to. They
don't buy — or, if they buy they don't recommend — romances in
which, for example, a heroine is raped: thus, in time, fewer and fewer
such plots find their way onto the racks by the supermarket checkout.

Radway's reading is typical of feminist cultural criticism in that it is
*political* but not exclusively about oppression. The subjectivities of
women may be "produced" by romances — the thinking of romance
readers may be governed by what is read — but the same women also
govern, to a great extent, what gets written or produced, thus performing "cultural work" of their own. Rather than seeing all forms of
popular culture as manifestations of ideology, soon to be remanifested
in the minds of victimized audiences, cultural critics tend to see a
sometimes disheartening but always dynamic synergy between cultural
forms and the culture's consumers. Their observations have increasingly led to an analysis of consumerism, from a feminist but also from
a more general point of view. This analysis owes a great deal to the
work of de Certeau, Hall, and, especially, Hebdige, whose 1979 book
*Subculture: The Meaning of Style* paved the way for critics like John
Fiske (*Television Culture*, 1987), Greil Marcus (*Dead Elvis*, 1991), and
Rachel Bowlby (*Shopping with Freud*, 1993). These later critics have
analyzed everything from the resistance tactics employed by television
audiences to the influence of consumers on rock music styles to the
psychology of consumer choice.

The overlap between feminist and cultural criticism is hardly surprising, especially given the recent evolution of feminism into various
femin*isms*, some of which remain focused on "majority" women of
European descent, others of which have focused instead on the lives
and writings of minority women in Western culture and of women living in Third World (now preferably called postcolonial) societies. The
culturalist analysis of value hierarchies within and between cultures has
inevitably focused on categories that include class, race, national origin, gender, and sexualities; the terms of its critique have proved useful

to contemporary feminists, many of whom differ from their predecessors insofar as they see *woman* not as a universal category but, rather,
as one of several that play a role in identity- or subject-formation. The
influence of cultural criticism (and, in some cases, Marxist class analysis) can be seen in the work of contemporary feminist critics such as
Gayatri Spivak, Trinh T. Minh-ha, and Gloria Anzaldúa, each of
whom has stressed that while all women are female, they are something else as well (such as working-class, lesbian, Native American,
Muslim Pakistani) and that that something else must be taken into account when their writings are read and studied.

The expansion of feminism and feminist literary criticism to include multicultural analysis, of course, parallels a transformation of education in general. On college campuses across North America, the
field of African-American studies has grown and flourished. African-
American critics have been influenced by and have contributed to the
cultural approach by pointing out that the white cultural elite of North
America has tended to view the oral-musical traditions of African
Americans (traditions that include jazz, the blues, sermons, and folk-
tales) as entertaining but nonetheless inferior. Black writers, in order
not to be similarly marginalized, have produced texts that, as Henry
Louis Gates has pointed out, fuse the language and traditions of the
white Western canon with a black vernacular and traditions derived
from African and Caribbean cultures. The resulting "hybridity" (to use
Homi K. Bhabha's word), although deplored by a handful of black
separatist critics, has proved both rich and complex — fertile ground
for many cultural critics practicing African-American criticism.

Interest in race and ethnicity at home has gone hand in hand with
a new, interdisciplinary focus on colonial and postcolonial societies
abroad, in which issues of race, class, and ethnicity also loom large.
Edward Said's book *Orientalism* (1978) is generally said to have inaugurated postcolonial studies, which in Bhabha's words "bears witness
to the unequal and uneven forces of cultural representation involved in
the contest for political and social authority within the modern world
order" ("Postcolonial Criticism" 437). *Orientalism* showed how Eastern and Middle Eastern peoples have for centuries been systematically
stereotyped by the West, and how that stereotyping facilitated the colonization of vast areas of the East and Middle East by Westerners.
Said's more recent books, along with postcolonial studies by Bhabha
and Patrick Brantlinger, are among the most widely read and discussed
works of literary scholarship. Brantlinger focuses on British literature
of the Victorian period, examining representations of the colonies in

WHAT IS CULTURAL CRITICISM? 357

works written during an era of imperialist expansion. Bhabha comple-
ments Brantlinger by suggesting that modern Western culture is best
understood from the postcolonial perspective.

Thanks to the work of scholars like Brantlinger, Bhabha, Said,
Gates, Anzaldúa, and Spivak, education in general and literary study in
particular is becoming more democratic, decentered (less patriarchal
and Eurocentric), and multicultural. The future of literary criticism
will owe a great deal indeed to those early cultural critics who demonstrated that the boundaries between high and low culture are at once
repressive and permeable, that culture is common and therefore includes all forms of popular culture, that cultural definitions are inevitably political, and that the world we see is seen through society's
ideology. In a very real sense, the future of education *is* cultural studies.

Peter Widdowson begins the essay that follows with a question:
"What is Forster making *Howards End* say?" He begins to answer that
question by suggesting that the house Howards End stands for England in the novel *Howards End*, and that the novel "proposes that the
traditional owners of England are being dispossessed and that the new
heirs should be furnished with the best possible values and advantages
for assuring the survival and vitality of the traditional culture."

The new heirs of Howards End are not, according to Widdowson,
Margaret Schlegel and Henry Wilcox, even though at the end of the
novel they are married and living together at the house, which Margaret has inherited from Ruth Wilcox. Rather, "the real heir" of
Howards End (and symbolically of the nation) is someone very different, namely, "the child of Helen [Schlegel's] and Leonard Bast's
union," a union that Widdowson sees as one uniting "complementary
representatives of the middle classes."

Thus, "at the 'conscious' or 'authorial' level," what Forster is
"making *Howards End* say" is, according to Widdowson, what liberals
of Forster's age *generally* said about the future of the nation, namely,
that it was in the hands of a middle class that would learn and preserve
the old ways while pursuing modern material interests. Widdowson
goes on to argue, however, that there is a "second, 'unconscious' significance of the book and another type of understanding" of English
society to be glimpsed between the lines of *Howards End*.

To suggest what that other "significance" or "understanding"
might be, Widdowson first critiques the late-nineteenth-century liberal
"vision" of England as an essentially (an idyllically) rural country of
reasonably prosperous farmers, pointing out that even Forster knew

that vision to be "'pastoral' . . . an idealized and largely literary myth." Yet in writing *Howards End*, Widdowson maintains, Forster perpetuated this literary construct, "exclud[ing] or neutraliz[ing] dynamic, if disruptive, aspects of society in favor of 'the past.'" London, for instance, is not only criticized but is even "dismissed as not 'England.'" And, as Widdowson points out, "the same dismissive tendency is apparent in Forster's treatment of the lower classes." (To quote the narrator of *Howards End*, "We are not concerned with the very poor.")

Widdowson is not, by the way, arguing that Forster's novel offers an entirely unrealistic representation of England. Quite to the contrary, he points out that "much of *Howards End* is brilliantly realistic." The hallmarks of the novel's undeniable realism include marvelously believable and revealing conversations and, especially, those passages that exude "wry wisdom" and a "complex and ironic perception of life that opposes the more rhetorical or vision-controlled passages." This realism is undercut, however, as "several aspects of the novel run counter" to it; in fact, "the novel as a whole implicitly rejects it in favor of 'vision.'"

Widdowson views *Howards End* as a bifurcated novel, a "sociomoral fable" that incompletely dominates the novel's realism. "There is a constant tension, therefore," Widdowson writes, "between the sketchy, underrealized but potent 'reality'" represented by the book's realistic tendencies "and the fictional attempts to realize the 'vision.'" This tension opens up chinks in the armor of the liberal vision, causing "fissures" to appear that allow us to see what Forster was unconsciously "making *Howards End* say," namely, that Edwardian life included "insistent realities" alien to the "myth of 'Liberal England,'" realities such as "suburban spread, socialism, female suffrage, Anglo-German hostility, urban living, speed, change."

Widdowson's argument is representative of cultural criticism in a number of ways. In stating that "the constant tendency" of *Howards End* is "a vision affirmed by Art," Widdowson connects Forster's novel with Edwardian Culture (with a capital *C*) and with a bright vision of England's future that hardly seems to have been borne out by reality, as any visitor to present-day Manchester, Leeds, or London's multicultural East End would readily attest. Widdowson also sees Forster's novel as one whose realistic mode subversively undercuts the "ideology" of the "liberal-humanist world-view," that is, the ideology that demands "the contrived resolution" of the novel's final chapters. Like Raymond Williams, Widdowson has been influenced by Marxist thinking about the ideological nature of literature. Like non-Marxist cul-

tural critics, however, he deftly resists viewing literature merely *as* ideology, arguing instead that *Howards End* has any number of things to
say to us today, some of them consciously intended by Forster; some
intended only subconsciously; others, perhaps, not intended at all.

Ross C Murfin

## CULTURAL CRITICISM:
## A SELECTED BIBLIOGRAPHY

### General Introductions to
### Cultural Criticism, Cultural Studies

Bathrick, David. "Cultural Studies." *Introduction to Scholarship in
Modern Languages and Literatures.* Ed. Joseph Gibaldi. New
York: MLA, 1992. 320–40.
Brantlinger, Patrick. *Crusoe's Footprints: Cultural Studies in Britain
and America.* New York: Routledge, 1990.
———. "Cultural Studies vs. the New Historicism." *English Studies/
Cultural Studies: Institutionalizing Dissent.* Ed. Isaiah Smithson
and Nancy Ruff. Urbana: U of Illinois P, 1994. 43–58.
Brantlinger, Patrick, and James Naremore, eds. *Modernity and Mass
Culture.* Bloomington: Indiana UP, 1991.
Brummett, Barry. *Rhetoric in Popular Culture.* New York: St. Mar-
tin's, 1994.
Desan, Philippe, Priscilla Parkhurst Ferguson, and Wendy Griswold.
"Editors' Introduction: Mirrors, Frames, and Demons: Reflections
on the Sociology of Literature." *Literature and Social Practice.*
Ed. Desan, Ferguson, and Griswold. Chicago: U of Chicago P,
1989. 1–10.
During, Simon, ed. *The Cultural Studies Reader.* New York: Rout-
ledge, 1993.
Eagleton, Terry. "Two Approaches in the Sociology of Literature."
*Critical Inquiry* 14 (1988): 469–76.
Easthope, Antony. *Literary into Cultural Studies.* New York: Rout-
ledge, 1991.
Fisher, Philip. "American Literary and Cultural Studies since the Civil
War." Greenblatt and Gunn 232–50.
Giroux, Henry, David Shumway, Paul Smith, and James Sosnoski.
"The Need for Cultural Studies: Resisting Intellectuals and
Oppositional Public Spheres." *Dalhousie Review* 64.2 (1984):
472–86.

Graff, Gerald, and Bruce Robbins. "Cultural Criticism." Greenblatt and Gunn 419–36.

Greenblatt, Stephen, and Giles Gunn, eds. *Redrawing the Boundaries: The Transformation of English and American Literary Studies.* New York: MLA, 1992.

Grossberg, Lawrence, Cary Nelson, and Paula A. Treichler, eds. *Cultural Studies.* New York: Routledge, 1992.

Gunn, Giles. *The Culture of Criticism and the Criticism of Culture.* New York: Oxford UP, 1987.

Hall, Stuart. "Cultural Studies: Two Paradigms." *Media, Culture and Society* 2 (1980): 57–72.

Humm, Peter, Paul Stigant, and Peter Widdowson, eds. *Popular Fictions: Essays in Literature and History.* New York: Methuen, 1986.

Hunt, Lynn, ed. *The New Cultural History: Essays.* Berkeley: U of California P, 1989.

Johnson, Richard. "What Is Cultural Studies Anyway?" *Social Text: Theory/Culture/Ideology* 16 (1986–87): 38–80.

Pfister, Joel. "The Americanization of Cultural Studies." *Yale Journal of Criticism* 4 (1991): 199–229.

Punter, David, ed. *Introduction to Contemporary Critical Studies.* New York: Longman, 1986. See especially Punter's "Introduction: Culture and Change" 1–18, Tony Dunn's "The Evolution of Cultural Studies" 71–91, and the essay "Methods for Cultural Studies Students" by Anne Beezer, Jean Grimshaw, and Martin Barker 95–118.

Storey, John. *An Introductory Guide to Cultural Theory and Popular Culture.* Athens: U of Georgia P, 1993.

Turner, Graeme. *British Cultural Studies: An Introduction.* Boston: Unwin Hyman, 1990.

**Cultural Studies:
Some Early British Examples**

Hoggart, Richard. *Speaking to Each Other.* 2 vols. London: Chatto, 1970.

———. *The Uses of Literacy: Changing Patterns in English Mass Culture.* Boston: Beacon, 1961.

Thompson, E. P. *The Making of the English Working Class.* New York: Harper, 1958.

———. *William Morris: Romantic to Revolutionary.* New York: Pantheon, 1977.

Williams, Raymond. *Culture and Society, 1780–1950.* 1958. New York: Harper, 1966.

———. *The Long Revolution.* New York: Columbia UP, 1961.

## Cultural Studies:
## Continental and Marxist Influences

Althusser, Louis. *For Marx.* Trans. Ben Brewster. New York: Pantheon, 1969.

———. "Ideology and Ideological State Apparatuses." *Lenin and Philosophy.* Trans. Ben Brewster. New York: Monthly Review P, 1971. 127–86.

Althusser, Louis, and Étienne Balibar. *Reading Capital.* Trans. Ben Brewster. New York: Pantheon, 1971.

Bakhtin, Mikhail. *The Dialogic Imagination: Four Essays.* Ed. Michael Holquist. Trans. Caryl Emerson. Austin: U of Texas P, 1981.

———. *Rabelais and His World.* Trans. Hélène Iswolsky. Cambridge: MIT P, 1968.

Baudrillard, Jean. *Simulations.* Trans. Paul Foss, Paul Patton, and Philip Beitchnan. 1981. New York: Semiotext(e), 1983.

Benjamin, Walter. *Illuminations.* Ed. with intro. Hannah Arendt. Trans. Harry H. Zohn. New York: Harcourt, 1968.

Bennett, Tony. "Marxism and Popular Fiction." Humm, Stigant, and Widdowson 237–65.

Bourdieu, Pierre. *Distinction: A Social Critique of the Judgment of Taste.* Trans. Richard Nice. Cambridge: Harvard UP, 1984.

de Certeau, Michel. *The Practice of Everyday Life.* Trans. Steven F. Rendall. Berkeley: U of California P, 1984.

Foucault, Michel. *Discipline and Punish: The Birth of the Prison.* Trans. Alan Sheridan. New York: Pantheon, 1978.

———. *The History of Sexuality.* Trans. Robert Hurley. Vol. 1. New York: Pantheon, 1978.

Gramsci, Antonio. *Selections from the Prison Notebooks.* Ed. Quintin Hoare and Geoffrey Nowell Smith. New York: International, 1971.

## Modern Cultural Studies:
## Selected British and American Examples

Bagdikian, Ben H. *The Media Monopoly.* Boston: Beacon, 1983.

Bowlby, Rachel. *Shopping with Freud.* New York: Routledge, 1993.

Chambers, Iain. *Popular Culture: The Metropolitan Experience.* New York: Methuen, 1986.

Colls, Robert, and Philip Dodd, eds. *Englishness: Politics and Culture, 1880–1920.* London: Croom Helm, 1986.

Denning, Michael. *Mechanic Accents: Dime Novels and Working-Class Culture in America.* New York: Verso, 1987.

Fiske, John. "British Cultural Studies and Television." *Channels of Discourse: Television and Contemporary Criticism.* Ed. Robert C. Allen. Chapel Hill: U of North Carolina P, 1987. 284–326.

———. *Television Culture.* New York: Methuen, 1987.

Hebdige, Dick. *Hiding the Light: On Images and Things.* New York: Routledge, 1988.

———. *Subculture: The Meaning of Style.* London: Methuen, 1979.

Huyssen, Andreas. *After the Great Divide: Modernism, Mass Culture, Postmodernism.* Bloomington: Indiana UP, 1986.

Marcus, Greil. *Dead Elvis: A Chronicle of a Cultural Obsession.* New York: Doubleday, 1991.

———. *Lipstick Traces: A Secret History of the Twentieth Century.* Cambridge: Harvard UP, 1989.

Modleski, Tania. *Loving with a Vengeance: Mass-Produced Fantasies for Women.* Hamden: Archon, 1982.

Poovey, Mary. *Uneven Developments: The Ideological Work of Gender in Mid-Victorian England.* Chicago: U of Chicago P, 1988.

Radway, Janice A. *Reading the Romance: Women, Patriarchy, and Popular Literature.* Chapel Hill: U of North Carolina P, 1984.

Reed, T. V. *Fifteen Jugglers, Five Believers: Literary Politics and the Poetics of American Social Movements.* Berkeley: U of California P, 1992.

## Ethnic and Minority Criticism, Postcolonial Studies

Anzaldúa, Gloria. *Borderlands = La Frontera: The New Mestiza.* San Francisco: Spinsters/Aunt Lute, 1987.

Baker, Houston. *Blues, Ideology, and Afro-American Literature: A Vernacular Theory.* Chicago: U of Chicago P, 1984.

———. *The Journey Back: Issues in Black Literature and Criticism.* Chicago: U of Chicago P, 1980.

Bhabha, Homi K. *The Location of Culture.* New York: Routledge, 1994.

———, ed. *Nation and Narration.* New York: Routledge, 1990.

———. "Postcolonial Criticism." Greenblatt and Gunn 437–65.

Brantlinger, Patrick. *Rule of Darkness: British Literature and Imperialism, 1830–1914.* Ithaca: Cornell UP, 1988.

Gates, Henry Louis, Jr. *Black Literature and Literary Theory.* New York: Methuen, 1984.

———, ed. *"Race," Writing, and Difference.* Chicago: U of Chicago P, 1986.

Gayle, Addison. *The Black Aesthetic.* Garden City: Doubleday, 1971.

———. *The Way of the New World: The Black Novel in America.* Garden City: Doubleday, 1975.

JanMohamed, Abdul. *Manichean Aesthetics: The Politics of Literature in Colonial Africa.* Amherst: U of Massachusetts P, 1983.

JanMohamed, Abdul, and David Lloyd, eds. *The Nature and Context of Minority Discourse.* New York: Oxford UP, 1991.

Kaplan, Amy, and Donald E. Pease, eds. *Cultures of United States Imperialism.* Durham: Duke UP, 1983.

*Neocolonialism.* Special issue, *Oxford Literary Review* 13 (1991).

Said, Edward. *After the Last Sky: Palestinian Lives.* New York: Pantheon, 1986.

———. *Culture and Imperialism.* New York: Knopf, 1993.

———. *Orientalism.* New York: Pantheon, 1978.

———. *The World, the Text, and the Critic.* Cambridge: Harvard UP, 1983.

Spivak, Gayatri Chakravorty. *In Other Worlds: Essays in Cultural Politics.* New York: Methuen, 1987.

Stepto, Robert B. *From Behind the Veil: A Study of Afro-American Narrative.* Urbana: U of Illinois P, 1979.

Young, Robert. *White Mythologies: Writing, History, and the West.* London: Routledge, 1990.

### Cultural Criticism and *Howards End*

Born, Daniel. "Private Gardens, Public Swamps: *Howards End* and the Revaluation of Liberal Guilt." *Novel* 25.2 (1992): 141–59.

Brooker, Peter, and Peter Widdowson. "A Literature for England." *Englishness: Politics and Culture, 1880–1920.* Ed. Robert Colls and Philip Dodd. London: Croom Helm, 1986. 116–63.

Delany, Paul. "'Islands of Money': Rentier Culture in E. M. Forster's *Howards End." English Literature in Transition, 1880–1920* 31 (1988): 285–96.

Dellamora, Richard. "Textual Politics/Sexual Politics." *Modern Language Quarterly* 54.1 (1993): 155–64.

A CULTURAL PERSPECTIVE

PETER WIDDOWSON

*Howards End:*
Fiction as History

What is Forster making *Howards End* say? The novel proposes that
the traditional owners of England are being dispossessed and that the
new heirs should be furnished with the best possible values and advantages for assuring the survival and vitality of the traditional culture.
But Forster recognizes both that powerful forces are inimical to the
traditional culture and that the new "heirs" will be modern; they will
not necessarily be "English to the backbone," nor will they be the
product of one social group. The necessary "connections" have to be
established between certain diverse, but indispensable, factors. At the
abstract level these are defined as "the passion" and "the prose," the
"inner" and the "outer" lives, the ability to see life "steadily" and
the ability to see it "whole" (where Henry wishes to "concentrate,"
Margaret wishes to "connect"). To put it another way, which Forster
himself almost makes explicit, there is to be a connection between the
"male" and "female" virtues. Margaret, early on, senses that their
house is "irrevocably feminine, even in father's time," and that the
Wilcoxes' is "irrevocably masculine." Both have weaknesses that their
owners must struggle against: the former against the "effeminate," the
latter against the "brutal" (54). The dissociation of the "virtues" is
clearly unnatural, and it is equally clear that they would be mutually
fortifying in association.

These abstractions, however, have individual and social definition
within the novel. Let us consider the various strands: Mrs. Wilcox, the
spirit of "Liberal England" and of "the Past," inhabits Howards End/
England but is about to leave it. That is the basic situation. But who is
it to be left to? The most suitable heirs are the Schlegel sisters, of part-
German origin but possessing the right values: idealism, a belief in
"personal relations," passion, culture, and so on. Of the two, Margaret
is the more down to earth, and she is the true "spiritual heir." But she
recognizes the need for a solid material base — the "great outer life"
of "telegrams and anger" (40) — on which to establish and propagate
their values. This the Wilcoxes supply, but they lack any sort of inner
life; they are all "prose" and no "poetry," public people whose inner-
most reality is "panic and emptiness." Howards End/England cannot

be left to them, but equally Margaret cannot inherit it alone, because she cannot survive without material and physical support. As part of Margaret's preparation for inheritance, therefore, she has to marry Henry Wilcox and become a new "Mrs. Wilcox," so inheriting "the house" on the basis of a connection between money and culture. Thus a base is secured. But who is the *actual* heir? Margaret does "not love children. . . . I can play with their beauty and charm, but that is all — nothing real, not one scrap of what there ought to be" (287). And Henry is too old and broken. Obviously Money and Culture are not enough; they leave too much out, and in particular the vital spark of life itself. The real heir, protected by the values already defined, is the child of Helen Schlegel and Leonard Bast's union — a union, it is worth noticing, between two complementary representatives of the middle classes. Helen's passion and idealism "connect" with the spirit of "adventure" and of unquenchable individual life in Leonard — that potential for true "wholeness" of culture hinted at, but unborn, in him and the huge class he represents. Unable to break out of the imprisoning poverty of his own life, Bast cannot achieve full being, but his son and Helen's — given money and the "life of values" — will be able to achieve this. The new heir of Howards End/England, then, is an amalgam of all the essential forces, with Margaret and her liberal-humanist culture as a sort of regent. Hence Forster's imperative: "Only connect. . . ".

All this, then, may be taken as the novel's "historical" significance at the "conscious" or "authorial" level: the way in which, through character, plot, action, pattern, and so forth, a historical situation is expressed. It is not, of course, a history of events or of "great men" but an attempt to recreate what the Welsh scholar and writer Raymond Williams calls "a structure of feeling"[1] as it is revealed by ordinary people acting out the ordinary business of their lives. What *is* enacted is Forster's vision, in 1910, of traditional Liberal England, beset by dangerous, destructive forces yet finally prevailing through a realistic, "modern" liberal humanism that makes "connections" with other powerful, supportive forces and leavens them with its values.

But it is precisely on the point of the victorious "vision" that another type of analysis is required that may reveal the second, "unconscious," significance of the book and another type of understanding.

---

[1]"Structure of feeling" is a common concept in Raymond Williams's work; see, for example, *The Country and the City*.

Certain questions posed by the curiously ambivalent effect of *Howards End* require consideration and answer: How is the "vision" victorious? How are the "connections" achieved? Is the movement of the book "convincing"? Is the "realism" sustained? The answers to these questions lie in the analysis of ostensibly "literary" matters, the novel's rhetoric, both linguistic and structural. We shall find, in fact, that the least accessible "historical" level of the book's total "statement" is contained in precisely these formal dimensions.

Let us begin with the base of the vision itself: "Liberal England." The England that Forster cherishes is actually that which the Georgian poets described and eulogized: "pastoral" England, an idealized and largely literary myth. (Forster himself, much later in his life, admitted that he carried "a ruck-sack of traditional nature-emotions" [*Two Cheers* 358]; and the opening paragraphs of his essay on the rural poet William Barnes [*Two Cheers* 204–05] suggest his "Georgian" proclivities.) This is not to deny that the English countryside can be idyllic but merely to suggest that the idyll is partial and exclusive because it ignores other aspects of rural life, let alone anything else. Forster's ideal England is itself something of a "poetical reality" and is not unlike that which Rupert Brooke evoked in "Grantchester." One can refer to the famous opening paragraph of chapter 19 of *Howards End*, with its undisguised rhetoric:

> If one wanted to show a foreigner England, perhaps the wisest course would be to take him to the final section of the Purbeck hills, and stand him on their summit, a few miles to the east of Corfe. Then system after system of our island would roll together under his feet. Beneath him is the valley of the Frome, and all the wild lands that come tossing down from Dorchester, black and gold, to mirror their gorse in the expanses of Poole. The valley of the Stour is beyond, unaccountable stream, dirty at Blandford, pure at Wimborne — the Stour, sliding out of fat fields, to marry the Avon beneath the tower of Christchurch. The valley of the Avon — invisible, but far to the north the trained eye may see Clearbury Ring that guards it, and the imagination may leap beyond that onto Salisbury Plain itself, and beyond the Plain to all the glorious downs of central England. Nor is suburbia absent. Bournemouth's ignoble coast cowers to the right, heralding the pine trees that mean, for all their beauty, red houses, and the Stock Exchange, and extend to the gates of London itself. So tremendous is the City's trail! But the cliffs of Freshwater it shall never touch, and the island will guard the Island's purity till the end of time. Seen from the west, the Wight is beautiful beyond all

laws of beauty. It is as if a fragment of England floated forward to
greet the foreigner — chalk of our chalk, turf of our turf, epitome
of what will follow. (152–53)

What is interesting here, apart from the poetic language, is the
recognition of "suburbia" and "the City's trail," followed by the significant shift into the future imperative tense: "the cliffs of Freshwater
it *shall* never touch." This is simply a rhetorical flourish, without a rational base, and it might well be described as shouting to keep one's
courage up. The novel is studded with passages of a similar nature in
which the most noteworthy features are the caressing tone and the
general imprecision of the language:

> In these English farms, if anywhere, one might see life steadily and
> see it whole, group in one vision its transitoriness and its eternal
> youth, connect — connect without bitterness until all men are
> brothers. (233)
>
> Here men had been up since dawn. Their hours were ruled, not by
> a London office, but by the movements of the crops and the sun.
> That they were men of the finest type only the sentimentalist can
> declare. But they kept to the life of daylight. They are England's
> hope. Clumsily they carry forward the torch of the sun, until such
> time as the nation sees fit to take it up. Half clodhopper, half
> board-school prig, they can still throw back to a nobler stock, and
> breed yeomen. (276)
>
> Hertfordshire is England at its quietest, with little emphasis of
> river and hill; it is England meditative. If Drayton were with us
> again to write a new edition of his incomparable poem, he would
> sing the nymphs of Hertfordshire as indeterminate of feature, with
> hair obfuscated by the London smoke. Their eyes would be sad,
> and averted from their fate towards the northern flats, their leader
> not Isis or Sabrina, but the slowly flowing Lea. No glory of rai-
> ment would be theirs, no urgency of dance; but they would be
> real nymphs. (176–77)

The problem with these pleasant images is that they are an idealization, and Forster's reliance on smooth cadences and vague rhetoric
to bolster it reveals how insubstantial the vision is. In the second passage quoted, he attempts to preempt the accusation of "sentimental-
ity" by mentioning it himself, but the imprecision and indulgent tone
of phrases like "they kept to the life of daylight," "a nobler stock,"
"England's hope," and "the torch of the sun" idealize and blur the
subject. But a vision such as this is necessarily vague and imprecise,

because its ability to idealize relies, simply, on the exclusion of all those aspects of England which it cannot assimilate. The Georgian poets were past masters at this, and Forster is guilty of it too. There is a telltale sign in the last passage quoted: "Their eyes would be sad, and averted from their fate. . . ." An "averting of the eyes" is one way of describing the Georgian view of England, and for Forster too "these English farms" are more essentially "England" than are London and the great towns — even in 1910. C. F. G. Masterman, in his widely read *The Condition of England* (1909), is, despite his own love of "the earth," very much more realistic than Forster:

> But no one to-day would seek in the ruined villages and dwindling population of the countryside the spirit of an "England" four-fifths of whose people have now crowded into the cities. The little red-roofed towns and hamlets, the labourer in the fields at noon-tide or evening, the old English service in the old English village church, now stand but as the historical survival of a once great and splendid past. Is "England" then to be discovered in the feverish industrial energy of the manufacturing cities? In the vast welter and chaos of the capital of Empire? Amongst the new Plutocracy? The middle classes? The artisan populations? The broken poor? All contribute their quota to the stream of the national life. (12)

The real danger of Forster's vision is that large areas of "England's" life and culture are dismissed as in some way "unreal." He excludes or neutralizes dynamic, even if disruptive, aspects of society in favor of "the past." I do not, of course, mean that Forster *should* have written about mining or public houses or factories or football or Pasteur or Marconi or the diet of the working class; I mean simply that there is a *dismissive* tone in his treatment of even those insistent realities that he is concerned with. London, for all its symbolic status, is dismissed as not "England." If we consider the long critique of London at the opening of chapter 13 (105–06), we will see how, in the second paragraph, Forster's passive despair makes the description general and reductive. The phrase "no pulsation of humanity" in London suggests a detachment that is really an elitist and alienated ignorance: "as I am out of tune with this place, it cannot be good."[2] It is symptomatic of a fundamental blind-spot in the liberal-humanist consciousness that it assumes its own values and its own form of "civilization" are absolute and for all time and that culture is static, having achieved

---

[2]It is interesting that, later in life, Forster changed his attitude toward London to a certain extent. See "London Is a Muddle" (1937) in *Two Cheers for Democracy.*

its apotheosis in the liberal-humanist image. Later in the novel, Margaret has an "epiphany" of London: "The mask fell off the city, and she saw it for what it really is — a caricature of infinity. The familiar barriers, the streets along which she moved, the houses between which she had made her little journeys for so many years, became negligible suddenly" (242). "For what it really *is*": had this been Margaret's reflection alone, the verb would have been "was," not "is." Once again the phrase implies Forster's Olympian rejection of the alien force. "London" does not fit into "Liberal England," but if one has the right values it can be dismissed, is "negligible suddenly." Hence the rhetoric.

The same dismissive tendency is apparent in Forster's treatment of the lower classes. Unlike Masterman, who devotes two sections to "the very poor," Forster regards them as "unthinkable," and therefore, "We are not concerned with the very poor" (55). This is not simple callousness; it is an honest admission that he knows nothing at all about them. And it is Forster's right as a novelist to delimit his objectives, to refuse to deal with them. All we may do is note that in a novel that seems to be concerned with the condition and future of England, the poor do not appear. It could, of course, be argued that the novel is only concerned with the condition of the middle classes and not with "England" after all. But this would both fail to take account of much of the novel's imagery and reference ("English farms," "English houses," "English trees," etc.), and would reinforce the exclusiveness of the liberal "future." Even if the middle classes set their own house in order, solidly founded on the "life of values," and establish a powerful enclave within society, they cannot be discrete; they must be related to other groups and forces. And if their values are to permeate and inform society, the means of "transmitting" private values into public good remains to be discovered. Willy-nilly, a novel concerned with the state of the middle classes in the early years of this century is concerned with "England," and Forster was too perceptive an intelligence to be unaware of it. Nevertheless, he did not deal with "the very poor."

The case of the Basts is rather different, and Forster *is* concerned to include them, and the class they represent, in the "new England." But as characters they are clearly "created" rather than known and observed. Jacky is one of the few really wooden caricatures in all of Forster's fiction and, she is significantly, little more than a necessary agent in the plot and pattern of the novel. Leonard is better, but he is still not convincing. He is described by Forster, rather than presented dramatically, and even when he is allowed to express himself, it is clearly in the terms that Forster *thought* a man would think:

"I'll tell you another thing too. I care a good deal about improving myself by means of Literature and Art, and so getting a wider outlook. For instance, when you came in I was reading Ruskin's *Stones of Venice*. I don't say this to boast, but just to show you the kind of man I am. I can tell you, I enjoyed that classical concert this afternoon." (62)

The Basts are poorly drawn characters, which suggests again that Forster is not very familiar with the class or its lifestyle. But what is more significant is the tone he adopts when discussing Leonard as "representative" of his class, especially at the opening of chapter 6:

> The boy, Leonard Bast, stood at the extreme verge of gentility. He was not in the abyss, but he could see it, and at times people whom he knew had dropped in, and counted no more. He knew that he was poor, and would admit it; he would have died sooner than confess any inferiority to the rich. This may be splendid of him. But he was inferior to most rich people, there is not the least doubt of it. He was not as courteous as the average rich man, nor as intelligent, nor as healthy, nor as lovable. His mind and his body had been alike underfed, because he was poor, and because he was modern they were always craving better food. Had he lived some centuries ago, in the brightly coloured civilizations of the past, he would have had a definite status, his rank and his income would have corresponded. But in his day the angel of Democracy had arisen, enshadowing the classes with leathern wings, and proclaiming, "All men are equal — all men, that is to say, who possess umbrellas," and so he was obliged to assert gentility, lest he slipped into the abyss where nothing counts, and the statements of Democracy are inaudible. (55–56)

It is again the detachment, and the condescension, which constitute the dismissal; the lack of understanding implies the absence of anything worthwhile to understand. If Leonard could stop being "poor," he would be "lovable"; as it is, his class's "culture" can be understood but not appreciated. And "Democracy," a liberal article of faith surely, is, *in practice*, guilty of engendering this "inferior" culture. The unconscious *elitism* of the Liberal position could not be better expressed than in the distaste this passage reveals for the *actual* results of its abstract principles. Forster's attitude to Bast, as the story develops, would seem to be that if his miserable being can be disregarded or eradicated, then his "spirit" will be invaluable. As for Helen, Bast is more a "cause" than a man and Forster has to kill him off to make his presence in "Liberal England" possible.

My general point, however, is that any vision of "England" in the early twentieth century that cannot or will not contain such realities as London or the huge battalions of the system's "prisoners" is partial to the point of being invalid. Indeed, the most revealing omission in *Howards End* is a detailed and extensive portrayal of the forces opposed to the realization of the vision. To be just to Forster, he constantly hints at the vulnerability of the vision: "London was but a foretaste of this nomadic civilization which is altering human nature so profoundly" (227); "'And London is only part of something else, I'm afraid. Life's going to be melted down, all over the world.' Margaret knew that her sister spoke truly" (288). Nevertheless, the overall movement and texture of the novel do not embody this vulnerability. It is withheld by the "positive" vision. For realities as potent as the forces of destructive change are suggested to be, they are scarcely realized in the world the novel defines. Sometimes they are the vague fears of the narrative voice or its representatives; sometimes they are the passing utterances of characters in conversation; at still other times they are presented symbolically, as "London," for example, or as the motorcars that cover things with dust and kill cats. Many of the insistent realities of Edwardian life — suburban spread, socialism, female suffrage, Anglo-German hostility, urban living, speed, change — hang in the air, but they are not allowed to obtrude. This is partly, no doubt, a result of the contemporary "satisfaction" (the "prophetic" tendencies of a period are always much clearer in retrospect), but it is also a result of the basic uncertainty of the vision. To allow full status to such elements would ipso facto destroy the myth of "Liberal England." They are fundamentally antithetical to it. So if the vision is to be achieved, forces hostile to it must be made to seem less formidable than they are in reality. This is not to suggest that Forster is incapable of "realistic writing." On the contrary, much of *Howards End* is brilliantly realistic. It is simply to suggest that by failing to give full realization to certain important aspects of the real world, Forster tacitly admits that his vision could not accommodate them. His vision represents, in fictional form, the liberal tendency to disconnect culture from society while still considering culture to have a crucial social function: "values" independent of a particular historical location.

In itself, the basis of the vision, "Liberal England," is something of a myth. But at the same time, the whole movement of the book affirms the validity of the vision: Howards End survives and is inherited by suitable heirs who have managed to "connect." As Virginia Woolf remarked in "The Novels of E. M. Forster" (1927), in Forster's work as a whole and in *Howards End* especially, "there is a vision which he is determined that we shall see" (166):

> We are tapped on the shoulder. We are to notice this, to take heed of that. Margaret or Helen, we are made to understand, is not speaking simply as herself; her words have another and a larger intention. So, exerting ourselves to find out the meaning, we step from the enchanted world of imagination, where our faculties work freely, to the twilight world of theory, where only our intellect functions dutifully. (172)

In other words, this is a legislative rather than a descriptive work; it says, for instance, who the inheritors of "England" *ought* to be, not who they *are*. *Howards End* is, in fact, a sociomoral fable, although the world the novel defines *purports* to be realistic, empirically perceived, equivalent to "the world out there." The "correct" resolution is known before the book begins, and Forster's task is to ensure that this resolution is actually effected. Much of the novel, therefore, is an artificial justification of the final "vision"; every scene of domestic comedy, every conversation, every event, every word, is controlled by its demands.

Despite the discernment and subtlety, the irony, the antipompous and skeptical tentativeness of *Howards End*'s style and manner, there is a resolute controlling mechanism that makes the novel "prove" Forster's conception; the material is cut and sewn to the approved design. Paradoxically, Forster was well aware of the problems of the overpatterned novel, and, although he is criticizing Henry James in terms of aesthetic, rather than moral, control, his comments in *Aspects of the Novel* (1927) suggest something of his own tendency:

> It is this question of the rigid pattern . . . Can it be combined with the immense richness of material which life provides? Wells and James would agree it cannot. Wells would go on to say that life should be given the preference, and must not be whittled or distended for a pattern's sake. My own prejudices are with Wells. . . . That then is the disadvantage of a rigid pattern. It may externalize the atmosphere, spring naturally from the plot, but it shuts the doors on life, and leaves the novelist doing exercises, generally in the drawing room. (164–65)

If Forster's prejudices were with Wells's ostensible openness to life, his practice was equally close to the didactic realism of Wells's fiction. But Forster might have added that pattern does not just exclude life but can actually falsify the "life" it is treating.

*Howards End,* however, is a complex work, and there remains a major complication: the novel is, of course, by no means unequivocally a "fable" or a "romance." As critics from Virginia Woolf onward have noticed, the novel is a mixture. The problems develop when the expectations of a realistic novel are aroused, and in *Howards End* they certainly are. The conversational opening of the novel, "One may as well begin with Helen's letters to her sister," with the letters appended, immediately suggests a novel aiming at verisimilitude. Forster continues throughout to be specific about time and place. The references to tariff reform, imperialism, female emancipation, the New English Art Club, Augustus John, suburban spread, and so on quite clearly establish the scene as Edwardian England between about 1908 and 1910. Equally carefully established — if sometimes not very knowledgeably — are the social matrices of the various characters, their heredity, class, attitudes, work, houses, and so on. The Basts' "background," for example, is attempted in considerable detail, and the treatment of their flat reads more like Arnold Bennett or H. G. Wells than "romance":

> The sitting-room contained, besides the armchair, two other chairs, a piano, a three-legged table and a cosy corner. Of the walls, one was occupied by the window, the other by a draped mantelshelf bristling with Cupids. Opposite the window was the door, and beside the door a bookcase, while over the piano there extended one of the masterpieces of Maude Goodman. (57)

Great care is taken also with the characterization and the dialogue. The former is, admittedly, done largely through the narrative voice (particularly in regard to the Wilcoxes and Schlegels), but then this, rather than the dramatic mode, has been the norm for most of the realist tradition. When Forster does present a dramatic "scene," the dialogue is generally handled in a masterly way and is entirely convincing, both in the comic and the serious veins. Margaret's luncheon party for Mrs. Wilcox (chapter 9) is a good example of the former, and Henry's "confession" to Margaret about his affair with Jacky Bast, of the latter:

> "Did Helen come?" [Margaret] asked.
> [Henry] shook his head.
> "But that won't do at all, at all! We don't want her gossiping with Mrs Bast."
> "Good god, no!" he exclaimed, suddenly natural. Then he caught himself up. "Let them gossip. My game's up, though I

thank you for your unselfishness — little as my thanks are
worth." . . .
"It is no good," said Henry. "Those things leak out; you cannot
stop a story once it has started. I have known cases of other
men — I despised them once, I thought that *I'm* different, *I* shall
never be tempted. Oh, Margaret —" He came and sat down near
her, improvising emotion. She could not bear to listen to him.
"We fellows all come to grief once in our time. Will you believe
that? There are moments when the strongest man — 'Let him
who standeth, take heed lest he fall.' That's true, isn't it? If you
knew all, you would excuse me. I was far from good influences —
far even from England. I was very, very lonely, and longed for a
woman's voice. That's enough. I have told you too much already
for you to forgive me now." (214–15)

What Forster is so good at doing in scenes of this sort is making a
"thematic" concern take on the timbre of an actual conversation; the
revelation here, in the tones and postures of Henry's speech, of what
Helen has earlier identified as the "panic and emptiness" at the heart
of "Wilcoxism," is brilliantly achieved. But even when the characterization is weak, as in the case of the Basts, it is because Forster does not
know about them, rather than because he is not trying to make them
"convincing." The very amount of effort he clearly puts into describing them suggests this.

Finally, one further aspect of the realistic texture of large sections
of *Howards End* is the wry wisdom of the authorial comment. Except
in certain ways, which I will explain in a moment, this technique is
both common to the realistic tradition and, to use Lionel Trilling's apt
word about Forster's wisdom, indelibly "worldly" (22). For example:

> The two men were gradually assuming the manner of the
> committee-room. They were both at their best when serving on
> committees. They did not make the mistake of handling human
> affairs in the bulk, but disposed of them item by item,
> sharply. . . . It is the best — perhaps the only — way of dodging
> emotion. They were the average human article, and had they con-
> sidered the note as a whole it would have driven them miserable
> or mad. Considered item by item, the emotional content was min-
> imized, and all went forward smoothly. (97–98)

Such passages are the result of observation and reflection, the quality
that makes Forster's essays so continuously stimulating. They imply
the "realism" he admires in Margaret Schlegel: "a profound vivacity, a
continual and sincere response to all that she encountered in her path

through life" (26). It is precisely this complex and ironic perception of life that opposes the more rhetorical or vision-controlled passages so that, despite their common theme, each calls into question the other's validity.

There would be little excuse in laboring what is perhaps an obvious point about Forster's realism were it not that several aspects of the novel run counter to this realism and that the novel as a whole implicitly rejects it in favor of "vision." The "precarious synthesis" of realism, romance, and allegory that David Lodge mentions (4) is upset by Forster's conflicting needs. On the one hand, Forster wishes to propagate a vision — which he partially recognizes to be inclusive and insecure and for which he needs myth, pattern, symbolism: "contrived" or "fabulous" modes. On the other hand, he must try to convince us of the "reality" of the vision: one can scarcely hope to make "England" credible if one ignores England. And for this he needs all the paraphernalia of realism, since the danger of plain fable, because of its manifest artificiality, is the option it grants the reader simply to disregard its "moral." But because the vision itself is partial, the realistic bolstering of it never really becomes credible; it is too closely tied to the symbolic and mythic elements and is too regulated and selective. Forster's eye is first and foremost on the vision, and the realism exists, therefore, in terms of that vision.

The mixed mode of *Howards End* is never quite synthesis. As Virginia Woolf remarked, "Elaboration, skill, wisdom, penetration, beauty — they are all there, but they lack fusion; they lack cohesion; the book as a whole lacks force. . . . His gifts in their variety and number tend to trip each other up" (171). Those critics who have attempted to justify Forster's romance or visionary apparatus as appropriate to his didactic purposes, in this novel at least, fail to recognize that the partial realism involves not just questions about literary coherence or "decorum," but also questions about the validity of the vision itself. A vision or a fable has to be absolute, totalizing, and assured; tiny fragments of doubt, or chinks through which an alternative world can be perceived, are likely to smash its all-embracing completeness. It must exist totally within the artificial but absolute walls of its convention. Forster's liberal vision is, almost by its nature, tentative and uncertain; realism creeps in, the certainty of the world of the fable is questioned, and the realistic elements in the novel set up a clamor for more *proof,* more application of vision to world. The walls have been breached, and when such fissures appear, an affirmation has to be made in symbolic or mythical terms. This uncertainty is significantly less evident in the earlier novels, where the social satire is firmly contained within the terms of the moral vision (Life against non-Life). But in *Howards End*, where the vision is to comprehend a social reality — England — the strains begin to show. The correlation between liberal dilemma and fictional form is most apparent here; just as the insistent realities of the real world undermine the liberal position so that it must begin to doubt itself, so the realistic elements in the novel call into question the self-sufficiency of the fable and, thus, the validity of the vision.

Were this paradox — vision juxtaposed with reality — the novel's intended subject, consciously realized and explored in the characters and the action, then the novel would be less questionable, less synthetic, less "finished." There would be no need for the "positive" ending, which reveals intensive structuring on behalf of the controlling idea. But the paradox is not a "subject" within *Howards End;* the whole novel is constructed to confirm the uncertain absolute of the vision. From the beginning it is geared to proving the *idea,* and prove the idea it does. The novel attempts, to borrow Margaret's thoughts, to reflect "the chaotic nature of our daily life," but it is finally bound by the "orderly sequence" of Forster's vision and its narrative formulation. In the search for harmony, for "connection," narrative and stylistic contrivance is used to justify vision against other, more realistic, elements that the novel's world itself contains.

This is the constant tendency of the novel: a vision affirmed by Art. The life that Forster might observe would scarcely support his vision of "England"; but before the Great War, for a man of Forster's persuasion, there was still the possibility of believing in Liberal England victorious. For Forster, as for Margaret (again their voices blend), Howards End and its wych elm were potent evidence of the truth and viability of the vision: "Their message was not of eternity, but of hope on this side of the grave" (183). The fact that for public expression "their message" required fictional manipulation is only further evidence of how complex a historical construct *Howards End* is.

At the very end of the novel occurs the following well-known passage, in which Margaret and Helen reflect on the changes taking place around them. Margaret speaks first:

". . . There are moments when I feel Howards End peculiarly our own."
"All the same, London's creeping."

[Helen] pointed over the meadow — over eight or nine meadows, but at the end of them was a red rust.

"You see that in Surrey and even Hampshire now," she continued. "I can see it from the Purbeck downs. And London is only
part of something else, I'm afraid. Life's going to be melted down,
all over the world."

Margaret knew that her sister spoke truly. Howards End, Oniton, the Purbeck downs, the Oderberge, were all survivals, and the
melting-pot was being prepared for them. Logically, they had no
right to be alive. One's hope was in the weakness of logic. Were
they possibly the earth beating time?

"Because a thing is going strong now, it need not go strong for
ever," she said. "This craze for motion has only set in during the
last hundred years. It may be followed by a civilization that won't
be a movement, because it will rest on the earth. All the signs are
against it now, but I can't help hoping, and very early in the
morning in the garden I feel that our house is the future as well as
the past." (288)

In a sense, this passage contains the essence of the whole novel: the
conscious ambivalence of Forster's recognition of imminent breakdown and, at the same time, the affirmation of the vision ("the earth
beating time") despite that recognition. But it also acts as a commentary on the mode of the novel as a whole: Margaret's "hope . . . in the
weakness of logic" is reflected in the "weakness of logic" in the fabric
of the book. And this weakness in turn is symptom and sign of the
weakness of logic in the vision.

Paradoxically, the structural weaknesses are the result of the intense control exercised by Forster and by the very completeness of the
"connections." Time and again, to achieve these connections, Forster
has to fall back on "illogical" fictional devices that claim exemption
from the laws of probability while their medium purports to be the
phenomenal world of Edwardian England. But Forster, before the war
made his Georgian utopianism totally untenable, could attempt to effect a solution that diminished the reality of his world while still employing techniques that caused that world to be inescapably intrusive.
There is a constant tension, therefore, between the sketchy, underrealized but potent "reality" and the fictional attempts to realize the "vision." And this results from the tension between the admission that
"It is impossible to see modern life steadily and see it whole" (148)
and the affirmation that "In these English farms, if anywhere, one

might see life steadily and see it whole" (233). The former represents
the realistic perception, the latter the contrived resolution. As the
liberal-humanist worldview lost potency, so did the cosmography of
the realistic novel seem to become redundant. For Forster in the pre-
war days of Liberal England, this cosmography could not substantiate
the visionary dream; for later writers in the postwar world, it could not
express a seemingly unreal reality. The emphasis is, of course, very different, but the implication is the same: traditional realism was the
expression of an assured and self-confident liberal-humanist world-
view. The primary ambivalence of *Howards End* is its uncertainty of
form. It is this tension that confirms its "historical" significance, symptomatic as the novel is of the "liberal crisis," both ideological and
literary.

## WORKS CITED

Forster, E. M. *Aspects of the Novel.* 1927. New York: Harcourt, 1954.
———. *Two Cheers for Democracy.* New York: Harcourt, 1951.
Lodge, David. *The Novelist at the Crossroads and Other Essays.* Lon-
don: Routledge, 1971.
Masterman, C. F. G. *The Condition of England.* London: Methuen,
1909.
Trilling, Lionel. *E. M. Forster.* London: Hogarth, 1944.
Williams, Raymond. *The Country and the City.* New York: Oxford UP,
1973.
Woolf, Virginia. "The Novels of E. M. Forster." 1927. *The Death of
the Moth and Other Essays.* New York: Harcourt, 1942.

# Feminist and Gender
# Criticism and
# *Howards End*

## WHAT ARE FEMINIST
## AND GENDER CRITICISM?

Among the most exciting and influential developments in the field of literary studies, feminist and gender criticism participate in a broad philosophical discourse that extends far beyond literature, far beyond the arts in general. The critical *practices* of those who explore the representation of women and men in works by male or female, lesbian or gay writers inevitably grow out of and contribute to a larger and more generally applicable *theoretical* discussion of how gender and sexuality are constantly shaped by and shaping institutional structures and attitudes, artifacts, and behaviors.

Feminist criticism was accorded academic legitimacy in American universities "around 1981," Jane Gallop claims in her book *Around 1981: Academic Feminist Literary Theory* (1992). With Gallop's title and approximation in mind, Naomi Schor has since estimated that "around 1985, feminism began to give way to what has come to be called gender studies" (275). Some would argue that feminist criticism became academically legitimate well before 1981. Others would take issue with the notion that feminist criticism and women's studies have been giving way to gender criticism and gender studies, and with the either/or distinction that such a claim implies. Taken together, however, Gallop and Schor provide us with a useful fact — that of feminist criticism's historical precedence — and a chronological focus on the early to mid-1980s, a period during which the feminist approach was unquestionably influential and during which new interests emerged, not all of which were woman centered.

During the early 1980s, three discrete strains of feminist theory and practice — commonly categorized as French, North American, and British — seemed to be developing. French feminists tended to focus their attention on language. Drawing on the ideas of the psychoanalytic philosopher Jacques Lacan, they argued that language as we commonly think of it — as public discourse — is decidedly phallocentric, privileging what is valued by the patriarchal culture. They also spoke of the possibility of an alternative, feminine language and of *l'écriture féminine:* women's writing. Julia Kristeva, who is generally seen as a pioneer of French feminist thought even though she dislikes the feminist label, suggested that feminine language is associated with the maternal and is derived from the pre-oedipal fusion between mother and child. Like Kristeva, Hélène Cixous and Luce Irigaray associated feminine writing with the female body. Both drew an analogy between women's writing and women's sexual pleasure, Irigaray arguing that just as a woman's *"jouissance"* is more diffuse and complex than a man's unitary phallic pleasure ("woman has sex organs just about everywhere"), so "feminine" language is more diffuse and less obviously coherent than its "masculine" counterpart (*This Sex* 101–03).

Kristeva, who helped develop the concept of *l'écriture féminine,* nonetheless urged caution in its use and advocacy. Feminine or feminist writing that resists or refuses participation in "masculine" discourse, she warned, risks political marginalization, relegation to the outskirts (pun intended) of what is considered socially and politically significant. Kristeva's concerns were not unfounded: the concept of *l'écriture féminine* did prove controversial, eliciting different kinds of criticism from different kinds of feminist and gender critics. To some, the concept appears to give writing a biological basis, thereby suggesting that there is an *essential* femininity and/or that women are *essentially* different from men. To others, it seems to suggest that men can write as women, so long as they abdicate authority, sense, and logic in favor of diffusiveness, playfulness, even nonsense.

While French feminists of the 1970s and early 1980s focused on language and writing from a psychoanalytic perspective, North American critics generally practiced a different sort of criticism.

Characterized by close textual reading and historical scholarship, it generally took one of two forms. Critics like Kate Millett, Carolyn Heilbrun, and Judith Fetterley developed what Elaine Showalter called the "feminist critique" of "male constructed literary history" by closely examining canonical works by male writers, exposing the patriarchal ideology implicit in such works and arguing that traditions of systematic masculine dominance are indelibly inscribed in our literary tradition. Fetterley urged women to become "resisting readers" — to notice how biased most of the classic texts by male authors are in their language, subjects, and attitudes and to actively reject that bias as they read, thereby making reading a different, less "immasculating" experience. Meanwhile, another group of North American feminists, including Showalter, Sandra Gilbert, Susan Gubar, and Patricia Meyer Spacks, developed a different feminist critical model — one that Showalter referred to as "gynocriticism." These critics analyzed great books by women from a feminist perspective, discovered neglected or forgotten women writers, and attempted to recover women's culture and history, especially the history of women's communities that nurtured female creativity.

The North American endeavor to recover women's history — for example, by emphasizing that women developed their own strategies to gain power within their sphere — was seen by British feminists like Judith Newton and Deborah Rosenfelt as an endeavor that "mystifies" male oppression, disguising it as something that has created a special world of opportunities for women. More important from the British standpoint, the universalizing and "essentializing" tendencies of French theory and a great deal of North American practice disguised women's oppression by highlighting sexual difference, thereby seeming to suggest that the dominant system may be impervious to change. As for the North American critique of male stereotypes that denigrate women, British feminists maintained that it led to counterstereotypes of female virtue that ignore real differences of race, class, and culture among women.

By now, the French, North American, and British approaches have so thoroughly critiqued, influenced, and assimilated one another that the work of most Western practitioners is no longer easily identifiable along national boundary lines. Instead, it tends to be characterized according to whether the category of *woman* is the major focus in the exploration of gender and gender oppression or, alternatively, whether the interest in sexual difference encompasses an interest in other differences that also define identity. The latter paradigm encompasses the work of feminists of color, Third World (preferably called post-colonial) feminists, and lesbian feminists, many of whom have asked whether the universal category of *woman* constructed by certain French and North American predecessors is appropriate to describe women in minority groups or non-Western cultures.

These feminists stress that, while all women are female, they are something else as well (such as African American, lesbian, Muslim Pakistani). This "something else" is precisely what makes them — including their problems and their goals — different from other women. As Armit Wilson has pointed out, Asian women living in Great Britain are expected by their families and communities to preserve Asian cultural traditions; thus, the expression of personal identity through clothing involves a much more serious infraction of cultural rules than it does for a Western woman. Gloria Anzaldúa has spoken personally and eloquently about the experience of many women on the margins of Eurocentric North American culture. "I am a border woman," she writes in *Borderlands* = *La Frontera: The New Mestiza* (1987). "I grew up between two cultures, the Mexican (with a heavy Indian influence) and the Anglo. . . . Living on the borders and in margins, keeping intact one's shifting and multiple identity and integrity is like trying to swim in a new element, an 'alien' element" (i).

Instead of being divisive and isolating, this evolution of feminism into femin*isms* has fostered a more inclusive, global perspective. The era of recovering women's texts, especially texts by white Western women, has been succeeded by a new era in which the goal is to recover entire cultures of women. Two important figures of this new era are Trinh T. Minh-ha and Gayatri Spivak. Spivak, in works such as *In Other Worlds: Essays in Cultural Politics* (1987) and *Outside in the Teaching Machine* (1993), has shown how political independence (generally looked upon by metropolitan Westerners as a simple and beneficial historical and political reversal) has complex implications for "subaltern" or subproletarian women.

The understanding of *woman* not as a single, deterministic category but rather as the nexus of diverse experiences has led some white, Western, "majority" feminists like Jane Tompkins and Nancy K. Miller to advocate and practice "personal" or "autobiographical" criticism. Once reluctant to reveal themselves in their analyses for fear of being labeled idiosyncratic, impressionistic, and subjective by men, some feminists are now openly skeptical of the claims to reason, logic, and objectivity that male critics have made in the past. With the advent of more personal feminist critical styles has come a powerful new interest in women's autobiographical writings, manifested in essays such as "Authorizing the Autobiographical" by Shari Benstock, which first appeared in her influential collection *The Private Self: Theory and Practice of Women's Autobiographical Writings* (1988).

Traditional autobiography, some feminists have argued, is a gendered, "masculinist" genre; its established conventions call for a life-plot that turns on action, triumph through conflict, intellectual self-discovery, and often public renown. The body, reproduction, children, and intimate interpersonal relationships are generally well in the background and often absent. Arguing that the lived experiences of women and men differ — women's lives, for instance, are often characterized by interruption and deferral — Leigh Gilmore has developed a theory of women's self-representation in her book *Autobiographics: A Feminist Theory of Self-Representation.*

*Autobiographics* was published in 1994, well after the chronological divide that, according to Schor, separates the heyday of feminist criticism and the rise of gender studies. Does that mean that Gilmore's book is a feminist throwback? Is she practicing gender criticism instead, the use of the word "feminist" in her book's subtitle notwithstanding? Or are both of these questions overly reductive? As implied earlier, many knowledgeable commentators on the contemporary critical scene are skeptical of the feminist/gender distinction, arguing that feminist criticism is by definition gender criticism and pointing out that one critic whose work *everyone* associates with feminism (Julia Kristeva) has problems with the feminist label while another critic whose name is continually linked with the gender approach (Teresa de Lauretis) continues to refer to herself and her work as feminist.

Certainly, feminist and gender criticism are not polar opposites but, rather, exist along a continuum of attitudes toward sex and sexism, sexuality and gender, language and the literary canon. There are, however, a few distinctions to be made between those critics whose writings are inevitably identified as being toward one end of the continuum or the other.

One distinction is based on focus: as the word implies, "feminists" have concentrated their efforts on the study of women and women's issues. Gender criticism, by contrast, has not been woman centered. It has tended to view the male and female sexes — and the masculine and feminine genders — in terms of a complicated continuum, much as we are viewing feminist and gender criticism. Critics like Diane K.

Lewis have raised the possibility that black women may be more like white men in terms of familial and economic roles, like black men in terms of their relationships with whites, and like white women in terms of their relationships with men. Lesbian gender critics have asked whether lesbian women are really more like straight women than they are like gay (or for that matter straight) men. That we refer to gay and lesbian studies as gender studies has led some to suggest that gender studies is a misnomer; after all, homosexuality is not a gender. This objection may easily be answered once we realize that one purpose of gender criticism is to criticize gender as we commonly conceive of it, to expose its insufficiency and inadequacy as a category.

Another distinction between feminist and gender criticism is based on the terms *gender* and *sex*. As de Lauretis suggests in *Technologies of Gender* (1987), feminists of the 1970s tended to equate gender with sex, gender difference with sexual difference. But that equation doesn't help us explain "the differences among women, . . . the differences *within women*." After positing that "we need a notion of gender that is not so bound up with sexual difference," de Lauretis provides just such a notion by arguing that "gender is not a property of bodies or something originally existent in human beings"; rather, it is "the product of various social technologies, such as cinema" (2). Gender is, in other words, a construct, an effect of language, culture, and its institutions. It is gender, not sex, that causes a weak old man to open a door for an athletic young woman. And it is gender, not sex, that may cause one young woman to expect old men to behave in this way, another to view this kind of behavior as chauvinistic and insulting, and still another to have mixed feelings (hence de Lauretis's phrase "differences *within women*") about "gentlemanly gallantry."

Still another, related distinction between feminist and gender criticism is based on the *essentialist* views of many feminist critics and the *constructionist* views of many gender critics (both those who would call themselves feminists and those who would not). Stated simply and perhaps too reductively, the term *essentialist* refers to the view that women are essentially different from men. *Constructionist*, by contrast, refers to the view that most of those differences are characteristics not of the male and female sex (nature) but, rather, of the masculine and feminine genders (nurture). Because of its essentialist tendencies, "radical feminism," according to the influential gender critic Eve Kosofsky Sedgwick, "tends to deny that the meaning of gender or sexuality has ever significantly changed; and more damagingly, it can make future change appear impossible" (*Between Men* 13).

Most obviously essentialist would be those feminists who emphasize the female body, its difference, and the manifold implications of that difference. The equation made by some avant-garde French feminists between the female body and the *maternal* body has proved especially troubling to some gender critics, who worry that it may paradoxically play into the hands of extreme conservatives and fundamentalists seeking to reestablish patriarchal family values. In her book *The Reproduction of Mothering* (1978), Nancy Chodorow, a sociologist of gender, admits that what we call "mothering" — not having or nursing babies but mothering more broadly conceived — is commonly associated not just with the feminine gender but also with the female sex, often considered nurturing by nature. But she critically interrogates the common assumption that it is in women's nature or biological destiny to "mother" in this broader sense, arguing that the separation of home and workplace brought about by the development of capitalism and the ensuing industrial revolution made mothering *appear* to be essentially a woman's job in modern Western society.

If sex turns out to be gender where mothering is concerned, what differences *are* grounded in sex — that is, nature? *Are* there *essential* differences between men and women — other than those that are purely anatomical and anatomically determined (for example, a man can exclusively take on the job of feeding an infant milk, but he may not do so from his own breast)? A growing number of gender critics would answer the question in the negative. Sometimes referred to as "extreme constructionists" and "postfeminists," these critics have adopted the viewpoint of philosopher Judith Butler, who in her book *Gender Trouble* (1990) predicts that "sex, by definition, will be shown to have been gender all along" (8). As Naomi Schor explains their position, "there is nothing outside or before culture, no nature that is not always and already enculturated" (278).

Whereas a number of feminists celebrate women's difference, postfeminist gender critics would agree with Chodorow's statement that men have an "investment in difference that women do not have" (Eisenstein and Jardine 14). They see difference as a symptom of oppression, not a cause for celebration, and would abolish it by dismantling gender categories and, ultimately, destroying gender itself. Since gender categories and distinctions are embedded in and perpetuated through language, gender critics like Monique Wittig have called for the wholesale transformation of language into a nonsexist, and nonheterosexist, medium.

Language has proved the site of important debates between

feminist and gender critics, essentialists and constructionists. Gender critics have taken issue with those French feminists who have spoken of a feminine language and writing and who have grounded differences in language and writing in the female body.[1] For much the same reason, they have disagreed with those French-influenced Anglo-American critics who, like Toril Moi and Nancy K. Miller, have posited an essential relationship between sexuality and textuality. (In an essentialist sense, such critics have suggested that when women write, they tend to break the rules of plausibility and verisimilitude that men have created to evaluate fiction.) Gender critics like Peggy Kamuf posit a relationship only between *gender* and textuality, between what most men and women *become* after they are born and the way in which they write. They are therefore less interested in the author's sexual "signature" — in whether the author was a woman writing — than in whether the author was (to borrow from Kamuf) "Writing like a Woman."

Feminists like Miller have suggested that no man could write the "female anger, desire, and selfhood" that Emily Brontë, for instance, inscribed in her poetry and in *Wuthering Heights* (*Subject* 72). In the view of gender critics, it is and has been possible for a man to write like a woman, a woman to write like a man. Shari Benstock, a noted feminist critic whose investigations into psychoanalytic and poststructuralist theory have led her increasingly to adopt the gender approach, poses the following question to herself in *Textualizing the Feminine* (1991): "Isn't it precisely 'the feminine' in Joyce's writings and Derrida's that carries me along?" (45). In an essay entitled "Unsexing Language: Pronomial Protest in Emily Dickinson's 'Lay this Laurel,'" Anna Shannon Elfenbein has argued that "like Walt Whitman, Emily Dickinson crossed the gender barrier in some remarkable poems," such as "We learned to like the Fire / By playing Glaciers — when a Boy —" (Berg 215).

It is also possible, in the view of most gender critics, for women to read as men, men as women. The view that women can, and indeed have been forced to, read as men has been fairly noncontroversial.

---

[1]Because feminist/gender studies, not unlike sex/gender, should be thought of as existing along a continuum of attitudes and not in terms of simple opposition, attempts to highlight the difference between feminist and gender criticism are inevitably prone to reductive overgeneralization and occasional distortion. Here, for instance, French feminism is made out to be more monolithic than it actually is. Hélène Cixous has said that a few men (such as Jean Genet) have produced "feminine writing," although she suggests that these are exceptional men who have acknowledged their own bisexuality.

Everyone agrees that the literary canon is largely "androcentric" and that writings by men have tended to "immasculate" women, forcing them to see the world from a masculine viewpoint. But the question of whether men can read as women has proved to be yet another issue dividing feminist and gender critics. Some feminists suggest that men and women have some essentially different reading strategies and outcomes, while gender critics maintain that such differences arise entirely out of social training and cultural norms. One interesting outcome of recent attention to gender and reading is Elizabeth A. Flynn's argument that women in fact make the best interpreters of imaginative literature. Based on a study of how male and female students read works of fiction, she concludes that women come up with more imaginative, open-ended readings of stories. Quite possibly the imputed hedging and tentativeness of women's speech, often seen by men as disadvantages, are transformed into useful interpretive strategies — receptivity combined with critical assessment of the text — in the act of reading (Flynn and Schweickart 286).

In singling out a catalyst of the gender approach, many historians of criticism have pointed to Michel Foucault. In his *History of Sexuality* (1976, tr. 1978), Foucault distinguished sexuality (that is, sexual behavior or practice) from sex, calling the former a "technology of sex." De Lauretis, who has deliberately developed her theory of gender "along the lines of . . . Foucault's theory of sexuality," explains his use of "technology" this way: "Sexuality, commonly thought to be a natural as well as a private matter, is in fact completely constructed in culture according to the political aims of the society's dominant class" (*Technologies* 2, 12). Foucault suggests that homosexuality as we now think of it was to a great extent an invention of the nineteenth century. In earlier periods there had been "acts of sodomy" and individuals who committed them, but the "sodomite" was, according to Foucault, "a temporary aberration," not the "species" he became with the advent of the modern concept of homosexuality (42–43). By historicizing sexuality, Foucault made it possible for his successors to consider the possibility that all of the categories and assumptions that currently come to mind when we think about sex, sexual difference, gender, and sexuality are social artifacts, the products of cultural discourses.

In explaining her reason for saying that feminism began to give way to gender studies "around 1985," Schor says that she chose that date "in part because it marks the publication of *Between Men*," a

seminal book in which Eve Kosofsky Sedgwick "articulates the insights
of feminist criticism onto those of gay-male studies, which had up to
then pursued often parallel but separate courses (affirming the existence of a homosexual or female imagination, recovering lost traditions, decoding the cryptic discourse of works already in the canon by
homosexual or feminist authors)" (276). Today, gay and lesbian criticism is so much a part of gender criticism that some people equate it
with the gender approach, while others have begun to prefer the
phrase "sexualities criticism" to "gender criticism."

Following Foucault's lead, some gay and lesbian gender critics
have argued that the heterosexual/homosexual distinction is as much
a cultural construct as is the masculine/feminine dichotomy. Arguing
that sexuality is a continuum, not a fixed and static set of binary oppositions, a number of gay and lesbian critics have critiqued heterosexuality as a norm, arguing that it has been an enforced corollary and consequence of what Gayle Rubin has referred to as the "sex/gender
system." (Those subscribing to this system assume that persons of the
male sex should be masculine, that masculine men are attracted to
women, and therefore that it is natural for masculine men to be attracted to women and unnatural for them to be attracted to men.)
Lesbian gender critics have also taken issue with their feminist counterparts on the grounds that they proceed from fundamentally heterosexual and even heterosexist assumptions. Particularly offensive to lesbians like the poet-critic Adrienne Rich have been those feminists who,
following Doris Lessing, have implied that to make the lesbian choice
is to make a statement, to act out feminist hostility against men. Rich
has called heterosexuality "a beachhead of male dominance" that, "like
motherhood, needs to be recognized and studied as a political institution" ("Compulsory Heterosexuality" 143, 145).

If there is such a thing as reading like a woman and such a thing as
reading like a man, how then do lesbians read? Are there gay and lesbian ways of reading? Many would say that there are. Rich, by reading
Emily Dickinson's poetry as a lesbian — by not assuming that "heterosexual romance is the key to a woman's life and work" — has introduced us to a poet somewhat different from the one heterosexual critics have made familiar (*Lies* 158). As for gay reading, Wayne
Koestenbaum has defined "the (male twentieth-century first world)
gay reader" as one who "reads resistantly for inscriptions of his condition, for texts that will confirm a social and private identity founded on
a desire for other men. . . . Reading becomes a hunt for histories that
deliberately foreknow or unwittingly trace a desire felt not by author

but by reader, who is most acute when searching for signs of himself" (qtd. in Boone and Cadden 176–77).

Lesbian critics have produced a number of compelling reinterpretations, or in-scriptions, of works by authors as diverse as Emily Dickinson, Virginia Woolf, and Toni Morrison. As a result of these provocative readings, significant disagreements have arisen between straight and lesbian critics and among lesbian critics as well. Perhaps the most famous and interesting example of this kind of interpretive controversy involves the claim by Barbara Smith and Adrienne Rich that Morrison's novel *Sula* can be read as a lesbian text — and author Toni Morrison's counterclaim that it cannot.

Gay male critics have produced a body of readings no less revisionist and controversial, focusing on writers as staidly classic as Henry James and Wallace Stevens. In Melville's *Billy Budd* and *Moby-Dick*, Robert K. Martin suggests, a triangle of homosexual desire exists. In the latter novel, the hero must choose between a captain who represents "the imposition of the male on the female" and a "Dark Stranger" (Queequeg) who "offers the possibility of an alternate sexuality, one that is less dependent upon performance and conquest" (5).

Masculinity as a complex construct producing and reproducing a constellation of behaviors and goals, many of them destructive (like performance and conquest) and most of them injurious to women, has become the object of an unprecedented number of gender studies. A 1983 issue of *Feminist Review* contained an essay entitled "Anti-Porn: Soft Issue, Hard World," in which B. Ruby Rich suggested that the "legions of feminist men" who examine and deplore the effects of pornography on women might better "undertake the analysis that can tell us why men like porn (not, piously, why this or that exceptional man does *not*)" (qtd. in Berg 185). The advent of gender criticism makes precisely that kind of analysis possible. Stephen H. Clark, who alludes to Ruby Rich's challenge, reads T. S. Eliot "as a man." Responding to "Eliot's implicit appeal to a specifically masculine audience — 'You! hypocrite lecteur! — mon semblable, — mon *frère!*'" — Clark concludes that poems like "Sweeney among the Nightingales" and "Gerontion," rather than offering what they are usually said to offer — "a social critique into which a misogynistic language accidentally seeps" — instead articulate a masculine "psychology of sexual fear and desired retaliation" (qtd. in Berg 173).

Some gender critics focusing on masculinity have analyzed "the anthropology of boyhood," a phrase coined by Mark Seltzer in an article in which he comparatively reads, among other things, Stephen

Crane's *Red Badge of Courage,* Jack London's *White Fang,* and the first Boy Scouts of America handbook (Boone and Cadden 150). Others have examined the fear men have that artistry is unmasculine, a guilty worry that surfaces perhaps most obviously in "The Custom-House," Hawthorne's lengthy preface to *The Scarlet Letter.* Still others have studied the representation in literature of subtly erotic disciple-patron relationships, relationships like the ones between Nick Carraway and Jay Gatsby, Charlie Marlow and Lord Jim, Doctor Watson and Sherlock Holmes, and any number of characters in Henry James's stories. Not all of these studies have focused on literary texts. Because the movies have played a primary role in gender construction during our lifetimes, gender critics have analyzed the dynamics of masculinity (vis-à-vis femininity and androgyny) in films from *Rebel without a Cause* to *Tootsie* to last year's Best Picture. One of the "social technologies" most influential in (re)constructing gender, film is one of the media in which today's sexual politics is most evident.

Necessary as it is, in an introduction such as this one, to define the difference between feminist and gender criticism, it is equally necessary to conclude by unmaking the distinction, at least partially. The two topics just discussed (film theory and so-called queer theory) give us grounds for undertaking that necessary deconstruction. The alliance I have been creating between gay and lesbian criticism on one hand and gender criticism on the other is complicated greatly by the fact that not all gay and lesbian critics are constructionists. Indeed, a number of them (Robert K. Martin included) share with many feminists the *essentialist* point of view; that is to say, they believe homosexuals and heterosexuals to be essentially different, different by nature, just as a number of feminists believe men and women to be different.

In film theory and criticism, feminist and gender critics have so influenced one another that their differences would be difficult to define based on any available criteria, including the ones outlined above. Cinema has been of special interest to contemporary feminists like Minh-ha (herself a filmmaker) and Spivak (whose critical eye has focused on movies including *My Beautiful Laundrette* and *Sammie and Rosie Get Laid*). Teresa de Lauretis, whose *Technologies of Gender* (1987) has proved influential in the area of gender studies, continues to publish film criticism consistent with earlier, unambiguously feminist works in which she argued that "the representation of woman as spectacle — body to be looked at, place of sexuality, and object of desire — so pervasive in our culture, finds in narrative cinema its most complex expression and widest circulation" (*Alice* 4).

Feminist film theory has developed alongside a feminist performance theory grounded in Joan Riviere's recently rediscovered essay "Womanliness as a Masquerade" (1929), in which the author argues that there is no femininity that is *not* masquerade. Marjorie Garber, a contemporary cultural critic with an interest in gender, has analyzed the constructed nature of femininity by focusing on men who have apparently achieved it — through the transvestism, transsexualism, and other forms of "cross-dressing" evident in cultural productions from Shakespeare to Elvis, from "Little Red Riding Hood" to *La Cage aux Folles*. The future of feminist and gender criticism, it would seem, is not one of further bifurcation but one involving a refocusing on femininity, masculinity, and related sexualities, not only as represented in poems, novels, and films but also as manifested and developed in video, on television, and along the almost infinite number of waystations rapidly being developed on the information highways running through an exponentially expanding cyberspace.

In the essay that follows, Elizabeth Langland admits that *Howards End* lacks the "stylistic resistance and technical virtuosity" typically associated with the great works of literary modernism. Nonetheless, she hastens to point out that "Forster accomplished something difficult and important in *Howards End*" by exposing "the constructed nature of gender and his own ambivalent relationship to traits coded 'masculine' and 'feminine' in his culture."

Langland grounds Forster's "textual politics" in the "sexual politics" of his day and, specifically, in the identity confusion that Forster, a homosexual, experienced as a result of his society's view of homosexuality. According to the Victorian view still prevalent in the early twentieth century, homosexuals were, in essence, women trapped in men's bodies; this perception, Langland argues, "precipitated a misogynistic homosexuality," one that pitted homosexuals against women in a destructive way.

Although hints of Forster's misogyny surface throughout the novel, Langland goes on to argue, so does "a desire for something other than the classical opposition between male and female, masculine and feminine." That desire results in Forster's obviously "embattled relationship" with the patriarchy that has for so long enforced and reinforced those overly simplistic oppositions. To expose the more "radical sexual politics" beneath the surface of *Howards End*,

Langland examines the way in which Forster's narrative is "focalized through the female protagonist, Margaret Schlegel." Through Margaret, Langland argues, Forster simultaneously subverts "essentialist conceptions of the female and . . . the social encoding of the feminine." (Here is a character "who can calmly state, for example, 'I do not love children. I am thankful to have none' . . . , thus debunking ideas of a natural, maternal female.") But it is through Margaret, too, Langland points out in an intricate and complex argument, that masculinity is debunked as well — and that both terms are integrated or, at least, reconciled.

The events of *Howards End*, of course, are not always seen from Margaret's perspective, nor do the sexual politics of the novel remain consistently radical throughout. Indeed, much as its author might have liked to live in a world without rigid conceptions of masculinity, *Howards End* is to a great extent built upon a dialectical opposition between masculine and feminine, an opposition under which several other oppositions are subsumed. In each of these subsidiary oppositions, which include rich/poor, logic/vision, and word/intuition, the first term is associated with masculinity and the second with femininity. Although Forster attempts to subvert the hierarchies implicit in these oppositions, he also perpetuates the oppositions in the process. As a result, Langland argues, Forster in many ways subtly reinforces the attendant masculinist value system.

Furthermore, what Forster accomplishes at the level of theme he often offsets via plot, which "appears to encode the very patriarchal structures that the novel seeks to escape." Thematically, his novel privileges vision and intuition and encourages sympathy with the poor, but, at the level of plot, traditional relationships between men and women and between the upper and lower classes persist. Thus, "Although the themes of the novel indicate a desire to deconstruct the patriarchal ideology," Langland writes,

> ultimately, it seems, Forster is forced to reconstruct that ideology in the structure of the novel, in Margaret's "victory" over Henry. Plot has demanded a hierarchical ordering of terms for a resolution of conflict even though the novel's themes have argued for replacement of conquest with connection. (411)

What makes Langland's essay unique and interesting is its conception of *Howards End* as both radical and reactionary, its author a Janus-faced figure simultaneously "imagin[ing] the 'inconceivable'" and preserving the old ways. This flexibility in reading Forster's novel may owe something to Langland's method, which combines the deconstructor's interest in and suspicion of binary oppositions and hierarchies with a feminist focus on the way in which women and the feminine are represented in novelistic discourse. Finally, and perhaps most tellingly, Langland's essay is grounded in the gender critic's conviction that femininity and masculinity are not essential or natural states but, rather — like Forster's version of homosexuality, like his *society's* definition of homosexuality — cultural constructs.

Ross C Murfin

## FEMINIST AND GENDER CRITICISM: A SELECTED BIBLIOGRAPHY

### French Feminist Theory

Cixous, Hélène. "The Laugh of the Medusa." Trans. Keith Cohen and Paula Cohen. *Signs* 1 (1976): 875–93.

Cixous, Hélène, and Catherine Clément. *The Newly Born Woman.* Trans. Betsy Wing. Minneapolis: U of Minnesota P, 1986.

Irigaray, Luce. *An Ethics of Sexual Difference.* Trans. Carolyn Burke and Gillian C. Gill. Ithaca: Cornell UP, 1993.

———. *This Sex Which Is Not One.* Trans. Catherine Porter. Ithaca: Cornell UP, 1985.

Jones, Ann Rosalind. "Inscribing Femininity: French Theories of the Feminine." *Making a Difference: Feminist Literary Criticism.* Ed. Gayle Green and Coppélia Kahn. London: Methuen, 1985. 80–112.

———. "Writing the Body: Toward an Understanding of *L'Écriture féminine.*" Showalter, *The New Feminist Criticism* 361–77.

Kristeva, Julia. *Desire in Language: A Semiotic Approach to Literature and Art.* Ed. Leon S. Roudiez. Trans. Thomas Gora, Alice Jardine, and Roudiez. New York: Columbia UP, 1980.

Marks, Elaine, and Isabelle de Courtivron, eds. *New French Feminisms: An Anthology.* Amherst: U of Massachusetts P, 1980.

Moi, Toril, ed. *French Feminist Thought: A Reader.* Oxford: Basil Blackwell, 1987.

### Feminist Theory: Classic Texts, General Approaches, Collections

Abel, Elizabeth, and Emily K. Abel, eds. *The "Signs" Reader: Women, Gender, and Scholarship.* Chicago: U of Chicago P, 1983.

Barrett, Michèle, and Anne Phillips. *Destabilizing Theory: Contemporary Feminist Debates.* Stanford: Stanford UP, 1992.

Beauvoir, Simone de. *The Second Sex.* 1953. Trans. and ed. H. M. Parshley. New York: Bantam, 1961.

Benstock, Shari. *Textualizing the Feminine: On the Limits of Genre.* Norman: U of Oklahoma P, 1991.

Butler, Judith. *Gender Trouble: Feminism and the Subversion of Identity.* New York: Routledge, 1990.

de Lauretis, Teresa, ed. *Feminist Studies/Critical Studies.* Bloomington: Indiana UP, 1986.

Felman, Shoshana. "Women and Madness: The Critical Phallacy." *Diacritics* 5 (1975): 2–10.

Fetterley, Judith. *The Resisting Reader: A Feminist Approach to American Fiction.* Bloomington: Indiana UP, 1978.

Fuss, Diana. *Essentially Speaking: Feminism, Nature and Difference.* New York: Routledge, 1989.

Gallop, Jane. *Around 1981: Academic Feminist Literary Theory.* New York: Routledge, 1992.

———. *The Daughter's Seduction: Feminism and Psychoanalysis.* Ithaca: Cornell UP, 1982.

Greenblatt, Stephen, and Giles Gunn, eds. *Redrawing the Boundaries: The Transformation of English and American Literary Studies.* New York: MLA, 1992.

hooks, bell. *Feminist Theory: From Margin to Center.* Boston: South End, 1984.

Kolodny, Annette. "Dancing through the Minefield: Some Observations on the Theory, Practice, and Politics of a Feminist Literary Criticism." Showalter, *The New Feminist Criticism* 144–67.

———. "Some Notes on Defining a 'Feminist Literary Criticism.'" *Critical Inquiry* 2 (1975): 78.

Lovell, Terry, ed. *British Feminist Thought: A Reader.* Oxford: Basil Blackwell, 1990.

Meese, Elizabeth, and Alice Parker, eds. *The Difference Within: Feminism and Critical Theory.* Philadelphia: John Benjamins, 1989.

Miller, Nancy K., ed. *The Poetics of Gender.* New York: Columbia UP, 1986.

Millett, Kate. *Sexual Politics.* Garden City: Doubleday, 1970.

Rich, Adrienne. *On Lies, Secrets, and Silence: Selected Prose, 1966–1979.* New York: Norton, 1979.

Showalter, Elaine. "Toward a Feminist Poetics." Showalter, *The New Feminist Criticism* 125–43.

————, ed. *The New Feminist Criticism: Essays on Women, Literature, and Theory*. New York: Pantheon, 1985.

Stimpson, Catherine R. "Feminist Criticism." Greenblatt and Gunn 251–70.

Warhol, Robyn, and Diane Price Herndl, eds. *Feminisms: An Anthology of Literary Theory and Criticism*. New Brunswick, NJ: Rutgers UP, 1991.

Weed, Elizabeth, ed. *Coming to Terms: Feminism, Theory, Politics*. New York: Routledge, 1989.

Woolf, Virginia. *A Room of One's Own*. New York: Harcourt, 1929.


### Women's Writing and Creativity

Abel, Elizabeth, ed. *Writing and Sexual Difference*. Chicago: U of Chicago P, 1982.

Berg, Temma F., ed. *Engendering the Word: Feminist Essays in Psychosexual Poetics*. Co-ed. Anna Shannon Elfenbein, Jeanne Larsen, and Elisa Kay Sparks. Urbana: U of Illinois P, 1989.

DuPlessis, Rachel Blau. *The Pink Guitar: Writing as Feminist Practice*. New York: Routledge, 1990.

Finke, Laurie. *Feminist Theory, Women's Writing*. Ithaca: Cornell UP, 1992.

Gilbert, Sandra M., and Susan Gubar. *The Madwoman in the Attic: The Woman Writer and the Nineteenth-Century Literary Imagination*. New Haven: Yale UP, 1979.

Homans, Margaret. *Bearing the Word: Language and Female Experience in Nineteenth-Century Women's Writing*. Chicago: U of Chicago P, 1986.

Jacobus, Mary, ed. *Women Writing and Writing about Women*. New York: Barnes, 1979.

Miller, Nancy K. *Subject to Change: Reading Feminist Writing*. New York: Columbia UP, 1988.

Newton, Judith Lowder. *Women, Power and Subversion: Social Strategies in British Fiction, 1778–1860*. Athens: U of Georgia P, 1981.

Poovey, Mary. *The Proper Lady and the Woman Writer: Ideology as Style in the Works of Mary Wollstonecraft, Mary Shelley, and Jane Austen*. Chicago: U of Chicago P, 1984.

Showalter, Elaine. *A Literature of Their Own: British Women Novelists from Brontë to Lessing*. Princeton: Princeton UP, 1977.

Spacks, Patricia Meyer. *The Female Imagination*. New York: Knopf, 1975.

### Feminism, Race, Class, and Nationality

Anzaldúa, Gloria. *Borderlands = La Frontera: The New Mestiza*. San Francisco: Spinsters/Aunt Lute, 1987.

Christian, Barbara. *Black Feminist Criticism: Perspectives on Black Women Writers*. New York: Pergamon, 1985.

hooks, bell. *Ain't I a Woman? Black Women and Feminism*. Boston: South End, 1981.

———. *Black Looks: Race and Representation*. Boston: South End, 1992.

Kaplan, Cora. *Sea Changes: Essays on Culture and Feminism*. London: Verso, 1986.

Moraga, Cherríe, and Gloria Anzaldúa. *This Bridge Called My Back: Writings by Radical Women of Color*. New York: Kitchen Table, 1981.

Newton, Judith, and Deborah Rosenfelt, eds. *Feminist Criticism and Social Change: Sex, Class, and Race in Literature and Culture*. New York: Methuen, 1985.

Pryse, Marjorie, and Hortense Spillers, eds. *Conjuring: Black Women, Fiction, and Literary Tradition*. Bloomington: Indiana UP, 1985.

Robinson, Lillian S. *Sex, Class, and Culture*. 1978. New York: Methuen, 1986.

Smith, Barbara. "Towards a Black Feminist Criticism." Showalter, *The New Feminist Criticism* 168–85.


### Feminism and Postcoloniality

Emberley, Julia. *Thresholds of Difference: Feminist Critique, Native Women's Writings, Postcolonial Theory*. Toronto: U of Toronto P, 1993.

Minh-ha, Trinh T. *Woman, Native, Other: Writing Postcoloniality and Feminism*. Bloomington: Indiana UP, 1989.

Mohanty, Chandra Talpade, Ann Russo, and Lourdes Torres, eds. *Third World Women and the Politics of Feminism*. Bloomington: Indiana UP, 1991.

Schipper, Mineke, ed. *Unheard Words: Women and Literature in Africa, the Arab World, Asia, the Caribbean, and Latin America*. London: Allison, 1985.

Spivak, Gayatri Chakravorty. *In Other Worlds: Essays in Cultural Politics*. New York: Methuen, 1987.

———. *Outside in the Teaching Machine*. New York: Routledge, 1993.

Wilson, Armit. *Finding a Voice: Asian Women in Britain*. 1979. London: Virago, 1980.

## Women's Self-Representation and Personal Criticism

Benstock, Shari, ed. *The Private Self: Theory and Practice of Women's Autobiographical Writings*. Chapel Hill: U of North Carolina P, 1988.

Gilmore, Leigh. *Autobiographics: A Feminist Theory of Self-Representation*. Ithaca: Cornell UP, 1994.

Martin, Biddy, and Chandra Talpade Mohanty. "Feminist Politics: What's Home Got to Do with It?" *Life/Lines: Theorizing Women's Autobiography*. Ed. Bella Brodski and Celeste Schenck. Ithaca: Cornell UP, 1988.

Miller, Nancy K. *Getting Personal: Feminist Occasions and Other Autobiographical Acts*. New York: Routledge, 1991.

Smith, Sidonie. *A Poetics of Women's Autobiography: Marginality and the Fictions of Self-Representation*. Bloomington: Indiana UP, 1988.


## Feminist Film Theory

de Lauretis, Teresa. *Alice Doesn't: Feminism, Semiotics, Cinema*. Bloomington: Indiana UP, 1986.

Doane, Mary Ann. *Re-vision: Essays in Feminist Film Criticism*. Frederick: U Publications of America, 1984.

Modleski, Tania. *Feminism without Women: Culture and Criticism in a "Postfeminist" Age*. New York: Routledge, 1991.

Mulvey, Laura. *Visual and Other Pleasures*. Bloomington: Indiana UP, 1989.

Penley, Constance, ed. *Feminism and Film Theory*. New York: Routledge, 1988.


## Studies of Gender and Sexuality

Boone, Joseph A., and Michael Cadden, eds. *Engendering Men: The Question of Male Feminist Criticism*. New York: Routledge, 1990.

Butler, Judith. *Gender Trouble: Feminism and the Subversion of Identity*. New York: Routledge, 1990.

Chodorow, Nancy. *The Reproduction of Mothering: Psychoanalysis and the Sociology of Gender*. Berkeley: U of California P, 1978.

Claridge, Laura, and Elizabeth Langland, eds. *Out of Bounds: Male Writing and Gender(ed) Criticism*. Amherst: U of Massachusetts P, 1990.

de Lauretis, Teresa. *Technologies of Gender: Essays on Theory, Film, and Fiction.* Bloomington: Indiana UP, 1987.

Doane, Mary Ann. "Masquerade Reconsidered: Further Thoughts on the Female Spectator." *Discourse* 11 (1988–89): 42–54.

Eisenstein, Hester, and Alice Jardine, eds. *The Future of Difference.* Boston: G. K. Hall, 1980.

Flynn, Elizabeth A., and Patrocinio P. Schweickart, eds. *Gender and Reading: Essays on Readers, Texts, and Contexts.* Baltimore: Johns Hopkins UP, 1986.

Foucault, Michel. *The History of Sexuality: Volume I: An Introduction.* Trans. Robert Hurley. New York: Random, 1978.

Kamuf, Peggy. "Writing like a Woman." *Women and Language in Literature and Society.* New York: Praeger, 1980. 284–99.

Laqueur, Thomas. *Making Sex: Body and Gender from the Greeks to Freud.* Cambridge: Harvard UP, 1990.

Riviere, Joan. "Womanliness as a Masquerade." 1929. *Formations of Fantasy.* Ed. Victor Burgin, James Donald, and Cora Kaplan. London: Methuen, 1986. 35–44.

Rubin, Gayle. "Thinking Sex: Notes for a Radical Theory of the Politics of Sexuality." Abelove, Barale, and Halperin 3–44.

———. "The Traffic in Women: Notes on the 'Political Economy' of Sex." *Toward an Anthropology of Women.* Ed. Rayna R. Reiter. New York: Monthly Review, 1975. 157–210.

Schor, Naomi. "Feminist and Gender Studies." *Introduction to Scholarship in Modern Languages and Literatures.* Ed. Joseph Gibaldi. New York: MLA, 1992. 262–87.

Sedgwick, Eve Kosofsky. *Between Men: English Literature and Male Homosocial Desire.* New York: Columbia UP, 1988.

———. "Gender Criticism." Greenblatt and Gunn 271–302.

### Lesbian and Gay Criticism

Abelove, Henry, Michèle Aina Barale, and David Halperin, eds. *The Lesbian and Gay Studies Reader.* New York: Routledge, 1993.

Butters, Ronald, John M. Clum, and Michael Moon, eds. *Displacing Homophobia: Gay Male Perspectives in Literature and Culture.* Durham: Duke UP, 1989.

Craft, Christopher. *Another Kind of Love: Male Homosexual Desire in English Discourse, 1850–1920.* Berkeley: U of California P, 1994.

de Lauretis, Teresa. *The Practice of Love: Lesbian Sexuality and Perverse Desire.* Bloomington: Indiana UP, 1994.

Dollimore, Jonathan. *Sexual Dissidence: Augustine to Wilde, Freud to Foucault.* Oxford: Clarendon, 1991.

Fuss, Diana, ed. *Inside/Out: Lesbian Theories, Gay Theories.* New York: Routledge, 1991.

Garber, Marjorie. *Vested Interests: Cross-Dressing and Cultural Anxiety.* New York: Routledge, 1992.

Halperin, David M. *One Hundred Years of Homosexuality and Other Essays on Greek Love.* New York: Routledge, 1990.

*The Lesbian Issue.* Special issue, *Signs* 9 (1984).

Martin, Robert K. *Hero, Captain, and Stranger: Male Friendship, Social Critique, and Literary Form in the Sea Novels of Herman Melville.* Chapel Hill: U of North Carolina P, 1986.

Munt, Sally, ed. *New Lesbian Criticism: Literary and Cultural Readings.* New York: Harvester Wheatsheaf, 1992.

Rich, Adrienne. "Compulsory Heterosexuality and Lesbian Existence." Abel and Abel 139–68.

Stimpson, Catherine R. "Zero Degree Deviancy: The Lesbian Novel in English." *Critical Inquiry* 8 (1981): 363–79.

Weeks, Jeffrey. *Sexuality and Its Discontents: Meanings, Myths, and Modern Sexualities.* London: Routledge, 1985.

Wittig, Monique. "The Mark of Gender." Miller, *The Poetics of Gender* 63–73.

———. "One Is Not Born a Woman." *Feminist Issues* 1.2 (1981): 47–54.

———. *The Straight Mind and Other Essays.* Boston: Beacon, 1992.

### Queer Theory

Butler, Judith. *Bodies That Matter: On the Discursive Limits of "Sex."* New York: Routledge, 1993.

Cohen, Ed. *Talk on the Wilde Side: Towards a Genealogy of Discourse on Male Sexualities.* New York: Routledge, 1993.

de Lauretis, Teresa, ed. Issue on Queer Theory. *differences* 3.2 (1991).

Sedgwick, Eve Kosofsky. *Epistemology of the Closet.* Berkeley: U of California P, 1991.

———. *Tendencies.* Durham: Duke UP, 1993.

Sinfield, Alan. *Cultural Politics — Queer Reading.* Philadelphia: U of Pennsylvania P, 1994.

———. *The Wilde Century: Effeminacy, Oscar Wilde, and the Queer Moment.* New York: Columbia UP, 1994.

FEMINIST AND GENDER CRITICISM

Warner, Michael, ed. *Fear of a Queer Planet: Queer Politics and Social Theory.* Minneapolis: U of Minnesota P, 1993.

## Feminist and Gender Criticism
## of *Howards End*

Dellamora, Richard. "Textual Politics/Sexual Politics." *Modern Language Quarterly* 54.1 (1993): 155–64.
Finkelstein, Bonnie Blumenthal. *Forster's Women: Eternal Differences.* New York: Columbia UP, 1975.
Heilbrun, Carolyn. *Toward a Recognition of Androgyny.* New York: Knopf, 1973.
Marcus, Jane. "Liberty, Sorority, Misogyny." *The Representation of Women in Fiction.* Ed. Carolyn G. Heilbrun and Margaret R. Higonnet. Baltimore: Johns Hopkins UP, 1983. 60–97.
Nelson, Scott R. "Narrative Inversion: The Textual Construction of Homosexuality in E. M. Forster's Novels." *Style* 26.2 (1992): 310–26.
Stubbs, Patricia. *Women and Fiction: Feminism and the Novel, 1880–1920.* New York: Barnes, 1979.

## A FEMINIST AND GENDER PERSPECTIVE

### ELIZABETH LANGLAND

### Gesturing toward an Open Space:
### Gender, Form, and Language in *Howards End*

E. M. Forster is a difficult writer to approach because he appears simple. His work presents none of the stylistic resistance and technical virtuosity characteristic of notable contemporaries such as Joyce and Woolf. Further, he seems to have recourse to a nineteenth-century liberal humanism in resolving his novels, an emphasis that sets at naught the complexities of literary modernism. So, at best, Forster claims a precarious stake in the twentieth-century canon. But Forster accomplished something difficult and important in *Howards End* that a gendered politics of reading can uncover. In his personal battle with gender and with patriarchal culture, Forster exposed the constructed nature of gender and his own ambivalent relationship to traits coded "masculine" and "feminine" in his culture.

This gendered politics of reading begins with an acknowledgment of Forster's homosexuality and outspoken misogyny, a textual politics that is tied to a sexual politics. There is substantial evidence that Forster was deeply troubled and preoccupied by his own gender identity during this period. He had spent his childhood largely in the female company and sheltering presence of his mother and aunt who no doubt gave him his "knowledge" of women and female friendship. At the same time, he was uncertain of his own sexual orientation and even of the basic facts of male-female reproduction, which Forster claimed he never fully grasped until his thirties. The conviction of his homosexuality came shortly after publication of *Howards End* when George Merrill, the working-class homosexual lover of Forster's friend Edward Carpenter, "touched Forster's backside — 'gently and just above the buttocks,'" Forster later recalled. "The sensation was unusual and I still remember it. . . . It seemed to go straight through the small of my back into my ideas, without involving my thoughts" (qtd. in King 57). That touch conceived *Maurice,* Forster's novel about homosexual love, published only posthumously.

It wasn't until 1916 that Forster found "total sexual fulfillment or, as he put it, 'parted with respectability — '" (King 64) — and not until 1917 that he experienced a loving homosexual relationship, with an Egyptian tram conductor, Mohammed el Adl. Of that relationship Forster wrote to Florence Barger: "It isn't happiness. . . . it's rather — offensive phrase — that I first feel a grown up man" (qtd. in Furbank 40). The offensiveness lies in the implication that a man becomes "grown-up" through sexual mastery.

Thus, in 1910, while composing *Howards End,* Forster was in a great deal of confusion, which we can understand more fully if we consider the Victorian notion of homosexuality: *anima mulieris in corpore virile inclusa,* or "a woman's soul trapped in a man's body" (Miller 154–55). Ironically, that confusion and dissatisfaction precipitated a misogynistic homosexuality, which I suggest we see in light of Forster's fear of the feminine in himself.[1] This understanding also gives us some insight into the process by which the confusions that produced this misogyny in Forster also fueled a desire for something other

---

[1]Eve Kosofsky Sedgwick, in *Between Men,* has made an important connection between misogyny and fear of the feminine. She argues that "homophobia directed by men against men is misogynistic, and perhaps transhistorically so. (By 'misogynistic' I mean not only that it is oppressive of the so-called feminine in men, but that it is oppressive of women)." Sedgwick also notes that, although antihomophobia and feminism are not the same forces, the bonds between them are "profound and intuitable" (20).

than the classical opposition between male and female, masculine and feminine, and so initiated his embattled relationship with patriarchy. In *Howards End* we see this relationship played out through the narrator, the leading female characters, certain thematic oppositions, and the connections between all of these and the dramatic structure of the novel.

At first glance, Forster appears to offer neither a radical literary practice nor a liberal sexual practice in this story of a younger woman's conventional marriage to an older and successful businessman who looks upon women as "recreation." But textual evidence suggests that this conventional image is an anamorphosis (an image that appears distorted unless it is viewed from a special angle) reflecting Forster's attempt to manage a site of conflict in himself. A close analysis of the textual maneuvers in *Howards End* discloses a radical sexual politics that has been obscured by psychobiographical approaches and by assumptions about Forster's literary allegiance to the nineteenth century. We may begin to excavate the layers of the text through its narrative stance, which is ambiguous, uneasy, and defensive. The following passage from the middle of the novel first brought me to examine *Howards End,* because of the ways it makes problematic the omniscient narrator's voice:

> Pity was at the bottom of her [Margaret's] actions all through this crisis. Pity, if one may generalize, is at the bottom of woman. When men like us, it is for our better qualities, and however tender their liking we dare not be unworthy of it, or they will quietly let us go. But unworthiness stimulates woman. It brings out her deeper nature, for good or for evil. (213)

The problem emerges from the "us," which initially appears to refer back to "woman," a term used to essentialize all women, with whom the narrator seems to identify. A closer reading suggests that "us" simply refers to all people, that is, "When men like people . . ." The temporary confusion arises here because previously the events have been focalized through the female protagonist, Margaret Schlegel, and "us," the first-person plural pronoun, invokes the feminine perspective.[2]

---

[2]Some early reviewers were persuaded that E. M. Forster must be a woman. Elia Pettie of the *Chicago Tribune* wrote, "In feeling the book is feminine" (qtd. in Gardner 160). Gardner also notes in his introduction that Pettie's conviction had British precedent: "The idea [that Forster was female] had already been whispered in passing" (5).

The "us" feels problematic, too, because the narrator's previous narrative intrusions have been characterized by an uneasy authority that hovers between irony and sympathy, creating an overall impression of indefiniteness. The narrator opens deferentially: "One may as well begin with Helen's letters to her sister" (21). Shortly thereafter we are told, "To Margaret — I hope that it will not set the reader against her — the station of King's Cross had always suggested infinity" (28). The special pleading is intrusive here and later: "That was 'how it happened,' or, rather, how Helen described it to her sister, using words even more unsympathetic than my own" (38). Comments on the underprivileged seem to attempt sarcasm but end up sounding defensive: "We are not concerned with the very poor. They are unthinkable . . ." (55); and "Take my word for it, that [poor woman's] smile was simply stunning, and it is only you and I who will be fastidious, and complain that true joy begins in the eyes . . ." (58). Later addresses to the reader fail to achieve either authority on the one hand or familiarity on the other: "It is rather a moment when the commentator should step forward. Ought the Wilcoxes to have offered their home to Margaret? I think not" (98); and "Margaret had expected the disturbance. . . . Good humour was the dominant note of her relations with Mr Wilcox, or, as I must now call him, Henry" (160).

Forster is more assured when he avoids omniscient comment and focuses on Margaret Schlegel, from whose perspective we see the events of the novel. It is not merely that we share the point of view of a woman here (although that is important to Forster's ends), but also that we tend to take her perspective as representative of the female point of view in general. As the novel develops, Forster complicates this identification of Margaret with the "female" or the "feminine," but initially it undergirds the binary oppositions informing the novel. The novel is built upon a dialectical opposition between male and female, under which several other oppositions are subsumed. The most significant oppositions for this analysis are those of class (rich and poor), those of philosophy (logic and vision), and those of language (word and intuition). On the male side of the equation fall wealth, logic, and the word; on the female, poverty, vision, and intuition. These oppositions are worked out on the levels of theme and plot.

On the level of theme, the resolution is fairly straightforward, although we should note that those terms subsumed under the aspects of male and female perpetuate a hierarchical tradition that relegates women to an inferior status. We may want to applaud Forster for attempting to redress the balance by privileging the feminine, but we are still caught in a net of stereotypes that perpetuate hierarchy and binary opposition, ideas that inscribe male perspectives in the world, as we shall see in a moment.

Although I have relegated wealth to the male side of the equation and poverty to the female, in fact the female protagonists of the novel, Margaret and Helen Schlegel, are well-to-do women. Their sympathy with the poor, however, initiates Forster's interrogation of class distinctions. The Schlegels are distinguished from the Wilcoxes, the masculine protagonists, by their recognition of the privilege that money confers. Margaret asserts that the rich "stand upon money as upon islands" in the sea of life (67). As a result of this perception, she and Helen are able to look beneath the social surface of a poor individual such as Leonard Bast to the "real man, who cared for adventure and beauty" (270).

Yet even as the novel attempts to redress the imbalance between rich and poor, it cannot transcend certain class attitudes that are implicit in Forster's uneven characterization of the workingman and explicit in Margaret's discovery that Jacky Bast has formerly been Henry Wilcox's mistress. Margaret writes to Helen that "the Basts are not at all the type we should trouble about" (211–12), and Helen, who is ready enough to sympathize with Leonard Bast, condemns Jacky as "ready enough to meet" Henry Wilcox and laments that such women "end in two ways: either they sink till the lunatic asylums and the workhouses are full of them . . . or else they entrap a boy into marriage before it is too late" (220). That Jacky is a victim of patriarchy is understood imperfectly, although Margaret strenuously criticizes Henry's double standard. Helen's disclaimer, "I can't blame her" (220), sounds unconvincing as the novel seeks to deconstruct sexist and class values on the level of theme, which it then reconstructs on the level of plot when Helen has a sexual relationship with Leonard — a woman's classic offering of her body in sympathy — and then arrogantly seeks to compensate him with cash, admitting that "I want never to see him again, though it sounds appalling. I wanted to give him money and feel finished" (267). Both of these episodes play out basic patriarchal expectations about relationships between men and women, between the rich and the poor. The pattern we see here, in which plot reconstructs what the theme interrogates so as to deconstruct, will be replicated in working out Forster's other binary oppositions.

Thematically, vision is privileged over logic, intuition over word. Of course, logic and the word are related: they are, in this novel, the *logos,* the word of the fathers. Forster is committed to an ideology that seeks to defy the phallic mode and, from the novel's opening, logic and the word are made to appear irrational. Charles Wilcox's blustering question to his brother, Paul, about Paul's engagement to Helen Schlegel — "Yes or no, man; plain question, plain answer. Did or didn't Miss Schlegel —" is corrected by his mother's response: "Charles, dear Charles, one doesn't ask plain questions. There aren't such things" (36). When Henry Wilcox confronts Margaret over Helen's seemingly irrational behavior at the end of the novel, he echoes his son: "Answer my question. Plain question, plain answer" (245). Henry's plan to trap Helen like some hunted animal and Margaret's resistance provoke her recognition that the plan "is impossible, because — . . . It's not the particular language that Helen and I talk" (244) and his counterclaim that "no education can teach a woman logic" (245). Margaret's later rejoinder, "Leave it that you don't see. . . . Call it fancy. But realize that fancy is a scientific fact" (262), refuses Henry's reductive dichotomies. Margaret is given the final word in the novel as she reflects that "Logically, they had no right to be alive. One's hope was in the weakness of logic" (288), and she is vindicated in the conclusion as the Wilcox clan gather to hear the word of the father ("And again and again fell the word, like the ebb of a dying sea" [290]), which belatedly yet inevitably affirms the intuitive vision of the mother in seeing that Margaret is the "spiritual heir" she seeks for Howards End.

And yet Margaret's "final word" is problematic, because definitive answers belong to the male-inscribed discourse the novel seeks to deconstruct. We might want to argue that the apparent difficulty is only a matter of semantics. But, in fact, my introduction of a teleology of final word here anticipates the deeper problems we discover on the level of plot.

Forster's central opposition between man and woman would seem, initially, to be played out between Henry Wilcox and Margaret Schlegel. It begins on the level of houses. Margaret recognizes that "ours is a female house. . . . it must be feminine, and all we can do is to see that it isn't effeminate. Just as another house that I can mention, but I won't, sounded irrevocably masculine, and all its inmates can do is to see that it isn't brutal" (54). This summary prepares us for the dialectic to follow, but Forster's feminist vision removes Margaret as a single term within the traditional dialectic, replaces her with Helen, and reinterprets Margaret as the principle that will complicate the hierarchical oppositions and provide a new kind of connection. That new connection is not the old androgyny, a merging or blurring of terms and traits; it is a condition that preserves difference.[3]

Whereas Forster's descriptions of Henry Wilcox leave him inscribed in a male mode of discourse, set within masculine imagery of dominance and conquest, his descriptions of Margaret transcend the traditionally feminine and reinscribe her within a rhetoric of reconciliation and connection. Through Margaret Schlegel, the traditional terms of masculinity and femininity are scrutinized and subjected to the demands of higher integration. Margaret's point of view, then, is ultimately not representative of a view we might code as essentially female or feminine. Forster is sensitive both to essentialist conceptions of the female and to the social encoding of the feminine. He subverts both in his characterization of Margaret Schlegel, who can calmly state, for example, "I do not love children. I am thankful to have none" (287), thus debunking ideas of a natural, maternal female.

And Margaret remains constantly alert to social expectations of feminine behavior, decoding those expectations. She turns the notion of "reading the feminine" into a lever against the men who are dependent on and limited by its convenient categories. When Henry proposes, Margaret has anticipated his action, but "she made herself give a little start. She must show surprise if he expected it" (151). Later, when a man hits a cat with his automobile and Margaret jumps out of the car, we learn that "Charles was absolutely honest. He described what he believed to have happened. . . . Miss Schlegel had lost her nerve, as any woman might." But the narrator reveals that "his father accepted this explanation, and neither knew that Margaret had artfully prepared the way for it. It fitted in too well with their view of feminine nature" (190). Later, in response to a question, Margaret "knew . . . but said that she did not know" (195), because "comment is unfeminine" (211).

Throughout the novel Margaret resists being controlled by this di-

---

[3]The subject of androgyny has become a vexed one in contemporary feminist discourse. In early stages of the feminist movement, the argument for equal treatment of women and men seemed to depend on detecting similarities, the masculine in the feminine and the feminine in the masculine. Then androgyny seemed the ideal. Subsequently, women have wanted to argue for the authority of the female perspective and values, and androgyny as a concept has become less attractive. It is interesting, in this light, that Forster doesn't advocate the merging of traits that androgyny implies, but instead insists on preserving distinctions. He is, in this regard, closer to the spirit of contemporary discourse that speaks of escaping hierarchies.

chotomous thinking and instead manipulates the terms with the goal of dismantling and transcending them. From the novel's beginning she is suspicious of hierarchies, as we discover in her mediation of the English and German claims to superiority. She announces, "To me one of two things is very clear: either God does not know his own mind about England and Germany, or else these do not know the mind of God" (43). The narrator pronounces Margaret, ironically, "a hateful little girl," acknowledging that "at thirteen she had grasped a dilemma that most people travel through life without perceiving" (43). That dilemma focuses on the logic of binary thinking. Margaret resists such dichotomous thought and chastises Helen's binary opposi- tions as "medieval," telling her, "Our business is not to contrast the two, but to reconcile them" (102). Not surprisingly, it is Margaret who is capable of concluding that "people are far more different than is pretended. All over the world men and women are worrying because they cannot develop as they are supposed to develop" (287).

In his reconceptualization of Margaret, Forster generates a new in- tegrative principle that is associated with a woman but not ideologi- cally encoded as feminine. Part of his success here depends, as I have suggested, on using Helen to reevaluate the traditionally feminine by associating her with emotion and the inner life.

Helen Schlegel, in contrast to Margaret, is emotional, impulsive, impatient of logic, impatient of all restraint on her generous impulses. She scoffs at moderation and is incapable of balance; she is first se- duced by the Wilcox men and then violently rejects them. She extols the "inner life" and, unlike Margaret, refuses to acknowledge the value of Wilcox energy, which has created a civilized world in which her sen- sibilities and the inner life can have free play. When Margaret must protect a pregnant and unmarried Helen from the interference of Wilcox men, Margaret herself codes the struggle as a sexual one: "A new feeling came over her: she was fighting for women against men. She did not care about rights, but if men came into Howards End it should be over her body" (249). Although Margaret prefers not to be locked into a struggle between opposed forces, under duress she will privilege what Helen represents. Forster has anticipated this moment earlier in the novel when Margaret and Helen disagree over the older sister's impending marriage to Henry Wilcox. "Their inner life was so safe," we are told, "that they could bargain over externals. . . . There are moments when the inner life actually 'pays', when years of self- scrutiny, conducted for no ulterior motive, are suddenly of practical use." The narrator adds that "Such moments are still rare in the West;

that they come at all promises a fairer future" (174–75). Forster codes the inner life within another set of oppositions — Eastern mysticism versus Western pragmatism — but he reverses the usual hierarchy to privilege the East and the inner life.

In contrast to Helen, Henry Wilcox is associated with an imagery of war, battle, and self-defense. When Margaret discovers that Jacky Bast had been Henry's mistress, the narrator claims that "expelled from his old fortress, Mr Wilcox was building a new one" (214). Margaret is forced to play "the girl, until he could rebuild his fortress and hide his soul from the world" (215). Henry believes that "man is for war, woman for the recreation of the warrior, but he does not dislike it if she makes a show of fight. She cannot win in a real battle, having no muscles, only nerves" (225). At the end of the novel, in the crisis over Helen, Henry speaks "straight from his fortress" (263), and Margaret at first fails to recognize that "to break him was her only hope." It is only when "Henry's fortress [gives] way" (284) that Margaret can initiate the process that leads to the integration, the connection, she enacts in the novel's conclusion by bringing Henry and Helen together at Howards End.

It is significant in *Howards End* that the most moving scene occurs between two women, Helen and Margaret.[4] When the sisters meet at Howards End and Margaret discovers that Helen is pregnant, Margaret asserts, "It all turns on affection now" (250). Although at first they feel themselves in antagonism, unconsciously they move toward communion:

> the triviality faded from their faces, though it left something behind — the knowledge that they never could be parted because their love was rooted in common things. Explanations and appeals had failed; they had tried for a common meeting-ground, and had only made each other unhappy. And all the time their salvation was lying round them — the past sanctifying the present; the present, with wild heart-throb, declaring that there would after all be a future, with laughter and the voices of children. Helen, still smiling, came up to her sister. She said: "It is always Meg." They looked into each other's eyes. The inner life had paid. (256)

---

[4]An early reviewer in the *Athenaeum* wrote: "the great thing in the book is the sisters' affection for each other . . . personal relationships . . . have never . . . been made more beautiful or more real" (qtd. in Gardner 151).

In stark contrast stands Charles Wilcox's relationship with his father:

> The Wilcoxes were not lacking in affection; they had it royally, but they did not know how to use it. It was the talent in the napkin, and, for a warm-hearted man, Charles had conveyed very little joy. As he watched his father shuffling up the road, he had a vague regret — a wish that something had been different somewhere — a wish (though he did not express it thus) that he had been taught to say "I" in his youth. He meant to make up for Margaret's defection, but knew that his father had been very happy with her until yesterday. How had she done it? By some dishonest trick, no doubt — but how? (280)

The traditionally feminine mode is clearly affirmed in these final contrasting scenes that sanction the inner life and "voiceless sympathy."

In privileging the inner life, as we have seen, Forster reverses the usual hierarchy in the oppositions of inner/outer, female/male, East/West, intuition/logic. This affirmation is a part of Forster's achievement. More significant, he takes a further step and sets up through Margaret a double reading in which the poles indecidably include each other and the *différance* of this irreducible difference. It is a process made familiar to us by Jacques Derrida. We are forced to think or to imagine the "inconceivable," that which we have seen as mutually exclusive; we are forced to form conceptions of that for which we have no concepts. The novel's epigraph, "Only connect," stands at the heart of this difficult process through which Margaret hopes to enable Henry's salvation: "Only connect! That was the whole of her sermon. Only connect the prose and the passion, and both will be exalted, and human love will be seen at its highest. Live in fragments no longer" (168). At Howards End, Margaret senses this connection of comrades between the house and the wych elm tree: "It was a comrade, bending over the house, strength and adventure in its roots, but in its utmost fingers tenderness. . . . It was a comrade. House and tree transcended any simile of sex" (183). Significantly, Forster has chosen representative terms, a house and a tree, that resist hierarchical placement and the classical oppositional structure of patriarchal thinking. Margaret reflects that "to compare either to man, to woman, always dwarfed the vision. Yet they kept within limits of the human. . . . As she stood in the one, gazing at the other, truer relationships had gleamed" (183). Margaret also argues for connection, this discovery of mutual inclusivity, in her conception of proportion: "truth, being alive, was not halfway between anything. It was only to be found by continuous excursions into either realm, and, though proportion is the final secret, to espouse it at the outset is to ensure sterility" (174). Finally, in the novel's conclusion, Margaret looks toward an "ultimate harmony" (281).

To summarize, the connection that Margaret seeks is obviously not born out of an attempt to merge or to blur or reverse oppositions. She fights the "daily gray" of life, the blending of black and white. Rather, she seeks to dismantle the hierarchical privileging of one term over another. She expresses her idea of connection as a celebration of "differences — eternal differences, planted by God in a single family, so that there may always be colour; sorrow perhaps, but colour in the daily gray" (287).

Ironically, however, although the resolution thematically insists on connections and although the patriarch Wilcox is unmanned, the plot appears to encode the very patriarchal structures that the novel seeks to escape. I began this essay with the narrator's ambiguous sexual identification. I then quoted a paragraph that is followed by one that reads:

> Here was the core of the question. Henry must be forgiven, and made better by love; nothing else mattered. . . . To her everything was in proportion now. . . . Margaret fell asleep, tethered by affection, and lulled by the murmurs of the river that descended all the night from Wales. She felt herself at one with her future home, colouring it and coloured by it, and awoke to see, for the second time, Oniton Castle conquering the morning mists. (213)

We notice the imagery of proportion, of connection, of mutuality monopolizing the paragraph which, nonetheless, concludes with an image of domination, "Oniton Castle conquering the morning mists." It is possible that Forster is being ironic because Oniton is not to be Margaret's home and she is, perhaps, mistaken in so valuing it. Yet, if this is irony, it is irony of a very subtle sort.

I suggest instead that the pattern is not ironic; rather, it anticipates the resolution of the novel, where the value of connection, represented by the presence of Henry and Helen at Howards End, is enacted in the plot by Margaret's conquest of Henry. Henry, in masculine style, has earlier told Margaret, "fix your price, and then don't budge," and she has responded, "But I do budge" (143). Nonetheless, on the issue of connection, she, like her masculine counterparts, won't budge: "he had refused to connect, on the clearest issue that can be laid before a man, and their love must take the consequences" (282). And in the novel's closing paragraphs, Margaret reflects that "there was something uncanny in her triumph. She, who had never expected to conquer anyone, had charged straight through these Wilcoxes and broken up their lives" (290). Margaret has triumphed, conquered, and broken up their lives. This conclusion to a novel about connection is ironic, although not, I would suggest, deliberately so.

The irony arises because Forster inscribes the value of connection within the patriarchal dialectic of conquest and defeat, domination and submission, and within a narrative form that demands a resolution instead of "continuous excursions into either realm" (174). Although the themes of the novel indicate a desire to deconstruct the patriarchal ideology, ultimately, it seems, Forster is forced to reconstruct that ideology in the structure of the novel, in Margaret's "victory" over Henry. Plot has demanded a hierarchical ordering of terms for a resolution of conflict even though the novel's themes have argued for replacement of conquest with connection. Forster's often trenchant interrogation of patriarchal language and perspectives appears to give way before the resistless temptation to expropriate the authority available to him in patriarchy. What he *wants* to assert, of course, is the value of the feminine perspective as a first step to dismantling hierarchy, but in the *act* of assertion, he affirms the value of the masculine mode, remaining dependent on patriarchy's hierarchical structures for authority, resolution, and conclusion. Ultimately, Forster recuperates an authority that would thematically seem to be repudiated.

Reaching this point in my argument — where the need to conclude an essay definitively is as imperative as the requirement to resolve a novel — I nonetheless stepped back from my own recuperation of authority, stepped from form to language. Perhaps Forster's critique of patriarchal modes and binary thinking was more trenchant and thoroughgoing than I first perceived. Forster had certainly appropriated the language of conquest, but he had also recontextualized it and, in the process, forestalled expropriation by that masculine terminology. A deep suspicion of conquest in its most notable manifestations, imperialism and war, lies at the very heart of *Howards End*. The narrator simply asserts, contrasting the yeoman who is "England's hope" to the Imperialist who "hopes to inherit the earth," that "the Imperialist is not what he thinks or seems. He is a destroyer. He prepares the way for cosmopolitanism, and though his ambitions may be fulfilled the earth that he inherits will be gray" (276). Strong biblical cadences underline this apocalyptic vision of a world shaped in a masculine mode.

Perhaps, then, Forster is having his joke when Margaret characterizes her success as a conquest: "she, who had never expected to conquer anyone, had charged straight through these Wilcoxes and broken up their lives" (290). In fact, she has not "charged through," she has simply done what "seemed easiest" (284); "No better plan had occurred to her" (285). She confesses, "I did the obvious things" (288). "To conquer," in this context, is not an act of self-assertion and dominance but is redefined as nonassertion, an opening up of space, a refusal to accept the exclusivity of opposition between Henry and Helen. "Everyone said [living together at Howards End] was impossible" (287), but Margaret defies this patriarchal logic.

The futility of binary thinking appears in the lives of both Henry and Helen, both of whom declare they are "ended." Henry confesses, "I don't know what to do — what to do. I'm broken — I'm ended" (284). As if in echo, Helen rejoins, "I'm ended. I used to be so dreamy about a man's love as a girl, and think that for good or evil love must be the great thing. But it hasn't been . . ." (286). The man of action and the woman of emotion reach the bankruptcy implicit in their exclusive positions. Margaret's conquest or victory, then, is not the patriarchal one demanding suppression of an other, but one that emerges as the traditional oppositions destroy themselves and clear a space for difference.

Forster has anticipated this conclusion, as we have seen earlier, in identifying a warfare mentality with Henry Wilcox. But we may now discover a further step Forster has taken. Whereas Henry Wilcox easily dismisses casualties such as Leonard Bast as "part of the battle of life" (171), as if such casualties were in the "nature" of things, and Helen angrily exposes how Henry uses his combat metaphor to shirk responsibility — "We upper classes have ruined him, and I suppose you'll tell me it's the battle of life" (198) — Margaret, in contrast, probes the way language inevitably involves power relations. She is a master of words, as we see in her first encounter with Leonard Bast when her speeches "flutter away from him like birds" (50). Margaret's strength lies in recognizing the way ideologies are encoded in language and in acknowledging the social privilege behind her "speech." She early argues, "all our thoughts are the thoughts of six-hundred-pounders, and all our speeches" (68), underlining both the intensity and the futility of Leonard Bast's desire "to form his style on Ruskin" (58). Ruskin's style cannot "speak" Leonard Bast's life.

When Margaret rejects Henry's language and metaphor of life as a battle, she rejects his patriarchal ideology and introduces new terms into the novel. She reflects that "life is indeed dangerous, but not in the way morality would have us believe. It is indeed unmanageable, but the essence of it is not a battle. It is unmanageable because it is a romance, and its essence is romantic beauty" (104). This passage informs the entire novel and encourages us to reread the metaphors of conquest that conclude the novel within a romance *topos* put into play by the figure of Ruth Wilcox, Henry's first wife.

Margaret's sense of victory is severely qualified when she learns that Ruth Wilcox had "willed" Howards End to her, had designated her as its "spiritual heir," many years earlier: "Something shook [Margaret's] life in its inmost recesses, and she shivered" (291). Ruth Wilcox is introduced into the novel as one who always "knew," although no one "told her a word" (40). Ruth Wilcox is represented as beyond language deployed as power, beyond the words that, implicated as they are in ideology, cripple communication among the other characters. Margaret ultimately asserts to Helen, "I feel that you and I and Henry are only fragments of that woman's mind. She knows everything. She is everything. She is the house, and the tree that leans over it" (268).

Miss Avery, who after Mrs. Wilcox's death becomes her representative, prophesies to Margaret, "You think that you won't come back to live here [at Howards End],...but you will" (235); and Margaret, who discounts Miss Avery's words, is disturbed to find them fulfilled when she and Helen sleep in the house: "It is disquieting to fulfil a prophecy, however superficially" (259). She will, of course, fulfill it much more deeply, making Howards End her permanent home as, increasingly, Margaret herself recognizes the power of the house: "it kills what is dreadful and makes what is beautiful live" (257).

As Margaret moves toward insight and vision, she, too, moves away from language. The narrator comments, for example, that Margaret's "mind trembled towards a conclusion which only the unwise have put into words" (182). And later we learn that Margaret "had outgrown stimulants, and was passing from words to things," an inevitable process "if the mind itself is to become a creative power" (227–28). Finally, Margaret admits to Helen, who calls Margaret's life "heroic": "No doubt I have done a little towards straightening the tangle, but things that I can't phrase have helped me" (288).

At best, because of its ideological nature, language can take characters to the brink of understanding, as it does when Margaret exposes Henry's hypocrisy in committing adultery himself and refusing to forgive it in Helen. Margaret confronts Henry: "I think you yourself recommended plain speaking"; and the narrator reveals that "they looked at each other in amazement. The precipice was at their feet now" (263). Language takes them to the abyss, but it cannot reconstruct their lives on a new basis because they cannot form conceptions of that for which there is no concept. Margaret simply relies on "the power of the house."

As we reconsider Forster's resolution in light of Mrs. Wilcox and the spiritual heir she seeks for Howards End, we notice that the novel moves toward resolution, but it is a resolution that existed from the beginning as a "part of Mrs Wilcox's mind" (269). In this respect, the plot subverts its own commitment to hierarchy and sequence, to prior and subsequent events. In addition, the power that has "defeated" Henry Wilcox, the patriarch, is diffused over the universe. At the end of the novel, Henry Wilcox lies suffering with hay fever, confined to the house, recalling Miss Avery's words with their echoes of battle imagery: "There's not one Wilcox that can stand up against a field in June . . ." (236). The patriarch is "shut up in the house," and his wife pronounces, "It has to be. . . . The hay fever is his chief objection against living here, but he thinks it worth while" (285).

As previously noted, the novel's last words belong to Helen, who rushes into the house with her child and the neighbor boy, accompanied by "shouts of infectious joy": "We've seen to the very end," she cries, "and it'll be such a crop of hay as never!" (291). To see "to the very end," in this scene and in the novel as a whole, is to discover the beginning of possibility: "such a crop of hay as never." The last phrase is appropriate, too, concluding with a "never" that has already been subverted. In its closure the novel gestures toward an open space, like a field in June, that "not one Wilcox . . . can stand up against." It is a "closure" that echoes Hélène Cixous on *l'écriture féminine*. Though Cixous is speaking of women writers, she describes what I am arguing that Forster has achieved:

> [Writers] must invent the impregnable language that will wreck partitions, classes, and rhetorics, regulations and codes, they must submerge, cut through, get beyond the ultimate reserve-discourse, including the one that laughs at the very idea of pronouncing the word "silence," the one that, aiming for the impossible, stops short before the word "impossible" and writes it as "the end." (256)

This reading seems more true to the narrative and linguistic procedures of Forster's *Howards End*. But it raises further questions. Can Forster thus evade the connection between discourse and power by postulating an unspoken knowledge? Indeed, the pressure of resolution may seem inevitably to produce an evasion as Forster gestures toward an alternative to binary thinking, a "conclusion that only the unwise will put into words." It is, at best, an uneasy truce. And this final, inaccessible metaphysics may leave us frustrated by our own continuing battle with language, power, and patriarchy.

## WORKS CITED

Cixous, Hélène. "The Laugh of the Medusa." *New French Feminisms: An Anthology.* Ed. Elaine Marks and Isabelle de Courtivron. New York: Schocken, 1981. 245–64.

Furbank, P. N. *E. M. Forster: A Life.* Vol. 2. New York: Harcourt, 1978.

Gardner, Philip, ed. *E. M. Forster: The Critical Heritage.* London: Routledge, 1973.

King, Francis. *E. M. Forster and His World.* New York: Scribner's, 1978.

Miller, D. A. *The Novel and the Police.* Berkeley: U of California P, 1988.

Sedgwick, Eve Kosofsky. *Between Men: English Literature and Male Homosocial Desire.* New York: Columbia UP, 1985.

# Marxist Criticism
# and
# *Howards End*

## WHAT IS MARXIST CRITICISM?

To the question "What is Marxist criticism?" it may be tempting to respond with another question: "What does it matter?" In light of the rapid and largely unanticipated demise of Soviet-style communism in the former USSR and throughout Eastern Europe, it is understandable to suppose that Marxist literary analysis would disappear too, quickly becoming an anachronism in a world enamored with full-market capitalism.

In fact, however, there is no reason why Marxist criticism should weaken, let alone disappear. It is, after all, a phenomenon distinct from Soviet and Eastern European communism, having had its beginnings nearly eighty years before the Bolshevik revolution and having thrived, since the 1940s, mainly in the West — not as a form of communist propaganda but rather as a form of critique, a discourse for interrogating *all* societies and their texts in terms of certain specific issues. Those issues — including race, class, and the attitudes shared within a given culture — are as much with us as ever, not only in contemporary Russia but also in the United States.

The argument could even be made that Marxist criticism has been strengthened by the collapse of Soviet-style communism. There was a time, after all, when few self-respecting Anglo-American journals would use Marxist terms or models, however illuminating, to analyze Western issues or problems. It smacked of sleeping with the enemy. With the collapse of the Kremlin, however, old taboos began to give way. Even the staid *Wall Street Journal* now seems comfortable using phrases like "worker alienation" to discuss the problems plaguing the American business world.

The assumption that Marxist criticism will die on the vine of a moribund political system rests in part on another mistaken assumption, namely, that Marxist literary analysis is practiced only by people who would like to see society transformed into a Marxist-communist state, one created through land reform, the redistribution of wealth, a tightly and centrally managed economy, the abolition of institutionalized religion, and so on. In fact, it has never been necessary to be a communist political revolutionary to be classified as a Marxist literary critic. (Many of the critics discussed in this introduction actually *fled* communist societies to live in the West.) Nor is it necessary to like only those literary works with a radical social vision or to dislike books that represent or even reinforce a middle-class, capitalist world-view. It is necessary, however, to adopt what most students of literature would consider a radical definition of the purpose and function of literary criticism.

More traditional forms of criticism, according to the Marxist critic Pierre Macherey, "set . . . out to deliver the text from its own silences by coaxing it into giving up its true, latent, or hidden meaning." Inevitably, however, non-Marxist criticism "intrude[s] its own discourse between the reader and the text" (qtd. in Bennett 107). Marxist critics, by contrast, do not attempt to discover hidden meanings in texts. Or if they do, they do so only after seeing the text, first and foremost, as a material product to be understood in broadly historical terms. That is to say, a literary work is first viewed as a product *of* work (and hence of the realm of production and consumption we call economics). Second, it may be looked upon as a work that *does* identifiable work of its own. At one level, that work is usually to enforce and reinforce the prevailing ideology, that is, the network of conventions, values, and opinions to which the majority of people uncritically subscribe.

This does not mean that Marxist critics merely describe the obvious. Quite the contrary: the relationship that the Marxist critic Terry Eagleton outlines in *Criticism and Ideology* (1978) among the soaring cost of books in the nineteenth century, the growth of lending libraries, the practice of publishing "three-decker" novels (so that three borrowers could be reading the same book at the same time), and the changing *content* of those novels is highly complex in its own way. But the complexity Eagleton finds is not that of the deeply buried meaning of the text. Rather, it is that of the complex web of social and economic relationships that were prerequisite to the work's production. Marxist criticism does not seek to be, in Eagleton's words, "a passage from text to reader." Indeed, "its task is to show the text as it cannot know itself, to manifest those conditions of its making (inscribed in its very letter) about which it is necessarily silent" (43).

As everyone knows, Marxism began with Karl Marx, the nineteenth-century German philosopher best known for writing *Das Kapital,* the seminal work of the communist movement. What everyone doesn't know is that Marx was also the first Marxist literary critic (much as Sigmund Freud, who psychoanalyzed E. T. A. Hoffmann's supernatural tale "The Sandman," was the first Freudian literary critic). During the 1830s Marx wrote critical essays on writers such as Goethe and Shakespeare (whose tragic vision of Elizabethan disintegration he praised).

The fact that Marxist literary criticism began with Marx himself is hardly surprising, given Marx's education and early interests. Trained in the classics at the University of Bonn, Marx wrote literary imitations, his own poetry, a failed novel, and a fragment of a tragic drama (*Oulanem*) before turning to contemplative and political philosophy. Even after he met Friedrich Engels in 1843 and began collaborating on works such as *The German Ideology* and *The Communist Manifesto,* Marx maintained a keen interest in literary writers and their works. He and Engels argued about the poetry of Heinrich Heine, admired Hermann Freiligrath (a poet critical of the German aristocracy), and faulted the playwright Ferdinand Lassalle for writing about a reactionary knight in the Peasants' War rather than about more progressive aspects of German history.

As these examples suggest, Marx and Engels would not — indeed, could not — think of aesthetic matters as being distinct and independent from such things as politics, economics, and history. Not surprisingly, they viewed the alienation of the worker in industrialized, capitalist societies as having grave consequences for the arts. How can people mechanically stamping out things that bear no mark of their producer's individuality (people thereby "reified," turned into things themselves) be expected to recognize, produce, or even consume things of beauty? And if there is no one to consume something, there will soon be no one to produce it, especially in an age in which production (even of something like literature) has come to mean *mass* (and therefore profitable) production.

In *The German Ideology* (1846), Marx and Engels expressed their sense of the relationship between the arts, politics, and basic economic reality in terms of a general social theory. Economics, they argued, provides the "base" or "infrastructure" of society, but from that base emerges a "superstructure" consisting of law, politics, philosophy, religion, and art.

Marx later admitted that the relationship between base and superstructure may be indirect and fluid: every change in economics may not be reflected by an immediate change in ethics or literature. In *The Eighteenth Brumaire of Louis Bonaparte* (1852), he came up with the word *homology* to describe the sometimes unbalanced, often delayed, and almost always loose correspondence between base and superstructure. And later in that same decade, while working on an introduction to his *Political Economy*, Marx further relaxed the base-superstructure relationship. Writing on the excellence of ancient Greek art (versus the primitive nature of ancient Greek economics), he conceded that a gap sometimes opens up between base and superstructure — between economic forms and those produced by the creative mind.

Nonetheless, *at* base the old formula was maintained. Economics remained basic and the connection between economics and superstructural elements of society was reaffirmed. Central to Marxism and Marxist literary criticism was and is the following "materialist" insight: consciousness, without which such things as art cannot be produced, is not the source of social forms and economic conditions. It is, rather, their most important product.

Marx and Engels, drawing upon the philosopher G. W. F. Hegel's theories about the dialectical synthesis of ideas out of theses and antitheses, believed that a revolutionary class war (pitting the capitalist class against a proletarian, antithetical class) would lead eventually to the synthesis of a new social and economic order. Placing their faith not in the idealist Hegelian dialectic but, rather, in what they called "dialectical materialism," they looked for a secular and material salvation of humanity — one in, not beyond, history — via revolution and not via divine intervention. And they believed that the communist society eventually established would be one capable of producing new forms of consciousness and belief and therefore, ultimately, great art.

The revolution anticipated by Marx and Engels did not occur in their century, let alone lifetime. When it finally did take place, it didn't happen in places where Marx and Engels had thought it might be successful: the United States, Great Britain, and Germany. It happened, rather, in 1917 Russia, a country long ruled by despotic czars but also enlightened by the works of powerful novelists and playwrights, including Chekhov, Pushkin, Tolstoy, and Dostoyevsky.

Perhaps because of its significant literary tradition, Russia produced revolutionaries like Nikolai Lenin, who shared not only Marx's interest in literature but also his belief in literature's ultimate importance. But it was not without some hesitation that Lenin endorsed the significance of texts written during the reign of the czars. Well before 1917 he had questioned what the relationship should be between a society undergoing a revolution and the great old literature of its bourgeois past.

Lenin attempted to answer that question in a series of essays on Tolstoy that he wrote between 1908 and 1911. Tolstoy — the author of *War and Peace* and *Anna Karenina* — was an important nineteenth-century Russian writer whose views did not accord with all of those of young Marxist revolutionaries. Continuing interest in a writer like Tolstoy may be justified, Lenin reasoned, given the primitive and unenlightened economic order of the society that produced him. Since superstructure usually lags behind base (and is therefore usually *more* primitive), the attitudes of a Tolstoy were relatively progressive when viewed in light of the monarchical and precapitalist society out of which they arose.

Moreover, Lenin also reasoned, the writings of the great Russian realists would *have* to suffice, at least in the short run. Lenin looked forward, in essays like "Party Organization and Party Literature," to the day in which new artistic forms would be produced by progressive writers with revolutionary political views and agendas. But he also knew that a great proletarian literature was unlikely to evolve until a thoroughly literate proletariat had been produced by the educational system.

Lenin was hardly the only revolutionary leader involved in setting up the new Soviet state who took a strong interest in literary matters. In 1924 Leon Trotsky published a book called *Literature and Revolution*, which is still acknowledged as a classic of Marxist literary criticism.

Trotsky worried about the direction in which Marxist aesthetic theory seemed to be going. He responded skeptically to groups like Proletkult, which opposed tolerance toward pre- and nonrevolutionary writers, and which called for the establishment of a new, proletarian culture. Trotsky warned of the danger of cultural sterility and risked unpopularity by pointing out that there is no necessary connection between the quality of a literary work and the quality of its author's politics.

In 1927 Trotsky lost a power struggle with Josef Stalin, a man who believed, among other things, that writers should be "engineers" of "human souls." After Trotsky's expulsion from the Soviet Union, views held by groups like Proletkult and the Left Front of Art (LEF), and by theorists such as Nikolai Bukharin and A. A. Zhdanov, became more prevalent. Speaking at the First Congress of the Union of Soviet Writers in 1934, the Soviet author Maxim Gorky called for writing that would "make labor the principal hero of our books." It was at the same writers' congress that "socialist realism," an art form glorifying workers and the revolutionary State, was made Communist party policy and the official literary form of the USSR.

Of those critics active in the USSR after the expulsion of Trotsky and the unfortunate triumph of Stalin, two critics stand out. One, Mikhail Bakhtin, was a Russian, later a Soviet, critic who spent much of his life in a kind of internal exile. Many of his essays were written in the 1930s and not published in the West or translated until the late 1960s. His work comes out of an engagement with the Marxist intellectual tradition as well as out of an indirect, even hidden, resistance to the Soviet government. It has been important to Marxist critics writing in the West because his theories provide a means to decode submerged social critique, especially in early modern texts. He viewed language — especially literary texts — in terms of discourses and dialogues. Within a novel written in a society in flux, for instance, the narrative may include an official, legitimate discourse, plus another infiltrated by challenging comments and even retorts. In a 1929 book on Dostoyevsky and a 1940 study titled *Rabelais and His World,* Bakhtin examined what he calls "polyphonic" novels, each characterized by a multiplicity of voices or discourses. In Dostoyevsky the independent status of a given character is marked by the difference of his or her language from that of the narrator. (The narrator's voice, too, can in fact be a dialogue.) In works by Rabelais, Bakhtin finds that the (profane) language of the carnival and of other popular festivals plays against and parodies the more official discourses, that is, of the king, church, or even socially powerful intellectuals. Bakhtin influenced modern cultural criticism by showing, in a sense, that the conflict between "high" and "low" culture takes place not only between classic and popular texts but also between the "dialogic" voices that exist within many books — whether "high" or "low."

The other subtle Marxist critic who managed to survive Stalin's dictatorship and his repressive policies was Georg Lukács. A Hungarian who had begun his career as an "idealist" critic, Lukács had converted to Marxism in 1919; renounced his earlier, Hegelian work shortly thereafter; visited Moscow in 1930–31; and finally emigrated to the USSR in 1933, just one year before the First Congress of the Union of Soviet Writers met. Lukács was far less narrow in his views than the most strident Stalinist Soviet critics of the 1930s and 1940s. He disliked much socialist realism and appreciated prerevolutionary, realistic novels that broadly reflected cultural "totalities" — and were populated with characters representing human "types" of the author's place and time. (Lukács was particularly fond of the historical canvasses painted by the early nineteenth-century novelist Sir Walter Scott.) But like his more rigid and censorious contemporaries, he drew the line at accepting nonrevolutionary, modernist works like James Joyce's *Ulysses*. He condemned movements like expressionism and symbolism, preferring works with "content" over more decadent, experimental works characterized mainly by "form."

With Lukács its most liberal and tolerant critic from the early 1930s until well into the 1960s, the Soviet literary scene degenerated to the point that the works of great writers like Franz Kafka were no longer read, either because they were viewed as decadent, formal experiments or because they "engineered souls" in "nonprogressive" directions. Officially sanctioned works were generally ones in which artistry lagged far behind the politics (no matter how bad the politics were).

Fortunately for the Marxist critical movement, politically radical critics *outside* the Soviet Union were free of its narrow, constricting policies and, consequently, able fruitfully to develop the thinking of Marx, Engels, and Trotsky. It was these non-Soviet Marxists who kept Marxist critical theory alive and useful in discussing all *kinds* of literature, written across the entire historical spectrum.

Perhaps because Lukács was the best of the Soviet communists writing Marxist criticism in the 1930s and 1940s, non-Soviet Marxists tended to develop their ideas by publicly opposing those of Lukács. German dramatist and critic Bertolt Brecht countered Lukács by arguing that art ought to be viewed as a field of production, not as a container of "content." Brecht also criticized Lukács for his attempt to enshrine realism at the expense not only of other "isms" but also of poetry and drama, both of which had been largely ignored by Lukács.

Even more outspoken was Brecht's critical champion Walter Benjamin, a German Marxist who, in the 1930s, attacked those conventional and traditional literary forms conveying a stultifying "aura" of culture. Benjamin praised dadaism and, more important, new forms of art ushered in by the age of mechanical reproduction. Those forms — including radio and film — offered hope, he felt, for liberation from capitalist culture, for they were too new to be part of its stultifyingly ritualistic traditions.

But of all the anti-Lukácsians outside the USSR who made a contribution to the development of Marxist literary criticism, the most important was probably Théodor Adorno. Leader since the early 1950s of the Frankfurt school of Marxist criticism, Adorno attacked Lukács for his dogmatic rejection of nonrealist modern literature and for his belief in the primacy of content over form. Art does not equal science, Adorno insisted. He went on to argue for art's autonomy from empirical forms of knowledge and to suggest that the interior monologues of modernist works (by Beckett and Proust) reflect the fact of modern alienation in a way that Marxist criticism ought to find compelling.

In addition to turning against Lukács and his overly constrictive canon, Marxists outside the Soviet Union were able to take advantage of insights generated by non-Marxist critical theories being developed in post–World War II Europe. One of the movements that came to be of interest to non-Soviet Marxists was structuralism, a scientific approach to the study of humankind whose proponents believed that all elements of culture, including literature, could be understood as parts of a system of signs. Using modern linguistics as a model, structuralists like Claude Lévi-Strauss broke down the myths of various cultures into "mythemes" in an attempt to show that there are structural correspondences, or homologies, between the mythical elements produced by various human communities across time.

Of the European structuralist Marxists, one of the most influential was Lucien Goldmann, a Rumanian critic living in Paris. Goldmann combined structuralist principles with Marx's base-superstructure model in order to show how economics determines the mental structures of social groups, which are reflected in literary texts. Goldmann rejected the idea of individual human genius, choosing to see works, instead, as the "collective" products of "trans-individual" mental structures. In early studies, such as *The Hidden God* (1955), he related

seventeenth-century French texts (such as Racine's *Phèdre*) to the ideology of Jansenism. In later works, he applied Marx's base-superstructure model even more strictly, describing a relationship between economic conditions and texts unmediated by an intervening, collective
consciousness.

In spite of his rigidity and perhaps because of his affinities with
structuralism, Goldmann came to be seen in the 1960s as the pro-
ponent of a kind of watered-down, "humanist" Marxism. He was
certainly viewed that way by the French Marxist Louis Althusser, a dis-
ciple not of Lévi-Strauss and structuralism but rather of the psychoanalytic theorist Jacques Lacan and of the Italian communist Antonio
Gramsci, famous for his writings about ideology and "hegemony."
(Gramsci used the latter word to refer to the pervasive, weblike system
of assumptions and values that shapes the way things look, what they
mean, and therefore what reality *is* for the majority of people within a
culture.)

Like Gramsci, Althusser viewed literary works primarily in terms of
their relationship to ideology, the function of which, he argued, is to
(re)produce the existing relations of production in a given society.
Dave Laing, in *The Marxist Theory of Art* (1978), has attempted to explain this particular insight of Althusser by saying that ideologies,
through the "ensemble of habits, moralities, and opinions" that can be
found in any literary text, "ensure that the work-force (and those responsible for re-producing them in the family, school, etc.) are maintained in their position of subordination to the dominant class" (91).
This is not to say that Althusser thought of the masses as a brainless
multitude following only the dictates of the prevailing ideology: Althusser followed Gramsci in suggesting that even working-class people
have some freedom to struggle against ideology and to change history.
Nor is it to say that Althusser saw ideology as being a coherent, consistent force. In fact, he saw it as being riven with contradictions that
works of literature sometimes expose and even widen. Thus Althusser
followed Marx and Gramsci in believing that although literature must
be seen in *relation* to ideology, it — like all social forms — has some
degree of autonomy.

Althusser's followers included Pierre Macherey, who in *A Theory of
Literary Production* (1978) developed Althusser's concept of the relationship between literature and ideology. A realistic novelist, he argued, attempts to produce a unified, coherent text, but instead ends
up producing a work containing lapses, omissions, gaps. This happens
because within ideology there are subjects that cannot be covered,

things that cannot be said, contradictory views that aren't recognized as contradictory. (The critic's challenge, in this case, is to supply what the text cannot say, thereby making sense of gaps and contradictions.)

But there is another reason why gaps open up and contradictions become evident in texts. Works don't just reflect ideology (which Goldmann had referred to as "myth" and which Macherey refers to as a system of "illusory social beliefs"); they are also "fictions," works of art, *products* of ideology that have what Goldmann would call a "world-view" to offer. What kind of product, Macherey implicitly asks, is identical to the thing that produced it? It is hardly surprising, then, that Balzac's fiction shows French peasants in two different lights, only one of which is critical and judgmental, only one of which is baldly ideological. Writing approvingly on Macherey and Macherey's mentor Althusser in *Marxism and Literary Criticism* (1976), Terry Eagleton says: "It is by giving ideology a determinate form, fixing it within certain fictional limits, that art is able to distance itself from [ideology], thus revealing . . . [its] limits" (19).

A follower of Althusser, Macherey is sometimes referred to as a "post-Althusserian Marxist." Eagleton, too, is often described that way, as is his American contemporary Fredric Jameson. Jameson and Eagleton, as well as being post-Althusserians, are also among the few Anglo-American critics who have closely followed and significantly developed Marxist thought.

Before them, Marxist interpretation in English was limited to the work of a handful of critics: Christopher Caudwell, Christopher Hill, Arnold Kettle, E. P. Thompson, and Raymond Williams. Of these, Williams was perhaps least Marxist in orientation: he felt that Marxist critics, ironically, tended too much to isolate economics from culture; that they overlooked the individualism of people, opting instead to see them as "masses"; and that even more ironically, they had become an elitist group. But if the least Marxist of the British Marxists, Williams was also by far the most influential. Preferring to talk about "culture" instead of ideology, Williams argued in works such as *Culture and Society 1780–1950* (1958) that culture is "lived experience" and, as such, an interconnected set of social properties, each and all grounded in and influencing history.

Terry Eagleton's *Criticism and Ideology* (1978) is in many ways a response to the work of Williams. Responding to Williams's statement in *Culture and Society* that "there are in fact no masses; there are only ways of seeing people as masses" (289), Eagleton writes:

That men and women really are now unique individuals was
Williams's (unexceptionable) insistence; but it was a proposition
bought at the expense of perceiving the fact that they must mass
and fight to achieve their full individual humanity. One has only
to adapt Williams's statement to "There are in fact no classes;
there are only ways of seeing people as classes" to expose its theoretical paucity. (*Criticism* 29)

Eagleton goes on, in *Criticism and Ideology,* to propose an elaborate theory about how history — in the form of "general," "authorial," and "aesthetic" ideology — enters texts, which in turn may reviv-
ify, open up, or critique those same ideologies, thereby setting in
motion a process that may alter history. He shows how texts by Jane
Austen, Matthew Arnold, Charles Dickens, George Eliot, Joseph Conrad, and T. S. Eliot deal with and transmute conflicts at the heart of
the general and authorial ideologies behind them: conflicts between
morality and individualism, and between individualism and social or-
ganicism and utilitarianism.

As all this emphasis on ideology and conflict suggests, a modern
British Marxist like Eagleton, even while acknowledging the work of a
British Marxist predecessor like Williams, is more nearly developing
the ideas of Continental Marxists like Althusser and Macherey. That
holds, as well, for modern American Marxists like Fredric Jameson.
For although he makes occasional, sympathetic references to the works
of Williams, Thompson, and Hill, Jameson makes far more *use* of
Lukács, Adorno, and Althusser as well as non-Marxist structuralist,
psychoanalytic, and poststructuralist critics.

In the first of several influential works, *Marxism and Form* (1971),
Jameson takes up the question of form and content, arguing that the
former is "but the working out" of the latter "in the realm of superstructure" (329). (In making such a statement Jameson opposes not
only the tenets of Russian formalists, for whom content had merely
been the fleshing out of form, but also those of so-called vulgar Marxists, who tended to define form as mere ornamentation or window-
dressing.) In his later work *The Political Unconscious* (1981), Jameson
uses what in *Marxism and Form* he had called "dialectical criticism" to
synthesize out of structuralism and poststructuralism, Freud and
Lacan, Althusser and Adorno, a set of complex arguments that can
only be summarized reductively.

The fractured state of societies and the isolated condition of individuals, he argues, may be seen as indications that there originally existed an unfallen state of something that may be called "primitive com-

munism." History — which records the subsequent divisions and alienations — limits awareness of its own contradictions and of that lost, Better State, via ideologies and their manifestation in texts whose strategies essentially contain and repress desire, especially revolutionary desire, into the collective unconscious. (In Conrad's *Lord Jim*, Jameson shows, the knowledge that governing classes don't *deserve* their power is contained and repressed by an ending that metaphysically blames Nature for the tragedy and that melodramatically blames wicked Gentleman Brown.)

As demonstrated by Jameson in analyses like the one mentioned above, textual strategies of containment and concealment may be discovered by the critic, but only by the critic practicing dialectical criticism, that is to say, a criticism aware, among other things, of its *own* status as ideology. All thought, Jameson concludes, is ideological; only through ideological thought that knows itself as such can ideologies be seen through and eventually transcended.

In the essay that follows, Judith Weissman begins by describing *Howards End* as a "strange," "unlikely," but nonetheless "compelling story of the transformation of modern urban liberals into farm-women." She then quickly moves on to discuss the novel's broader political and economic contexts. "Within this apparently gentle novel," Weissman writes,

> "there is always the knowledge that England and Germany are about to go to war because they are both empires. . . . Men like the Wilcoxes are making their fortunes from Africa's riches; neither England nor Germany has enough raw materials from which powerful and greedy men can make their money." (432)

Although Forster represents neither the war between imperialist powers nor the devastating effects of imperialism, he does show us the "insensitivity" of the Wilcoxes, their "incapacity for personal relationships," and, above all, their "wastefulness."

The Schlegel sisters, as well as Forster's narrator, are liberal enough to disapprove of the Wilcoxes, their destructive cars, and their "new attitude toward the earth." But liberalism, Weissman argues, ultimately proves to be "exactly what both Forster's narrator and his young heroines . . . must learn to recognize as inadequate." The realization that "the values of a feminist, intellectual, domestic, personal, benevolent life" amount to an "articulate but ineffectual opposition to the imperialistic life of the Wilcoxes" stems, in Weissman's view, from a growing familiarity with Ruth Wilcox and Leonard Bast, characters who "finally force the Schlegel sisters — and the reader — to recognize that women like them do not offer any resistance to what men like the Wilcoxes stand for, and that real resistance, in the form of a new economy, remains a possibility."

The new economy to which Weissman refers is, of course, that of the village community in which Ruth Wilcox has long led "a double life, that of the businessman's wife who has a country place and, secretly, that of the village woman." This "secret life," the life of an agricultural worker, "is still a real and good possible life, a genuine basis for an economy, and a radical hope for England." Henry Wilcox and the Schlegels only reach this understanding, however, through the supernatural interventions of the dead Ruth Wilcox, who ultimately assumes the status of a goddess in the novel.

Weissman's argument is a sweeping one. It discusses everything from what the Schlegel sisters learn through their bungled attempts to help Leonard Bast to the role played by the automobile in Forster's novel. The argument, however, is perhaps most interesting when focused on yet another subject — namely, the sexual double standard that permits Margaret to forgive Henry his dalliance with Jacky Bast but does *not* permit Henry to allow Margaret to spend a night at Howards End with her own sister, Helen, who is pregnant with an illegitimate child. Suffice it to say that Weissman views the end of the novel — which brings together "an old man [Henry], his youngish, childless wife [Margaret], her younger sister [Helen], and the sister's illegitimate son" at Howards End — as one that prophesies a sexual as well as an economic revolution: "Unwelcome in the rest of England," Weissman writes, "at Howards End they suggest the possibilities of both personal transformation and sexual openness."

Weissman's approach to *Howards End,* which is wonderfully attentive to the text and full of insights into its subtleties, may seem different from some of the Marxist thought described in this introduction. If it does, that is a tribute to Weissman's well-articulated love of her subject and, to some extent, a shortcoming of this introduction, which must necessarily cite and summarize the most general and theoretical Marxist writings. Weissman's work is by no means an unusual example of the Marxist approach; owing as much to literary and social critics such as John Ruskin and William Morris as to Marx, it typifies Marxist criticism as it was developed by Raymond Williams. That is to say, Weissman approaches the text in terms of political and economic contexts, analyzing it through the lens of radical social and economic theory but always with the conviction that the literary text is itself important — that, indeed, it is through the text's subtleties that readers may first discover the cracked and crazed nature of the ideologies limiting our lives.

Ross C Murfin

## MARXIST CRITICISM: A SELECTED BIBLIOGRAPHY

### Marx, Engels, Lenin, and Trotsky

Engels, Friedrich. *The Condition of the Working Class in England.* Ed. and trans. W. O. Henderson and W. H. Chaloner. Stanford: Stanford UP, 1968.

Lenin, V. I. *On Literature and Art.* Moscow: Progress, 1967.

Marx, Karl. *Selected Writings.* Ed. David McLellan. Oxford: Oxford UP, 1977.

Trotsky, Leon. *Literature and Revolution.* New York: Russell, 1967.

### General Introductions to and Reflections on Marxist Criticism

Bennett, Tony. *Formalism and Marxism.* London: Methuen, 1979.

Demetz, Peter. *Marx, Engels, and the Poets.* Chicago: U of Chicago P, 1967.

Eagleton, Terry. *Literary Theory: An Introduction.* Minneapolis: U of Minnesota P, 1983.

———. *Marxism and Literary Criticism.* Berkeley: U of California P, 1976.

Elster, Jon. *An Introduction to Karl Marx.* Cambridge: Cambridge UP, 1985.

———. *Nuts and Bolts for the Social Sciences.* Cambridge: Cambridge UP, 1989.

Fokkema, D. W., and Elrud Kunne-Ibsch. *Theories of Literature in the Twentieth Century: Structuralism, Marxism, Aesthetics of Reception, Semiotics.* New York: St. Martin's, 1977. See ch. 4, "Marxist Theories of Literature."

Frow, John. *Marxism and Literary History.* Cambridge: Harvard UP, 1986.

Jefferson, Ann, and David Robey. *Modern Literary Theory: A Critical Introduction.* Totowa: Barnes, 1982. See the essay "Marxist Literary Theories," by David Forgacs.

Laing, Dave. *The Marxist Theory of Art.* Brighton, Eng.: Harvester, 1978.

Selden, Raman. *A Readers' Guide to Contemporary Literary Theory.* Lexington: U of Kentucky P, 1985. See ch. 2, "Marxist Theories."

Slaughter, Cliff. *Marxism, Ideology, and Literature.* Atlantic Highlands: Humanities, 1980.

## Some Classic Marxist Studies and Statements

Adorno, Théodor. *Prisms: Cultural Criticism and Society.* Trans. Samuel Weber and Sherry Weber. Cambridge: MIT P, 1982.

Althusser, Louis. *For Marx.* Trans. Ben Brewster. New York: Pantheon, 1969.

Althusser, Louis, and Étienne Balibar. *Reading Capital.* Trans. Ben Brewster. New York: Pantheon, 1971.

Bakhtin, Mikhail. *The Dialogic Imagination: Four Essays.* Ed. Michael Holquist. Trans. Caryl Emerson. Austin: U of Texas P, 1981.

———. *Rabelais and His World.* Trans. Hélène Iswolsky. Cambridge: MIT P, 1968.

Benjamin, Walter. *Illuminations.* Ed. with introd. by Hannah Arendt. Trans. H. Zohn. New York: Harcourt, 1968.

Caudwell, Christopher. *Illusion and Reality.* 1935. New York: Russell, 1955.

———. *Studies in a Dying Culture.* London: Lawrence, 1938.

Goldmann, Lucien. *The Hidden God.* New York: Humanities, 1964.

———. *Towards a Sociology of the Novel.* London: Tavistock, 1975.

Gramsci, Antonio. *Selections from the Prison Notebooks.* Ed. Quintin Hoare and Geoffrey Nowell Smith. New York: International UP, 1971.

Kettle, Arnold. *An Introduction to the English Novel.* New York: Harper, 1960.

Lukács, Georg. *The Historical Novel.* Trans. H. Mitchell and S. Mitchell. Boston: Beacon, 1963.

———. *Studies in European Realism.* New York: Grosset, 1964.

———. *The Theory of the Novel.* Cambridge: MIT P, 1971.

Marcuse, Herbert. *One-Dimensional Man.* Boston: Beacon, 1964.

Thompson, E. P. *The Making of the English Working Class.* New York: Pantheon, 1964.

————. *William Morris: Romantic to Revolutionary.* New York: Pantheon, 1977.

Williams, Raymond. *Culture and Society 1780–1950.* New York: Harper, 1958.

————. *The Long Revolution.* New York: Columbia UP, 1961.

————. *Marxism and Literature.* Oxford: Oxford UP, 1977.

Wilson, Edmund. *To the Finland Station.* Garden City: Doubleday, 1953.

### Studies by and of Post-Althusserian Marxists

Dowling, William C. *Jameson, Althusser, Marx: An Introduction to "The Political Unconscious."* Ithaca: Cornell UP, 1984.

Eagleton, Terry. *Criticism and Ideology: A Study in Marxist Literary Theory.* London: Verso, 1978.

————. *Exiles and Émigrés.* New York: Schocken, 1970.

Goux, Jean-Joseph. *Symbolic Economies after Marx and Freud.* Trans. Jennifer Gage. Ithaca: Cornell UP, 1990.

Jameson, Fredric. *Marxism and Form: Twentieth-Century Dialectical Theories of Literature.* Princeton: Princeton UP, 1971.

————. *The Political Unconscious: Narrative as a Socially Symbolic Act.* Ithaca: Cornell UP, 1981.

Macherey, Pierre. *A Theory of Literary Production.* Trans. G. Wall. London: Routledge, 1978.

### Marxist Criticism Relating to *Howards End*

Eagleton, Terry. "Evelyn Waugh and the Upper-Class Novel." *Exiles and Émigrés: Studies in Modern Literature.* New York: Schocken, 1970. 33–40.

Henke, Suzette A. "*Howards End*: E. M. Forster without Marx or Sartre." *Moderna Sprak* (Stockholm) 80 (1986): 116–20.

Mirsky, Dmitri. *The Intelligentsia of Great Britain.* Trans. Alec Brown. London: Gollancz, 1935.

# A MARXIST PERSPECTIVE

## JUDITH WEISSMAN

### *Howards End:*
### Gasoline and Goddesses

Like Trollope and Hardy, E. M. Forster asks his readers to discover an unknown rural world as a source of radical hope for women. The difference is that in *Howards End*, unlike the Barsetshire chronicles and *Tess of the D'Urbervilles*, that world has already died, killed by the full-fledged forces of urban culture, machines, and now, in 1910, British imperialism. Rural culture has died (or dies, with Ruth Wilcox, about a third of the way through *Howards End*); however, this culture can be and is reborn, in a strange, apparently unlikely, and ultimately compelling story of the transformation of modern urban liberals into farmwomen with the help of a dead woman who may be, if we believe in her, a ghost or even a Greek goddess.

Within this apparently gentle novel there is always the knowledge that England and Germany are about to go to war because they are both empires; the world is not big enough for both of them. Men like the Wilcoxes are making their fortunes from Africa's riches; neither England nor Germany has enough raw materials from which powerful and greedy men can make their money. Men like the Wilcoxes make their money from countries outside England, and what they do with their money changes England as well as the countries they victimize. Henry Wilcox's office contains a map of Africa: he has worked in Cyprus; his son Paul, in Nigeria. By choosing imperialism as the most destructive form of English capitalism, Forster leaves what is commonly called liberalism and allies himself with English radicals such as William Morris, who wrote in his last article,

> Look how the whole capitalist world is stretching out long arms towards the barbarous world and grabbing and clutching in eager competition at countries whose inhabitants don't want them. . . . It is for the opening of fresh markets to take in all the fresh profit-producing wealth which is growing greater and greater every day; in other words, to make fresh opportunities for *waste;* the waste of our labour and our lives. (qtd. in Thompson 632)

What the English and the Germans are doing to Africa is not only bad for Africans, it is bad for the English and the Germans.

In *Howards End* Forster shows us not the suffering of Africans but the wastefulness of the Wilcoxes. Their insensitivity, their lack of appreciation for art and music, their incapacity for personal relationships — these are the flaws liberal women see in them, and these are the least of their faults. Waste is much more important in the action of this novel; English imperialists are laying waste to both Africa and their own country. At home they are rigid in their assumed superiority to women; they are social Darwinists who believe that the fittest will survive in the business world, "progressives" who believe that bigger is better and more efficient and that there is nothing to value in the village.

The Wilcoxes have a new instrument of disruption in their new means of transportation, the automobile. The narrator keeps the presence, and the meaning, of this new machine, new mode of transportation, new economic fact, and, emblematically, new attitude toward the earth, before us at all times, perpetually enlarging its meaning. In 1910, automobiles were the exclusive property of rich men, and in this book they become weapons against women and the poor. Very early in the novel, when the Schlegels' Aunt Juley is rushing from London to Howards End to supervise her niece Helen's short-lived engagement to Paul Wilcox, her railroad train runs beside a road that has come back into use since the car replaced the horse. She finds herself in Charles Wilcox's automobile when she arrives, and the narrator lets us know what the car is doing to the remaining villagers of Hilton: "Some [of the dust raised by the car] had percolated through the open windows, some had whitened the roses and gooseberries of the wayside gardens, while a certain proportion had entered the lungs of the villagers" (33).

Later on, the Wilcoxes say that they and their car were "fit as a fiddle . . . as far as Ripon," where their motorcar hit "a wretched horse and cart [with] a fool of a driver" (89). The collision is an emblem of an ancient life of agricultural labor increasingly vulnerable to the new economic world of machines. Finally, on the way to Evie Wilcox's wedding at Oniton, a car in the wedding party runs over a village girl's cat, usually considered a more "feminine" pet than a dog. Here the narrator, through Margaret Schlegel, steps forward and warns us that this accident, which the men want to dismiss because the victim is not a dog, is serious. "But she felt their whole journey from London had been unreal. They had no part with the earth and its emotions. They were dust, and a stink, and cosmopolitan chatter, and the girl whose cat had been killed had lived more deeply than they" (190).

The Wilcoxes cannot be themselves without their cars. Cars and empire and the destruction of the English village are inseparable. There was no North Sea oil in 1910; the English needed their empire to get the oil to run their cars. And once they had their cars, they could treat their own country as they treated Africa and India. The Wilcoxes travel around England buying and selling houses with new ease and abandon. Places such as Ducie Street and Oniton come easy and go easy; the Wilcoxes think nothing of rushing into the country for a wedding and then rushing out. The narrator, however, takes such behavior very seriously and tells us things that cannot begin to enter the minds of the Wilcoxes. After the hurried wedding at Oniton, for example, he says: "But the Wilcoxes have no part in the place, nor in any place. It is not their names that recur in the parish register. It is not their ghosts that sigh among the alders at evening. They have swept into the valley and swept out of it, leaving a little dust and a little money behind" (218).

The Wilcoxes see themselves, their imperialism, and their automobiles as facts of life, economic necessities, the inevitable results of progress. Forster presents them all as facts, but as alterable and wrong facts, part of an economy to which his two heroines are at least superficially alien. He is supported today not by literary critics, who have usually ignored the meaning of the automobile in *Howards End,* but by radical social critics such as historian Christopher Lasch, who observes that the "automobile did not simply add another form of transportation to existing forms; it achieved its preeminence at the expense of canals, railways, streetcars, and horse-drawn carriages, thereby forcing the population to depend almost exclusively on automotive transport even for those purposes for which it is obviously unsuited, such as commuting back and forth to work" (43–44). Forster's vision of the form that economic power would take in our century has proved prophetic, hardly the stuff of wishy-washy liberalism.

Liberalism is exactly what both Forster's narrator and his young heroines, the Schlegels, must learn to recognize as inadequate. The cozy familiarity that Forster's narrator establishes among himself, the reader, and the liberal characters begins as a genuine affirmation of shared values, the values of a feminist, intellectual, domestic, personal, benevolent life that exists in articulate but ineffectual opposition to the imperialistic life of the Wilcoxes. The Schlegels' virtues and their political inadequacy are based on their economic situation, their nice nest eggs of secure stocks, about which they and the narrator are refreshingly open. The Marxist historian E. J. Hobsbawm describes this class: "The era of railway, iron and foreign investment also provided the economic base for the Victorian spinster and the Victorian aesthete" (119).

The first indication of the limitations of their class is an event more serious than the Schlegels first realize: they lose their lease at Wickham Place and have to move. Travel and movement have been part of their freedom; now they suddenly find out that, rich as they are, movement has been thrust upon them. The Schlegels cannot understand the true meaning of their forced move until their complacently liberated lives have been repeatedly jolted by two apparently unconnected, but actually deeply connected, people: Ruth Wilcox and Leonard Bast. Between them, these two characters will finally force the Schlegel sisters — and the reader — to realize that women like them do not offer any resistance to what men like the Wilcoxes stand for, and that real resistance, in the form of a new economy, remains a possibility. The Schlegels must encounter both Ruth Wilcox and Leonard Bast several times, however, before they begin to understand this; neither realization is fully understood until the Schlegels come together again at Howards End.

Ruth Wilcox is at first merely beautiful, odd, and a little out of place for the Schlegels; Margaret cannot really hear her when she reveals the true importance of their move from Wickham Place: "It is worse than dying. I would rather die than — oh, poor girls! Can what they call civilization be right, if people mayn't die in the room where they were born?" (86). Over and over, Mrs. Wilcox unconsciously challenges Margaret's bastion of literary, liberal behavior, the tail end of cultured nineteenth-century Romanticism. She says almost nothing at the literary luncheon Margaret gives in her honor, and leaves Margaret with the feeling that some undreamed-of possibility, something more than a single odd woman, exists, though she does not know what it is: "[Mrs. Wilcox] and daily life were out of focus: one or the other must show blurred. And at lunch she seemed more out of focus than usual, and nearer the line that divides daily life from a life that may be of greater importance" (80–81). Margaret spends the rest of the book learning what that life is, that it is not an eerie mystery but a solid economy.

Margaret finally has a moment of true friendship with Ruth Wilcox and impulsively, unconsciously, chooses a new life. She comes close to losing her friend when she carelessly answers, "some other day" (86) to Ruth's suggestion that they go to Howards End together; but soon conquered by her wiser self, she rushes to meet Ruth at the train station and says she will still come if she may. Ruth answers, "You are coming to sleep, dear, too. It is in the morning that my house is most beautiful. You are coming to stop" (88). Though the trip is cut off by the sudden appearance of Evie and Mr. Wilcox, the choice has been made. Ruth Wilcox has told Margaret another truth that she cannot yet hear. Ruth Wilcox dies soon after, before Margaret can make her trip, but leaves a codicil to her will: "I should like Miss Schlegel (Margaret) to have Howards End" (96). Because the Wilcoxes understand neither the house nor Ruth Wilcox nor Margaret, they destroy the note without telling Margaret. But Margaret's destiny is settled: she is to begin a new rural life, a life of true Romantic radicalism.

The urgent need for a new life, something different from both the life of the Wilcoxes and the life of the Schlegels, is forced upon the consciousness of both the Schlegels and the reader by the repeated encounters with Leonard Bast. He surprises only by his suffering. He is the most vivid victim of the Wilcoxes' imperialistic economy, and he is the bearer of bad news to the Schlegels, the news that no social plan available to them can help him. They first meet him at a concert, and Margaret invites him home to retrieve his umbrella, which Helen has carelessly taken. Good liberals, they hope to be generous to someone of a class below their own. He is uncomfortable, of course, and disappoints them by running away.

Leonard comes back several years later to explain why his bedraggled, pathetic wife had come searching for him at Wickham Place: she had found Margaret's visiting card among his books and had been looking for him when he disappeared for a night and a day. The Schlegels are ecstatic when he tells them he spent the night walking out of the city, into the woods; they want to take him a few steps further, to strengthen him, purify him, stop his obeisant references to the inspiring books he has read, the remnants of Romanticism.

Because we, unlike the Schlegels, have seen Leonard at home, we know better than they how little good the remains of Romanticism are doing him:

> They began with a soup square, which Leonard had just dissolved in some hot water. It was followed by the tongue — a freckled cylinder of meat, with a little jelly at the top, and a great deal of yellow fat at the bottom — ending with another square dissolved in water (jelly: pineapple), which Leonard had prepared earlier in the day. (62)

Food is precisely what the Schlegels do not have to think about. But food is at the heart of Leonard's degradation, and food is at the heart of the true, radical Romanticism that the Schlegels will have to discover. Hobsbawm says of a man like Leonard, the new urban worker, "His sheer material ignorance of the best way to live in a city, or to eat industrial food (so very different from village food) might actually make his poverty worse than it 'need have been'; that is, than it might have been if he had not been the sort of person he inevitably was" (87–88). Leonard's terrible food is one of the hidden by-products of the imperialistic capitalism of the Wilcoxes. As Wendell Berry says of the American imperialism that has devastated both our country and the rest of the world: "by now the revolution has deprived the mass of consumers of any independent access to the staples of life: clothing, shelter, food, even water" (6).

The Schlegels soon discover how very worthless all their ideas are to Leonard, how very bankrupt their economic theories are, how very empty their politics have become. In all liberal, helpful good faith, the Schlegels have passed on to Leonard a business tip from Henry Wilcox, now attached to Margaret, that Leonard should clear out of the Porphyrion Fire Insurance Company because it is sure to "smash." He clears out; the company does not smash; he takes a job in a bank; he gets fired; and he finds himself in a uniquely modern urban class, the unemployable. When Margaret suggests that his luck will change, Leonard answers,

> You don't know what you're talking about . . . I shall never get work now. If rich people fail at one profession, they can try another. Not I. I had my groove, and I've got out of it. I could do one particular branch of insurance in one particular office well enough to command a salary, but that's all. . . . I mean, if a man over twenty once loses his own particular job, it's all over with him. I have seen it happen to others. Their friends give them money for a little, but in the end they fall over the edge. (200)

Leonard is right. Neither Henry Wilcox nor the Schlegels meant to hurt him with their advice; having given it, they cannot help him. The very nature of the new forms of urban work has made Leonard unemployable. Henry might have taken him in, but he will not, for the ethics of capitalism do not allow for charity. Henry believes that men like Leonard must fend for themselves, and the Schlegels have no job to give him. Leonard's unemployment, like his food, is a new economic fact for which neither he nor his would-be benefactors are prepared. As Hobsbawm observes, "This conflict between the 'moral economy' of the past and the economic rationality of the capitalist present was particularly clear in the realm of social security" (88).

Leonard's difficulties are compounded by another victim of the Wilcox imperialism, his wife. Jacky, sweet, stupid, uneducated, vulgar, a fallen woman, has wheedled poor young Leonard first into sex and then into marriage. This is what the Schlegels know before Helen brings the newly unemployed Basts into Evie Wilcox's country wedding for a showdown with Henry. At the wedding the Schlegels find out Jacky's past, for she recognizes and greets Henry as an old lover. On one of his imperialist ventures, a long stay in Cyprus, he had had his fling with her; presumably she is the daughter of another Englishman out of England. Helen sums up the life that remained to women like Jacky after men like Henry: "either they sink till the lunatic asylums and the workhouses are full of them, and cause Mr Wilcox to write letters to the papers complaining of our national degeneracy, or else they entrap a boy into marriage before it is too late" (220). Jacky, back in England, has trapped Leonard into marriage merely from economic desperation. Both are part of the underclass produced by the Wilcox economy; both are problems for which the intellectual politics and intellectual feminism of the Schlegels offer no solution.

The only solution is the revelation to which both the Schlegels and the reader must finally come: the economic radicalism that remains possible at Howards End. There is a secret affinity between the two discordant characters in the Schlegels' life, Leonard Bast and Ruth Wilcox: both still are linked to the old "moral economy" of rural England, though Leonard does not know it. When Helen presses him to tell her about his family on the night of Evie's wedding, "Leonard told her a secret that he had held shameful up to now. 'They were just nothing at all,' he said — 'agricultural labourers and that sort'" (208). Leonard, a victim of the economy that has been destroying the culture of rural England, has bought that economy's lies, believing that agricultural laborers are nothing and that their life is necessarily degraded. Only Ruth Wilcox knows better in this novel, and she is already dead.

Ruth Wilcox triumphs nevertheless. The strange plot that brings everyone to Ruth's family home must be read in two ways, both as the realistically explicable convergence of people who are in one kind of trouble or another, and as the workings of a woman who is a ghost and perhaps a goddess, who is calling people back to an ancient, holy life. Neither the Wilcoxes nor the Schlegels have ever thought seriously about the life that Mrs. Wilcox, Ruth Howard, had lived as a girl on a small farm outside the village of Hilton. The inhabitants of the modern world — characters, readers, and perhaps even the narrator of the beginning — have forgotten about a life that was, until recently, considered important.

After Ruth dies and Margaret becomes engaged to Henry, Margaret visits Howards End on various errands and learns how recently Hilton was a living village, a good place to live. Later, Miss Avery, the last living link with the old life in the novel, tells Margaret more about the Howards: "Old Mrs Howard never spoke against anybody, nor let anyone be turned away without food. Then it was never 'Trespassers will be prosecuted' in their land, but would people please not come in?" Miss Avery recognizes that more than such kindness is needed: "Mrs Howard was never created to run a farm. . . . Things went on until there were no men" (237). Neither sex can run a rural, agricultural community alone. Though the Howards had been generous, hospitable village women still living by the code of the "moral economy," they had been doomed when men kept leaving the country for the city. Though Henry Wilcox had saved what was left of the farm when he married Ruth Howard, he had no intention of becoming a country man. As Henry's wife, Ruth leads a double life, that of the businessman's wife who has a country place and, secretly, that of the village woman. Until the end of the novel, neither her husband, who is now Margaret's husband, nor the Schlegels understand that her secret life is still a real and good possible life, a genuine basis for an economy, and a radical hope for England. No one makes the intellectual choice of agriculture as the basis of radical change, but all the characters come to Howards End. They come because they have to. They come because they are hurt, wretched, broken. Proud male imperialists, liberated literary women, poor cast-off clerk — none can survive in London.

The person who comes to Howards End most willingly is Margaret, Ruth Wilcox's chosen heir, and even she must learn by stages that she belongs there. On her first visit she begins to recognize the meaning of the land and the house. The land is fertile, and the house is modest and useful, not a palatial monument to Victorian greed. William Morris and Raymond Williams, both country men and both radicals, help us understand the meaning of the cultivated, fertile land and the small house Margaret discovers. Morris writes about the small scale, which the English, at their best, have made into a moral idea:

This land is a little land. . . . all is measured, mingled, varied, glid-
ing easily one thing into another: little rivers, little plains, swelling,
speedily changing uplands, all beset with handsome, orderly trees;
little hills, little mountains, netted over with the walls of sheep-
walks; all is little, yet not foolish and blank, but serious rather, and
abundant of meaning, for such as choose to seek it; it is neither
prison nor palace, but a decent home. (qtd. in Thompson 728)

Williams illuminates the meaning of this decent home, the small
house, by exposing the meaning of the big house:

Think it through as labour and see how long and systematic the
exploitation and seizure must have been, to rear that many houses,
on that scale. See by contrast what any ancient, isolated farm, in
uncounted generations of labour, has managed to become, by the
efforts of any single real family, however prolonged. (105)

Howards End is potentially the home of a single agricultural family
with enough land to produce its own food. It is the kind of house with
an amount of land that could easily be made available to large numbers
of people in a reordered agricultural economy. It is a shelter for friends;
it is a remnant of the ancient "moral economy" of the country.

But only disaster, an apparently unsolvable problem, brings Margaret to action. She and Helen converge at Howards End because of
Helen's illegitimate pregnancy, her violation of England's deepest sexual rules. Neither likes the terms on which they come to Howards
End: Helen comes unwillingly, tricked and trapped; and Margaret
comes guiltily, part of the trick and the trap. Helen abruptly left England a few days after Evie's wedding and has avoided all contact with
her family since; she has come back only because Margaret thinks their
Aunt Juley is dying. By the time Helen arrives, Margaret knows her
aunt is recovering, but after sending the good news to Helen, she
allows Henry to talk her into plotting to trap her sister, whom they
both call "sick." Margaret's intentions are bad, because she lies to
Helen, telling her that she can go to Howards End to get her books
without meeting anyone; Henry's intentions are also bad, because he
wants to lie to his sister-in-law as he lied to his first wife, denying her
the right to die in the room where she had been born. But Ruth
Wilcox is getting her way in spite of all, bringing a pregnant woman to
her home to start a new family.

The intellectual radicalism that Margaret felt as a London spinster
but that has grown dormant in her as Henry's wife reawakens and becomes active as soon as she sees her sister, who is eight months preg-

nant. For the first time, Margaret takes her stand at Howards End and tells Henry and the doctor to leave: "A new feeling came over her: she was fighting for women against men. She did not care about rights, but if men came into Howards End it should be over her body" (249).

When Henry denies Helen's request to spend one night at Howards End with her sister, Margaret's anger finally becomes articulate, the rage that has to go along with Romantic, radical hope. Henry implies that Helen's immoral presence will depreciate the value of his property and despoil his dear wife's memory, and insists that her sexual behavior is entirely different from his own with Jacky Bast. In response, Margaret explodes: "'Not any more of this!' she cried. 'You shall see the connection if it kills you, Henry! You have had a mistress — I forgave you. My sister has a lover — you drive her from the house. Do you see the connection? Stupid, hypocritical, cruel — oh, contemptible! . . .'" (263–64). She leaves Henry, intending to spend one night at Howards End with Helen and then go back with her to Europe. Once inside the house, however, brought by the most human and painful of causes, they are powerless to leave; they are caught by a power of which they — and we — are only dimly aware.

Henry, Charles, and Leonard must also come to Howards End for the final cataclysm that must precede rebirth. The Wilcox men come to oust the women and to find out how to track the man they call Helen's "seducer." Leonard, meanwhile, has been tracking Margaret, to whom he wants to confess what he — poor, self-tormented Victorian — considers his terrible crime against Helen. Everything misguided and wrong in Victorian sexuality brings the men to Howards End, just as deception brought the women. Leonard's shame is unwarranted, for Helen, after all, seduced him, having the advantages of age, class, and money; and the Wilcoxes' vengefulness against both Helen and her "seducer" is prudery and misogyny masquerading as chivalry.

The final bit of British wrongness necessary to keep the new family at Howards End is the blind legal system that condemns Charles Wilcox for the death of Leonard Bast even though Leonard was about to die of heart trouble, misery, and poverty. He dies when Charles exacts his vengeance by hitting Leonard with the Schlegels' father's sword: "'Yes, murder's enough,' said Miss Avery, coming out of the house with the sword" (277). In Charles's cruel heart, it is murder, though the English legal system calls it manslaughter, sentencing Charles to three years in prison. This injustice also has its part in the

mysterious plot: Charles's punishment keeps Henry at Howards End
so that it will no longer be inhabited only by women: "Then Henry's
fortress gave way. He could bear no one but his wife, he shambled up
to Margaret afterwards and asked her to do what she could with him.
She did what seemed easiest — she took him down to recruit at
Howards End" (284). At the end he is still sick, broken, afflicted by
the hay fever that has always alienated him from the land, but he is
there, part of a new family. Crime, poverty, and sexual taboos have
brought two women, an old man — and soon, a baby boy — to an
abandoned small farm both to suffer and to begin again. A whole
world of wrong, a world run by the Wilcoxes in England, cannot be
gently adjusted into ease and comfort; Forster's plot asks us to believe
that it will finally precipitate its own destruction. For it has been
human, believable, predictable wrong that has brought everyone to
the crisis at Howards End. The wrongs seem irremediable to ordinary
English ways of thinking, but all along, another plot, another narrative, another vision has been working.

Reading through *Howards End*, we can see that the natural disasters built into the English urban economy and Victorian sexual morality have brought everyone together at Howards End; yet upon re-
thinking and rereading, we have to acknowledge the possibility of a
simultaneous supernatural cause: Ruth Wilcox, though dead, has had
her way. At the very end we share Margaret's sense of revelation when
Dolly discloses the family secret that Mrs. Wilcox left Howards End to
Margaret. After Henry tells Margaret the story, "Margaret was silent.
Something shook her life in its inmost recesses, and she shivered. 'I
didn't do wrong, did I?' he asked, bending down. 'You didn't, darling. Nothing has been done wrong'" (291). Nothing has been done
wrong, even though the realistic plot is compounded of wrongs.
Nothing has been done wrong, because a divinity has been using the
Wilcoxes and the Schlegels for her own ends, bringing them back to
an ancient agricultural life not as the fanciful choice of dilettantes but
as an economic and moral necessity.

Forster suggests very slowly, very delicately, the idea that this life
might also include a lost divinity, yet he always offers the reader the
possibility of rational disbelief, as Emily Brontë and Nathaniel
Hawthorne do in *Wuthering Heights* and *The House of the Seven
Gables*, respectively. The supernatural creatures whom the narrator of
*Howards End* introduces gradually increase in seriousness and power.
The narrator brings in the idea of ghosts with a mere simile: "the
fog — we are in November now — pressed against the windows like

an excluded ghost" (72). After Ruth Wilcox dies, he keeps suggesting that she may be alive as a ghost. When Henry proposes to Margaret, "Mrs Wilcox strayed in and out, ever a welcome ghost; surveying the scene, thought Margaret, without one hint of bitterness" (152). Having learned about Henry's affair with Jacky, Margaret thinks that "Mrs Wilcox, that unquiet yet kindly ghost, must be left to her own wrong" (213). After this, we must consider the possibility that the narrator is serious when he says of the Wilcoxes, "It is not their ghosts that sigh among the alders at evening" (218). All this prepares us for Margaret's eventual belief that Ruth Wilcox and her house and farm are both divine and powerful, capable of propelling a group of characters through a painful plot: "I feel that you and I and Henry are only fragments of that woman's mind. She knows everything. She is everything. She is the house, and the tree that leans over it" (268).

Meanwhile, the narrator has been providing another clue to the nature of Ruth Wilcox's divinity and the plot she is weaving. Both the narrator and the characters keep referring to ancient Greece, first in ways that can be dismissed as more of the literary playfulness with which Forster wrote about gods and Greece in his earlier novels and stories: "The tragedy of preparedness has scarcely been handled, save by the Greeks" (104; "You mean to keep proportion, and that's heroic, it's Greek . . ." (174); "Remorse is not among the eternal verities. The Greeks were right to dethrone her" (270). Even Helen's favorite saying, "Death destroys a man; the idea of Death saves him" (210), is more Greek than Christian. The Greece of these comments is the Greece of Matthew Arnold's Victorian essays. It is the Greece dearest to young university men, a literary ideal of the balanced, humane, secular life, so much healthier and more sensible than the life of Christian repression. But beyond this there is another Greece, the Greece of the mystery religions, the Greece of Demeter and Persephone.

This is the Greece of Sophocles' last play, *Oedipus at Colonus,* a hidden source of the final magic in *Howards End.* Forster is so subtle, so determined not to alienate his audience of educated, sophisticated, secular people, that he reveals his unfamiliar, shattering source in Sophocles through the familiar, comfortable voice of Matthew Arnold. The narrator speaks repeatedly about "seeing life steadily and seeing it whole," borrowing a phrase from Arnold's "To a Friend." The line sounds so utterly Victorian! But read in context, it offers another way of reading *Howards End.* Arnold gives special thanks in his poem to Sophocles,

> Who saw life steadily, and saw it whole
> The mellow glory of the Attic stage,
> Singer of sweet Colonus and its child. (12–14)

Once we understand the source of Forster's echoing line, we can see that *Howards End* is more than an English novel; it is a Greek drama reborn in England, a drama of magic and salvation.

There are deep similarities between *Oedipus at Colonus* and *Howards End*. Both reflect the last days of a destructive empire; both are desperate exhortations to a damaged citizenry to come home to their best selves, to the beautiful lands that they are no longer really seeing, and to the old divinities that give both shelter and justice. Just as Ruth Wilcox draws everyone to Howards End to receive justice — blessings and punishments — so the Eumenides, the kindly ones, the transformed Furies, draw everyone to their beautiful fertile shrine at Colonus. Old blind Oedipus comes there to die and to be transformed, after all his suffering, into a divinity; Theseus, his Athenian host, comes there to welcome Oedipus in the best spirit of his city, a place that gives refuge to the wretched of other lands, and to receive Oedipus's blessing in return; Oedipus's brother-in-law and son, who have cruelly banished and repeatedly wronged him, come there to receive his curse. The blessing for both sets of characters and both audiences, ancient Greek and modern English, is the spiritual recovery of a lost life. It is the agricultural life of beautiful, fertile lands, sacred places, female goddesses, justice, and shelter — the moral economy of the country.

Once we come to believe that the agricultural life awaiting Margaret and Helen is both the beginning of a radical new economic order that can subvert the Wilcoxes and their empire, and also a reborn ancient divine order, we can reread or remember the novel and realize that Forster's narrator has been hinting all along that his heroines are involved in something more than ordinary life. In an inobtrusive subordinate clause he tells us that Howards End is a temple; he also lets us know that Miss Avery, the guardian of the place, sees its destiny:

> They went into the dining-room, where the sunlight poured in
> upon her mother's chiffonier, and upstairs, where many an old
> god peeped from a new niche. The furniture fitted extraordinarily
> well. In the central room — over the hall, the room that Helen
> had slept in four years ago — Miss Avery had placed Tibby's old
> bassinette.
> "The nursery," she said. (236)

And we have to look twice at the child who will occupy that nursery, Helen's child. First we can see that Howards End is still ruled by the welcoming spirit of Ruth Wilcox's ancestors; it is a shelter and a sanctuary for Helen, the wandering sexual sinner who would be cast out of the prudish world of English imperialists. Our second vision of her reveals that she, like the Greek wandering sexual sinner Oedipus, is bringing the place a blessing. Forster's narrator has hinted prophetically that Helen will bear a savior, but the hint is so subtle that we can recognize it only in retrospect. After her night with Leonard, she goes to see her brother, Tibby, to ask him to give Leonard five thousand pounds. Tibby understands neither her request nor her state of mind, yet even his dim eyes can see that she has changed in some way. She is "ceaselessly beautiful," as pregnant women often are; at the last, "her eyes, the hand laid on the mouth, quite haunted him, until they were absorbed into the figure of St Mary the Virgin, before whom he paused for a moment on the walk home" (223). He sees the truth, though he does not recognize it. Unmarried Helen is bringing salvation to a hurt world, not peace but a sword, a new man who will turn the old world upside down.

That these hurt people who have gathered at Howards End to survive have in fact been saved bursts upon us as a revelation in the last, joyful, sunlit chapter: "Tom's father was cutting the big meadow. He passed again and again amid whirring blades and sweet odours of grass, encompassing with narrowing circles the sacred centre of the field" (284). Forster tosses the idea off lightly, hoping that we have finally understood the holiness of this place, a holiness that the Greeks found in their sacred groves. Howards End is more than a beautiful landscape; it is holy because it is productive. On the first night Helen and Margaret spend there, Tom, their neighbor, brings milk and eggs — country food, what pregnant women are supposed to eat, country hospitality, no Jell-O and soup cubes. And the last chapter opens with a harvest of hay, a crop to feed animals. This farm is not a retirement home; it is the beginning of a reborn agricultural economy.

In 1910 the Schlegels must do more than join a village community, for there is virtually nothing left to join. Drained of its wealth and its artists, intellectuals, artisans, and proud laborers, the country has become a vacation place for the rich and a place of drudgery for the poor. The village of Hilton needs the dignity, the intelligence, the culture, and the money that the Schlegels bring; they are restoring what it possessed in the relatively recent past. They are also bringing a hope that belongs to the future, not the past. The Schlegels and Wilcoxes make up an unusual family: an old man, his youngish, childless wife, her younger sister, and the sister's illegitimate son. Unwelcome in the rest of England, at Howards End they suggest the possibilities of both personal transformation and sexual openness.

Forster's most daring hope for the future of England — especially of English women — lies beyond economic change. The confessions that Margaret and Helen make to each other contain a new sexual liberty. Helen confesses that she no longer wants the love of a man; Margaret, that she does not love children. Margaret says, "It is only that people are far more different than is pretended. All over the world men and women are worrying because they cannot develop as they are supposed to develop" (287). Forster, a homosexual, dares to combine an ancient economic life of villages and small farms with radical hopes for personal and sexual liberty, liberty for all women and all men who are different. Forster reveals how utopian this hope is in an exchange between Margaret and Helen:

". . . Men don't know what we want —"
"And never will."
"I don't agree. In two thousand years they'll know." (255)

The idea that the world must wait two thousand years is very humbling, a firm reminder that we are a long way from knowing how to make each other happy. But two thousand years is not forever. It is a figure that asks us to take the radical leap into hope.

## WORKS CITED

Arnold, Matthew. *Arnold, Poetical Works.* London: Oxford UP, 1950.

Berry, Wendell. *The Unsettling of America: Culture and Agriculture.* New York: Avon, 1977.

Hobsbawm, Eric J. *Industry and Empire.* Harmondsworth: Penguin, 1969.

Lasch, Christopher. *The Minimal Self: Psychic Survival in Troubled Times.* New York: Norton, 1984.

Thompson, E. P. *William Morris.* New York: Pantheon, 1955.

Williams, Raymond. *The Country and the City.* New York: Oxford UP, 1973.

# Deconstruction
# and
# *Howards End*

## WHAT IS DECONSTRUCTION?

Deconstruction has a reputation for being the most complex and forbidding of contemporary critical approaches to literature, but in fact almost all of us have, at one time, either deconstructed a text or badly wanted to deconstruct one. Sometimes when we hear a lecturer effectively marshal evidence to show that a book means primarily one thing, we long to interrupt and ask what he or she would make of other, conveniently overlooked passages that seem to contradict the lecturer's thesis. Sometimes, after reading a provocative critical article that *almost* convinces us that a familiar work means the opposite of what we assumed it meant, we may wish to make an equally convincing case for our former reading of the text. We may not think that the poem or novel in question better supports our interpretation, but we may recognize that the text can be used to support *both* readings. And sometimes we simply want to make that point: texts can be used to support seemingly irreconcilable positions.

To reach this conclusion is to feel the deconstructive itch. J. Hillis Miller, the preeminent American deconstructor, puts it this way: "Deconstruction is not a dismantling of the structure of a text, but a demonstration that it has already dismantled itself. Its apparently solid ground is no rock but thin air" ("Stevens' Rock" 341). To deconstruct a text isn't to show that all the high old themes aren't there to be found in it. Rather, it is to show that a text — not unlike DNA with its double helix — can have intertwined, opposite "discourses" — strands of narrative, threads of meaning.

Ultimately, of course, deconstruction refers to a larger and more complex enterprise than the practice of demonstrating that a text can have contradictory meanings. The term refers to a way of reading texts practiced by critics who have been influenced by the writings of the French philosopher Jacques Derrida. It is important to gain some understanding of Derrida's project and of the historical backgrounds of his work before reading the deconstruction that follows, let alone attempting to deconstruct a text.

Derrida, a philosopher of language who coined the term *deconstruction*, argues that we tend to think and express our thoughts in terms of opposites. Something is black but not white, masculine and therefore not feminine, a cause rather than an effect, and so forth. These mutually exclusive pairs or dichotomies are too numerous to list but would include beginning/end, conscious/unconscious, presence/ absence, and speech/writing. If we think hard about these dichotomies, Derrida suggests, we will realize that they are not simply oppositions; they are also hierarchies in miniature. In other words, they contain one term that our culture views as being superior and one term viewed as negative or inferior. Sometimes the superior term seems only subtly superior (*speech, cause*), but at other times we know immediately which term is culturally preferable (*presence, beginning,* and *consciousness* are easy choices). But the hierarchy always exists.

Of particular interest to Derrida, perhaps because it involves the language in which all the other dichotomies are expressed, is the hierarchical opposition "speech/writing." Derrida argues that the "privileging" of speech, that is, the tendency to regard speech in positive terms and writing in negative terms, cannot be disentangled from the privileging of presence. (Postcards are written by absent friends; we read Plato because he cannot speak from beyond the grave.) Furthermore, according to Derrida, the tendency to privilege both speech and presence is part of the Western tradition of *logocentrism*, the belief that in some ideal beginning were creative *spoken* words, such as "Let there be light," spoken by an ideal, *present* God.[1] According to logocentric

---

[1]Derrida sometimes uses the word *phallogocentrism* to indicate that there is "a certain indissociability" between logocentrism and the "phallocentrism" (Derrida, *Acts* 57) of a culture whose God created light, the world, and man before creating woman — from Adam's rib. "Phallocentrism" is another name for patriarchy. The role that deconstruction has played in feminist analysis will be discussed later.

tradition, these words can now be represented only in unoriginal speech or writing (such as the written phrase in quotation marks above). Derrida doesn't seek to reverse the hierarchized opposition between speech and writing, or presence and absence, or early and late, for to do so would be to fall into a trap of perpetuating the same forms of thought and expression that he seeks to deconstruct. Rather, his goal is to erase the boundary between oppositions such as speech and writing, and to do so in such a way as to throw into question the order and values implied by the opposition.

Returning to the theories of Ferdinand de Saussure, who invented the modern science of linguistics, Derrida reminds us that the association of speech with present, obvious, and ideal meaning — and writing with absent, merely pictured, and therefore less reliable meaning — is suspect, to say the least. As Saussure demonstrated, words are *not* the things they name and, indeed, they are only arbitrarily associated with those things. A word, like any sign, is what Derrida has called a "deferred presence"; that is to say, "the signified concept is never present in itself," and "every concept is necessarily . . . inscribed in a chain or system, within which it refers to another and to other concepts" ("Différance" 138, 140). Neither spoken nor written words have present, positive, identifiable attributes themselves. They have meaning only by virtue of their difference from other words (*red, read, reed*) and, at the same time, their contextual relationship to those words. Take *read* as an example. To know whether it is the present or past tense of the verb — whether it rhymes with *red* or *reed* — we need to see it in relation to some other words (for example, *yesterday*).

Because the meanings of words lie in the differences between them and in the differences between them and the things they name, Derrida suggests that all language is constituted by *différance*, a word he has coined that puns on two French words meaning "to differ" and "to defer": words are the deferred presences of the things they "mean," and their meaning is grounded in difference. Derrida, by the way, changes the *e* in the French word *différence* to an *a* in his neologism *différance;* the change, which can be seen in writing but cannot be heard in spoken French, is itself a playful, witty challenge to the notion that writing is inferior or "fallen" speech.

In *Dissemination* (1972) and *De la grammatologie* [*Of Grammatology*] (1967), Derrida begins to redefine writing by deconstructing some old definitions. In *Dissemination*, he traces logocentrism back to Plato, who in the *Phaedrus* has Socrates condemn writing and who, in all the great dialogues, powerfully postulates that metaphysical longing for origins and ideals that permeates Western thought. "What Derrida does in his reading of Plato," Barbara Johnson points out in her translator's introduction to *Dissemination*, "is to unfold dimensions of Plato's *text* that work against the grain of (Plato's own) Platonism" (xxiv). Remember: that is what deconstruction does, according to Miller; it shows a text dismantling itself.

In *Of Grammatology*, Derrida turns to the *Confessions* of Jean-Jacques Rousseau and exposes a grain running against the grain. Rousseau — who has often been seen as another great Western idealist and believer in innocent, noble origins — on one hand condemned writing as mere representation, a corruption of the more natural, childlike, direct, and therefore undevious speech. On the other hand, Rousseau acknowledged his own tendency to lose self-presence and blurt out exactly the wrong thing in public. He confesses that by writing at a distance from his audience he often expressed himself better: "If I were present, one would never know what I was worth," Rousseau admitted (Derrida, *Of Grammatology* 142). Thus, Derrida shows that one strand of Rousseau's discourse made writing seem a secondary, even treacherous supplement, while another made it seem necessary to communication.

Have Derrida's deconstructions of *Confessions* and the *Phaedrus* explained these texts, interpreted them, opened them up and shown us what they mean? Not in any traditional sense. Derrida would say that anyone attempting to find a single, homogeneous or universal meaning in a text is simply imprisoned by the structure of thought that would oppose two readings and declare one to be right and not wrong, correct rather than incorrect. In fact, any work of literature that we interpret defies the laws of Western logic, the laws of opposition and noncontradiction. From deconstruction's point of view, texts don't say "A and not B." They say "A and not-A." "Instead of a simple 'either/or' structure," Johnson explains,

> deconstruction attempts to elaborate a discourse that says *neither* "either/or" *nor* "both/and" nor even "neither/nor," while at the same time not totally abandoning these logics either. The word deconstruction is meant to undermine the either/or logic of the opposition "construction/destruction." Deconstruction is both, it is neither, and it reveals the way in which both construction and destruction are themselves not what they appear to be. (Johnson, *World* 12–13)

Although its ultimate aim may be to criticize Western idealism and logic, deconstruction began as a response to structuralism and to for-

WHAT IS DECONSTRUCTION? 451

malism, another structure-oriented theory of reading. Using Saussure's theory as Derrida was to do later, European structuralists attempted to create a *semiology*, or science of signs, that would give humankind at once a scientific and a holistic way of studying the world
and its human inhabitants. Roland Barthes, a structuralist who later
shifted toward poststructuralism, hoped to recover literary language
from the isolation in which it had been studied and to show that the
laws that govern it govern all signs, from road signs to articles of clothing. Claude Lévi-Strauss, a structural anthropologist who studied
everything from village structure to the structure of myths, found in
myths what he called *mythemes*, or building blocks, such as basic plot
elements. Recognizing that the same mythemes occur in similar myths
from different cultures, he suggested that all myths may be elements of
one great myth being written by the collective human mind.

Derrida did not believe that structuralists had the concepts that
would someday explain the laws governing human signification and
thus provide the key to understanding the form and meaning of everything from an African village to Greek myth to Rousseau's *Confessions*.
In his view, the scientific search by structural anthropologists for what
unifies humankind amounts to a new version of the old search for the
lost ideal, whether that ideal be Plato's bright realm of the Idea or the
Paradise of Genesis or Rousseau's unspoiled Nature. As for the structuralist belief that texts have "centers" of meaning, in Derrida's view
that derives from the logocentric belief that there is a reading of the
text that accords with "the book as seen by God." Jonathan Culler,
who thus translates a difficult phrase from Derrida's *L'Écriture et la
différence* [*Writing and Difference*] (1967) in his book *Structuralist
Poetics* (1975), goes on to explain what Derrida objects to in structuralist literary criticism:

> [When] one speaks of the structure of a literary work, one does so
> from a certain vantage point: one starts with notions of the mean-
> ing or effects of a poem and tries to identify the structures respon-
> sible for those effects. Possible configurations or patterns that make
> no contribution are rejected as irrelevant. That is to say, an intu-
> itive understanding of the poem functions as the "centre". . . :
> it is both a starting point and a limiting principle. (244)

Deconstruction calls into question assumptions made about literature by formalist, as well as by structuralist, critics. Formalism, or the
New Criticism as it was once commonly called, assumes a work of literature to be a freestanding, self-contained object, its meanings found
in the complex network of relations that constitute its parts (images,

sounds, rhythms, allusions, and so on). To be sure, deconstruction is
somewhat like formalism in several ways. Both formalism and deconstruction are text-oriented approaches whose practitioners pay a great
deal of attention to rhetorical *tropes* (forms of figurative language including allegory, symbol, metaphor, and metonymy). And formalists,
long before deconstructors, discovered counterpatterns of meaning in
the same text. Formalists find ambiguity: deconstructors find undecidability. On close inspection, however, the formalist understanding of
rhetorical tropes or figures is quite different from that of deconstruction, and undecidability turns out to be different from the ambiguity
formalists find in texts.

Formalists, who associated literary with figurative language, made
qualitative distinctions between types of figures of speech; for instance,
they valued symbols and metaphors over metonyms. (A metonym is a
term standing for something with which it is commonly associated or
contiguous; we use metonymy when we say we had "the cold plate"
for lunch.) From the formalist perspective, metaphors and symbols are
less arbitrary figures than metonyms and thus rank more highly in the
hierarchy of tropes: a metaphor ("I'm feeling blue") supposedly involves a special, intrinsic, nonarbitrary relationship between its two
terms (the feeling of melancholy and the color blue); a symbol ("the
river of life") allegedly involves a unique fusion of image and idea.

From the perspective of deconstruction, however, these distinctions
are suspect. In "The Rhetoric of Temporality" Paul de Man deconstructs the distinction between symbol and allegory; elsewhere, he,
Derrida, and Miller have similarly questioned the metaphor/metonymy
distinction, arguing that all figuration is a process of linguistic substitu-
tion. In the case of a metaphor (or symbol), they claim, we have forgotten what juxtaposition or contiguity gave rise to the association that
now seems mysteriously special. Derrida, in "White Mythology," and
de Man, in "Metaphor (*Second Discourse*)," have also challenged the
priority of literal over figurative language, and Miller has gone so far as
to deny the validity of the literal/figurative distinction, arguing that all
words are figures because all language involves *catachresis*, "the violent,
forced, or abusive importation of a term from another realm to name
something which has no proper name" (Miller, *Ariadne* 21).

The difference between the formalist concept of literary ambiguity
and the deconstructive concept of undecidability is as significant as the
gap between formalist and deconstructive understandings of figurative
language. Undecidability, as de Man came to define it, is a complex
notion easily misunderstood. There is a tendency to assume it refers to

readers who, when forced to decide between two or more equally plausible and conflicting readings, throw up their hands and decide that the choice can't be made. But undecidability in fact debunks this whole notion of reading as a decision-making process carried out on texts by readers. To say we are forced to choose or decide, or that we are unable to do so, is to locate the problem of undecidability falsely within ourselves, rather than recognizing that it is an intrinsic feature of the text.

Undecidability is thus different from ambiguity, as understood by formalists. Formalists believed that a complete understanding of a literary work is possible, an understanding in which ambiguities will be resolved objectively by the reader, even if only in the sense that they will be shown to have definite, meaningful functions. Deconstructors do not share that belief. They do not accept the formalist view that a work of literary art is demonstrably unified from beginning to end, in one certain way, or that it is organized around a single center that ultimately can be identified and defined. Neither do they accept the concept of irony as simply saying one thing and meaning another thing that will be understood with certainty by the reader. As a result, deconstructors tend to see texts as more radically heterogeneous than do formalists. The formalist critic ultimately makes sense of ambiguity; undecidability, by contrast, is never reduced, let alone mastered by deconstructive reading, although the incompatible possibilities between which it is impossible to decide can be identified with certainty.

For critics practicing deconstruction, a literary text is neither a sphere with a center nor an unbroken line with a definite beginning and end. In fact, many assumptions about the nature of texts have been put in question by deconstruction, which in Derrida's words "dislocates the borders, the framing of texts, everything which should preserve their immanence and make possible an internal reading or merely reading in the classical sense of the term" ("Some Statements" 86). A text consists of words inscribed in and inextricable from the myriad discourses that inform it; from the point of view of deconstruction, the boundaries between any given text and that larger text we call language are always shifting.

It was that larger text that Derrida was referring to when he made his famous statement *"there is nothing outside the text"* (*Grammatology* 158). To understand what Derrida meant by that statement, consider the following: we know the world through language, and the acts and practices that constitute that "real world" (the Oklahoma City bombing, the decision to marry) are inseparable from the discourses out of which they arise and as open to interpretation as any work of literature. Derrida is not alone in deconstructing the world/text opposition. De Man viewed language as something that has great power in individual, social, and political life. Geoffrey Hartman, who was closely associated with deconstruction during the 1970s, wrote that "nothing can lift us out of language" (xii).

Once we understand deconstruction's view of the literary text — as words that are part of and that resonate with an immense linguistic structure in which we live and move and have our being — we are in a better position to understand why deconstructors reach points in their readings at which they reveal, but cannot decide between, incompatible interpretive possibilities. A text is not a unique, hermetically sealed space. Perpetually open to being seen in the light of new contexts, any given text has the potential to be different each time it is read. Furthermore, as Miller has shown in *Ariadne's Thread: Story Lines* (1992), the various "terms" and "famil[ies]" of terms" we use in performing our readings invariably affect the results. Whether we choose to focus on a novel's characters or its realism, for instance, leads us to different views of the same text. "No one thread," Miller asserts, "can be followed to a central point where it provides a means of overseeing, controlling, and understanding the whole" (21).

Complicating matters still further is the fact that the individual words making up narratives — the words out of which we make our mental picture of a character or place — usually have several (and often have conflicting) meanings due to the complex histories of their usage. (If your professor tells the class that you have written a "fulsome report" and you look up the word *fulsome* in a contemporary dictionary, you will learn that it can mean either "elaborate" or "offensive"; if, for some reason, you don't know what *offensive* means, you will find out that it can equally well describe your favorite quarterback and a racist joke.) "Each word," as Miller puts it, "inheres in a labyrinth of branching interverbal relationships"; often there are "forks in the etymological line leading to bifurcated or trifurcated roots." Deconstructors often turn to etymology, not to help them decide whether a statement means this or that, but rather as a way of revealing the coincidence of several meanings in the same text. "The effect of etymological retracing," Miller writes, "is not to ground the work solidly but to render it unstable, equivocal, wavering, groundless" (*Ariadne* 19).

Deconstruction is not really interpretation, the act of choosing between or among possible meanings. Derrida has glossed de Man's statement that "there is no need to deconstruct Rousseau" by saying that "this was another way of saying: there is always already deconstruction, at work *in* works, especially *literary* works. It cannot be applied, after the fact and from outside, as a technical instrument. Texts deconstruct *themselves* by themselves" (Derrida, *Memoires* 123). If deconstruction is not interpretation, then what is it? Deconstruction may be defined as reading, as long as reading is defined as de Man defined it — as a process involving moments of what he called *aporia* or terminal uncertainty, and as an act performed with full knowledge of the fact that all texts are ultimately unreadable (if reading means reducing a text to a single, homogeneous meaning). Miller explains unreadability by saying that although there are moments of great lucidity in reading, each "lucidity will in principle contain its own blind spot requiring a further elucidation and exposure of error, and so on, ad infinitum. . . . One should not underestimate, however, the productive illumination produced as one moves through these various stages of reading" (*Ethics* 42, 44).

Miller's point is important because, in a sense, it deconstructs or erases the boundary between the readings of deconstructors and the interpretations of more traditional critics. It suggests that all kinds of critics have had their moments of lucidity; it also suggests that critics practicing deconstruction know that their *own* insights — even their insights into what is or isn't contradictory, undecidable, or unreadable in a text — are hardly the last word. As Art Berman writes,

> In *Blindness and Insight* de Man demonstrates that the apparently well-reasoned arguments of literary critics contain contradiction at their core; yet there is no alternative path to insight. . . . The readers of criticism recognize the blindness of their predecessors, reorganize it, and thereby gain both the insight of the critics and a knowledge of the contradiction that brings forth insight. Each reader, of course, has his own blindness; and the criticism of criticism is not a matter of rectifying someone else's mistakes. (Berman 239–40)

When de Man spoke of the resistance to theory he referred generally to the antitheoretical bias in literary studies. But he might as well have been speaking specifically of the resistance to deconstruction, as expressed not only in academic books and journals but also in popular magazines such as *Newsweek*. Attacks on deconstruction became more common and more personal some four years after de Man's death in

1983. That was the year that a Belgian scholar working on a doctoral thesis discovered ninety-two articles that de Man had written during World War II for the Brussels newspaper *Le Soir,* a widely read French-language daily that had fallen under Nazi control during the German occupation of Belgium. Ultimately, one hundred and seventy articles by de Man were found in *Le Soir;* another ten were discovered in *Het Vlaamsche Land,* a collaborationist newspaper published in Flemish. These writings, which date from 1941 (when de Man was twenty-one years old), ceased to appear before 1943, by which time it had become clear to most Belgians that Jews were being shipped to death camps such as Auschwitz.

De Man's wartime journalism consists mainly, but not entirely, of inoffensive literary pieces. In one article de Man takes Germany's triumph in World War II as a given, places the German people at the center of Western civilization, and foresees a mystical era involving suffering but also faith, exaltation, and rapture. In another article, entitled *"Les Juifs dans la littérature actuelle"* ["Jews in Present-Day Literature"], de Man scoffs at the notion that Jewish writers have significantly influenced the literature of his day and, worse, considers the merits of creating a separate Jewish colony that would be isolated from Europe.

No one who had known de Man since his immigration to the United States in 1948 had found him to be illiberal or anti-Semitic. Furthermore, de Man had spent his career in the United States demystifying or, as he would have said, "debunking" the kind of ideological assumptions (about the relationship between aesthetics and national cultures) that lie behind his most offensive Belgian newspaper writings. The critic who in *The Resistance to Theory* (1986) argued that literature must not become "a substitute for theology, ethics, etc." (de Man 24) had either changed radically since writing of the magical integrity and wholeness of the German nation and its culture or had not deeply believed what he had written as a young journalist.

These points have been made in various ways by de Man's former friends and colleagues. Geoffrey Hartman has said that de Man's later work, the work we associate with deconstruction, "looks like a belated, but still powerful, act of conscience" (26–31). Derrida, who like Hartman is a Jew, has read carefully de Man's wartime discourse, showing it to be "split, disjointed, engaged in incessant conflicts" (Hamacher, Hertz, and Keenan 135). "On the one hand," Derrida finds *"unpardonable"* de Man's suggestion that a separate Jewish colony be set up; "on the other hand," he notes that of the four writers de Man praises in the same article (André Gide, Franz Kafka, D. H. Lawrence, and Ernest Hemingway), not one was German, one (Kafka) *was* Jewish, and all four "represent everything that Nazism . . . would have liked to extirpate from history and the great tradition" (Hamacher, Hertz, and Keenan 145).

While friends asserted that some of de Man's statements were unpardonable, deconstruction's severest critics tried to use a young man's sometimes deplorable statements as evidence that a whole critical movement was somehow morally as well as intellectually flawed. As Andrej Warminski summed it up, "the 'discovery' of the 1941–42 writings is being used to perpetuate the old myths about so-called 'deconstruction'" (Hamacher, Hertz, and Keenan 389). Knowing what some of those myths are — and why, in fact, they *are* myths — aids our understanding in an indirect, contrapuntal way that is in keeping with the spirit of deconstruction.

In his book *The Ethics of Reading* (1987), Miller refutes two notions commonly repeated by deconstruction's detractors. One is the idea that deconstructors believe a text means nothing in the sense that it means whatever the playful reader *wants* it to mean. The other is the idea that deconstruction is "immoral" insofar as it refuses to view literature in the way it has traditionally been viewed, namely, "as the foundation and embodiment, the means of preserving and transmitting, the basic humanistic values of our culture" (9). Responding to the first notion, Miller points out that neither Derrida nor de Man "has ever asserted the freedom of the reader to make the text mean anything he or she wants it to mean. Each has in fact asserted the reverse" (10). As for the second notion — that deconstructors are guilty of shirking an ethical responsibility because their purpose is not to (re)discover and (re)assert the transcendent and timeless values contained in great books — Miller argues that "this line of thought" rests "on a basic misunderstanding of the way the ethical moment enters into the act of reading" (9). That "ethical moment," Miller goes on to argue, "is not a matter of response to a thematic content asserting this or that idea about morality. It is a much more fundamental 'I must' responding to the language of literature in itself. . . . Deconstruction is nothing more or less than good reading as such" (9–10). Reading itself, in other words, is an act that leads to further ethical acts, decisions, and behaviors in a real world involving relations to other people and to society at large. For these, the reader must take responsibility, as for any other ethical act.

A third commonly voiced objection to deconstruction is to its playfulness, to the evident pleasure its practitioners take in teasing out all the contradictory interpretive possibilities generated by the words in a text, their complex etymologies and contexts, and their potential to be read figuratively or even ironically. Certainly, playfulness and pleasure are aspects of deconstruction. In his book *The Post Card* (1987), Derrida specifically associates deconstruction with pleasure; in an interview published in a collection of his essays entitled *Acts of Literature* (1992), he speculates that "it is perhaps this *jouissance* which most irritates the all-out adversaries of deconstruction" (56). But such adversaries misread deconstruction's "jouissance," its pleasurable playfulness. Whereas they see it as evidence that deconstructors view texts as tightly enclosed fields on which they can play delightfully useless little word games, Derrida has said that the "subtle and intense pleasure" of deconstruction arises from the "dismantl[ing]" of repressive assumptions, representations, and ideas — in short, from the "lifting of repression" (*Acts* 56–57). As Gregory S. Jay explains in his book *America the Scrivener: Deconstruction and the Subject of Literary History* (1990), "Deconstruction has been not only a matter of reversing binary oppositions but also a matter of disabling the hierarchy of values they enable and of speculating on alternative modes of knowing and of acting" (xii).

Far from viewing literature as a word-playground, Derrida, in Derek Attridge's words, "emphasizes . . . literature as an institution," one "not given in nature or the brain but brought into being by processes that are social, legal, and political, and that can be mapped historically and geographically" (*Acts* 23). By thus characterizing Derrida's emphasis, Attridge counters the commonest of the charges that have been leveled at deconstructors, namely, that they divorce literary texts from historical, political, and legal institutions.

In *Memoires for Paul de Man* (1986), Derrida argues that, where history is concerned, "deconstructive discourses" have pointedly and effectively questioned "the classical assurances of history, the genealogical narrative, and periodizations of all sorts" (15) — in other words, the tendency of historians to view the past as the source of (lost) truth and value, to look for explanations in origins, and to view as unified epochs (for example, the Victorian period, 1837–1901) what are in fact complex and heterogeneous times in history. As for politics, Derrida points out that de Man invariably "says something about institutional structures and the political stakes of hermeneutic conflicts," which is to say that de Man's commentaries acknowledge that conflicting interpretations reflect and are reflected in the politics of institutions (such as the North American university).

In addition to history and politics, the law has been a subject on which deconstruction has had much to say of late. In an essay on Franz Kafka's story "Before the Law," Derrida has shown that for Kafka the law as such exists but can never be confronted by those who would do so and fulfill its commands. Miller has pointed out that the law "may only be confronted in its delegates or representatives or by its effects on us or others" (*Ethics* 20). What or where, then, is the law itself? The law's presence, Miller suggests, is continually deferred by narrative, that is, writing about or on the law which constantly reinterprets the law in the attempt to reveal what it really is and means. This very act of (re)interpretation, however, serves to "defer" or distance the law even further from the case at hand, since the (re)interpretation takes precedence (and assumes prominence) over the law itself. (As Miller defines it, narrative would include everything from a Victorian novel that promises to reveal moral law, to the opinion of a Supreme Court justice regarding the constitutionality of a given action, however different these two documents are in the conventions they follow and the uses to which they are put.) Miller likens the law to a promise, "the validity of [which] does not lie in itself but in its future fulfillment," and to a story "divided against itself" that in the end "leaves its readers . . . still in expectation" (*Ethics* 33).

Because the facts about deconstruction are very different from the myth of its playful irreverence and irrelevance, a number of contemporary thinkers have found it useful to adapt and apply deconstruction in their work. For instance, a deconstructive theology has been developed. Architects have designed and built buildings grounded, as it were, in deconstructive architectural theory. In the area of law, the critical legal studies movement has, in Christopher Norris's words, effectively used "deconstructive thinking" of the kind de Man used in analyzing Rousseau's *Social Contract* "to point up the blind spots, conflicts, and antinomies that plague the discourse of received legal wisdom." Critical legal theorists have debunked "the formalist view of law," that is, the "view which holds law to be a system of neutral precepts and principles," showing instead how the law "gives rise to various disabling contradictions," such as "the problematic distinction between 'private' and 'public' domains." They have turned deconstruction into "a sophisticated means of making the point that all legal discourse is performative in character, i.e., designed to secure assent through its rhetorical power to convince or persuade" (Norris,

*Deconstruction and the Interests* 17). Courtroom persuasion, Gerald
Lopez has argued in a 1989 article in the *Michigan Law Review*, consists of storytelling as much as argument (Clayton 13).

In the field of literary studies, the influence of deconstruction may
be seen in the work of critics ostensibly taking some other, more political approach. Barbara Johnson has put deconstruction to work for the
feminist cause. She and Shoshana Felman have argued that chief
among those binary oppositions "based on repression of differences
with entities" is the opposition man/woman (Johnson, *Critical* x). In
a reading of the "undecidability" of "femininity" in Balzac's story
"The Girl with the Golden Eyes," Felman puts it this way: "the
rhetorical hierarchization of the . . . opposition between the sexes
is . . . such that woman's *difference* is suppressed, being totally subsumed by the reference of the feminine to masculine identity"
("Rereading" 25).

Elsewhere, Johnson, Felman, and Gayatri Spivak have combined
Derrida's theories with the psychoanalytic theory of Jacques Lacan to
analyze the way in which gender and sexuality are ultimately textual,
grounded in language and rhetoric. In an essay on Edmund Wilson's
reading of Henry James's story *The Turn of the Screw*, Felman has
treated sexuality as a form of rhetoric that can be deconstructed,
shown to contain contradictions and ambiguities that more traditional
readings of sexuality have masked. Gay and lesbian critics have seen
the positive implications of this kind of analysis, hence Eve Kosofsky
Sedgwick's admission in the early pages of her book *Epistemology of the
Closet* (1990): "One main strand of argument in this book is deconstructive, in a fairly specific sense. The analytic move it makes is to
demonstrate that categories presented in a culture as symmetrical binary oppositions . . . actually subsist in a more unsettled and dynamic
tacit relation" (9–10).

In telling "The Story of Deconstruction" in his book on contemporary American literature and theory, Jay Clayton assesses the current
status of this unique approach. Although he notes how frequently deconstructive critics have been cited for their lack of political engagement, he concludes that deconstruction, "a movement accused of formalism and arid intellectualism, participates in the political turn of
contemporary culture" (34). He suggests that what began as theory in
the late 1960s and 1970s has, over time, developed into a method employed by critics taking a wide range of approaches to literature — ethnic, feminist, new historicist, Marxist — in addition to critics outside
of literary studies per se who are involved in such areas as critical legal

studies and critical race theory, which seeks to "sustain a complementary relationship between the deconstructive energies of Critical Legal Studies and the constructive energies of civil rights activism" (58).

Clayton cites the work of Edward Said as a case in point. Through 1975, the year that his *Beginnings: Intention and Method* was published, Said was employing a form of deconstructive criticism that, in Clayton's words, emphasized the "power" of texts "to initiate projects in the real world" (45–46). Said became identified with cultural and postcolonial criticism, however, beginning in 1978 with the publication of his book *Orientalism*, in which he deconstructs the East/West, Orient/Occident opposition. Said argues that Eastern and Middle Eastern peoples have for centuries been stereotyped by the Western discourses of "orientalism," a textuality that in no way reflects the diversity and differences that exist among the peoples it claims to represent. According to Said, that stereotyping not only facilitated the colonization of vast areas of the globe by the so-called West but also still governs, to a great extent, relations with the Arab and the so-called Eastern world. The expansion of Said's field of vision to include not just literary texts but international relations is powerfully indicative of the expanding role that deconstruction currently plays in developing contemporary understandings of politics and culture, as well as in active attempts to intervene in these fields.

In the essay that follows, the noted American deconstructor J. Hillis Miller argues that "a just reading of *Howards End* all depends on how you take the word *unseen* and its synonyms" in the novel, including *invisible, unknown,* and *infinity.* The novel "measures" its characters according to "their openness or lack of openness to the unseen," valuing as superior those who sense and respond to it. Miller goes on to point out, however, that Forster also "places his characters in relation to gender, class, nation, and race. . . . These two forms of placement are related, but they also conflict." For instance, although Englishness, maleness, and the upper class often seem the privileged terms in Forster's Edwardian hierarchy of values, openness to the unseen turns out to be a German, female, and lower-to-middle-class characteristic in the world depicted in *Howards End.*

Another example of the subtle kind of conflict Miller finds in Forster's novel is the way in which the "narrator gives the Wilcoxes their due for the efficient exercise of patriarchal power . . . while at the same time [displaying] abundantly and with evident relish what havoc these 'virile' men wreak. . . ." Given the subtle crosscurrents in

*Howards End,* Miller argues that "it is not all that easy to figure out just where Forster stands."

Miller ultimately argues that openness and responsiveness to "the unseen" are more reliable yardsticks for measuring character in *Howards End* than are markers such as gender, nationality, and class. He associates "the unseen" with "the other," a term sometimes used by multicultural critics to refer to sexual, racial, and/or socioeconomic difference. But Miller distinguishes between two versions of otherness, between an "other" that can ultimately be assimilated by a tolerant and sympathetic society and another "other" that is irreducible and unassimilable, what French philosopher Jacques Derrida has called "wholly other."

Forster's "unseen," Miller argues, is the latter type. Grounded in "the infinite," it calls characters to action and imposes responsibilities that are impossible to fulfill. What it is, finally, is unknowable: "The unseen is like a black hole at the center of *Howards End.*" Mrs. Wilcox, for whom the house Howards End is a mediator of the unseen, is herself such a mediator in *Howards End,* a novel which, in turn, "is a further mediator in this chain of mediation." Arguing that readers are "on [their] own in response to the unseen," left free by the novel to "negotiate [their] own reaction[s]," Miller poses a hypothetical question. "Might it not be possible," he asks,

> . . . to claim that the strand of *Howards End* that refers to the unseen is no more than another part of conservative, white, Western, male ideology, something that functions as a bogus absolute keeping the other ideological elements concerning race, gender, and the uneven distribution of privilege and goods firmly in place, the lines of power unchanged? Yes, it would be possible to claim that. You are free to do so. It would also be possible to take the unseen seriously as something that works against the various elements of that conservative ideology in *Howards End.* Then you would have an obligation to respond in some way to the unseen. (481)

Written especially for this edition of Forster's novel, Miller's essay typifies deconstruction as it was practiced in the 1980s while at the same time reflecting its more recent turn toward questions of ethics, politics, and religion. In exposing two strands of discourse — one of which is patriarchal and patriotic in its assumptions, the other of which radically critiques those conservative assumptions — Miller shows us ways in which the text contradicts itself by saying both "A" and "not-A." But he also suggests that, in spite of the text's "undecidability," we are not only free but also called on to decide what "the unseen" means (and whether its force is liberating or repressive). He thus writes the kind of deconstruction he unveiled in *The Ethics of Reading,* where he wrote of how "the ethical moment enters into the act of reading" (9). That moment and act combine to produce what Miller here calls "just reading," that is, a reading that "does justice to the text" while at the same time "fulfill[ing] the demand" to "act" that "the novel makes on me when I read it."

Ross C Murfin

## DECONSTRUCTION:
## A SELECTED BIBLIOGRAPHY

### Writings on Deconstruction

Arac, Jonathan, Wlad Godzich, and Wallace Martin, eds. *The Yale Critics: Deconstruction in America.* Minneapolis: U of Minnesota P, 1983. See especially the essays by Bové, Godzich, Pease, and Corngold.

Berman, Art. *From the New Criticism to Deconstruction: The Reception of Structuralism and Post-Structuralism.* Urbana: U of Illinois P, 1988.

Butler, Christopher. *Interpretation, Deconstruction, and Ideology: An Introduction to Some Current Issues in Literary Theory.* Oxford: Oxford UP, 1984.

Clayton, Jay. *The Pleasure of Babel: Contemporary American Literature and Theory.* New York: Oxford UP, 1993.

Culler, Jonathan. *On Deconstruction: Theory and Criticism after Structuralism.* Ithaca: Cornell UP, 1982.

———. *Structuralist Poetics: Structuralism, Linguistics, and the Study of Literature.* Ithaca: Cornell UP, 1975. See especially ch. 10.

Esch, Deborah. "Deconstruction." *Redrawing the Boundaries: The Transformation of English and American Literary Studies.* Ed. Stephen Greenblatt and Giles Gunn. New York: MLA, 1992. 374–91.

*Feminist Studies* 14 (1988). Special issue on deconstruction and feminism.

Hamacher, Werner, Neil Hertz, and Thomas Keenan. *Responses: On Paul de Man's Wartime Journalism.* Lincoln: U of Nebraska P, 1989.

Hartman, Geoffrey. "Blindness and Insight." *The New Republic,* 7 Mar. 1988: 26–31.

Jay, Gregory S. *America the Scrivener: Deconstruction and the Subject of Literary History.* Ithaca: Cornell UP, 1990.

Leitch, Vincent B. *American Literary Criticism from the Thirties to the Eighties.* New York: Columbia UP, 1988. See especially ch. 10, "Deconstructive Criticism."

——. *Cultural Criticism, Literary Theory, Poststructuralism.* New York: Columbia UP, 1992.

Loesberg, Jonathan. *Aestheticism and Deconstruction: Pater, Derrida, and de Man.* Princeton: Princeton UP, 1991.

Melville, Stephen W. *Philosophy beside Itself: On Deconstruction and Modernism.* Theory and History of Lit. 27. Minneapolis: U of Minnesota P, 1986.

Norris, Christopher. *Deconstruction and the Interests of Theory.* Oklahoma Project for Discourse and Theory 4. Norman: U of Oklahoma P, 1989.

——. *Deconstruction: Theory and Practice.* London: Methuen, 1982. Rev. ed. London: Routledge, 1991.

——. *Paul de Man, Deconstruction and the Critique of Aesthetic Ideology.* New York: Routledge, 1988.

Weber, Samuel. *Institution and Interpretation.* Minneapolis: U of Minnesota P, 1987.

### Works by de Man, Derrida, and Miller

de Man, Paul. *Allegories of Reading.* New Haven: Yale UP, 1979. See especially ch. 1, "Semiology and Rhetoric," and ch. 7, "Metaphor (*Second Discourse*)."

——. *Blindness and Insight.* New York: Oxford UP, 1971. Minneapolis: U of Minnesota P, 1983. The 1983 edition contains important essays not included in the original edition.

——. "Phenomenality and Materiality in Kant." *Hermeneutics: Questions and Prospects.* Ed. Gary Shapiro and Alan Sica. Amherst: U of Massachusetts P, 1984. 121–44.

——. *The Resistance to Theory.* Minneapolis: U of Minnesota P, 1986.

——. *Romanticism and Contemporary Culture.* Ed. E. S. Burt, Kevin Newmarkj, and Andrzej Warminski. Baltimore: Johns Hopkins UP, 1993.

———. *Wartime Journalism, 1939–1943.* Lincoln: U of Nebraska P, 1989.

Derrida, Jacques. *Acts of Literature.* Ed. Derek Attridge. New York: Routledge, 1992.

———. "Différance." *Speech and Phenomena.* Trans. David B. Alison. Evanston: Northwestern UP, 1973. 129–60.

———. *Dissemination.* 1972. Trans. Barbara Johnson. Chicago: U of Chicago P, 1981. See especially the concise, incisive "Translator's Introduction," which provides a useful point of entry into this work and others by Derrida.

———. "Force of Law: The 'Mystical Foundation of Authority.'" Trans. Mary Quaintance. *Deconstruction and the Possibility of Justice.* Ed. Drucilla Cornell, Michel Rosenfeld, and David Gray Carlson. New York: Routledge, 1992. 3–67.

———. *Given Time: I. Counterfeit Money.* Trans. Peggy Kamuf. Chicago: U of Chicago P, 1992.

———. *Margins of Philosophy.* Trans. Alan Bass. Chicago: U of Chicago P, 1982. Contains the essay "White Mythology: Metaphor in the Text of Philosophy."

———. *Memoires for Paul de Man.* Wellek Library Lectures. Trans. Cecile Lindsay, Jonathan Culler, and Eduardo Cadava. New York: Columbia UP, 1986.

———. *Of Grammatology.* Trans. Gayatri C. Spivak. Baltimore: Johns Hopkins UP, 1976. Trans. *of De la grammatologie.* 1967.

———. "Passions." *Derrida: A Critical Reader.* Ed. David Wood. Cambridge: Basil Blackwell, 1992. 5–35.

———. *The Post Card: From Socrates to Freud and Beyond.* Trans. with intro. Alan Bass. Chicago: U of Chicago P, 1987.

———. "Some Statements and Truisms about Neo-logisms, Newisms, Postisms, and Other Small Seisisms." *The States of "Theory."* New York: Columbia UP, 1990. 63–94.

———. *Specters of Marx.* Trans. Peggy Kamuf. New York: Routledge, 1994.

———. *Writing and Difference.* 1967. Trans. Alan Bass. Chicago: U of Chicago P, 1978.

Miller, J. Hillis. *Ariadne's Thread: Story Lines.* New Haven: Yale UP, 1992.

———. *The Ethics of Reading: Kant, de Man, Eliot, Trollope, James, and Benjamin.* New York: Columbia UP, 1987.

———. *Fiction and Repetition: Seven English Novels.* Cambridge: Harvard UP, 1982.

————. *Hawthorne and History: Defacing It.* Cambridge: Basil Blackwell, 1991. Contains a bibliography of Miller's work from 1955 to
1990.

————. *Illustrations.* Cambridge: Harvard UP, 1992.

————. "Stevens' Rock and Criticism as Cure." *Georgia Review* 30
(1976): 3–31, 330–48.

————. *Topographies.* Stanford: Stanford UP, 1995.

————. *Versions of Pygmalion.* Cambridge: Harvard UP, 1990.


## Essays on Deconstruction
## and Poststructuralism

Barthes, Roland. *S/Z.* Trans. Richard Miller. New York: Hill, 1974. In
this influential work, Barthes turns from a structuralist to a poststructuralist approach.

Benstock, Shari. *Textualizing the Feminine: On the Limits of Genre.*
Norman: U of Oklahoma P, 1991.

Bloom, Harold, et al., eds. *Deconstruction and Criticism.* New York:
Seabury, 1979. Includes essays by Bloom, de Man, Derrida,
Miller, and Hartman.

Chase, Cynthia. *Decomposing Figures.* Baltimore: Johns Hopkins UP,
1986.

Cohen, Tom. *Anti-Mimesis: From Plato to Hitchcock.* Cambridge:
Cambridge UP, 1994.

Elam, Diane. *Feminism and Deconstruction: Ms. en Abyme.* New York:
Routledge, 1994.

Felman, Shoshana. "Rereading Femininity." Special Issue on "Feminist Readings: French Texts/American Contexts," *Yale French
Studies* 62 (1981): 19–44.

————. "Turning the Screw of Interpretation." *Literature and Psycho-
analysis: The Question of Reading: Otherwise.* Special issue, *Yale
French Studies* 55–56 (1978): 3–508. Baltimore: Johns Hopkins
UP, 1982.

Harari, Josué, ed. *Textual Strategies: Perspectives in Post-Structuralist
Criticism.* Ithaca: Cornell UP, 1979.

Johnson, Barbara. *The Critical Difference: Essays in the Contemporary
Rhetoric of Reading.* Baltimore: Johns Hopkins UP, 1980.

————. *A World of Difference.* Baltimore: Johns Hopkins UP, 1987.

Krupnick, Mark, ed. *Displacement: Derrida and After.* Bloomington:
Indiana UP, 1987.

Meese, Elizabeth, and Alice Parker, eds. *The Difference Within: Feminism and Critical Theory.* Philadelphia: John Benjamins, 1989.

Sedgwick, Eve Kosofsky. *Epistemology of the Closet.* Berkeley: U of California P, 1990.

Ulmer, Gregory L. *Applied Grammatology.* Baltimore: Johns Hopkins UP, 1985.

————. *Teletheory: Grammatology in the Age of Video.* New York: Routledge, 1989.

# A DECONSTRUCTIVE PERSPECTIVE

## J. HILLIS MILLER

## Just Reading *Howards End*

A place, as well as a person, may catch the glow.

(*Howards End* 287)

A just reading of *Howards End* all depends on how you take the word *unseen* and its synonyms, "invisible" (25), "unknown" (101), "infinity" (28), "the obscure borderland" (67), "the submerged" (77), "a more inward light" (91), "the inconceivable" (182), "the glow" (287), the "idea of Death" (210), and so on. These words and phrases recur. An adept reader of *Howards End* soon comes to notice repetitions and to assume they are probably important. Among other such repetitions, the word *unseen* echoes discreetly and unostentatiously through the novel like a musical motif. It occurs repeatedly in different contexts. The word is especially associated with Margaret Schlegel. She, for example, is said to have concluded that "any human being lies nearer to the unseen than any organization" (43). Later she asserts that for the Germans, "literature and art have what one might call the kink of the unseen about them" (81). The narrator observes of Mrs. Wilcox's strange decision on her deathbed to leave Howards End to Margaret Schlegel, "The desire for a more inward light had found expression at last, the unseen had impacted on the seen" (99). Margaret writes to her sister Helen, "Don't brood too much . . . on the superiority of the unseen to the seen" (102). Later she thinks, "All vistas close in the unseen — no one doubts it — but Helen closed them rather too quickly for her [Margaret's] taste" (174), whereas for

Charles Wilcox's shallow wife, Dolly, "'spooks' and 'going to church' summarized the unseen" (180). What does the word *unseen* mean in these sentences? To what does it refer? Should we as readers take it seriously, or does it name no more than a personal "kink" ascribed ironically to the characters, especially to Margaret, by a demystified narrator?

By "you" in "all depends on how you take the word *unseen*" I mean *you*, the reader of these words, the person to whom they are addressed. In the same way, the narrator of *Howards End* speaks to you, to me, or to any other reader in a way that seems unique in each case. The narrator is speaking to *me*, and I must respond as best I can. Just who or what that narrator is, what he, she, or it invokes, demands, requests, or obliges me to do is another question, to which I shall return.

The absence of the narrator makes the film of *Howards End*, faithful as it is to the novel and admirable as it is as a film, fundamentally different. The linguistic texture of the novel is made up to a considerable degree by the narrator's constant, ruminative, slightly ironic commentary. The narrator also speaks for the characters' interior thoughts in that locution called "indirect discourse." In indirect discourse the narrator speaks in the third-person past tense for what the characters think to themselves in the first-person present tense. Forster's narrator, like the narrators of many Victorian novels, is anonymous and ubiquitous. He, she, or it can enter at will into the thoughts and feelings of the characters. Film, which has its own strong visual resources not available to the novel,[1] has no easy equivalent for either the narrator's commentary or indirect discourse. Two other differences between the novel and the film are that the film is by necessity much briefer, omitting or shortening many episodes, and that the film leaves out many of those verbal repetitions (for example, of the word *unseen* or of references to hay and hay fever) that generate so much of the meaning of the novel.

By a "just reading" in my title I mean one that does justice to the text, one that fulfills the demand the novel makes on me when I read it. A just reading does not simply get the novel right, that is, understand it correctly. It also responds in a responsible way and acts rightly on the basis of the reading. A just reading is as much a matter of doing

[1]Alistair Duckworth identifies these resources succinctly apropos of the film *Howards End:* "(1) The film is a visual medium that gives imagistic representation to what is verbal description in the novel, and (2) the film uses sound both diegetically and mimetically and thus either performs or 'underscores' Forster's words" (personal letter).

as of knowing. Doing what? This doing might be behaving differently in your daily life as a result of the reading, or it might be bearing witness to other people about your reading, for example, in talking, teaching, or even in writing about the novel, as in this present essay. Just as Jane Austen's novels measure their characters on a scale of intelligence, on their ability to reconcile the claims of both sense and sensibility, and just as Anthony Trollope's novels measure their characters on a scale of faithfulness to the commitment made by falling in love, so *Howards End*, like Forster's other novels, measures the characters by their responses to the unseen. The reader of all these novels is put on trial in relation to the different scale of evaluation set up in each case.

I mention Jane Austen and Anthony Trollope because their novels, like Forster's *Howards End*, deal with courtship and marriage among the middle and upper classes at specific moments in English history. The novels of all three have as central themes the redistribution of money and property through marriage. They place these transactions within a given social context and locate them at a given historical moment. *Howards End*, it could be said, is the story of how possession of a house in the country, Howards End, is passed from the first Mrs. Wilcox to the second. Perhaps it would be better to say "possession *by* the house," since the house is the novel's most material and powerful mediator of the unseen. For Jane Austen the historical moment is the Napoleonic era, the aftermath of the French Revolution, a period of reaction in England. For Trollope it is the high Victorian period, the period of an imperialism so taken for granted that it is only obliquely a question in his novels. For Forster in *Howards End*, the time is that high moment of English prosperity, at least for the ruling classes,[2] just before the First World War, a time when the British Empire was in its last phase of flourishing but when the justice or injustice of imperialism was, a little more overtly, an uneasy question.

Henry Wilcox, we are told, has made his fortune first in Cyprus and now in African rubber plantations. He is "the man who had carved money out of Greece and Africa, and bought forests from the natives for a few bottles of gin" (244). A map of Africa is on the wall at his firm's offices. The firm is called the Imperial and West African Rubber Company. His son Paul goes out to do his "duty," as

---

[2]This prosperity for the rich went along with increasing poverty and ill health for the lower classes, especially in the cities. The Basts are the example of this in *Howards End*.

Margaret calls it, in Nigeria: "beastly work — dull country, dishonest natives, an eternal fidget over fresh water and food. A nation who can produce men of that sort may well be proud. No wonder England has become an Empire" (108). Forster is much more overt than Trollope in specifying his complex feelings about the British Empire. Trollope thought it was, on the whole, a very good thing. Forster is, on the whole, opposed, though it is hardly the case that *Howards End* is simply anti-imperialist. He quotes Margaret's words and Henry Wilcox's, but does not pass overt judgment on them, though the awfulness of the Wilcox men is a kind of indirect judgment. This is what imperialists are like, for better or for worse, the narrator in effect says, but it is up to the reader to pass judgment. Ultimately, the narrator does say straightforwardly enough that "the Imperialist is not what he thinks or seems. He is a destroyer. He prepares the way for cosmopolitanism, and though his ambitions may be fulfilled the earth that he inherits will be gray" (276). Nevertheless, Henry Wilcox's virtues are consistently praised in the teeth of the demonstration of his limitations. One difference between the novel and the film, at least in my sense of it, is that Anthony Hopkins's performance as Henry Wilcox makes Wilcox rather more attractive than he is in the novel.

*Howards End* carries on the long tradition of the English novel in its exact specification of the characters' social placement. He tells the reader just how rich or poor the characters are, where their money comes from, what work they do or what professions they follow, what foods they like, what sorts of houses or flats they live in, what servants they have, whether they have country houses as well as houses in London, what their furniture is like, whether or not they have motorcars or travel by underground and train. Forster has an extraordinary ability to convey economically the sense of a setting, as in his descriptions of Howards End, modeled on a house in Hertfordshire, Rooksnest, where Forster himself had lived as a child. Though Forster writes in prose, his name could be added to William Wordsworth's and others' as one of England's great topographical "poets."

My mention of Wordsworth is not fortuitous. For both Wordsworth and Forster, topographical features — trees, houses, fields, and so on — are chief mediators of the unseen, while certain persons — such as Wordsworth's old leechgatherer and Forster's Mrs. Wilcox — are valued as specially initiated mediators of the unseen as it is mediated by the landscape. Toward the end of the novel, long after Mrs. Wilcox's death, she has become, at least in Margaret Schlegel's mind, a ubiquitous, all-knowing, all-encompassing spirit. "I feel," Margaret tells Helen, "that you and I and Henry are only fragments of that woman's mind. She knows everything. She is everything. She is the house, and the tree that leans over it" (268).

Readers today are trained to be sensitive to assumptions about class, gender, nation, and race (those four leitmotifs of contemporary cultural studies). These, it is presumed, govern a given literary work and form its presupposed ideology. By "ideology" I mean what both Louis Althusser and Paul de Man mean by the word: unspoken and often unconscious assumptions that are taken to be natural and universal though they are social or linguistic and could be otherwise.[3] Though *Howards End* makes some perhaps unconscious ideological assumptions of its own, it is at the same time, like most great English novels, a critical exposure of the ideologies of its characters and of the community to which they belong. Exposure of ideological assumptions, knowledge of them, does not, however, free one from them, as both Althusser and de Man, in their different ways, stress. For that, the "just reading" I began by advocating would be necessary, that is, a "materialist" reading that does something, that leads to action in the real world rather than merely to knowledge.[4]

I have said that Forster places his characters in relation to gender, class, nation, and race. I have also said that he measures them by their openness or lack of openness to the unseen. These two forms of placement are related, but they also conflict. Let me explain how.

Part of the difficulty *Howards End* presents to an American reader is the complexity of social discriminations in the Edwardian England that Forster depicts, to which may be added the complexity of the narrator's response to those complexities. Forster is wonderfully adept at catching subtle nuances of clashes between sexes or between classes. It is not that present-day United States culture is not complex and finely reticulated but that the lines go in different places. England was in 1910 still a class society in a way the United States has never been. In the United States we still assume, as a deeply held ideological presupposition, an almost unlimited possibility of social mobility. As a multicultural and multiracial country, we are divided more along economic, racial, and ethnic lines than along anything like class lines in the

<hr/>

[3]Louis Althusser defines ideology as "the imaginary relation of individuals to the real relations in which they live" (165). "What we call ideology," writes Paul de Man, "is precisely the confusion of linguistic with natural reality, of reference with phenomenalism" (11).

[4]"Materialist practice assumes language acts on the real world and . . . continually credits the possibility that literature acts on historical reality" (Scarry xxiii).

English sense. An American's expectations are defined by being Caucasian, African American, Hispanic, or Asian American, by being male or female, by being rich or poor, not by inherited class placement. England is presented in *Howards End* as a uniracial and unicultural country. Race appears only peripherally in the novel, as in Margaret's remark about "dishonest natives" in Nigeria (108). The almost complete omission of racial difference is significant. That all middle-class English men and women are white and that the British Empire rests on the exploitation of Indians and Africans are assumptions so taken for granted that race is hardly an overt issue. In place of racial difference is put national difference, about which I shall have more to say later.

Divisions of class, on the other hand, are in *Howards End* relatively fixed and highly discriminated. It is not all that easy for an American reader to get the hang of these discriminations, particularly when Forster is to some degree putting in question the nominal class distinctions that were assumed in England in his time. Class distinctions in Edwardian England depended on money, but not just on money, though Forster by no means minimizes the difference that having money or not having it can make. The Schlegel sisters have less money than the Wilcoxes but still enough to relieve them of the necessity of working. They are by inheritance members of an emancipated group of intellectuals, whereas the Wilcox men are frozen in the ideological complacencies of the commercial middle class. This puts the Schlegels in a class above the Wilcoxes, according to the subtle discriminations the novel makes. It also deliberately puts in question the class discriminations that members of the new plutocracy like the Wilcoxes make. As Helen says about a moment of insight into this plutocracy, "I felt for a moment that the whole Wilcox family was a fraud, just a wall of newspapers and motor-cars and golf-clubs, and that if it fell I should find nothing behind it but panic and emptiness" (39). Helen and Margaret Schlegel, on the other hand, "know that personal relations are the real life, for ever and ever" (41). Mrs. Wilcox is in a class above them all, or rather her superiority is not a matter of class but rather a matter of superior sensitivity to the unseen. Her superiority is beyond class distinctions. Miss Avery, in spite of her low class status, is also superior to the Wilcoxes by virtue of the uncanny awareness of the unseen that she shares with Mrs. Wilcox. Mrs. Wilcox has brought to her marriage only the house in which she was born, Howards End, but her attachment to the house and to the immemorial tradition it embodies puts her at the top of the social hierarchy in the novel:

She seemed to belong not to the young people and their motor, but to the house, and to the tree that overshadowed it. One knew that she worshipped the past, and that the instinctive wisdom the past can alone bestow had descended upon her — that wisdom to which we give the clumsy name of aristocracy. High-born she might not be. But assuredly she cared about her ancestors, and let them help her. (36)

Much further down in the social hierarchy, so taken for granted as to be almost invisible, is the class of servants. Whether or not they have any sensitivity to the unseen is impossible to say. All the main characters in the novel but the Basts have servants: chauffeurs, housemaids, cooks, gardeners, boot cleaners, and so on. Only the Basts cook their own meals, or rather, Leonard Bast cooks them. Forster's description makes this a sordid and unattractive event (62).

In Forster's England a person tended to remain permanently placed in whatever class he or she was born into. Class, moreover, determined one's capabilities, an assumption that will seem absurd to most American readers today. Leonard Bast is a clerk in an insurance company, grandson of agricultural laborers. He marries a vulgar woman of loose morals. He is fixed on the thin edge between respectability and depths of poverty that are "unthinkable"[5] and not narratable. He can move only slightly, to one side or the other of that thin edge. However hard Leonard Bast tries to get "culture" by reading books and going to concerts, he will never get it right. All his reading of John Ruskin, George Henry Borrow, Richard Jefferies, Robert Louis Stevenson, and Henry David Thoreau has only put him in "a swamp of books" (115) without raising him one inch above his fixed class status. In America we tend to assume that ability to read depends on an innate intelligence that crosses economic lines and on education, which in principle is open to everyone. In America in 1994, you cannot so easily blame an inability to read on class heritage, but in *Howards End* in 1910, you could.

*Howards End* still belongs to the high period of the nationalism that was about to lead to the First World War and subsequently to the Second World War. Nationalism assumes that England is filled with

[5]"We are not concerned with the very poor," says the narrator, in a remarkably condescending assertion, an assertion that is hardly redeemed by whatever irony it may have. "They are unthinkable, and only to be approached by the statistician or the poet" (55).

English men and women, Germany with Germans, Russia with Rus-
sians, and so on. Minorities do not count, and a national heritage is a
prime determinant of identity. An Englishman will be — well, like an
Englishman. Germans will be Germans. The characteristics of each nationality can be precisely defined.

If on the one hand it is implied in *Howards End* that nationalist assumptions are ideological delusions, on the other hand the novel itself
seems to some degree to depend on them. The characterization of the
Schlegel sisters as divided between two cultural heritages depends on
the distinction between English and German nationality traits. Since
*Howards End* centers on this self-division in the two main protagonists, one could claim that the novel as a whole relies on assumptions
about national identity. Margaret, in particular, is torn between her allegiance to the Germanic unseen and her allegiance to the practicality,
grit, and manliness she admires in Henry Wilcox. Of her father the
narrator says, "If one classed him at all it would be as the countryman
of Hegel and Kant, as the idealist, inclined to be dreamy, whose Imperialism was the Imperialism of the air" (41).[6] On the question of the
reality or the ideological mystification of nationalist assumptions,
*Howards End* is once more somewhat contradictory, as in its attitudes
toward imperialism and in the way Forster both shows up class assumptions and uses them to place the characters. The reader must
make a judgment. The book will not clearly decide.

The same thing can be said for the treatment of gender and sexual
difference in *Howards End*. This is perhaps the most elaborately refined element in the system of ideological assumptions that the novel
both criticizes and employs to place the characters. The novel is a
powerful exposure and implicit condemnation of what today we would
call "patriarchy," as embodied in Henry Wilcox and his two sons.
Their insensitivity, their blatant assumption of male superiority, their
acceptance of a double standard that allows marital infidelity in men
while ostracizing any woman who has sex outside of marriage, their
unconquerable and insufferable condescension to women — these are

[6]*Schlegel* is not just a random, German-sounding name. It was the name of the two
Schlegel brothers, Friedrich and August Wilhelm, countrymen and contemporaries of
Hegel and Kant, who were, in their different ways, important spokespersons for the un-
seen in German Romanticism. An earlier manuscript version of the passage about Mar-
garet and Helen's father confirms this: "Their father, a distant relation of the great critic
. . ." (Forster 26). There is no way to tell whether Forster had in mind Friedrich
Schlegel or August Wilhelm Schlegel as "the great critic." August Wilhelm may have
had greater importance in Forster's day, whereas today, Friedrich is more admired.

shown again and again in wonderfully adroit little touches. Women in this society have little choice between marrying (thereby becoming subordinate to their husbands) and not marrying (thereby remaining celibate). The possibility that the Schlegel sisters, who are intelligent and well educated, might have a job or a profession is never really considered as an option possible under present social conditions, any more than it would have been in the Victorian period. Only men are supposed to work. The Schlegel sisters are emancipated in their thinking. They believe in "temperance, tolerance and sexual equality" (41). Nevertheless, even though Helen has a child out of wedlock, the lives of these two women are for the most part determined by Edwardian assumptions that those around them make about the place of women.

All of the elements for a strong feminist reading are present in *Howards End*, but as with the treatment of other ideological elements, it is not all that easy to figure out just where Forster stands. His narrator gives the Wilcoxes their due for the efficient exercise of patriarchal power. He shows Margaret as genuinely in love with Henry, while at the same time he displays abundantly and with evident relish what havoc these "virile" men wreak all around them, most melodramatically in causing the death of Leonard Bast. Perhaps the climax of the novel for many readers is the moment when Margaret speaks out at last in fierce condemnation of Henry Wilcox, now her husband:

"You shall see the connection if it kills you, Henry! You have had a mistress — I forgave you. My sister has a lover — you drive her from the house. Do you see the connection? Stupid, hypocritical, cruel — oh, contemptible! — a man who insults his wife when she's alive and cants with her memory when she's dead. A man who ruins a woman for his pleasure, and casts her off to ruin other men. And gives bad financial advice, and then says he is not responsible. These men are you. . . . No one has ever told you what you are — muddled, criminally muddled." (263–64)

The matter of gender treatment is made even more complicated if the reader knows that Forster became a practicing homosexual and wrote in 1914 an overtly homosexual novel, *Maurice,* published in 1971 after his death. What difference does this knowledge make to a reading of *Howards End*? Is *Howards End* a covertly homosexual novel? It is not all that easy to answer these questions. For one thing, "being homosexual" is not an absolute condition, like having red hair or even like being biologically male or female, though the latter has its ambiguities too. An infinite variety of ways to be gay, as of ways to be

straight, exists. Every person is to some degree bisexual. Homosexual
behavior and feelings, moreover, like heterosexual ones, are embedded
in each individual case in a complex social, cultural, personal, psychological, and physiological matrix. Saying "Forster was homosexual"
does not so much solve problems in the reading of *Howards End* as
raise new ones. The social history of homosexuality in England has
been quite different from its history in the United States, different in
the process of its legalization, in the degree of its acceptance or rejection in different classes, and in the distinctions made between gay and
lesbian. Homosexuality between men was always much more tolerated
in the English professional and governing class than was lesbianism, as
feminist interpreters of Virginia Woolf, a contemporary of Forster,
have lamented.[7]

Does Forster's "homosexuality," whatever that means exactly, explain the rather cool and distant treatment heterosexual passion gets in
this novel, as in others by him or as in novels by Henry James, another
supposedly homosexual novelist? The reader is told that Henry
Wilcox's proposal of marriage to Margaret Schlegel "was not to rank
among the world's great love scenes" (150). They do not even shake
hands to mark the event, much less kiss. The film version deviates significantly from the novel in having Margaret kiss Henry in acknowledgment and acceptance of his proposal, as well as in showing a good
bit of overt physical affection later on between them. The sexual encounter between Helen Schlegel and Leonard Bast has been found im-
plausible. Katherine Mansfield wondered in her diary "whether Helen
was got with child by Leonard Bast or by his fatal...umbrella" (121).
The film's interpolations make the seduction of Helen by Leonard (or
of Leonard by Helen) more believable; in any case, it fits Helen's
slightly defiant recklessness as presented in the novel. I find more inex-
plicable the attraction of Margaret to Henry and have difficulty imagining them making love, in spite of the care with which Forster builds
up Margaret's admiration for conventional, domineering males. Henry
is presented as so despicable, so inhabited by "panic and emptiness,"
so incapable of "saying 'I,'" — that is, of taking responsibility for a
personal commitment or action — that Helen's reaction of dislike and

---

[7]There may be a discreet hint of lesbianism in the description of Monica, the
woman with whom Helen shares an apartment in Munich after she has fled England,
having been got with child by Leonard Bast: "Margaret guessed at Monica's type —
'Italiano inglesiato' they had named it: the crude feminist of the South, whom one respects but avoids. And Helen had turned to it in her need!" (252).

distaste (she says his eyes are like "brandy-balls" [148]) seems more plausible than Margaret's love. Nevertheless, Henry Wilcox, like Leonard Bast, is praised for being a "real man" (137), whereas their brother Tibby is not a real man. Tibby's apparent asexuality is presented as part of his weakness as a person, whereas Henry's virility is part of his attraction for Margaret, part of his general possession of male mastery. Margaret's marriage to Henry is necessary to put her ultimately in triumphant matriarchal possession of Howards End, firmly in control of her broken and subdued husband, as much so as Jane Eyre is in control of a mutilated and blinded Rochester at the end of Charlotte Brontë's *Jane Eyre*. Perhaps there is some wish fulfillment in both cases.

Does Forster's homosexuality explain why conventional marriages in his novels are generally such disasters, why he has such distaste for "patriarchal males" like Henry and Charles Wilcox, why strong and mysterious older women — for example, Mrs. Wilcox in this novel and Mrs. Moore in *A Passage to India* — play such a role in his novels? To suppose that we are incapable of understanding the sexual feeling of the other sex or of those with different sexual preferences than our own might involve putting in question the ability of apparently "straight" nineteenth-century novelists such as Trollope, Thackeray, Meredith, or Hardy to do what they spend much of their time in their novels doing, that is, presenting the feelings and thoughts of female protagonists. Henry James said that Trollope made the English girl his special province. Many of James's protagonists are also English or American girls, as are those of the other novelists I have mentioned. Forster joins this long tradition in the English novel by centering *Howards End* on the Schlegel sisters and primarily on heterosexual love.

*Howards End,* in any case, remains very much in the closet. There are only moments here and there of what Eve Sedgwick calls "male homosociality" — for example, in the tight bond between Henry Wilcox and his son Charles. It breaks Henry's spirit when his son is sent to prison for manslaughter. One of the warmest moments in the novel, a bright moment in an array of tense and never wholly satisfying relations between the sexes, is the episode of Leonard Bast's casual encounter with an undergraduate on a train (117). The warmth of this brief encounter anticipates the more overtly homosexual tenderness between Fielding and Aziz in *A Passage to India*. Nothing matches it for warmth in the novel except the affection and understanding between the two Schlegel sisters and that between Ruth Wilcox and

Margaret Schlegel. The latter are powerfully presented examples of female homosociality.

As with class, race, and nationalism, so the attempt to read *Howards End* rightly on the issue of gender leads the reader into a labyrinth of somewhat conflicting evidence. That leaves the *unseen*. I began by saying that the characters in *Howards End* are measured on a scale of their responsiveness, or lack of it, to the unseen. Is the unseen, like class, race, nationality, and gender, just one way more of measuring the characters in relation to a prevailing ideology? Well, not exactly. For one thing, it is an absolute, not an ambiguous, yardstick of measurement. Those who are sensitive to the unseen are unequivocally superior to those who are not. Ability to respond to the unseen cuts across all the other measures. Leonard Bast has this ability, but his wife, Jacky, certainly does not. Margaret Schlegel does, as does her sister, Helen, though in a somewhat different way. Mrs. Wilcox has it to a supreme degree. None of the other Wilcoxes, including Henry's daughter, Evie, have it at all. Nor does the Schlegel sisters' Aunt Juley, nor their cousin Frieda from Germany. Response to the unseen is not a matter of female against male, nor of lower against middle classes, nor of Germany against England, because not all women or Germans or members of any class are aware that there is any unseen to respond to. Yet to have this awareness is, for Forster, the one thing needful.

Just what does it mean to have or not to have awareness of the unseen? One word that might be used today for the unseen is the *other*. The word or the concept of *otherness* has great force in many forms of current literary and cultural studies. It is used as a name for those of a different race, nationality, ethnic culture, gender, or sexual orientation. A hegemonic culture, we have been told, defines itself by naming subordinate or minority cultures, whether those of the colonized or those of minorities within their own borders, as "other." Proust's Marcel in *Remembrance of Things Past* finds Albertine's supposed lesbianism bewilderingly, fascinatingly other. Jacques Lacan, in a celebrated formula, defined the unconscious as "the discourse of the other." The concept of the other also has great importance, though with a different meaning in each case, for influential theorists such as Jacques Derrida, Emmanuel Levinas, and Jean-François Lyotard. A self may find its own depths — for example, its unconscious — other to itself. Or another person may be other. Or another nation or ethnic group may be other.

In all these diverse and conflicting uses of the word *other*, as Levinas and Derrida (*Psyché*) have argued, two different concepts of otherness govern as the chief alternatives. On the one hand, the other may be another version of the same, in one way or another assimilable, comprehensible, able to be appropriated and understood. On the other hand, the other may be truly and radically other. In the latter case, the other cannot be turned into some version of the same. It cannot be made transparent to the understanding and thereby be dominated and controlled. It remains, whatever effort we make to deal with it, irreducibly other. As Jacques Derrida puts this, "Tout autre est tout autre" [Every other is wholly other].[8] For Forster, or perhaps it would be better to say for Forster's narrator in *Howards End*, the otherness of race, nationality, class, and gender can in one way or another, by tolerance and sympathy, be reduced to the same. This is true in spite of Forster's celebration of difference.[9] The national, class, and gender other can be comprehended and so assimilated, at least in principle, into an ideal society such as Margaret and Helen Schlegel imagine as their utopian goal. The happy ending of the novel is a miniature version of this ideal society. Forster's belief in this possibility is what is meant by his "liberal humanism."

Forster's notion of the "unseen," on the other hand, what he calls the "glow," a responsiveness to which leads some few persons "outside humanity" (287), puts him outside liberal humanism. The unseen remains just that: unseen. It is therefore unknown, submerged, obscure, invisible. It cannot be returned to the same. It remains heterogeneous to any act of understanding. It is "wholly other." Because the unseen remains invisible, there is no way to adjudicate between those who are aware of it and those who are not. You are either aware of it or you are not aware. The appeal that the unseen makes is therefore in

---

[8]Derrida, *Aporias* 22; I have changed Dutoit's "completely" to "wholly."

[9]Margaret Schlegel makes an eloquent defense of difference in a speech to her sister at the end of the novel:

> It is only that people are far more different than is pretended. All over the world men and women are worrying because they cannot develop as they are supposed to develop. . . . And others — others go further still, and move outside humanity altogether. A place, as well as a person, may catch the glow. Don't you see that all this leads to comfort in the end? It is part of the battle against sameness. Differences — eternal differences, planted by God in a single family, so that there may always be colour; sorrow perhaps, but colour in the daily gray. (287)

This recognition of difference (perhaps even a difference in sexual preference, as is here intimated) is not incompatible, however, in Margaret, and in Forster's narrator too, with a confidence that sympathy and tolerance will make the different understandable, even though difference, as the reader can see, is a response to the unseen, the "glow."

principle different from the appeal that another person makes, even though another person may mediate the unseen, as Mrs. Wilcox does for Margaret Schlegel. Margaret's phrase, "Only connect!" (uttered when she still hopes to change Henry Wilcox to something nearer her own vision), by which she means "Only connect the prose and the passion, and both will be exalted" (168), is often taken as the pinnacle of wisdom in *Howards End*. This consoling and optimistic slogan is not, however, compatible with the irreconcilable opposition shown everywhere in the novel between "life's daily gray" (135) and the urgent demand made by the unseen. The latter leads to action that can be only with difficulty, if at all, reconciled with the prose of everyday life. The prose and the passion remain in conflict. Attempts to connect them are rarely successful. Margaret conspicuously fails in getting her husband to connect the prose and the passion or to have even a glimpse of the unseen.

Being called to an awareness of the unseen is the highest vocation, the most demanding, the most absolute, even though it lays on those called a responsibility impossible to fulfill. It is impossible to fulfill because it comes from the "infinite" and so puts an infinite obligation on the one who receives the call. It is not a demand to do this or that, but a demand to be and to feel in a certain way that then leads spontaneously to right action. That the action is right, however, cannot be verified by any preexisting code of ethics or moral behavior. You can never know for sure that you have responded rightly to the demand that the unseen makes. No voice of commendation comes down from heaven to tell you that you have done right.

Examples of right actions in *Howards End* in response to the unseen are Mrs. Wilcox's decision to bequeath Howards End to Margaret Schlegel; Leonard Bast's taking a night's walk in the woods; Helen's sleeping with Leonard Bast; Margaret's jumping out of the car in sympathy for the flattened cat and its owner; and Margaret's taking over of Howards End, in place of the first Mrs. Wilcox, at the end of the novel. This is a heterogeneous list. All these acts, however, are in one way or another acts of transgression. They defy ordinary morals and rules of behavior. They go against the dictates of those ideological assumptions I have identified.

The German cousin Frieda, of all people, expresses in a sentence a key to understanding what it means to measure people by their sensitivity to the unseen: "One is certain of nothing but the truth of one's own emotions." The narrator comments that this aphorism, though "not an original remark" (it recalls a sentence in one of Keats's letters), "betrayed that interest in the universal [the manuscript at first had *unseen* here] which the average Teuton possesses and the average Englishman does not" (155). Emotions are the result of a response to the unseen; reason has little to do with it. The unseen is unknowable, not amenable to reason or understanding. Its truth cannot be spoken rationally. It does, however, generate emotions that have their own kind of truth. It is a truth of corresponding to the unseen. That emotional truth is the only thing of which we can be certain. It carries its own guarantee and validation. The emotions then determine the appropriate action, without reference to ordinary codes of morality or behavior. Mrs. Wilcox leaves her house to someone who is almost a stranger. Margaret jumps out of the motorcar. Leonard Bast spends a night walking in the woods. Helen sleeps with Leonard Bast.

The unseen is like a black hole at the center of *Howards End*. The other chief thematic elements, distinctions of class, nation, gender, and so on, could be measured as true or false by comparison with other accounts of Edwardian society. Nothing can measure or validate the black hole of the unseen. It is not even possible to prove that the unseen exists, that it is not a subjective fantasy. The Wilcoxes have no understanding, no possibility of understanding, the actions I have listed, all of which follow in one way or another from an encounter with the unseen. The Wilcoxes have panic and emptiness at the center, not a responsible "I" aware of the unseen.

The reader's right response to *Howards End* is like the actions I have named. Just as Mrs. Wilcox is a mediator of the unseen that is embodied in Howards End, so *Howards End* is a further mediator in this chain of mediation. The novel presents models of correct behavior in response to the obligation laid on those who are sensitive to the unseen, but the reader is by no means supposed to copy these. You are on your own in response to the unseen. Each reader must negotiate his or her own reaction. Might it not be possible, for example, to claim that the strand of *Howards End* that refers to the unseen is no more than another part of conservative, white, Western, male ideology, something that functions as a bogus absolute keeping the other ideological elements concerning race, gender, and the uneven distribution of privilege and goods firmly in place, the lines of power unchanged? Yes, it would be possible to claim that. You are free to do so. It would also be possible to take the unseen seriously as something that works against the various elements of that conservative ideology in *Howards End*. Then you would have an obligation to respond in some way to the unseen. It is up to you. Or rather, if Forster is right, it is a matter of the spontaneous truth of your own emotions in response to the unseen as it is mediated by *Howards End*. This is the only truth of which you can be certain. On the basis of that certain truth you must then act rightly.

## WORKS CITED

Althusser, Louis. "Ideology and Ideological State Apparatuses." *Lenin and Philosophy*. Trans. Ben Brewster. London: Verso, 1971. 127–86.

de Man, Paul. "The Resistance to Theory." *The Resistance to Theory*. Minneapolis: U of Minnesota P, 1986. 3–20.

Derrida, Jacques. *Aporias*. Trans. Thomas Dutoit. Stanford: Stanford UP, 1993.

———. "Psyché: Invention de l'autre." *Psyché: Inventions de l'autre*. Paris: Galilee, 1987. 11–61.

Forster, E. M. *The Manuscripts of "Howards End."* Ed. Oliver Stallybrass. London: Edward Arnold, 1973.

Levinas, Emmanuel. "The Trace of the Other." 1963. Trans. Alphonso Lingis. *Deconstruction in Context*. Ed. Mark Taylor. Chicago: U of Chicago P, 1986. 345–59.

Mansfield, Katherine. *Journal*. Ed. J. Middleton Murry. London: Constable, 1954.

Scarry, Elaine. Introduction. *Literature and the Body: Essays on Population and Persons*. Ed. Scarry. Baltimore: Johns Hopkins UP, 1988.

Sedgwick, Eve Kosofsky. *Between Men: English Literature and Male Homosocial Desire*. New York: Columbia UP, 1985.

# Glossary of Critical and Theoretical Terms

Most terms have been glossed parenthetically where they first appear in the text. Mainly, the glossary lists terms that are too complex to define in a phrase or a sentence or two. A few of the terms listed are discussed at greater length elsewhere (*feminist criticism*, for instance); these terms are defined succinctly, and a page reference to the longer discussion is provided.

**AFFECTIVE FALLACY**   First used by William K. Wimsatt and Monroe C. Beardsley to refer to what they regarded as the erroneous practice of interpreting texts according to the psychological responses of readers. "The Affective Fallacy," they wrote in a 1946 essay later republished in *The Verbal Icon* (1954), "is a confusion between the poem and its *results* (what it *is* and what it *does*). . . . It begins by trying to derive the standards of criticism from the psychological effects of a poem and ends in impressionism and relativism." The affective fallacy, like the intentional fallacy (confusing the meaning of a work with the author's expressly intended meaning), was one of the main tenets of the New Criticism, or formalism. The affective fallacy has recently been contested by reader-response critics, who have deliberately dedicated their efforts to describing the way individual readers and "interpretive communities" go about "making sense" of texts.

*See also:* Authorial Intention, Formalism, Reader-Response Criticism.

**AUTHORIAL INTENTION**   Defined narrowly, an author's intention in writing a work, as expressed in letters, diaries, interviews, and conversations. Defined more broadly, "intentionality" involves unexpressed motivations, designs, and purposes, some of which may have remained unconscious.

The debate over whether critics should try to discern an author's intentions (conscious or otherwise) is an old one. William K. Wimsatt and Monroe C. Beardsley, in an essay first published in the 1940s, coined the term "intentional fallacy" to refer to the practice of basing interpretations on the expressed or implied intentions of authors, a practice they judged to be erroneous. As proponents of the New Criticism, or formalism, they argued that a work of literature is an object in itself and should be studied as such. They believed that it is sometimes helpful to learn what an author intended, but the critic's real purpose is to show what is actually in the text, not what an author intended to put there.

*See also:* Affective Fallacy, Formalism.

**BASE** *See* Marxist Criticism.

**BINARY OPPOSITIONS** *See* Oppositions.

**BLANKS** *See* Gaps.

**CANON** Since the fourth century, used to refer to those books of the Bible that the Christian church accepts as being Holy Scripture. The term has come to be applied more generally to those literary works given special status, or "privileged," by a culture. Works we tend to think of as "classics" or the "Great Books" produced by Western culture — texts that are found in every anthology of American, British, and world literature — would be among those that constitute the canon.

Recently, Marxist, feminist, minority, and postcolonial critics have argued that, for political reasons, many excellent works never enter the canon. Canonized works, they claim, are those that reflect—and respect—the culture's dominant ideology and/or perform some socially acceptable or even necessary form of "cultural work." Attempts have been made to broaden or redefine the canon by discovering valuable texts, or versions of texts, that were repressed or ignored for political reasons. These have been published both in traditional and in nontraditional anthologies. The most outspoken critics of the canon, especially radical critics practicing cultural criticism, have called into question the whole concept of canon or "canonicity." Privileging no form of artistic expression that reflects and revises the culture, these critics treat cartoons, comics, and soap operas with the same cogency and respect they accord novels, poems, and plays.

*See also:* Cultural Criticism, Feminist Criticism, Ideology, Marxist Criticism.

**CONFLICTS, CONTRADICTIONS** *See* Gaps.

**CULTURAL CRITICISM** A critical approach that is sometimes referred to as "cultural studies" or "cultural critique." Practitioners of cultural criticism oppose "high" definitions of culture and take seriously popular cultural forms. Grounded in a variety of continental European influences, cultural criticism nonetheless gained institutional force in England, in 1964, with the founding of the Centre for Contemporary Cultural Studies at Birmingham University. Broadly interdisciplinary in its scope and approach, cultural criticism views the text as the locus and catalyst of a complex network of political and economic discourses. Cultural critics share with Marxist critics an interest in the ideological contexts of cultural forms. *See* "What Is Cultural Criticism?" pp. 345–59.

**DECONSTRUCTION** A poststructuralist approach to literature that is strongly influenced by the writings of the French philosopher Jacques Derrida. Deconstruction, partly in response to structuralism and formalism, posits the undecidability of meaning for all texts. In fact, as the deconstructionist critic J. Hillis Miller points out, "deconstruction is not a dismantling of the structure of a text but a demonstration that it has already dismantled itself." See "What Is Deconstruction?" pp. 447–63.

**DIALECTIC** Originally developed by Greek philosophers, mainly Socrates and Plato, as a form and method of logical argumentation; the term later came to denote a philosophical notion of evolution. The German philosopher G. W. F. Hegel described dialectic as a process whereby a thesis, when countered by an antithesis, leads to the synthesis of a new idea. Karl Marx and Friedrich Engels, adapting Hegel's idealist theory, used the phrase "dialectical materialism" to discuss the way in which a revolutionary class war might lead to the synthesis of a new social economic order. The American Marxist critic Fredric Jameson has coined the phrase "dialectical criticism" to refer to a Marxist critical approach that synthesizes structuralist and poststructuralist methodologies.
See also: Marxist Criticism, Poststructuralism, Structuralism.

**DIALOGIC** See Discourse.

**DISCOURSE** Used specifically, can refer to (1) spoken or written discussion of a subject or area of knowledge; (2) the words in, or text of, a narrative as opposed to its story line; or (3) a "strand" within a given narrative that argues a certain point or defends a given value system.

More generally, "discourse" refers to the language in which a subject or area of knowledge is discussed or a certain kind of business is transacted. Human knowledge is collected and structured in discourses. Theology and medicine are defined by their discourses, as are politics, sexuality, and literary criticism.

A society is generally made up of a number of different discourses or "discourse communities," one or more of which may be dominant or serve the dominant ideology. Each discourse has its own vocabulary, concepts, and rules, knowledge of which constitutes power. The psychoanalyst and psychoanalytic critic Jacques Lacan has treated the unconscious as a form of discourse, the patterns of which are repeated in literature. Cultural critics, following Mikhail Bakhtin, use the word "dialogic" to discuss the dialogue *between* discourses that takes place within language or, more specifically, a literary text.
See also: Cultural Criticism, Ideology, Narrative, Psychoanalytic Criticism.

**FEMINIST CRITICISM** An aspect of the feminist movement whose primary goals include critiquing masculine-dominated language and literature by showing how they reflect a masculine ideology; writing the history of unknown or undervalued women writers, thereby earning them their rightful place in the literary canon; and helping create a climate in which women's creativity may be fully realized and appreciated. See "What Are Feminist and Gender Criticism?" pp. 379–93.

**FIGURE** See Metaphor, Metonymy, Symbol.

**FORMALISM** Also referred to as the New Criticism, formalism reached its height during the 1940s and 1950s, but it is still practiced today. Formalists treat a work of literary art as if it were a self-contained, self-referential object. Rather than basing their interpretations of a text on the reader's response, the author's stated intentions, or parallels between the text and historical contexts (such as the author's life), formalists concentrate on the relationships *within* the text that give it its own distinctive character or form. Special attention is paid to repetition, particularly of images or symbols, but also of sound effects and rhythms in poetry.

Because of the importance placed on close analysis and the stress on the text as a carefully crafted, orderly object containing observable formal patterns, formalism has often been seen as an attack on Romanticism and impressionism, particularly impressionistic criticism. It has sometimes even been called an "objective" approach to literature. Formalists are more likely than certain other critics to believe and say that the meaning of a text can be known objectively. For instance, reader-response critics see meaning as a function either of each reader's experience or of the norms that govern a particular "interpretive community," and deconstructors argue that texts mean opposite things at the same time.

Formalism was originally based on essays written during the 1920s and 1930s by T. S. Eliot, I. A. Richards, and William Empson. It was significantly developed later by a group of American poets and critics, including R. P. Blackmur, Cleanth Brooks, John Crowe Ransom, Allen Tate, Robert Penn Warren, and William K. Wimsatt. Although we associate formalism with certain principles and terms (such as the "affective fallacy" and the "intentional fallacy" as defined by Wimsatt and Monroe C. Beardsley), formalists were trying to make a cultural statement rather than establish a critical dogma. Generally southern, religious, and culturally conservative, they advocated the inherent value of literary works (particularly of literary works regarded as beautiful art objects) because they were sick of the growing ugliness of modern life and contemporary events. Some recent theorists even suggest that the rising popularity of formalism after World War II was a feature of American isolationism, the formalist tendency to isolate literature from biography and history being a manifestation of the American fatigue with wider involvements.

*See also:* Affective Fallacy, Authorial Intention, Deconstruction, Reader-Response Criticism, Symbol.

**GAPS**   When used by reader-response critics familiar with the theories of Wolfgang Iser, refers to "blanks" in texts that must be filled in by readers. A gap may be said to exist whenever and wherever a reader perceives something to be missing between words, sentences, paragraphs, stanzas, or chapters. Readers respond to gaps actively and creatively, explaining apparent inconsistencies in point of view, accounting for jumps in chronology, speculatively supplying information missing from plots, and resolving problems or issues left ambiguous or "indeterminate" in the text.

Reader-response critics sometimes speak as if a gap actually exists in a text; a gap is, of course, to some extent a product of readers' perceptions. Different readers may find gaps in different texts, and different gaps in the same text. Furthermore, they may fill these gaps in different ways, which is why, a reader-response critic might argue, works are interpreted in different ways.

Although the concept of the gap has been used mainly by reader-response critics, it has also been used by critics taking other theoretical approaches. Practitioners of deconstruction might use "gap" when speaking of the radical contradictoriness of a text. Marxists have used the term to speak of everything from the gap that opens up between economic base and cultural superstructure to the two kinds of conflicts or contradictions to be found in literary texts. The first of these, they would argue, results from the fact that texts reflect ideology, within which certain subjects cannot be covered, things cannot be said, contradictory views cannot be recognized as contradictory. The second kind of conflict, contradiction, or gap within a text results from the fact that works don't just reflect ideology; they are also fictions that, consciously or unconsciously, distance themselves from the same ideology.

See also: Deconstruction, Ideology, Marxist Criticism, Reader-Response Criticism.

GENDER CRITICISM Developing out of feminist criticism in the mid-1980s, this fluid and inclusive movement by its nature defies neat definition. Its practitioners include, but are not limited to, self-identified feminists, gay and lesbian critics, queer and performance theorists, and poststructuralists interested in deconstructing oppositions such as masculine/feminine, heterosexual/homosexual. This diverse group of critics shares an interest in interrogating categories of gender and sexuality and exploring the relationships between them, though it does not necessarily share any central assumptions about the nature of these categories. For example, some gender critics insist that all gender identities are cultural constructions, but others have maintained a belief in essential gender identity. Often gender critics are more interested in examining gender issues through a literary text than a literary text through gender issues. See "What Are Feminist and Gender Criticism?" pp. 379–93.

GENRE A French word referring to a kind or type of literature. Individual works within a genre may exhibit a distinctive form, be governed by certain conventions, and/or represent characteristic subjects. Tragedy, epic, and romance are all genres.

Perhaps inevitably, the term *genre* is used loosely. Lyric poetry is a genre, but so are characteristic *types* of the lyric, such as the sonnet, the ode, and the elegy. Fiction is a genre, as are detective fiction and science fiction. The list of genres grows constantly as critics establish new lines of connection between individual works and discern new categories of works with common characteristics. Moreover, some writers form hybrid genres by combining the characteristics of several in a single work. Knowledge of genres helps critics to understand and explain what is conventional and unconventional, borrowed and original, in a work.

HEGEMONY Given intellectual currency by the Italian communist Antonio Gramsci, the word (a translation of *egemonia*) refers to the pervasive system of assumptions, meanings, and values—the web of ideologies, in other word—that shapes the way things look, what they mean, and therefore what reality *is* for the majority of people within a given culture.

See also: Ideology, Marxist Criticism.

IDEOLOGY A set of beliefs underlying the customs, habits, and/or practices common to a given social group. To members of that group, the beliefs seem obviously true, natural, and even universally applicable. They may seem just as obviously arbitrary, idiosyncratic, and even false to outsiders or members of another group who adhere to another ideology. Within a society, several ideologies may coexist, or one or more may be dominant. Ideologies may be forcefully imposed or willingly subscribed to. Their component beliefs may be held consciously or unconsciously. In either case, they come to form what Johanna M. Smith has called "the unexamined ground of our experience." Ideology governs our perceptions, judgments, and prejudices—our sense of what is acceptable, normal, and deviant. Ideology may cause a revolution; it may also allow discrimination and even exploitation.

Ideologies are of special interest to sociologically oriented critics of literature because of the way in which authors reflect or resist prevailing views in their texts. Some Marxist critics have argued that literary texts reflect and reproduce the ideologies that produced them; most, however, have shown how ideologies are riven with contradictions that works of literature manage to expose and widen. Still other Marxists have focused on the way in which texts themselves are characterized by gaps, conflicts, and contradictions between their ideological and anti-ideological functions.

Feminist critics have addressed the question of ideology by seeking to expose (and thereby call into question) the patriarchal ideology mirrored or inscribed in works written by men—even men who have sought to counter sexism and break down sexual stereotypes. New historicists have been interested in demonstrating the ideological underpinnings not only of literary representations but also of our interpretations of them. Fredric Jameson, an American Marxist critic, argues that all thought is ideological, but that ideological thought that knows itself as such stands the chance of seeing through and transcending ideology.

*See also:* Cultural Criticism, Feminist Criticism, Marxist Criticism, New Historicism.

**IMAGINARY ORDER**    One of the three essential orders of the psychoanalytic field (*see* Real and Symbolic Order), it is most closely associated with the senses (sight, sound, touch, taste, and smell). The infant, who by comparison to other animals is born premature and thus is wholly dependent on others for a prolonged period, enters the Imaginary order when it begins to experience a unity of body parts and motor control that is empowering. This usually occurs between six and eighteen months, and is called by Lacan the "mirror stage" or "mirror phase," in which the child anticipates mastery of its body. It does so by identifying with the *image* of wholeness (that is, seeing its own image in the mirror, experiencing its mother as a whole body, and so on). This sense of oneness, and also difference from others (especially the mother or primary caretaker), is established through an image or a vision of harmony that is both a mirroring and a "mirage of maturation" or false sense of individuality and independence. The Imaginary is a metaphor for unity, is related to the visual order, and is always part of human subjectivity. Because the subject is fundamentally separate from others and also internally divided (conscious/unconscious), the apparent coherence of the Imaginary, its fullness and grandiosity, is always false, a *mis*recognition that the ego (or "me") tries to deny by imagining itself as coherent and empowered. The Imaginary operates in conjunction with the Real and the Symbolic and is not a "stage" of development equivalent to Freud's "pre-oedipal stage," nor is it prelinguistic.

*See also:* Psychoanalytic Criticism, Real, Symbolic Order.

**IMPLIED READER**   A phrase used by some reader-response critics in place of the phrase "the reader." Whereas "the reader" could refer to any idiosyncratic individual who happens to have read or to be reading the text, "the implied reader" is *the* reader intended, even created, by the text. Other reader-response critics seeking to describe this more generally conceived reader have spoken of the "informed reader" or the "narratee," who is "the necessary counterpart of a given narrator."

   *See also:* Reader-Response Criticism.

**INTENTIONAL FALLACY**   *See* Authorial Intention.

**INTENTIONALITY**   *See* Authorial Intention.

**INTERTEXTUALITY**   The condition of interconnectedness among texts. Every author has been influenced by others, and every work contains explicit and implicit references to other works. Writers may consciously or unconsciously echo a predecessor or precursor; they may also consciously or unconsciously disguise their indebtedness, making intertextual relationships difficult for the critic to trace.

   Reacting against the formalist tendency to view each work as a freestanding object, some poststructuralist critics suggested that the meaning of a work emerges only intertextually, that is, within the context provided by other works. But there has been a reaction, too, against this type of intertextual criticism. Some new historicist critics suggest that literary history is itself too narrow a context and that works should be interpreted in light of a larger set of cultural contexts.

   There is, however, a broader definition of intertextuality, one that refers to the relationship between works of literature and a wide range of narratives and discourses that we don't usually consider literary. Thus defined, intertextuality could be used by a new historicist to refer to the significant interconnectedness between a literary text and nonliterary discussions of or discourses about contemporary culture. Or it could be used by a poststructuralist to suggest that a work can only be recognized and read within a vast field of signs and tropes that is *like* a text and that makes any single text self-contradictory and "undecidable."

   *See also:* Discourse, Formalism, Narrative, New Historicism, Poststructuralism, Trope.

**MARXIST CRITICISM**   An approach that treats literary texts as material products, describing them in broadly historical terms. In Marxist criticism, the text is viewed in terms of its production and consumption, as a product *of* work that does identifiable cultural work of its own. Following Karl Marx, the founder of communism, Marxist critics have used the terms *base* to refer to economic reality and *superstructure* to refer to the corresponding or "homologous" infrastructure consisting of politics, law, philosophy, religion, and the arts. Also following Marx, they have used the word *ideology* to refer to that set of cultural beliefs that literary works at once reproduce, resist, and revise. *See* "What Is Marxist Criticism?" pp. 416–29.

**METAPHOR**   The representation of one thing by another related or similar thing. The image (or activity or concept) used to represent or "figure" something else is known as the "vehicle" of the metaphor; the thing represented is called the "tenor." In other words, the vehicle is what we substitute for the tenor. The relationship between vehicle and tenor can provide much additional meaning. Thus, instead of saying, "Last night I read a book," we might say, "Last night I plowed through a book." "Plowed through" (or the activity of plowing) is the vehicle of our metaphor; "read" (or the act of reading) is the tenor, the thing being figured. The increment in meaning through metaphor is fairly obvious. Our audience knows not only *that* we read but also *how* we read, because to read a book in the way that a plow rips through earth is surely to read in a relentless, unreflective way. Note that in the sentence above, a new metaphor—"rips through"—has been used to explain an old one. This serves (which is a metaphor) as an example of just how thick (another metaphor) language is with metaphors!

Metaphor is a kind of "trope" (literally, a "turning," that is, a figure of speech that alters or "turns" the meaning of a word or phrase). Other tropes include allegory, conceit, metonymy, personification, simile, symbol, and synecdoche. Traditionally, metaphor and symbol have been viewed as the principal tropes; minor tropes have been categorized as *types* of these two major ones. Similes, for instance, are usually defined as simple metaphors that usually employ *like* or *as* and state the tenor outright, as in "My love is like a red, red rose." Synecdoche involves a vehicle that is a *part* of the tenor, as in "I see a sail" meaning "I see a boat." Metonymy is viewed as a metaphor involving two terms commonly if arbitrarily associated with (but not fundamentally or intrinsically related to) each other. Recently, however, deconstructors such as Paul de Man and J. Hillis Miller have questioned the "privilege" granted to metaphor and the metaphor/metonymy distinction or "opposition." They have suggested that all metaphors are really metonyms and that all figuration is arbitrary.

*See also:* Deconstruction, Metonymy, Oppositions, Symbol.

**METONYMY** The representation of one thing by another that is commonly and often physically associated with it. To refer to a writer's handwriting as his or her "hand" is to use a metonymic "figure" or "trope." The image or thing used to represent something else is known as the "vehicle" of the metonym; the thing represented is called the "tenor."

Like other tropes (such as metaphor), metonymy involves the replacement of one word or phrase by another. Liquor may be referred to as "the bottle," a monarch as "the crown." Narrowly defined, the vehicle of a metonym is arbitrarily, not intrinsically, associated with the tenor. In other words, the bottle just happens to be what liquor is stored in and poured from in our culture. The hand may be involved in the production of handwriting, but so are the brain and the pen. There is no special, intrinsic likeness between a crown and a monarch; it's just that crowns traditionally sit on monarchs' heads and not on the heads of university professors. More broadly, *metonym* and *metonymy* have been used by recent critics to refer to a wide range of figures and tropes. Deconstructors have questioned the distinction between metaphor and metonymy.

*See also:* Deconstruction, Metaphor, Trope.

**NARRATIVE** A story or a telling of a story, or an account of a situation or of events. A novel and a biography of a novelist are both narratives, as are Freud's case histories.

Some critics use the word narrative even more generally; Brook Thomas, a new historicist, has critiqued "narratives of human history that neglect the role human labor has played."

**NEW CRITICISM**   *See* Formalism.

**NEW HISTORICISM**   First practiced and articulated in the late 1970s and early 1980s in the work of critics such as Stephen Greenblatt—who named this movement in contemporary critical theory—and Louis Montrose, its practitioners share certain convictions, primarily that literary critics need to develop a high degree of historical consciousness and that literature should not be viewed apart from other human creations, artistic or otherwise. They share a belief in referentiality—a belief that literature refers to and is referred to by things outside itself—that is fainter in the works of formalist, poststructuralist, and even reader-response critics. Discarding old distinctions between literature, history, and the social sciences, new historicists agree with Greenblatt that the "central concerns" of criticism "should prevent it from permanently sealing off one type of discourse from another, or decisively separating works of art from the minds and lives of their creators and their audiences."

*See also:* Authorial Intention, Deconstruction, Formalism, Ideology, Poststructuralism, Psychoanalytic Criticism.

**OPPOSITIONS**   A concept highly relevant to linguistics, inasmuch as linguists maintain that words (such as *black* and *death*) have meaning not in themselves but in relation to other words (*white* and *life*). Jacques Derrida, a poststructuralist philosopher of language, has suggested that in the West we think in terms of these "binary oppositions" or dichotomies, which on examination turn out to be evaluative hierarchies. In other words, each opposition—beginning/end, presence/absence, or consciousness/unconsciousness—contains one term that our culture views as superior and one term that we view as negative or inferior.

Derrida has "deconstructed" a number of these binary oppositions, including two—speech/writing and signifier/signified—that he believes to be central to linguistics in particular and Western culture in general. He has concurrently critiqued the "law" of noncontradiction, which is fundamental to Western logic. He and other deconstructors have argued that a text can contain opposed strands of discourse and, therefore, can mean opposite things: reason *and* passion, life *and* death, hope *and* despair, black *and* white. Traditionally, criticism has involved choosing between opposed or contradictory meanings and arguing that one is present in the text and the other absent.

French feminists have adopted the ideas of Derrida and other deconstructors, showing not only that we think in terms of such binary oppositions as male/female, reason/emotion, and active/passive, but that we also associate reason and activity with masculinity and emotion and passivity with femininity. Because of this, they have concluded that language is "phallocentric," or masculine-dominated.

*See also:* Deconstruction, Discourse, Feminist Criticism, Poststructuralism.

**PHALLUS**   The symbolic value of the penis that organizes libidinal development and that Freud saw as a stage in the process of human subjectivity. Lacan viewed the Phallus as the representative of a fraudulent power (male over female) whose "Law" is a principle of psychic division (conscious/

unconscious) and sexual difference (masculine/feminine). The Symbolic order (*see* Symbolic Order) is ruled by the Phallus, which of itself has no inherent meaning *apart from* the power and meaning given to it by individual cultures and societies, and represented by the name of the father as lawgiver and namer.

**POSTSTRUCTURALISM**    The general attempt to contest and subvert structuralism initiated by deconstructors and certain other critics associated with psychoanalytic, Marxist, and feminist theory. Structuralists, using linguistics as a model and employing semiotic (sign) theory, posit the possibility of knowing a text systematically and revealing the "grammar" behind its form and meaning. Poststructuralists argue against the possibility of such knowledge and description. They counter that texts can be shown to contradict not only structuralist accounts of them but also themselves. In making their adversarial claims, they rely on close readings of texts and on the work of theorists such as Jacques Derrida and Jacques Lacan.

Poststructuralists have suggested that structuralism rests on distinctions between "signifier" and "signified" (signs and the things they point toward), "self" and "language" (or "text"), texts and other texts, and text and world that are overly simplistic, if not patently inaccurate. Poststructuralists have shown how all signifieds are also signifiers, and they have treated texts as "intertexts." They have viewed the world as if it *were* a text (we desire a certain car because it *symbolizes* achievement) and the self as the subject, as well as the user, of language; for example, we may shape and speak through language, but it also shapes and speaks through us.

*See also:* Deconstruction, Feminist Criticism, Intertextuality, Psychoanalytic Criticism, Semiotics, Structuralism.

**PSYCHOANALYTIC CRITICISM**    Grounded in the psychoanalytic theories of Sigmund Freud, it is one of the oldest critical methodologies still in use. Freud's view that works of literature, like dreams, express secret, unconscious desires led to criticism and interpreted literary works as manifestations of the authors' neuroses. More recently, psychoanalytic critics have come to see literary works as skillfully crafted artifacts that may appeal to *our* neuroses by tapping into our repressed wishes and fantasies. Other forms of psychological criticism that diverge from Freud, although they ultimately derive from his insights, include those based on the theories of Carl Jung and Jacques Lacan. *See* "What is Psychoanalytic Criticism?" pp. 313–24.

**READER-RESPONSE CRITICISM**    An approach to literature that, as its name implies, considers the way readers respond to texts as they read. Stanley Fish describes the method by saying that it substitutes for one question, "What does this sentence mean?" a more operational question, "What does this sentence do?" Reader-response criticism shares with deconstruction a strong textual orientation and a reluctance to define a single meaning for a work. Along with psychoanalytic criticism, it shares an interest in the dynamics of mental response to textual cues.

**REAL**    One of the three orders of subjectivity (*see* Imaginary Order and Symbolic Order), the Real is the intractable and substantial world that resists and exceeds interpretation. The Real cannot be imagined, symbolized, or known directly. It constantly eludes our efforts to name it (death, gravity, the physicality of objects are examples of the Real), and thus challenges both the Imaginary and the Symbolic orders. The Real is fundamentally "Other," the mark of the divide between conscious and unconscious, and is signaled in language by gaps, slips, speechlessness, and the sense of the uncanny. The Real is not what we call "reality." It is the stumbling block of the Imaginary (which thinks it can "imagine" anything, including the Real) and of the Symbolic, which tries to bring the Real under its laws (the Real exposes the "phallacy" of the Law of the Phallus). The Real is frightening; we try to tame it with laws and language and call it "reality."

*See also:* Imaginary Order, Psychoanalytic Criticism, Symbolic Order.

**SEMIOLOGY, SEMIOTIC**   *See* Semiotics.

**SEMIOTICS**   The study of signs and sign systems and the way meaning is derived from them. Structuralist anthropologists, psychoanalysts, and literary critics developed semiotics during the decades following 1950, but much of the pioneering work had been done at the turn of the century by the founder of modern linguistics, Ferdinand de Saussure, and the American philosopher Charles Sanders Peirce.

Semiotics is based on several important distinctions, including the distinction between "signifier" and "signified" (the sign and what it points toward) and the distinction between "langue" and "parole." *Langue* (French for "tongue," as in "native tongue," meaning language) refers to the entire system within which individual utterances or usages of language have meaning; *parole* (French for "word") refers to the particular utterances or usages. A principal tenet of semiotics is that signs, like words, are not significant in themselves, but instead have meaning only in relation to other signs and the entire system of signs, or *langue.*

The affinity between semiotics and structuralist literary criticism derives from this emphasis placed on langue, or system. Structuralist critics, after all, were reacting against formalists and their procedure of focusing on individual words as if meanings didn't depend on anything external to the text.

Poststructuralists have used semiotics but questioned some of its underlying assumptions, including the opposition between signifier and signified. The feminist poststructuralist Julia Kristeva, for instance, has used the word *semiotic* to describe feminine language, a highly figurative, fluid form of discourse that she sets in opposition to rigid, symbolic, masculine language.

*See also:* Deconstruction, Feminist Criticism, Formalism, Oppositions, Poststructuralism, Structuralism, Symbol.

**SIMILE**   *See* Metaphor.

**SOCIOHISTORICAL CRITICISM**   *See* New Historicism.

**STRUCTURALISM**   A science of humankind whose proponents attempted to show that all elements of human culture, including literature, may be understood as parts of a system of signs. Structuralism, according to Robert Scholes, was a reaction to "'modernist' alienation and despair."

Using Ferdinand de Saussure's linguistic theory, European structuralists such as Roman Jakobson, Claude Lévi-Strauss, and Roland Barthes (before his shift toward poststructuralism) attempted to develop a "semiology" or "semiotics" (science of signs). Barthes, among others, sought to recover literature and even language from the isolation in which they had been studied and to show that the laws that govern them govern all signs, from road signs to articles of clothing.

Particularly useful to structuralists were two of Saussure's concepts: the idea of "phoneme" in language and the idea that phonemes exist in two kinds of relationships: "synchronic" and "diachronic." A phoneme is the smallest consistently significant unit in language; thus, both "a" and "an" are phonemes, but "n" is not. A diachronic relationship is that which a phoneme has with those that have preceded it in time and those that will follow it. These "horizontal" relationships produce what we might call discourse or narrative and what Saussure called "parole." The synchronic relationship is the "vertical" one that a word has in a given instant with the entire system of language ("langue") in which it may generate meaning. "An" means what it means in English because those of us who speak the language are using it in the same way at a given time.

Following Saussure, Lévi-Strauss studied hundreds of myths, breaking them into their smallest meaningful units, which he called "mythemes." Removing each from its diachronic relations with other mythemes in a single myth (such as the myth of Oedipus and his mother), he vertically aligned those mythemes that he found to be homologous (structurally correspondent). He then studied the relationships within as well as between vertically aligned columns, in an attempt to understand scientifically, through ratios and proportions, those thoughts and processes that humankind has shared, both at one particular time and across time. One could say, then, that structuralists followed Saussure in preferring to think about the overriding langue or language of myth, in which each mytheme and mytheme-constituted myth fits meaningfully, rather than about isolated individual paroles or narratives. Structuralists followed Saussure's lead in believing what the poststructuralist Jacques Derrida later decided he could not subscribe to—that sign systems must be understood in terms of binary oppositions. In analyzing myths and texts to find basic structures, structuralists tended to find that opposite terms modulate until they are finally resolved or reconciled by some intermediary third term. Thus, a structuralist reading of *Paradise Lost* would show that the war between God and the bad angels becomes a rift between God and sinful, fallen man, the rift then being healed by the Son of God, the mediating third term.

*See also:* Deconstruction, Discourse, Narrative, Poststructuralism, Semiotics.

**SUPERSTRUCTURE**   *See* Marxist Criticism.

**SYMBOL**   A thing, image, or action that, although it is of interest in its own right, stands for or suggests something larger and more complex—often an idea or a range of interrelated ideas, attitudes, and practices.

Within a given culture, some things are understood to be symbols: the flag of the United States is an obvious example. More subtle cultural symbols might be the river as a symbol of time and the journey as a symbol of life and its manifold experiences.

Instead of appropriating symbols generally used and understood within their culture, writers often create symbols by setting up, in their works, a complex but identifiable web of associations. As a result, one object, image, or action suggests others, and often, ultimately, a range of ideas.

A symbol may thus be defined as a metaphor in which the "vehicle," the thing, image, or action used to represent something else, represents many related things (or "tenors") or is broadly suggestive. The urn in Keats's "Ode on a Grecian Urn" suggests many interrelated concepts, including art, truth, beauty, and timelessness.

Symbols have been of particular interest to formalists, who study how meanings emerge from the complex, patterned relationships between images in a work, and psychoanalytic critics, who are interested in how individual authors and the larger culture both disguise and reveal unconscious fears and desires through symbols. Recently, French feminists have also focused on the symbolic. They have suggested that, as wide-ranging as it seems, symbolic language is ultimately rigid and restrictive. They favor semiotic language and writing, which, they contend, is at once more rhythmic, unifying, and feminine.

*See also:* Feminist Criticism, Metaphor, Psychoanalytic Criticism, Trope.

**SYMBOLIC ORDER** One of the three orders of subjectivity (*see* Imaginary Order and Real), it is the realm of law, language, and society; it is the repository of generally held cultural beliefs. Its symbolic system is language, whose agent is the father or lawgiver, the one who has the power of naming. The human subject is commanded into this preestablished order by language (a process that begins long before a child can speak) and must submit to its orders of communication (grammar, syntax, and so on). Entrance into the Symbolic order determines subjectivity according to a primary law of referentiality that takes the male sign (phallus; *see* Phallus) as its ordering principle. Lacan states that both sexes submit to the Law of the Phallus (the law of order, language, and differentiation) but that their individual relation to the law determines whether they see themselves as—and are seen by others to be—either "masculine" or "feminine." The Symbolic institutes repression (of the Imaginary), thus creating the unconscious, which itself is structured like the language of the symbolic. The unconscious, a timeless realm, cannot be known directly, but it can be understood by a kind of translation that takes place in language—psychoanalysis is the "talking cure." The Symbolic is not a "stage" of development (as is Freud's "oedipal stage"), nor is it set in place once and for all in human life. We constantly negotiate its threshold (in sleep, in drunkenness) and can "fall out" of it altogether in psychosis.

*See also:* Imaginary Order, Psychoanalytic Criticism, Real.

**SYNECDOCHE** *See* Metaphor, Metonymy.

**TENOR** *See* Metaphor, Metonymy, Symbol.

**TROPE** A figure, as in "figure of speech." Literally a "turning," that is, a turning or twisting of a word or phrase to make it mean something else. Principal tropes include metaphor, metonymy, personification, simile, and synecdoche.

*See also:* Metaphor, Metonymy.

**VEHICLE** *See* Metaphor, Metonymy, Symbol.

# About the Contributors

## THE VOLUME EDITOR

**Alistair M. Duckworth,** professor of English at the University of Florida, Gainesville, is the author of *"Howards End": E. M. Forster's House of Fiction* (1992) and *The Improvement of the Estate: A Study of Jane Austen's Novels* (1971), which Johns Hopkins reissued in 1994 as a paperback, with a new introduction by the author.

## THE CRITICS

**Elizabeth Langland** is professor of English and associate dean of the College of Liberal Arts and Sciences at the University of Florida, Gainesville. She is the author of *Anne Brontë: The Other One* (1989) and *Nobody's Angels: Middle-Class Women and Domestic Ideology in Victorian Culture* (1995) and coeditor of *Out of Bounds: Male Writers and Gender(ed) Criticism* (1990).

**J. Hillis Miller** is professor of English and comparative literature at the University of California, Irvine. He is the author of many books, including studies of Dickens and Hardy and *The Ethics of Reading: Kant, de Man, Eliot, Trollope, James, and Benjamin* (1987), *Tropes, Parables, Performatives: Essays on Twentieth-Century Literature* (1990),

*Versions of Pygmalion* (1990), *Hawthorne and History: Defacing It* (1991), *Ariadne's Thread: Story Lines* (1992), and *Topographies* (1995).

**J. H. Stape,** professor of English literature at Japan Women's University in Tokyo, has written frequently on Conrad and the modern novel. He is the author of *E. M. Forster: A Chronology* (1993) and the editor of *E. M. Forster: Interviews and Recollections* (1993). His *E. M. Forster: Critical Assessments* is forthcoming.

**Judith Weissman** is a member of the Department of English at Washington University, St. Louis, and the author of *Half Savage and Hardy and Free: Women and Rural Radicalism in the Nineteenth-Century Novel* (1987) and *Of Two Minds: Poets Who Hear Voices* (1993).

**Peter Widdowson** is a professor in the Department of Humanities and Religious Studies at Cheltenham and Gloucester College of Higher Education, Cheltenham, England. He has written articles on "Englishness" in modern fiction and the future of the English department, and is the author of *"Howards End": Fiction as History* (1977) and *Hardy in History: A Study of the Sociology of Literature* (1989).

## THE SERIES EDITOR

**Ross C Murfin,** general editor of the Case Studies in Contemporary Criticism and volume editor of Conrad's *Heart of Darkness* and Hawthorne's *The Scarlet Letter* in the series, is provost and vice president for Academic Affairs at Southern Methodist University. He has taught at the University of Miami, Yale University, and the University of Virginia and has published scholarly studies of Joseph Conrad, Thomas Hardy, and D. H. Lawrence.

*Acknowledgments (continued from page iv)*

J. Hillis Miller, "Just Reading *Howards End.*" Copyright © 1997 by J. Hillis Miller.

Judith Weissman, "*Howards End:* Gasoline and Goddesses." Excerpt from chapter 11, *Half-Savage and Hardy and Free,* © 1987 by Judith Weissman, Wesleyan University Press. Reprinted by permission of the University Press of New England.

Peter Widdowson, "*Howards End:* Fiction as History." Revised excerpt from *Howards End: Fiction as History.* Copyright © 1977 by Peter Widdowson.